TRUCKUS MAXIMUS

Story by
SCOTT PETERSON

Art by
JOSÉ GARCÍA

First Second
New York

To my creative partners-in-crime, Jordan B. Gorfinkel and Darren J. Vincenzo: There couldn't possibly be better guys with whom to hang out on a racetrack in the Roman Empire for countless hours.

For Lissa, who taught me everything about the only things that matter.

—S.P.

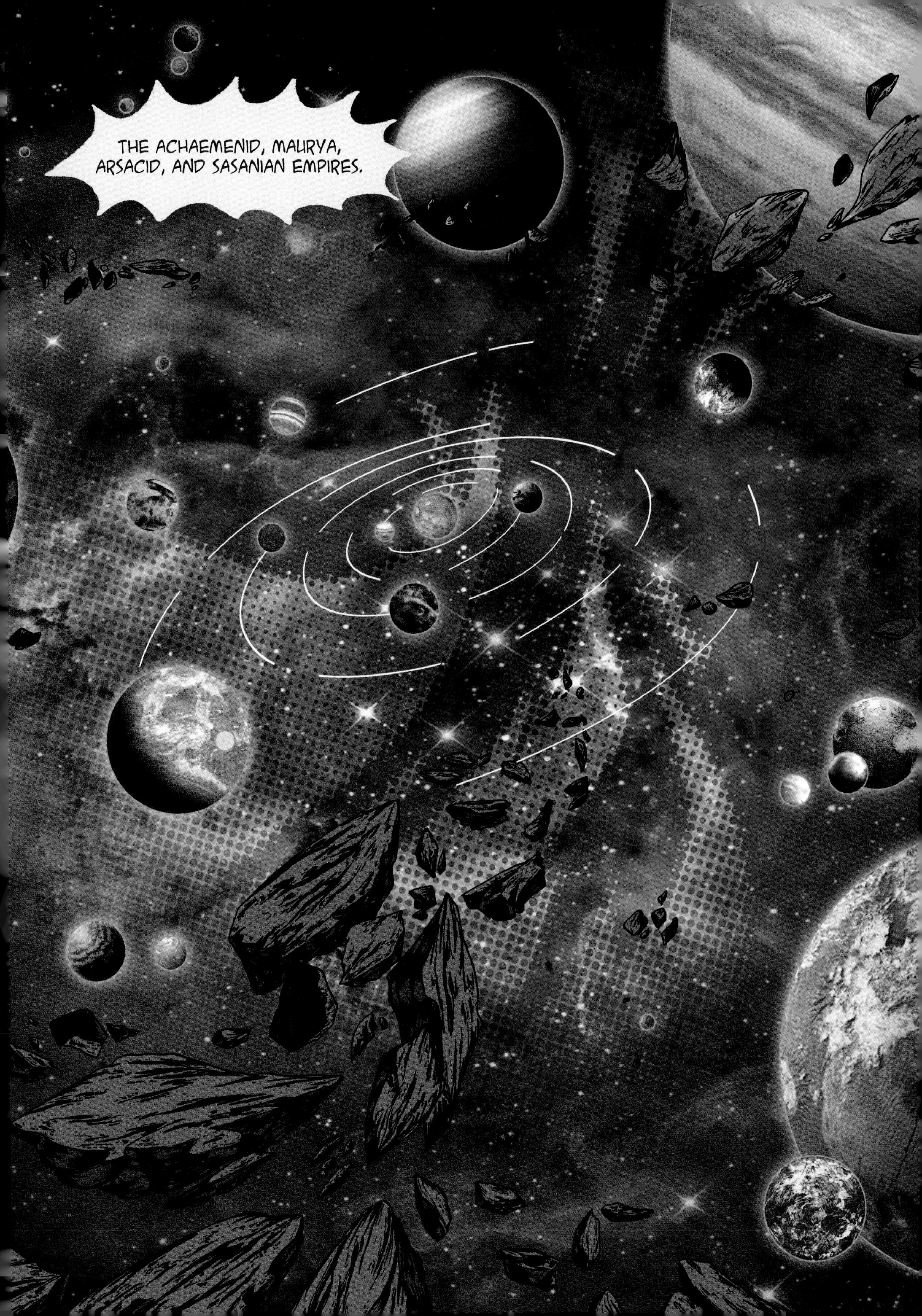
THE ACHAEMENID, MAURYA, ARSACID, AND SASANIAN EMPIRES.

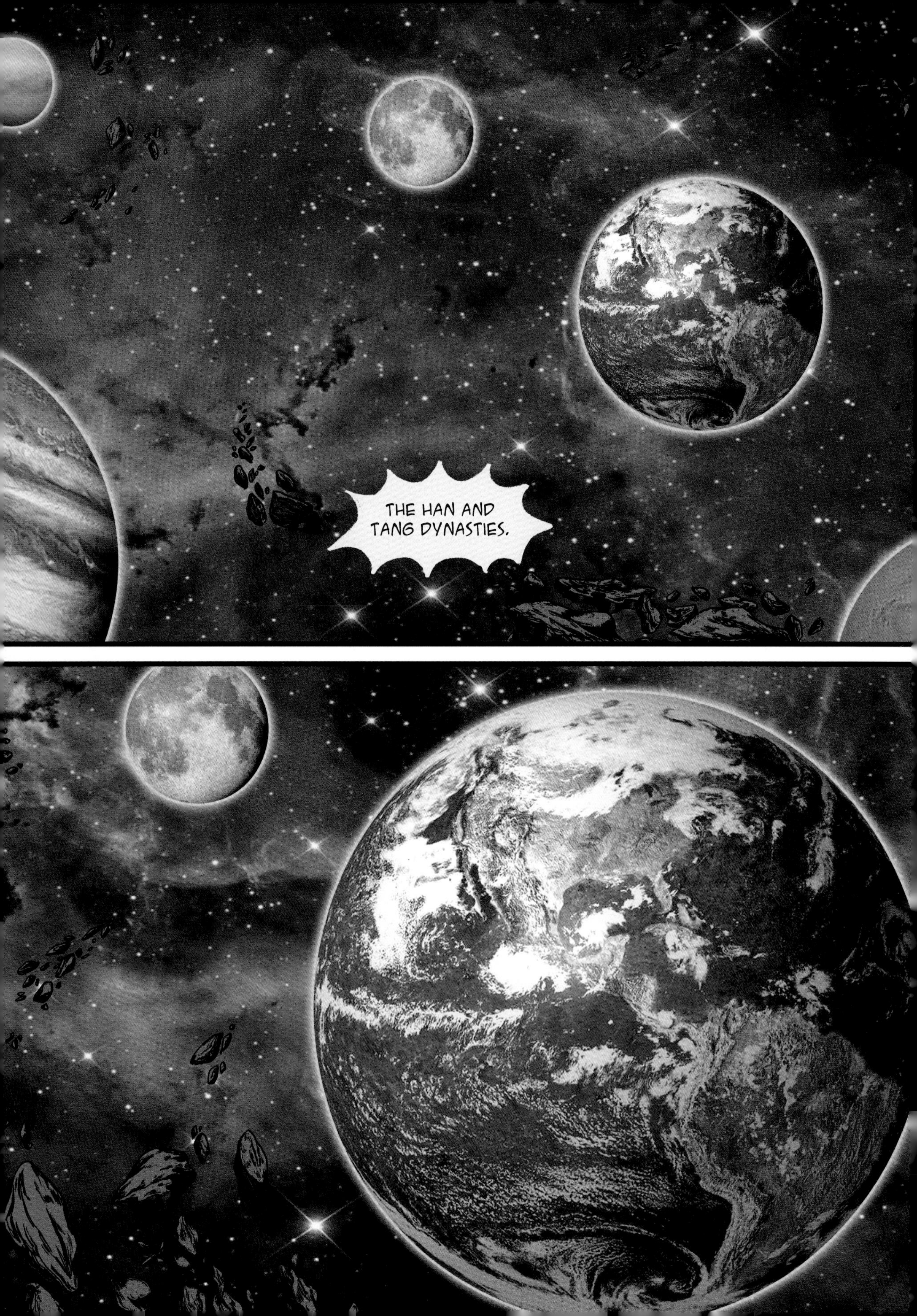
THE HAN AND TANG DYNASTIES.

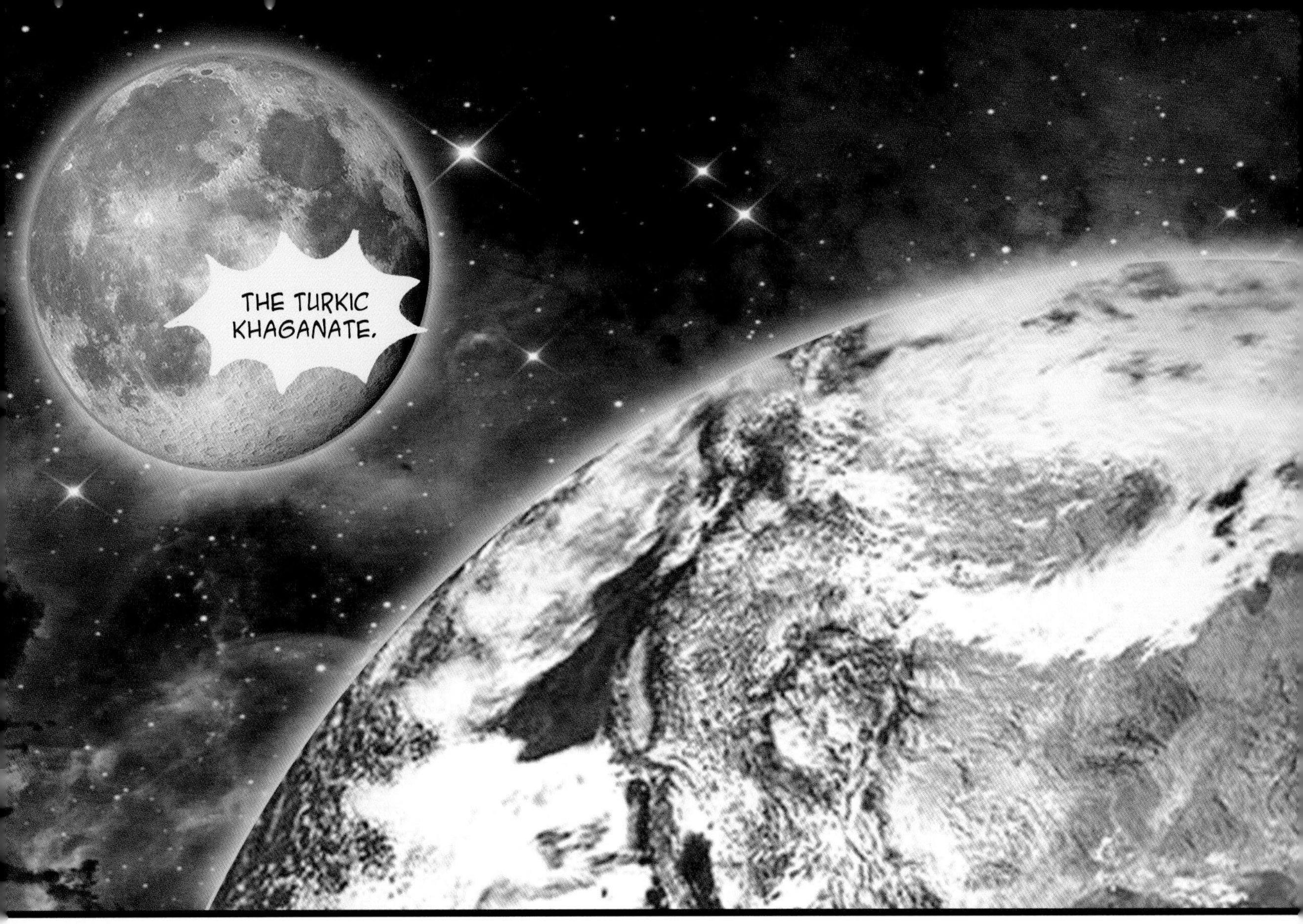
THE TURKIC KHAGANATE.
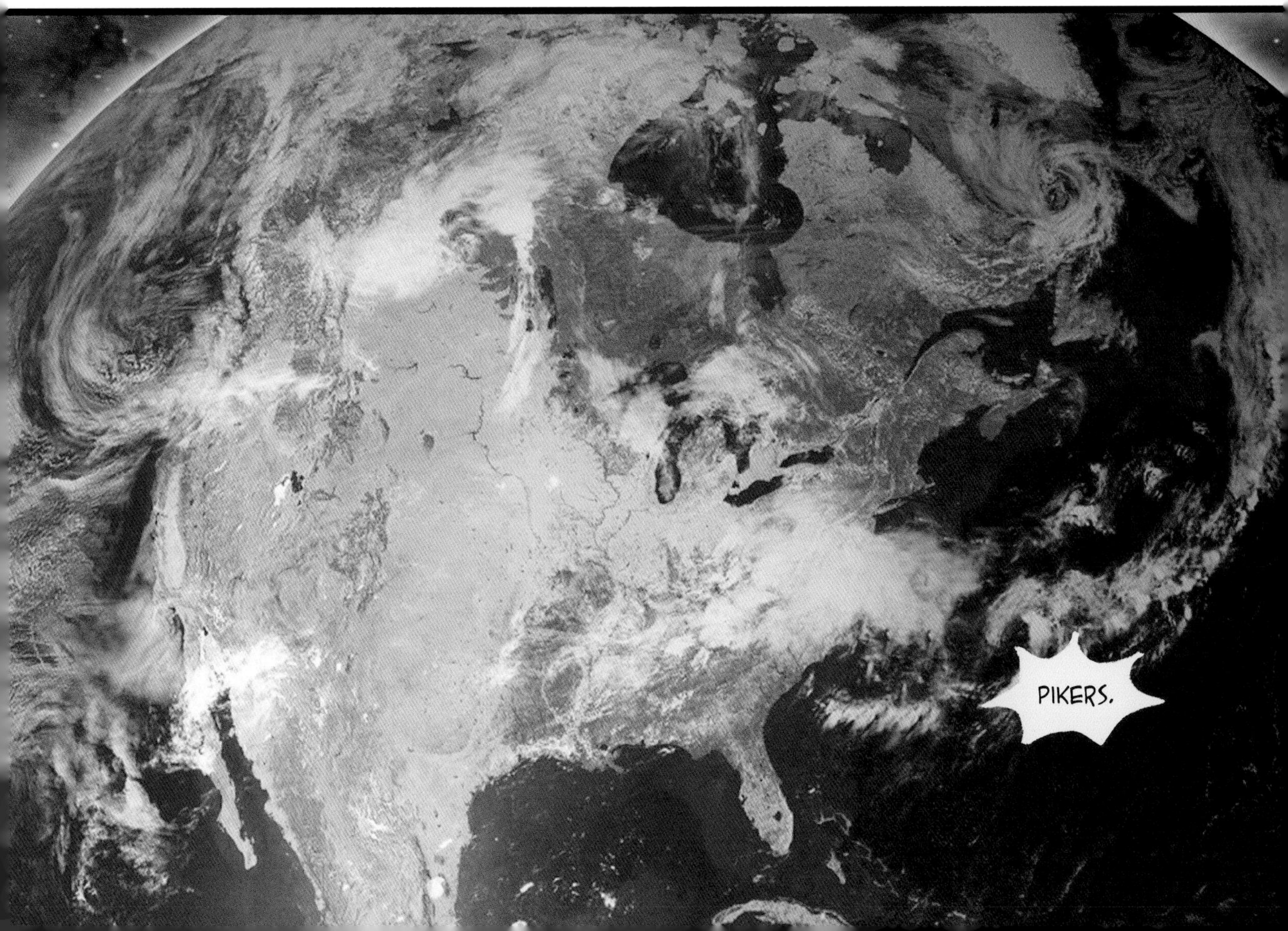
PIKERS.

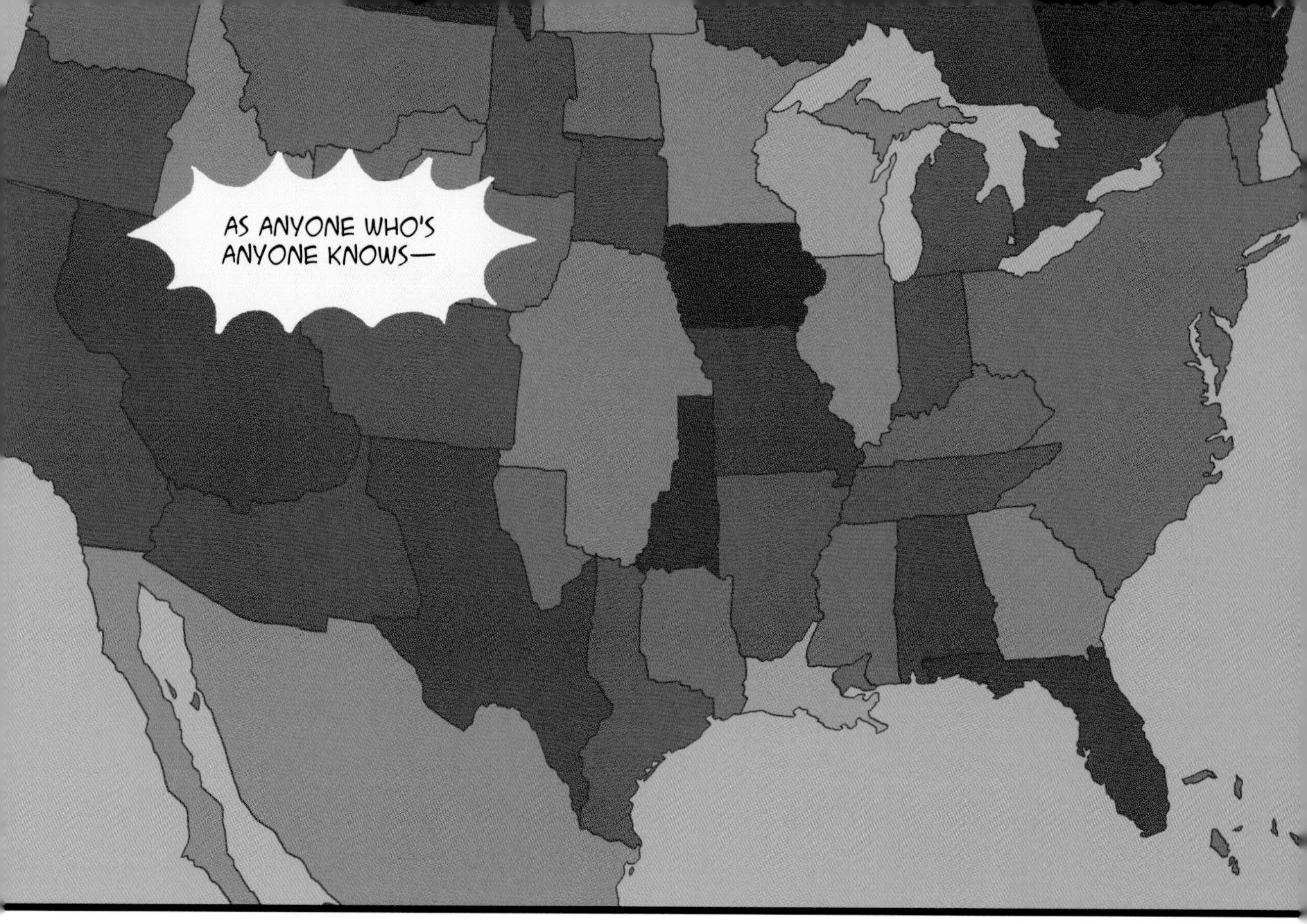
AS ANYONE WHO'S
ANYONE KNOWS—

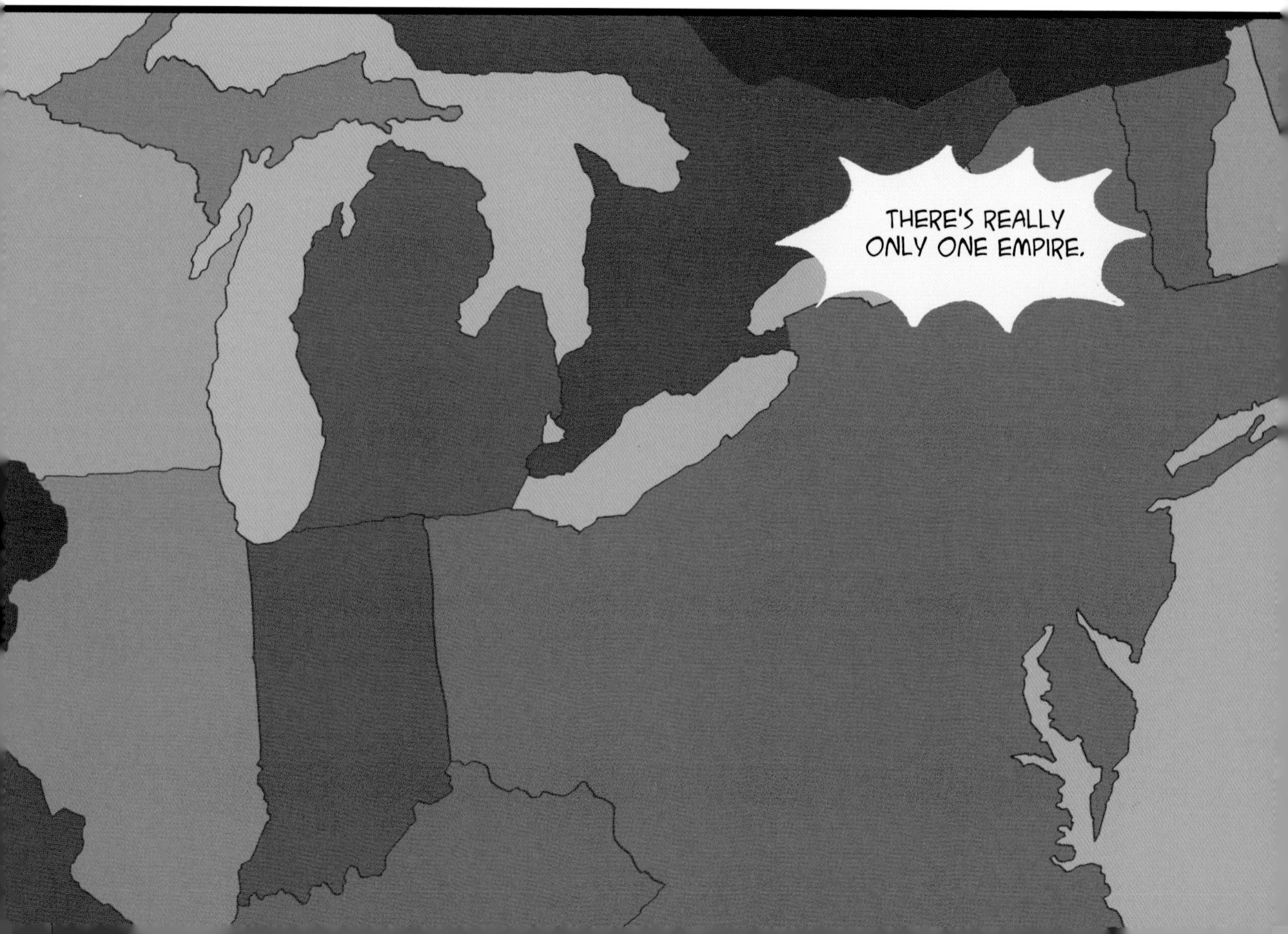
THERE'S REALLY
ONLY ONE EMPIRE.

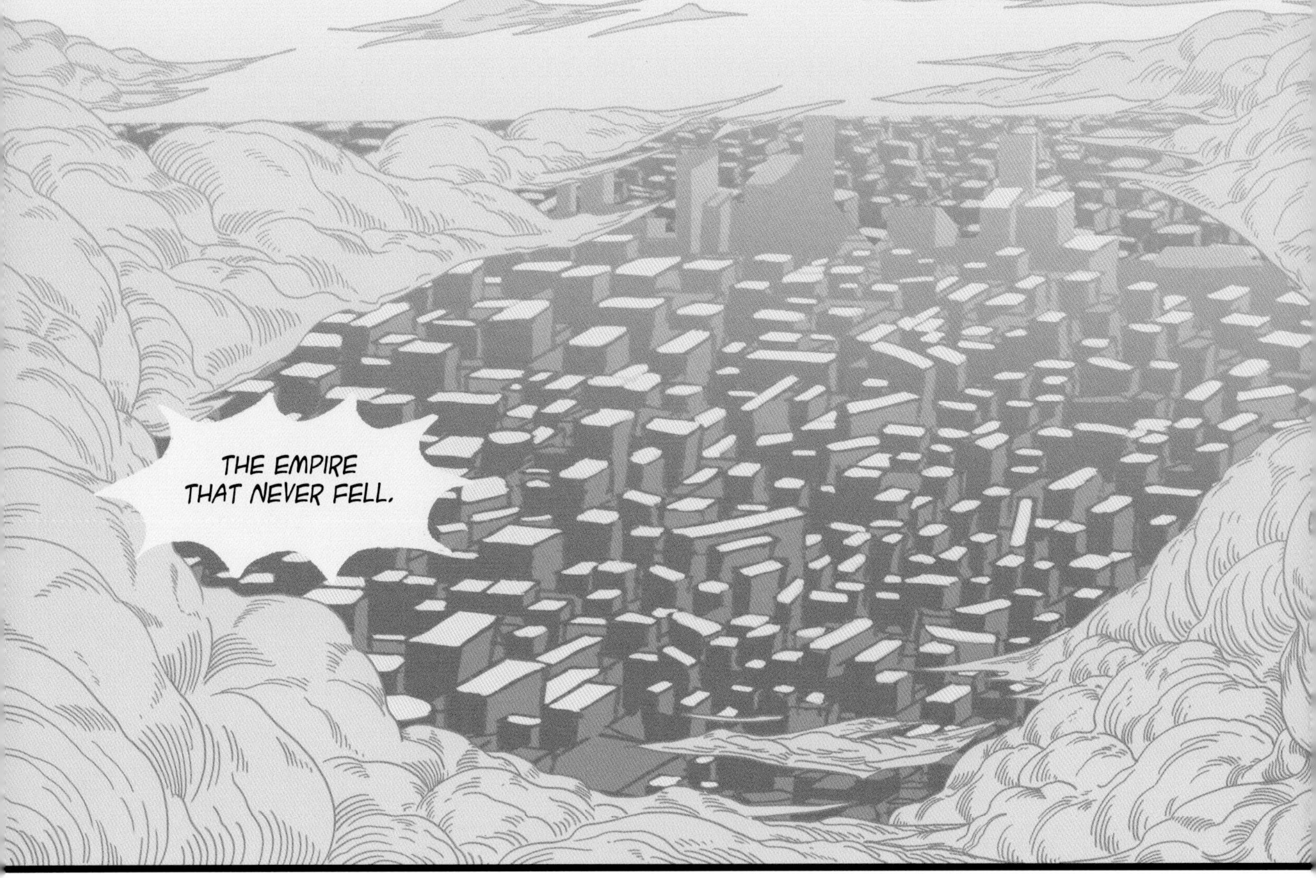
THE EMPIRE THAT NEVER FELL.

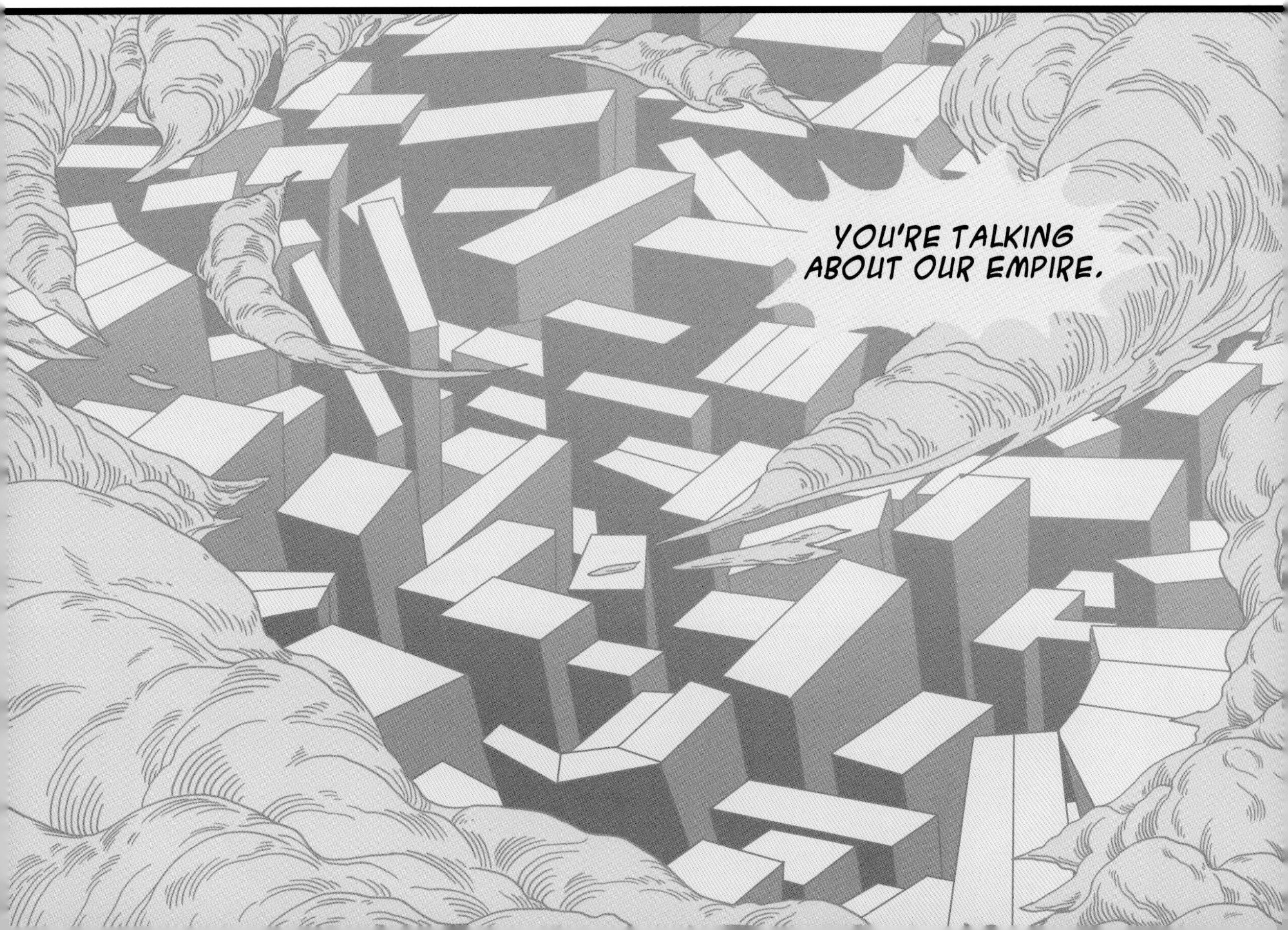
YOU'RE TALKING ABOUT OUR EMPIRE.

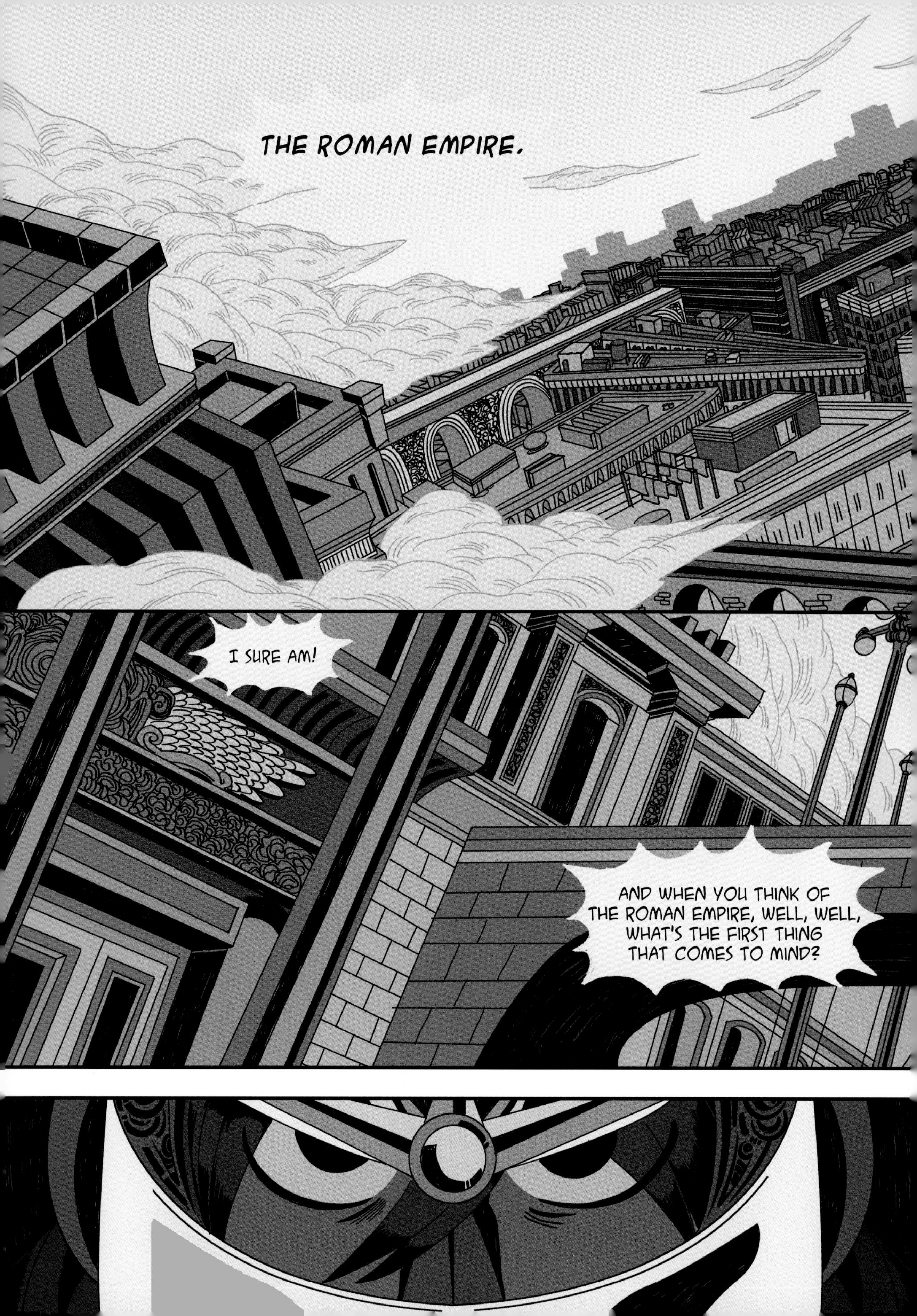
THE ROMAN EMPIRE.
I SURE AM!
AND WHEN YOU THINK OF THE ROMAN EMPIRE, WELL, WELL, WHAT'S THE FIRST THING THAT COMES TO MIND?

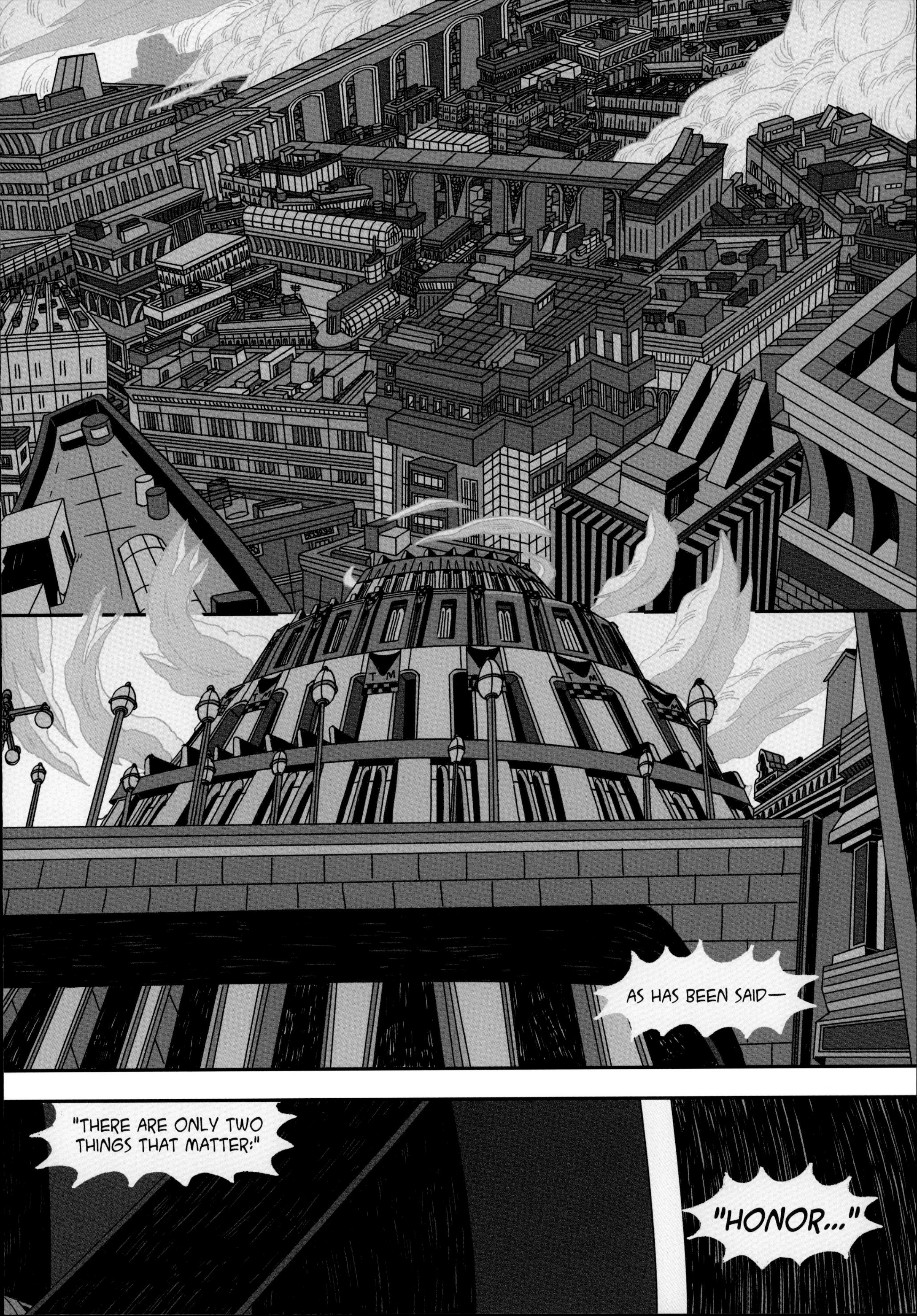
AS HAS BEEN SAID—
"THERE ARE ONLY TWO THINGS THAT MATTER:"
"HONOR..."

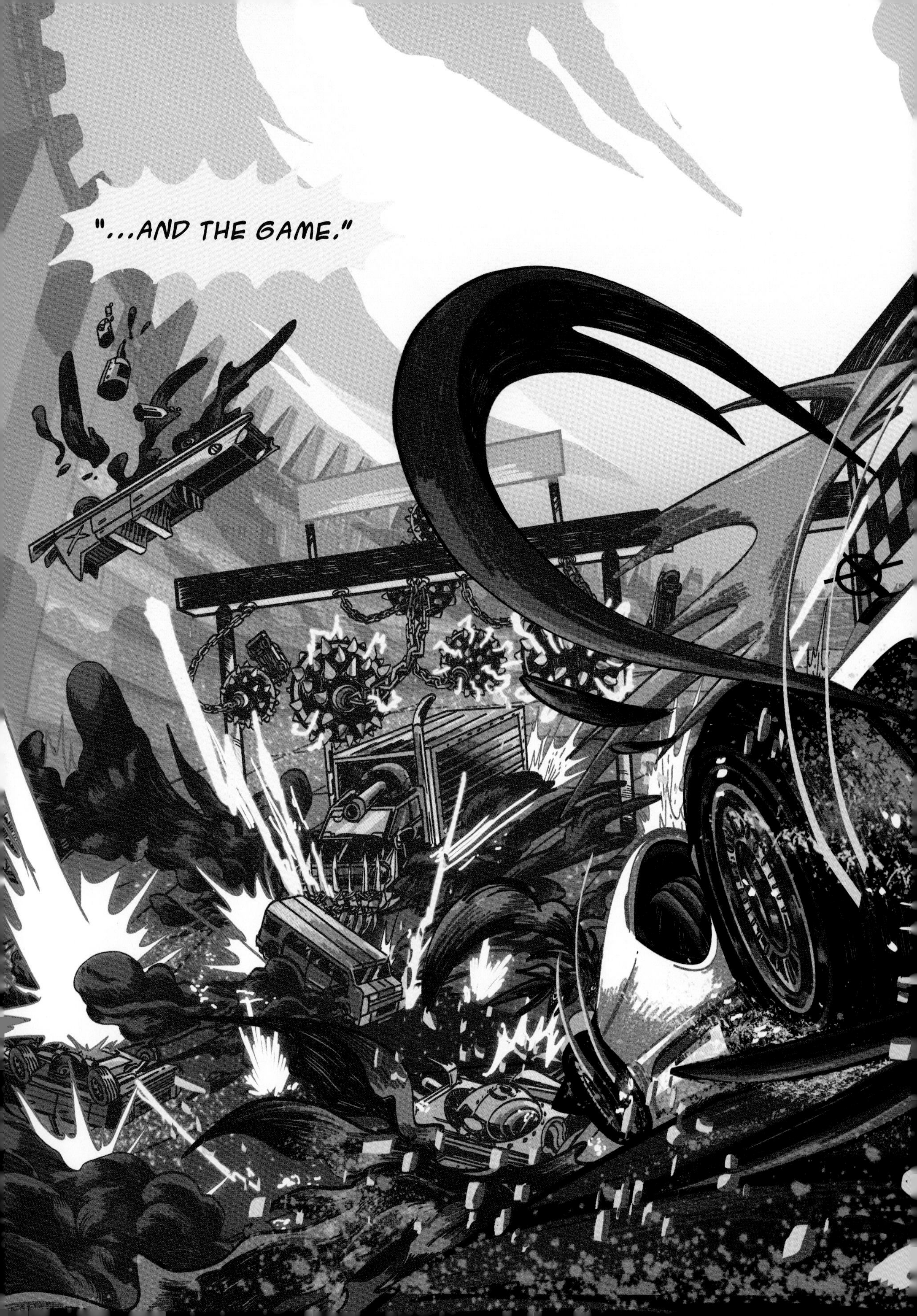
"...AND THE GAME."

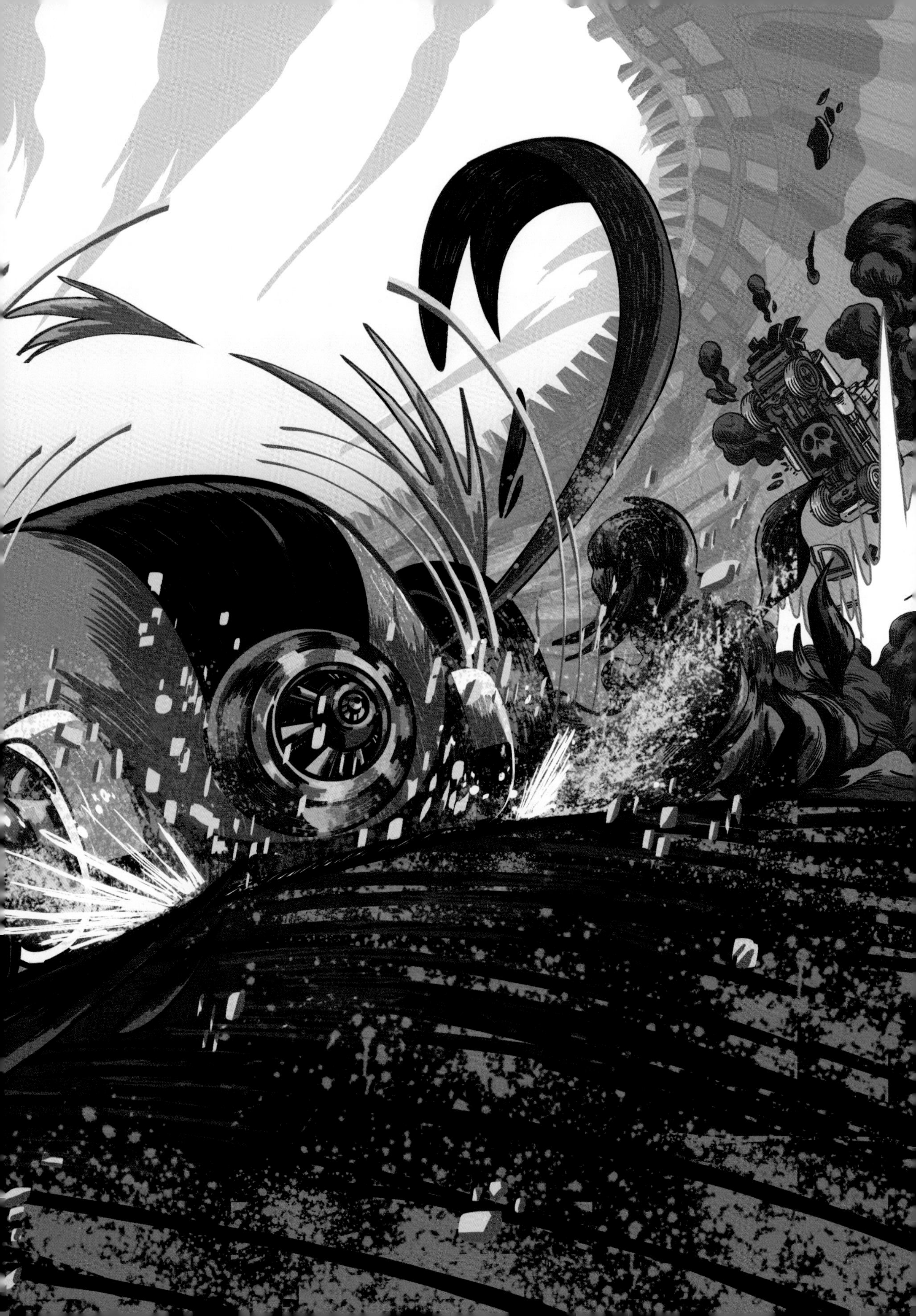

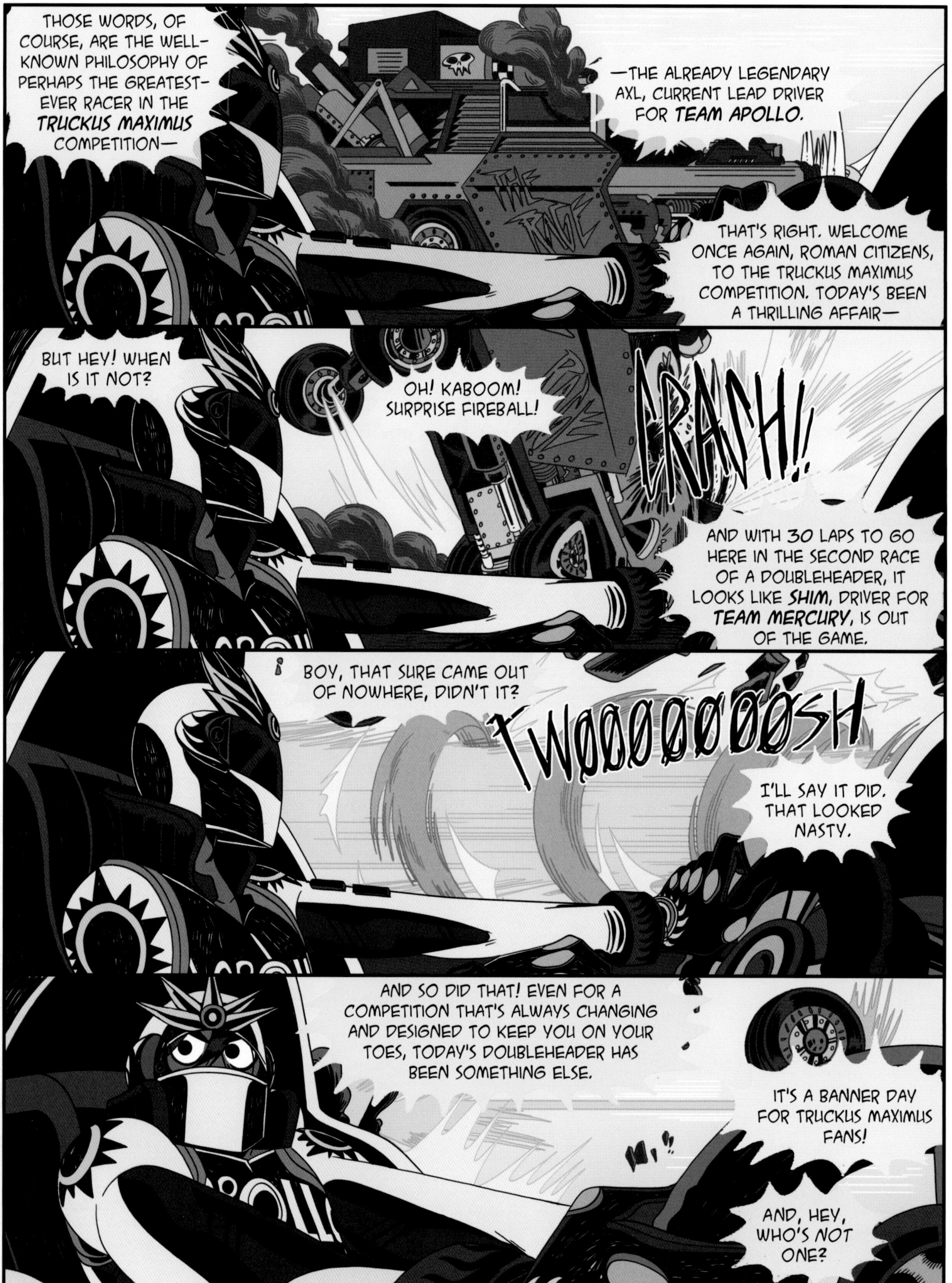
THOSE WORDS, OF COURSE, ARE THE WELL-KNOWN PHILOSOPHY OF PERHAPS THE GREATEST-EVER RACER IN THE TRUCKUS MAXIMUS COMPETITION—
—THE ALREADY LEGENDARY AXL, CURRENT LEAD DRIVER FOR TEAM APOLLO.
THAT'S RIGHT. WELCOME ONCE AGAIN, ROMAN CITIZENS, TO THE TRUCKUS MAXIMUS COMPETITION. TODAY'S BEEN A THRILLING AFFAIR—
BUT HEY! WHEN IS IT NOT?
OH! KABOOM! SURPRISE FIREBALL!
CRASH!!
AND WITH 30 LAPS TO GO HERE IN THE SECOND RACE OF A DOUBLEHEADER, IT LOOKS LIKE SHIM, DRIVER FOR TEAM MERCURY, IS OUT OF THE GAME.
BOY, THAT SURE CAME OUT OF NOWHERE, DIDN'T IT?
TWOOOOOOOSH
I'LL SAY IT DID. THAT LOOKED NASTY.
AND SO DID THAT! EVEN FOR A COMPETITION THAT'S ALWAYS CHANGING AND DESIGNED TO KEEP YOU ON YOUR TOES, TODAY'S DOUBLEHEADER HAS BEEN SOMETHING ELSE.
IT'S A BANNER DAY FOR TRUCKUS MAXIMUS FANS!
AND, HEY, WHO'S NOT ONE?

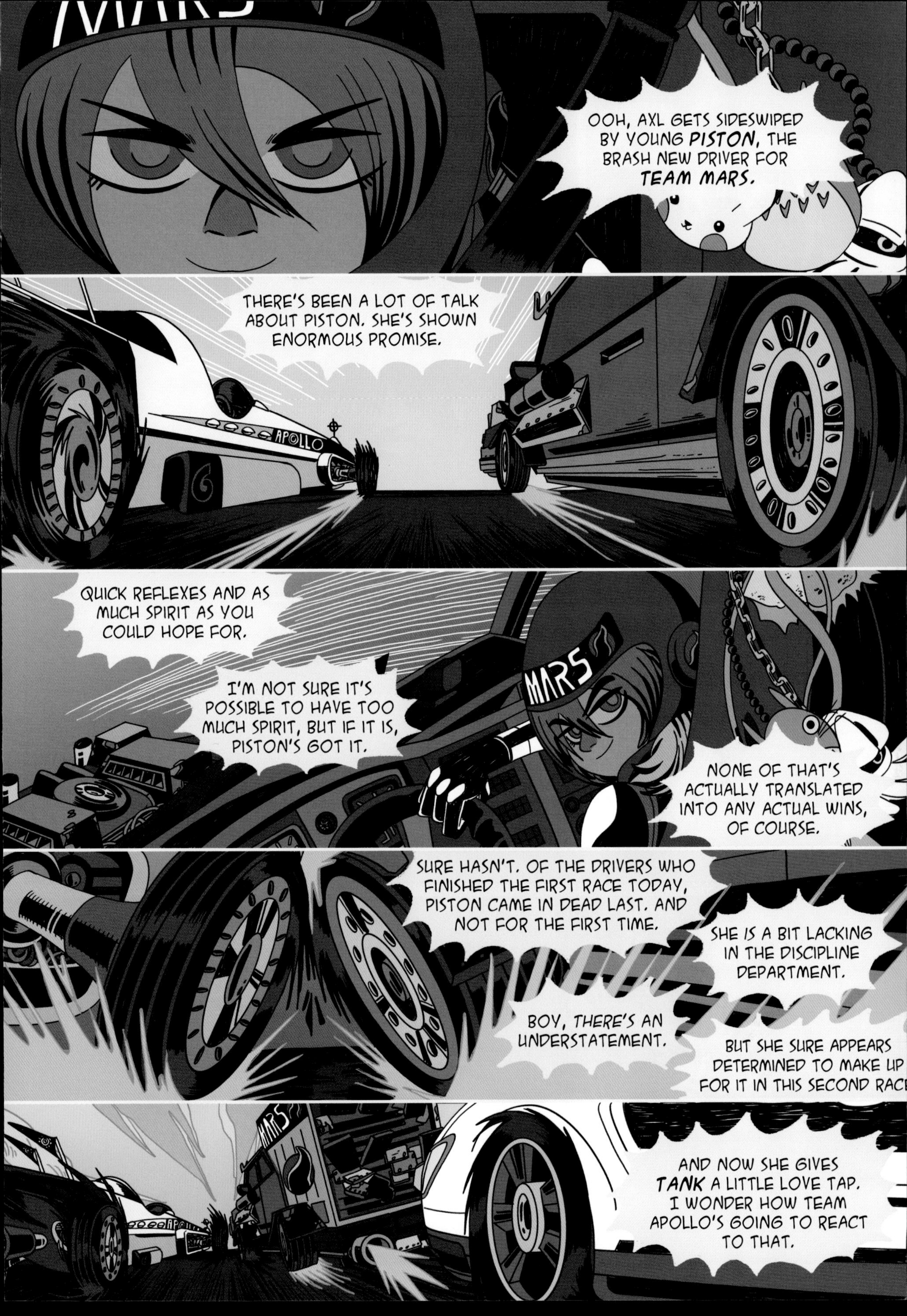
MARS
OOH, AXL GETS SIDESWIPED BY YOUNG PISTON, THE BRASH NEW DRIVER FOR TEAM MARS.
THERE'S BEEN A LOT OF TALK ABOUT PISTON. SHE'S SHOWN ENORMOUS PROMISE.
APOLLO
QUICK REFLEXES AND AS MUCH SPIRIT AS YOU COULD HOPE FOR.
I'M NOT SURE IT'S POSSIBLE TO HAVE TOO MUCH SPIRIT, BUT IF IT IS, PISTON'S GOT IT.
MARS
NONE OF THAT'S ACTUALLY TRANSLATED INTO ANY ACTUAL WINS, OF COURSE.
SURE HASN'T. OF THE DRIVERS WHO FINISHED THE FIRST RACE TODAY, PISTON CAME IN DEAD LAST. AND NOT FOR THE FIRST TIME.
SHE IS A BIT LACKING IN THE DISCIPLINE DEPARTMENT.
BOY, THERE'S AN UNDERSTATEMENT.
BUT SHE SURE APPEARS DETERMINED TO MAKE UP FOR IT IN THIS SECOND RAC
MARS
APOLLO
AND NOW SHE GIVES TANK A LITTLE LOVE TAP. I WONDER HOW TEAM APOLLO'S GOING TO REACT TO THAT.

ALL GOOD, TANK?

I THINK SO, AXL. FEELS LIKE THAT NEW KID LOCKED OUR BUMPERS TOGETHER. IF SHE GIVES ME A SECOND, I THINK I CAN UNHOOK US.

OH! PISTON HITS THE BRAKES AND CRANKS THE WHEEL!

TANK'S STILL STUCK TO PISTON'S VEHICLE.

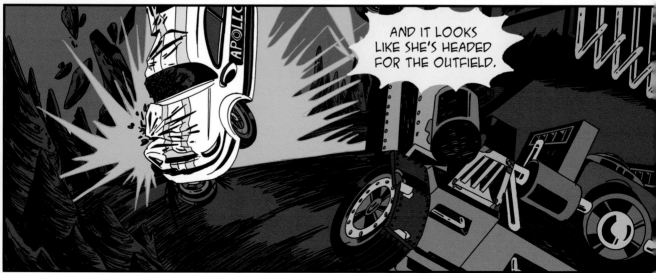

AND IT LOOKS LIKE SHE'S HEADED FOR THE OUTFIELD.

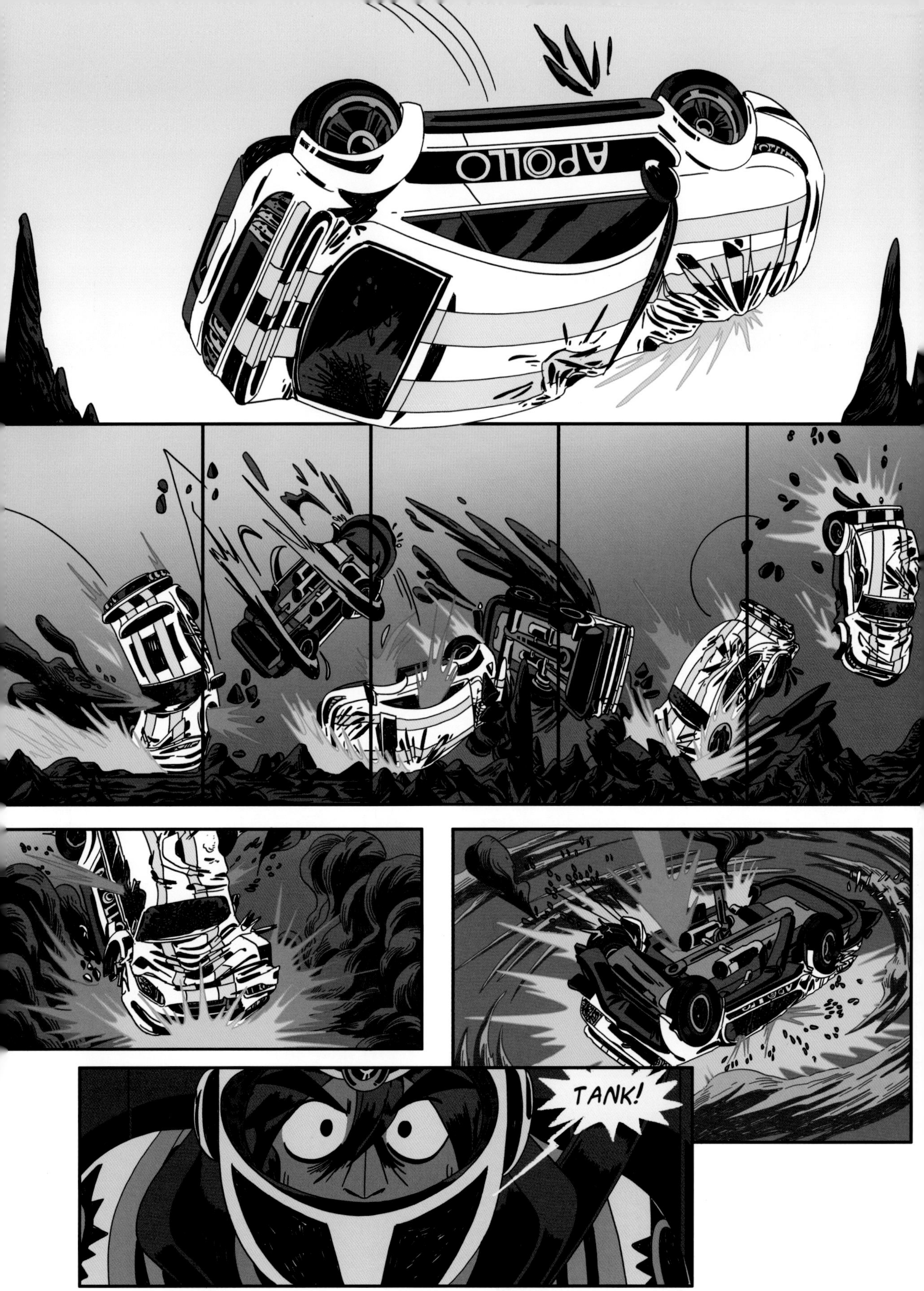
APOLLO
TANK!

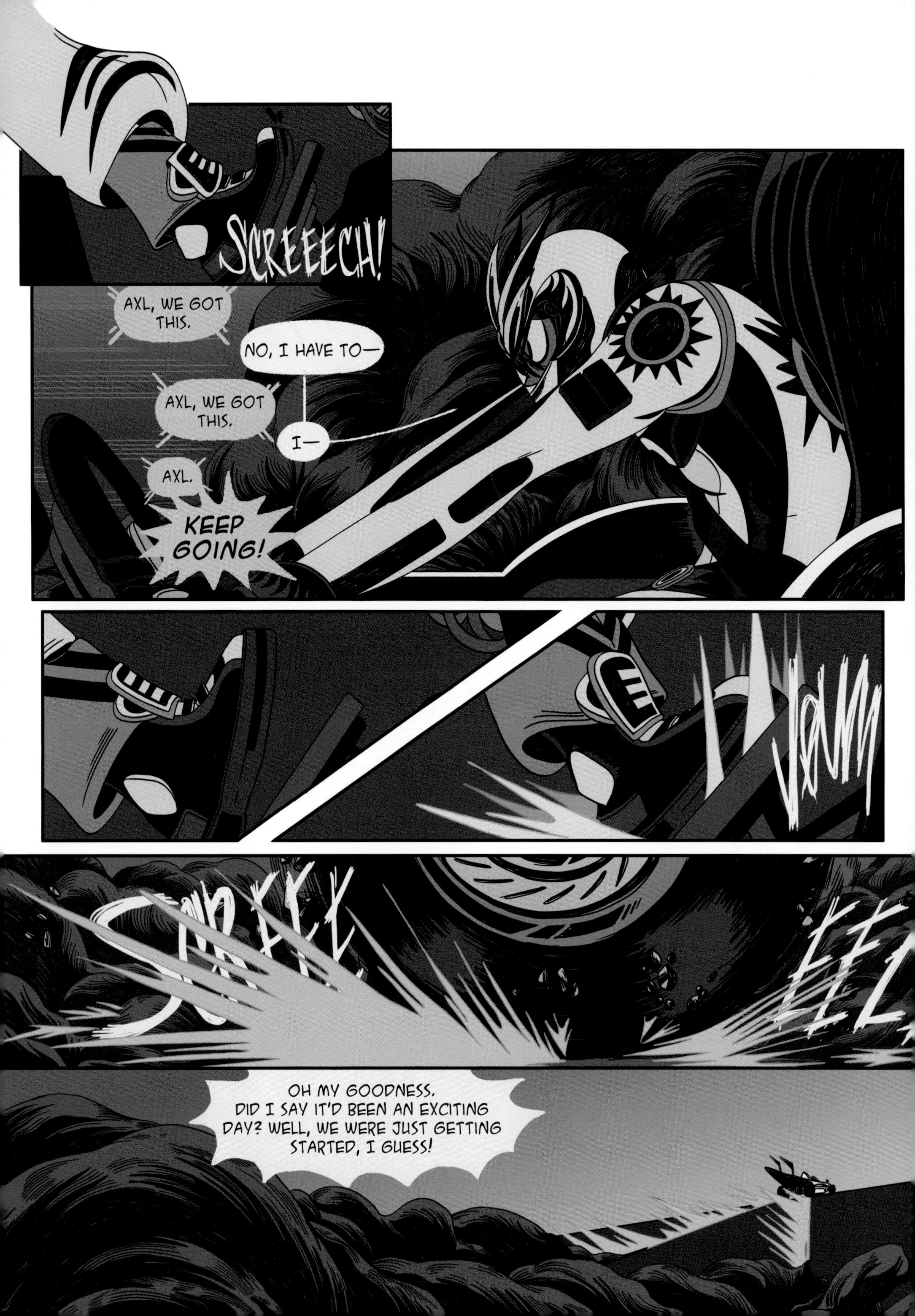
SCREEECH!
AXL, WE GOT THIS.
NO, I HAVE TO—
AXL, WE GOT THIS.
I—
AXL.
KEEP GOING!
OH MY GOODNESS. DID I SAY IT'D BEEN AN EXCITING DAY? WELL, WE WERE JUST GETTING STARTED, I GUESS!

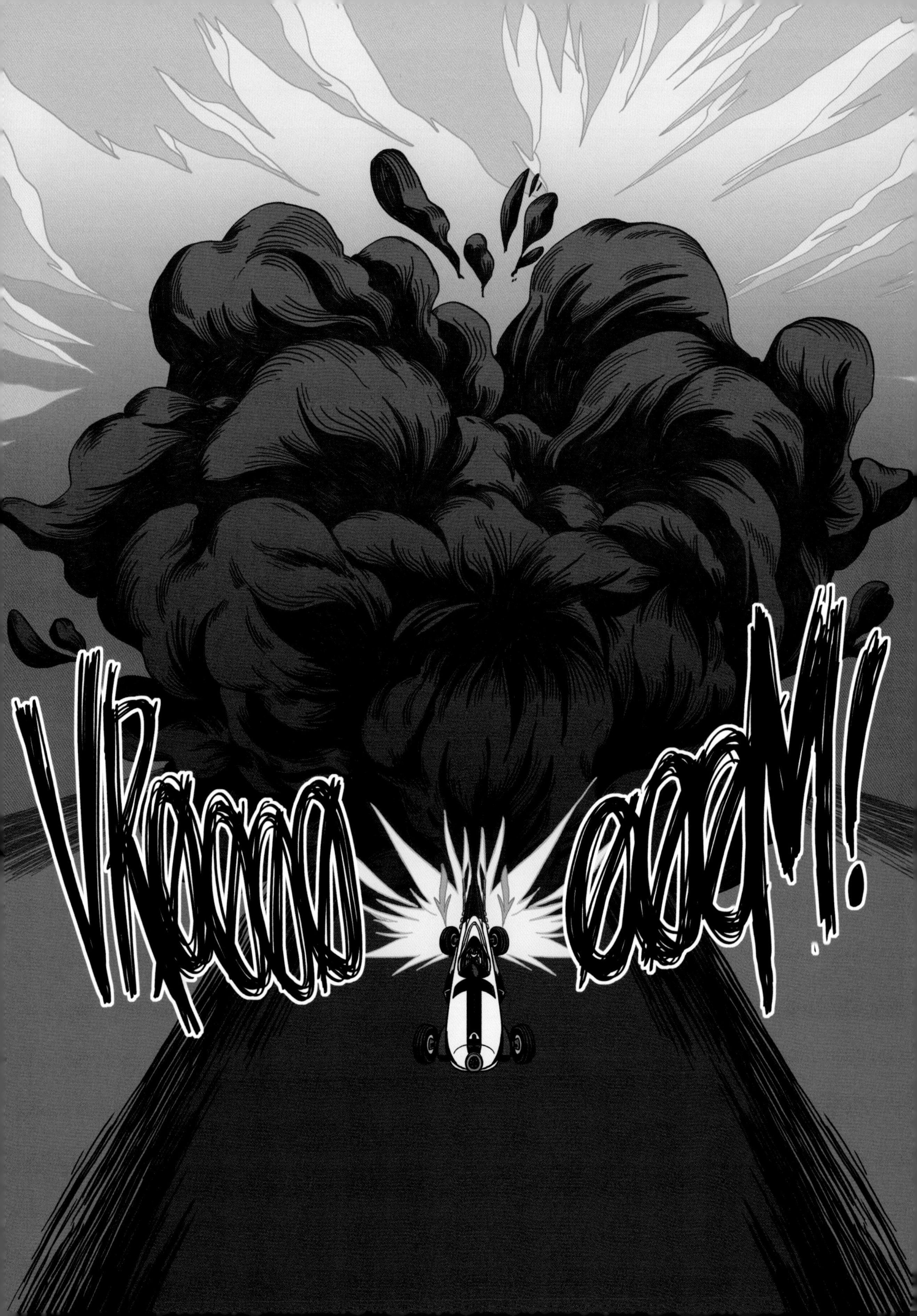
VRoooo ooooM!

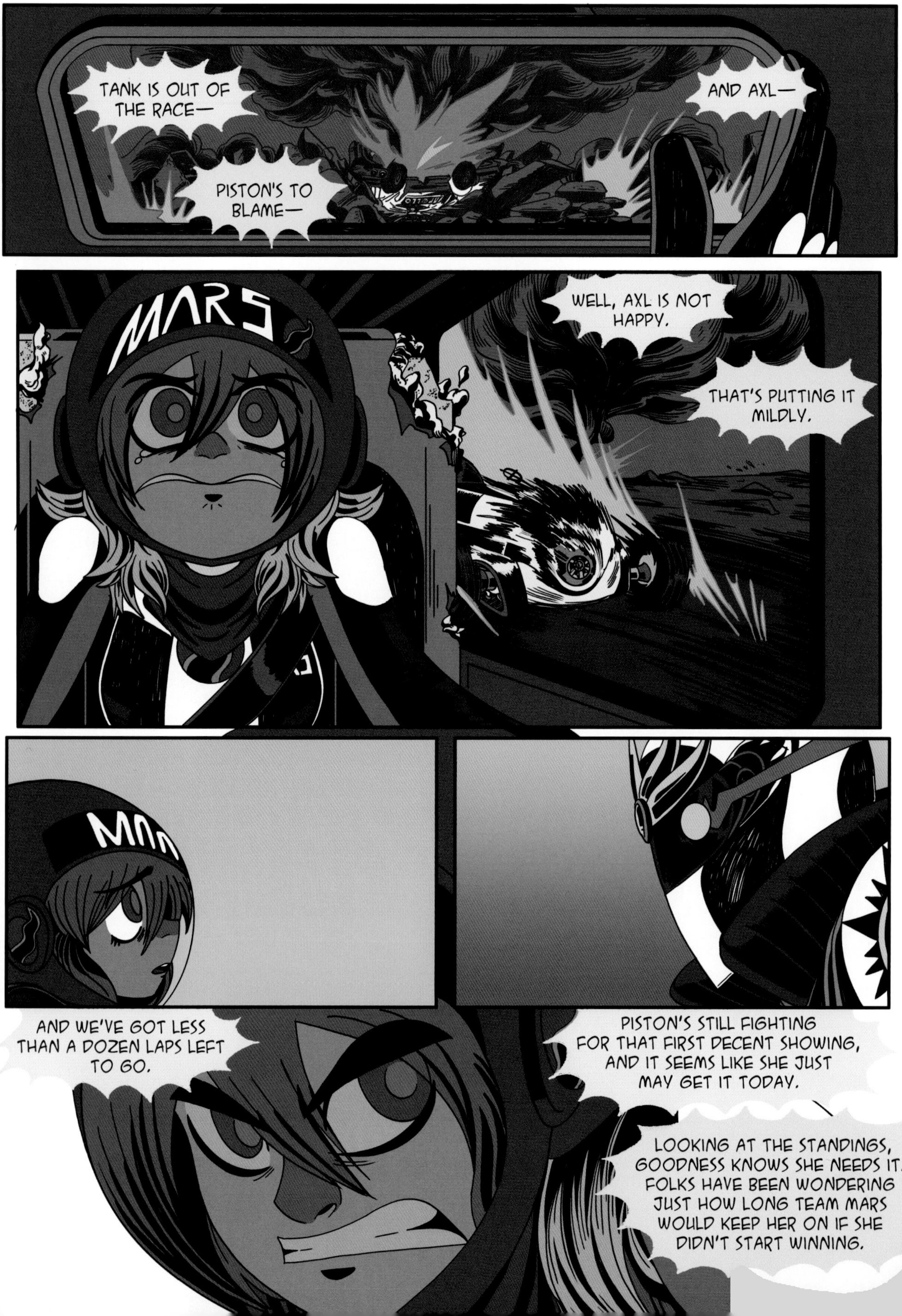
TANK IS OUT OF THE RACE—
PISTON'S TO BLAME—
AND AXL—
WELL, AXL IS NOT HAPPY.
THAT'S PUTTING IT MILDLY.
MARS
MARS
AND WE'VE GOT LESS THAN A DOZEN LAPS LEFT TO GO.
PISTON'S STILL FIGHTING FOR THAT FIRST DECENT SHOWING, AND IT SEEMS LIKE SHE JUST MAY GET IT TODAY.
LOOKING AT THE STANDINGS, GOODNESS KNOWS SHE NEEDS IT. FOLKS HAVE BEEN WONDERING JUST HOW LONG TEAM MARS WOULD KEEP HER ON IF SHE DIDN'T START WINNING.

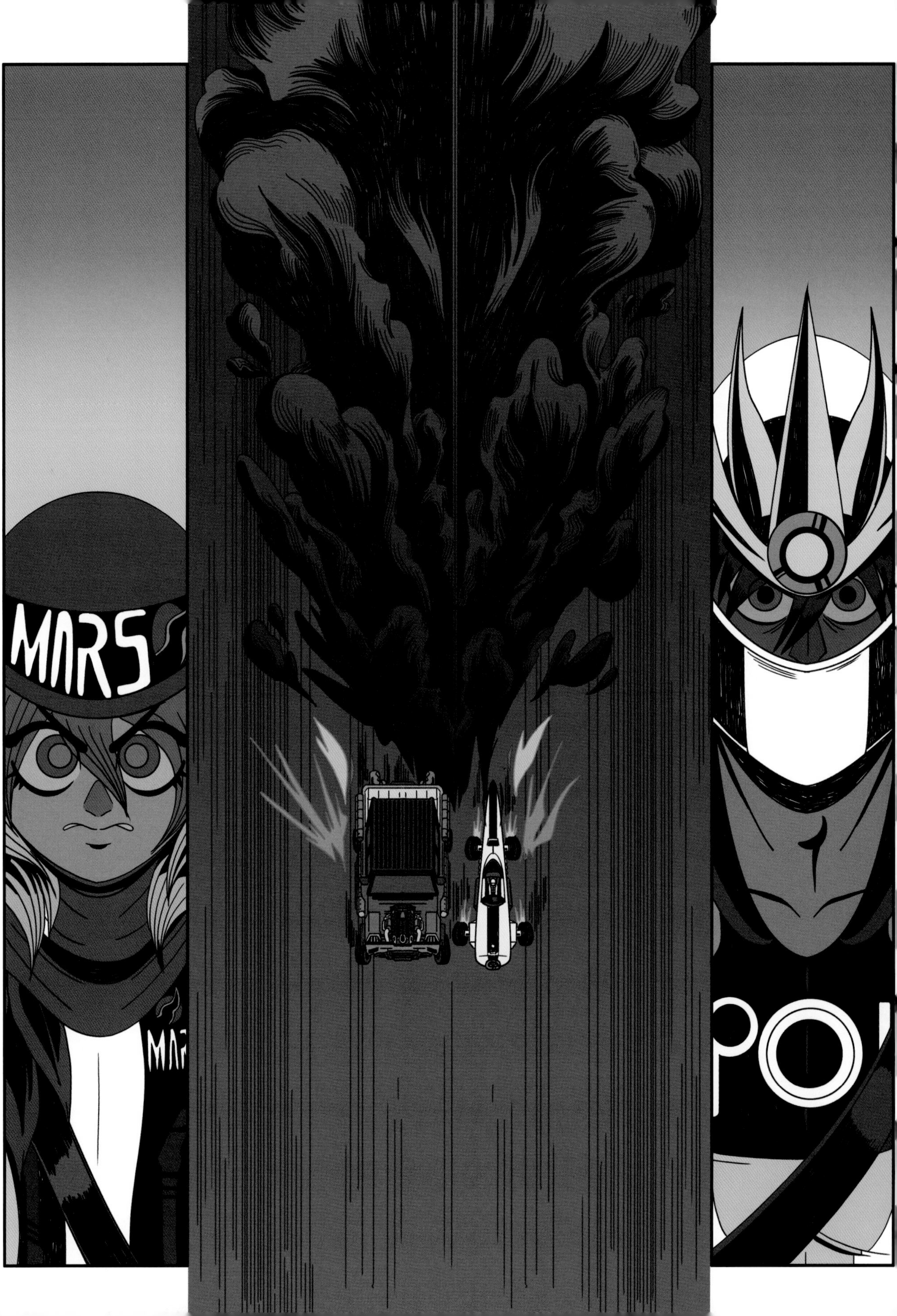
MARS

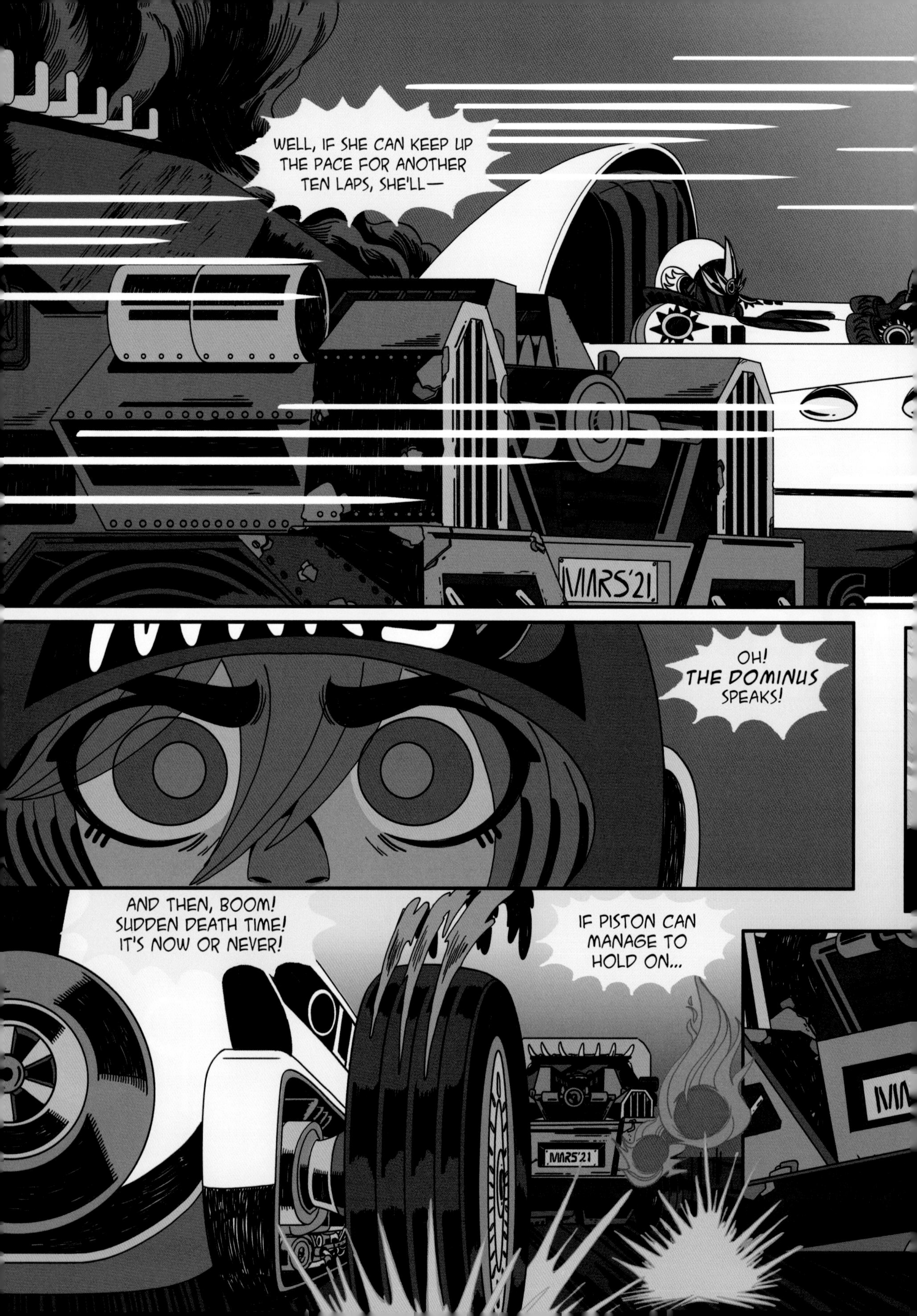
WELL, IF SHE CAN KEEP UP THE PACE FOR ANOTHER TEN LAPS, SHE'LL—
MARS'21
OH! THE DOMINUS SPEAKS!
AND THEN, BOOM! SUDDEN DEATH TIME! IT'S NOW OR NEVER!
IF PISTON CAN MANAGE TO HOLD ON...
MARS'21

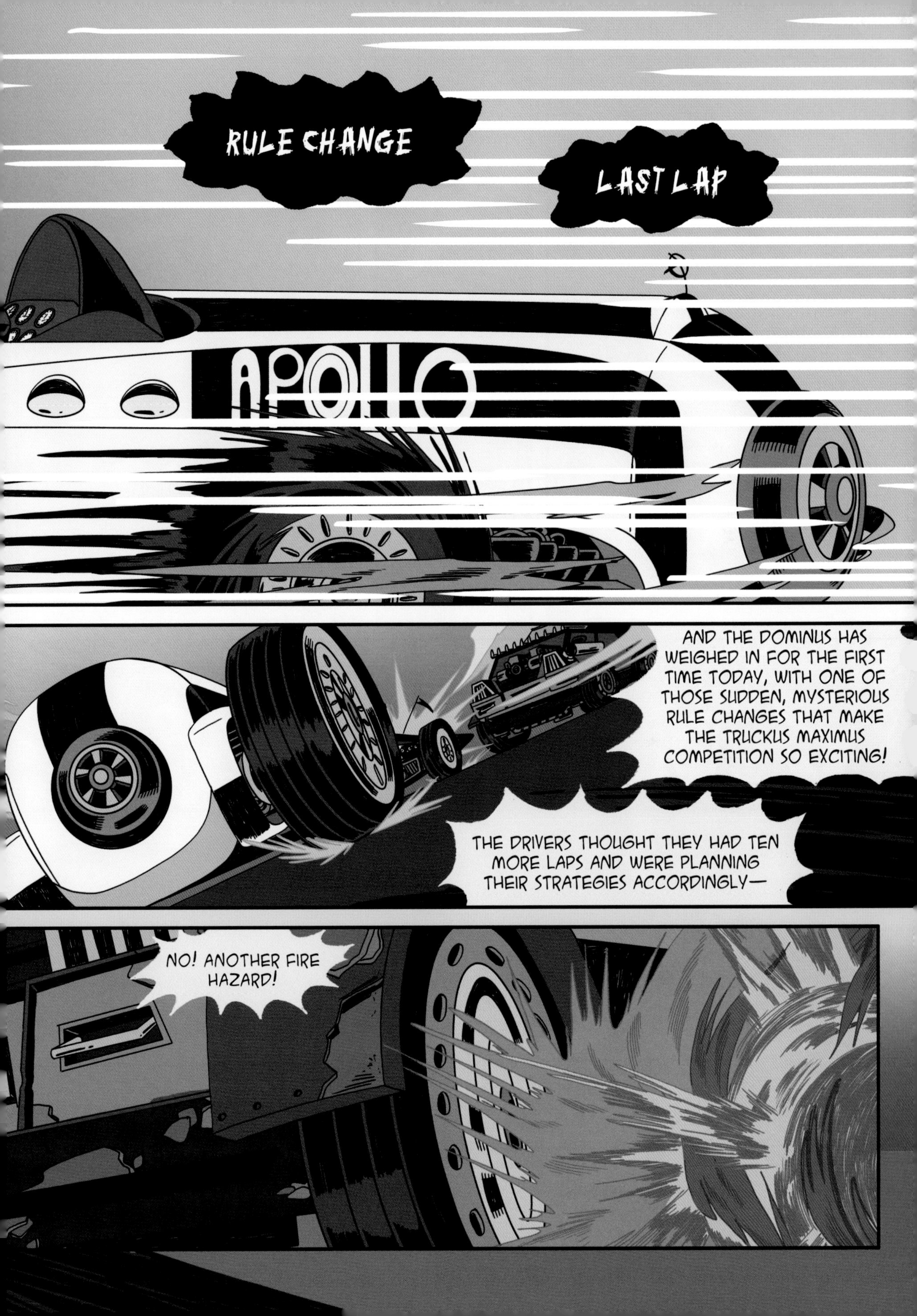
RULE CHANGE
LAST LAP
APOLLO
AND THE DOMINUS HAS WEIGHED IN FOR THE FIRST TIME TODAY, WITH ONE OF THOSE SUDDEN, MYSTERIOUS RULE CHANGES THAT MAKE THE TRUCKUS MAXIMUS COMPETITION SO EXCITING!
THE DRIVERS THOUGHT THEY HAD TEN MORE LAPS AND WERE PLANNING THEIR STRATEGIES ACCORDINGLY—
NO! ANOTHER FIRE HAZARD!

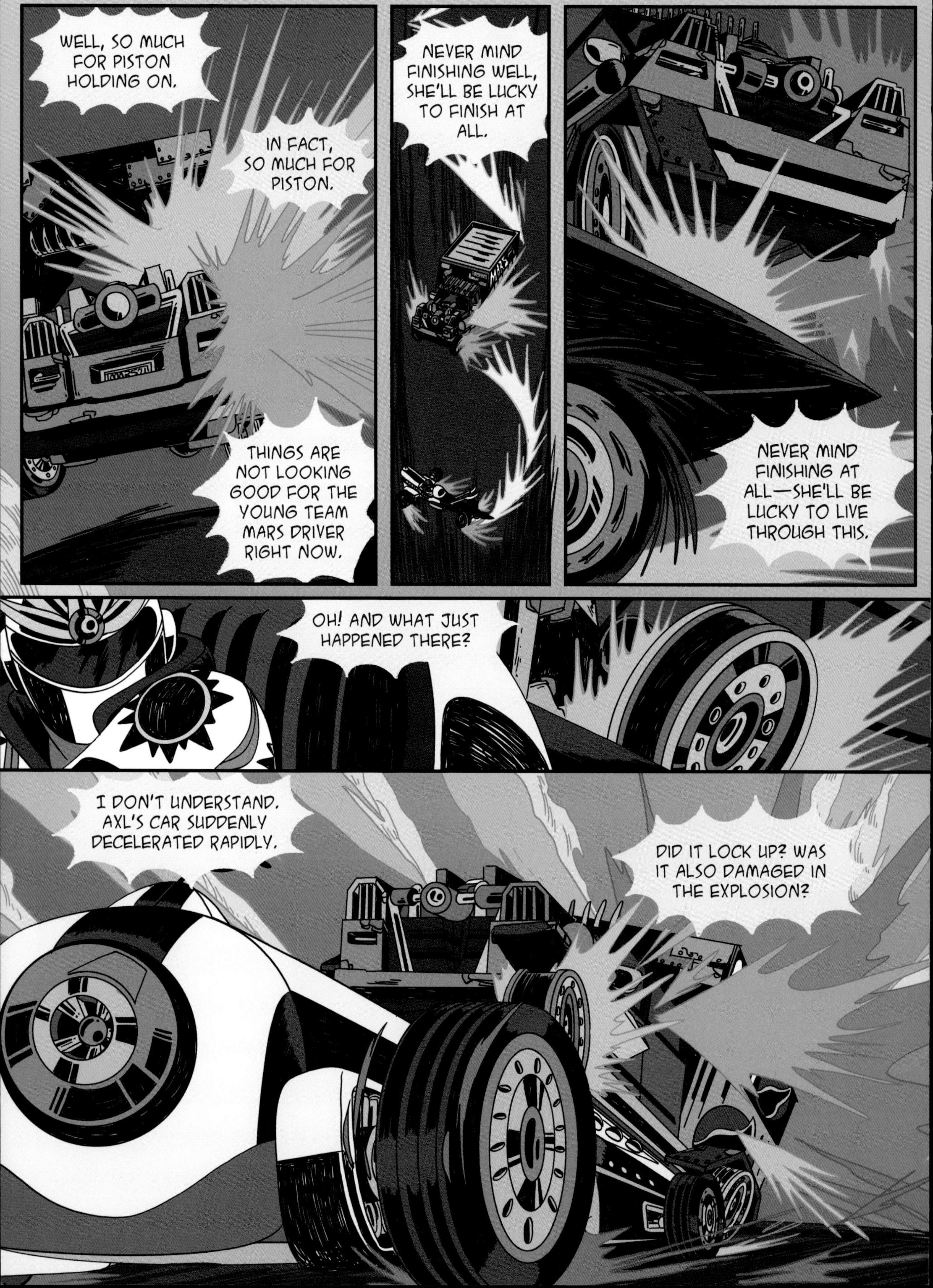
WELL, SO MUCH FOR PISTON HOLDING ON.
IN FACT, SO MUCH FOR PISTON.
THINGS ARE NOT LOOKING GOOD FOR THE YOUNG TEAM MARS DRIVER RIGHT NOW.
NEVER MIND FINISHING WELL, SHE'LL BE LUCKY TO FINISH AT ALL.
NEVER MIND FINISHING AT ALL—SHE'LL BE LUCKY TO LIVE THROUGH THIS.
OH! AND WHAT JUST HAPPENED THERE?
I DON'T UNDERSTAND. AXL'S CAR SUDDENLY DECELERATED RAPIDLY.
DID IT LOCK UP? WAS IT ALSO DAMAGED IN THE EXPLOSION?

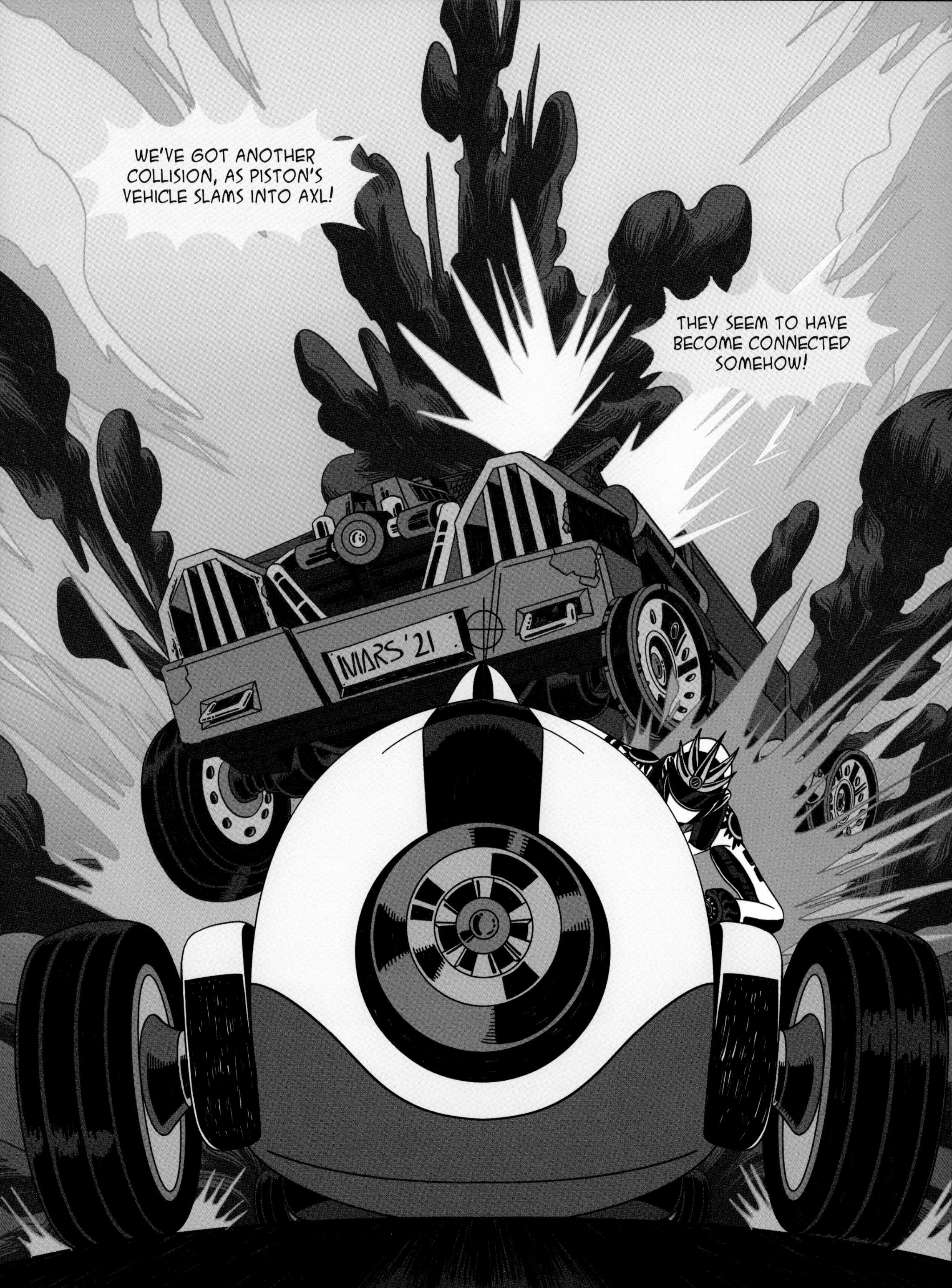
WE'VE GOT ANOTHER COLLISION, AS PISTON'S VEHICLE SLAMS INTO AXL!
THEY SEEM TO HAVE BECOME CONNECTED SOMEHOW!
MARS '21

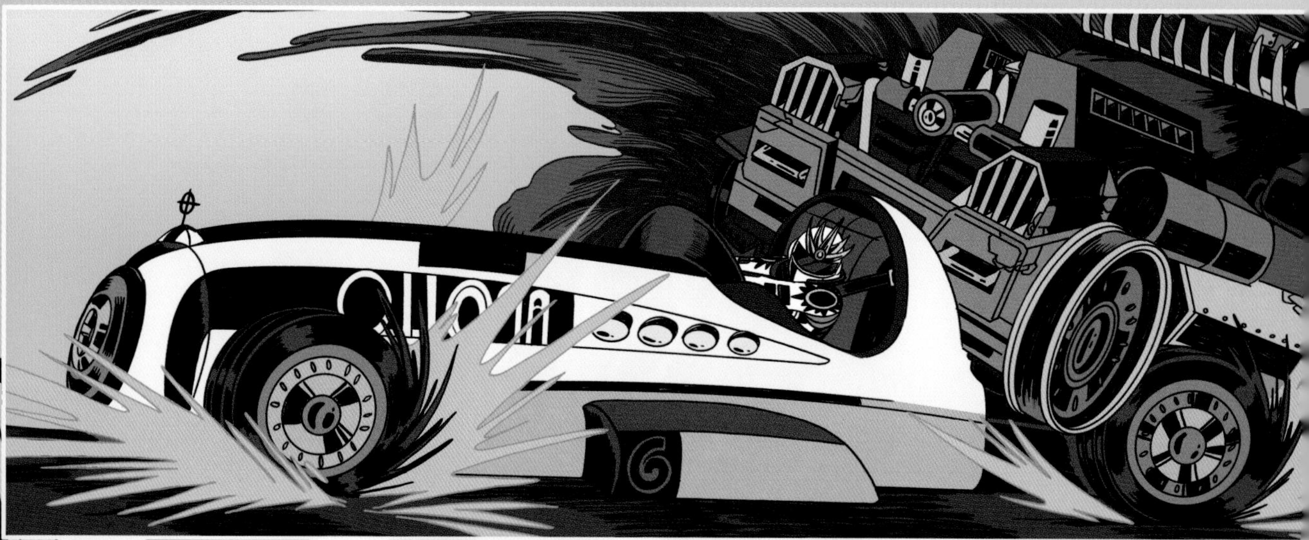

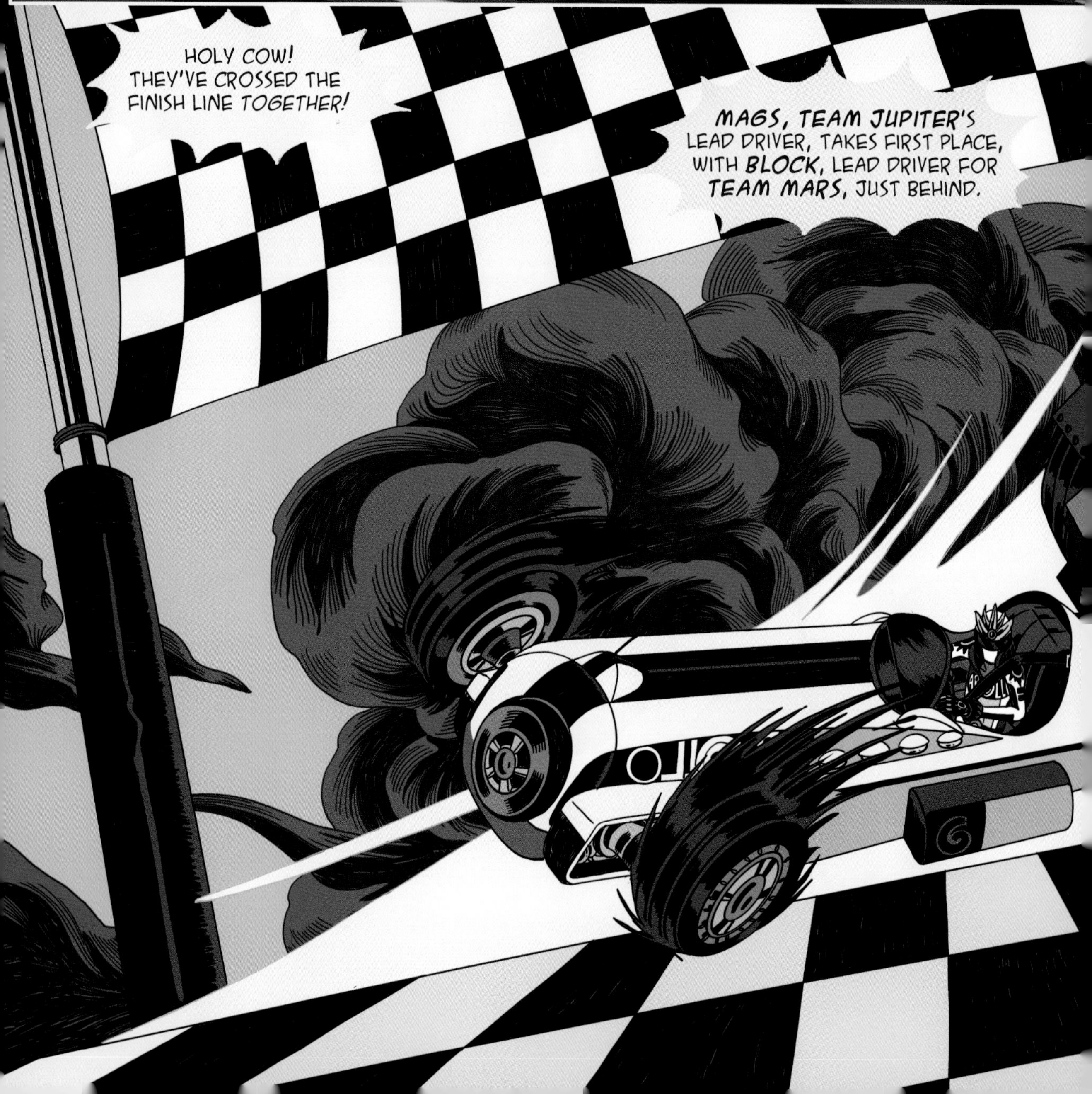
HOLY COW! THEY'VE CROSSED THE FINISH LINE TOGETHER!
MAGS, TEAM JUPITER'S LEAD DRIVER, TAKES FIRST PLACE, WITH BLOCK, LEAD DRIVER FOR TEAM MARS, JUST BEHIND.

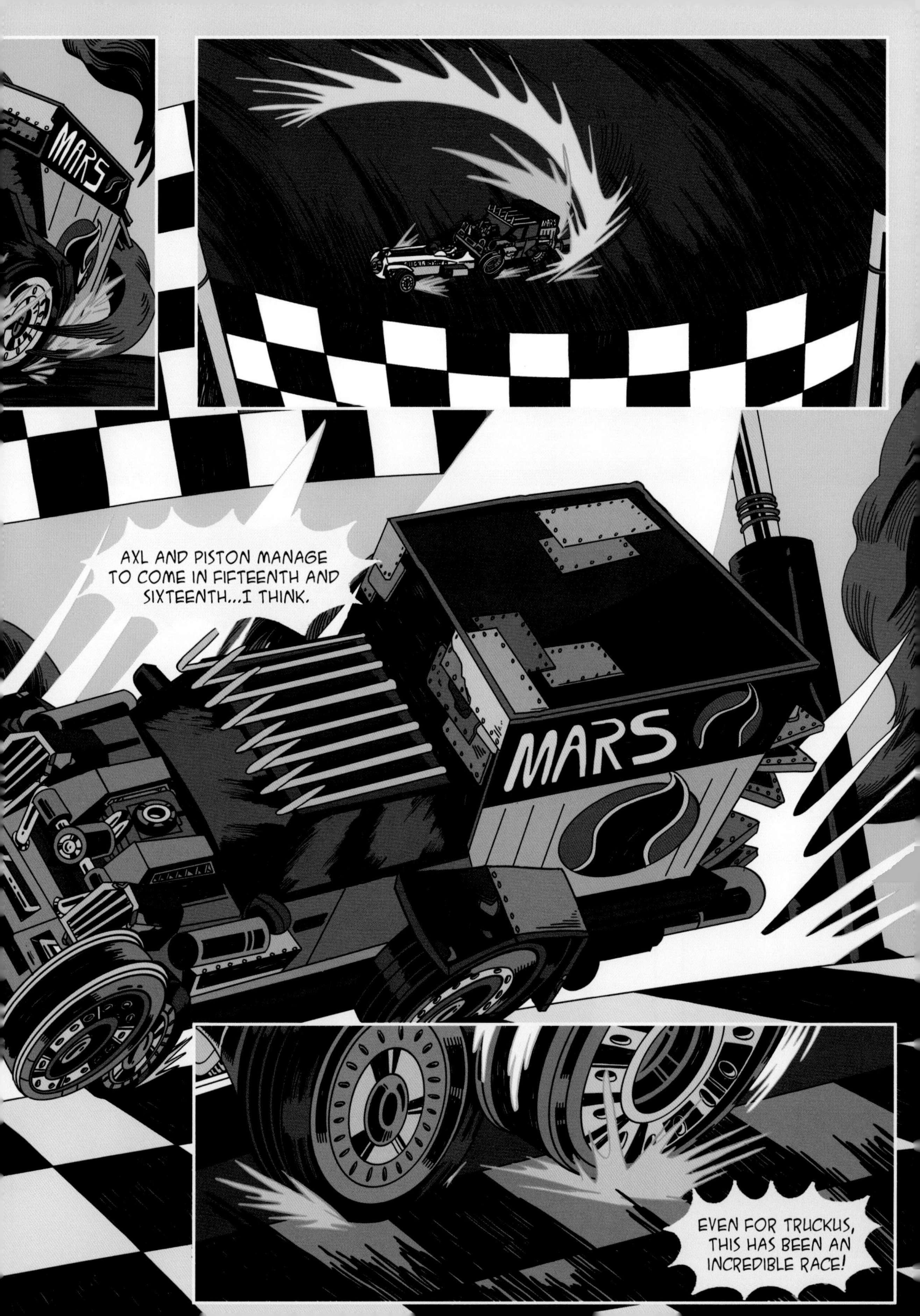
MARS
AXL AND PISTON MANAGE TO COME IN FIFTEENTH AND SIXTEENTH...I THINK.
MARS
EVEN FOR TRUCKUS, THIS HAS BEEN AN INCREDIBLE RACE!

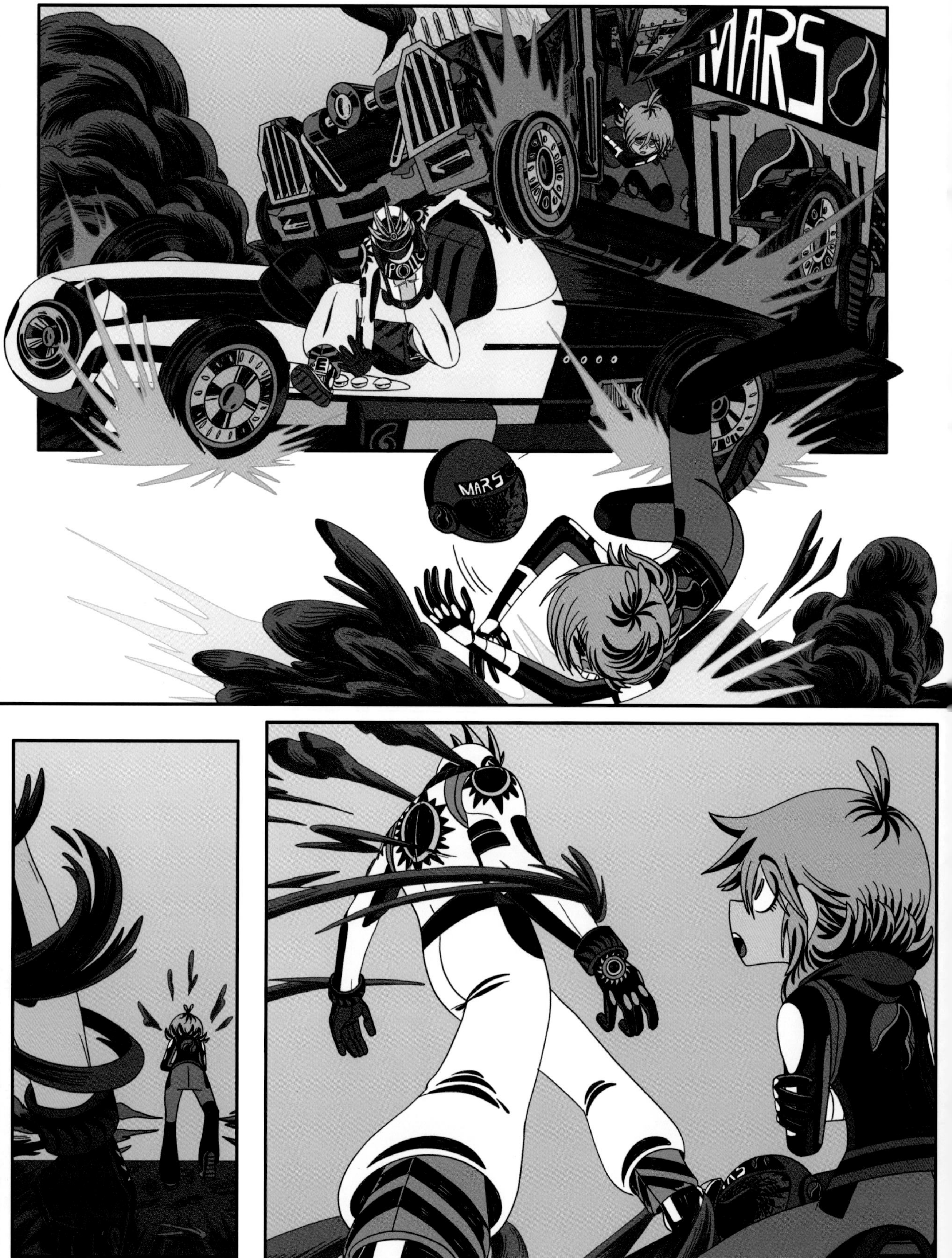
MARS
MARS

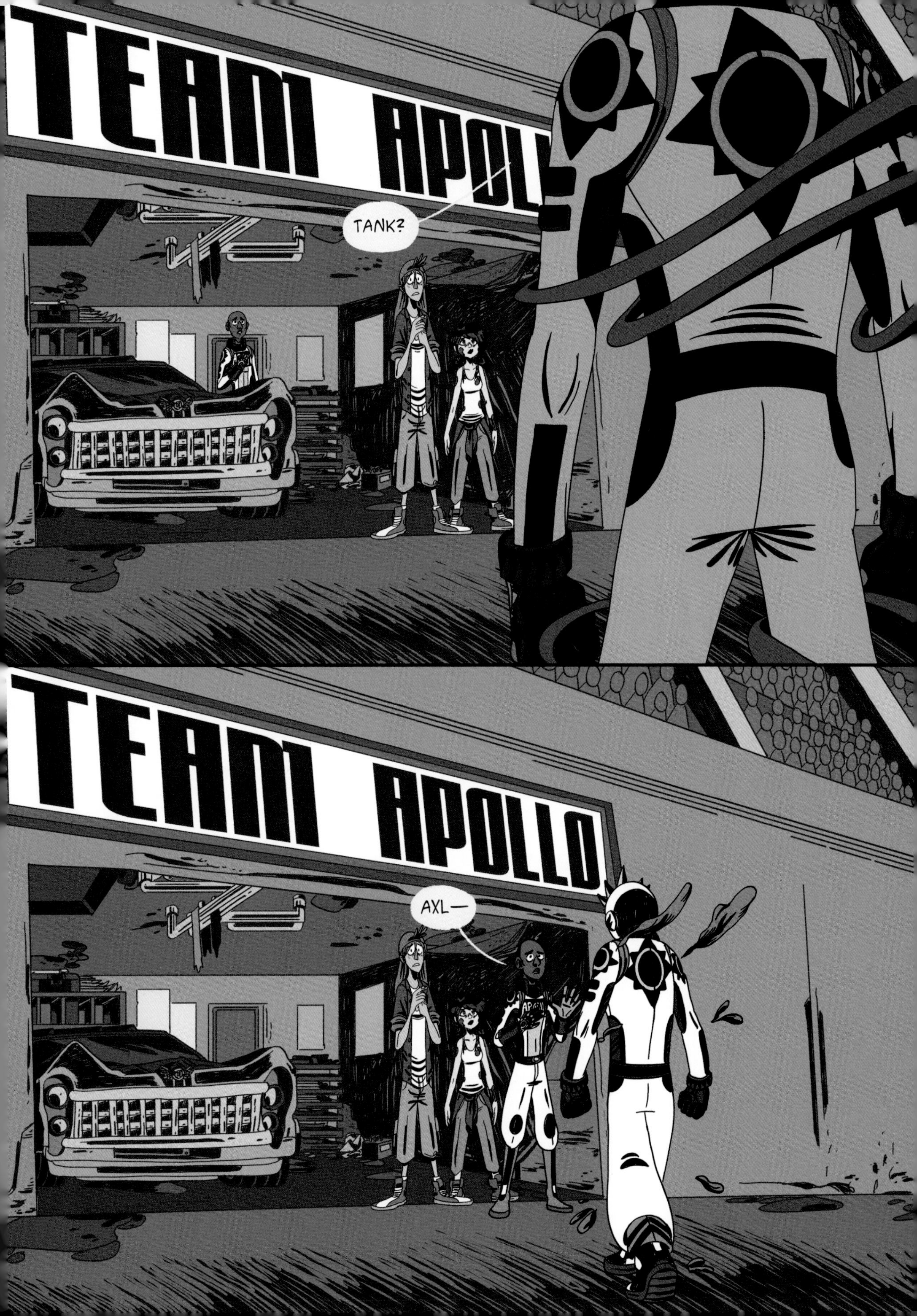
TEAM APOLL
TANK?
TEAM APOLLO
AXL—

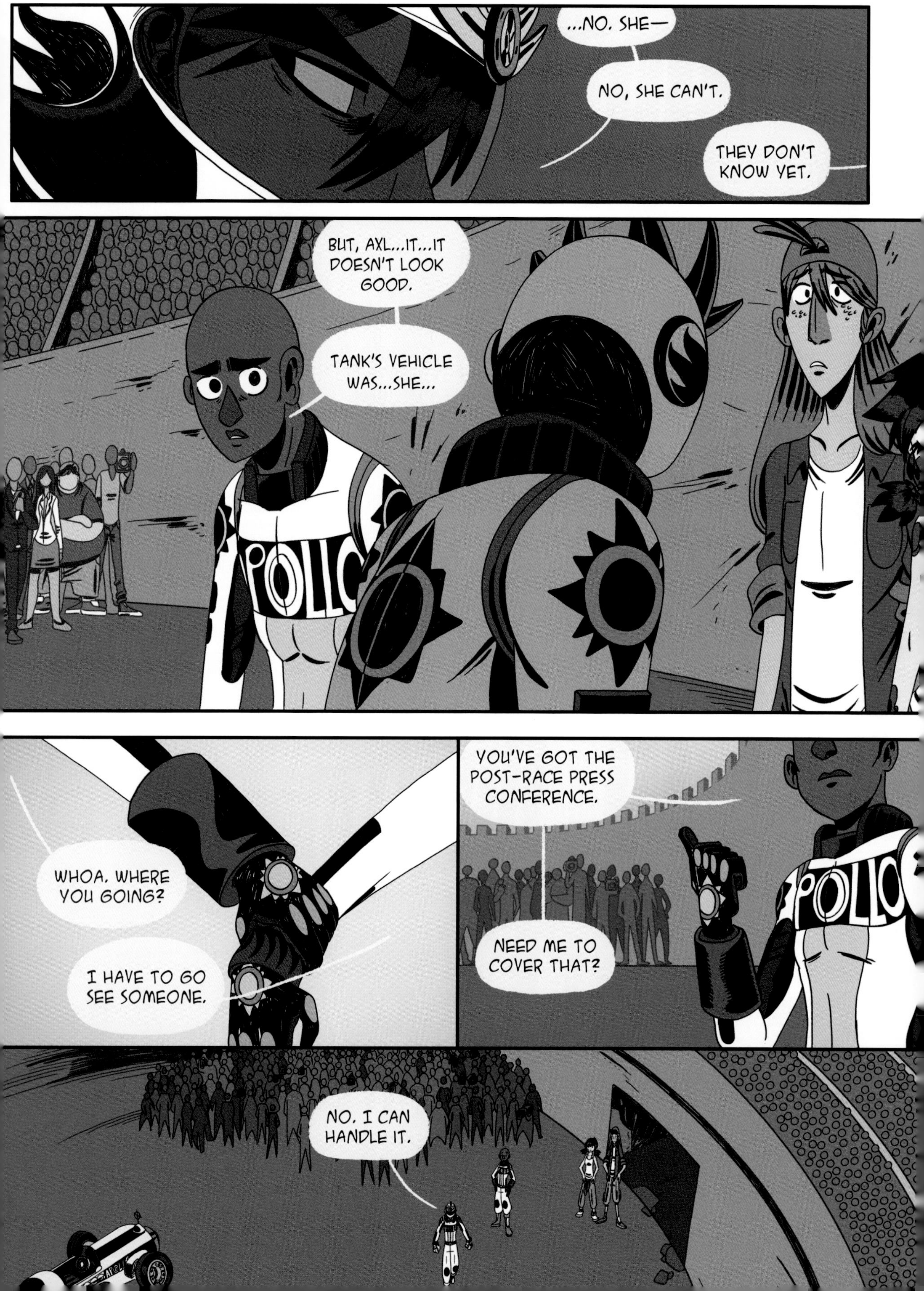
...NO. SHE—
NO, SHE CAN'T.
THEY DON'T KNOW YET.
BUT, AXL...IT...IT DOESN'T LOOK GOOD.
TANK'S VEHICLE WAS...SHE...
POLLO
WHOA. WHERE YOU GOING?
I HAVE TO GO SEE SOMEONE.
YOU'VE GOT THE POST-RACE PRESS CONFERENCE.
NEED ME TO COVER THAT?
POLLO
NO. I CAN HANDLE IT.

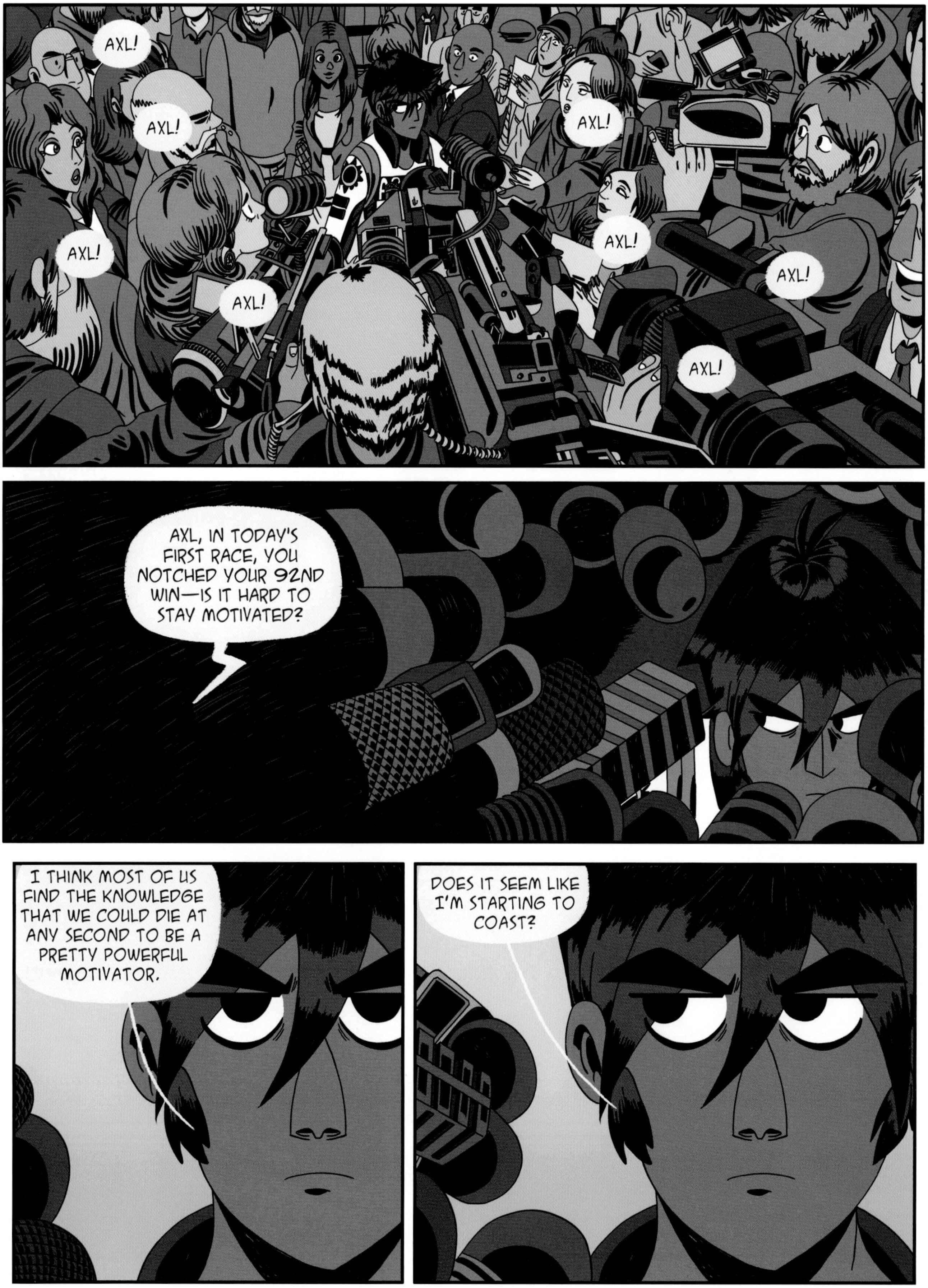
AXL!
AXL!
AXL!
AXL!
AXL!
AXL!
AXL!
AXL!
AXL, IN TODAY'S FIRST RACE, YOU NOTCHED YOUR 92ND WIN—IS IT HARD TO STAY MOTIVATED?
I THINK MOST OF US FIND THE KNOWLEDGE THAT WE COULD DIE AT ANY SECOND TO BE A PRETTY POWERFUL MOTIVATOR.
DOES IT SEEM LIKE I'M STARTING TO COAST?

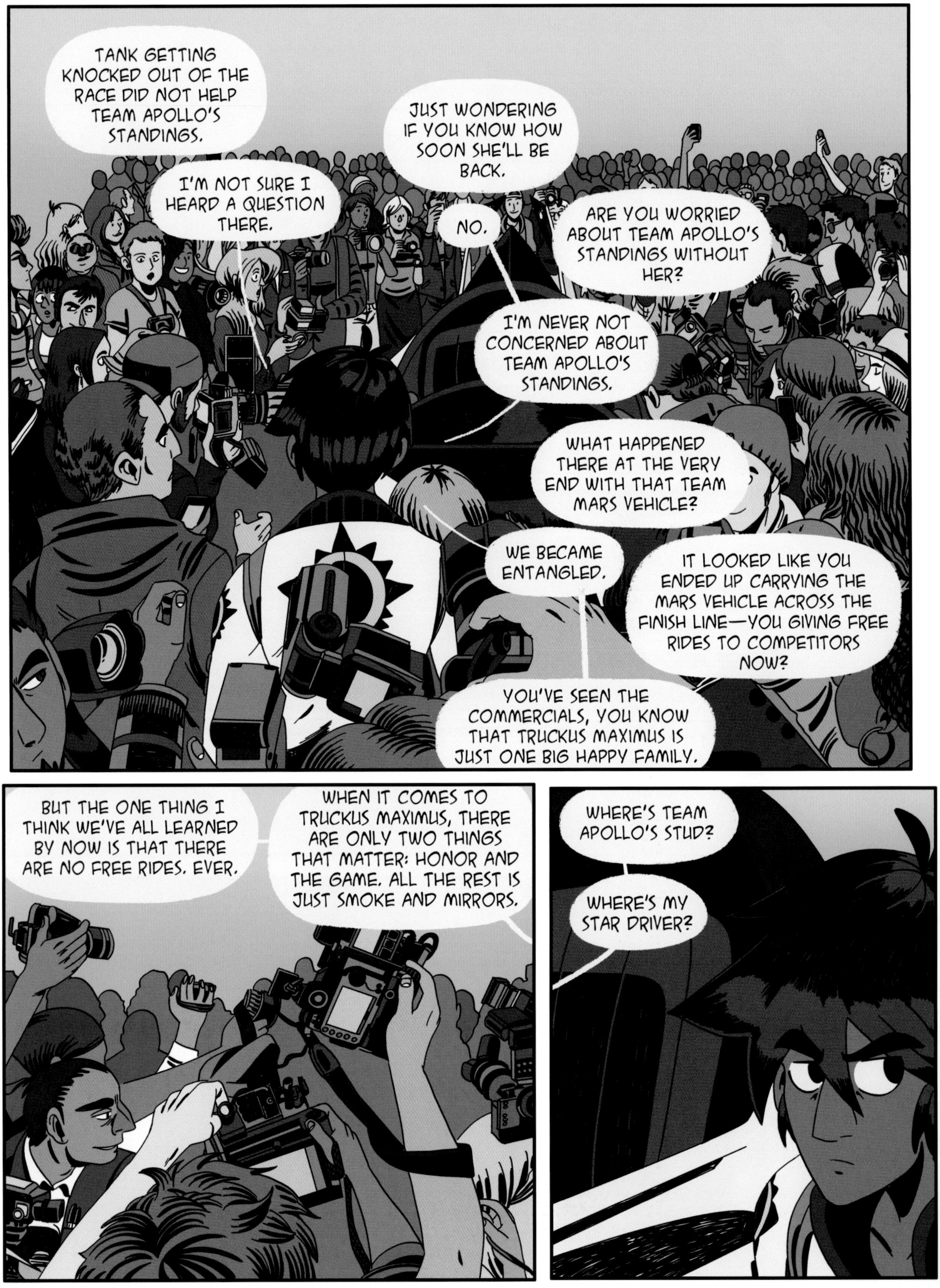
TANK GETTING KNOCKED OUT OF THE RACE DID NOT HELP TEAM APOLLO'S STANDINGS.
I'M NOT SURE I HEARD A QUESTION THERE.
JUST WONDERING IF YOU KNOW HOW SOON SHE'LL BE BACK.
NO.
ARE YOU WORRIED ABOUT TEAM APOLLO'S STANDINGS WITHOUT HER?
I'M NEVER NOT CONCERNED ABOUT TEAM APOLLO'S STANDINGS.
WHAT HAPPENED THERE AT THE VERY END WITH THAT TEAM MARS VEHICLE?
WE BECAME ENTANGLED.
IT LOOKED LIKE YOU ENDED UP CARRYING THE MARS VEHICLE ACROSS THE FINISH LINE—YOU GIVING FREE RIDES TO COMPETITORS NOW?
YOU'VE SEEN THE COMMERCIALS, YOU KNOW THAT TRUCKUS MAXIMUS IS JUST ONE BIG HAPPY FAMILY.
BUT THE ONE THING I THINK WE'VE ALL LEARNED BY NOW IS THAT THERE ARE NO FREE RIDES. EVER.
WHEN IT COMES TO TRUCKUS MAXIMUS, THERE ARE ONLY TWO THINGS THAT MATTER: HONOR AND THE GAME. ALL THE REST IS JUST SMOKE AND MIRRORS.
WHERE'S TEAM APOLLO'S STUD?
WHERE'S MY STAR DRIVER?

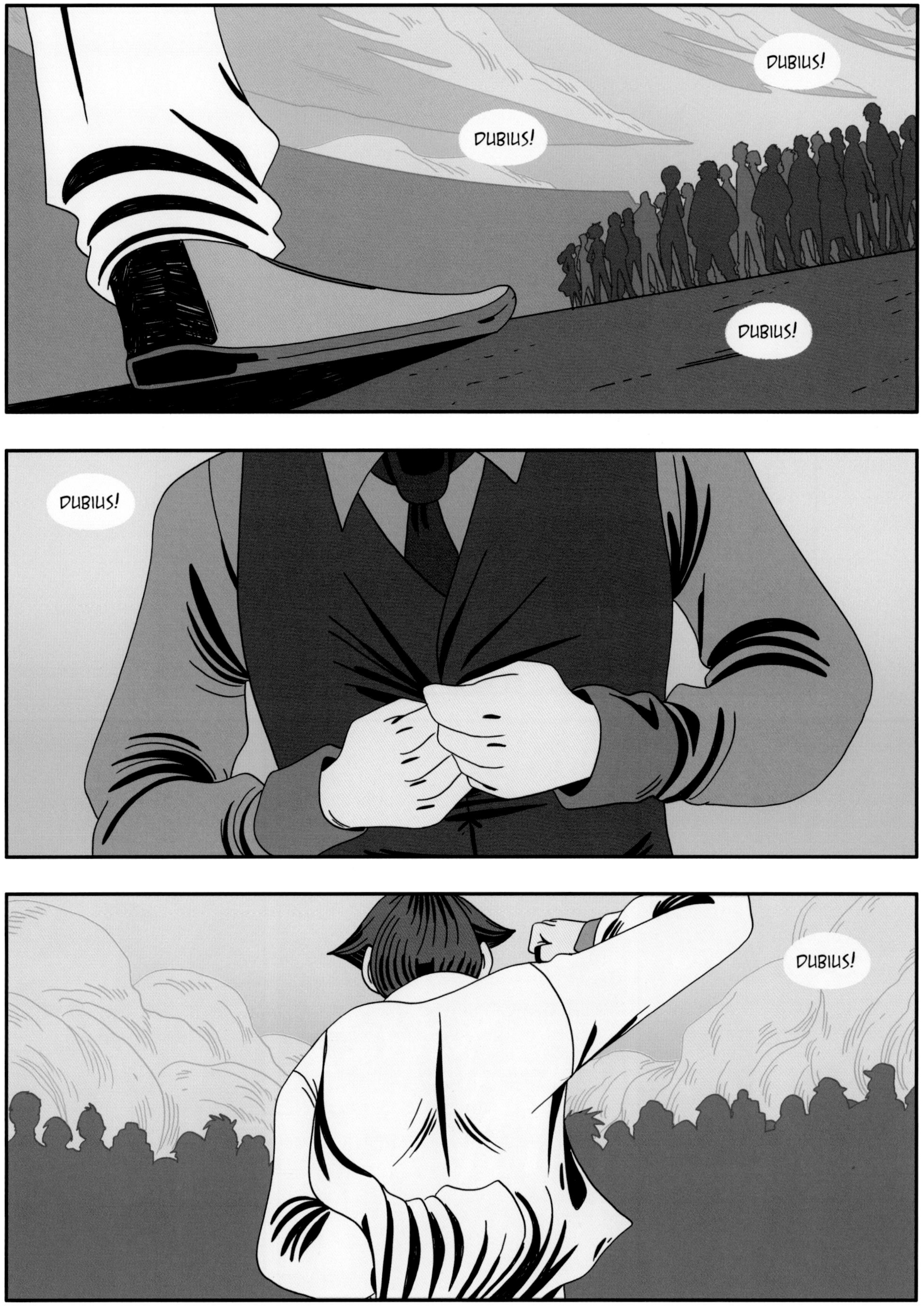
DUBIUS!
DUBIUS!
DUBIUS!
DUBIUS!
DUBIUS!

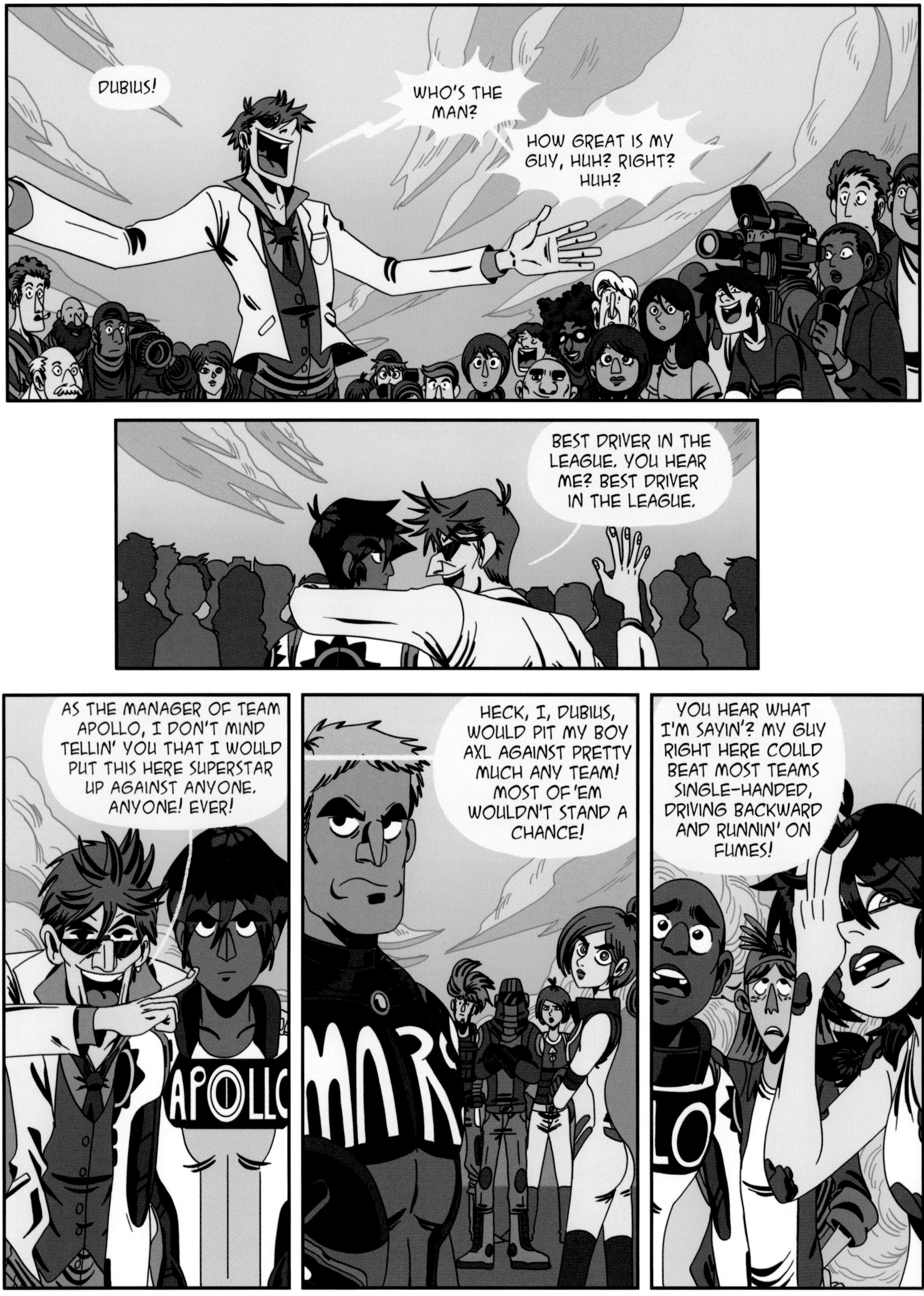
DUBIUS!
WHO'S THE MAN?
HOW GREAT IS MY GUY, HUH? RIGHT? HUH?
BEST DRIVER IN THE LEAGUE. YOU HEAR ME? BEST DRIVER IN THE LEAGUE.
AS THE MANAGER OF TEAM APOLLO, I DON'T MIND TELLIN' YOU THAT I WOULD PUT THIS HERE SUPERSTAR UP AGAINST ANYONE. ANYONE! EVER!
APOLLO
HECK, I, DUBIUS, WOULD PIT MY BOY AXL AGAINST PRETTY MUCH ANY TEAM! MOST OF 'EM WOULDN'T STAND A CHANCE!
YOU HEAR WHAT I'M SAYIN'? MY GUY RIGHT HERE COULD BEAT MOST TEAMS SINGLE-HANDED, DRIVING BACKWARD AND RUNNIN' ON FUMES!

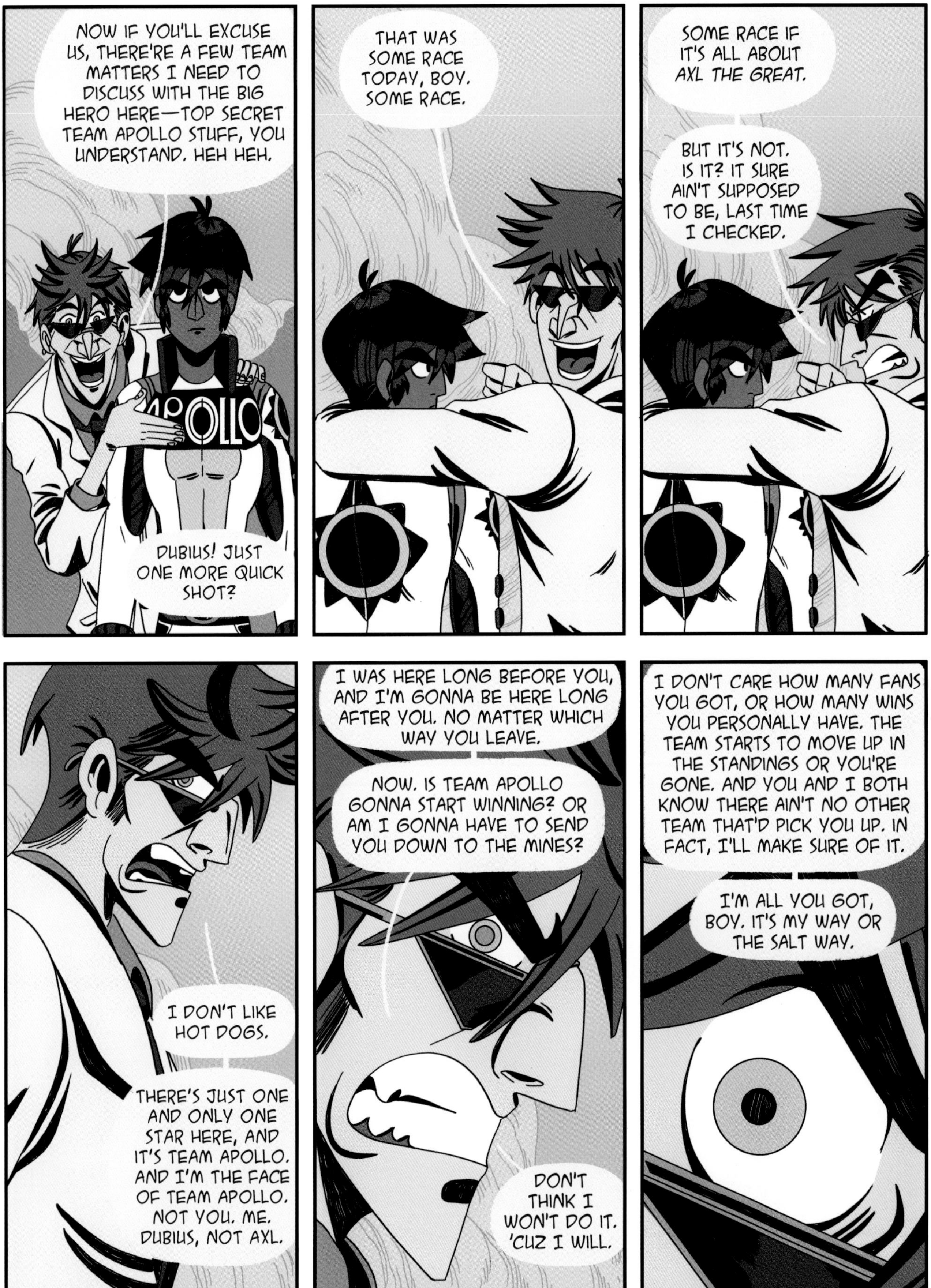
NOW IF YOU'LL EXCUSE US, THERE'RE A FEW TEAM MATTERS I NEED TO DISCUSS WITH THE BIG HERO HERE—TOP SECRET TEAM APOLLO STUFF, YOU UNDERSTAND. HEH HEH.
APOLLO
DUBIUS! JUST ONE MORE QUICK SHOT?
THAT WAS SOME RACE TODAY, BOY. SOME RACE.
SOME RACE IF IT'S ALL ABOUT AXL THE GREAT.
BUT IT'S NOT. IS IT? IT SURE AIN'T SUPPOSED TO BE, LAST TIME I CHECKED.
I DON'T LIKE HOT DOGS.
THERE'S JUST ONE AND ONLY ONE STAR HERE, AND IT'S TEAM APOLLO. AND I'M THE FACE OF TEAM APOLLO. NOT YOU. ME. DUBIUS, NOT AXL.
I WAS HERE LONG BEFORE YOU, AND I'M GONNA BE HERE LONG AFTER YOU. NO MATTER WHICH WAY YOU LEAVE.
NOW. IS TEAM APOLLO GONNA START WINNING? OR AM I GONNA HAVE TO SEND YOU DOWN TO THE MINES?
DON'T THINK I WON'T DO IT. 'CUZ I WILL.
I DON'T CARE HOW MANY FANS YOU GOT, OR HOW MANY WINS YOU PERSONALLY HAVE. THE TEAM STARTS TO MOVE UP IN THE STANDINGS OR YOU'RE GONE. AND YOU AND I BOTH KNOW THERE AIN'T NO OTHER TEAM THAT'D PICK YOU UP. IN FACT, I'LL MAKE SURE OF IT.
I'M ALL YOU GOT, BOY. IT'S MY WAY OR THE SALT WAY.

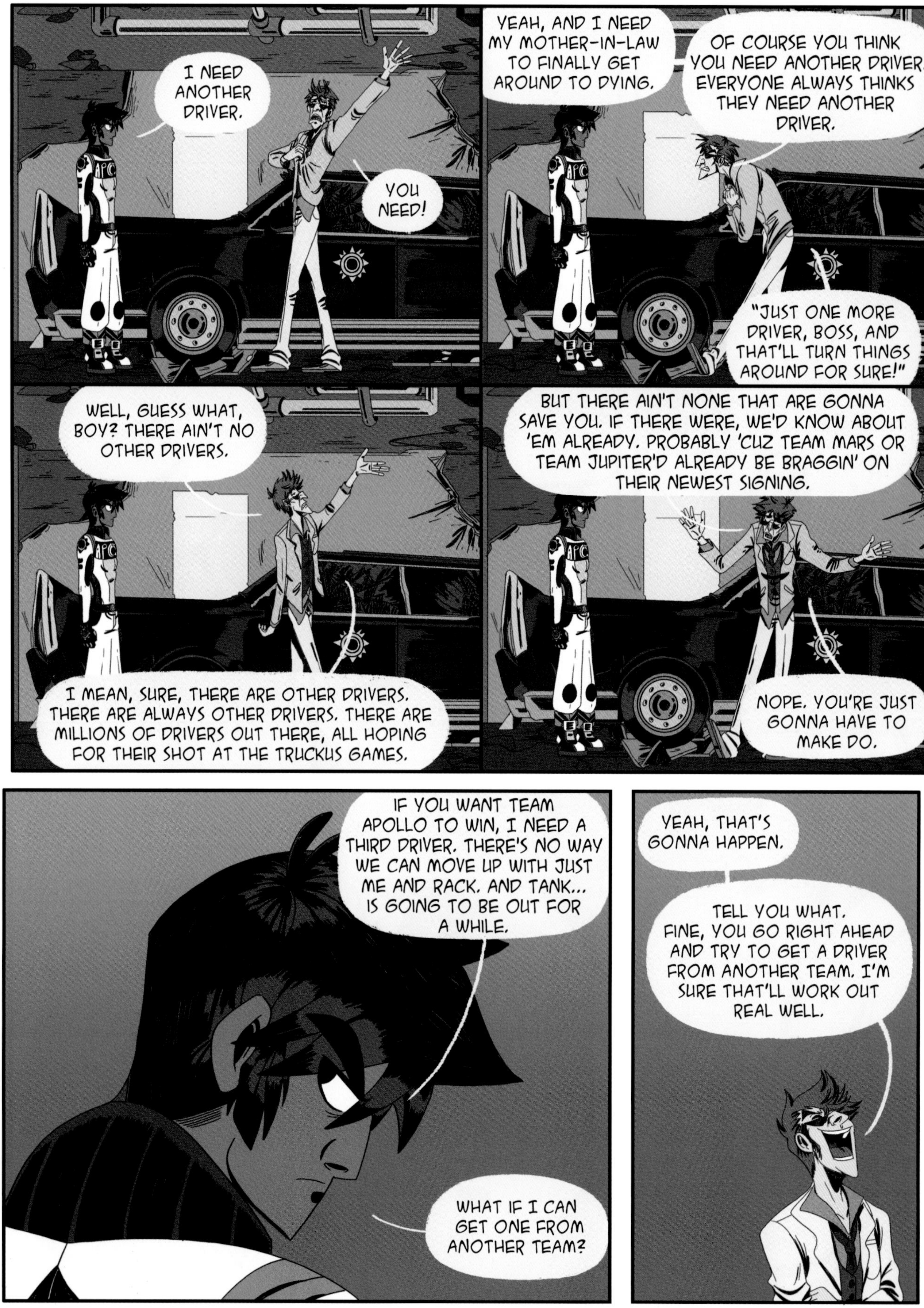
I NEED ANOTHER DRIVER.
YOU NEED!
YEAH, AND I NEED MY MOTHER-IN-LAW TO FINALLY GET AROUND TO DYING.
OF COURSE YOU THINK YOU NEED ANOTHER DRIVER. EVERYONE ALWAYS THINKS THEY NEED ANOTHER DRIVER.
"JUST ONE MORE DRIVER, BOSS, AND THAT'LL TURN THINGS AROUND FOR SURE!"
WELL, GUESS WHAT, BOY? THERE AIN'T NO OTHER DRIVERS.
I MEAN, SURE, THERE ARE OTHER DRIVERS. THERE ARE ALWAYS OTHER DRIVERS. THERE ARE MILLIONS OF DRIVERS OUT THERE, ALL HOPING FOR THEIR SHOT AT THE TRUCKUS GAMES.
BUT THERE AIN'T NONE THAT ARE GONNA SAVE YOU. IF THERE WERE, WE'D KNOW ABOUT 'EM ALREADY. PROBABLY 'CUZ TEAM MARS OR TEAM JUPITER'D ALREADY BE BRAGGIN' ON THEIR NEWEST SIGNING.
NOPE. YOU'RE JUST GONNA HAVE TO MAKE DO.
IF YOU WANT TEAM APOLLO TO WIN, I NEED A THIRD DRIVER. THERE'S NO WAY WE CAN MOVE UP WITH JUST ME AND RACK. AND TANK... IS GOING TO BE OUT FOR A WHILE.
WHAT IF I CAN GET ONE FROM ANOTHER TEAM?
YEAH, THAT'S GONNA HAPPEN.
TELL YOU WHAT. FINE, YOU GO RIGHT AHEAD AND TRY TO GET A DRIVER FROM ANOTHER TEAM. I'M SURE THAT'LL WORK OUT REAL WELL.
APC
APC
APC
APC

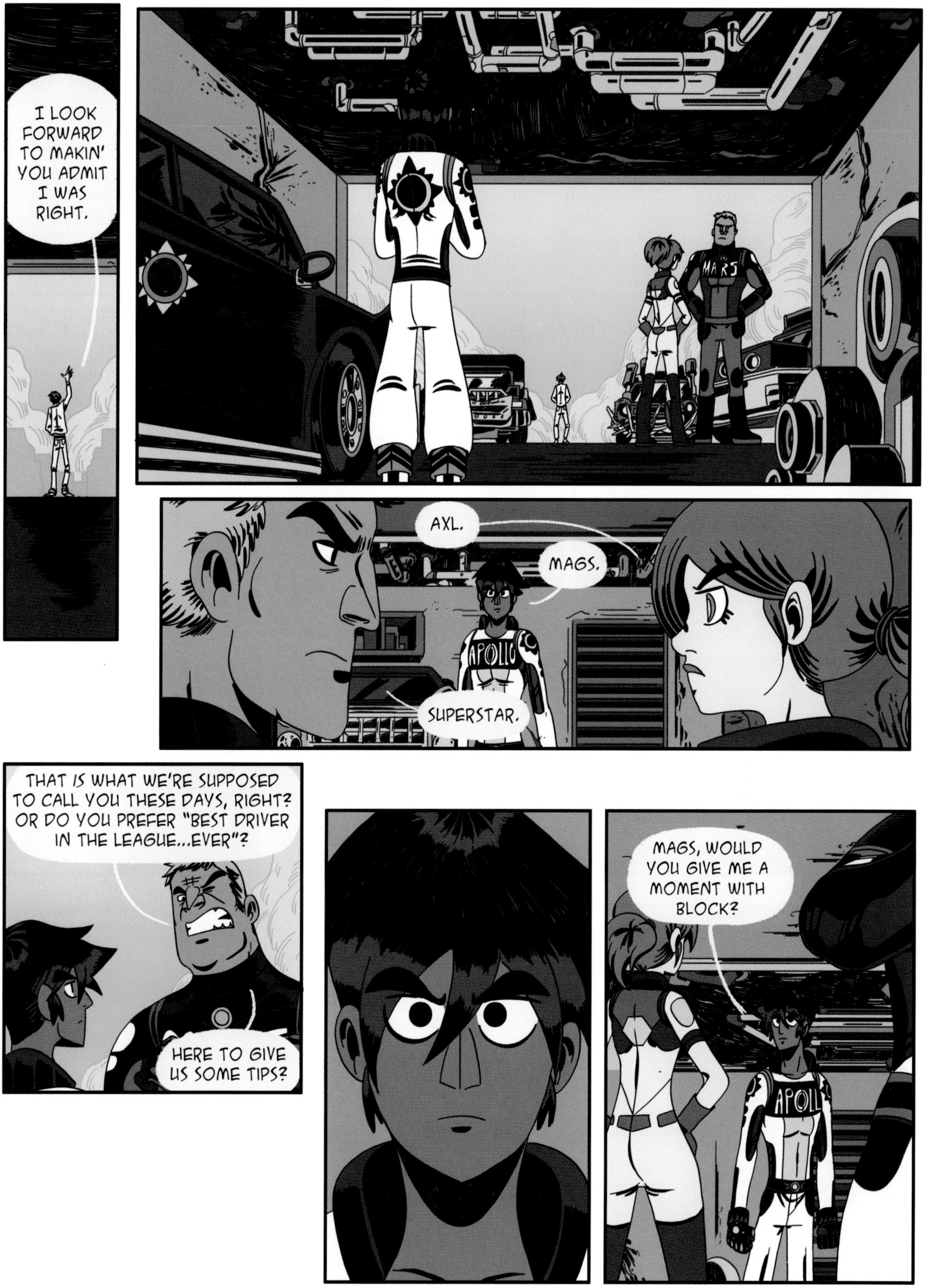

I LOOK FORWARD TO MAKIN' YOU ADMIT I WAS RIGHT.
MARS
AXL.
MAGS.
APOLLO
SUPERSTAR.
THAT IS WHAT WE'RE SUPPOSED TO CALL YOU THESE DAYS, RIGHT? OR DO YOU PREFER "BEST DRIVER IN THE LEAGUE...EVER"?
HERE TO GIVE US SOME TIPS?
MAGS, WOULD YOU GIVE ME A MOMENT WITH BLOCK?
APOLL

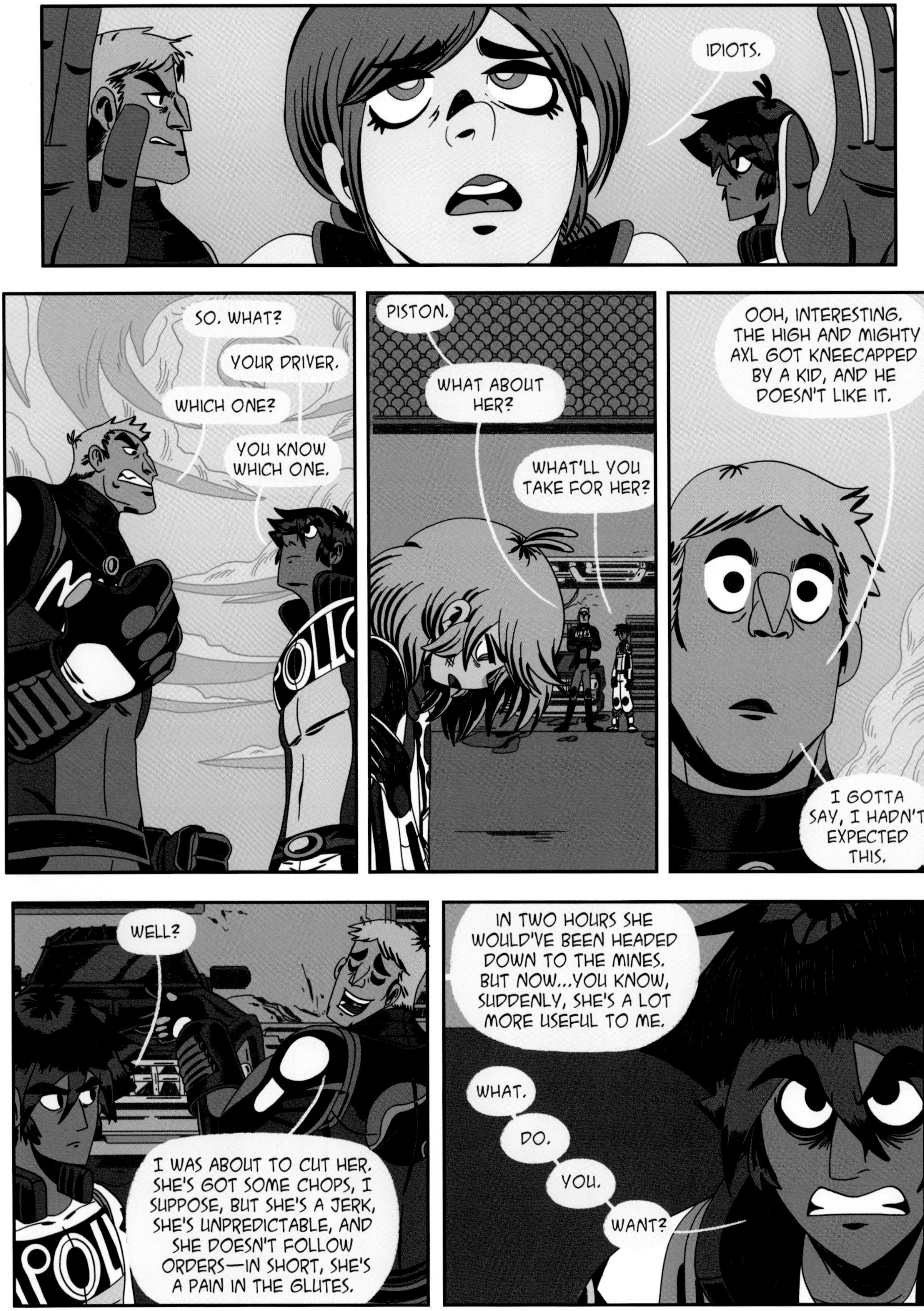
IDIOTS.
SO. WHAT?
YOUR DRIVER.
WHICH ONE?
YOU KNOW WHICH ONE.
PISTON.
WHAT ABOUT HER?
WHAT'LL YOU TAKE FOR HER?
OOH, INTERESTING. THE HIGH AND MIGHTY AXL GOT KNEECAPPED BY A KID, AND HE DOESN'T LIKE IT.
I GOTTA SAY, I HADN'T EXPECTED THIS.
WELL?
I WAS ABOUT TO CUT HER. SHE'S GOT SOME CHOPS, I SUPPOSE, BUT SHE'S A JERK, SHE'S UNPREDICTABLE, AND SHE DOESN'T FOLLOW ORDERS—IN SHORT, SHE'S A PAIN IN THE GLUTES.
IN TWO HOURS SHE WOULD'VE BEEN HEADED DOWN TO THE MINES. BUT NOW...YOU KNOW, SUDDENLY, SHE'S A LOT MORE USEFUL TO ME.
WHAT.
DO.
YOU.
WANT?

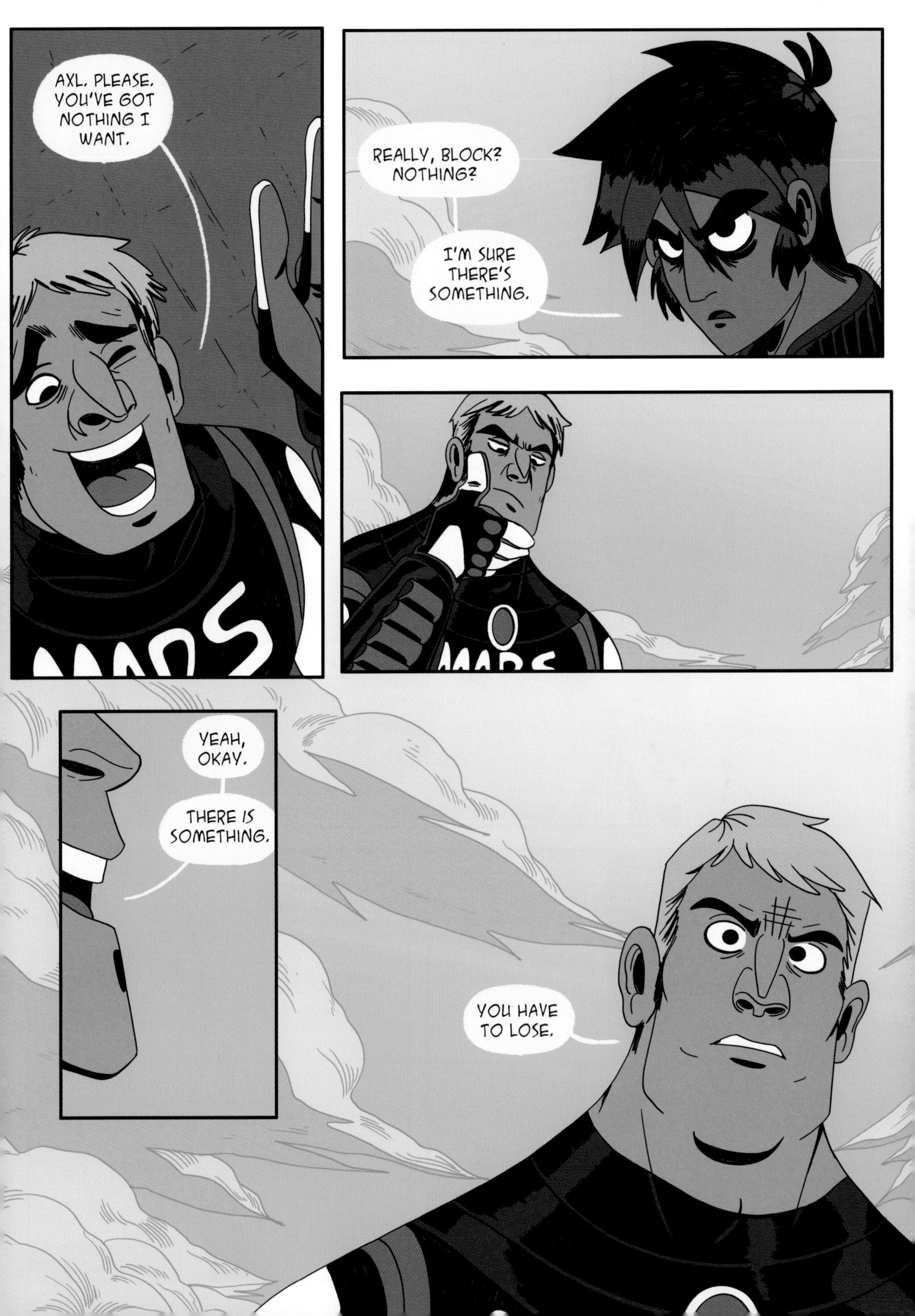
AXL, PLEASE. YOU'VE GOT NOTHING I WANT.
REALLY, BLOCK? NOTHING?
I'M SURE THERE'S SOMETHING.
YEAH, OKAY.
THERE IS SOMETHING.
YOU HAVE TO LOSE.

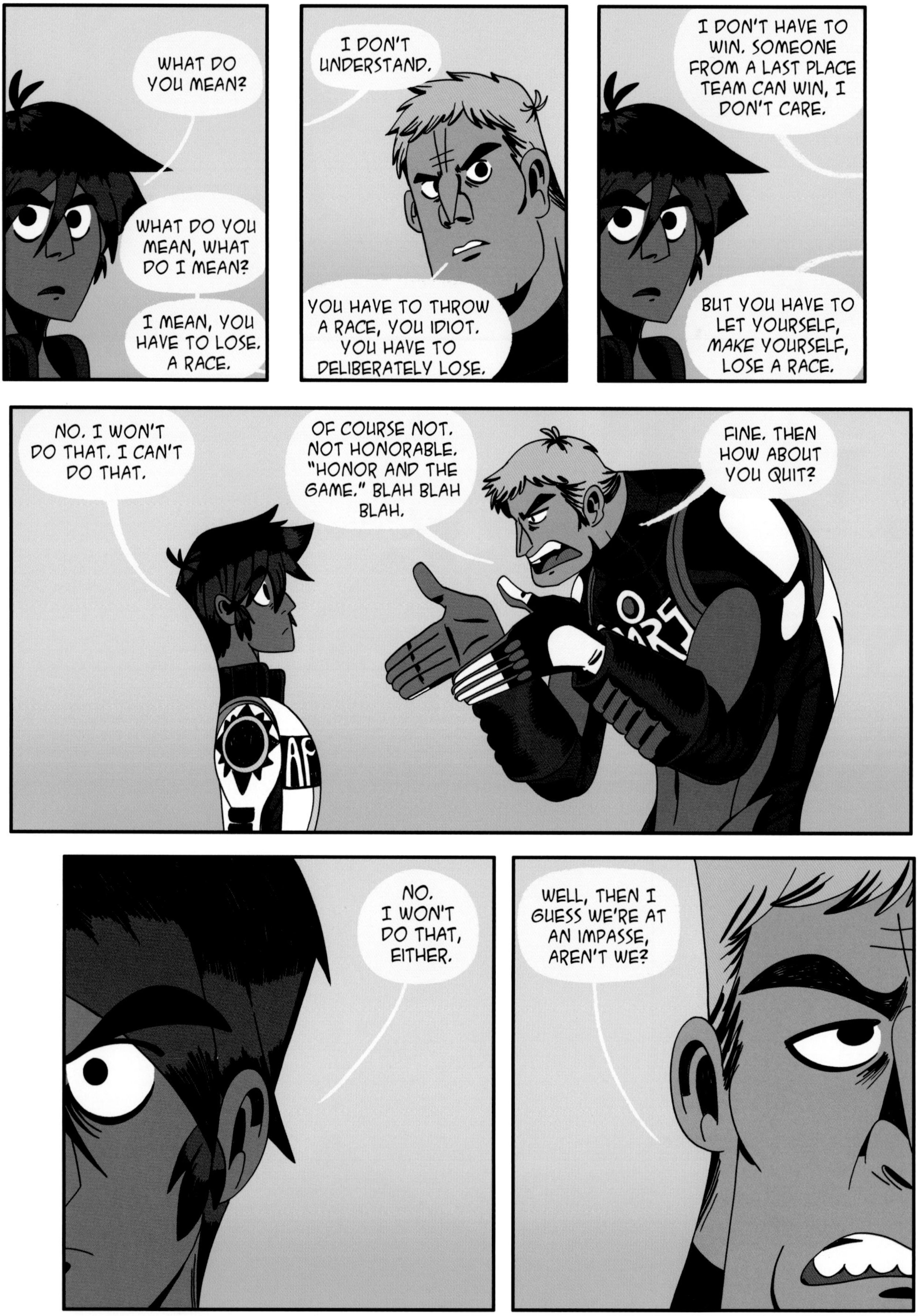
WHAT DO YOU MEAN?
WHAT DO YOU MEAN, WHAT DO I MEAN?
I MEAN, YOU HAVE TO LOSE. A RACE.
I DON'T UNDERSTAND.
YOU HAVE TO THROW A RACE, YOU IDIOT. YOU HAVE TO DELIBERATELY LOSE.
I DON'T HAVE TO WIN. SOMEONE FROM A LAST PLACE TEAM CAN WIN, I DON'T CARE.
BUT YOU HAVE TO LET YOURSELF, MAKE YOURSELF, LOSE A RACE.
NO. I WON'T DO THAT. I CAN'T DO THAT.
OF COURSE NOT. NOT HONORABLE. "HONOR AND THE GAME." BLAH BLAH BLAH.
FINE. THEN HOW ABOUT YOU QUIT?
NO. I WON'T DO THAT, EITHER.
WELL, THEN I GUESS WE'RE AT AN IMPASSE, AREN'T WE?

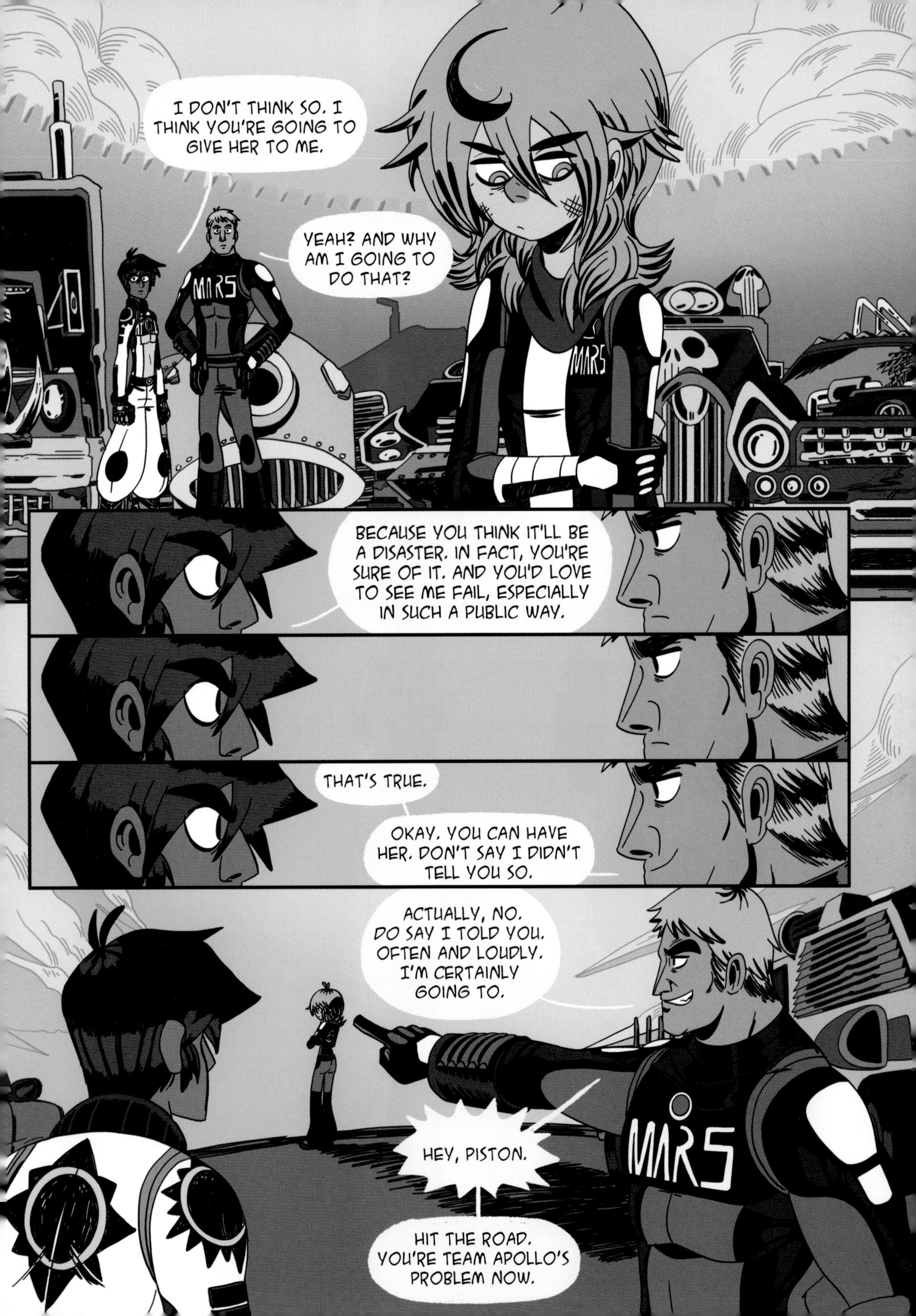
I DON'T THINK SO. I THINK YOU'RE GOING TO GIVE HER TO ME.
YEAH? AND WHY AM I GOING TO DO THAT?
BECAUSE YOU THINK IT'LL BE A DISASTER. IN FACT, YOU'RE SURE OF IT. AND YOU'D LOVE TO SEE ME FAIL, ESPECIALLY IN SUCH A PUBLIC WAY.
THAT'S TRUE.
OKAY. YOU CAN HAVE HER. DON'T SAY I DIDN'T TELL YOU SO.
ACTUALLY, NO. DO SAY I TOLD YOU. OFTEN AND LOUDLY. I'M CERTAINLY GOING TO.
HEY, PISTON.
HIT THE ROAD. YOU'RE TEAM APOLLO'S PROBLEM NOW.

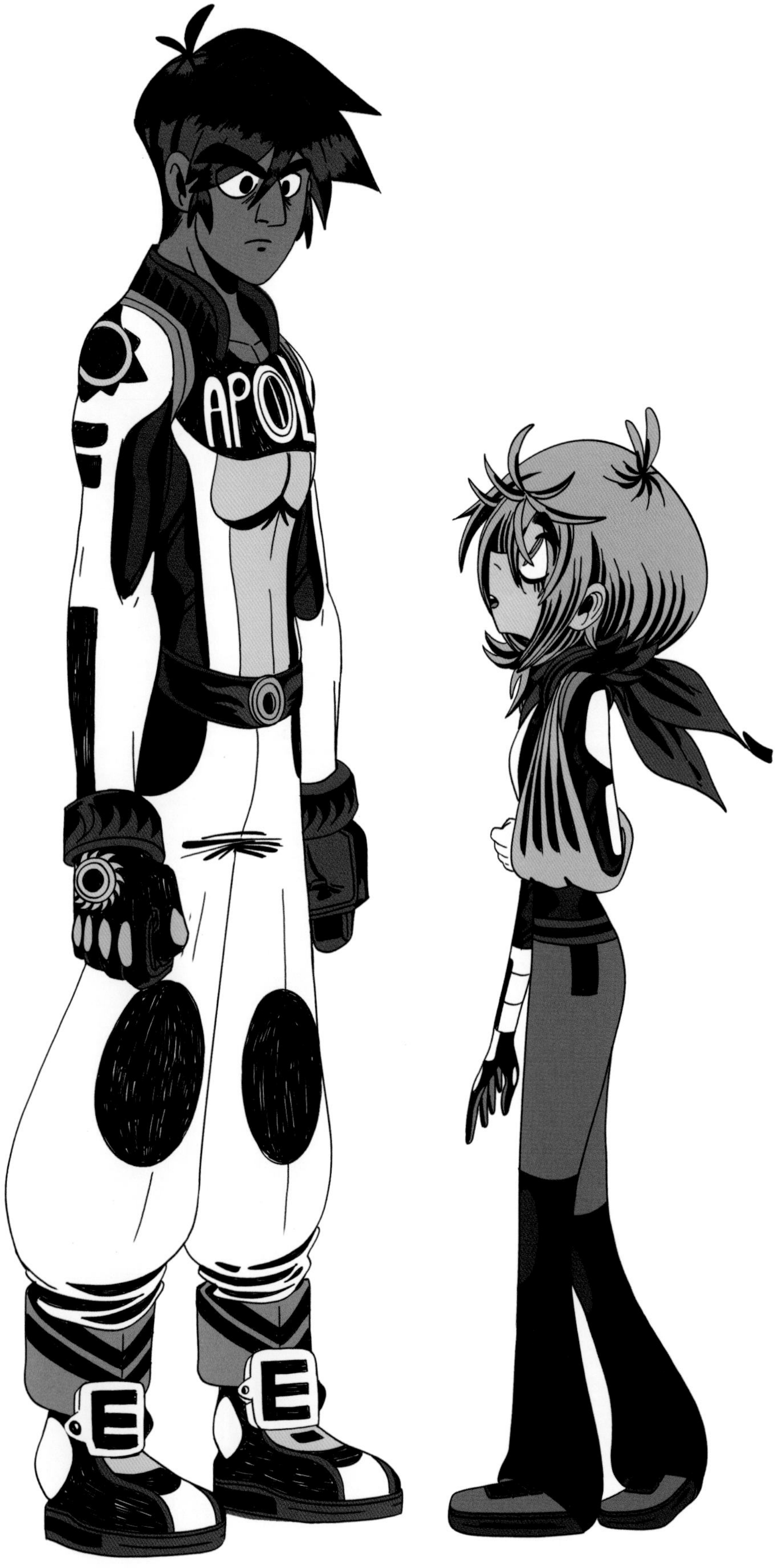
APOL
E
E

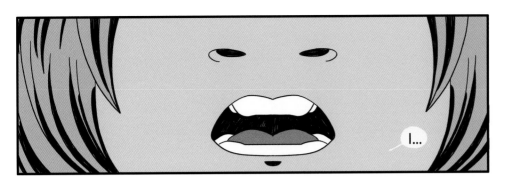

I...

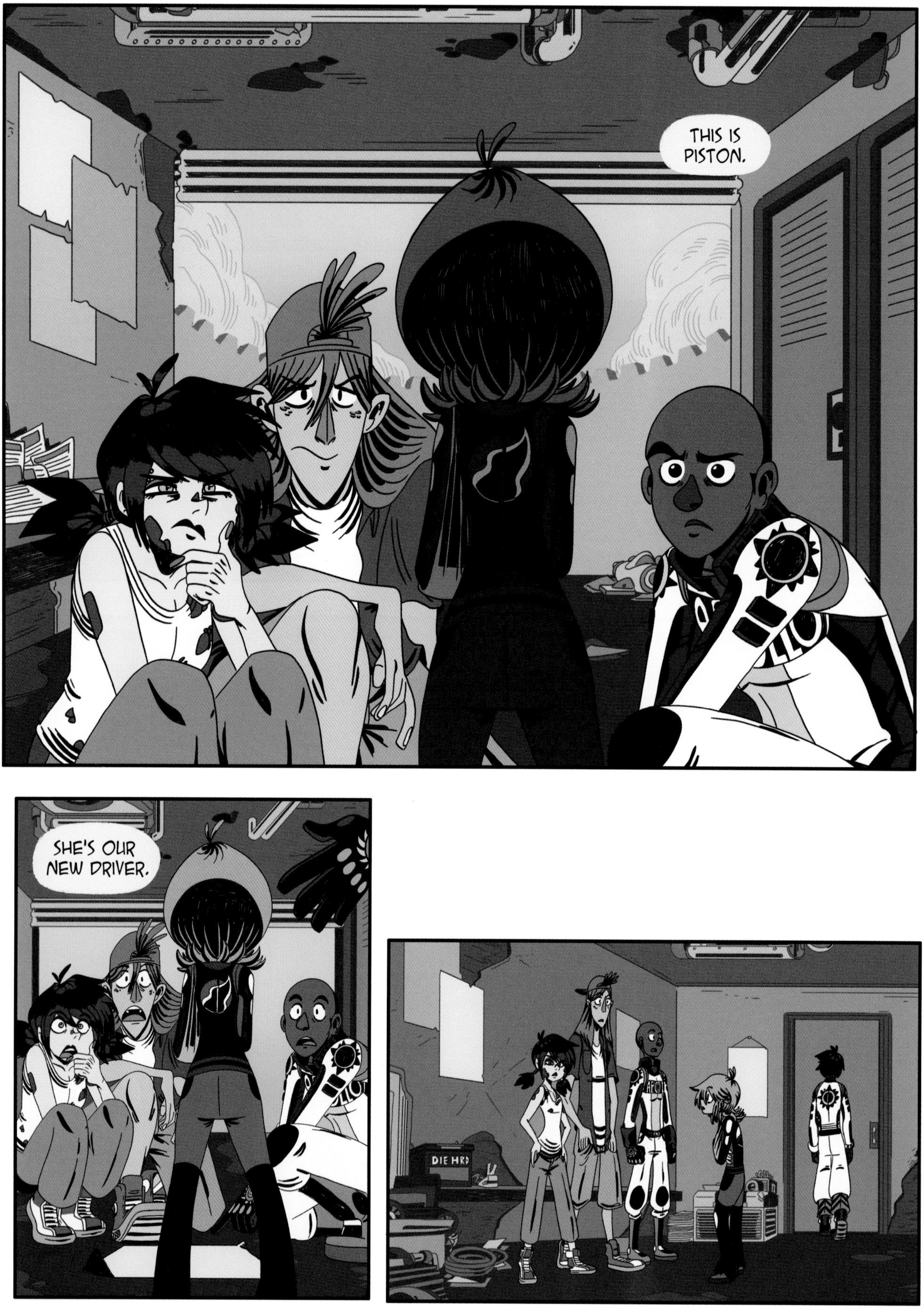
THIS IS PISTON.
SHE'S OUR NEW DRIVER.
DIE HRD

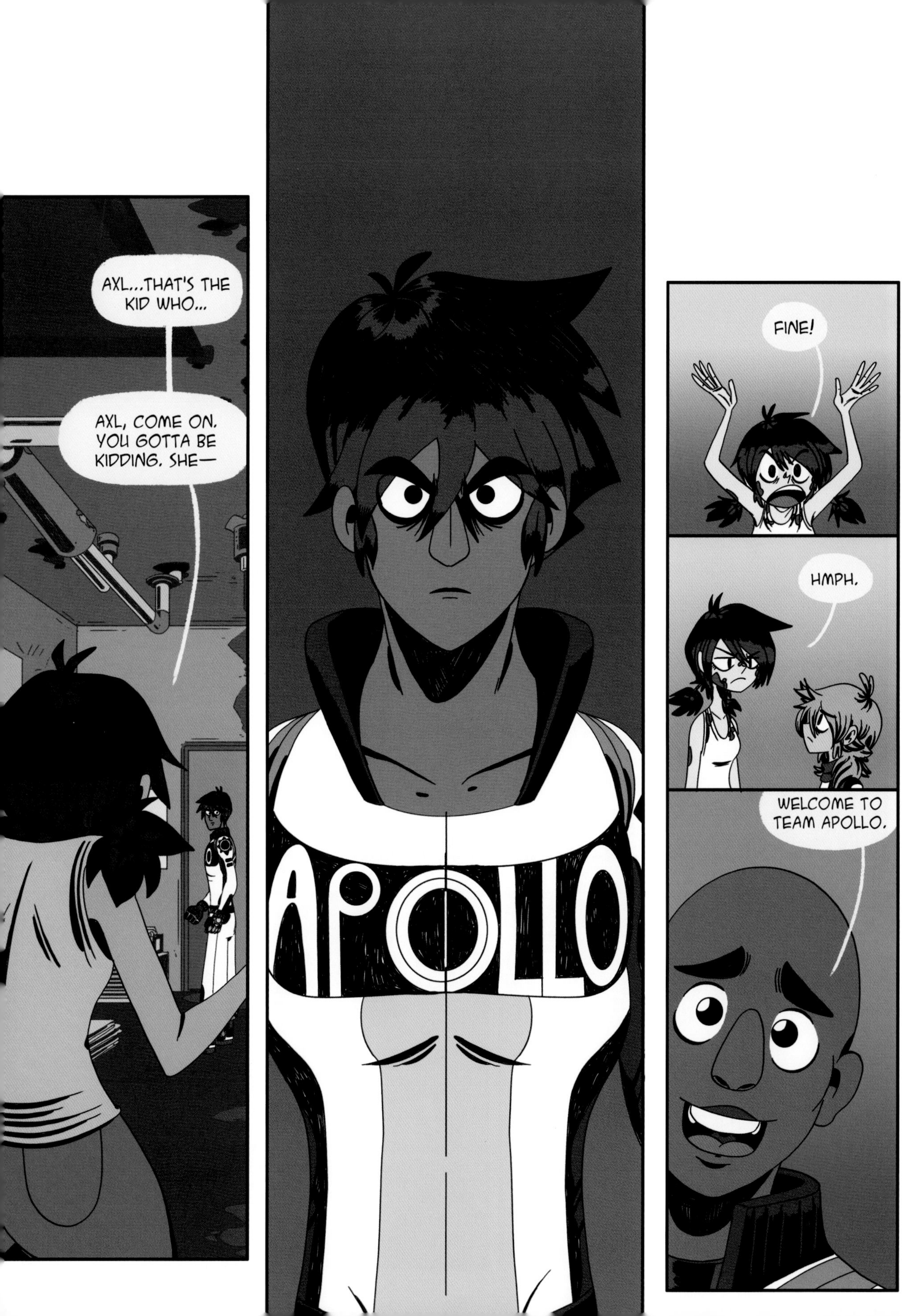
AXL...THAT'S THE KID WHO...
AXL, COME ON. YOU GOTTA BE KIDDING. SHE—
APOLLO
FINE!
HMPH.
WELCOME TO TEAM APOLLO.

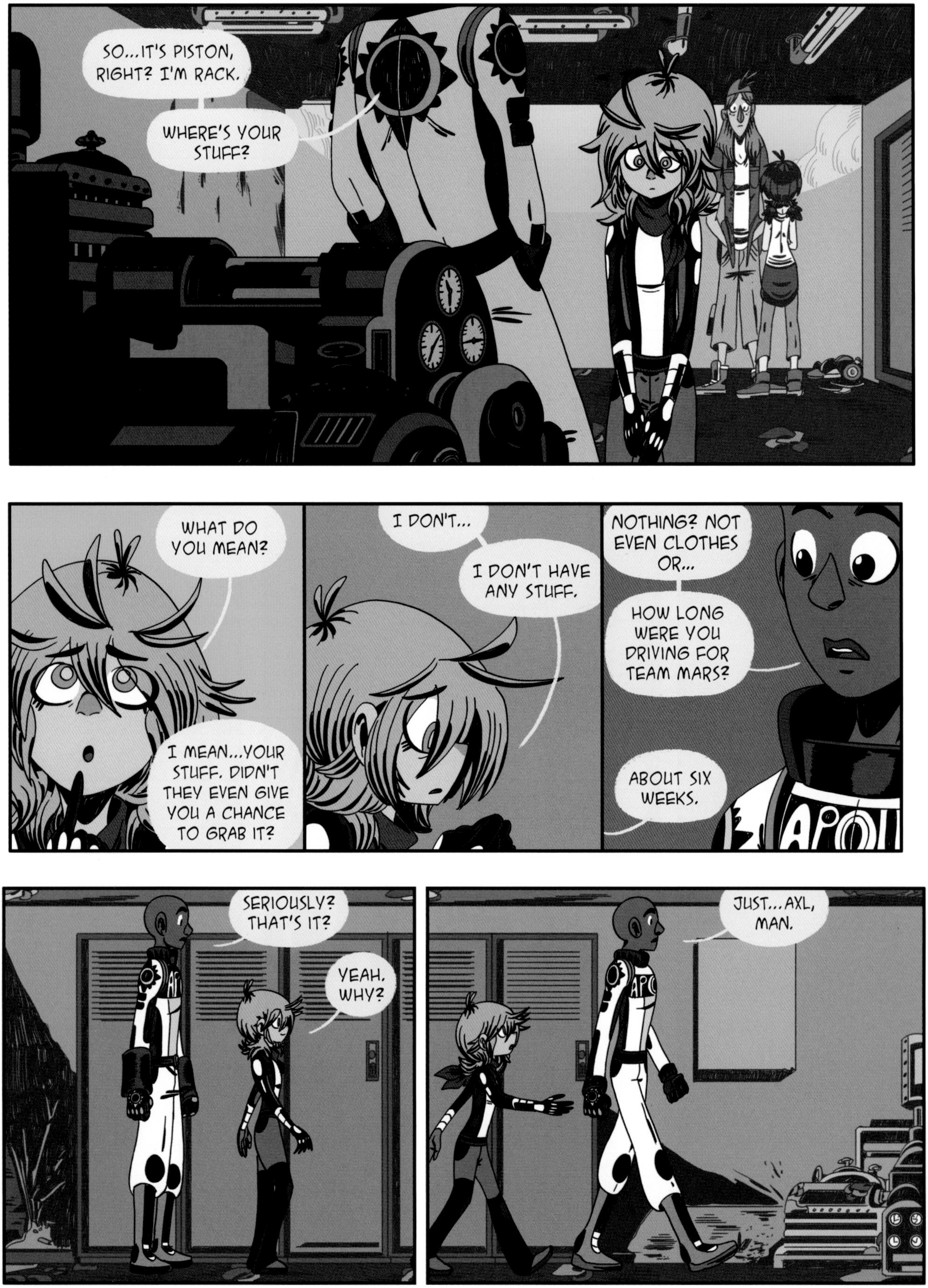
SO...IT'S PISTON, RIGHT? I'M RACK.
WHERE'S YOUR STUFF?
WHAT DO YOU MEAN?
I MEAN...YOUR STUFF. DIDN'T THEY EVEN GIVE YOU A CHANCE TO GRAB IT?
I DON'T...
I DON'T HAVE ANY STUFF.
NOTHING? NOT EVEN CLOTHES OR...
HOW LONG WERE YOU DRIVING FOR TEAM MARS?
ABOUT SIX WEEKS.
APOL
SERIOUSLY? THAT'S IT?
YEAH. WHY?
JUST...AXL, MAN.

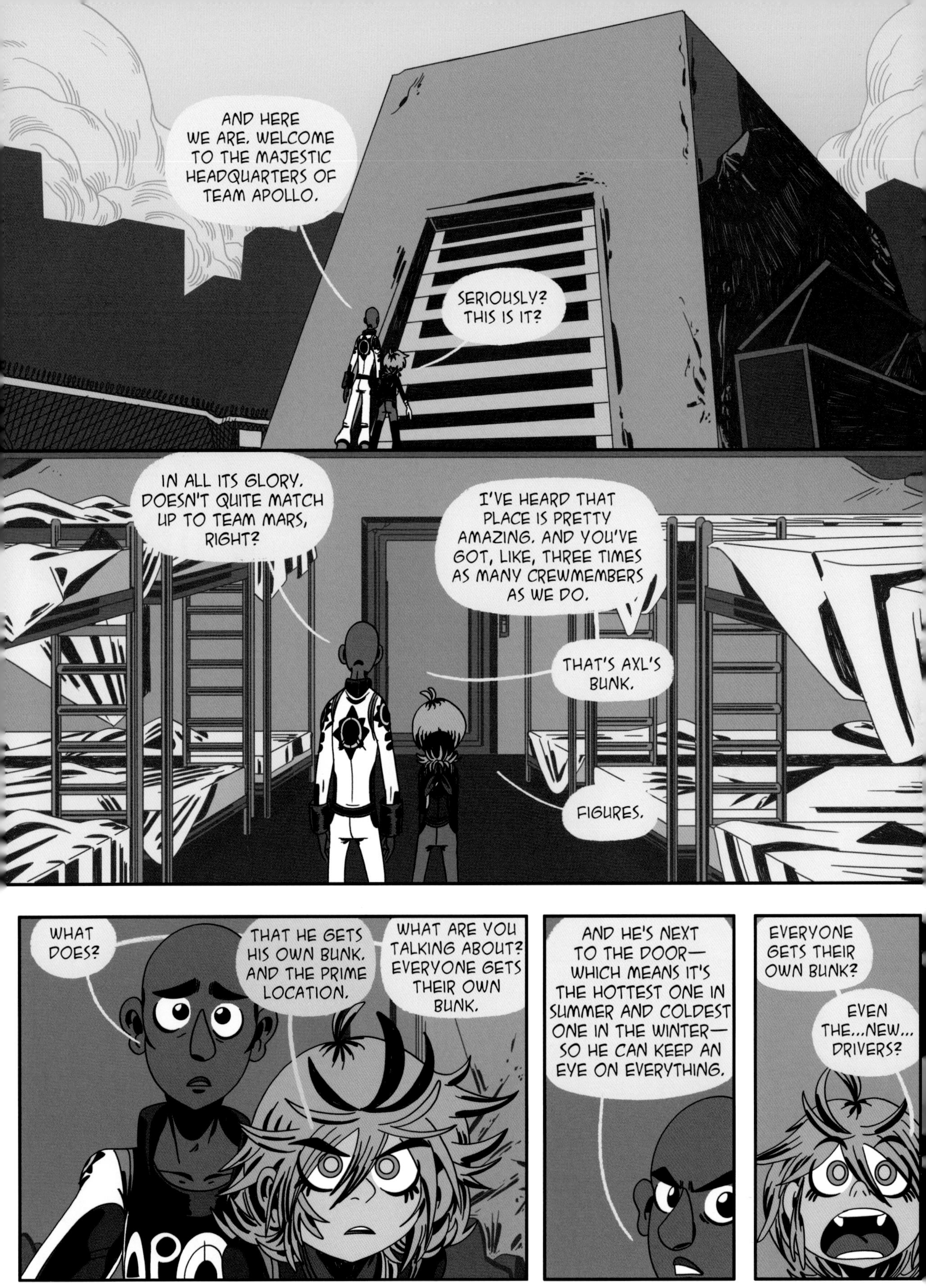
AND HERE WE ARE. WELCOME TO THE MAJESTIC HEADQUARTERS OF TEAM APOLLO.
SERIOUSLY? THIS IS IT?
IN ALL ITS GLORY. DOESN'T QUITE MATCH UP TO TEAM MARS, RIGHT?
I'VE HEARD THAT PLACE IS PRETTY AMAZING. AND YOU'VE GOT, LIKE, THREE TIMES AS MANY CREWMEMBERS AS WE DO.
THAT'S AXL'S BUNK.
FIGURES.
WHAT DOES?
THAT HE GETS HIS OWN BUNK. AND THE PRIME LOCATION.
WHAT ARE YOU TALKING ABOUT? EVERYONE GETS THEIR OWN BUNK.
AND HE'S NEXT TO THE DOOR—WHICH MEANS IT'S THE HOTTEST ONE IN SUMMER AND COLDEST ONE IN THE WINTER—SO HE CAN KEEP AN EYE ON EVERYTHING.
EVERYONE GETS THEIR OWN BUNK?
EVEN THE...NEW... DRIVERS?

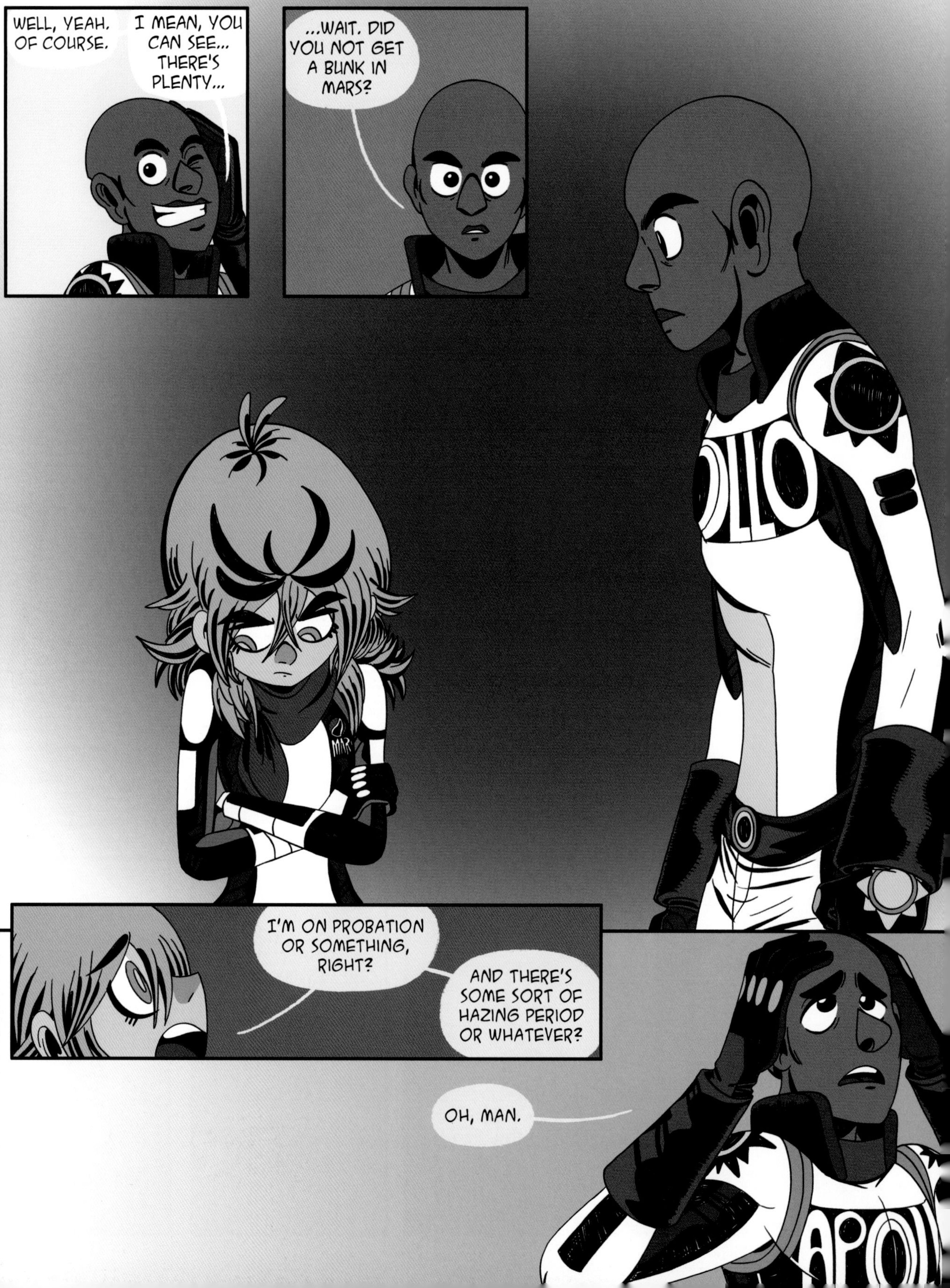
WELL, YEAH. OF COURSE.
I MEAN, YOU CAN SEE... THERE'S PLENTY...
...WAIT. DID YOU NOT GET A BUNK IN MARS?
I'M ON PROBATION OR SOMETHING, RIGHT?
AND THERE'S SOME SORT OF HAZING PERIOD OR WHATEVER?
OH, MAN.

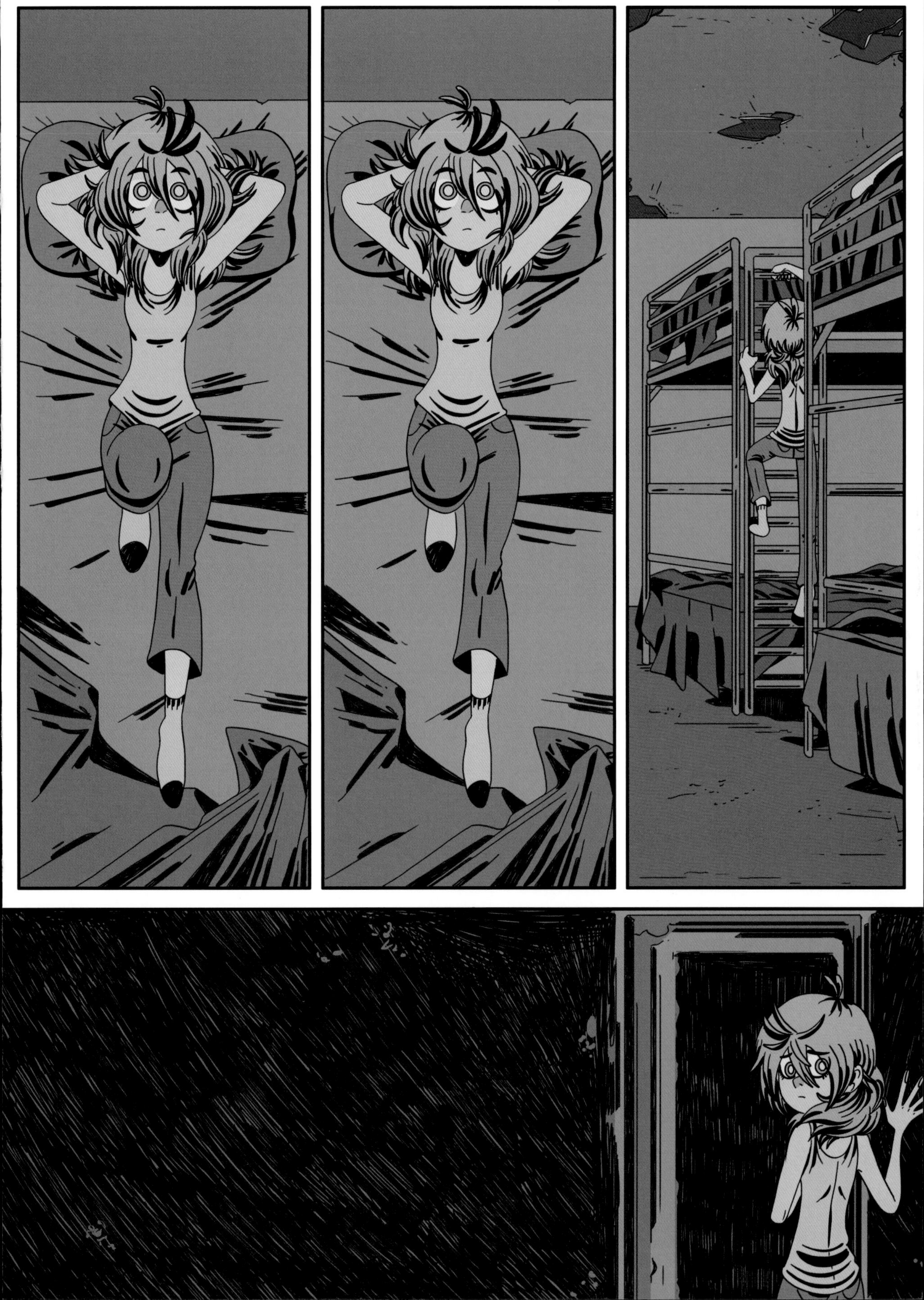

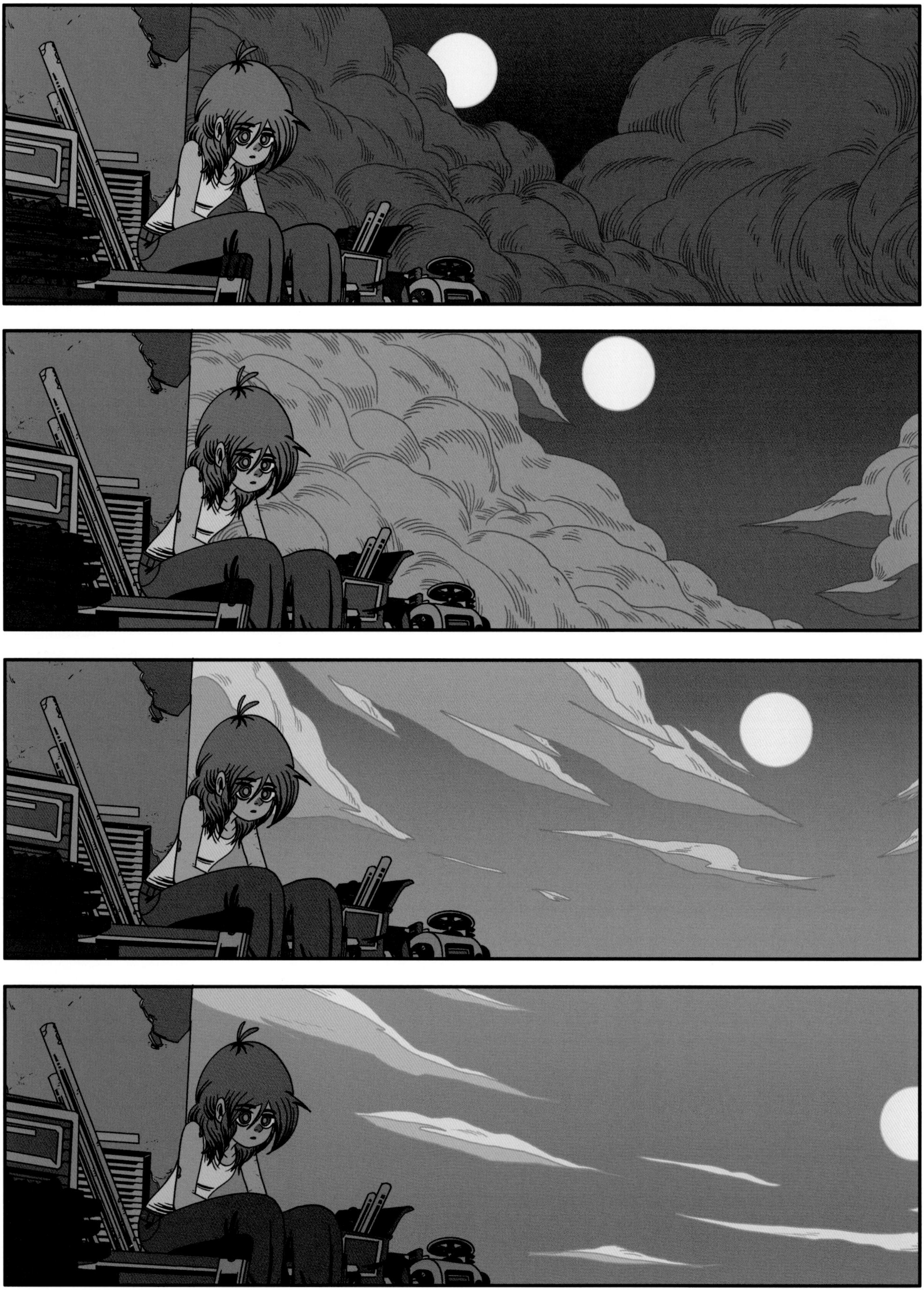

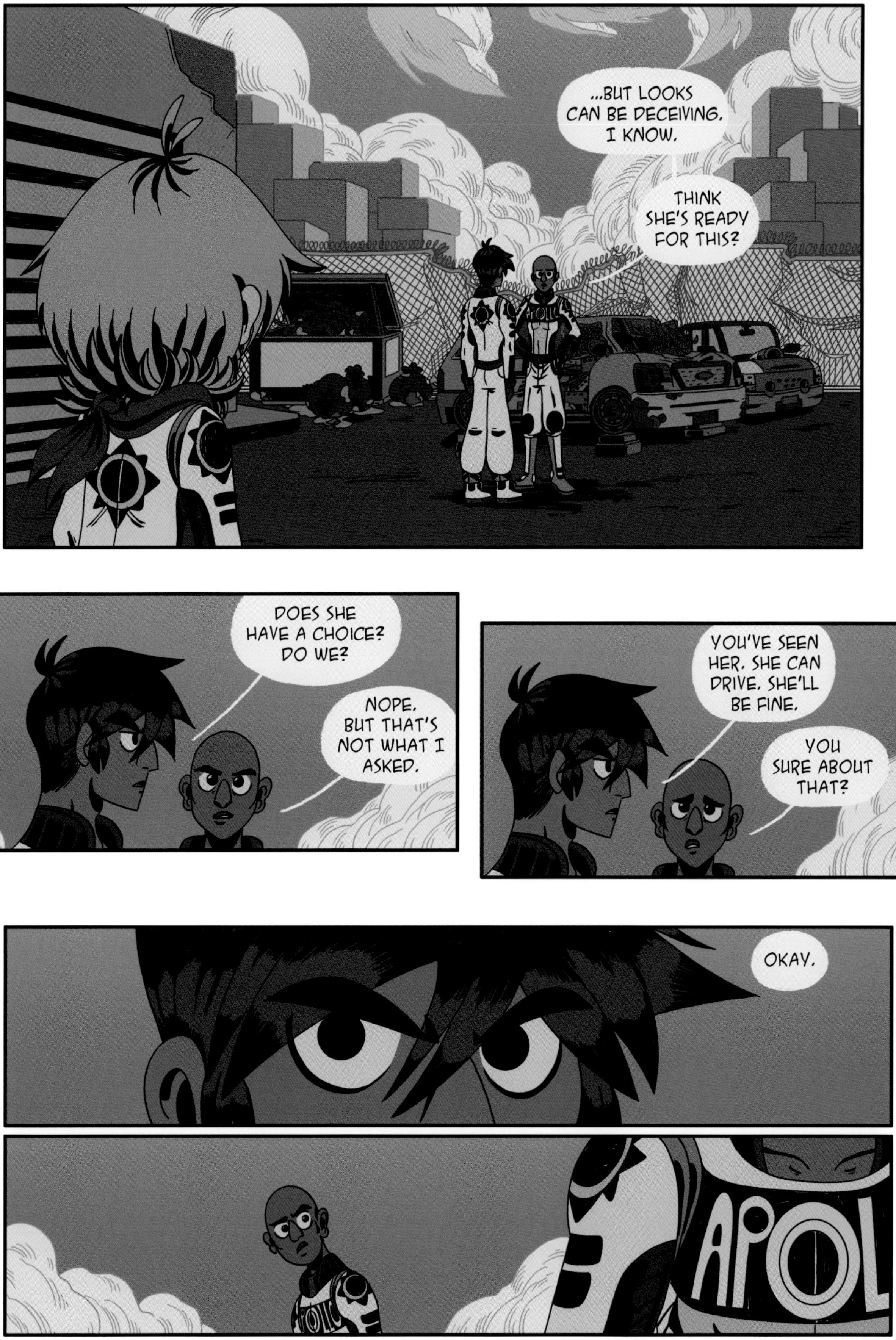
...BUT LOOKS CAN BE DECEIVING. I KNOW.
THINK SHE'S READY FOR THIS?
DOES SHE HAVE A CHOICE? DO WE?
NOPE. BUT THAT'S NOT WHAT I ASKED.
YOU'VE SEEN HER. SHE CAN DRIVE. SHE'LL BE FINE.
YOU SURE ABOUT THAT?
OKAY.
APOL

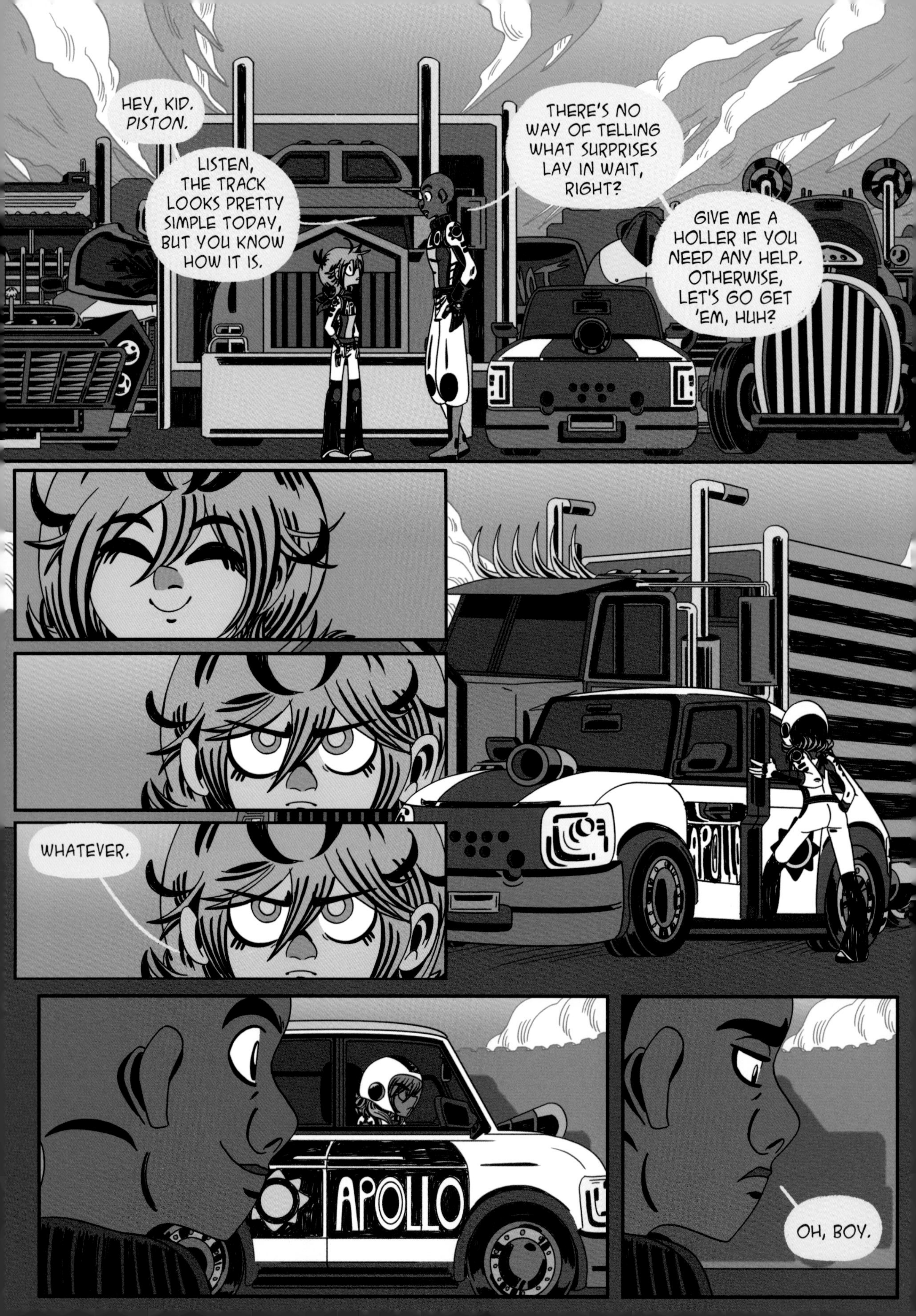
HEY, KID. PISTON.
LISTEN, THE TRACK LOOKS PRETTY SIMPLE TODAY, BUT YOU KNOW HOW IT IS.
THERE'S NO WAY OF TELLING WHAT SURPRISES LAY IN WAIT, RIGHT?
GIVE ME A HOLLER IF YOU NEED ANY HELP. OTHERWISE, LET'S GO GET 'EM, HUH?
WHATEVER.
APOLLO
APOLLO
OH, BOY.

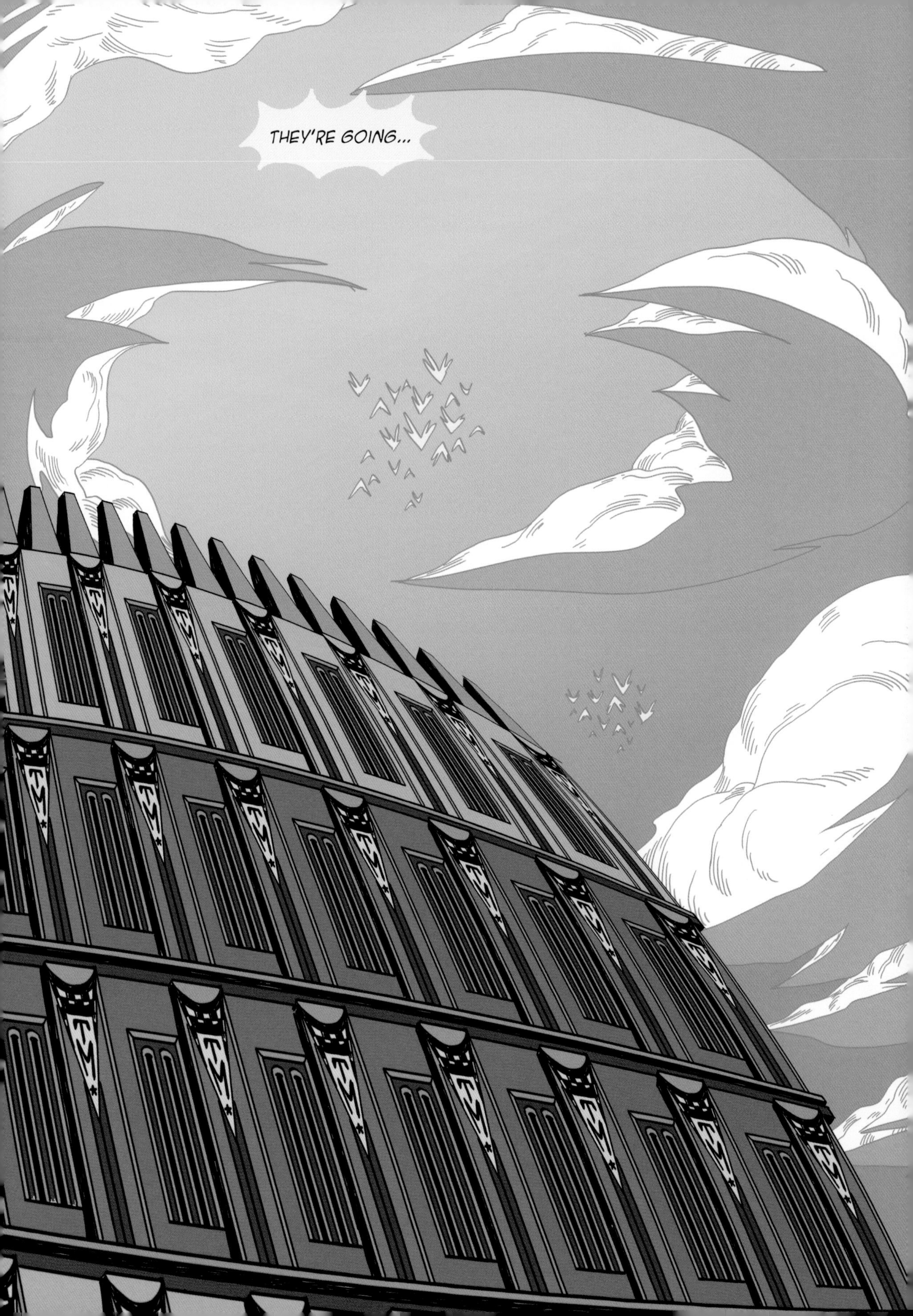
THEY'RE GOING...

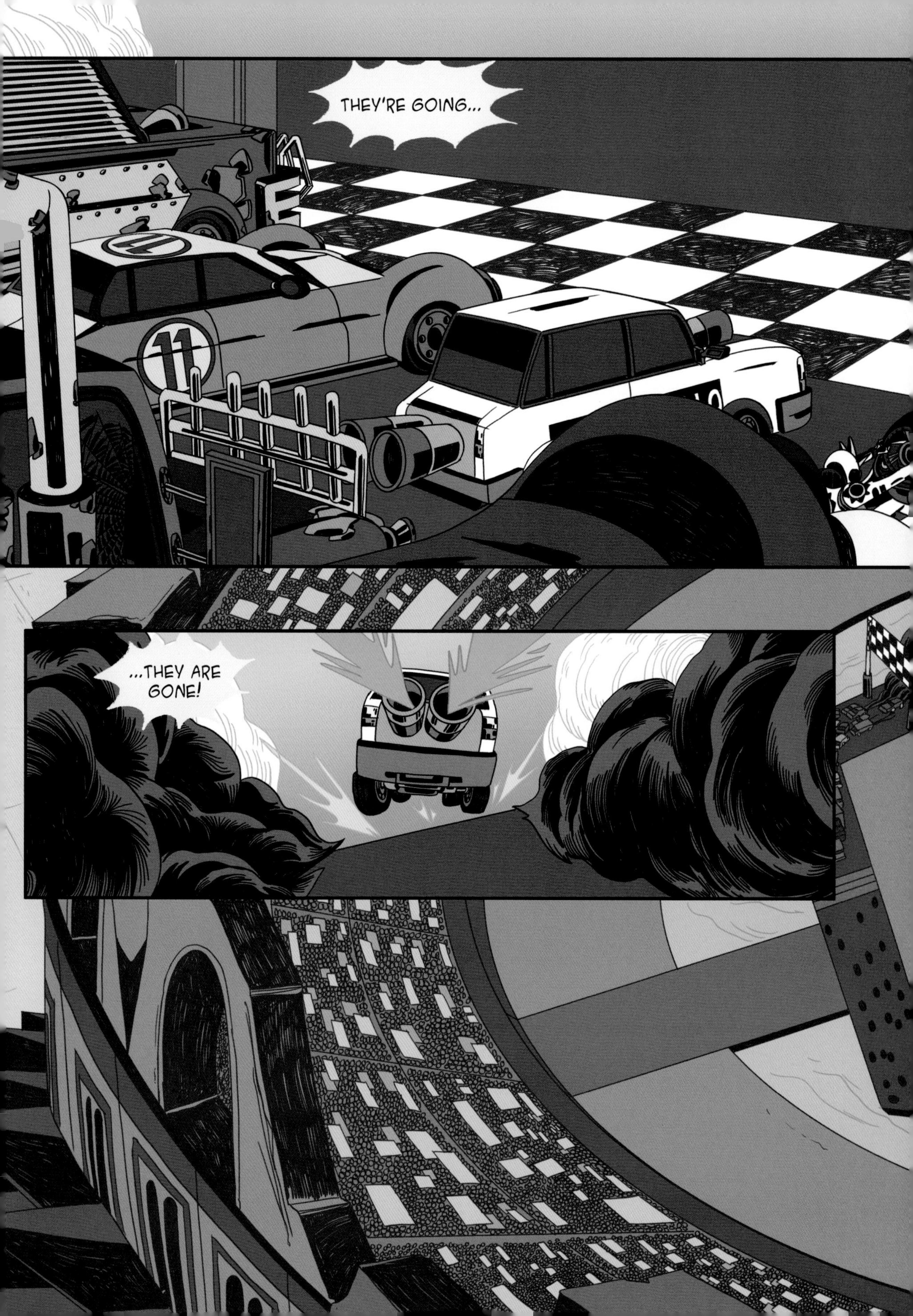
THEY'RE GOING...
...THEY ARE GONE!

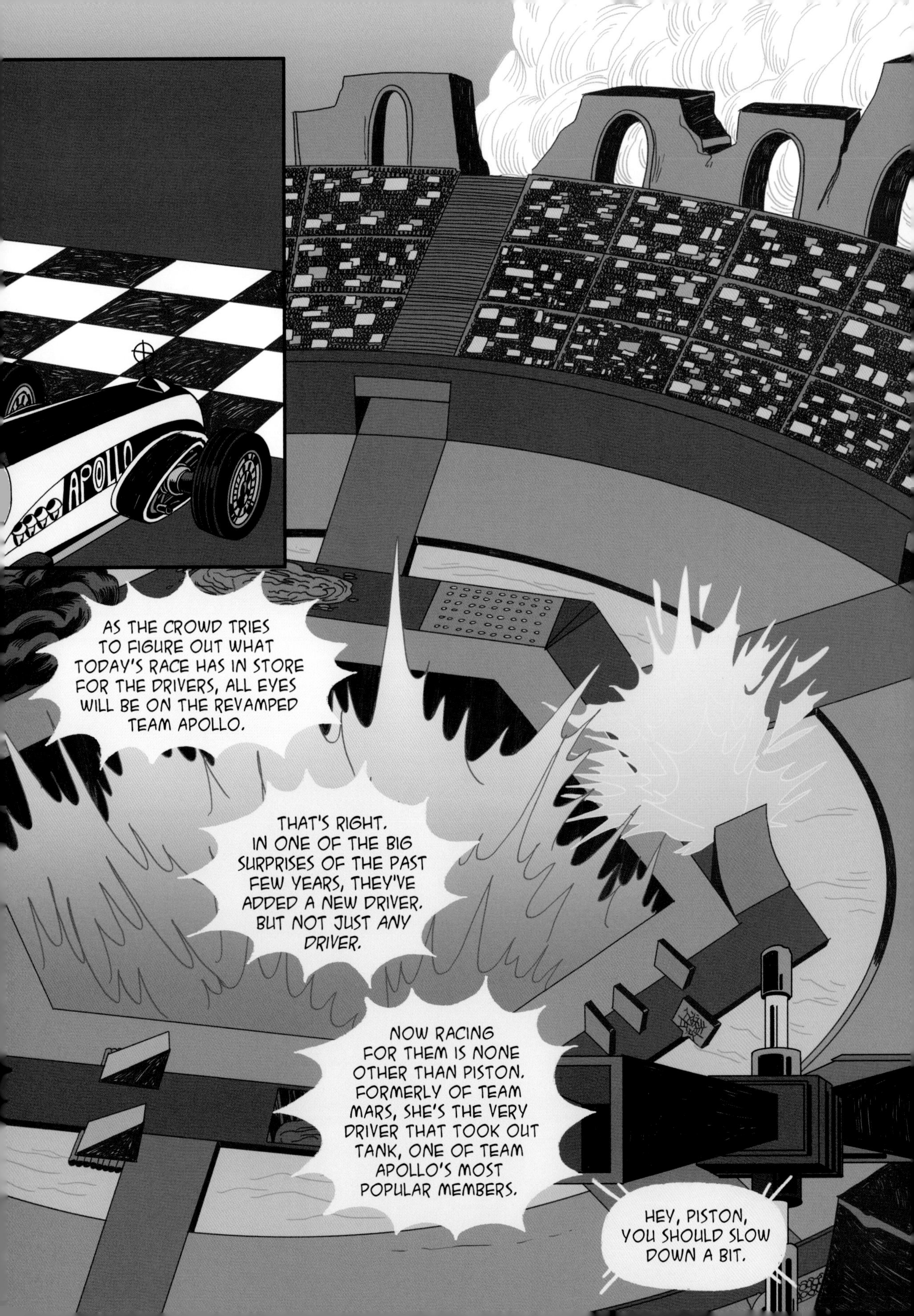
APOLLO
AS THE CROWD TRIES TO FIGURE OUT WHAT TODAY'S RACE HAS IN STORE FOR THE DRIVERS, ALL EYES WILL BE ON THE REVAMPED TEAM APOLLO.
THAT'S RIGHT. IN ONE OF THE BIG SURPRISES OF THE PAST FEW YEARS, THEY'VE ADDED A NEW DRIVER. BUT NOT JUST ANY DRIVER.
NOW RACING FOR THEM IS NONE OTHER THAN PISTON. FORMERLY OF TEAM MARS, SHE'S THE VERY DRIVER THAT TOOK OUT TANK, ONE OF TEAM APOLLO'S MOST POPULAR MEMBERS.
HEY, PISTON, YOU SHOULD SLOW DOWN A BIT.

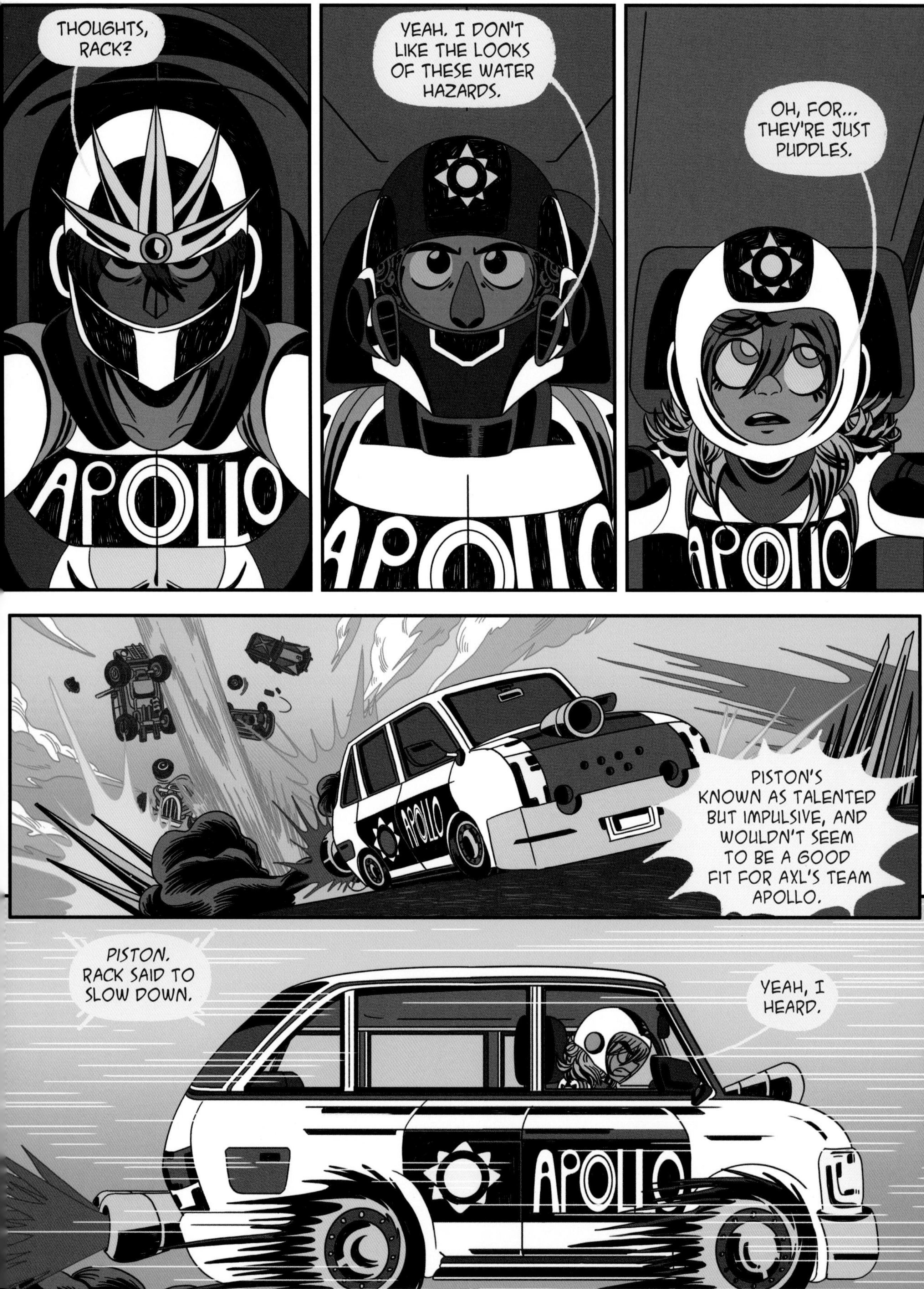
THOUGHTS, RACK?
YEAH. I DON'T LIKE THE LOOKS OF THESE WATER HAZARDS.
OH, FOR... THEY'RE JUST PUDDLES.
APOLLO
APOLLO
APOLLO
APOLLO
PISTON'S KNOWN AS TALENTED BUT IMPULSIVE, AND WOULDN'T SEEM TO BE A GOOD FIT FOR AXL'S TEAM APOLLO.
PISTON. RACK SAID TO SLOW DOWN.
YEAH, I HEARD.
APOLLO

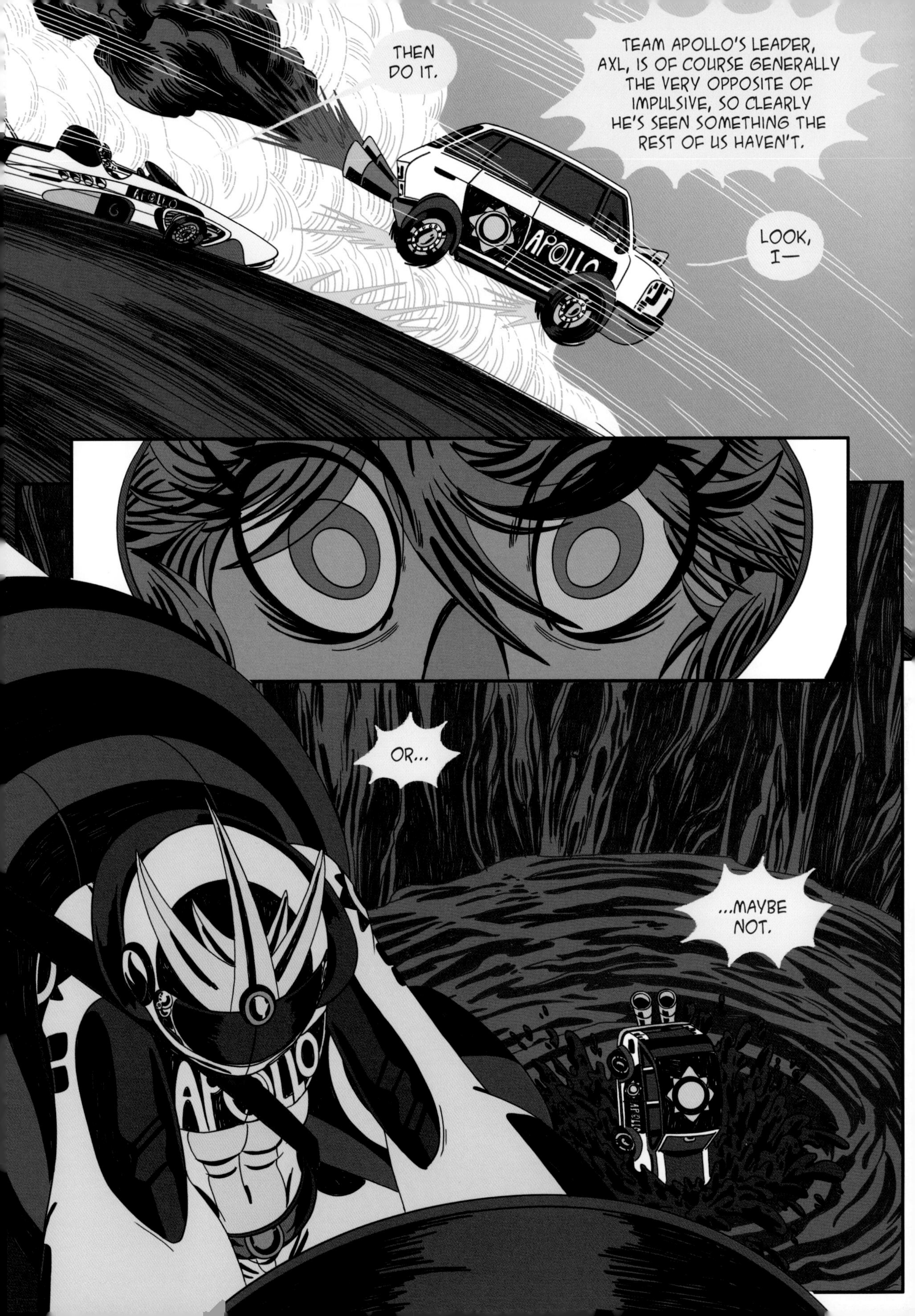
THEN DO IT.
TEAM APOLLO'S LEADER, AXL, IS OF COURSE GENERALLY THE VERY OPPOSITE OF IMPULSIVE, SO CLEARLY HE'S SEEN SOMETHING THE REST OF US HAVEN'T.
LOOK, I—
APOLLO
OR...
...MAYBE NOT.
APOLLO

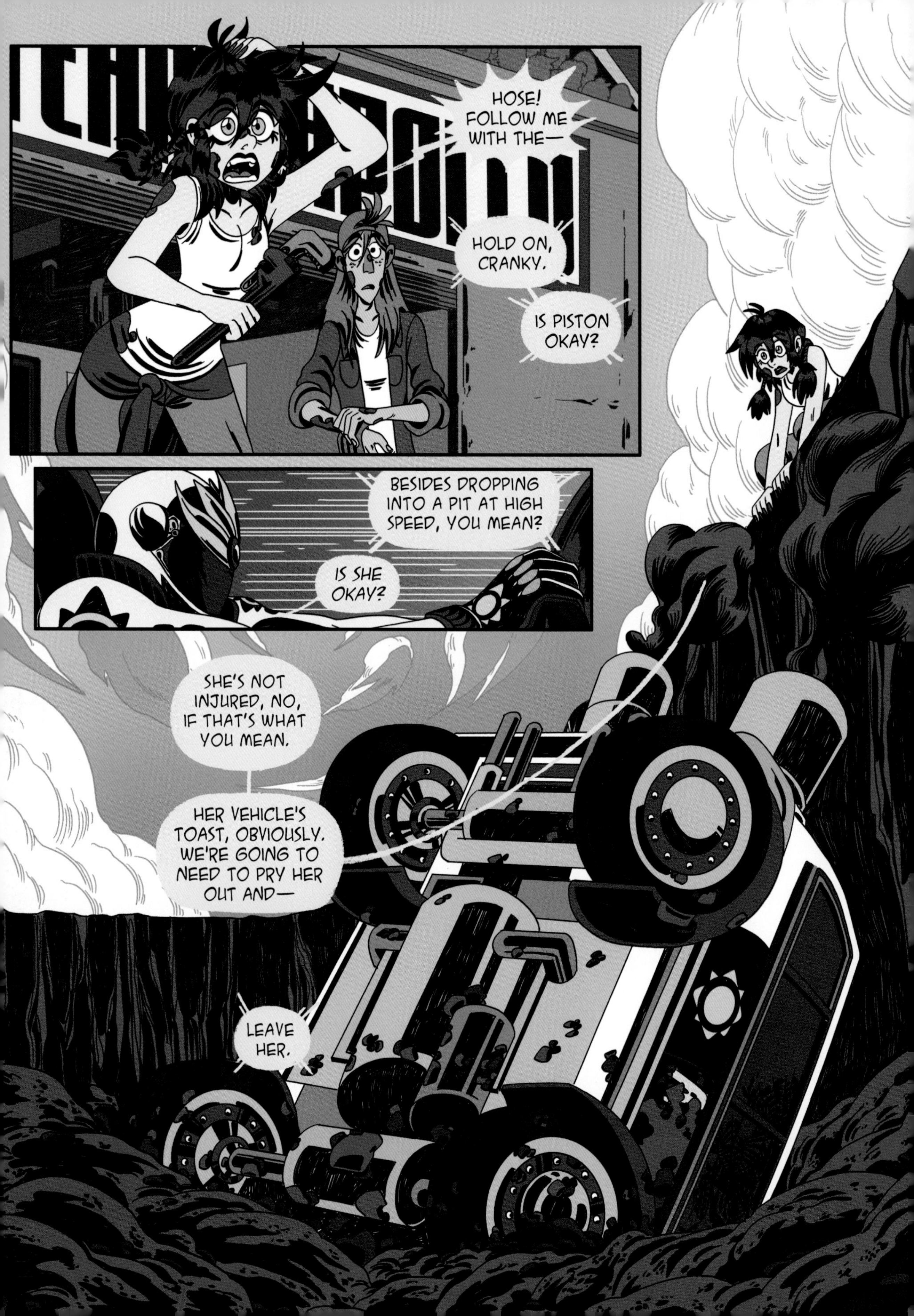
HOSE! FOLLOW ME WITH THE—
HOLD ON, CRANKY.
IS PISTON OKAY?
BESIDES DROPPING INTO A PIT AT HIGH SPEED, YOU MEAN?
IS SHE OKAY?
SHE'S NOT INJURED, NO, IF THAT'S WHAT YOU MEAN.
HER VEHICLE'S TOAST, OBVIOUSLY. WE'RE GOING TO NEED TO PRY HER OUT AND—
LEAVE HER.

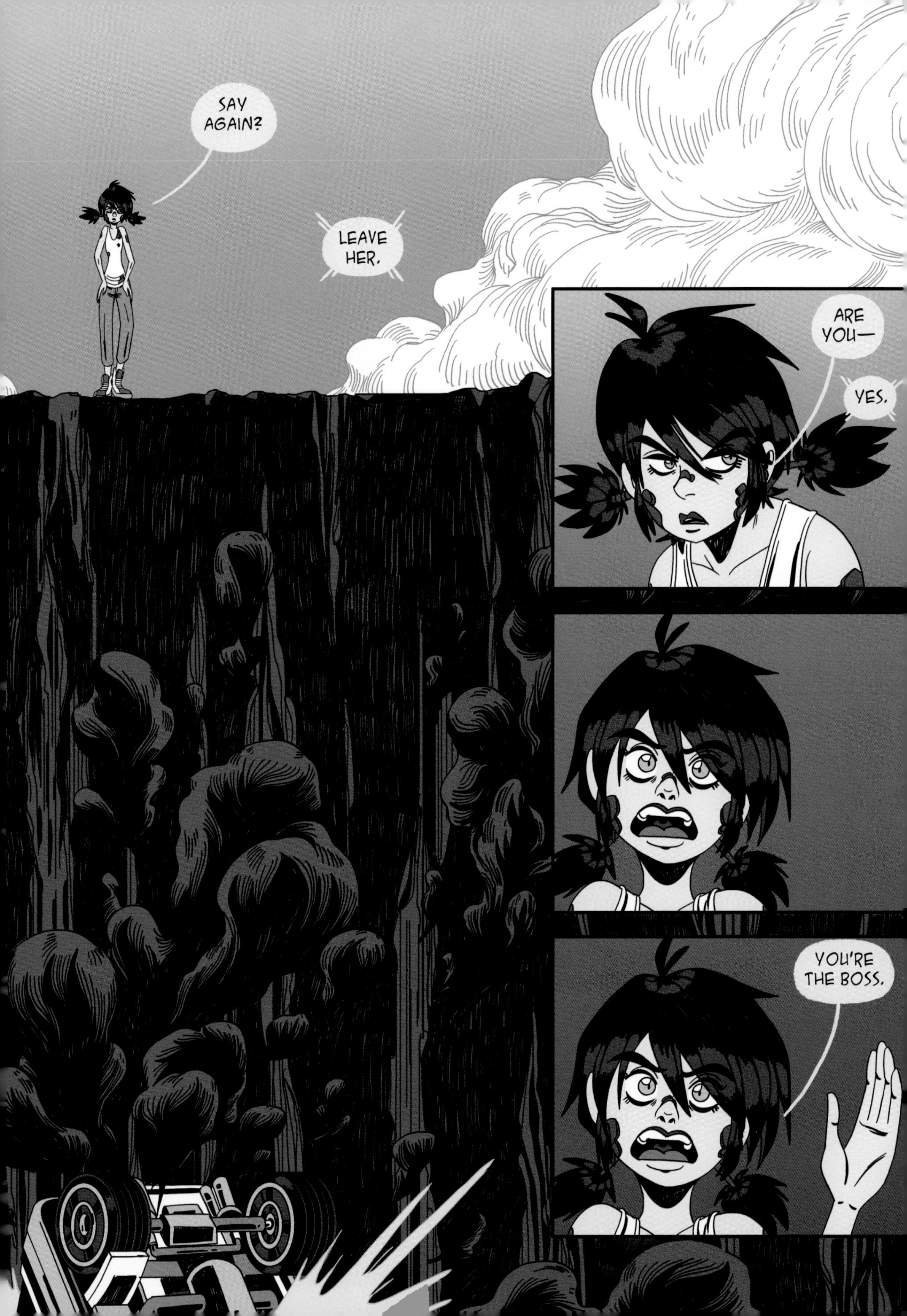

SAY AGAIN?
LEAVE HER.
ARE YOU—
YES.
YOU'RE THE BOSS.

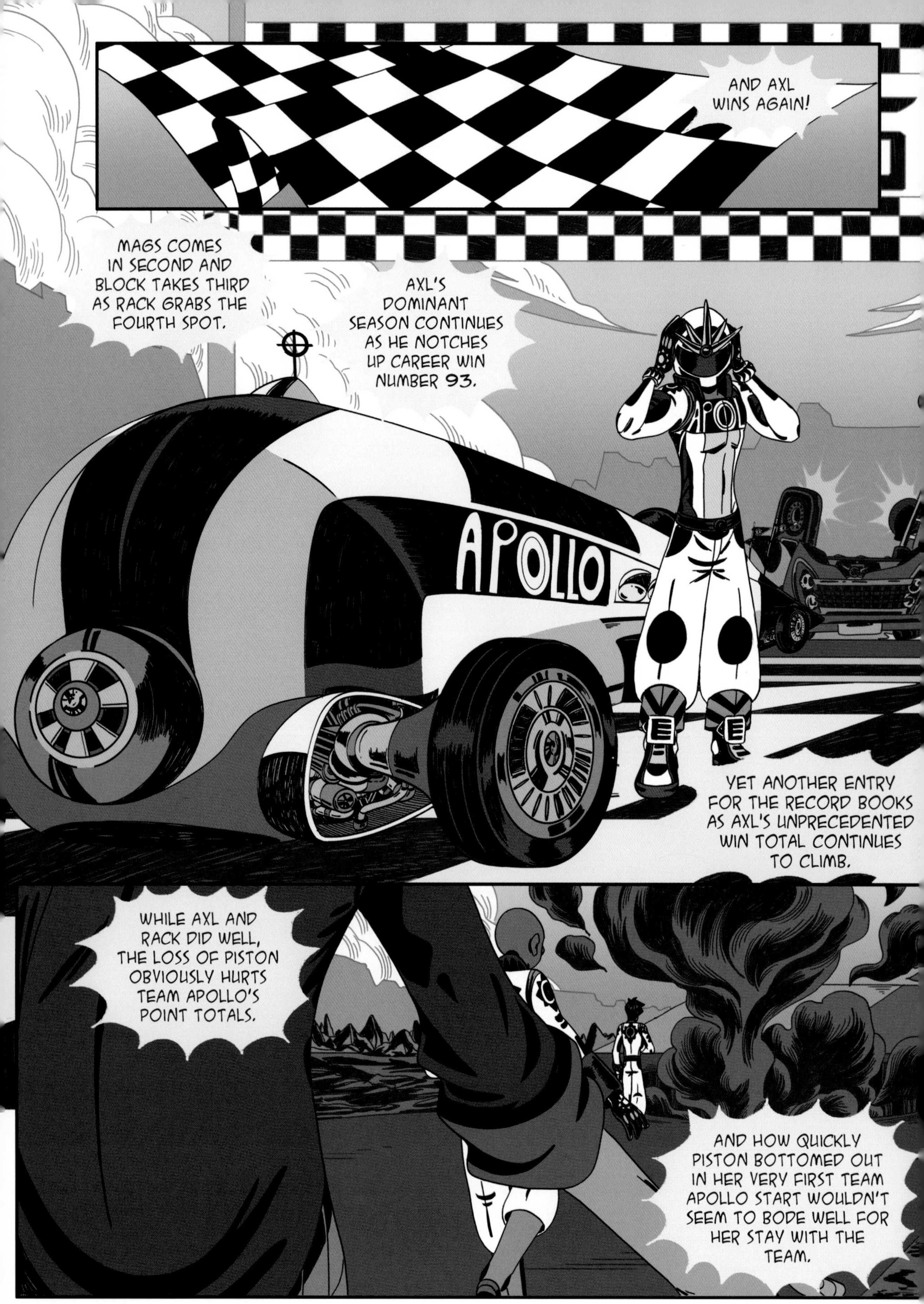
AND AXL WINS AGAIN!
MAGS COMES IN SECOND AND BLOCK TAKES THIRD AS RACK GRABS THE FOURTH SPOT.
AXL'S DOMINANT SEASON CONTINUES AS HE NOTCHES UP CAREER WIN NUMBER 93.
APOLLO
APOLLO
YET ANOTHER ENTRY FOR THE RECORD BOOKS AS AXL'S UNPRECEDENTED WIN TOTAL CONTINUES TO CLIMB.
WHILE AXL AND RACK DID WELL, THE LOSS OF PISTON OBVIOUSLY HURTS TEAM APOLLO'S POINT TOTALS.
AND HOW QUICKLY PISTON BOTTOMED OUT IN HER VERY FIRST TEAM APOLLO START WOULDN'T SEEM TO BODE WELL FOR HER STAY WITH THE TEAM.

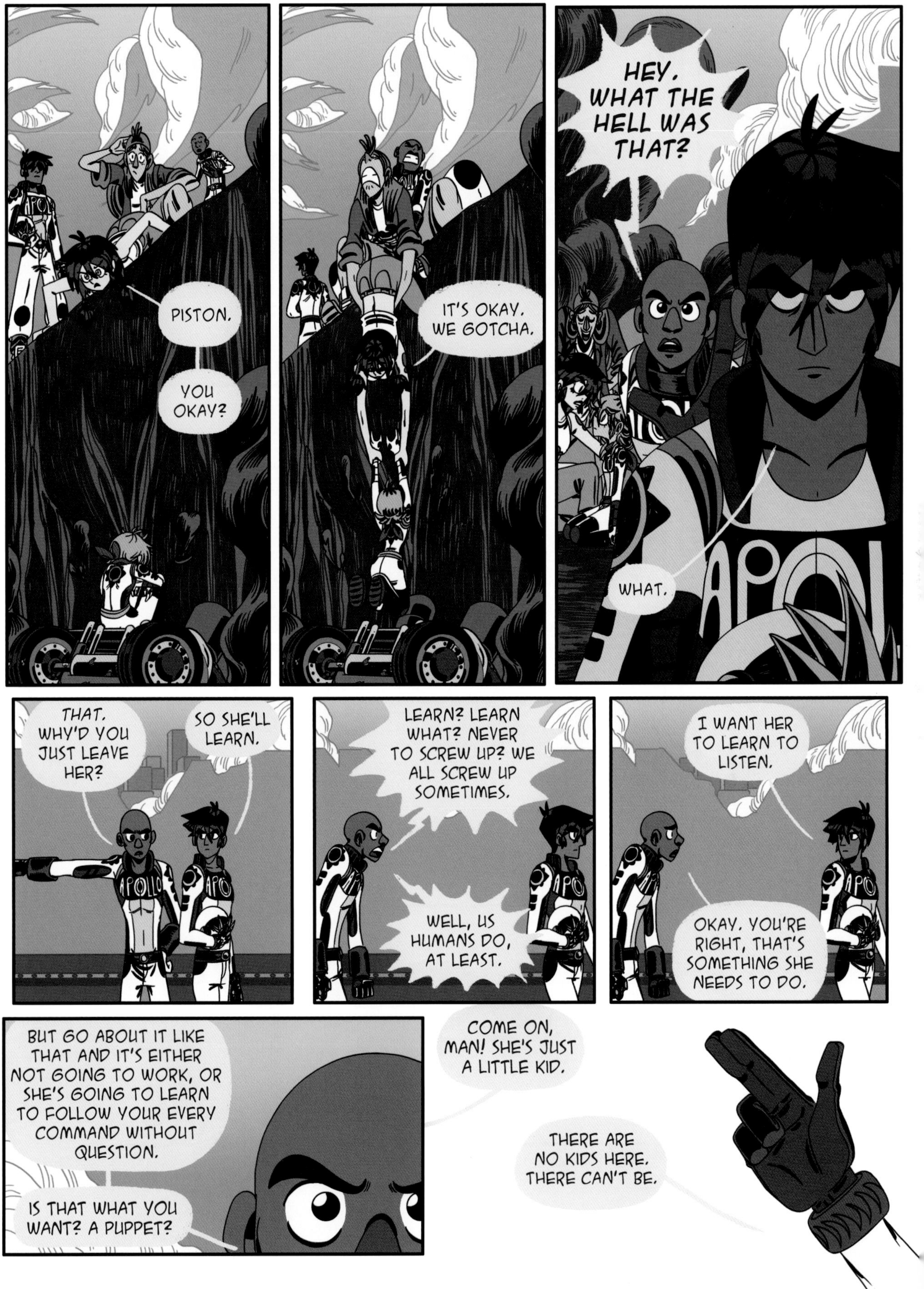
PISTON.
YOU OKAY?
IT'S OKAY. WE GOTCHA.
HEY. WHAT THE HELL WAS THAT?
WHAT.
THAT. WHY'D YOU JUST LEAVE HER?
SO SHE'LL LEARN.
LEARN? LEARN WHAT? NEVER TO SCREW UP? WE ALL SCREW UP SOMETIMES.
WELL, US HUMANS DO, AT LEAST.
I WANT HER TO LEARN TO LISTEN.
OKAY. YOU'RE RIGHT, THAT'S SOMETHING SHE NEEDS TO DO.
BUT GO ABOUT IT LIKE THAT AND IT'S EITHER NOT GOING TO WORK, OR SHE'S GOING TO LEARN TO FOLLOW YOUR EVERY COMMAND WITHOUT QUESTION.
IS THAT WHAT YOU WANT? A PUPPET?
COME ON, MAN! SHE'S JUST A LITTLE KID.
THERE ARE NO KIDS HERE. THERE CAN'T BE.

THAT WAS LITERALLY THE STUPIDEST THING I'VE EVER SEEN ANYONE DO, EVER.

I—

YEAH, YEAH, YOU. I'VE SEEN YOUR TYPE BEFORE. IT'S YOU. ALWAYS YOU.

NOW IF YOU DON'T MIND.

I'M GOING TO BE UP ALL NIGHT TRYING TO FIX WHAT YOU DID TO *OUR* VEHICLE, SO I'D LIKE TO GET STARTED.

JEEZ.

NOT HARD TO GUESS WHY SHE'S CALLED CRANKY.

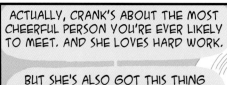

ACTUALLY, CRANK'S ABOUT THE MOST CHEERFUL PERSON YOU'RE EVER LIKELY TO MEET. AND SHE LOVES HARD WORK.

BUT SHE'S ALSO GOT THIS THING ABOUT, YOU KNOW, LOVED ONES— SHE LOVES THEM. SO WHEN SOMEONE MAYBE KILLS ONE OF 'EM, WELL, IT PUTS HER A BIT ON EDGE.

AND WHEN THAT PERSON THEN GOES ON TO DO SOMETHING *ELSE* STUPID, WELL...

I'M SORRY, I DIDN'T...

...WAIT. SERIOUSLY?

NO, SHE'S PRETTY MUCH ALWAYS THAT WAY.

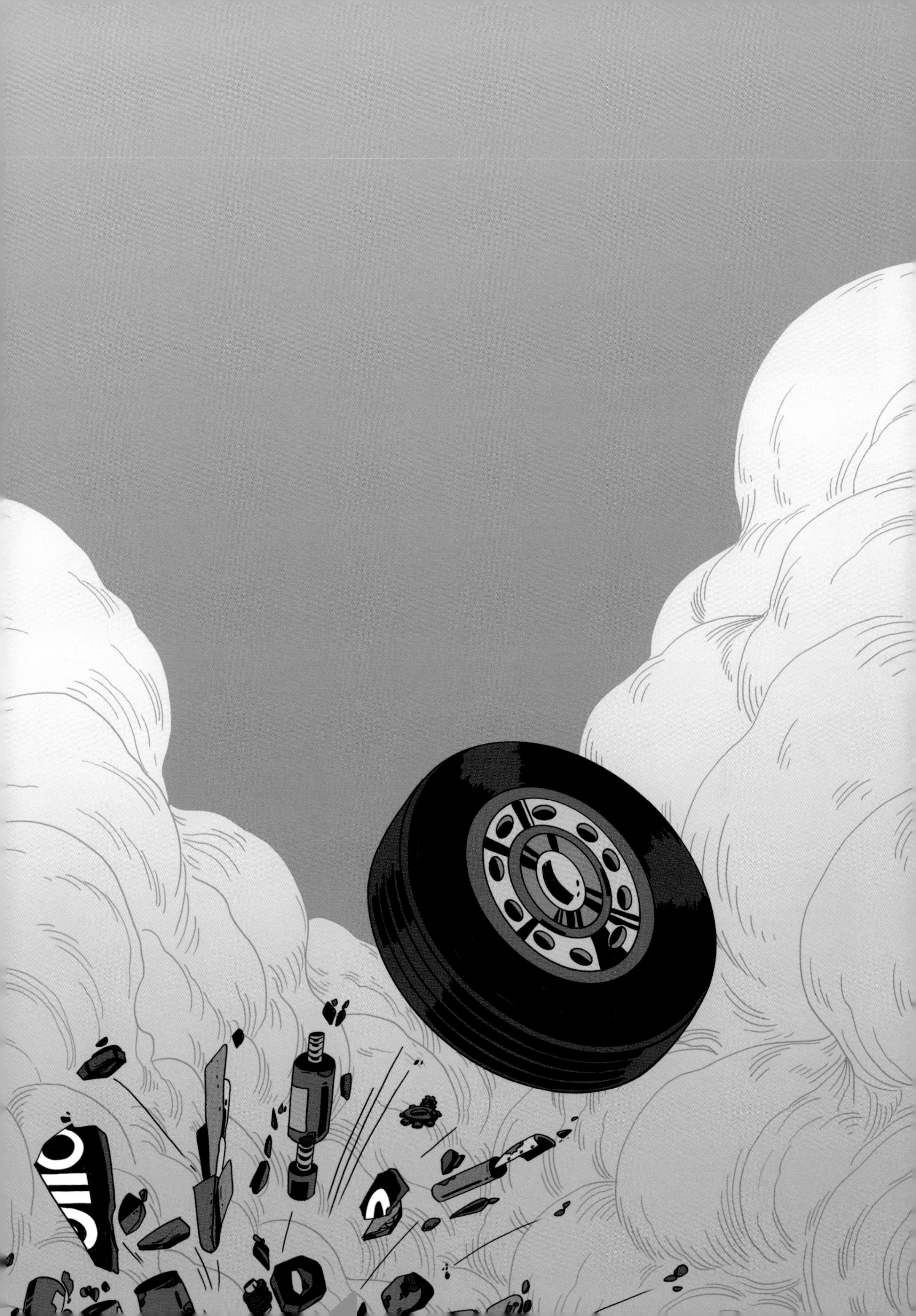

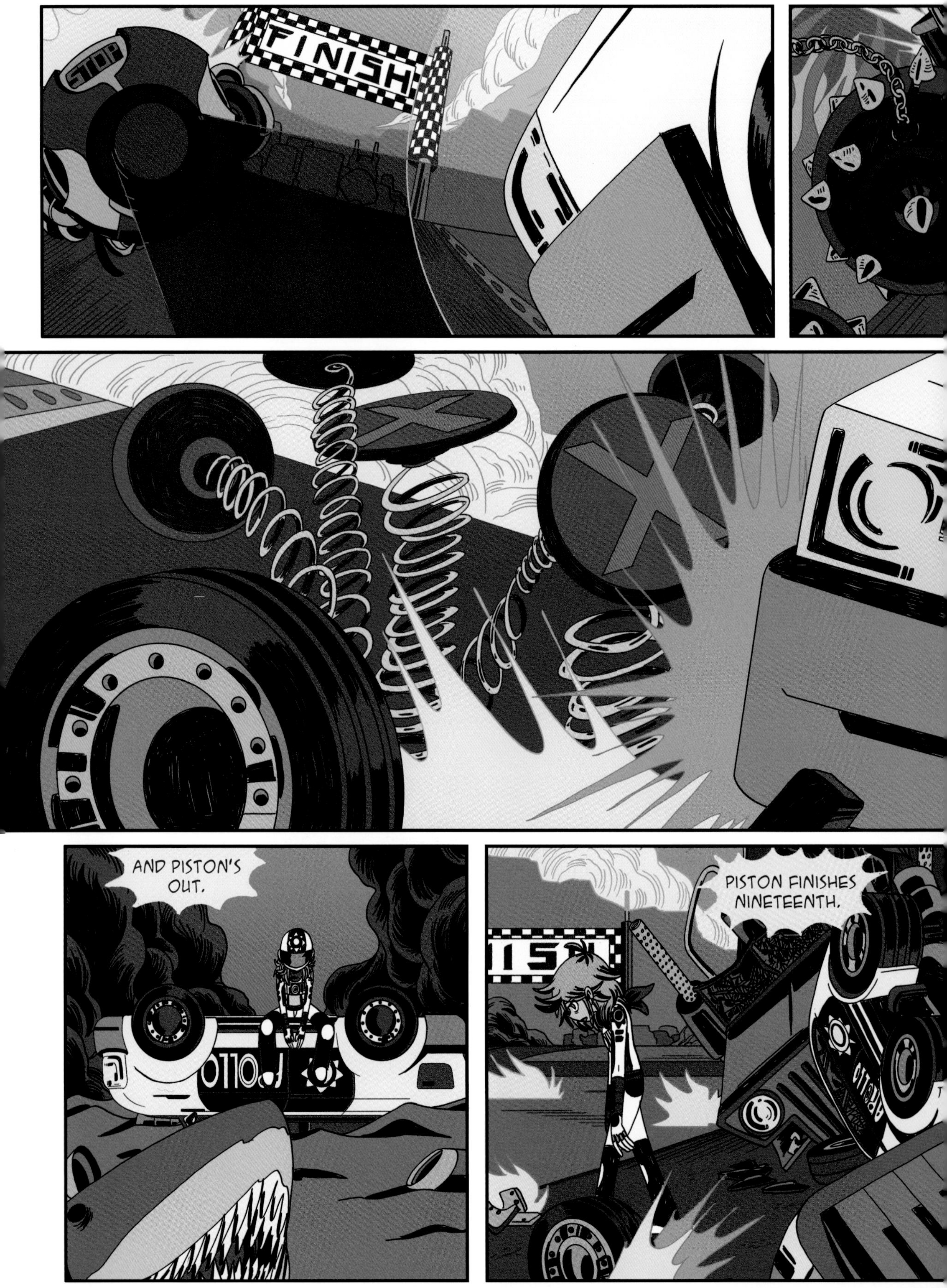
STOP
FINISH
AND PISTON'S OUT.
PISTON FINISHES NINETEENTH.

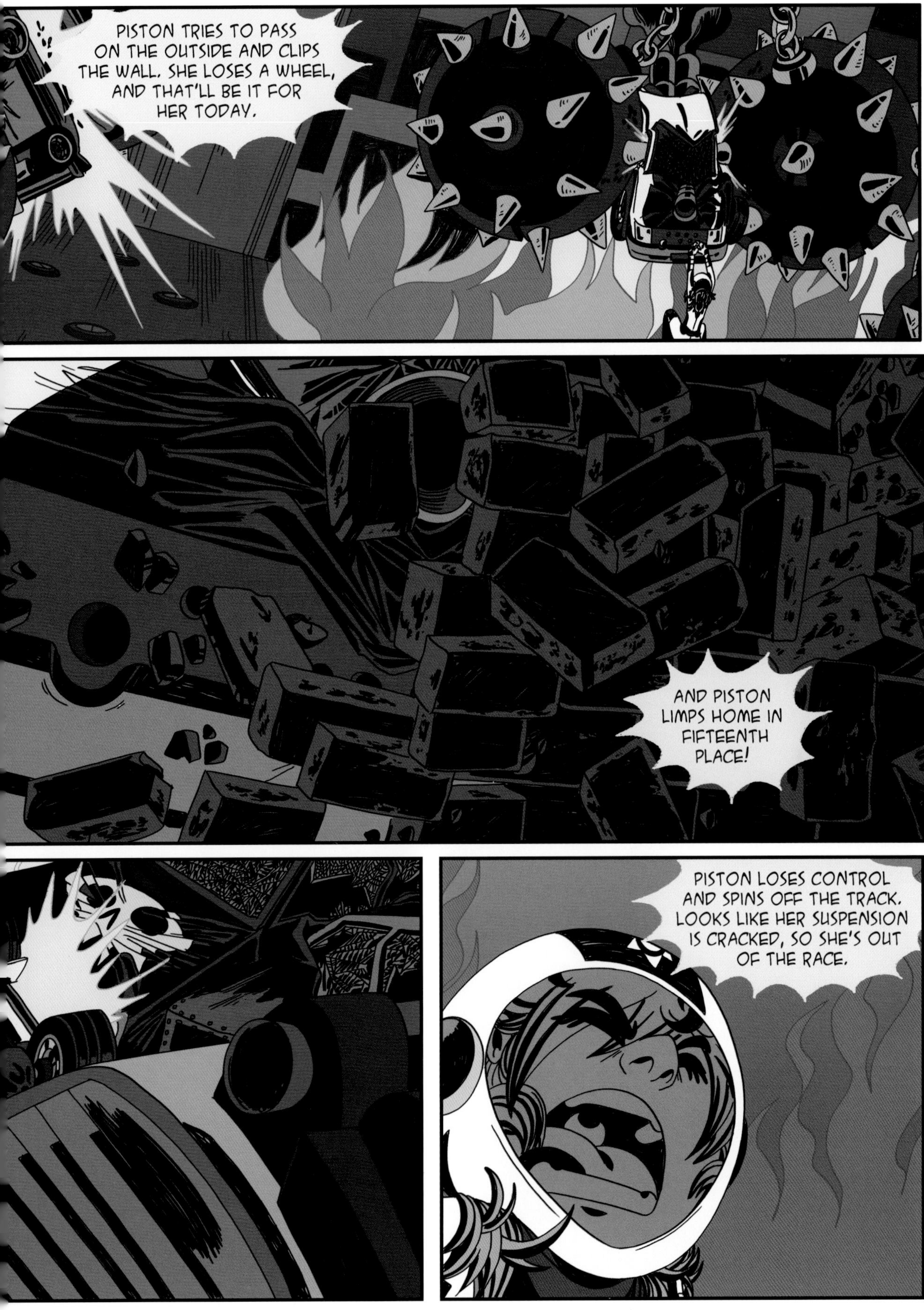
PISTON TRIES TO PASS ON THE OUTSIDE AND CLIPS THE WALL. SHE LOSES A WHEEL, AND THAT'LL BE IT FOR HER TODAY.
AND PISTON LIMPS HOME IN FIFTEENTH PLACE!
PISTON LOSES CONTROL AND SPINS OFF THE TRACK. LOOKS LIKE HER SUSPENSION IS CRACKED, SO SHE'S OUT OF THE RACE.

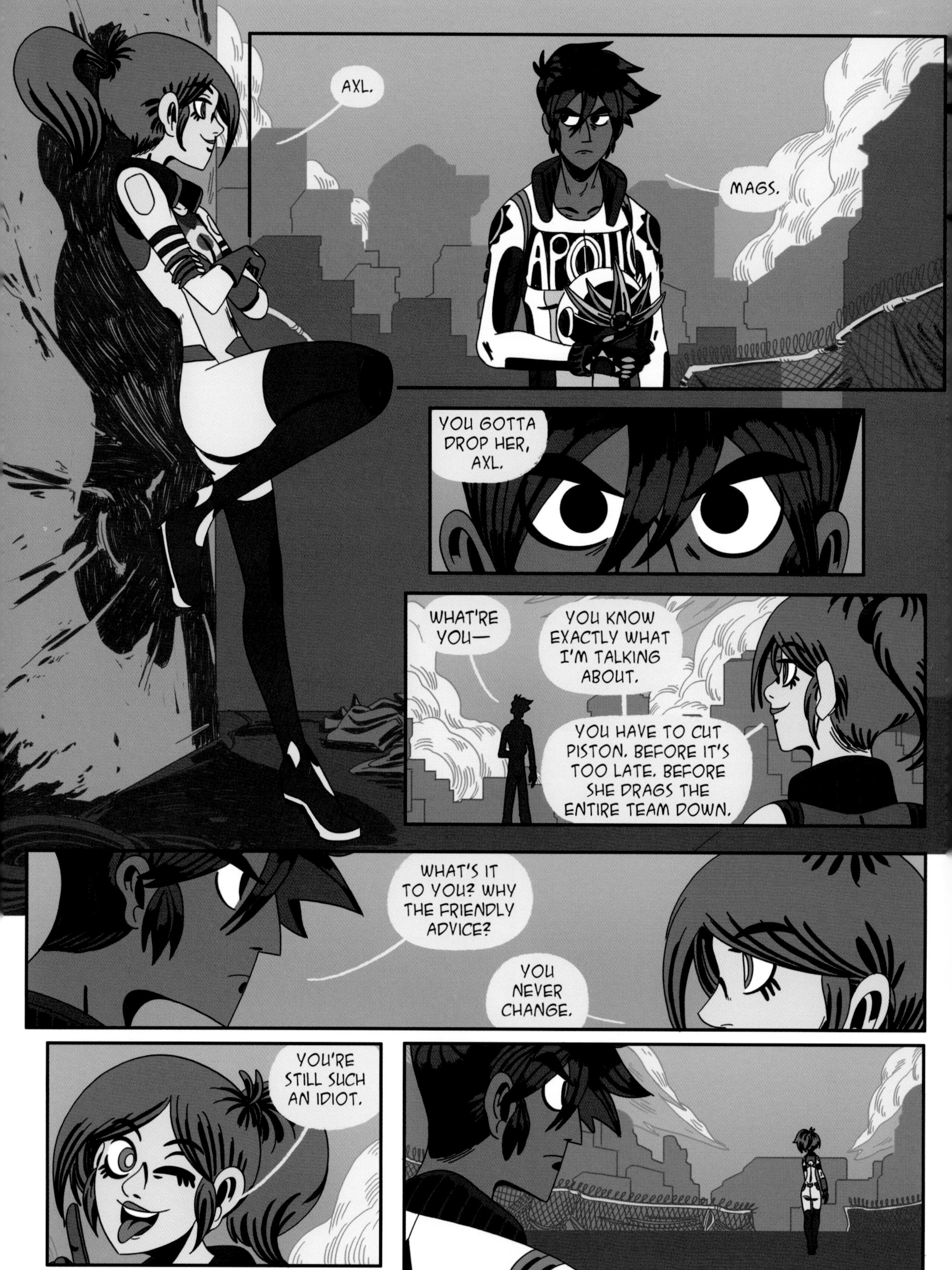
AXL.
MAGS.
APOLLO
YOU GOTTA DROP HER, AXL.
WHAT'RE YOU—
YOU KNOW EXACTLY WHAT I'M TALKING ABOUT.
YOU HAVE TO CUT PISTON. BEFORE IT'S TOO LATE. BEFORE SHE DRAGS THE ENTIRE TEAM DOWN.
WHAT'S IT TO YOU? WHY THE FRIENDLY ADVICE?
YOU NEVER CHANGE.
YOU'RE STILL SUCH AN IDIOT.

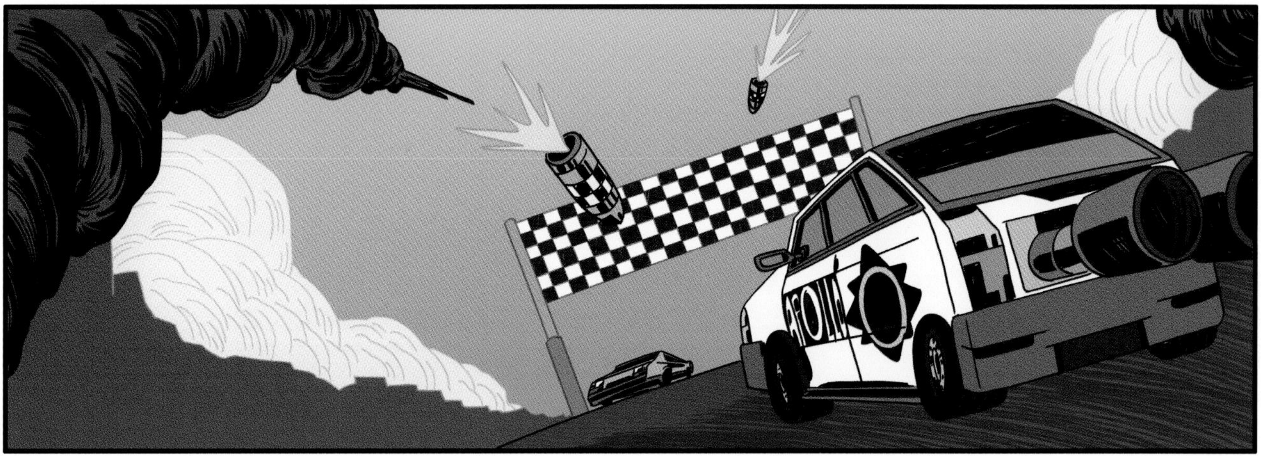

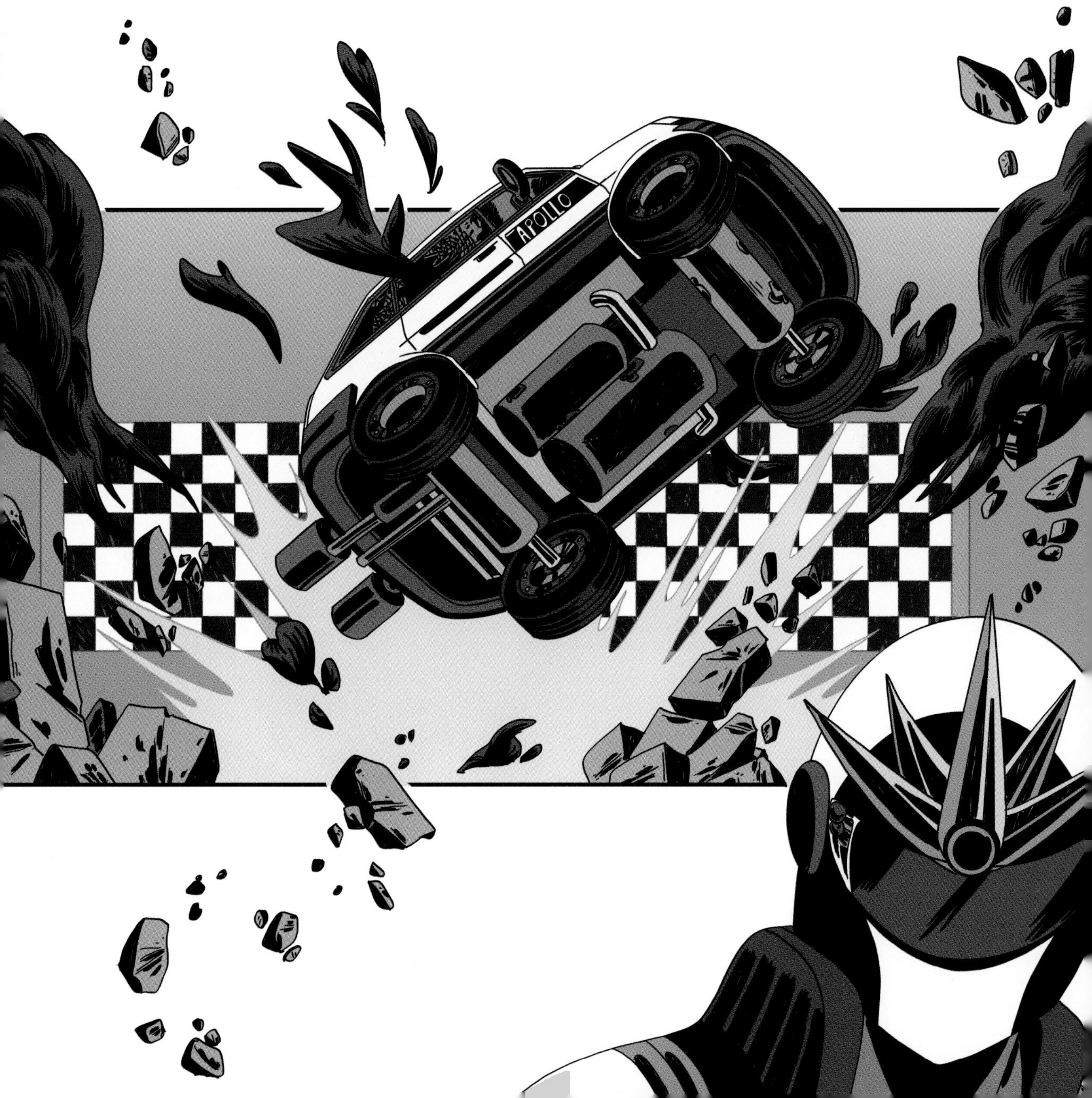
APOLLO

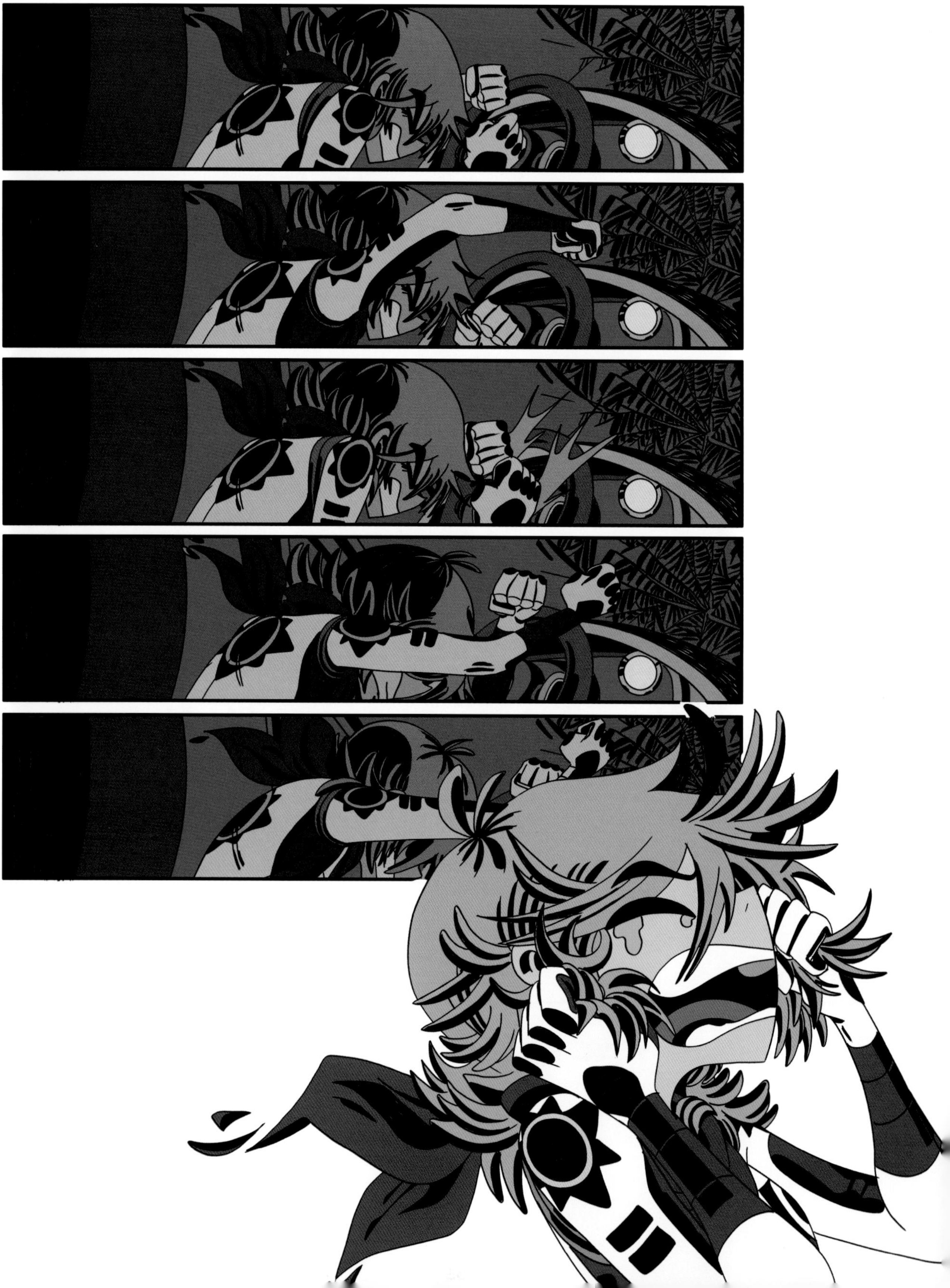

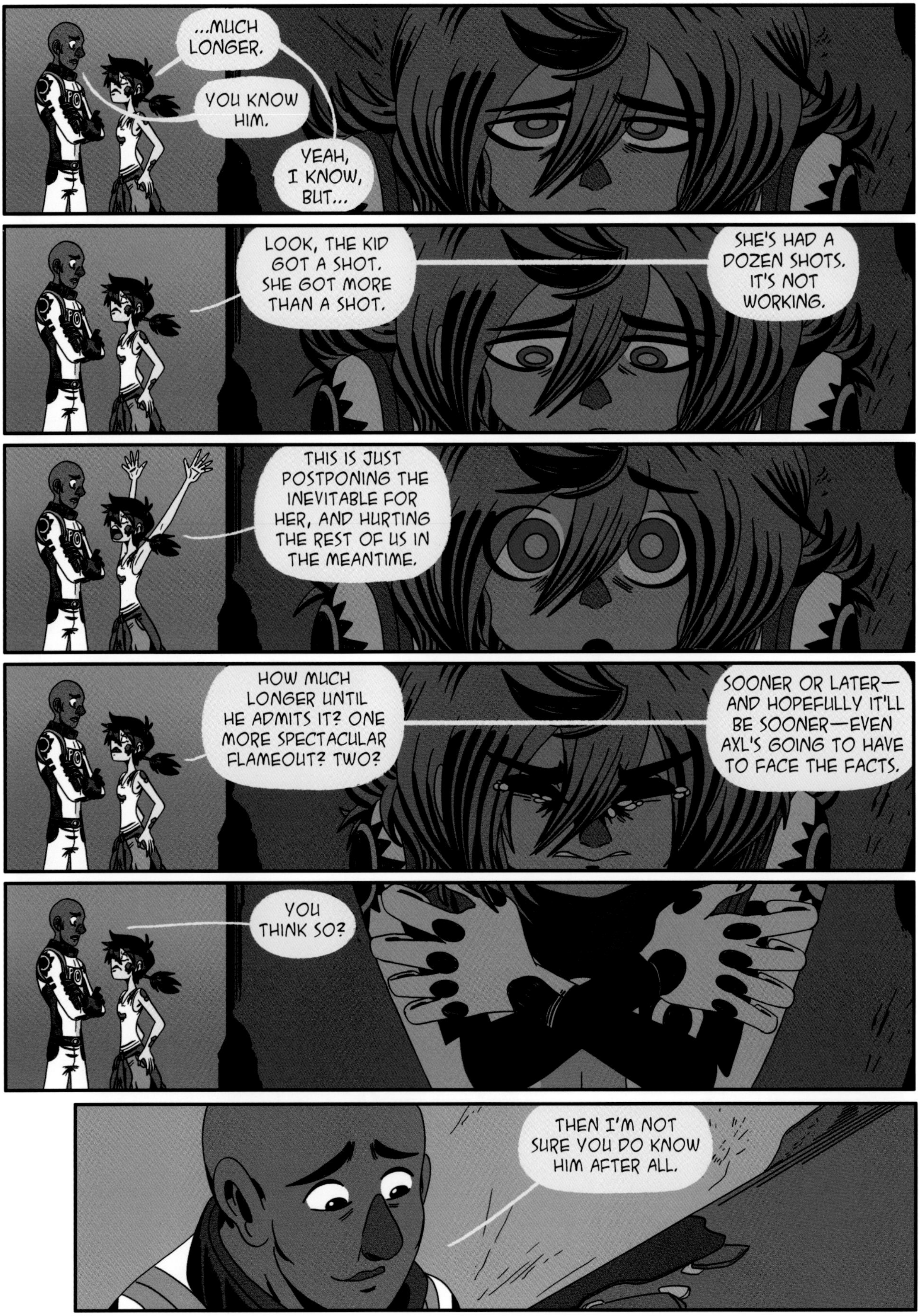
...MUCH LONGER.
YOU KNOW HIM.
YEAH, I KNOW, BUT...
LOOK, THE KID GOT A SHOT. SHE GOT MORE THAN A SHOT.
SHE'S HAD A DOZEN SHOTS. IT'S NOT WORKING.
THIS IS JUST POSTPONING THE INEVITABLE FOR HER, AND HURTING THE REST OF US IN THE MEANTIME.
HOW MUCH LONGER UNTIL HE ADMITS IT? ONE MORE SPECTACULAR FLAMEOUT? TWO?
SOONER OR LATER—AND HOPEFULLY IT'LL BE SOONER—EVEN AXL'S GOING TO HAVE TO FACE THE FACTS.
YOU THINK SO?
THEN I'M NOT SURE YOU DO KNOW HIM AFTER ALL.

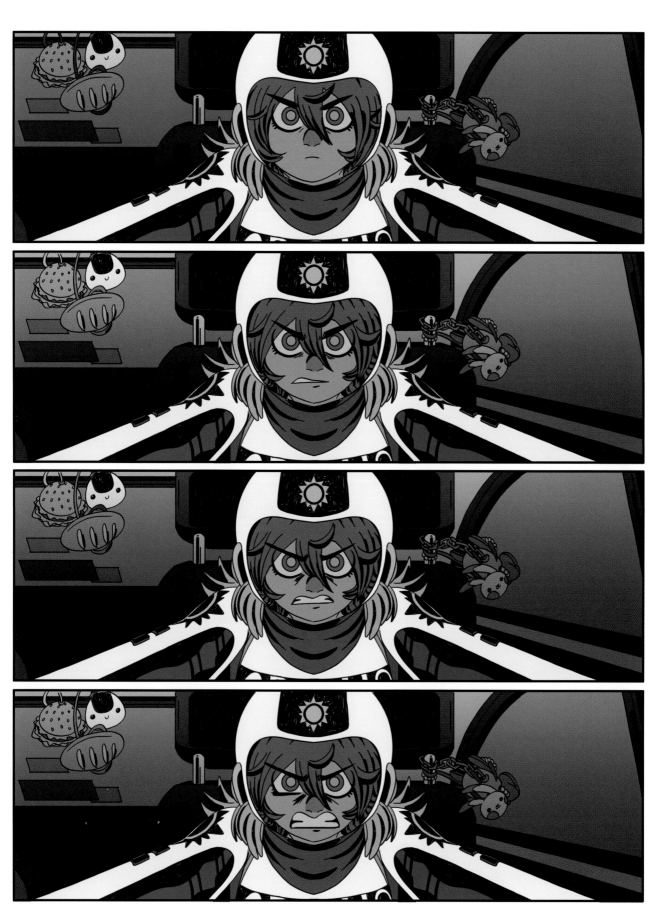

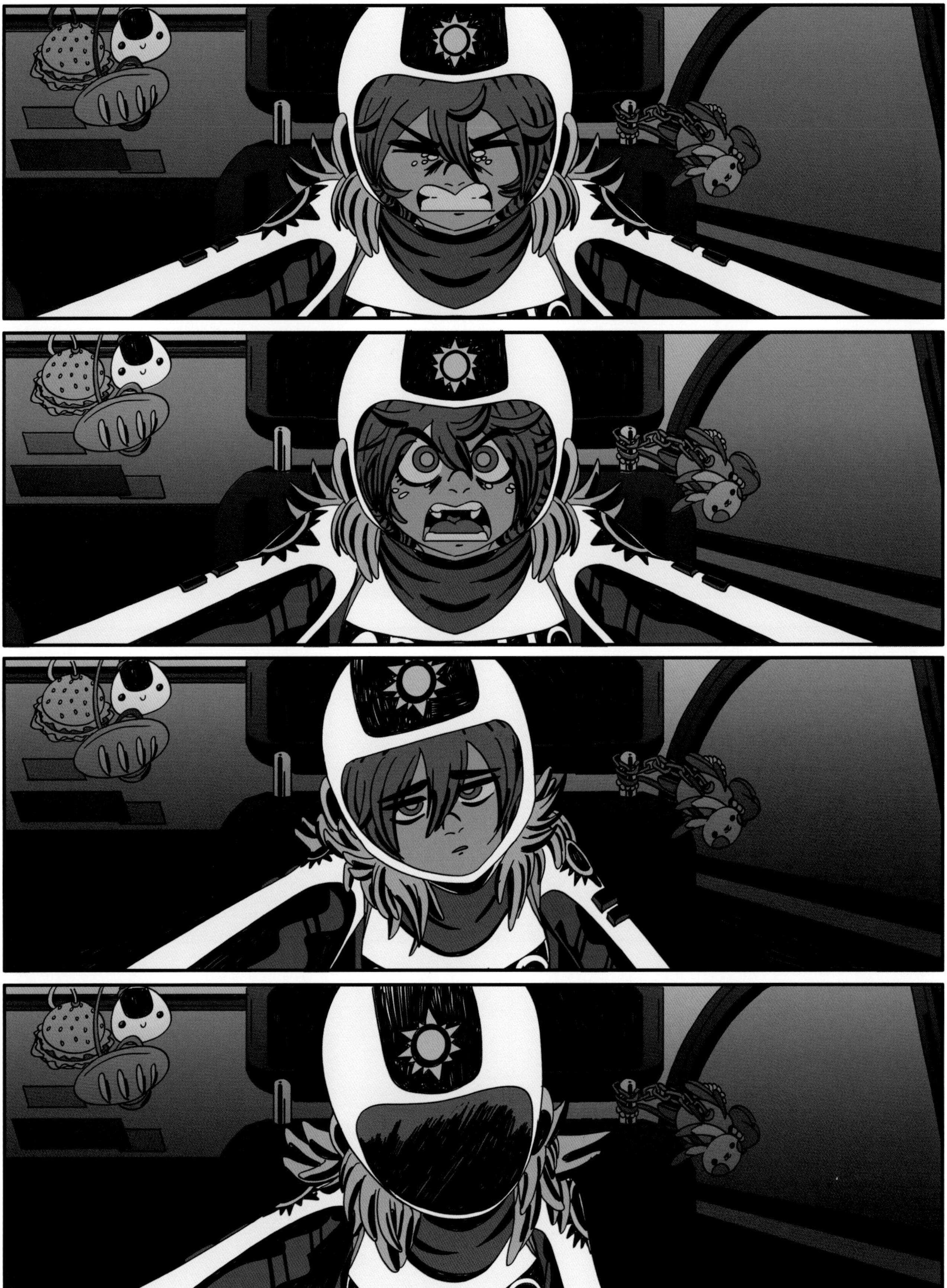

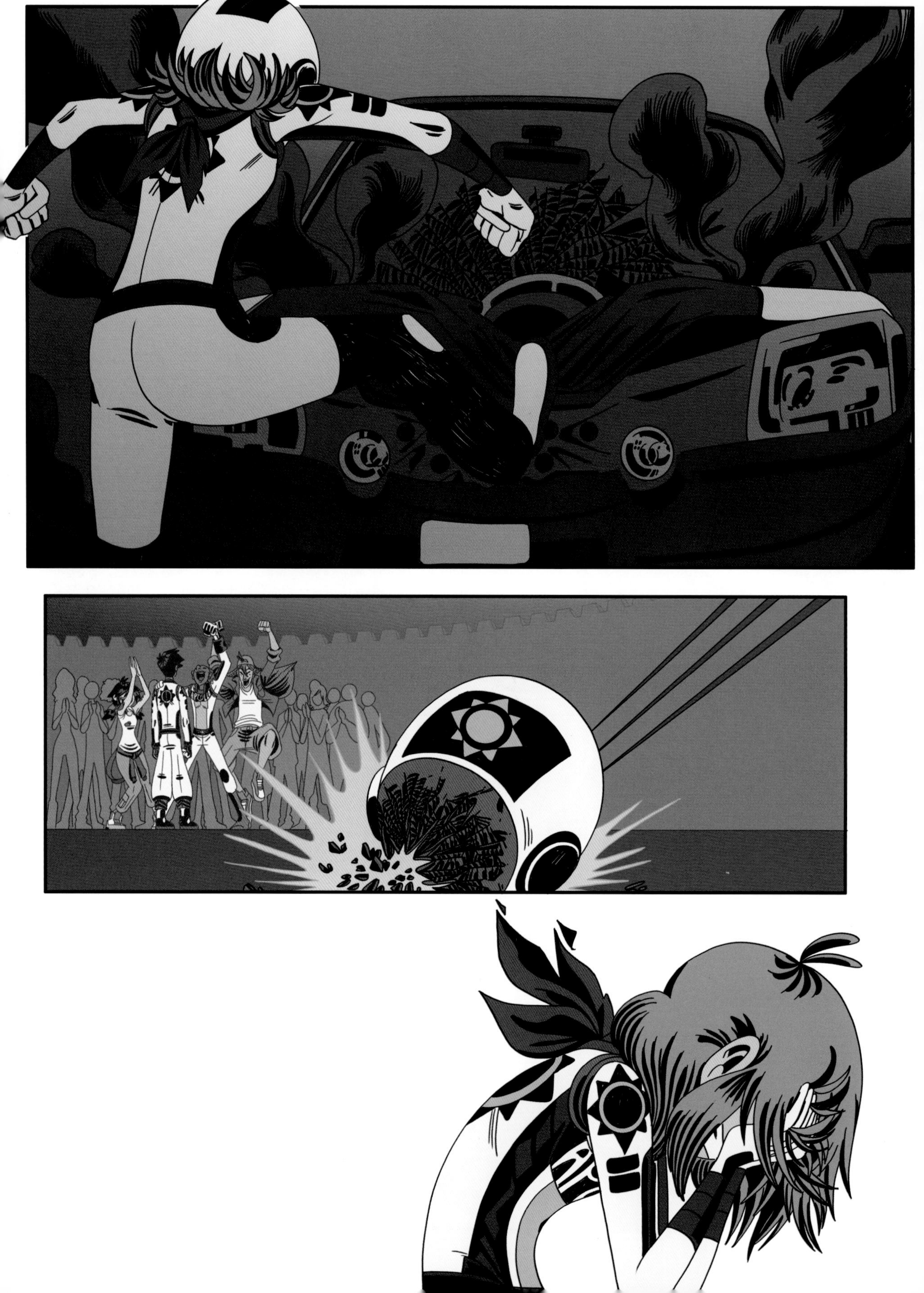

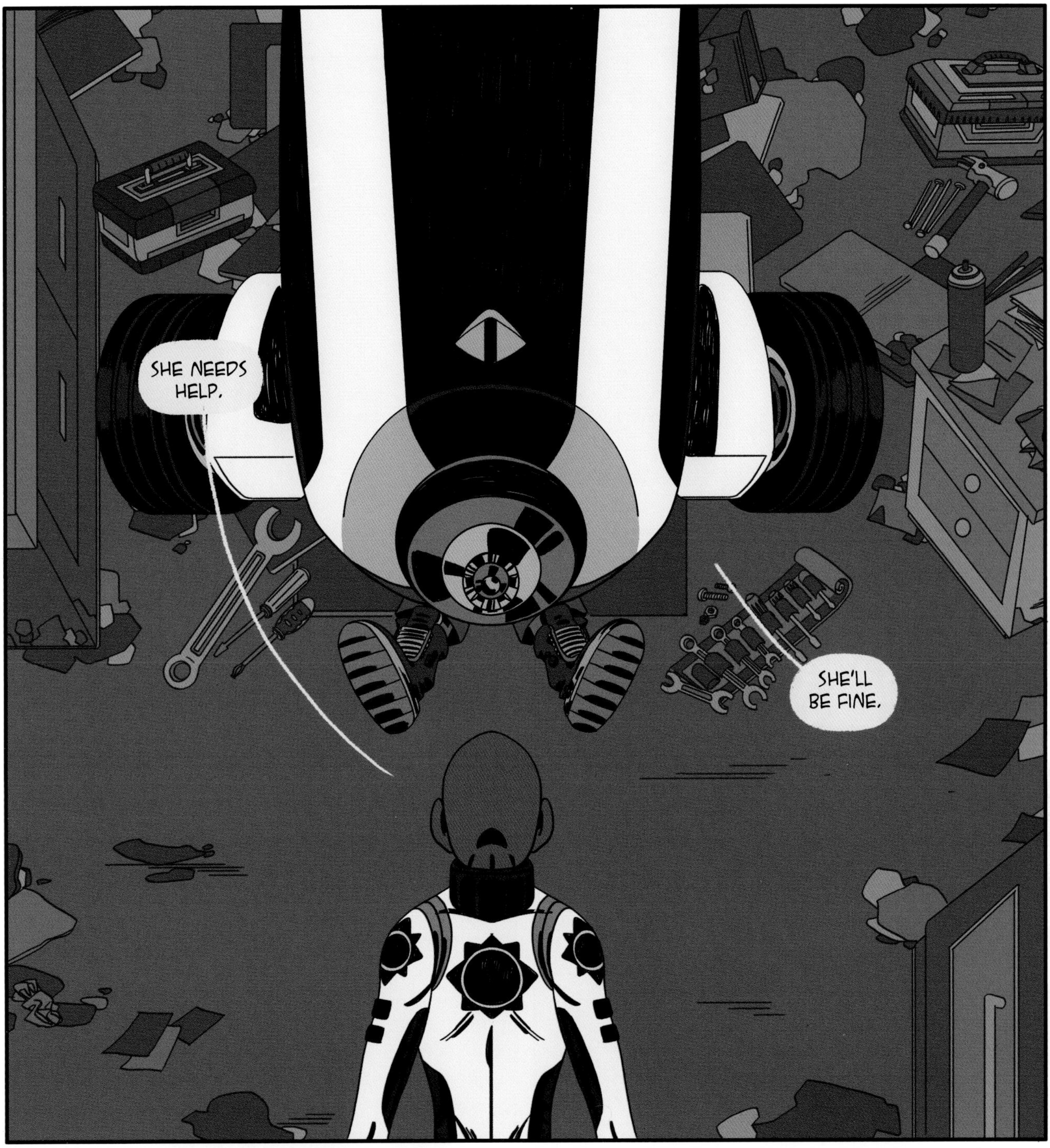
SHE NEEDS HELP.
SHE'LL BE FINE.

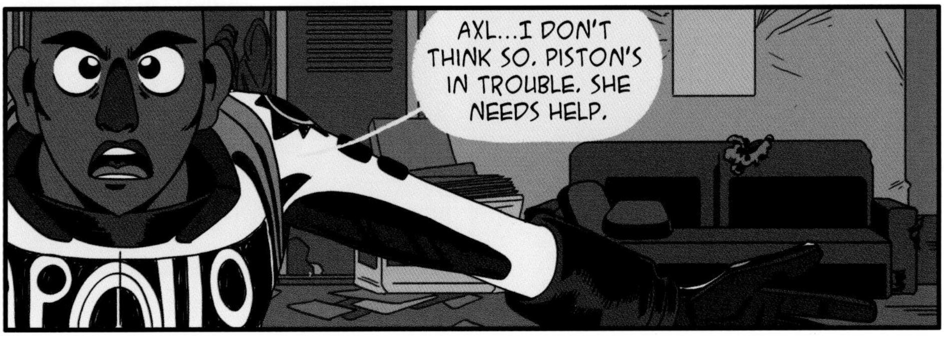
AXL...I DON'T THINK SO. PISTON'S IN TROUBLE. SHE NEEDS HELP.

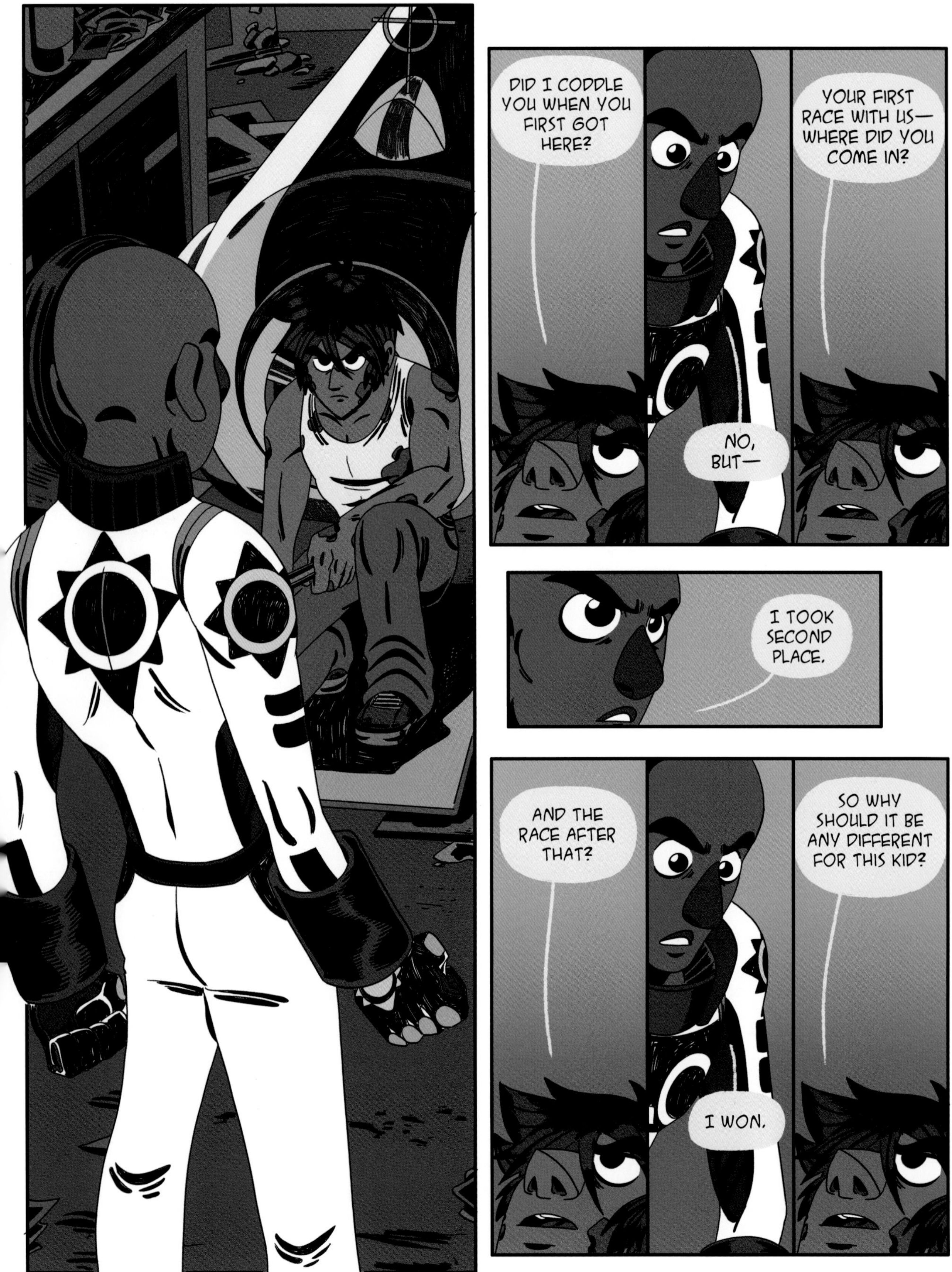

DID I CODDLE YOU WHEN YOU FIRST GOT HERE?
NO, BUT—
YOUR FIRST RACE WITH US—WHERE DID YOU COME IN?
I TOOK SECOND PLACE.
AND THE RACE AFTER THAT?
I WON.
SO WHY SHOULD IT BE ANY DIFFERENT FOR THIS KID?

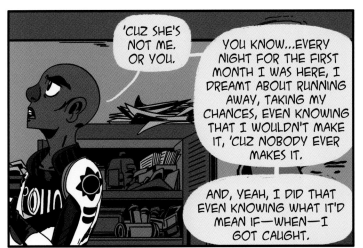

'CUZ SHE'S NOT ME. OR YOU.

YOU KNOW...EVERY NIGHT FOR THE FIRST MONTH I WAS HERE, I DREAMT ABOUT RUNNING AWAY, TAKING MY CHANCES, EVEN KNOWING THAT I WOULDN'T MAKE IT, 'CUZ NOBODY EVER MAKES IT.

AND, YEAH, I DID THAT EVEN KNOWING WHAT IT'D MEAN IF—WHEN—I GOT CAUGHT.

AND I THINK YOU'RE FORGETTING SOMETHING IMPORTANT.

YEAH, THAT'S RIGHT, AXL WITH HIS AMAZING MEMORY IS FORGETTING SOMETHING—OR HE JUST DOESN'T KNOW I KNOW.

YOU CARRIED ME TO THAT SECOND-PLACE FINISH.

AND THEN YOU LET ME WIN THAT NEXT RACE.

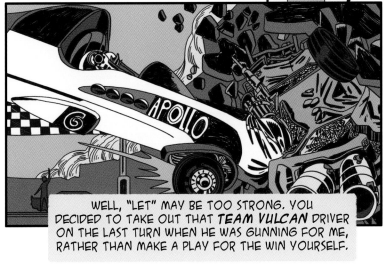

WELL, "LET" MAY BE TOO STRONG. YOU DECIDED TO TAKE OUT THAT *TEAM VULCAN* DRIVER ON THE LAST TURN WHEN HE WAS GUNNING FOR ME, RATHER THAN MAKE A PLAY FOR THE WIN YOURSELF.

DON'T TRY TO DENY IT, MAN. I WAS THERE, AND I MAY HAVE BEEN YOUNG, BUT I'M NOT STUPID, AND I KNOW WHAT I KNOW.

PISTON'S SCARED. SHE'S GOT NO IMPULSE CONTROL AND SHE LOST ALL HER CONFIDENCE AND SHE FEELS TOTALLY ALONE.

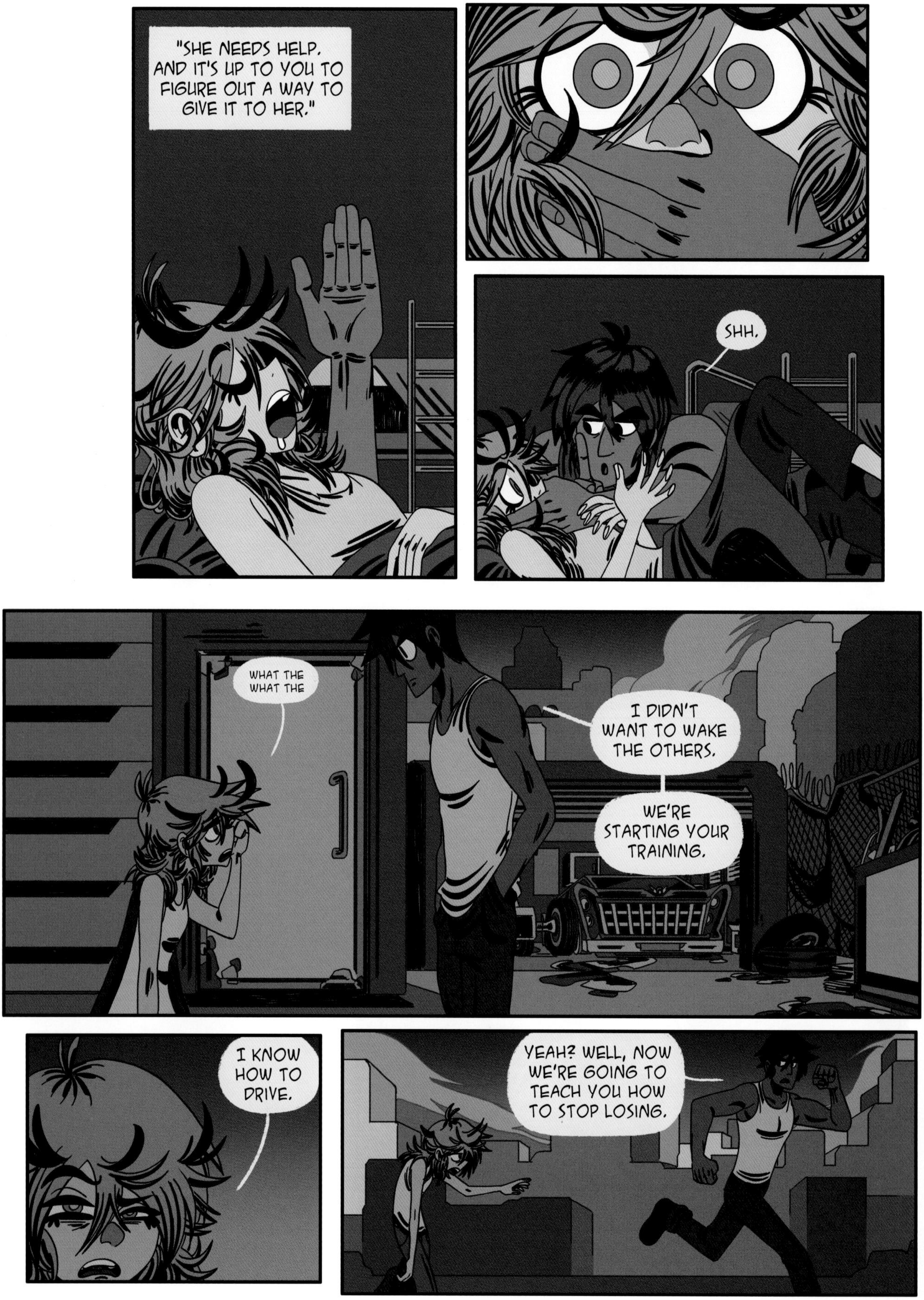
"SHE NEEDS HELP. AND IT'S UP TO YOU TO FIGURE OUT A WAY TO GIVE IT TO HER."
SHH.
WHAT THE WHAT THE
I DIDN'T WANT TO WAKE THE OTHERS.
WE'RE STARTING YOUR TRAINING.
I KNOW HOW TO DRIVE.
YEAH? WELL, NOW WE'RE GOING TO TEACH YOU HOW TO STOP LOSING.

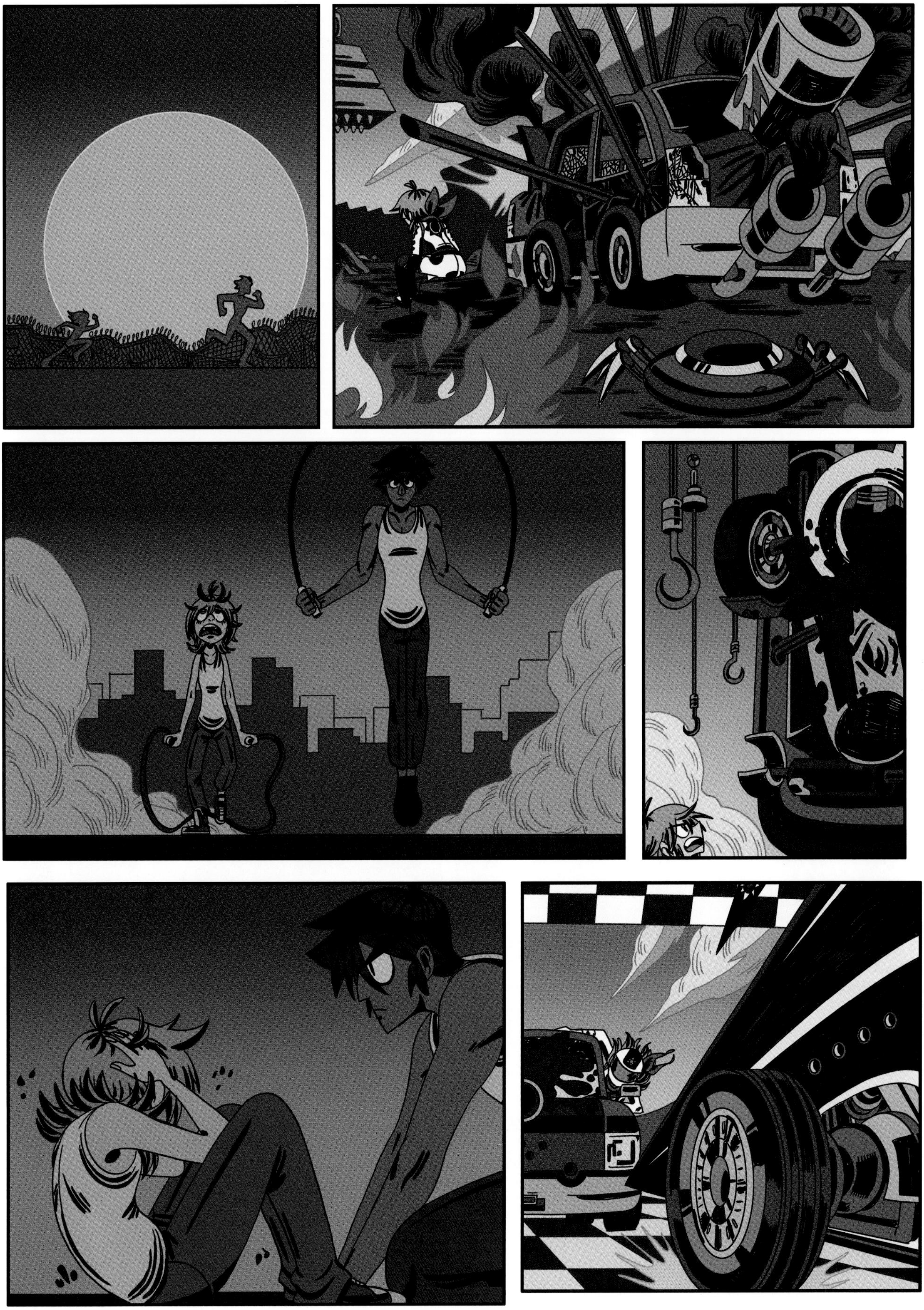

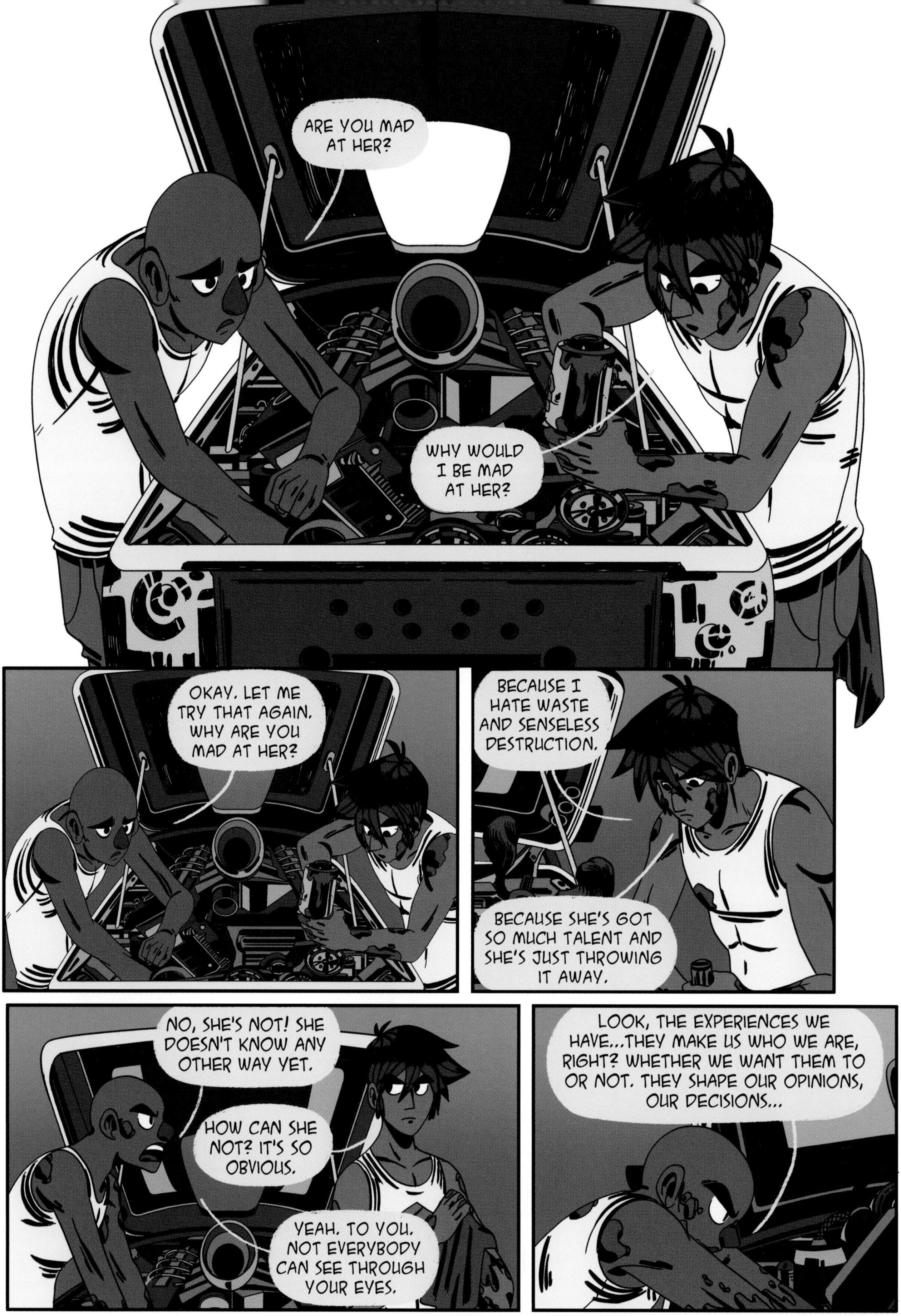
ARE YOU MAD AT HER?
WHY WOULD I BE MAD AT HER?
OKAY. LET ME TRY THAT AGAIN. WHY ARE YOU MAD AT HER?
BECAUSE I HATE WASTE AND SENSELESS DESTRUCTION.
BECAUSE SHE'S GOT SO MUCH TALENT AND SHE'S JUST THROWING IT AWAY.
NO, SHE'S NOT! SHE DOESN'T KNOW ANY OTHER WAY YET.
HOW CAN SHE NOT? IT'S SO OBVIOUS.
YEAH. TO YOU. NOT EVERYBODY CAN SEE THROUGH YOUR EYES.
LOOK, THE EXPERIENCES WE HAVE...THEY MAKE US WHO WE ARE, RIGHT? WHETHER WE WANT THEM TO OR NOT. THEY SHAPE OUR OPINIONS, OUR DECISIONS...

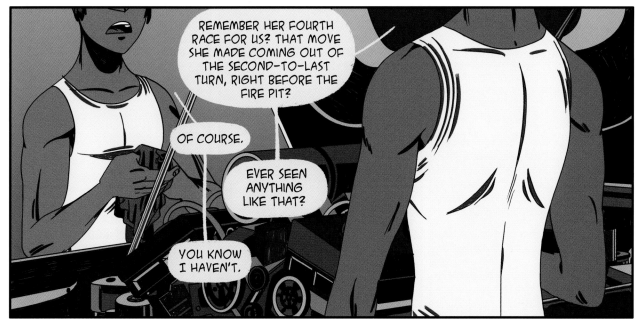

REMEMBER HER FOURTH RACE FOR US? THAT MOVE SHE MADE COMING OUT OF THE SECOND-TO-LAST TURN, RIGHT BEFORE THE FIRE PIT?

OF COURSE.

EVER SEEN ANYTHING LIKE THAT?

YOU KNOW I HAVEN'T.

RIGHT. IN THE WHOLE LONG HISTORY OF TRUCKUS MAXIMUS, NO ONE'S EVER THOUGHT OF DOING SOMETHING LIKE THAT.

THAT'S MY POINT. SHE'S GOT SO MUCH POTENTIAL AND—

NO. HOLD ON.

YOU'RE THE WINNINGEST DRIVER IN THE HISTORY OF THE COMPETITION. AND YET THAT MOVE HAD NEVER OCCURRED TO YOU— WOULD NEVER HAVE OCCURRED TO YOU.

SO WHY CAN'T YOU TURN THAT AROUND?

WHY CAN'T YOU SEE HOW THINGS THAT ARE SO OBVIOUS TO YOU MIGHT JUST BE TOTALLY INVISIBLE TO HER? HOW STUFF THAT WOULD WORK FOR YOU OR ME WON'T NECESSARILY WORK FOR HER?

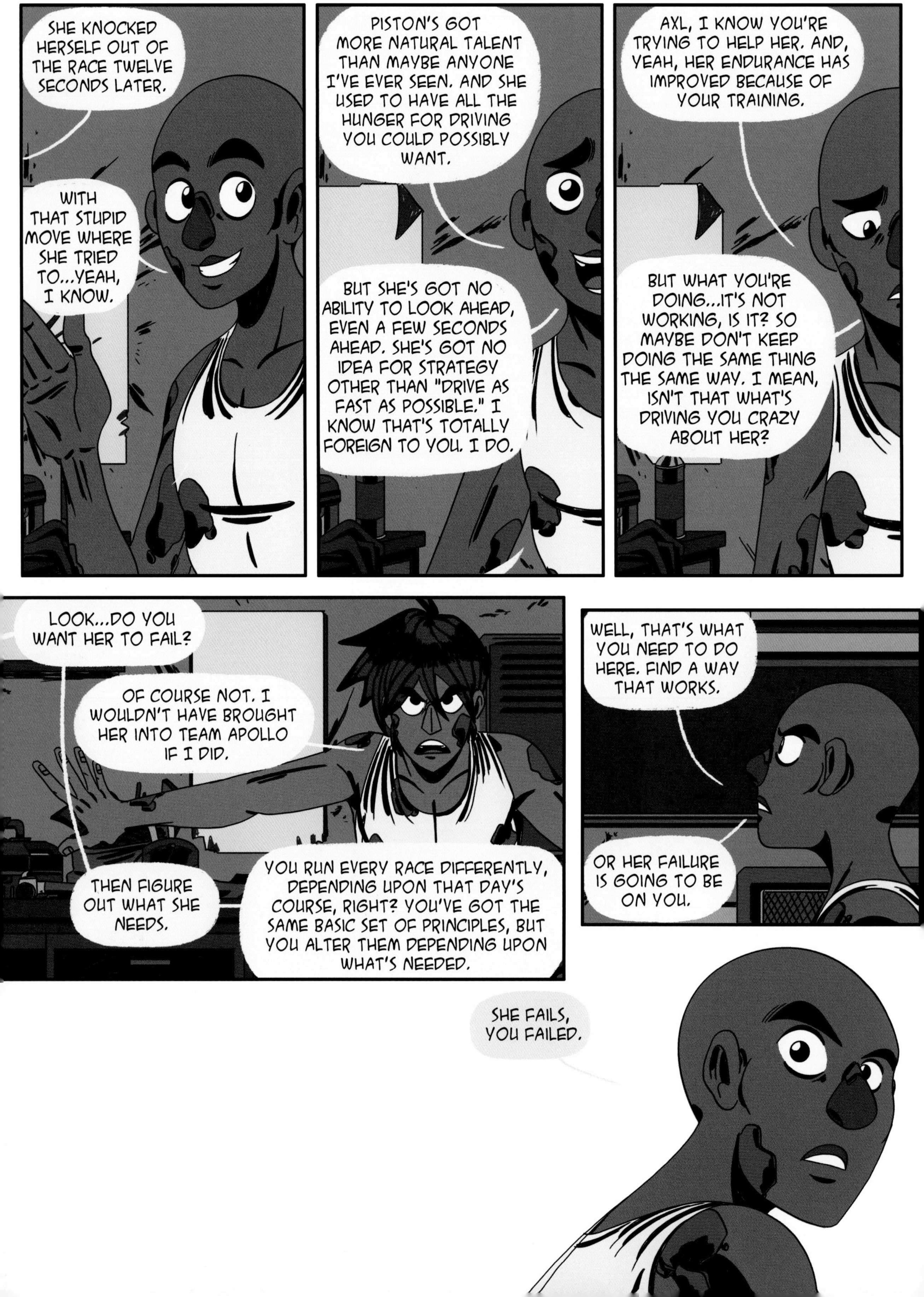
SHE KNOCKED HERSELF OUT OF THE RACE TWELVE SECONDS LATER.
WITH THAT STUPID MOVE WHERE SHE TRIED TO...YEAH, I KNOW.
PISTON'S GOT MORE NATURAL TALENT THAN MAYBE ANYONE I'VE EVER SEEN. AND SHE USED TO HAVE ALL THE HUNGER FOR DRIVING YOU COULD POSSIBLY WANT.
BUT SHE'S GOT NO ABILITY TO LOOK AHEAD, EVEN A FEW SECONDS AHEAD. SHE'S GOT NO IDEA FOR STRATEGY OTHER THAN "DRIVE AS FAST AS POSSIBLE." I KNOW THAT'S TOTALLY FOREIGN TO YOU. I DO.
AXL, I KNOW YOU'RE TRYING TO HELP HER. AND, YEAH, HER ENDURANCE HAS IMPROVED BECAUSE OF YOUR TRAINING.
BUT WHAT YOU'RE DOING...IT'S NOT WORKING, IS IT? SO MAYBE DON'T KEEP DOING THE SAME THING THE SAME WAY. I MEAN, ISN'T THAT WHAT'S DRIVING YOU CRAZY ABOUT HER?
LOOK...DO YOU WANT HER TO FAIL?
OF COURSE NOT. I WOULDN'T HAVE BROUGHT HER INTO TEAM APOLLO IF I DID.
THEN FIGURE OUT WHAT SHE NEEDS.
YOU RUN EVERY RACE DIFFERENTLY, DEPENDING UPON THAT DAY'S COURSE, RIGHT? YOU'VE GOT THE SAME BASIC SET OF PRINCIPLES, BUT YOU ALTER THEM DEPENDING UPON WHAT'S NEEDED.
WELL, THAT'S WHAT YOU NEED TO DO HERE. FIND A WAY THAT WORKS.
OR HER FAILURE IS GOING TO BE ON YOU.
SHE FAILS, YOU FAILED.

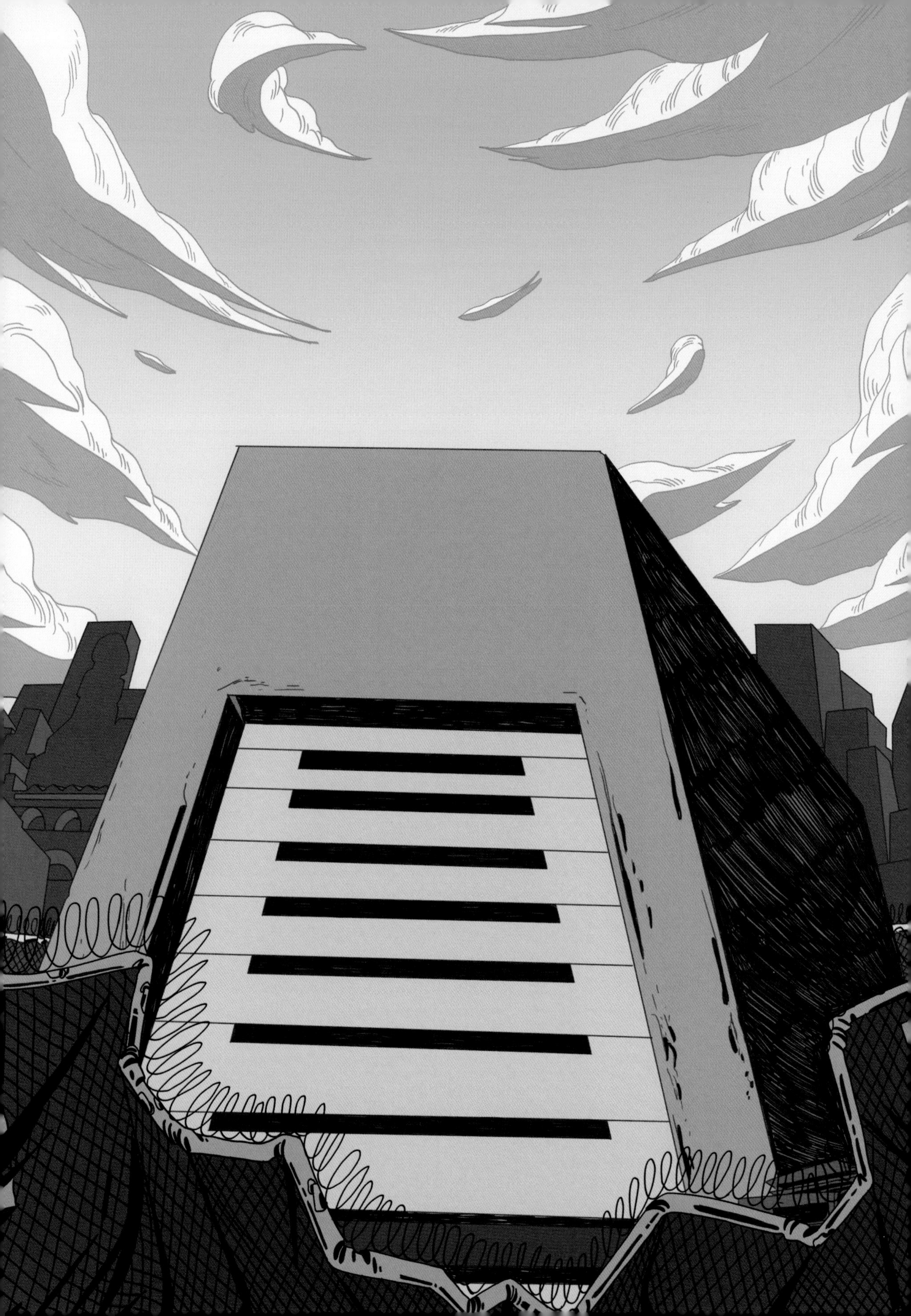

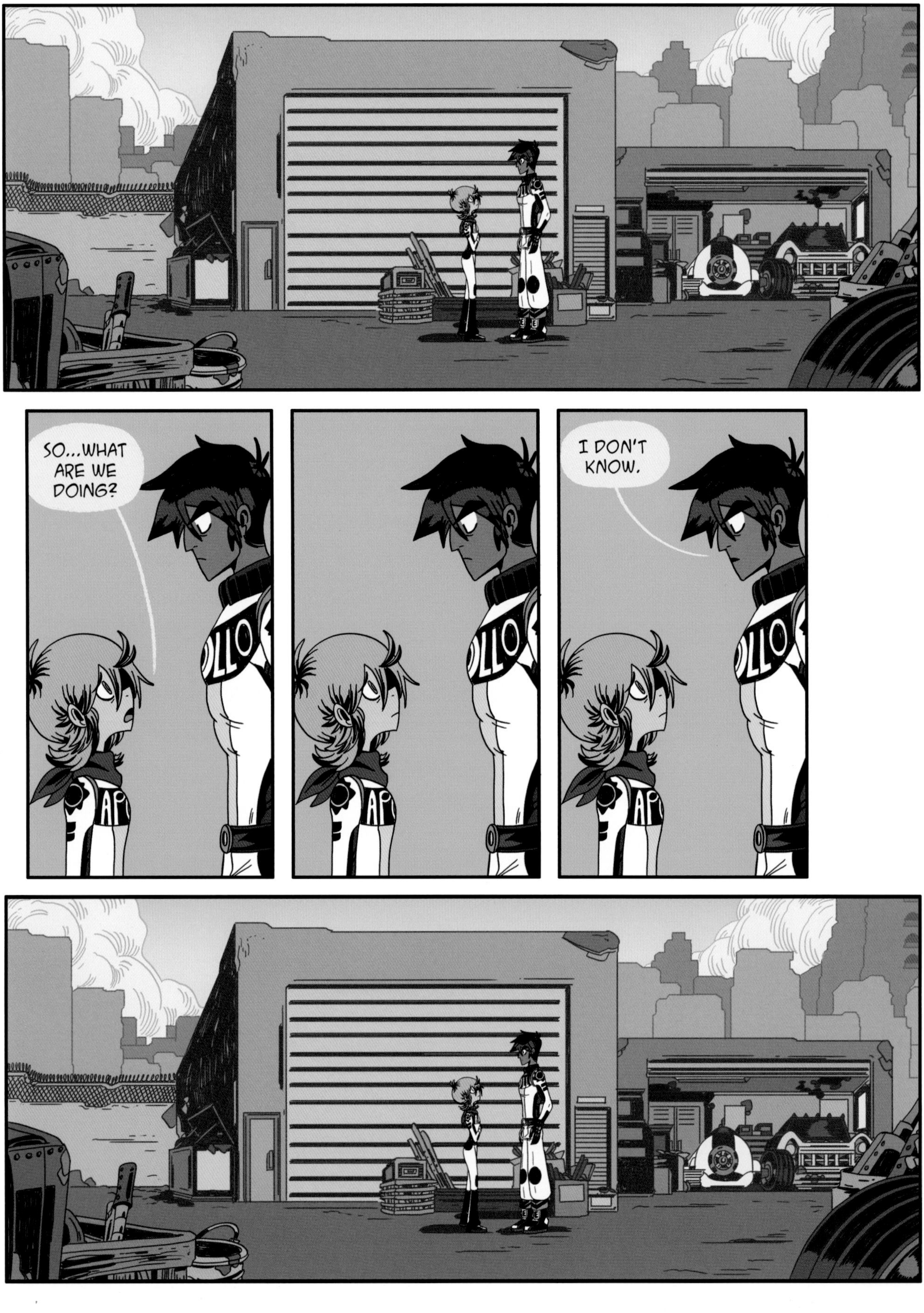
SO...WHAT ARE WE DOING?
I DON'T KNOW.

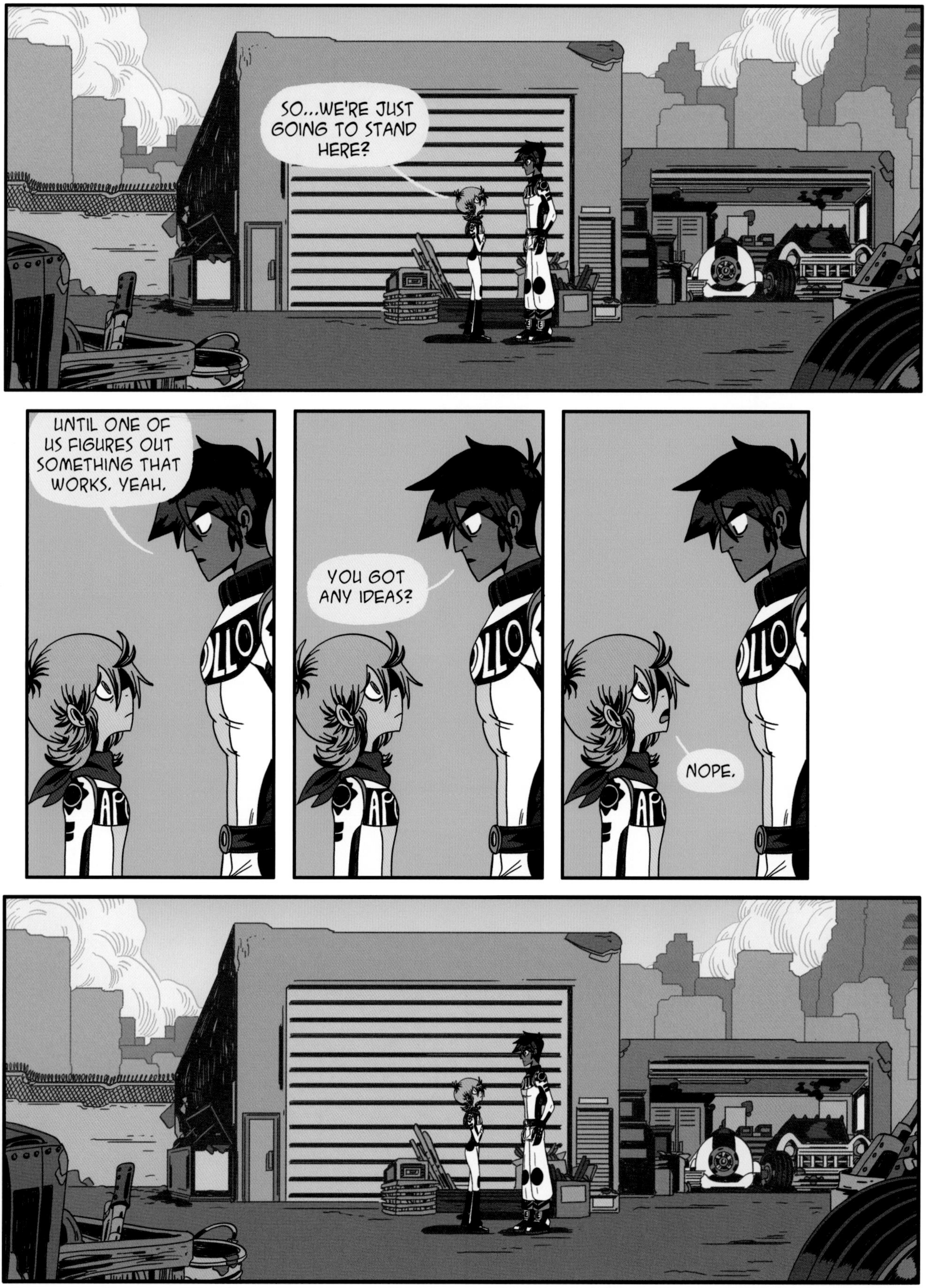
SO...WE'RE JUST GOING TO STAND HERE?
UNTIL ONE OF US FIGURES OUT SOMETHING THAT WORKS. YEAH.
YOU GOT ANY IDEAS?
NOPE.

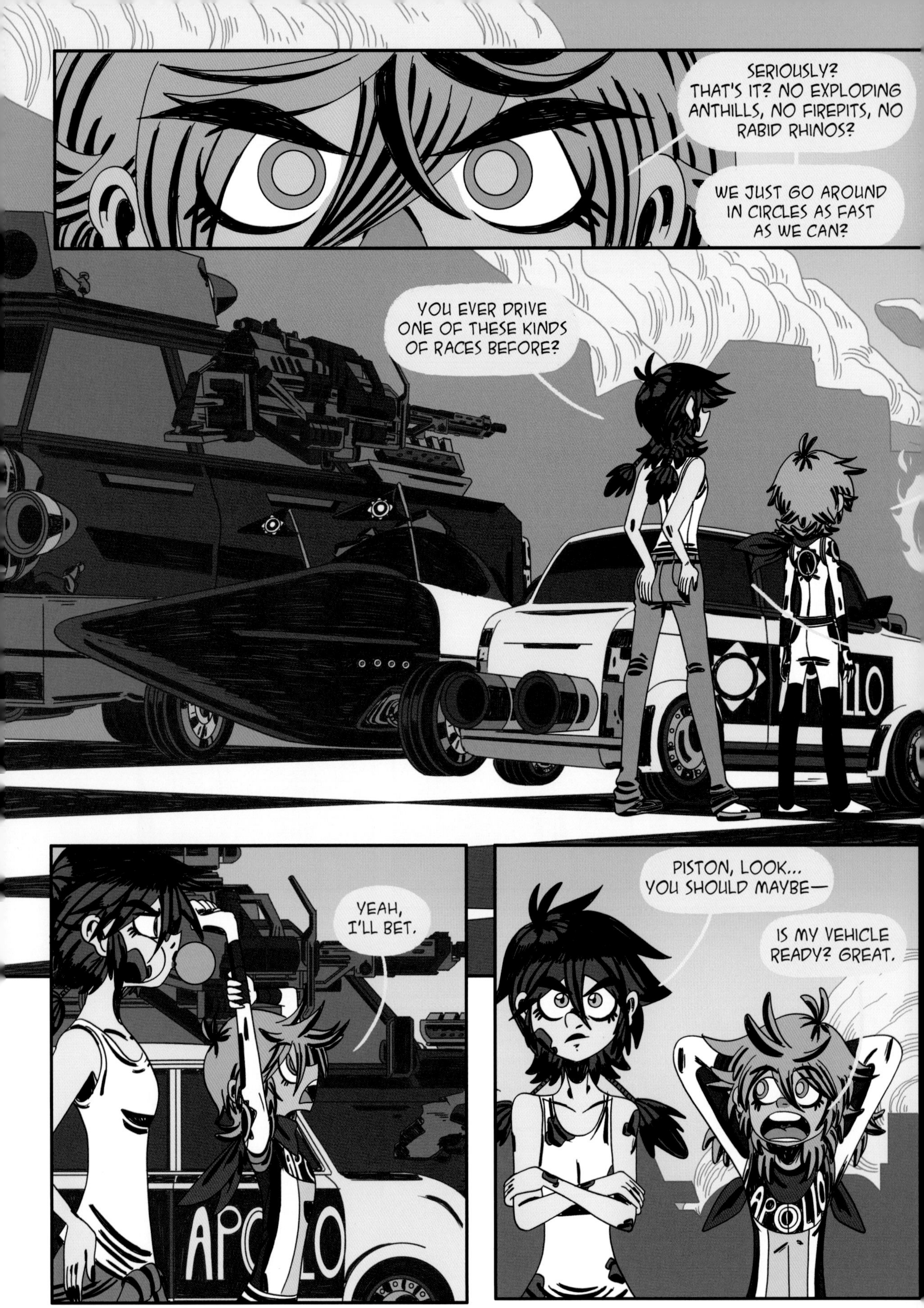
SERIOUSLY? THAT'S IT? NO EXPLODING ANTHILLS, NO FIREPITS, NO RABID RHINOS?
WE JUST GO AROUND IN CIRCLES AS FAST AS WE CAN?
YOU EVER DRIVE ONE OF THESE KINDS OF RACES BEFORE?
APOLLO
YEAH, I'LL BET.
APOLLO
PISTON, LOOK... YOU SHOULD MAYBE—
IS MY VEHICLE READY? GREAT.
APOLLO

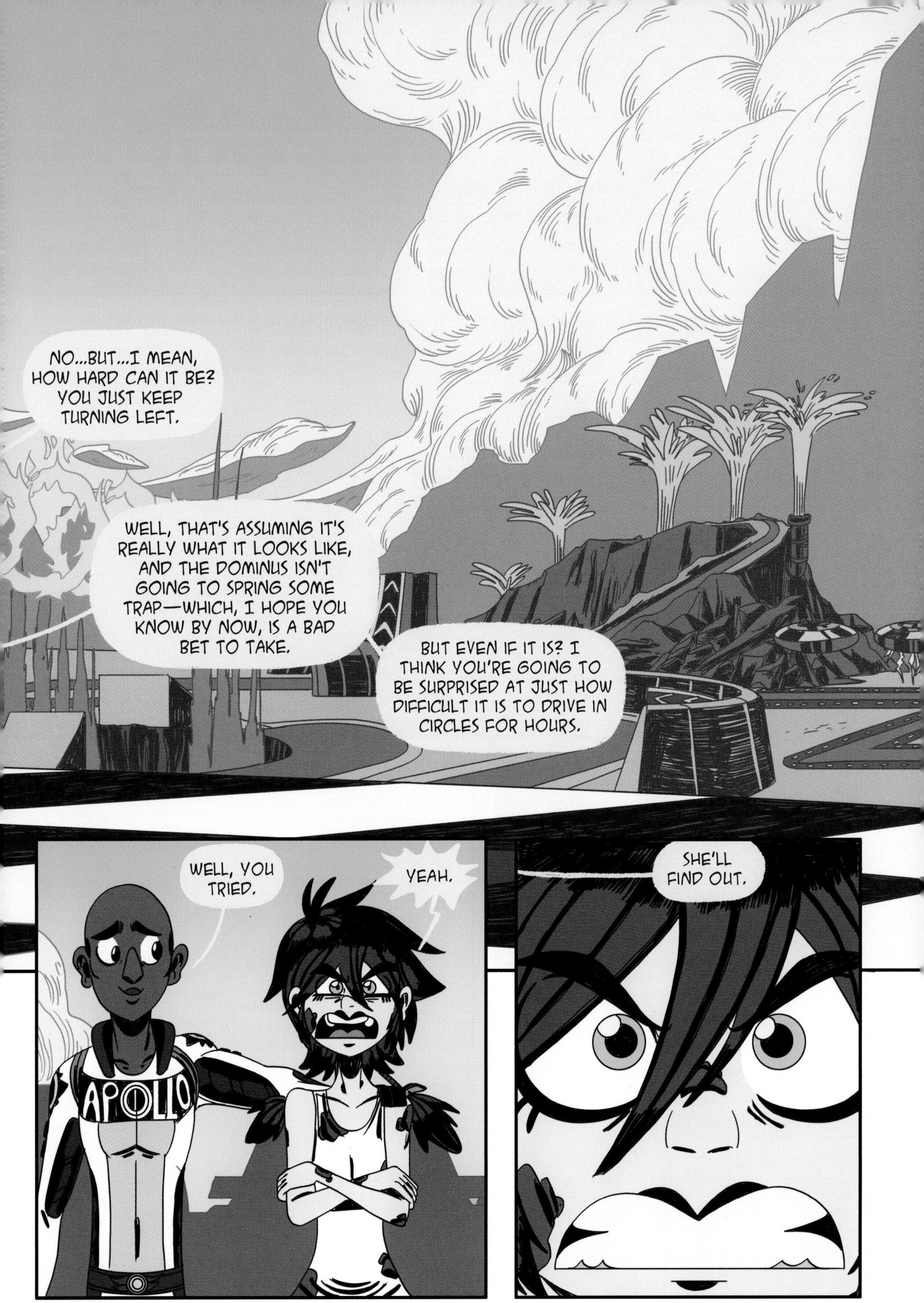
NO...BUT...I MEAN, HOW HARD CAN IT BE? YOU JUST KEEP TURNING LEFT.
WELL, THAT'S ASSUMING IT'S REALLY WHAT IT LOOKS LIKE, AND THE DOMINUS ISN'T GOING TO SPRING SOME TRAP—WHICH, I HOPE YOU KNOW BY NOW, IS A BAD BET TO TAKE.
BUT EVEN IF IT IS? I THINK YOU'RE GOING TO BE SURPRISED AT JUST HOW DIFFICULT IT IS TO DRIVE IN CIRCLES FOR HOURS.
WELL, YOU TRIED.
YEAH.
APOLLO
SHE'LL FIND OUT.

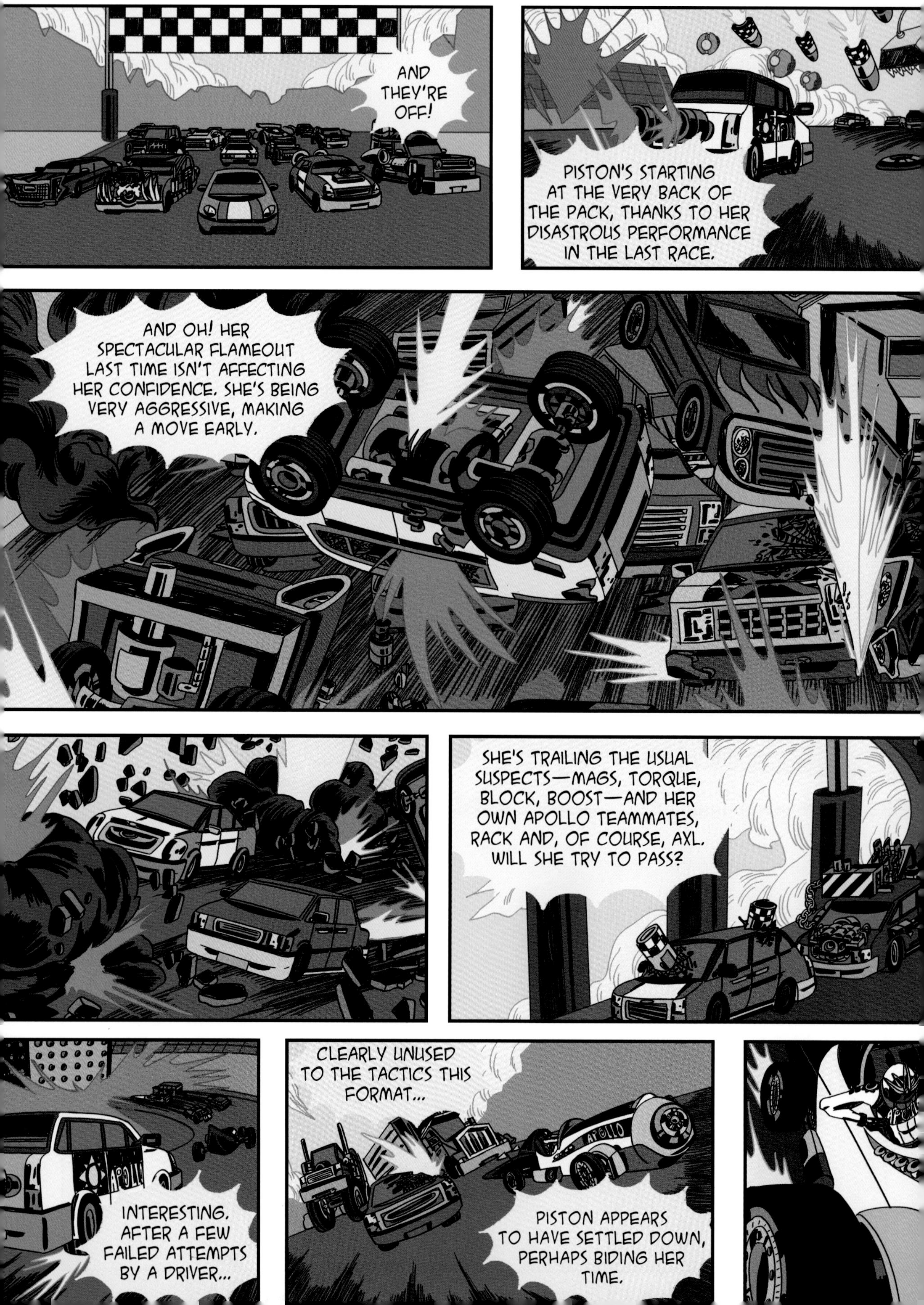
AND THEY'RE OFF!
PISTON'S STARTING AT THE VERY BACK OF THE PACK, THANKS TO HER DISASTROUS PERFORMANCE IN THE LAST RACE.
AND OH! HER SPECTACULAR FLAMEOUT LAST TIME ISN'T AFFECTING HER CONFIDENCE. SHE'S BEING VERY AGGRESSIVE, MAKING A MOVE EARLY.
SHE'S TRAILING THE USUAL SUSPECTS—MAGS, TORQUE, BLOCK, BOOST—AND HER OWN APOLLO TEAMMATES, RACK AND, OF COURSE, AXL. WILL SHE TRY TO PASS?
INTERESTING. AFTER A FEW FAILED ATTEMPTS BY A DRIVER...
CLEARLY UNUSED TO THE TACTICS THIS FORMAT...
PISTON APPEARS TO HAVE SETTLED DOWN, PERHAPS BIDING HER TIME.

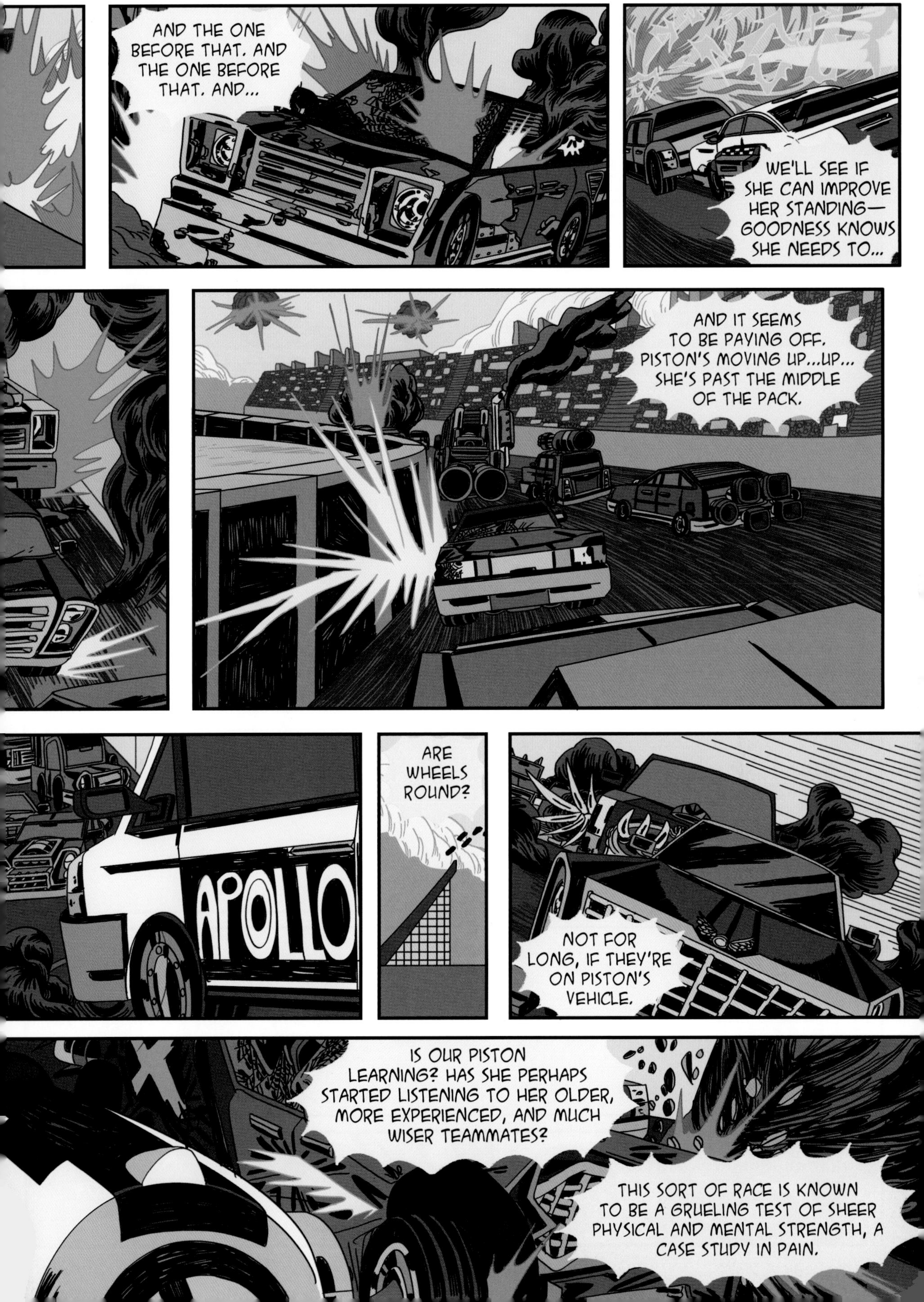
AND THE ONE BEFORE THAT. AND THE ONE BEFORE THAT. AND...
WE'LL SEE IF SHE CAN IMPROVE HER STANDING—GOODNESS KNOWS SHE NEEDS TO...
AND IT SEEMS TO BE PAYING OFF. PISTON'S MOVING UP...UP... SHE'S PAST THE MIDDLE OF THE PACK.
APOLLO
ARE WHEELS ROUND?
NOT FOR LONG, IF THEY'RE ON PISTON'S VEHICLE.
IS OUR PISTON LEARNING? HAS SHE PERHAPS STARTED LISTENING TO HER OLDER, MORE EXPERIENCED, AND MUCH WISER TEAMMATES?
THIS SORT OF RACE IS KNOWN TO BE A GRUELING TEST OF SHEER PHYSICAL AND MENTAL STRENGTH, A CASE STUDY IN PAIN.

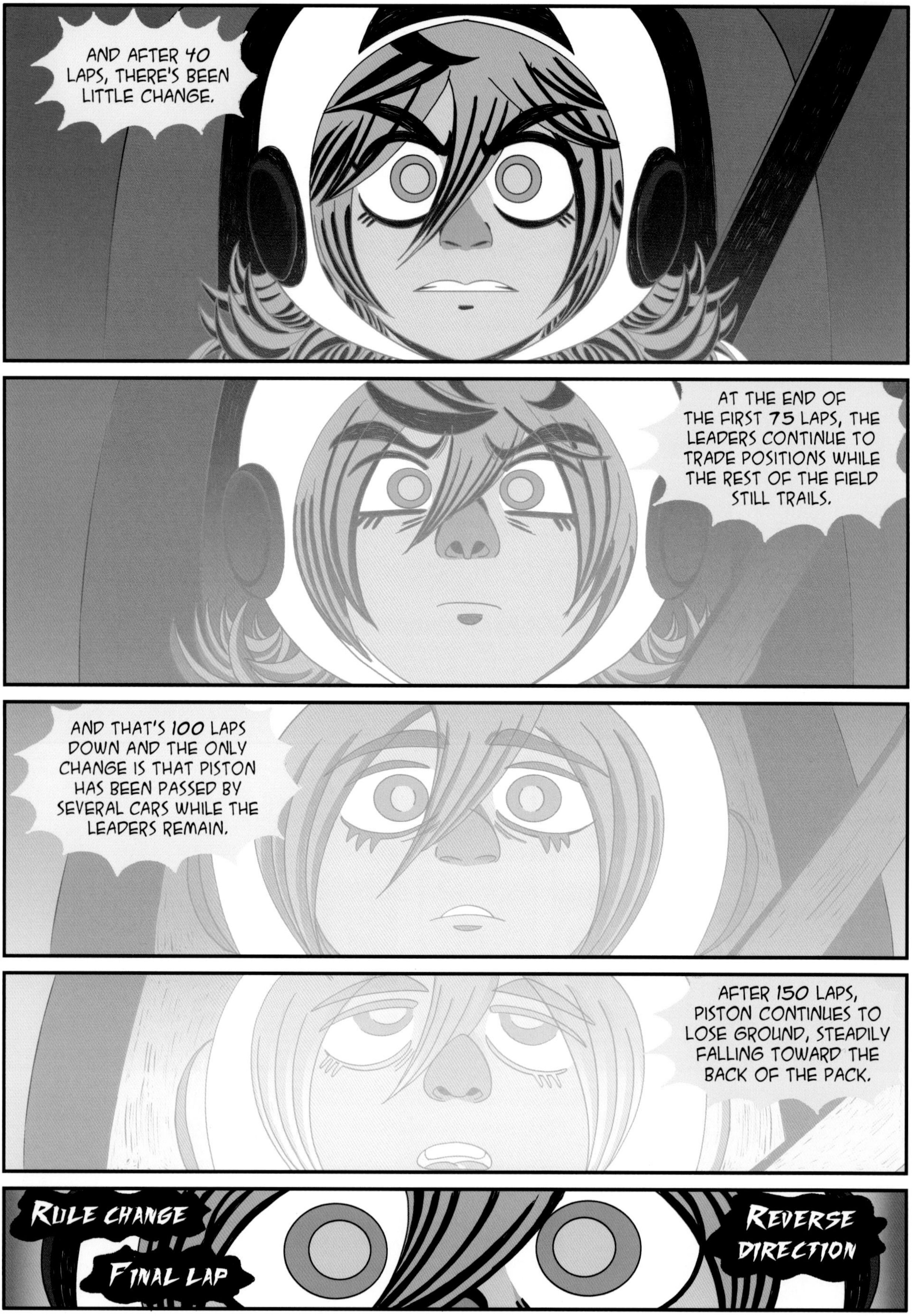
AND AFTER 40 LAPS, THERE'S BEEN LITTLE CHANGE.
AT THE END OF THE FIRST 75 LAPS, THE LEADERS CONTINUE TO TRADE POSITIONS WHILE THE REST OF THE FIELD STILL TRAILS.
AND THAT'S 100 LAPS DOWN AND THE ONLY CHANGE IS THAT PISTON HAS BEEN PASSED BY SEVERAL CARS WHILE THE LEADERS REMAIN.
AFTER 150 LAPS, PISTON CONTINUES TO LOSE GROUND, STEADILY FALLING TOWARD THE BACK OF THE PACK.
RULE CHANGE
FINAL LAP
REVERSE DIRECTION

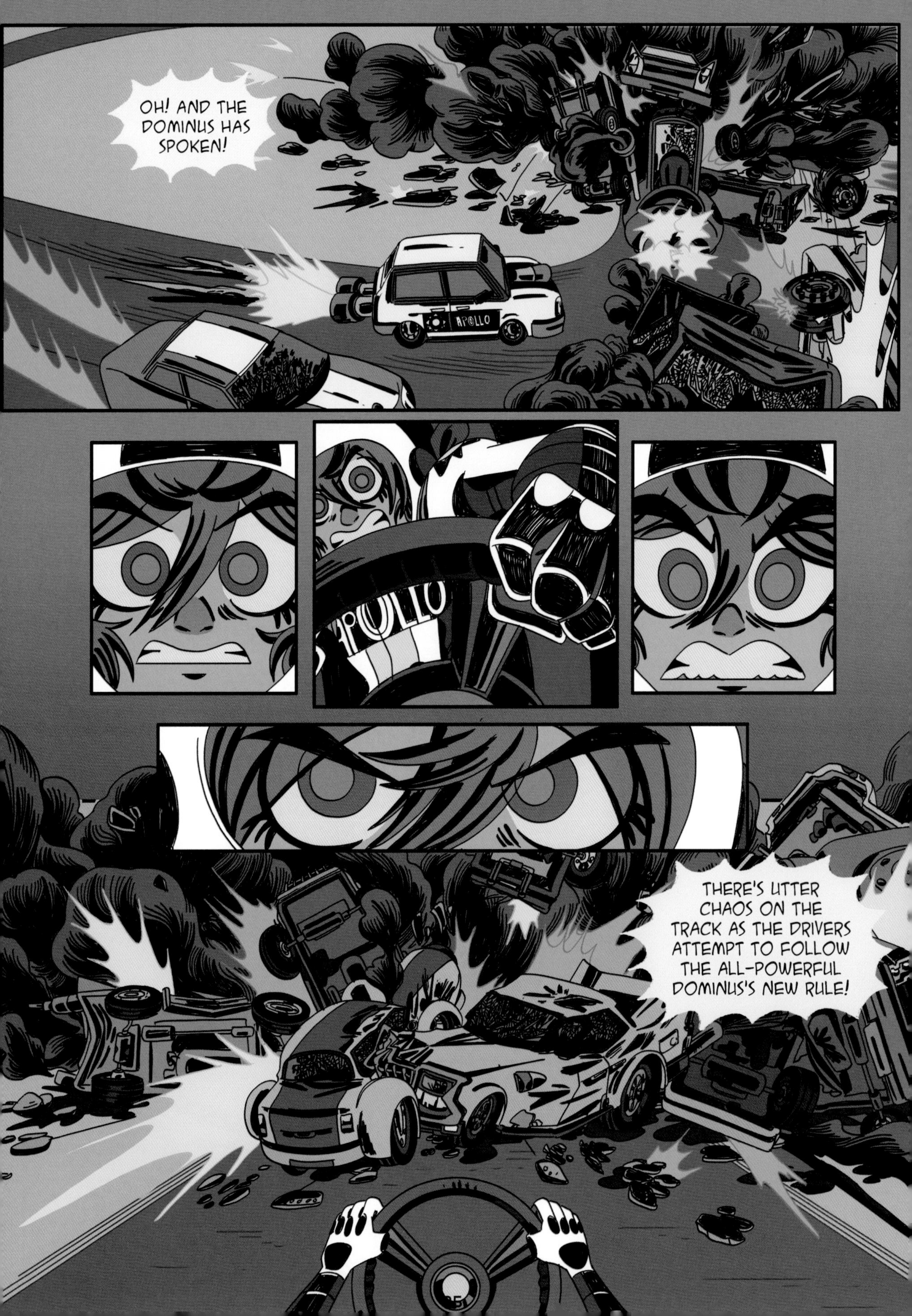
OH! AND THE DOMINUS HAS SPOKEN!
APOLLO
APOLLO
THERE'S UTTER CHAOS ON THE TRACK AS THE DRIVERS ATTEMPT TO FOLLOW THE ALL-POWERFUL DOMINUS'S NEW RULE!

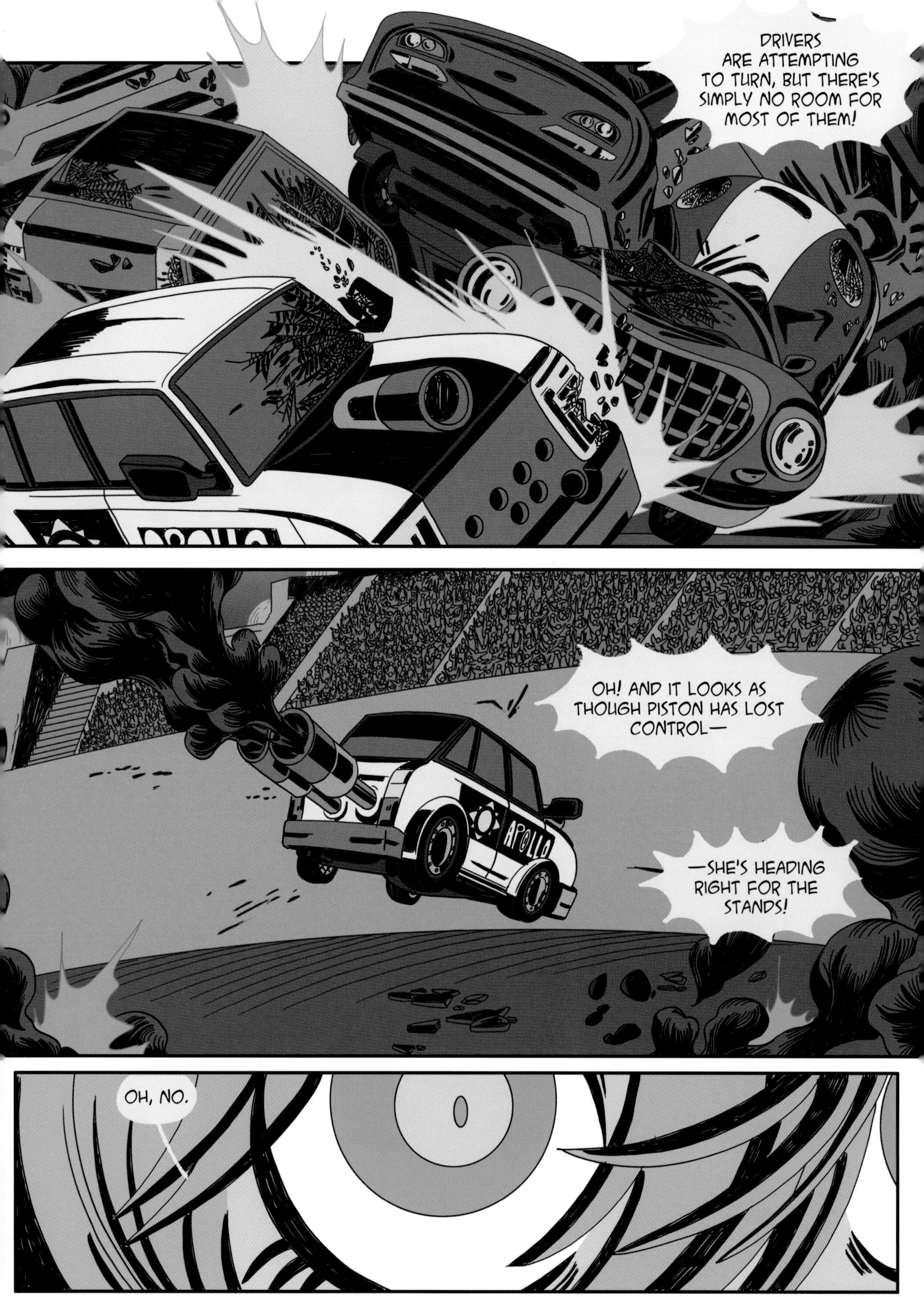
DRIVERS ARE ATTEMPTING TO TURN, BUT THERE'S SIMPLY NO ROOM FOR MOST OF THEM!
APOLLO
OH! AND IT LOOKS AS THOUGH PISTON HAS LOST CONTROL—
—SHE'S HEADING RIGHT FOR THE STANDS!
OH, NO.

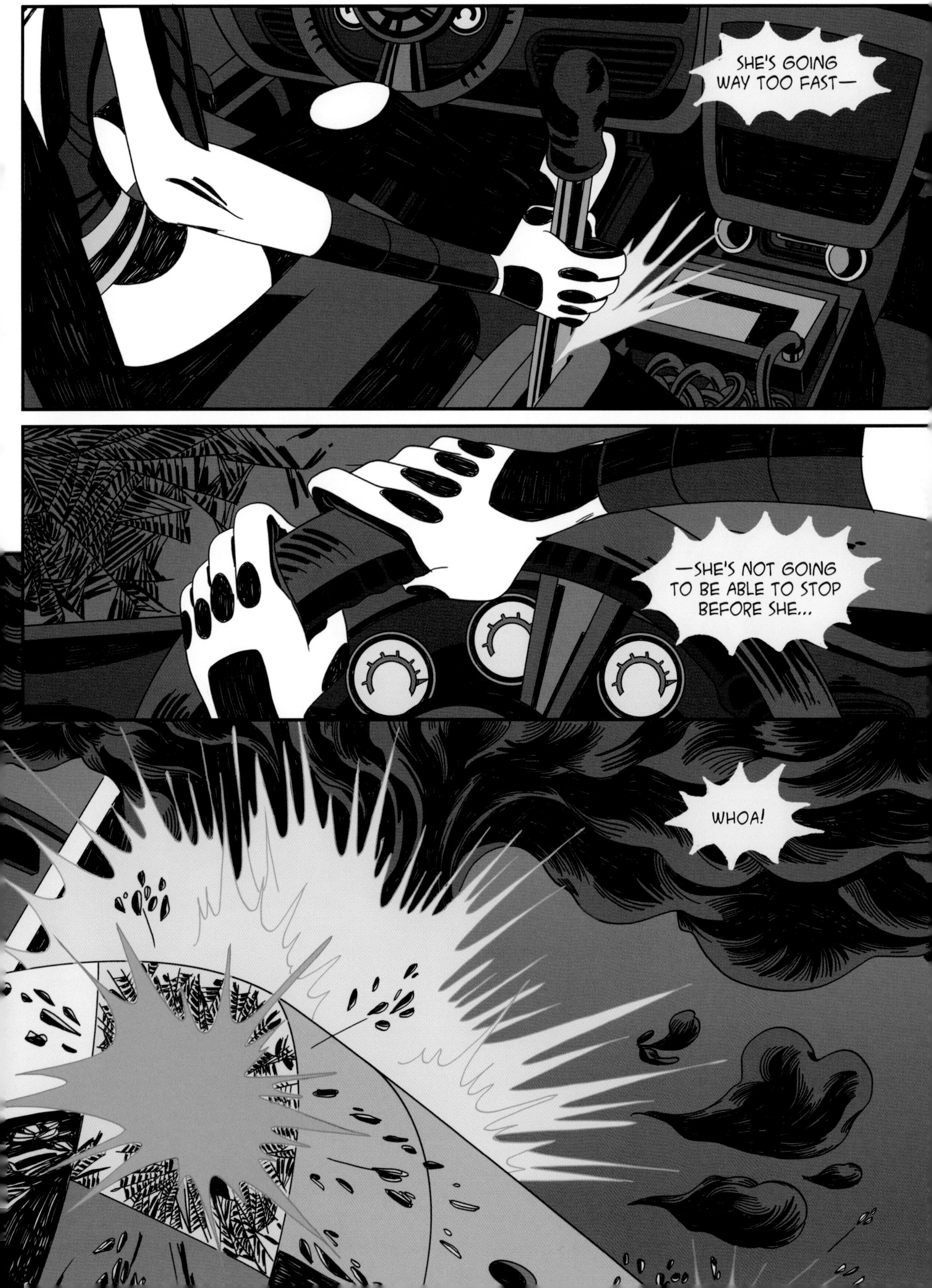
SHE'S GOING WAY TOO FAST—
—SHE'S NOT GOING TO BE ABLE TO STOP BEFORE SHE...
WHOA!

WHAT WAS...

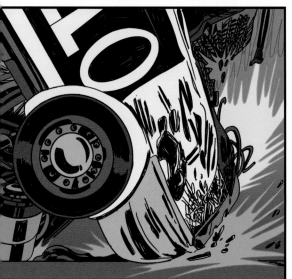

...DID...DID PISTON'S ENGINE JUST FALL OUT OF HER VEHICLE?

SURE LOOKS LIKE IT.

AND THAT'S THE LEAST OF PISTON'S WORRIES.

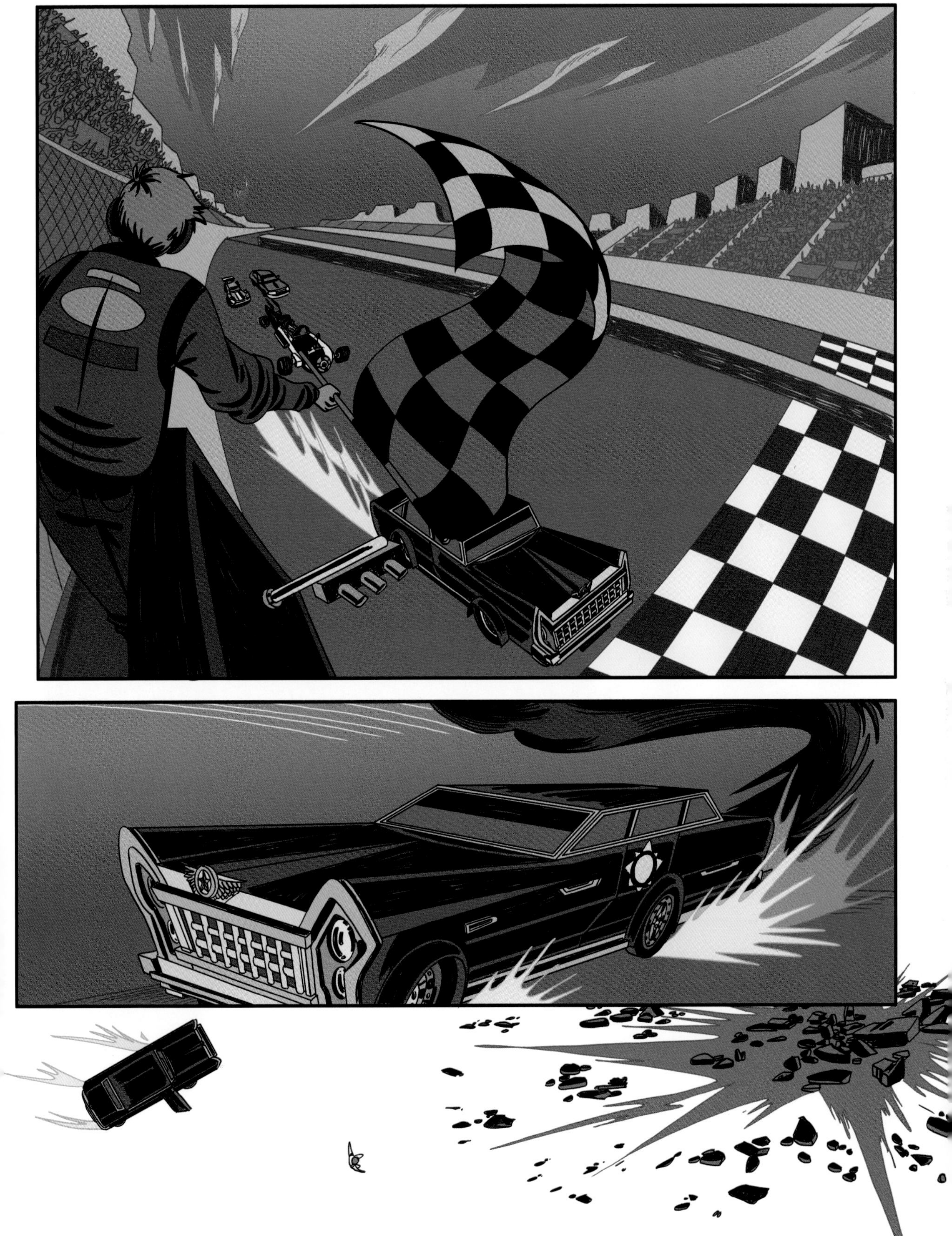

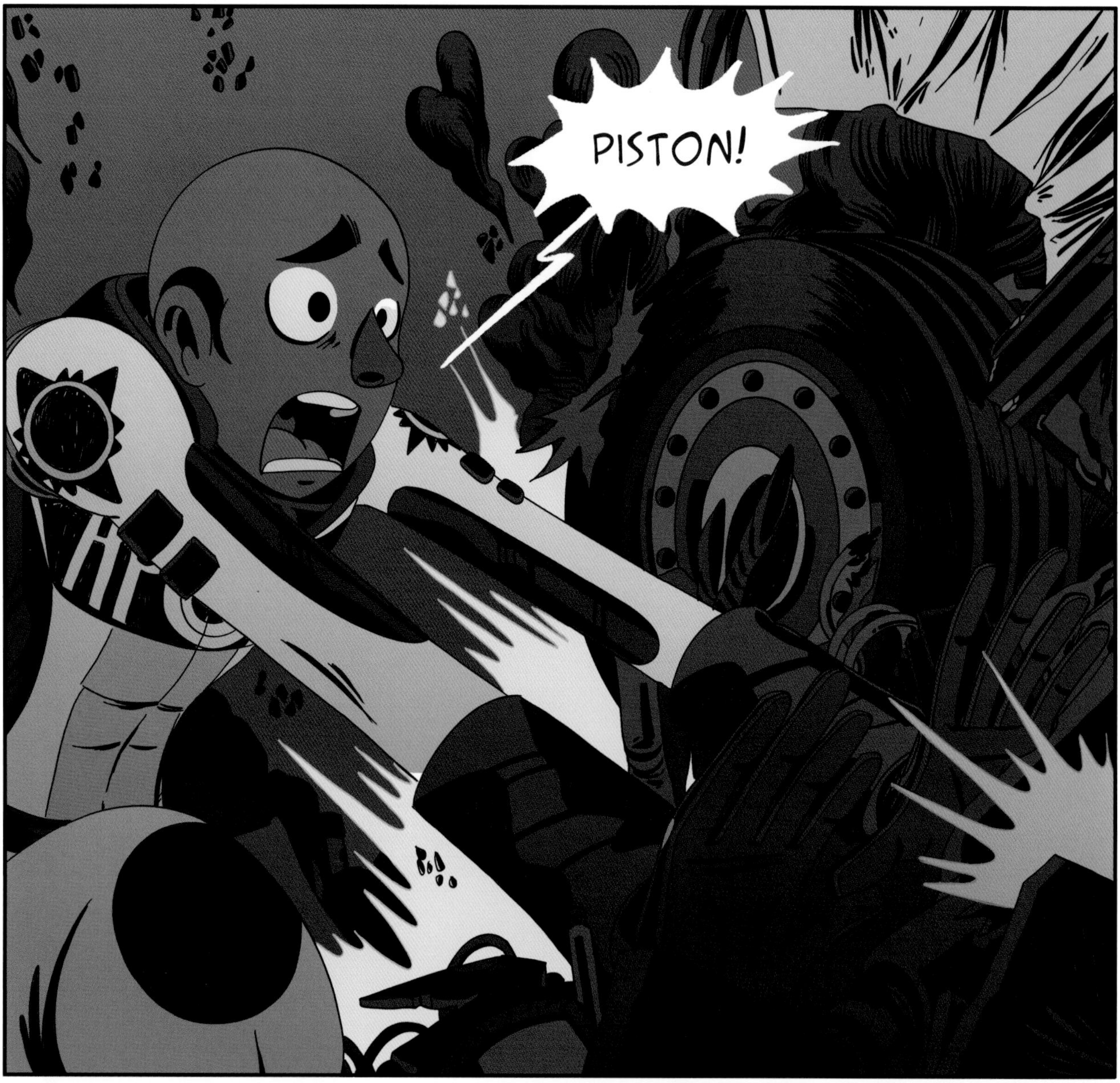
PISTON!

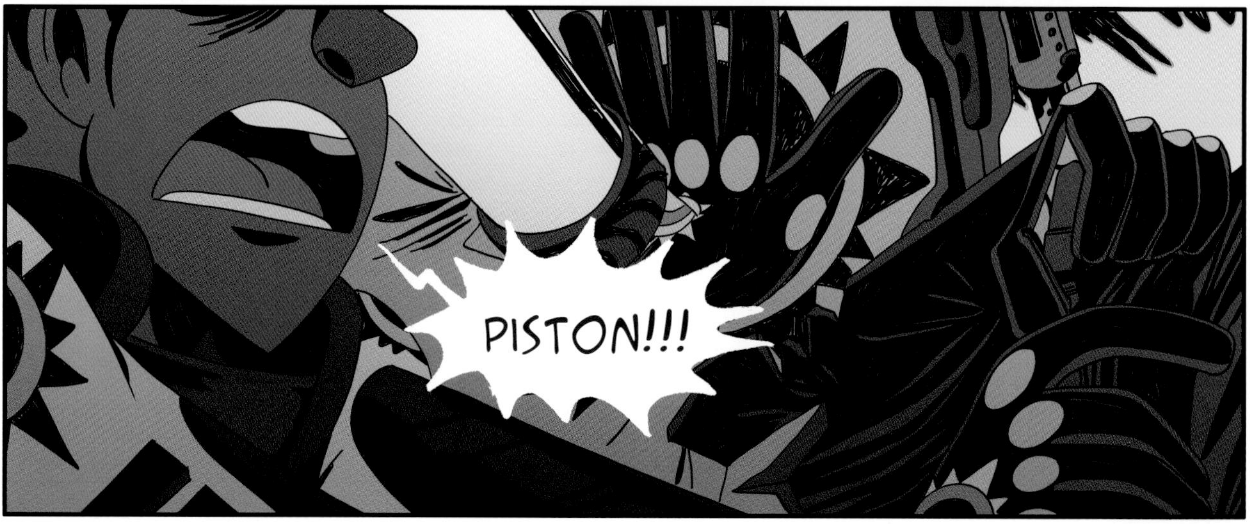
PISTON!!!

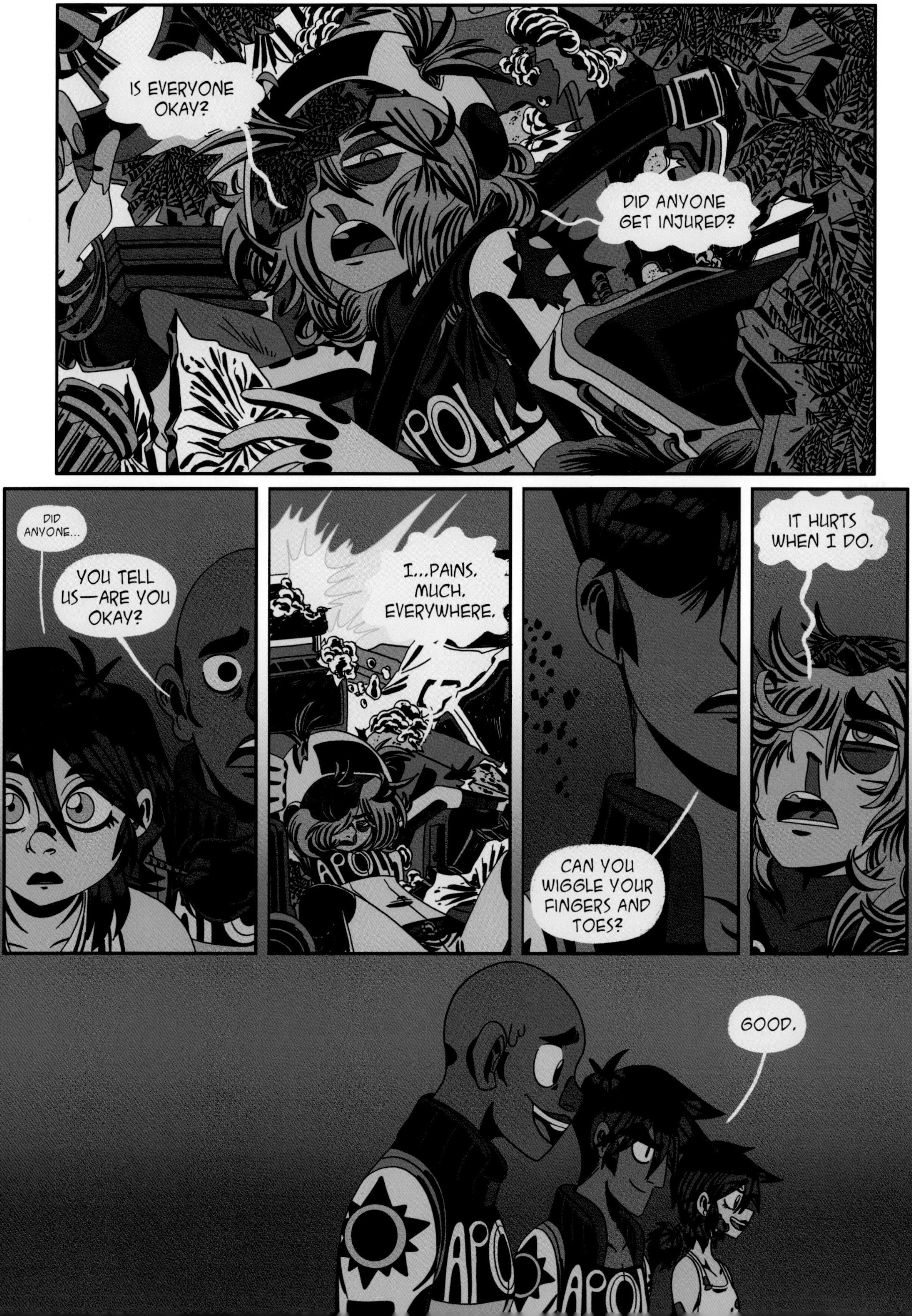
IS EVERYONE OKAY?
DID ANYONE GET INJURED?
APOLLO
DID ANYONE...
YOU TELL US—ARE YOU OKAY?
I...PAINS. MUCH. EVERYWHERE.
CAN YOU WIGGLE YOUR FINGERS AND TOES?
IT HURTS WHEN I DO.
GOOD.

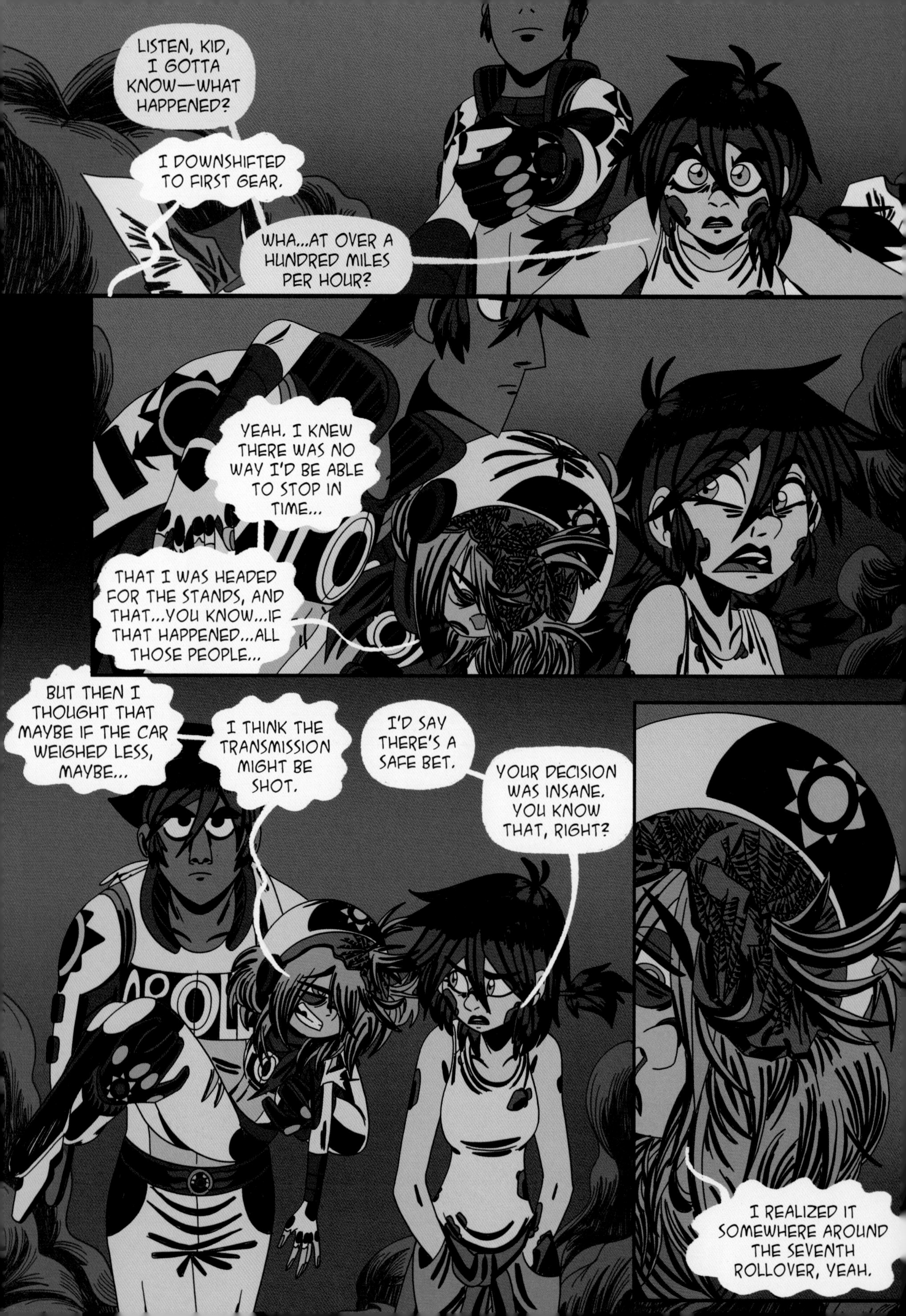
LISTEN, KID, I GOTTA KNOW—WHAT HAPPENED?
I DOWNSHIFTED TO FIRST GEAR.
WHA...AT OVER A HUNDRED MILES PER HOUR?
YEAH. I KNEW THERE WAS NO WAY I'D BE ABLE TO STOP IN TIME...
THAT I WAS HEADED FOR THE STANDS, AND THAT...YOU KNOW...IF THAT HAPPENED...ALL THOSE PEOPLE...
BUT THEN I THOUGHT THAT MAYBE IF THE CAR WEIGHED LESS, MAYBE...
I THINK THE TRANSMISSION MIGHT BE SHOT.
I'D SAY THERE'S A SAFE BET.
YOUR DECISION WAS INSANE. YOU KNOW THAT, RIGHT?
I REALIZED IT SOMEWHERE AROUND THE SEVENTH ROLLOVER, YEAH.

COOL.

NICE JOB, KID.

PISTON.

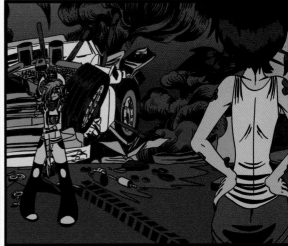

HEY, UH...THANKS. FOR, YOU KNOW. BEING SO GOOD AT...THE CAR AND ALL.

I MEAN...THANK YOU FOR ME STILL BEING NOT DEAD.

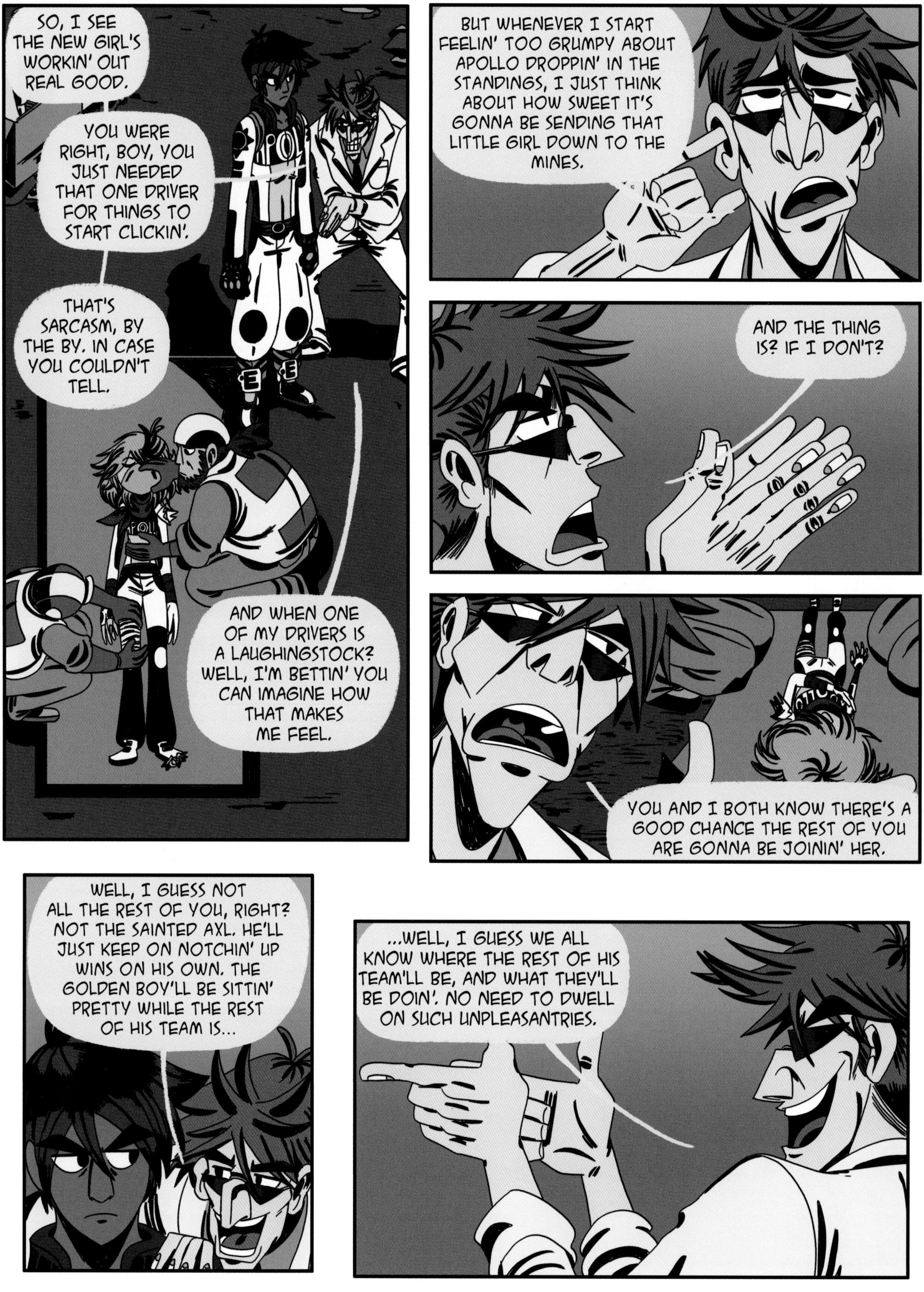
SO, I SEE THE NEW GIRL'S WORKIN' OUT REAL GOOD.
YOU WERE RIGHT, BOY, YOU JUST NEEDED THAT ONE DRIVER FOR THINGS TO START CLICKIN'.
THAT'S SARCASM, BY THE BY. IN CASE YOU COULDN'T TELL.
AND WHEN ONE OF MY DRIVERS IS A LAUGHINGSTOCK? WELL, I'M BETTIN' YOU CAN IMAGINE HOW THAT MAKES ME FEEL.
BUT WHENEVER I START FEELIN' TOO GRUMPY ABOUT APOLLO DROPPIN' IN THE STANDINGS, I JUST THINK ABOUT HOW SWEET IT'S GONNA BE SENDING THAT LITTLE GIRL DOWN TO THE MINES.
AND THE THING IS? IF I DON'T?
YOU AND I BOTH KNOW THERE'S A GOOD CHANCE THE REST OF YOU ARE GONNA BE JOININ' HER.
WELL, I GUESS NOT ALL THE REST OF YOU, RIGHT? NOT THE SAINTED AXL. HE'LL JUST KEEP ON NOTCHIN' UP WINS ON HIS OWN. THE GOLDEN BOY'LL BE SITTIN' PRETTY WHILE THE REST OF HIS TEAM IS...
...WELL, I GUESS WE ALL KNOW WHERE THE REST OF HIS TEAM'LL BE, AND WHAT THEY'LL BE DOIN'. NO NEED TO DWELL ON SUCH UNPLEASANTRIES.

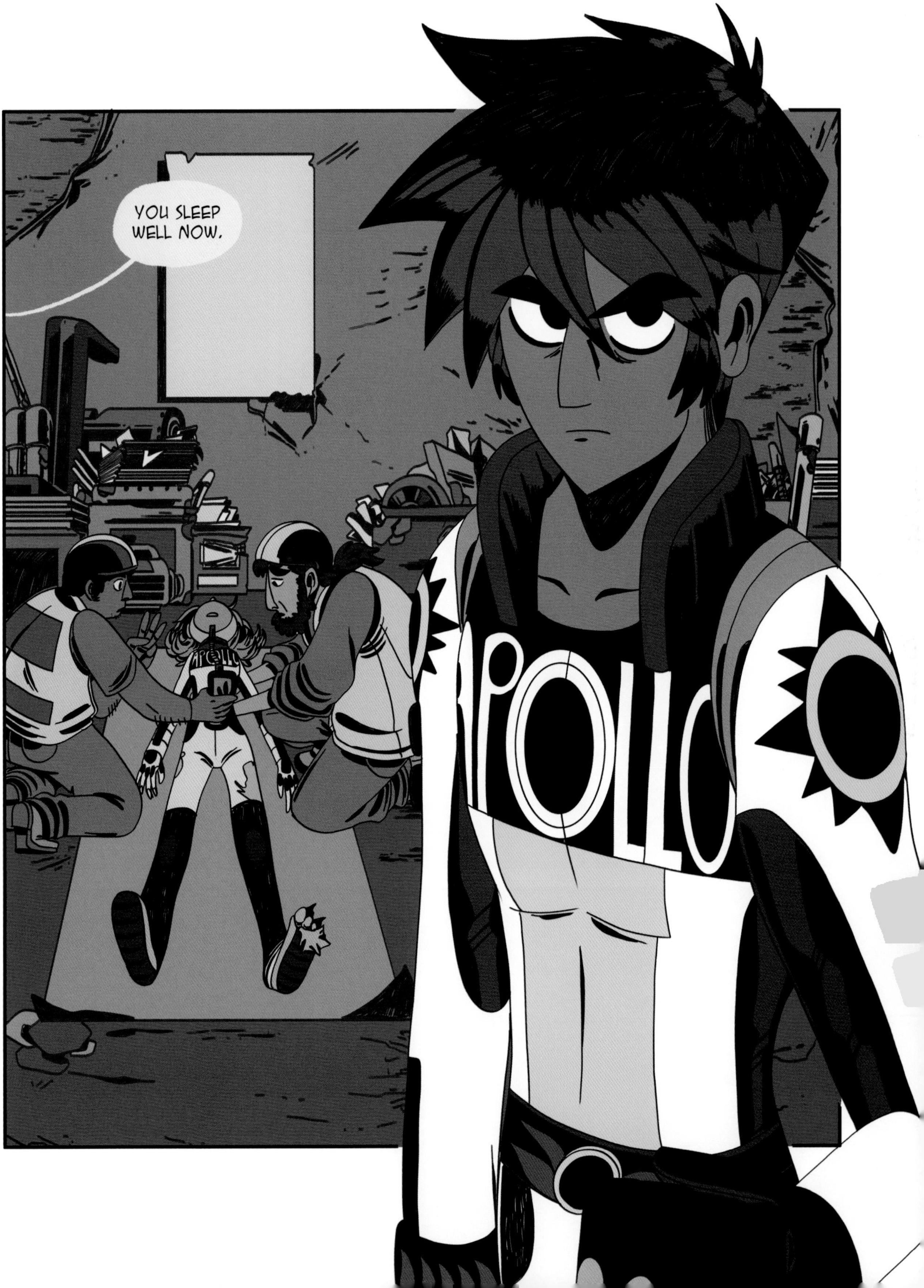
YOU SLEEP WELL NOW.
APOLLO

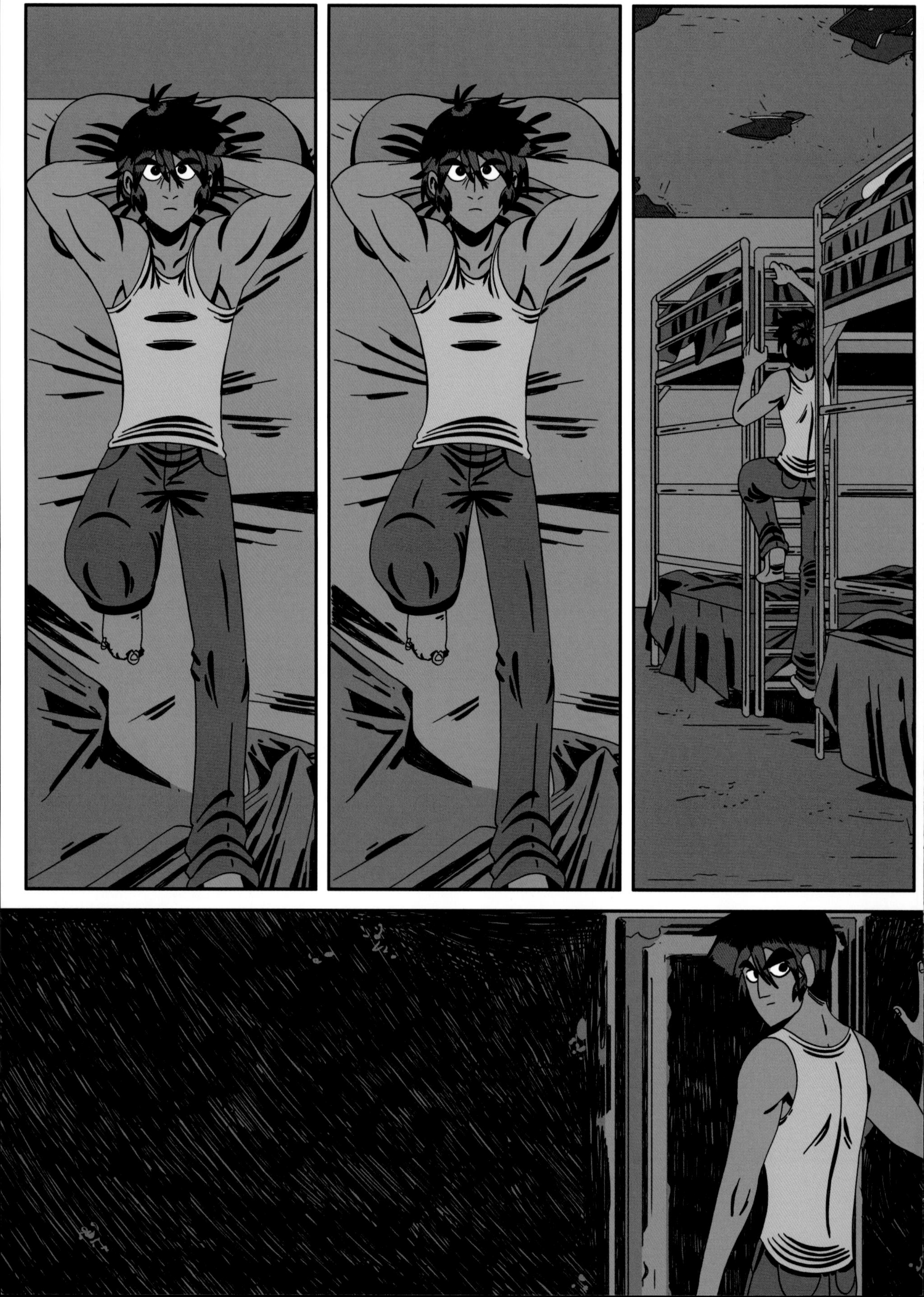

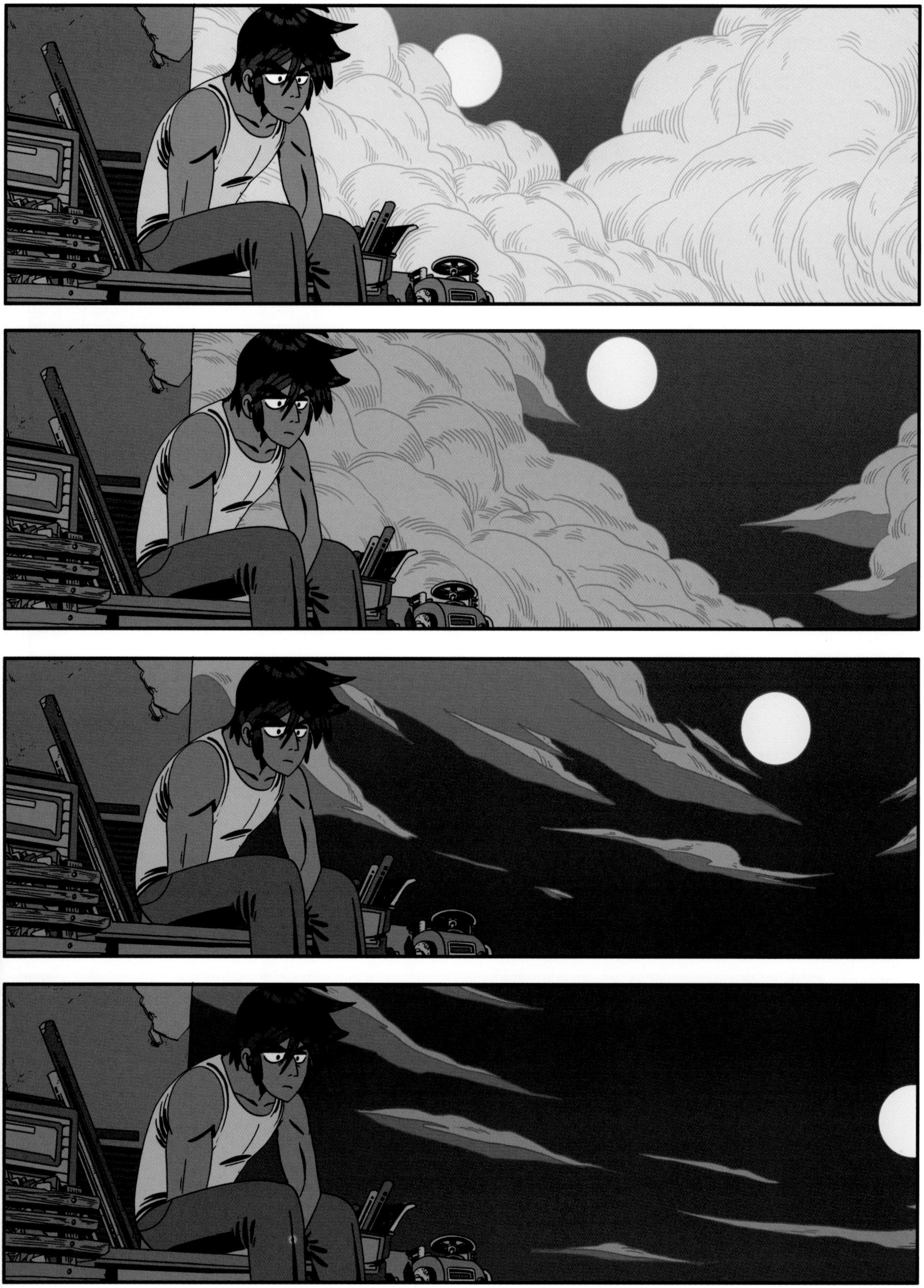

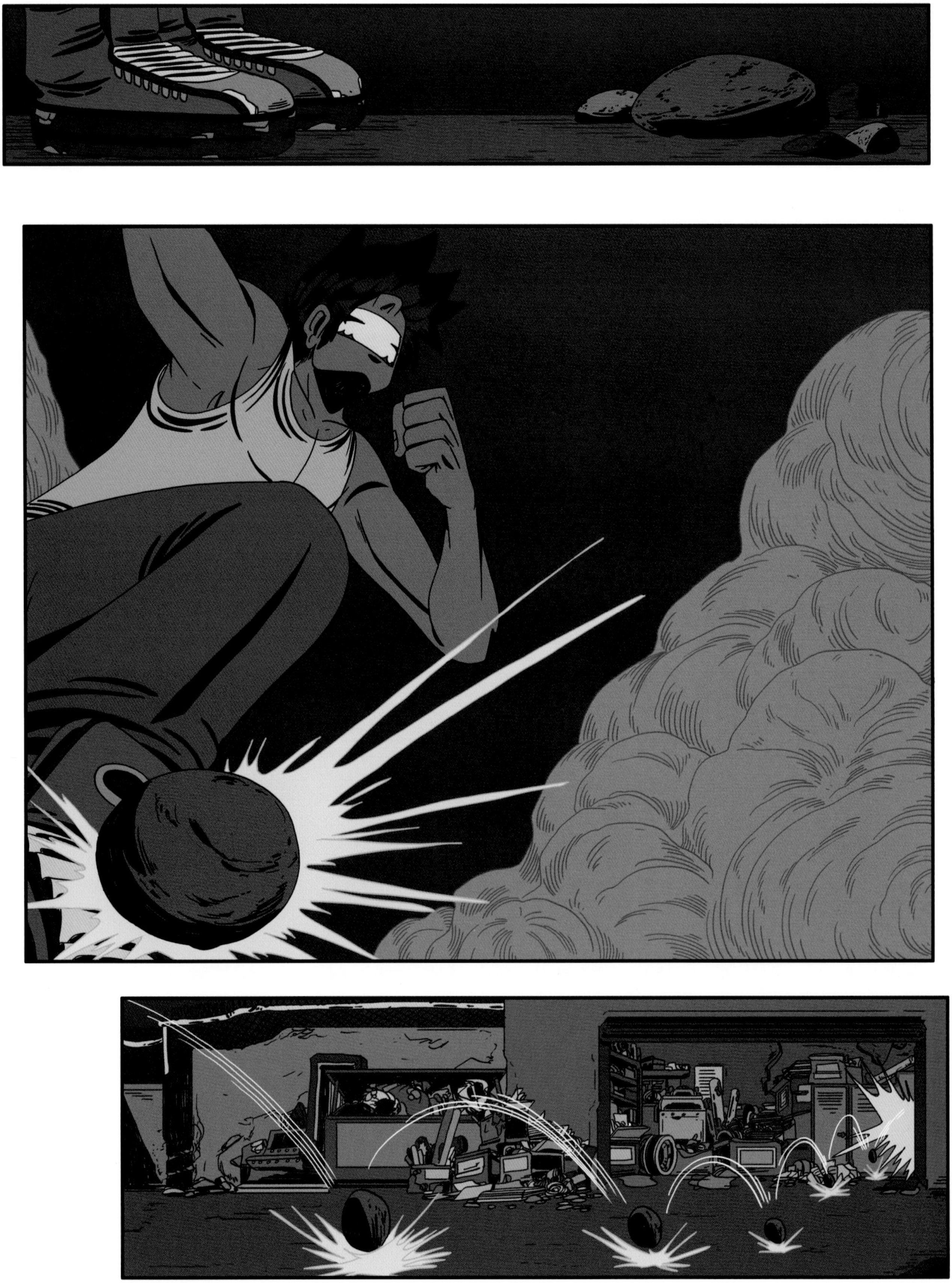

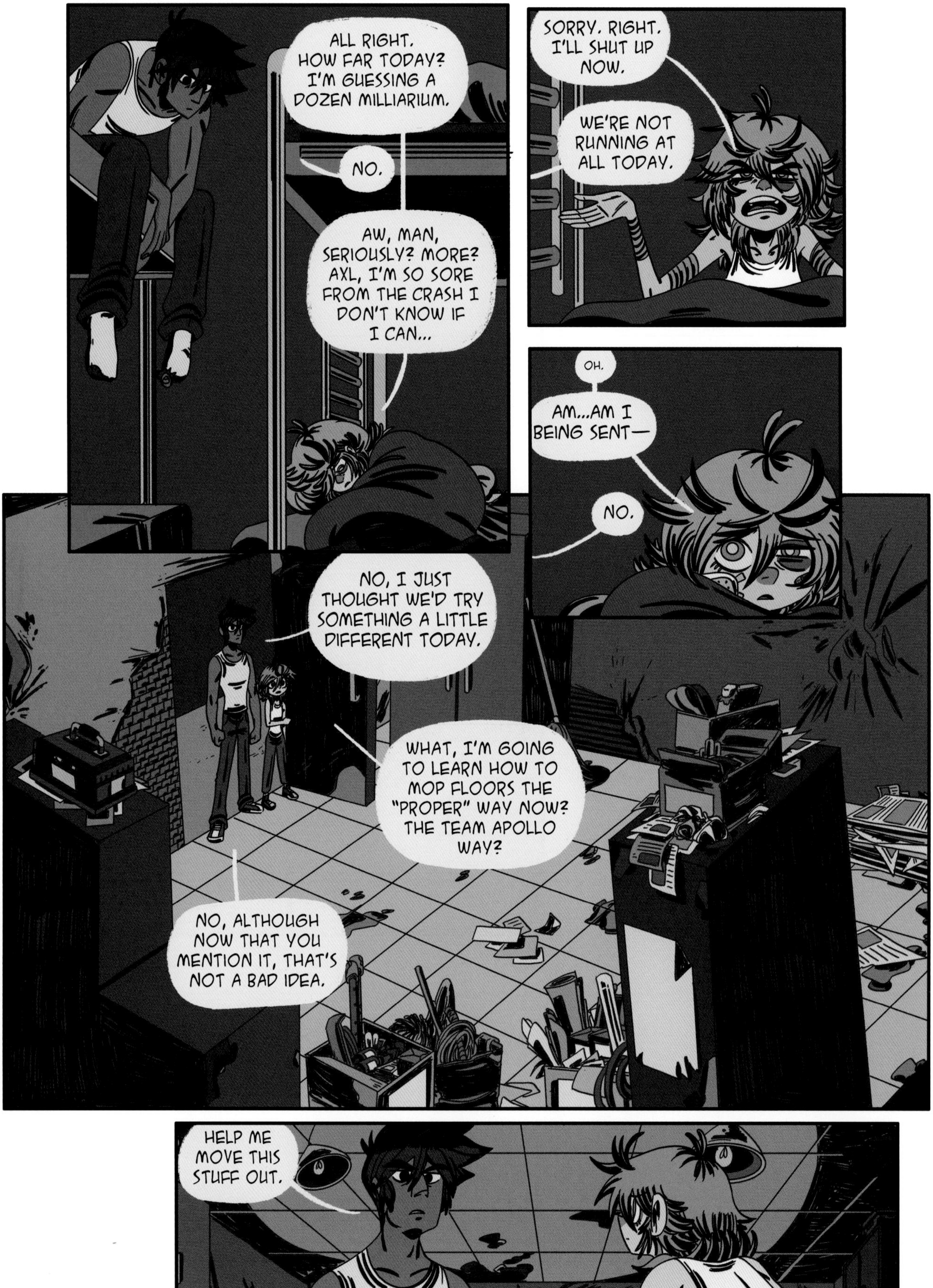
ALL RIGHT. HOW FAR TODAY? I'M GUESSING A DOZEN MILLIARIUM.
NO.
AW, MAN, SERIOUSLY? MORE? AXL, I'M SO SORE FROM THE CRASH I DON'T KNOW IF I CAN...
SORRY. RIGHT. I'LL SHUT UP NOW.
WE'RE NOT RUNNING AT ALL TODAY.
OH.
AM...AM I BEING SENT—
NO.
NO, I JUST THOUGHT WE'D TRY SOMETHING A LITTLE DIFFERENT TODAY.
WHAT, I'M GOING TO LEARN HOW TO MOP FLOORS THE "PROPER" WAY NOW? THE TEAM APOLLO WAY?
NO, ALTHOUGH NOW THAT YOU MENTION IT, THAT'S NOT A BAD IDEA.
HELP ME MOVE THIS STUFF OUT.

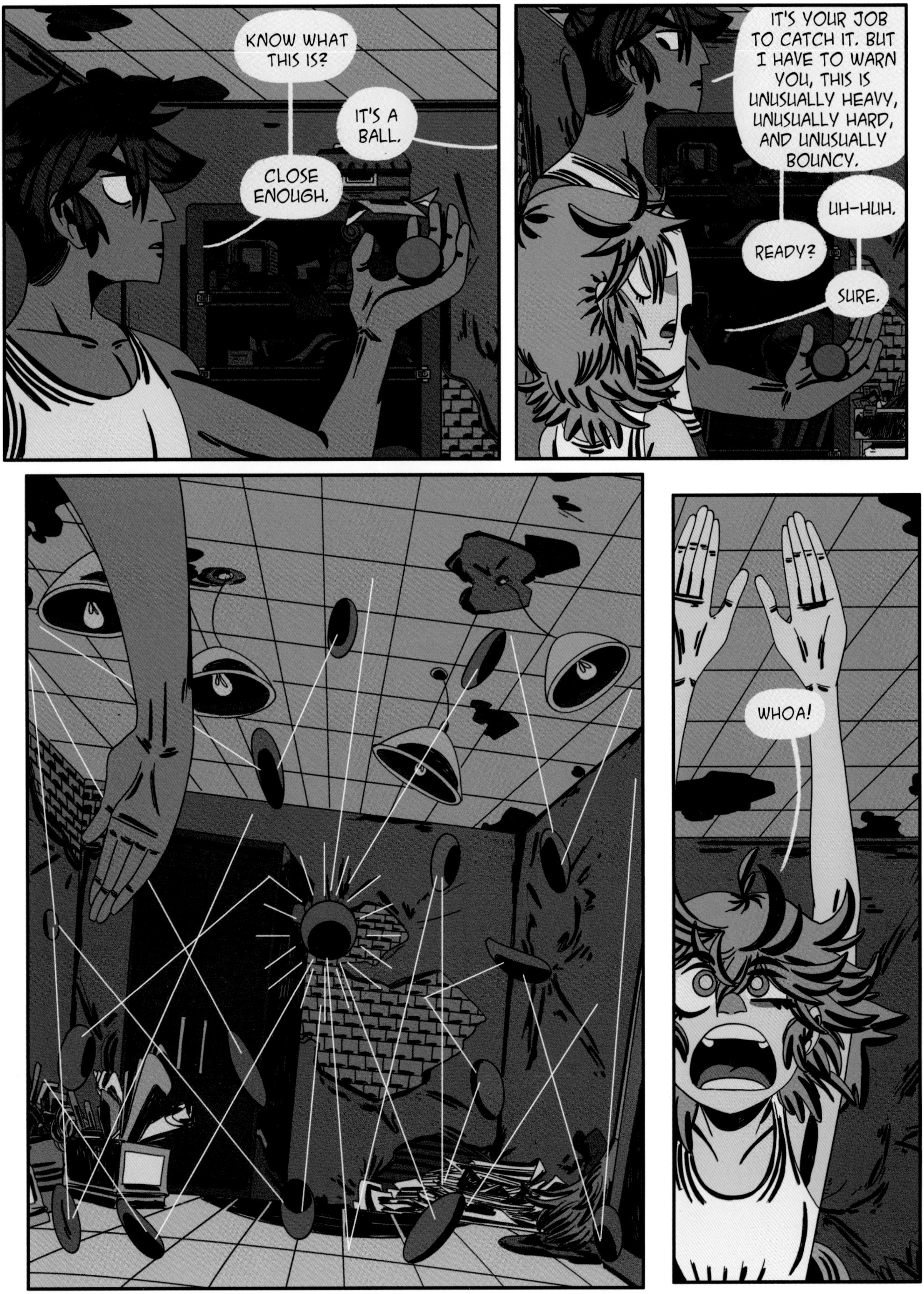
KNOW WHAT THIS IS?
IT'S A BALL.
CLOSE ENOUGH.
IT'S YOUR JOB TO CATCH IT. BUT I HAVE TO WARN YOU, THIS IS UNUSUALLY HEAVY, UNUSUALLY HARD, AND UNUSUALLY BOUNCY.
UH-HUH.
READY?
SURE.
WHOA!

AH!

OOF.

READY TO TRY AGAIN?

LET'S GO.

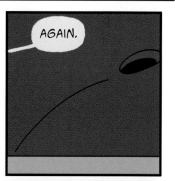

AGAIN.

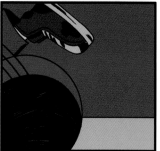

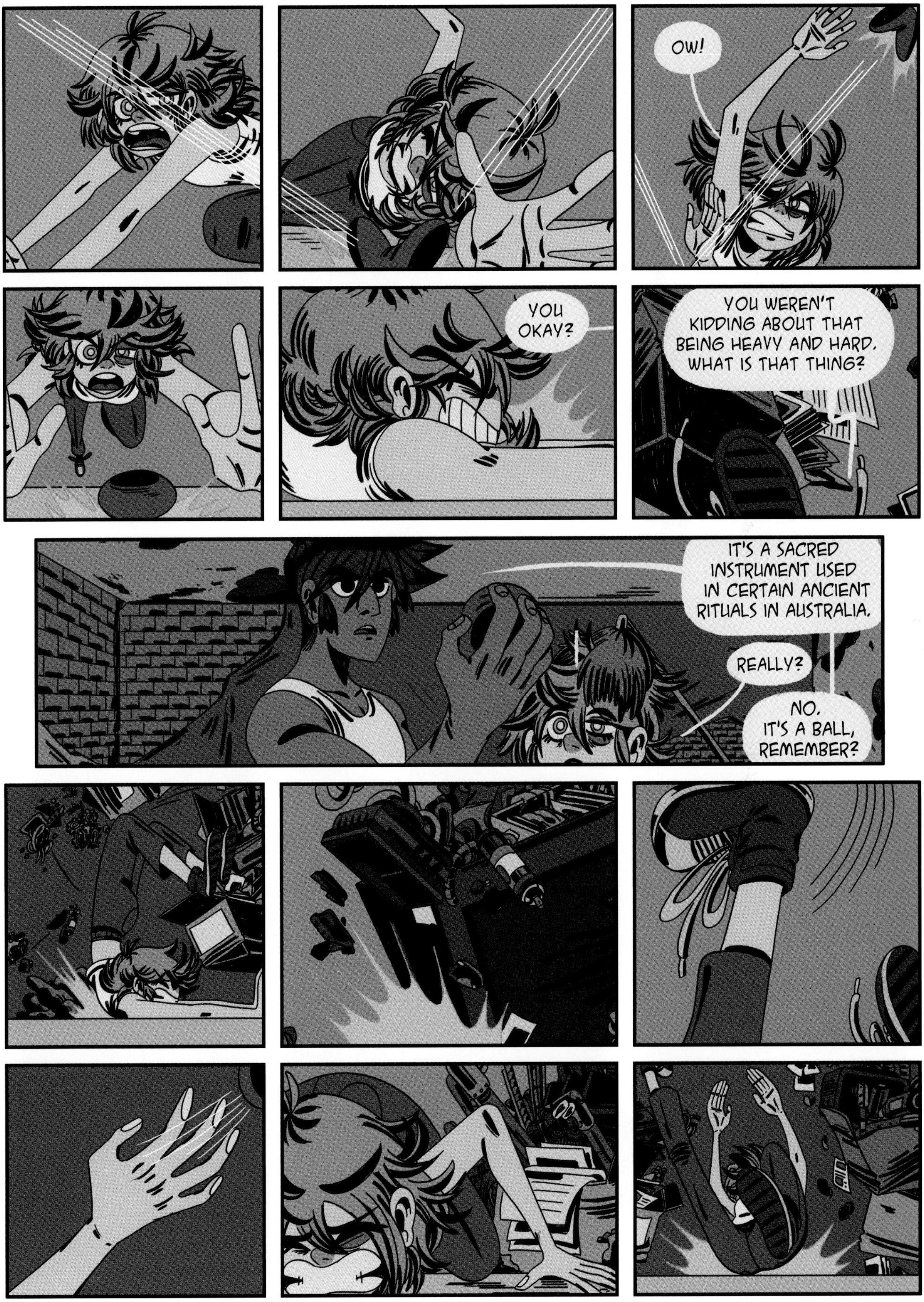
OW!
YOU OKAY?
YOU WEREN'T KIDDING ABOUT THAT BEING HEAVY AND HARD. WHAT IS THAT THING?
IT'S A SACRED INSTRUMENT USED IN CERTAIN ANCIENT RITUALS IN AUSTRALIA.
REALLY?
NO. IT'S A BALL, REMEMBER?

DON'T TRY TO GRAB THE BALL.

WATCH ITS PATH.

NOTE WHERE IT'S BEEN, THEN FIGURE OUT WHERE IT'S GOING TO BE...

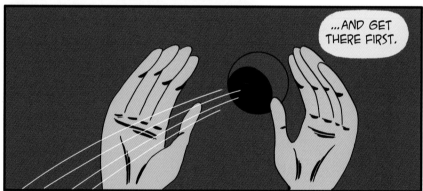

...AND GET THERE FIRST.

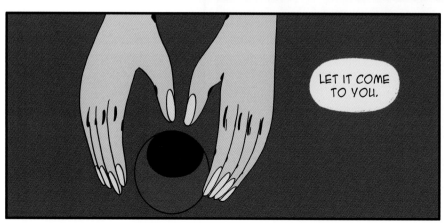

LET IT COME TO YOU.

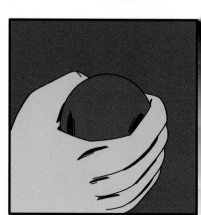

GOOD. READY?

FOR WHAT? I DID IT.

ONCE. YOU NEED TO DO IT EVERY TIME.

BRING IT.

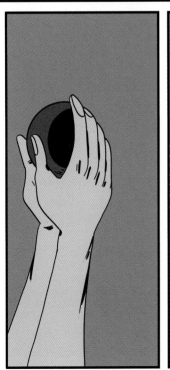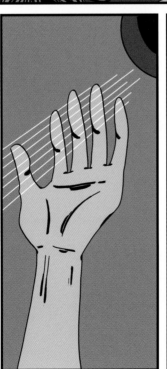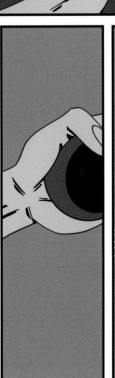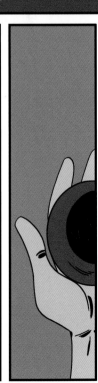

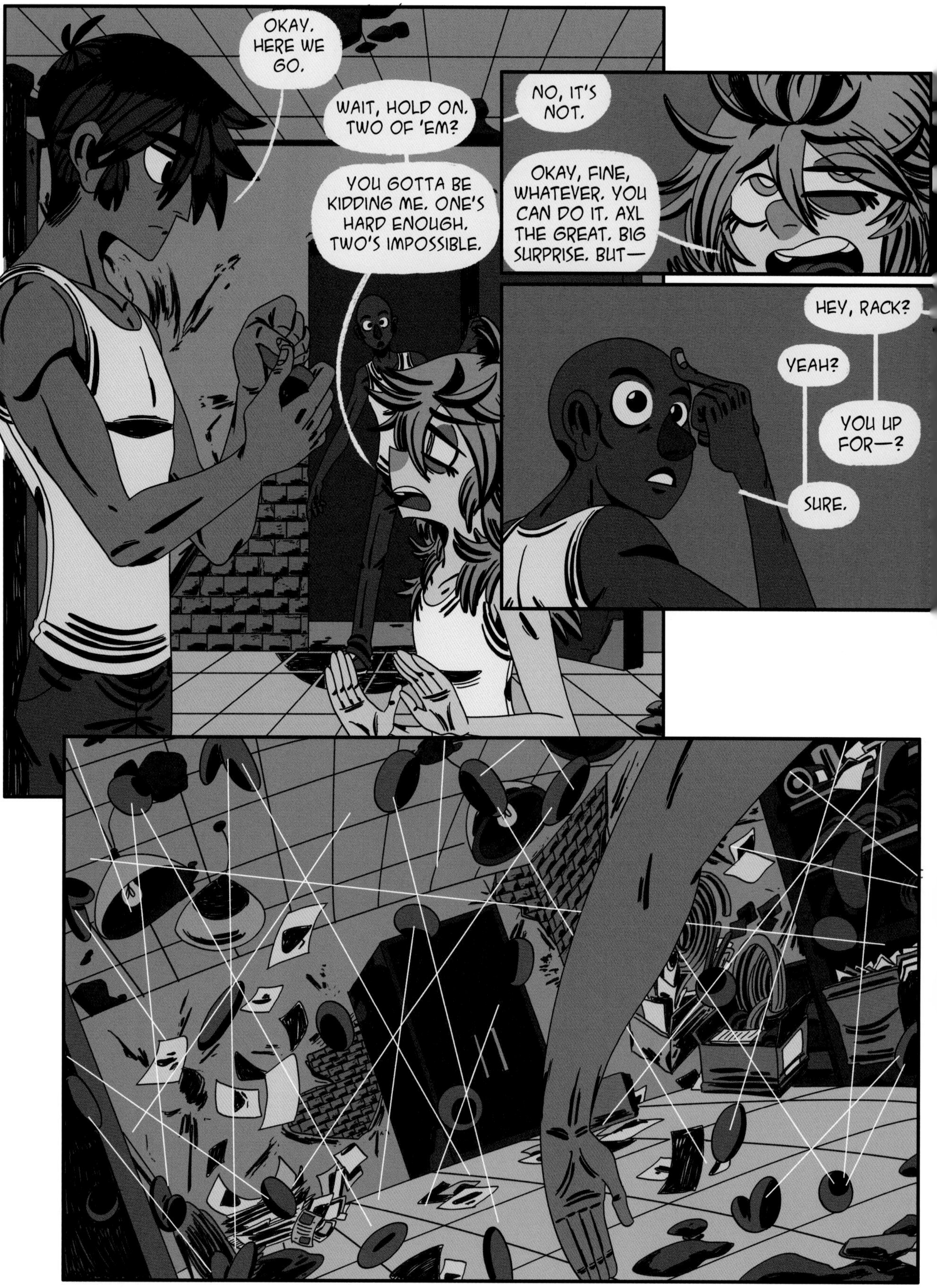
OKAY. HERE WE GO.
WAIT, HOLD ON. TWO OF 'EM?
YOU GOTTA BE KIDDING ME. ONE'S HARD ENOUGH. TWO'S IMPOSSIBLE.
NO, IT'S NOT.
OKAY, FINE, WHATEVER. YOU CAN DO IT. AXL THE GREAT. BIG SURPRISE. BUT—
HEY, RACK?
YEAH?
YOU UP FOR—?
SURE.

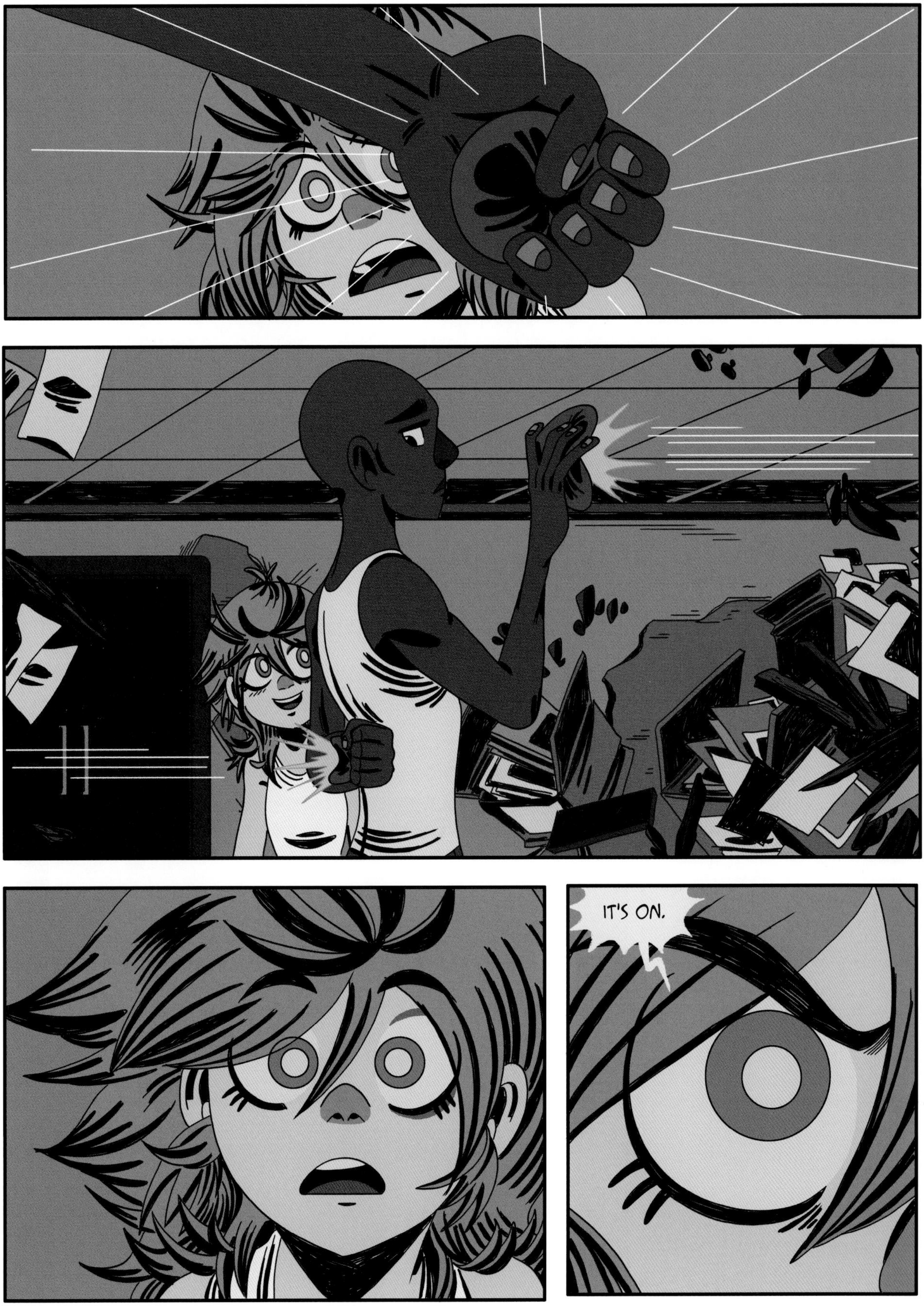
IT'S ON.

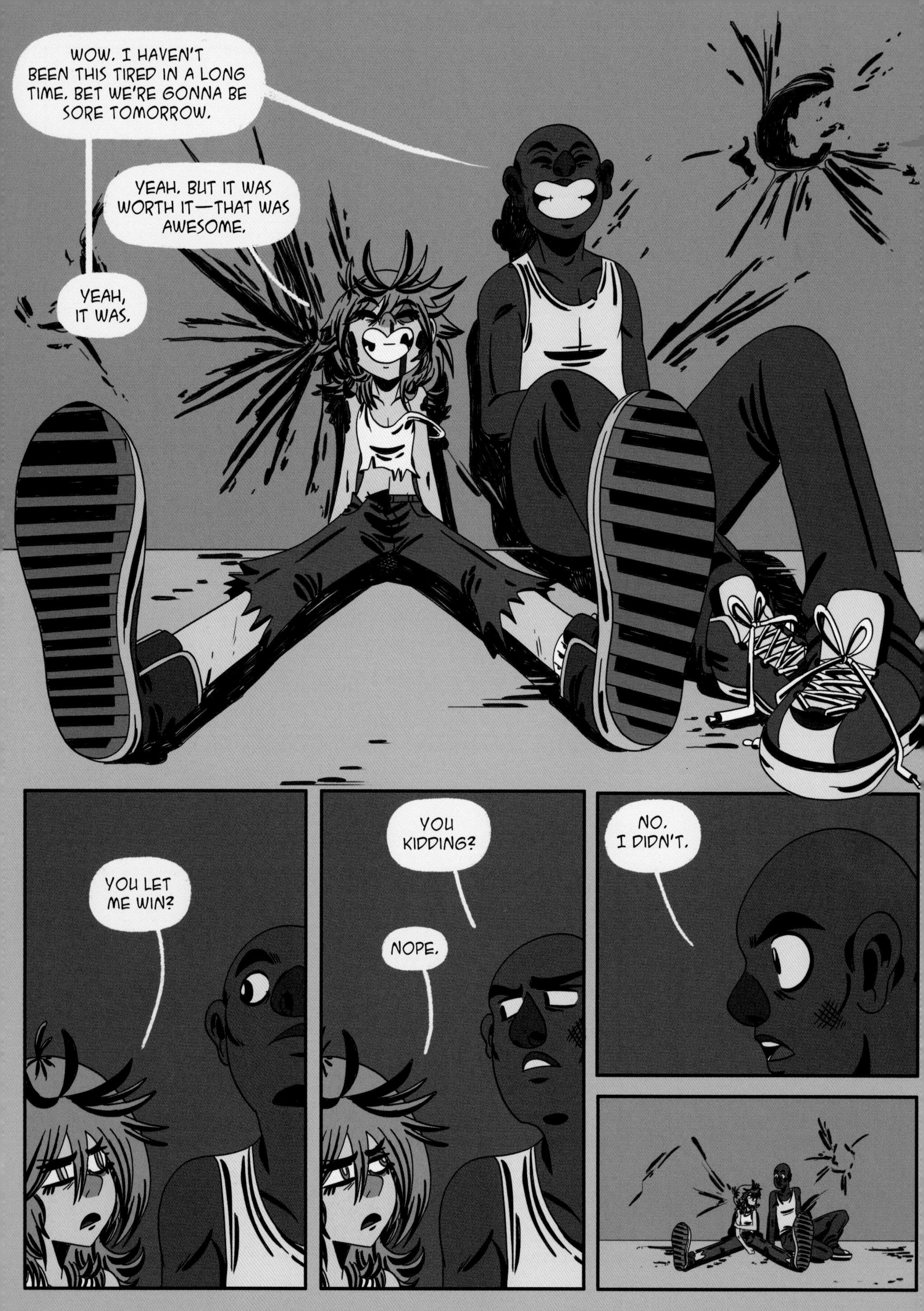
WOW. I HAVEN'T BEEN THIS TIRED IN A LONG TIME. BET WE'RE GONNA BE SORE TOMORROW.
YEAH. BUT IT WAS WORTH IT—THAT WAS AWESOME.
YEAH, IT WAS.
YOU LET ME WIN?
YOU KIDDING?
NOPE.
NO. I DIDN'T.

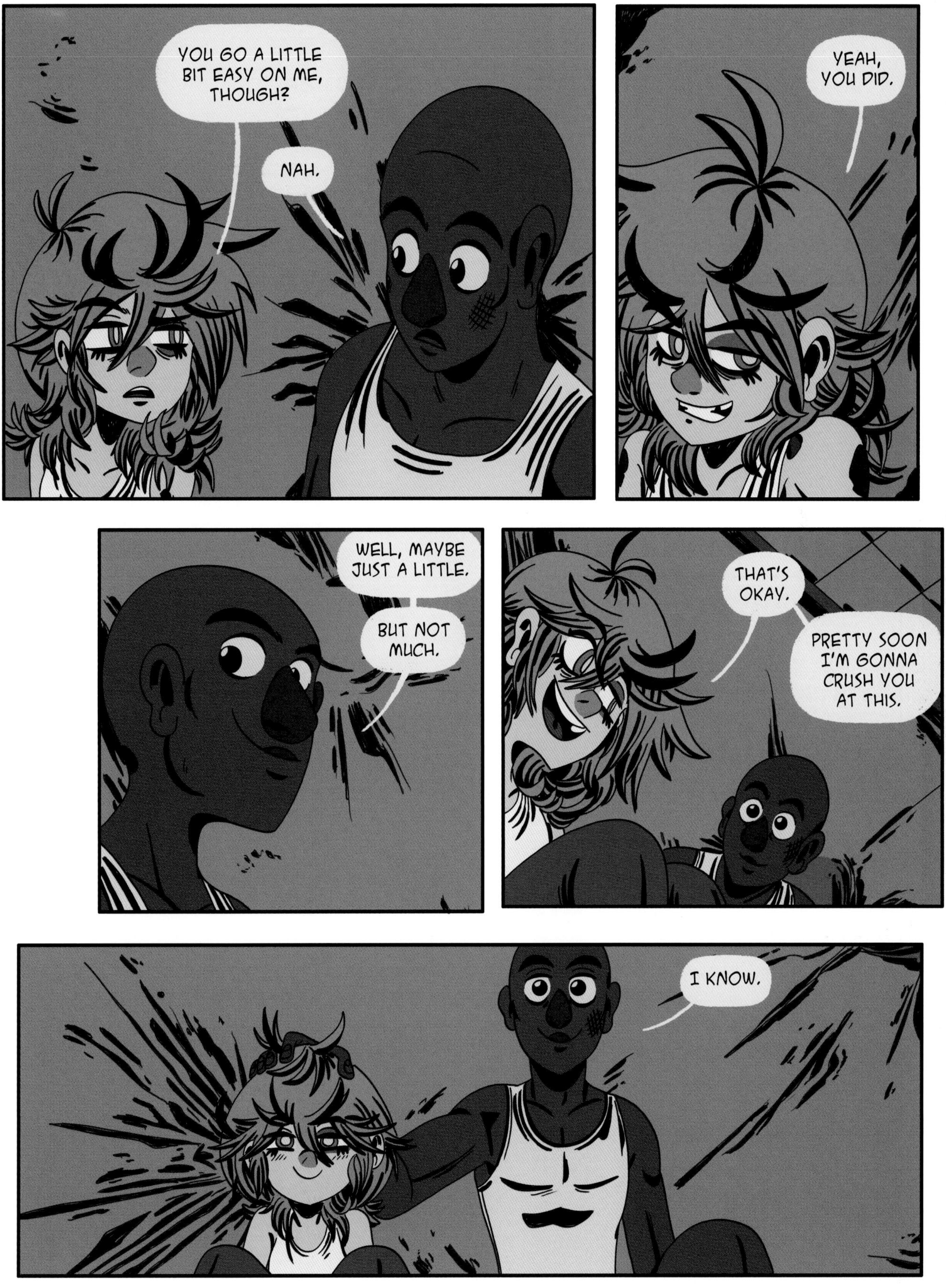
YOU GO A LITTLE BIT EASY ON ME, THOUGH?
NAH.
YEAH, YOU DID.
WELL, MAYBE JUST A LITTLE.
BUT NOT MUCH.
THAT'S OKAY.
PRETTY SOON I'M GONNA CRUSH YOU AT THIS.
I KNOW.

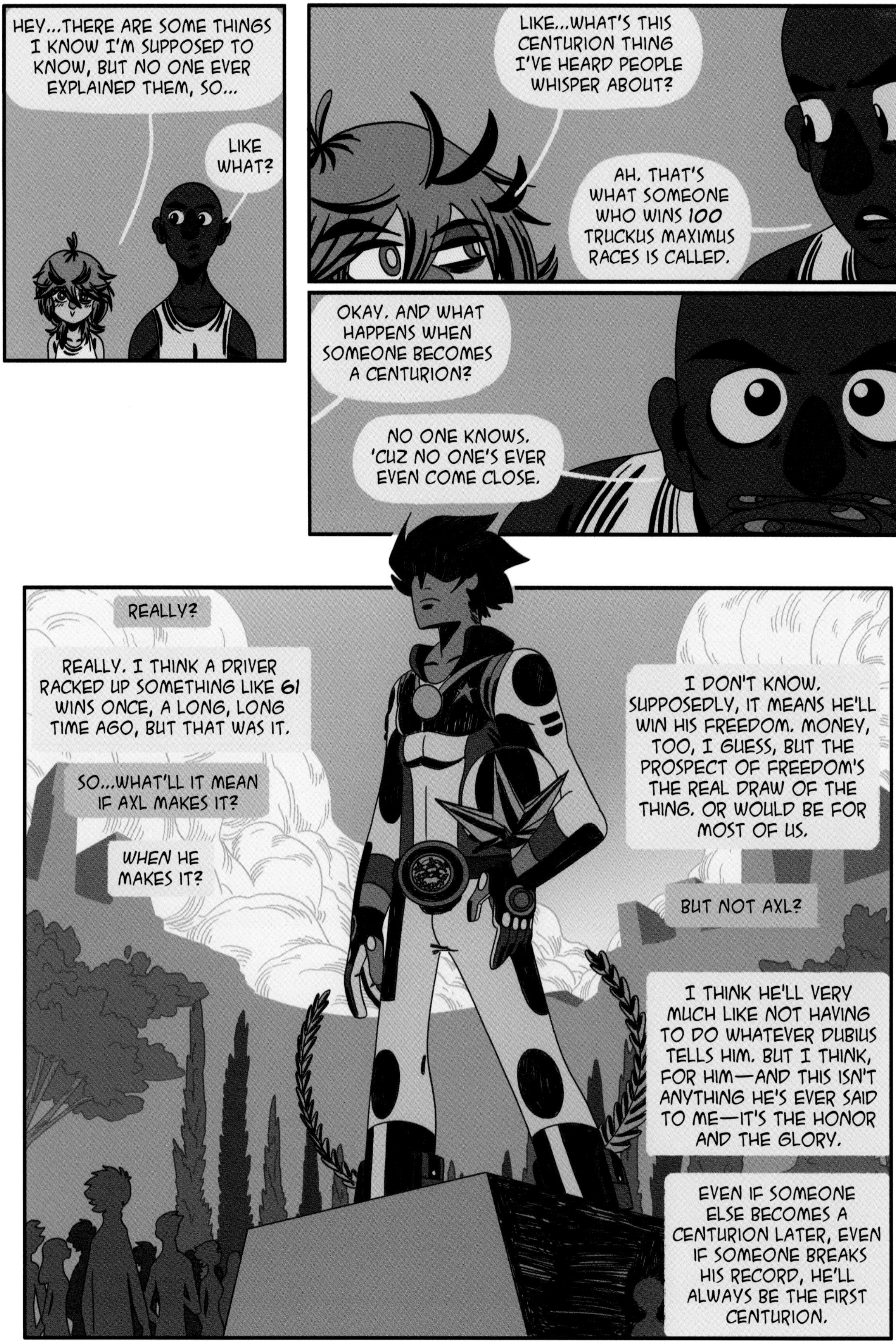
HEY...THERE ARE SOME THINGS I KNOW I'M SUPPOSED TO KNOW, BUT NO ONE EVER EXPLAINED THEM, SO...
LIKE WHAT?
LIKE...WHAT'S THIS CENTURION THING I'VE HEARD PEOPLE WHISPER ABOUT?
AH. THAT'S WHAT SOMEONE WHO WINS 100 TRUCKUS MAXIMUS RACES IS CALLED.
OKAY. AND WHAT HAPPENS WHEN SOMEONE BECOMES A CENTURION?
NO ONE KNOWS. 'CUZ NO ONE'S EVER EVEN COME CLOSE.
REALLY?
REALLY. I THINK A DRIVER RACKED UP SOMETHING LIKE 61 WINS ONCE, A LONG, LONG TIME AGO, BUT THAT WAS IT.
SO...WHAT'LL IT MEAN IF AXL MAKES IT?
WHEN HE MAKES IT?
I DON'T KNOW. SUPPOSEDLY, IT MEANS HE'LL WIN HIS FREEDOM. MONEY, TOO, I GUESS, BUT THE PROSPECT OF FREEDOM'S THE REAL DRAW OF THE THING. OR WOULD BE FOR MOST OF US.
BUT NOT AXL?
I THINK HE'LL VERY MUCH LIKE NOT HAVING TO DO WHATEVER DUBIUS TELLS HIM. BUT I THINK, FOR HIM—AND THIS ISN'T ANYTHING HE'S EVER SAID TO ME—IT'S THE HONOR AND THE GLORY.
EVEN IF SOMEONE ELSE BECOMES A CENTURION LATER, EVEN IF SOMEONE BREAKS HIS RECORD, HE'LL ALWAYS BE THE FIRST CENTURION.

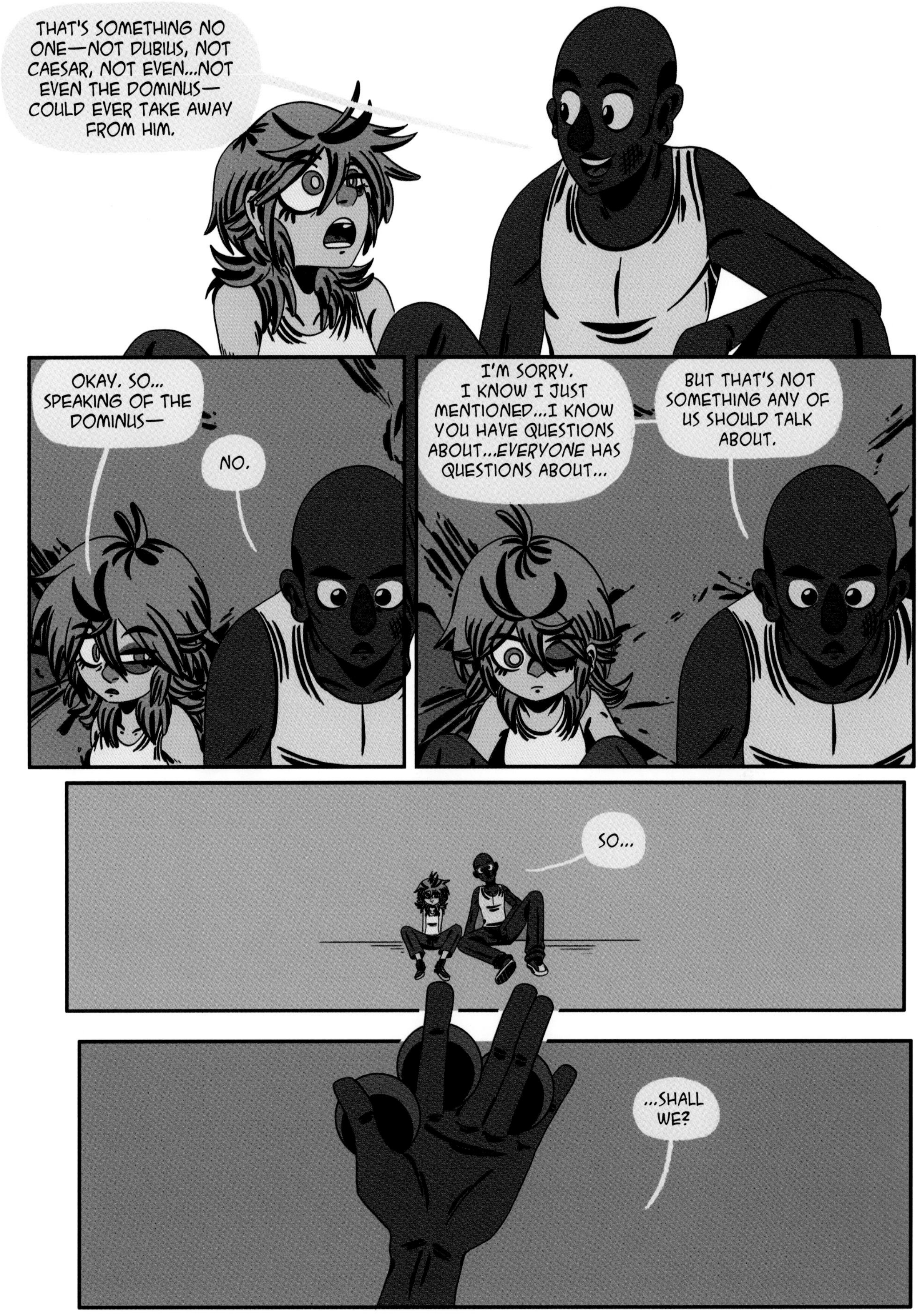
THAT'S SOMETHING NO ONE—NOT DUBIUS, NOT CAESAR, NOT EVEN...NOT EVEN THE DOMINUS—COULD EVER TAKE AWAY FROM HIM.
OKAY. SO... SPEAKING OF THE DOMINUS—
NO.
I'M SORRY. I KNOW I JUST MENTIONED...I KNOW YOU HAVE QUESTIONS ABOUT...*EVERYONE* HAS QUESTIONS ABOUT...
BUT THAT'S NOT SOMETHING ANY OF US SHOULD TALK ABOUT.
SO...
...SHALL WE?

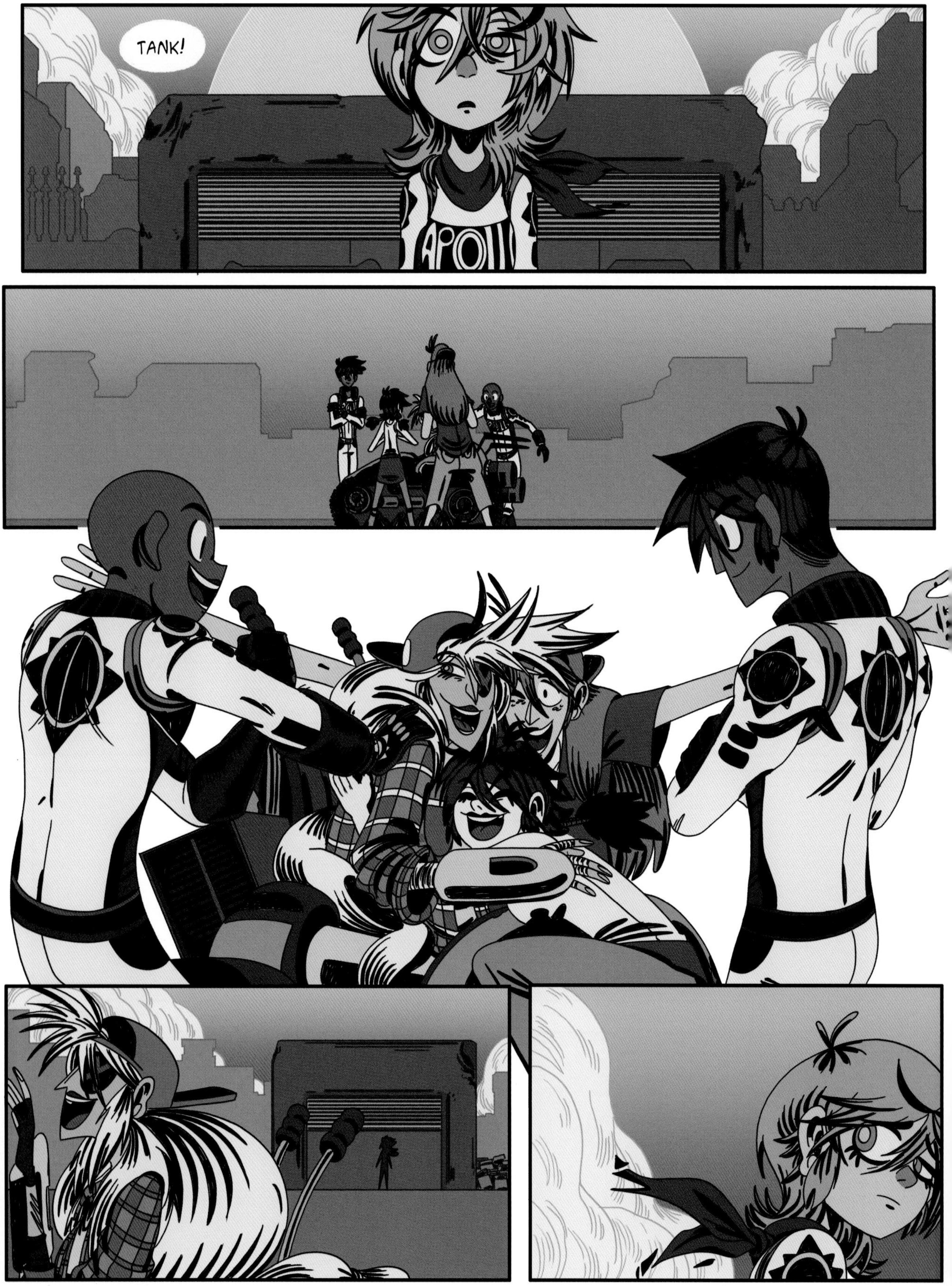
TANK!

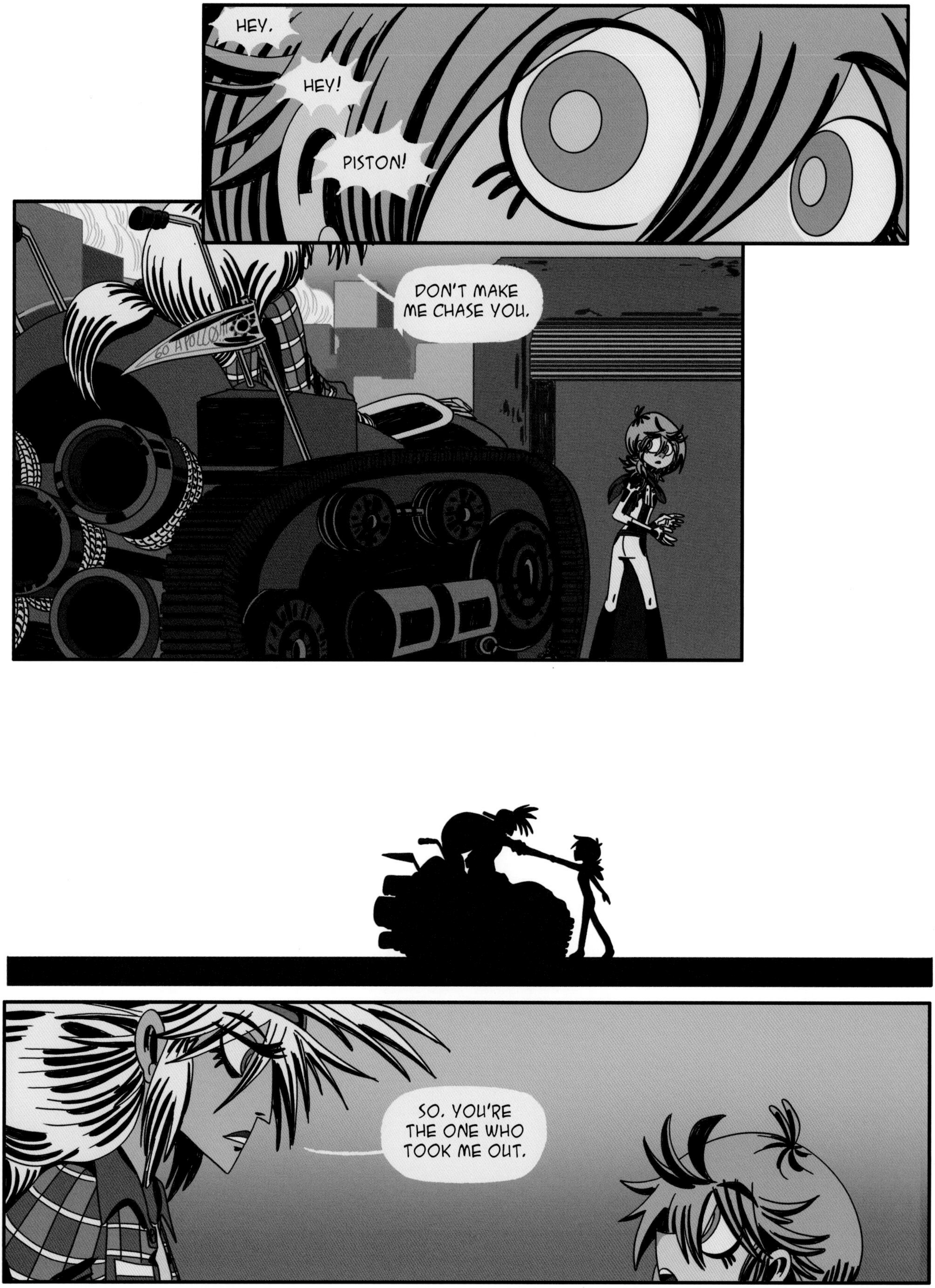
HEY.
HEY!
PISTON!
DON'T MAKE ME CHASE YOU.
GO APOLLO
SO. YOU'RE THE ONE WHO TOOK ME OUT.

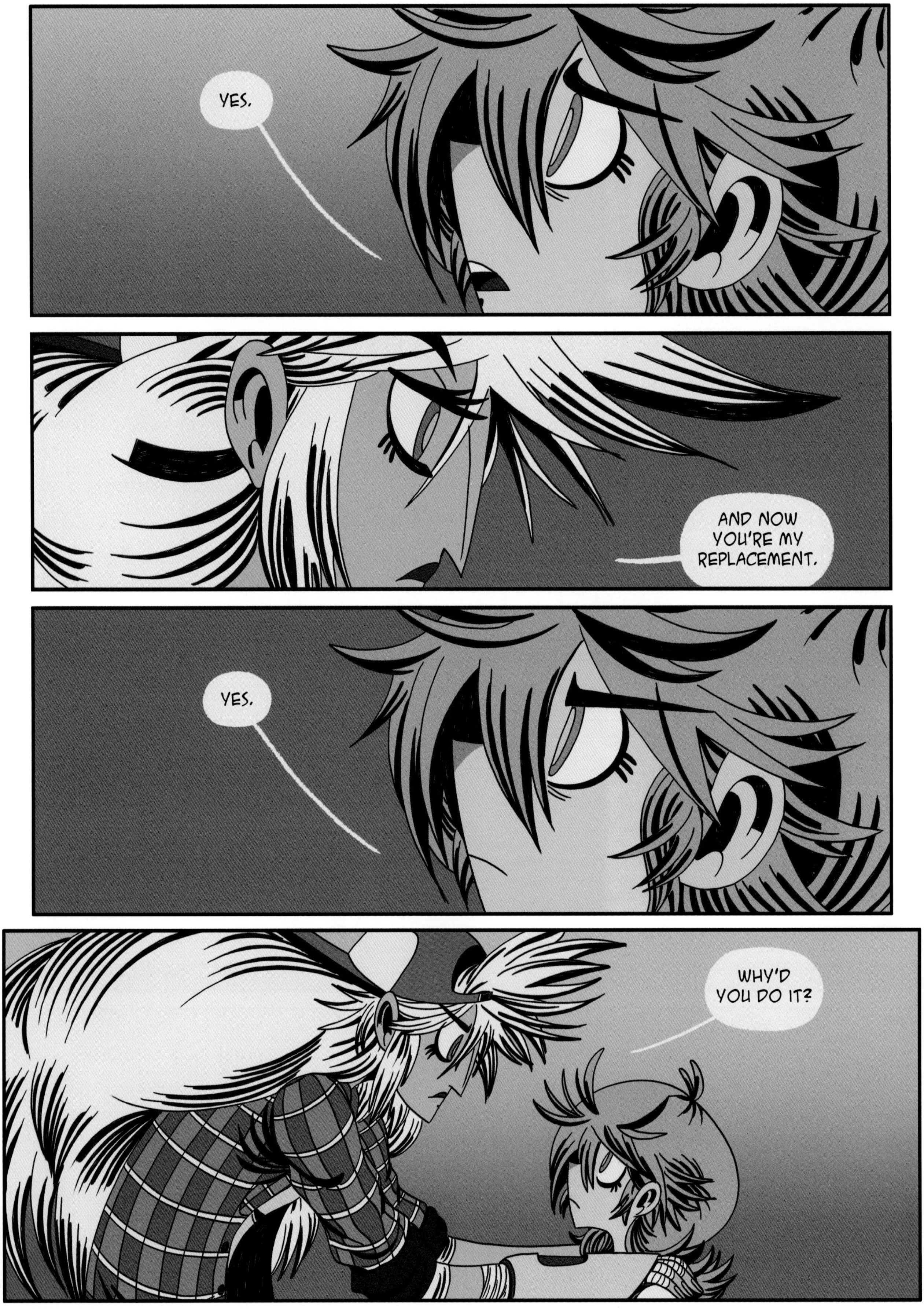
YES.
AND NOW YOU'RE MY REPLACEMENT.
YES.
WHY'D YOU DO IT?

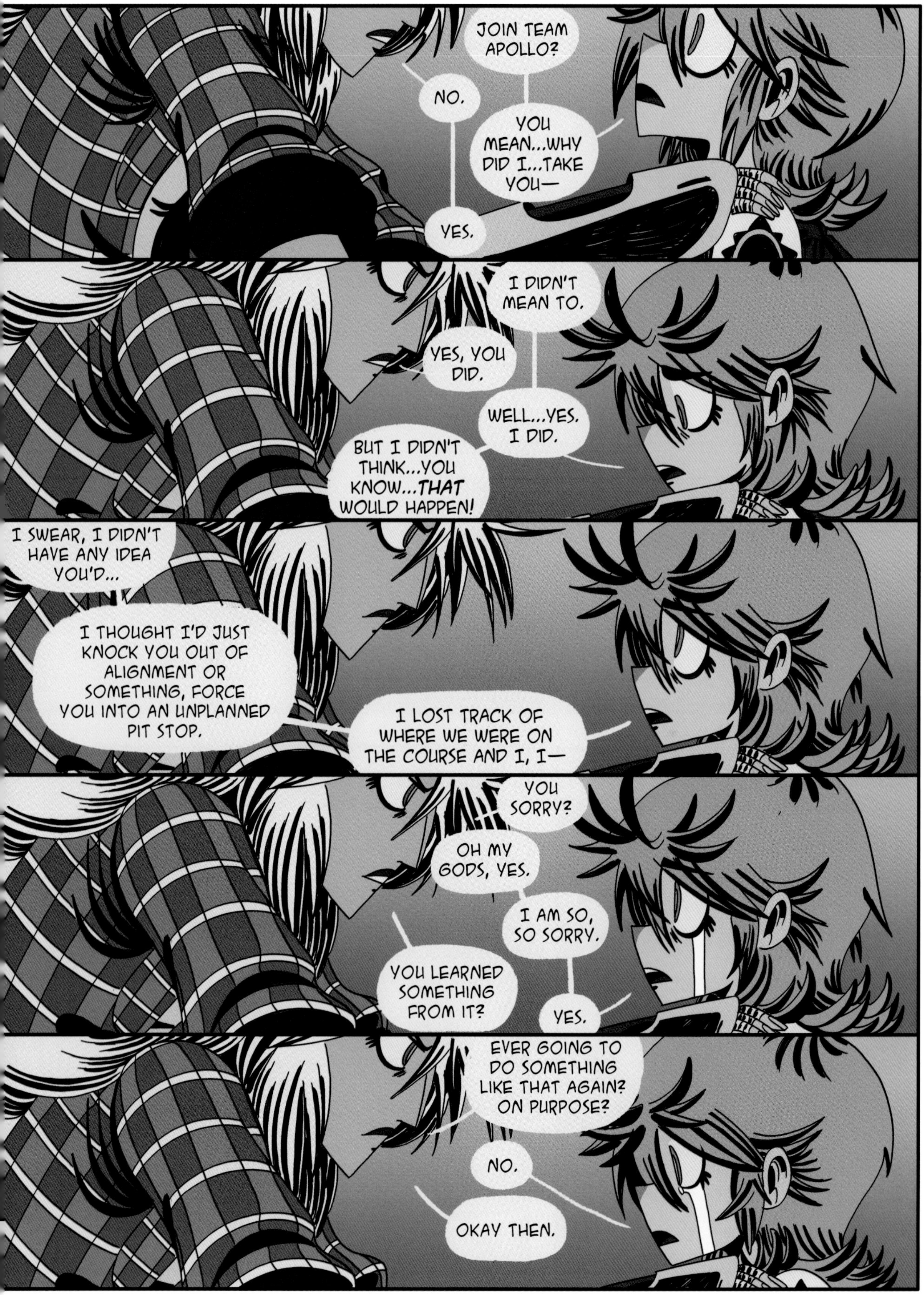
JOIN TEAM APOLLO?
NO.
YOU MEAN...WHY DID I...TAKE YOU—
YES.
I DIDN'T MEAN TO.
YES, YOU DID.
WELL...YES. I DID.
BUT I DIDN'T THINK...YOU KNOW...**THAT** WOULD HAPPEN!
I SWEAR, I DIDN'T HAVE ANY IDEA YOU'D...
I THOUGHT I'D JUST KNOCK YOU OUT OF ALIGNMENT OR SOMETHING, FORCE YOU INTO AN UNPLANNED PIT STOP.
I LOST TRACK OF WHERE WE WERE ON THE COURSE AND I, I—
YOU SORRY?
OH MY GODS, YES.
I AM SO, SO SORRY.
YOU LEARNED SOMETHING FROM IT?
YES.
EVER GOING TO DO SOMETHING LIKE THAT AGAIN? ON PURPOSE?
NO.
OKAY THEN.

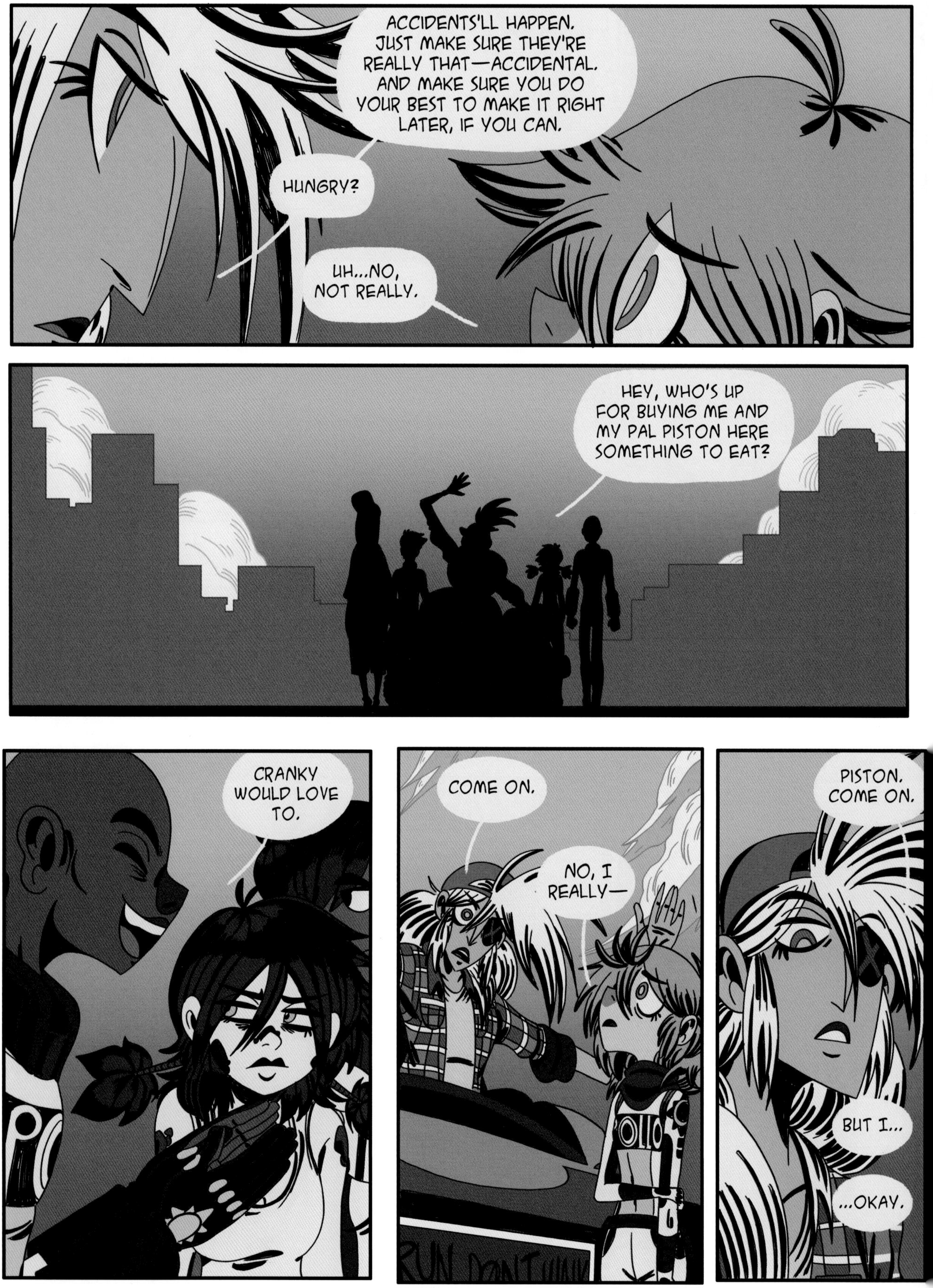
ACCIDENTS'LL HAPPEN. JUST MAKE SURE THEY'RE REALLY THAT—ACCIDENTAL. AND MAKE SURE YOU DO YOUR BEST TO MAKE IT RIGHT LATER, IF YOU CAN.
HUNGRY?
UH...NO, NOT REALLY.
HEY, WHO'S UP FOR BUYING ME AND MY PAL PISTON HERE SOMETHING TO EAT?
CRANKY WOULD LOVE TO.
COME ON.
NO, I REALLY—
PISTON. COME ON.
BUT I...
...OKAY.
RUN DON'T

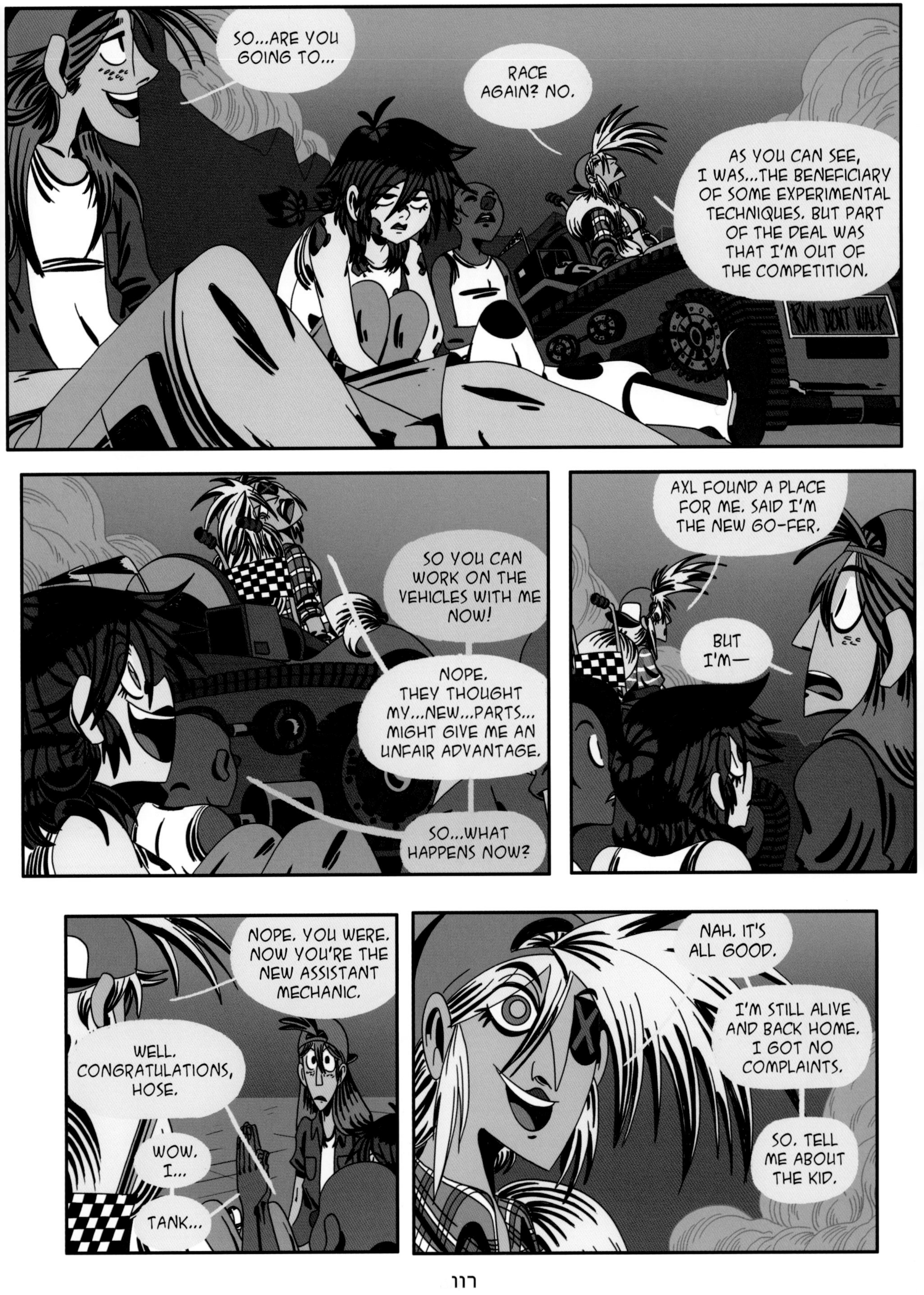
SO...ARE YOU GOING TO...
RACE AGAIN? NO.
AS YOU CAN SEE, I WAS...THE BENEFICIARY OF SOME EXPERIMENTAL TECHNIQUES. BUT PART OF THE DEAL WAS THAT I'M OUT OF THE COMPETITION.
RUN DONT WALK
SO YOU CAN WORK ON THE VEHICLES WITH ME NOW!
NOPE. THEY THOUGHT MY...NEW...PARTS... MIGHT GIVE ME AN UNFAIR ADVANTAGE.
SO...WHAT HAPPENS NOW?
AXL FOUND A PLACE FOR ME. SAID I'M THE NEW GO-FER.
BUT I'M—
NOPE. YOU WERE. NOW YOU'RE THE NEW ASSISTANT MECHANIC.
WELL. CONGRATULATIONS, HOSE.
WOW. I...
TANK...
NAH. IT'S ALL GOOD.
I'M STILL ALIVE AND BACK HOME. I GOT NO COMPLAINTS.
SO. TELL ME ABOUT THE KID.

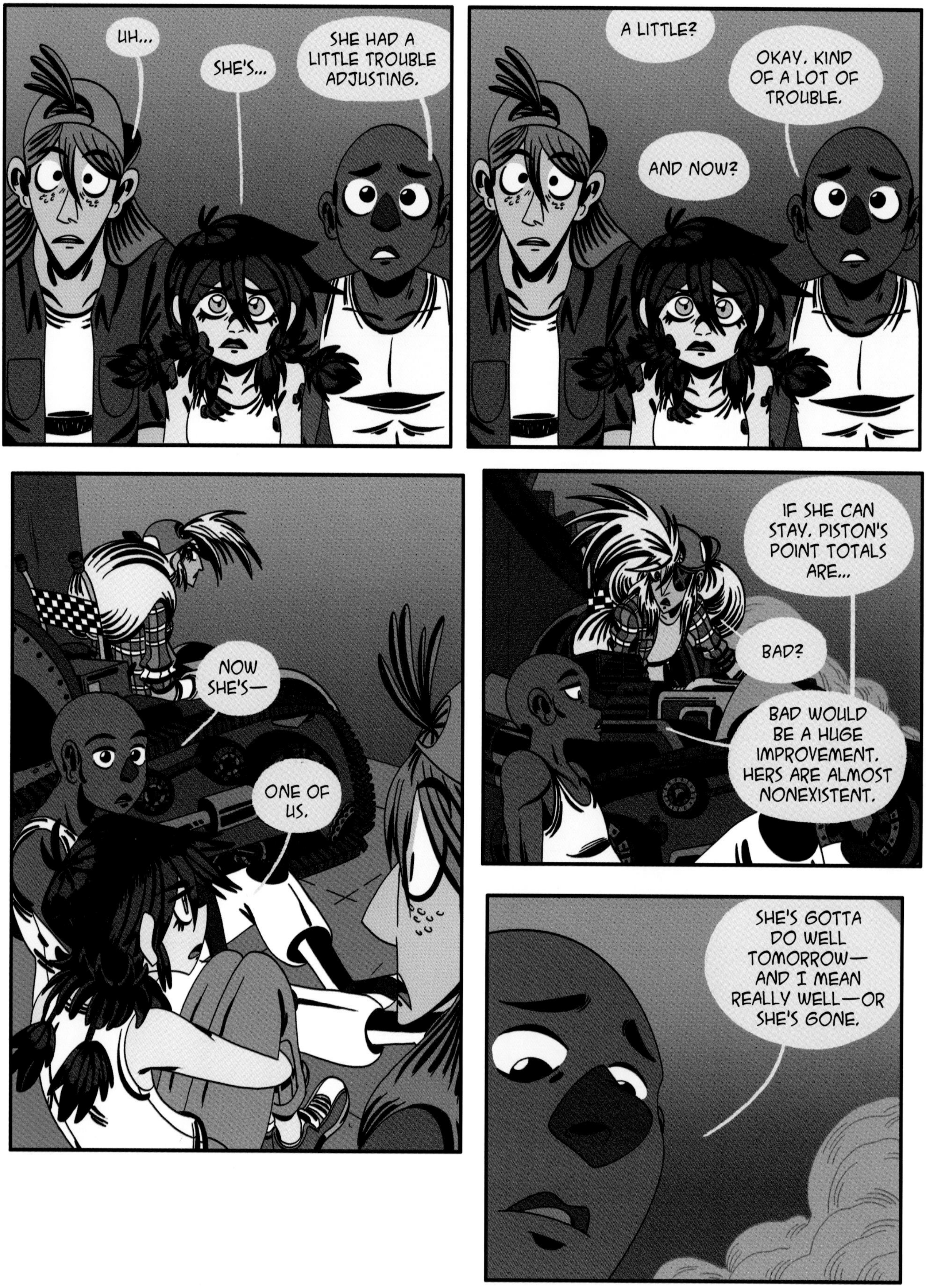
UH...
SHE'S...
SHE HAD A LITTLE TROUBLE ADJUSTING.
A LITTLE?
OKAY. KIND OF A LOT OF TROUBLE.
AND NOW?
NOW SHE'S—
ONE OF US.
IF SHE CAN STAY, PISTON'S POINT TOTALS ARE...
BAD?
BAD WOULD BE A HUGE IMPROVEMENT. HERS ARE ALMOST NONEXISTENT.
SHE'S GOTTA DO WELL TOMORROW— AND I MEAN REALLY WELL—OR SHE'S GONE.

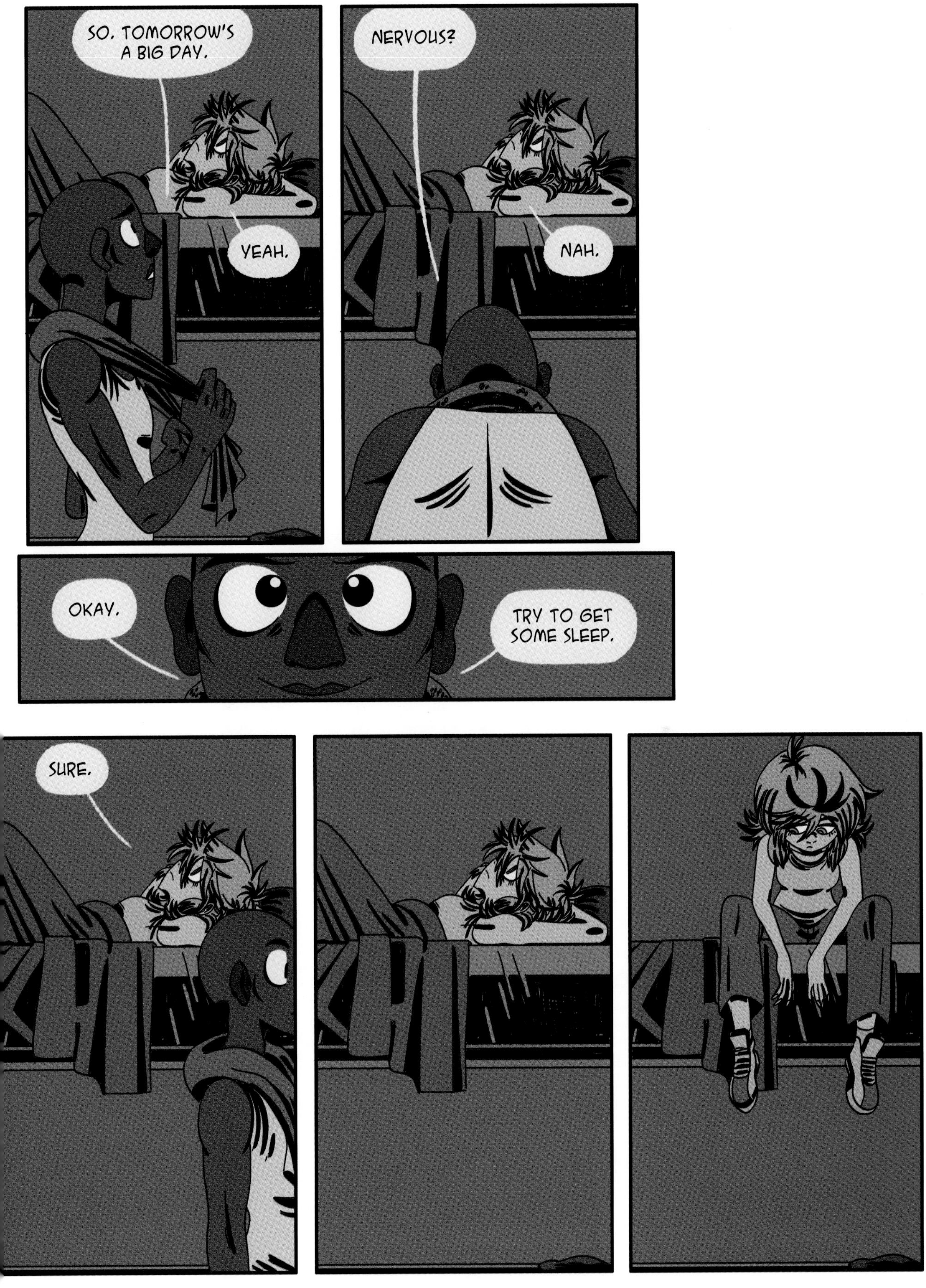
SO. TOMORROW'S A BIG DAY.
YEAH.
NERVOUS?
NAH.
OKAY.
TRY TO GET SOME SLEEP.
SURE.

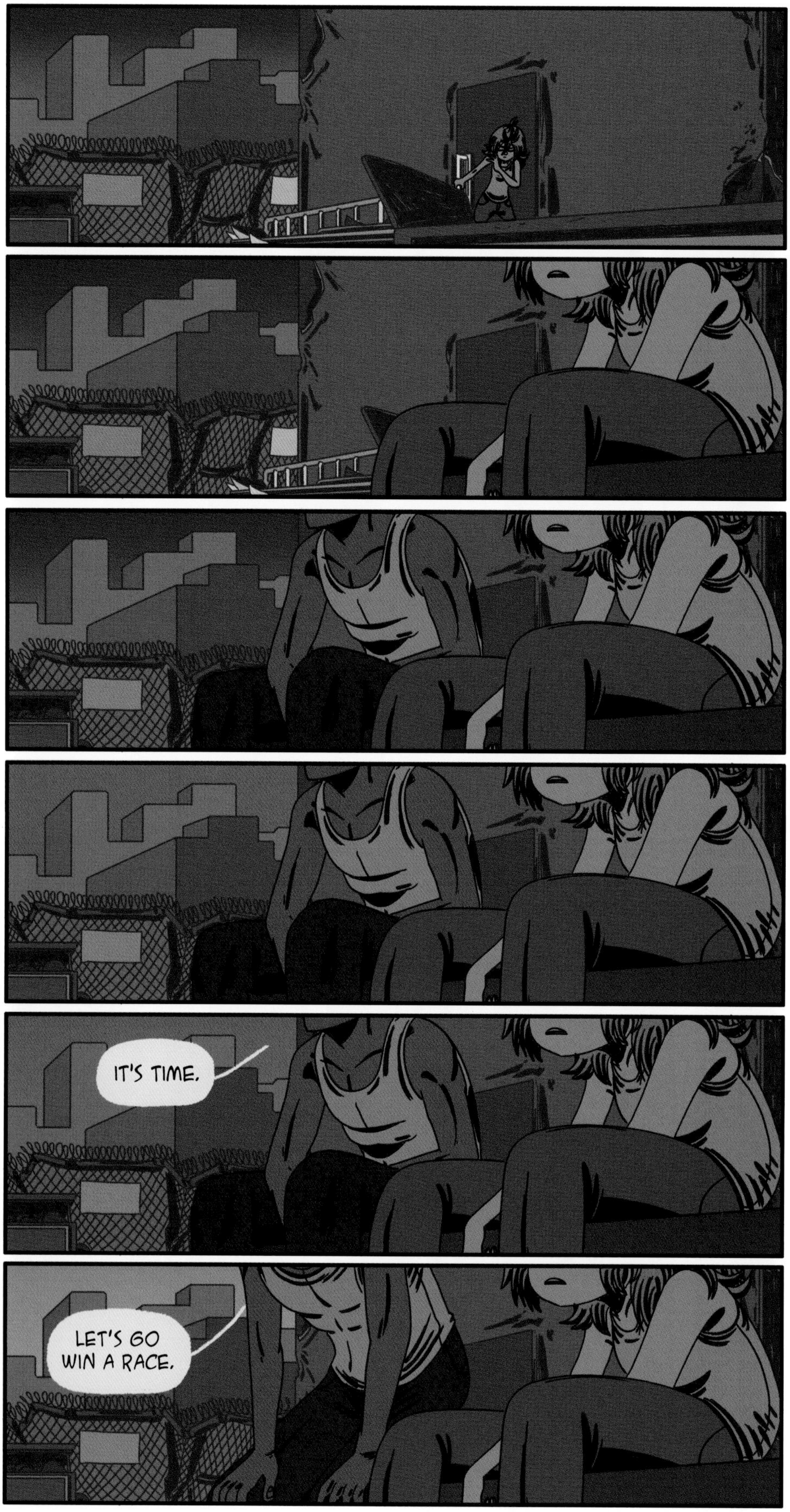
IT'S TIME.
LET'S GO WIN A RACE.

OKAY. I GUESS YOU KNOW THIS RACE IS PRETTY IMPORTANT.

YOU MEAN BECAUSE MY ENTIRE CAREER— MY WHOLE LIFE— IS PRETTY MUCH DEPENDENT ON THIS ONE RACE?

AND IF I DON'T FINISH WELL, I'M OUT OF THE TRUCKUS MAXIMUS COMPETITION FOR GOOD AND I'LL BE SPENDING THE REST OF MY LIFE WORKING IN A SALT MINE?

YEAH, THAT'S PRETTY MUCH IT.

OKAY. GOT IT.

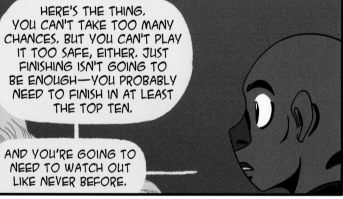

HERE'S THE THING. YOU CAN'T TAKE TOO MANY CHANCES. BUT YOU CAN'T PLAY IT TOO SAFE, EITHER. JUST FINISHING ISN'T GOING TO BE ENOUGH—YOU PROBABLY NEED TO FINISH IN AT LEAST THE TOP TEN.

AND YOU'RE GOING TO NEED TO WATCH OUT LIKE NEVER BEFORE.

SOME OF THE OTHERS ARE GOING TO BE GUNNING FOR YOU. BUT YOU CAN'T DRIVE TOO DEFENSIVELY, EITHER. BUT DON'T GET OVERLY AGGRESSIVE.

YOU KNOW, YOU'RE STARTING TO MAKE THIS SOUND LIKE IT'S NOT GOING TO BE EASY.

IT'S NOT. IT NEVER IS. YOU KNOW THAT. IT'S WHY THERE ARE ONLY A FEW DOZEN TRUCKUS DRIVERS OUT OF THE MILLIONS WHO DREAM OF IT.

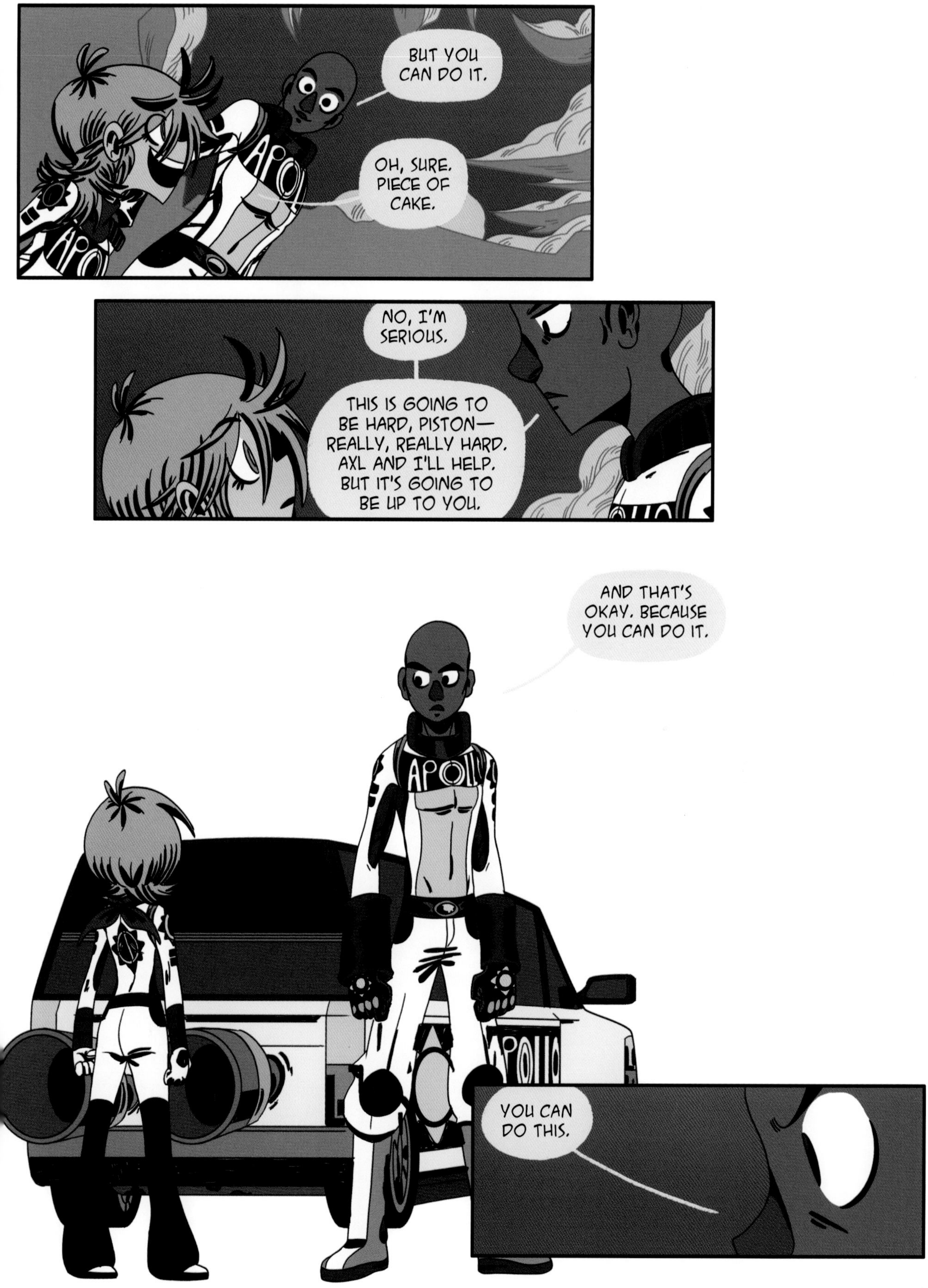
BUT YOU CAN DO IT.
OH, SURE. PIECE OF CAKE.
NO, I'M SERIOUS.
THIS IS GOING TO BE HARD, PISTON— REALLY, REALLY HARD. AXL AND I'LL HELP. BUT IT'S GOING TO BE UP TO YOU.
AND THAT'S OKAY. BECAUSE YOU CAN DO IT.
YOU CAN DO THIS.

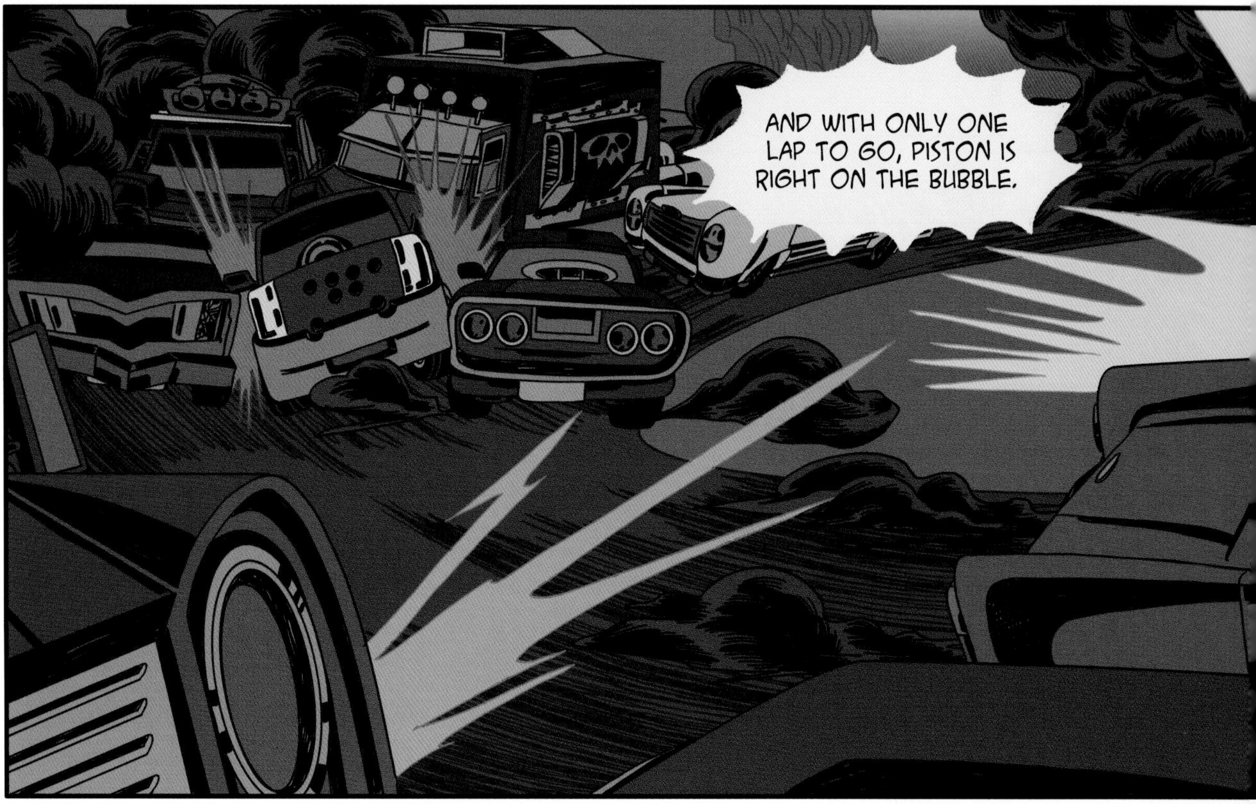
AND WITH ONLY ONE LAP TO GO, PISTON IS RIGHT ON THE BUBBLE.

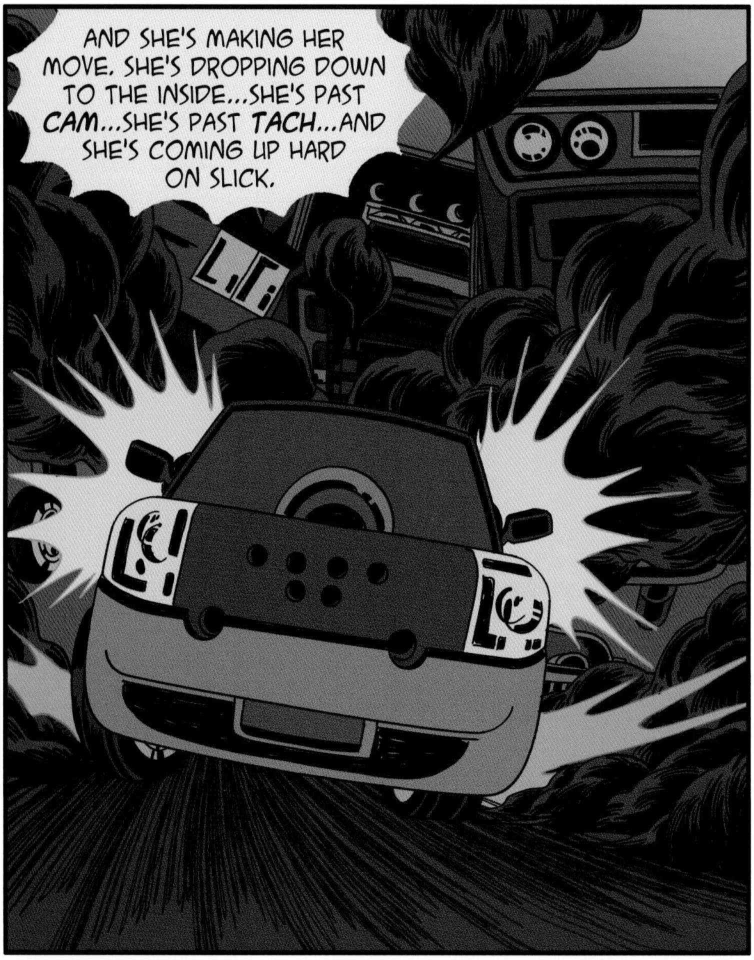
AND SHE'S MAKING HER MOVE. SHE'S DROPPING DOWN TO THE INSIDE...SHE'S PAST CAM...SHE'S PAST TACH...AND SHE'S COMING UP HARD ON SLICK.

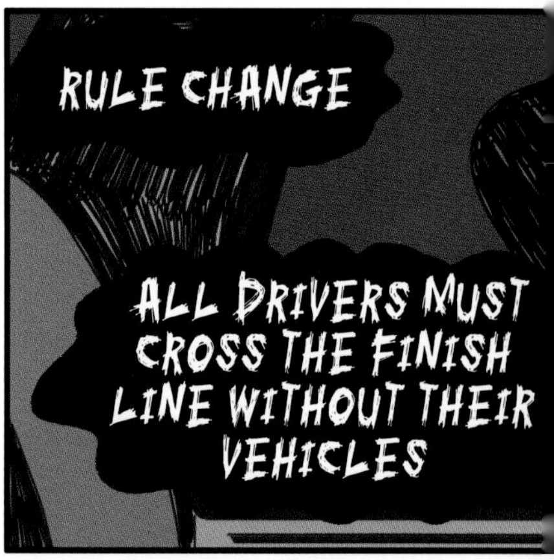
RULE CHANGE
ALL DRIVERS MUST CROSS THE FINISH LINE WITHOUT THEIR VEHICLES

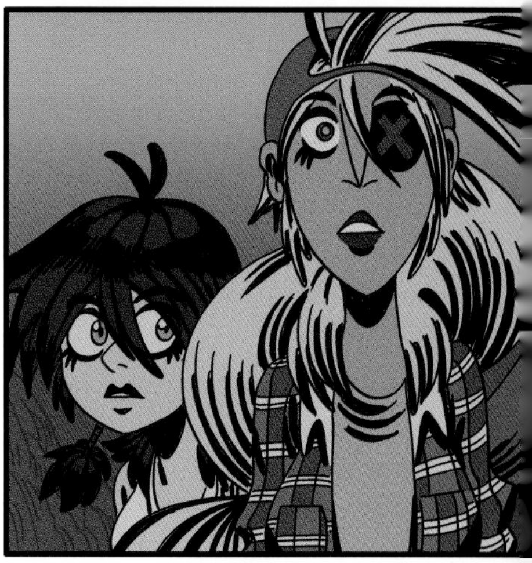

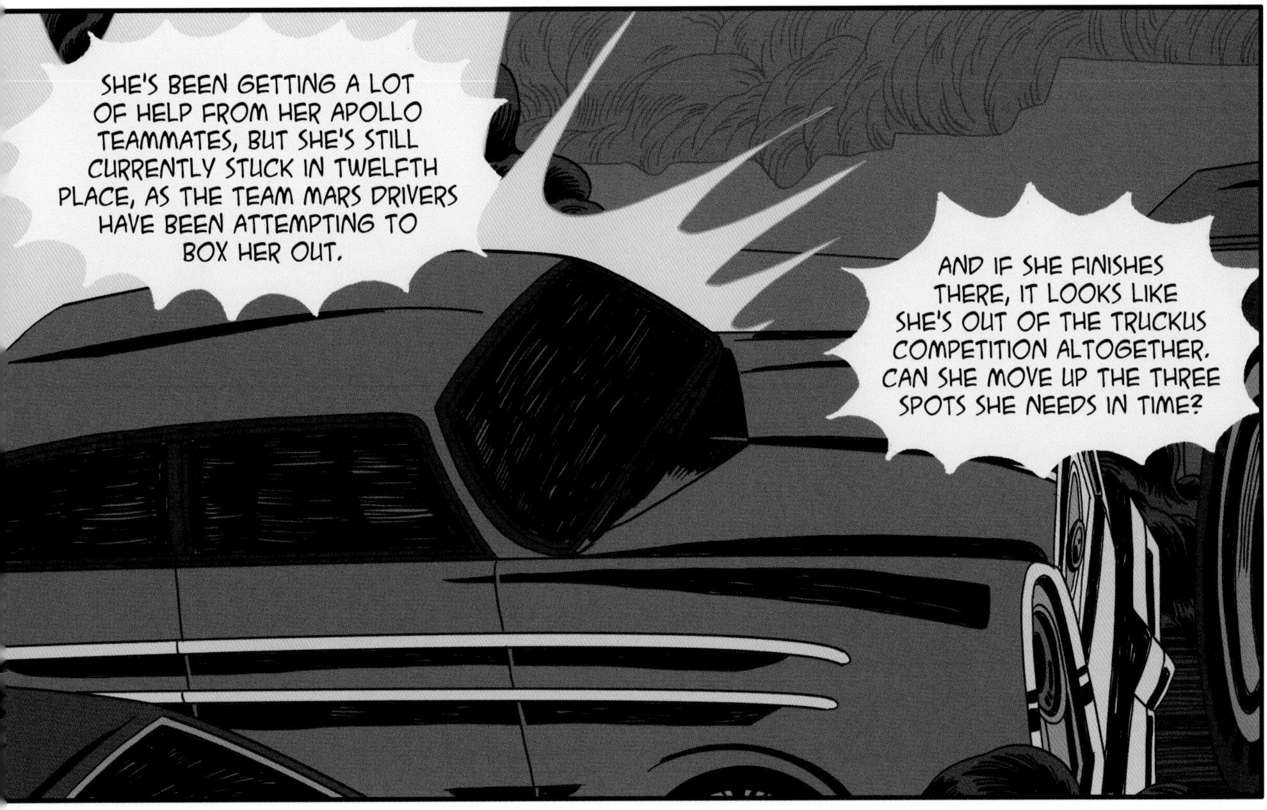
SHE'S BEEN GETTING A LOT OF HELP FROM HER APOLLO TEAMMATES, BUT SHE'S STILL CURRENTLY STUCK IN TWELFTH PLACE, AS THE TEAM MARS DRIVERS HAVE BEEN ATTEMPTING TO BOX HER OUT.
AND IF SHE FINISHES THERE, IT LOOKS LIKE SHE'S OUT OF THE TRUCKUS COMPETITION ALTOGETHER. CAN SHE MOVE UP THE THREE SPOTS SHE NEEDS IN TIME?

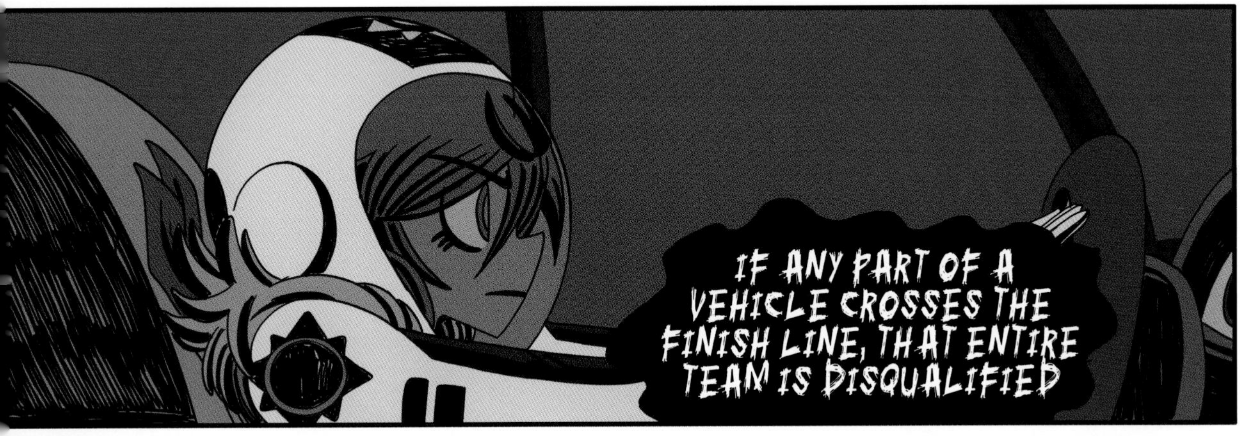
IF ANY PART OF A VEHICLE CROSSES THE FINISH LINE, THAT ENTIRE TEAM IS DISQUALIFIED

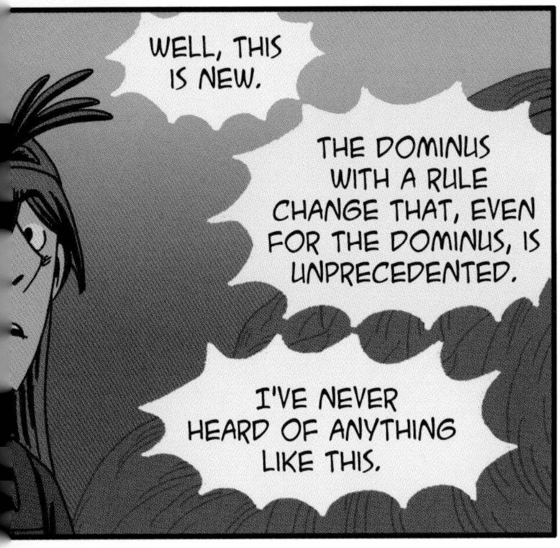
WELL, THIS IS NEW.
THE DOMINUS WITH A RULE CHANGE THAT, EVEN FOR THE DOMINUS, IS UNPRECEDENTED.
I'VE NEVER HEARD OF ANYTHING LIKE THIS.

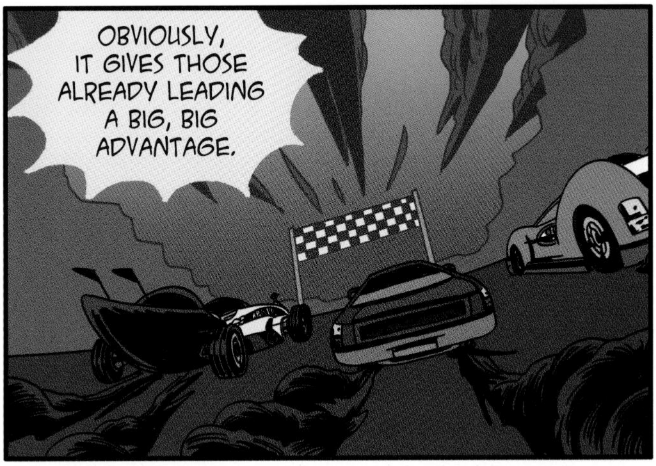
OBVIOUSLY, IT GIVES THOSE ALREADY LEADING A BIG, BIG ADVANTAGE.

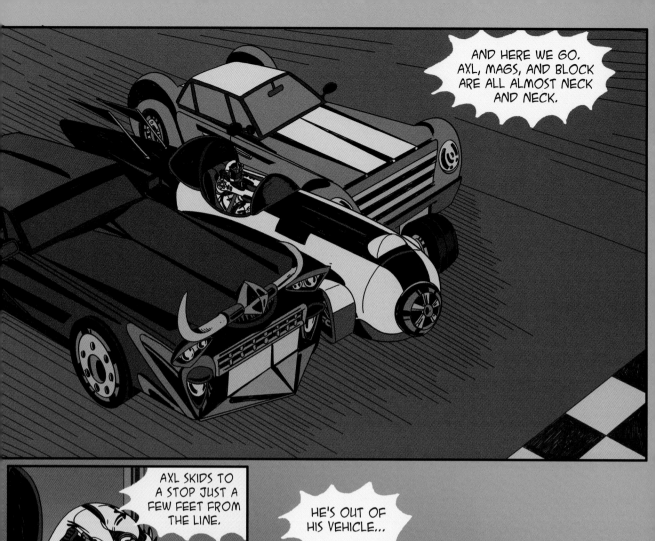

AND HERE WE GO. AXL, MAGS, AND BLOCK ARE ALL ALMOST NECK AND NECK.

AXL SKIDS TO A STOP JUST A FEW FEET FROM THE LINE.

HE'S OUT OF HIS VEHICLE...

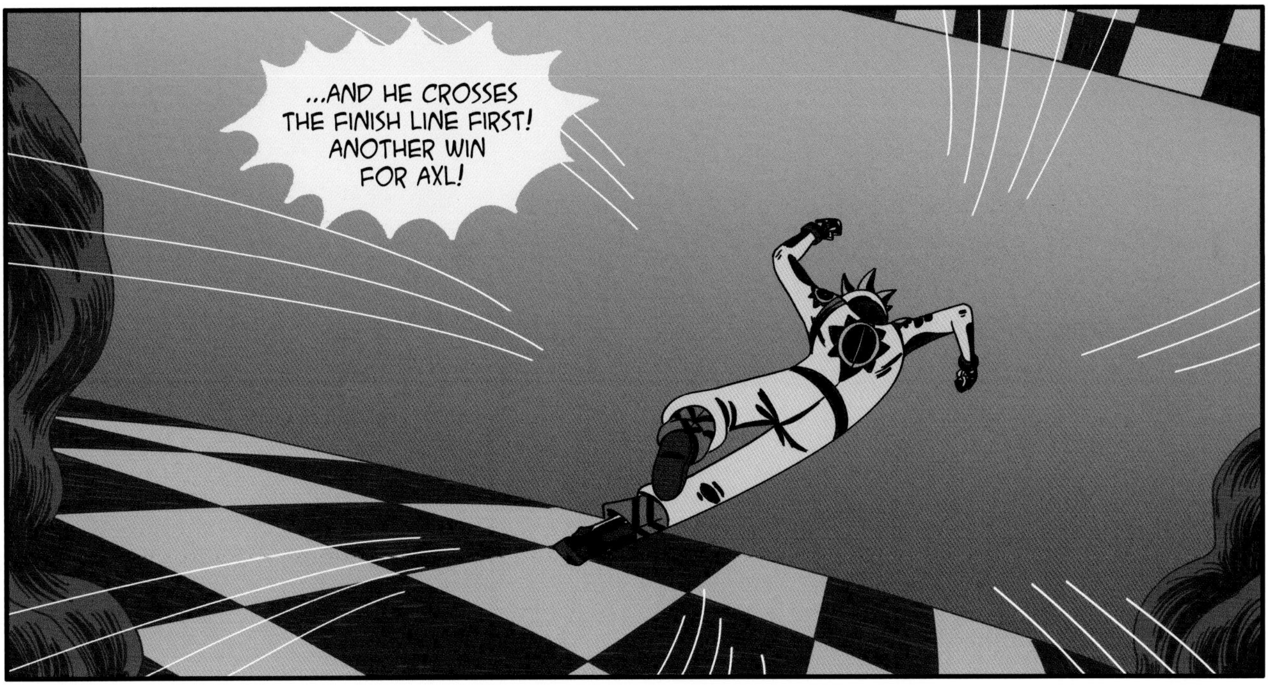
...AND HE CROSSES THE FINISH LINE FIRST! ANOTHER WIN FOR AXL!

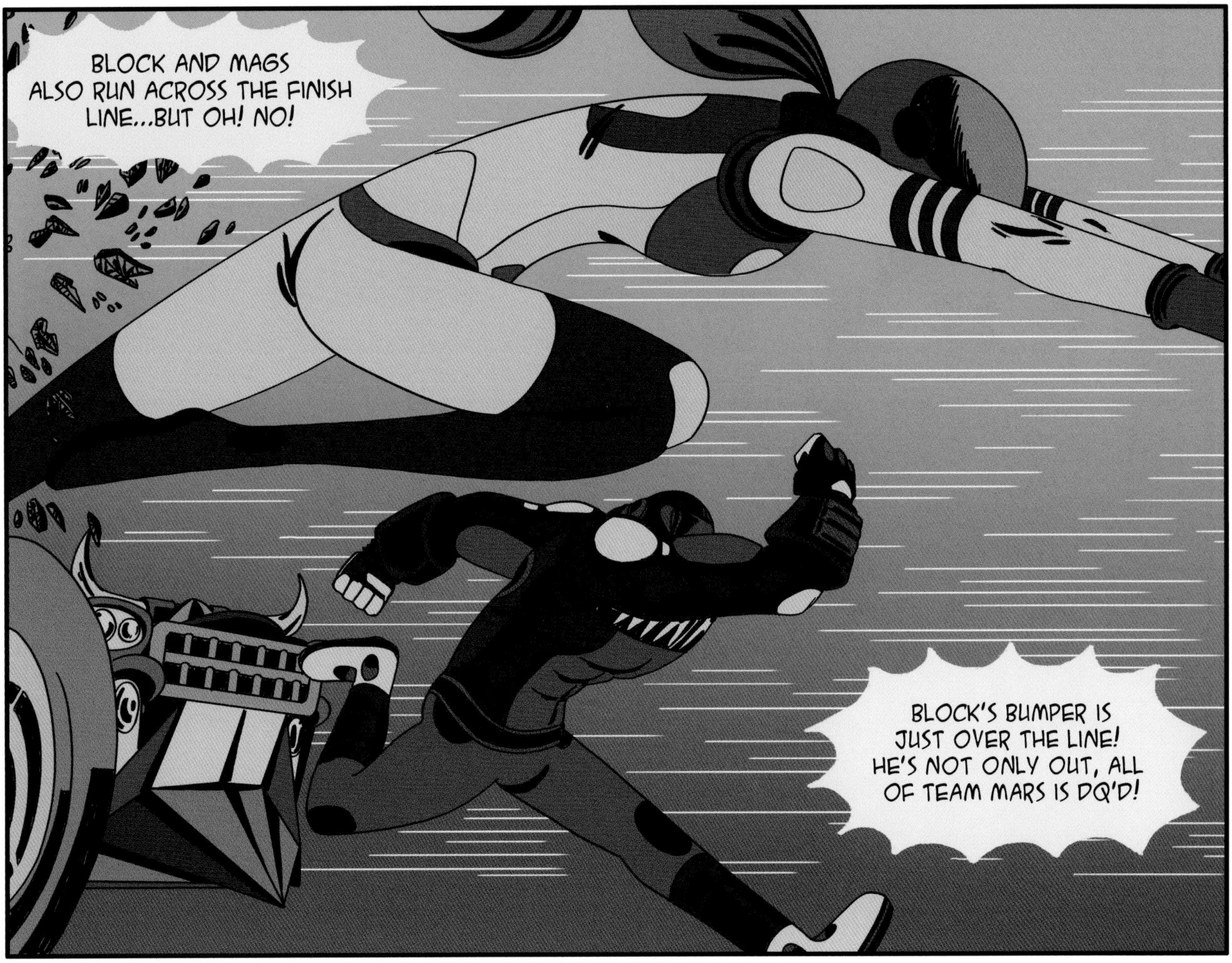
BLOCK AND MAGS ALSO RUN ACROSS THE FINISH LINE...BUT OH! NO!
BLOCK'S BUMPER IS JUST OVER THE LINE! HE'S NOT ONLY OUT, ALL OF TEAM MARS IS DQ'D!

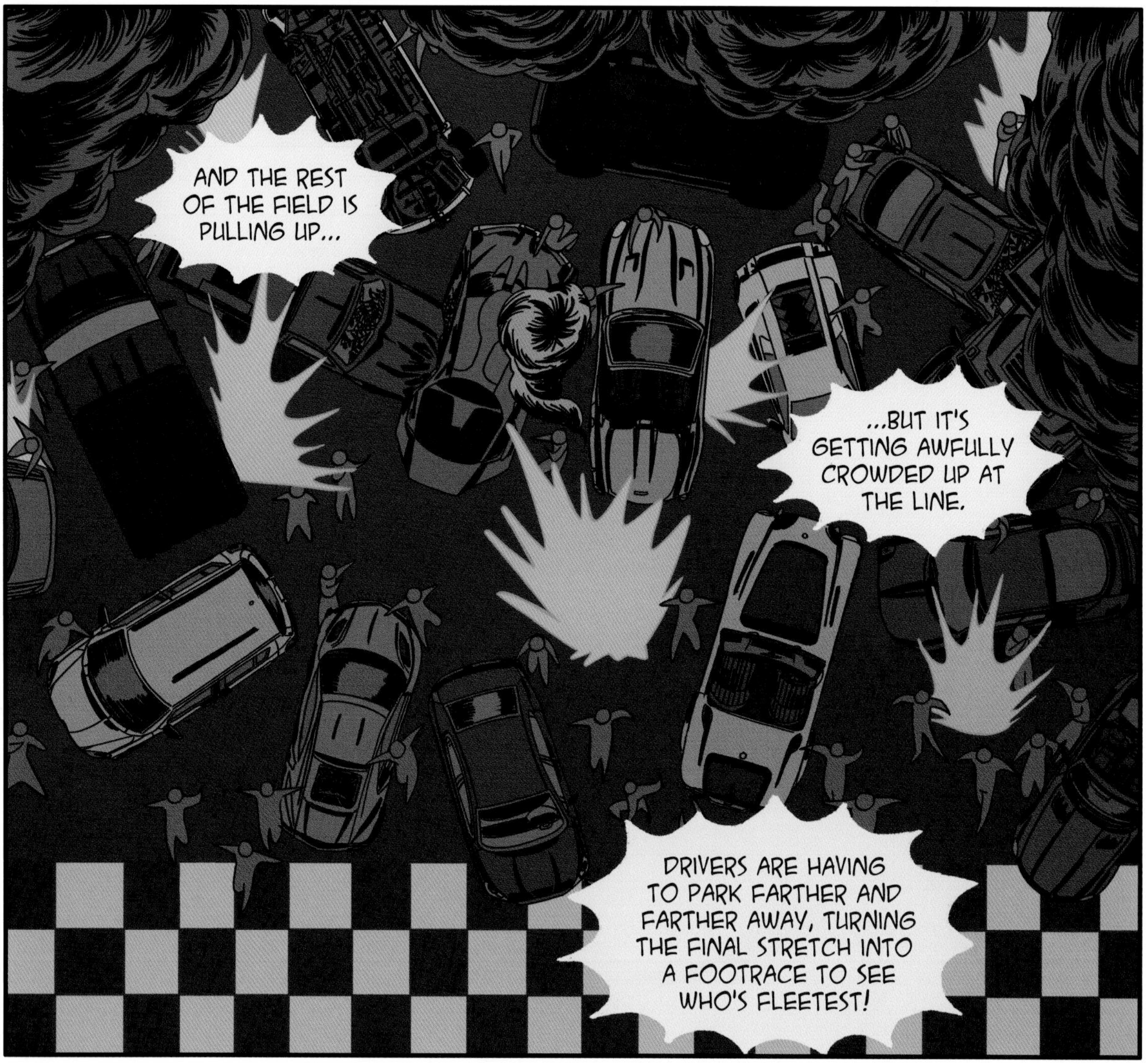
AND THE REST OF THE FIELD IS PULLING UP...
...BUT IT'S GETTING AWFULLY CROWDED UP AT THE LINE.
DRIVERS ARE HAVING TO PARK FARTHER AND FARTHER AWAY, TURNING THE FINAL STRETCH INTO A FOOTRACE TO SEE WHO'S FLEETEST!

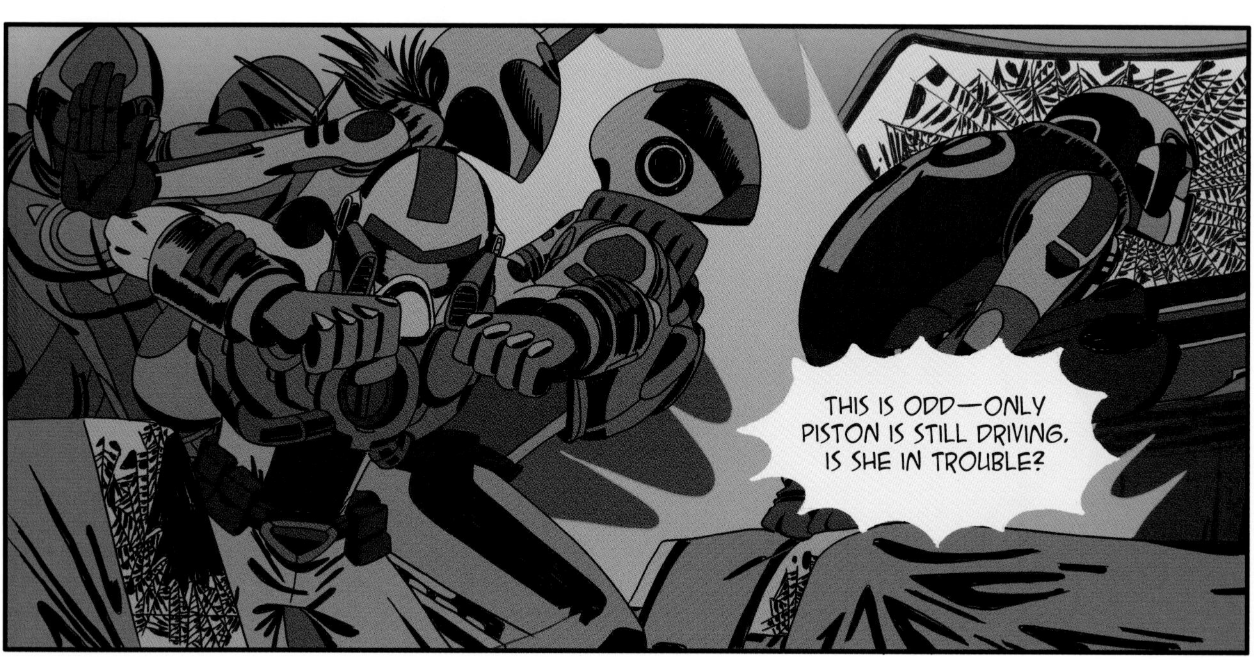
THIS IS ODD—ONLY PISTON IS STILL DRIVING. IS SHE IN TROUBLE?

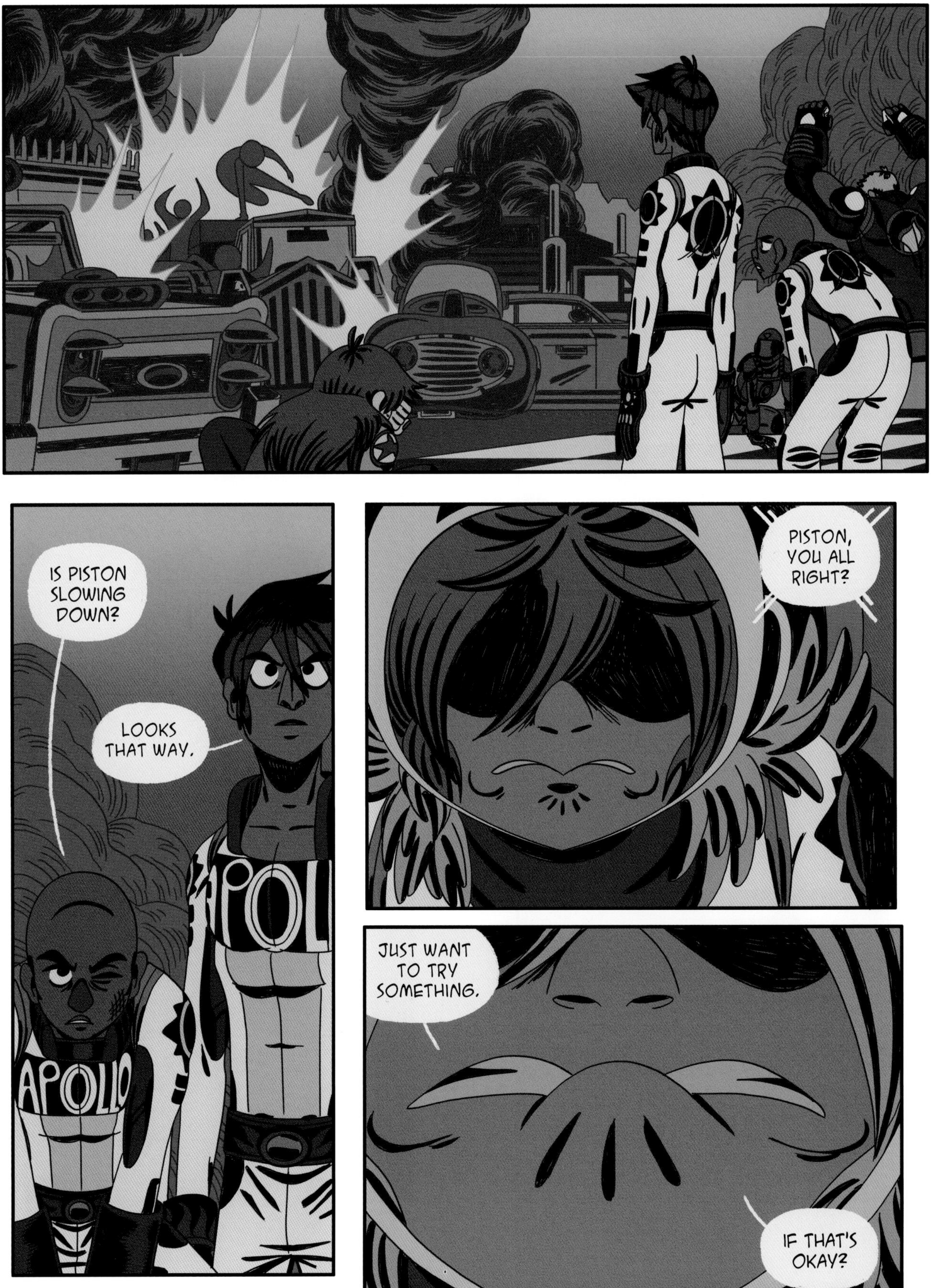
IS PISTON SLOWING DOWN?
LOOKS THAT WAY.
APOLLO
APOLLO
PISTON, YOU ALL RIGHT?
JUST WANT TO TRY SOMETHING.
IF THAT'S OKAY?

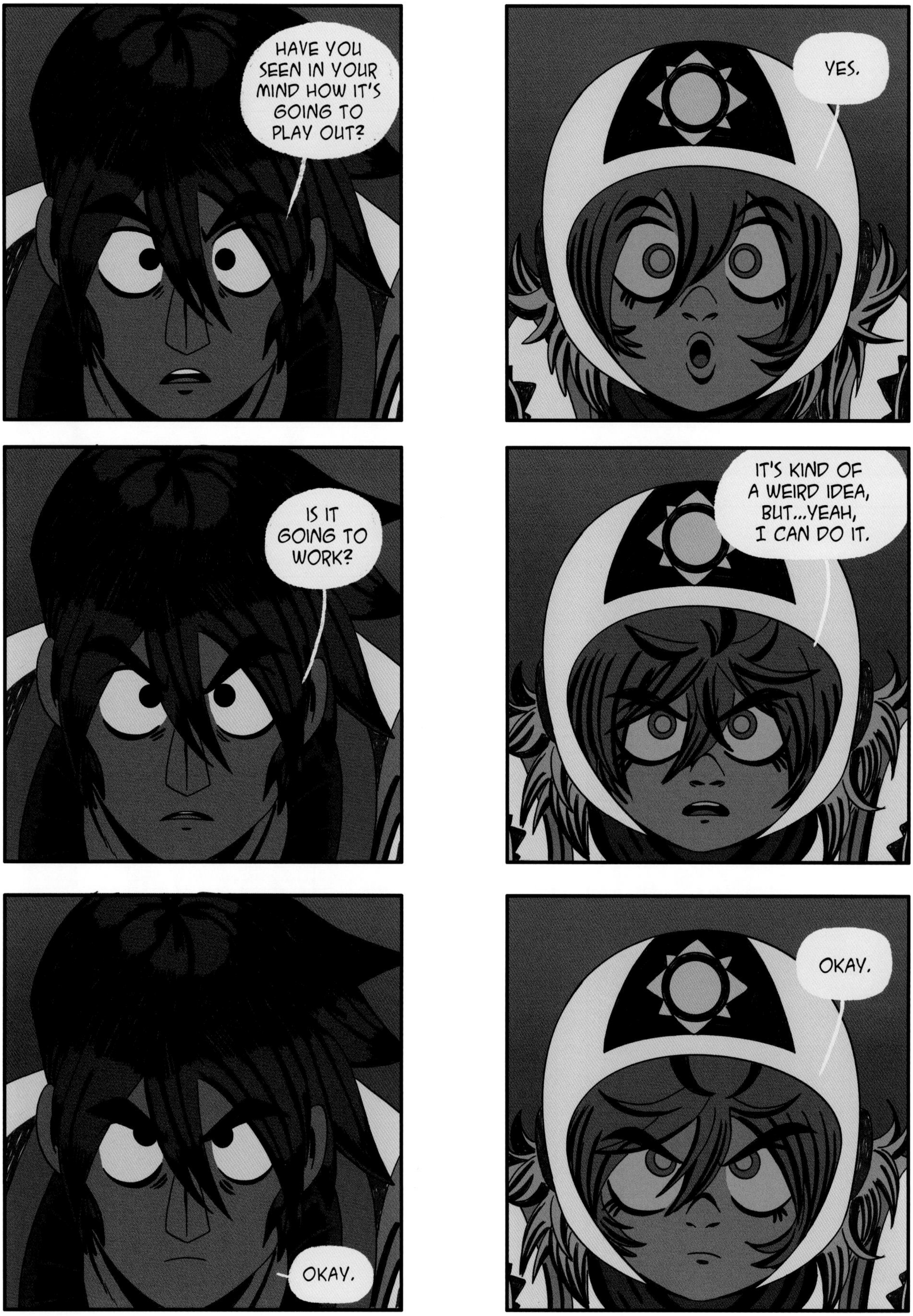
HAVE YOU SEEN IN YOUR MIND HOW IT'S GOING TO PLAY OUT?
YES.
IS IT GOING TO WORK?
IT'S KIND OF A WEIRD IDEA, BUT...YEAH, I CAN DO IT.
OKAY.
OKAY.

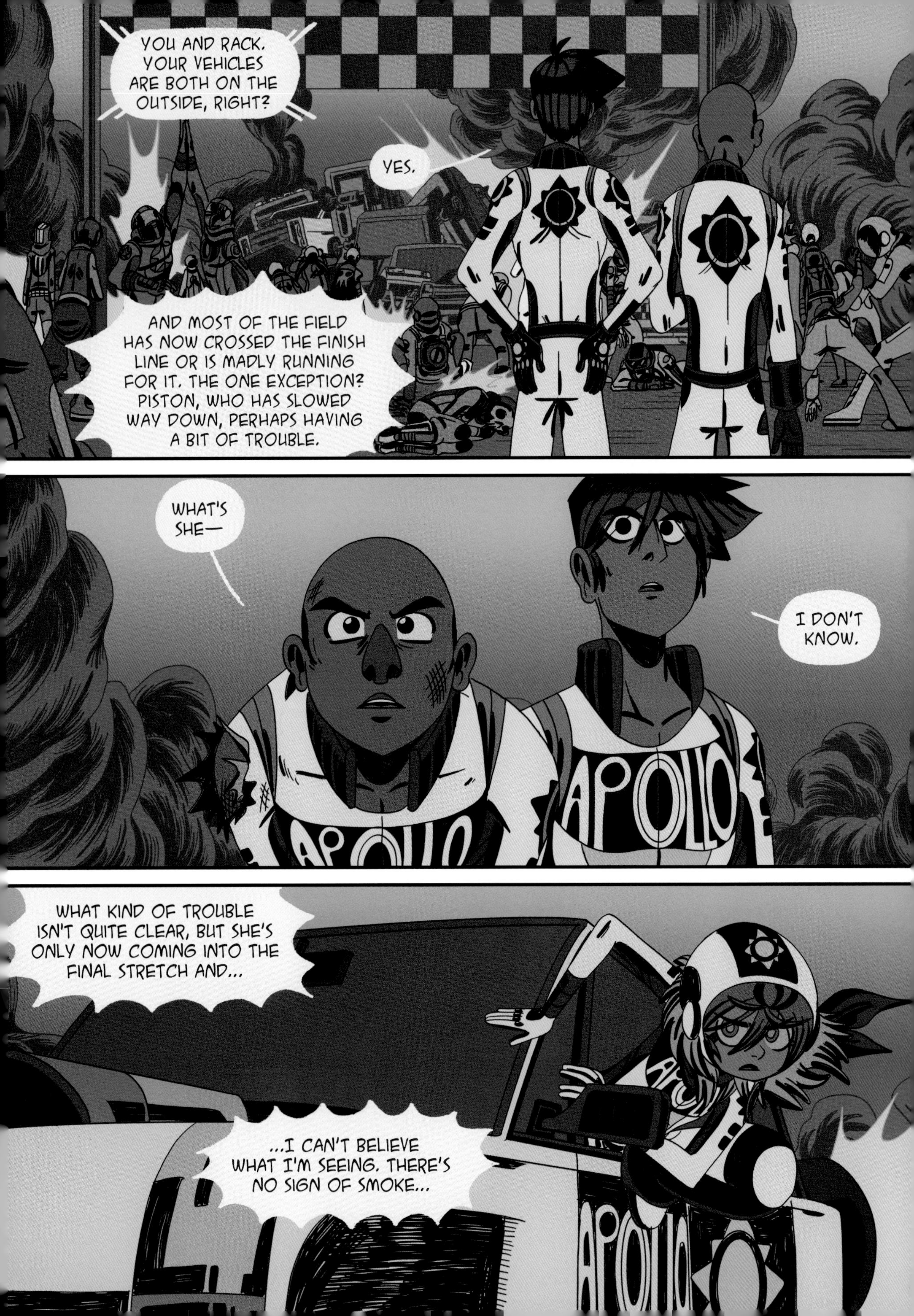
YOU AND RACK. YOUR VEHICLES ARE BOTH ON THE OUTSIDE, RIGHT?
YES.
AND MOST OF THE FIELD HAS NOW CROSSED THE FINISH LINE OR IS MADLY RUNNING FOR IT. THE ONE EXCEPTION? PISTON, WHO HAS SLOWED WAY DOWN, PERHAPS HAVING A BIT OF TROUBLE.
WHAT'S SHE—
I DON'T KNOW.
APOLLO
APOLLO
WHAT KIND OF TROUBLE ISN'T QUITE CLEAR, BUT SHE'S ONLY NOW COMING INTO THE FINAL STRETCH AND...
...I CAN'T BELIEVE WHAT I'M SEEING. THERE'S NO SIGN OF SMOKE...
APOLLO

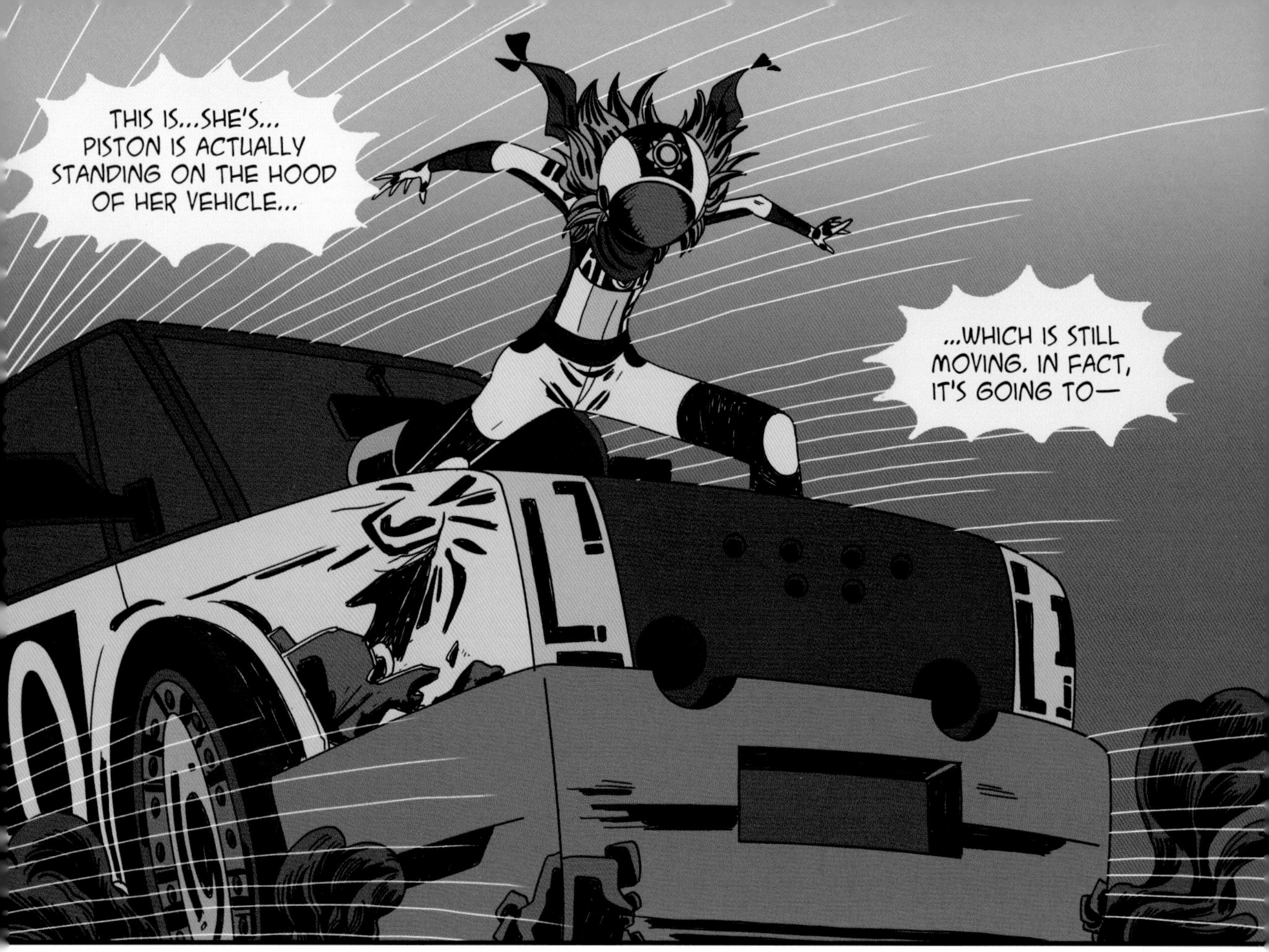
THIS IS...SHE'S... PISTON IS ACTUALLY STANDING ON THE HOOD OF HER VEHICLE...
...WHICH IS STILL MOVING. IN FACT, IT'S GOING TO—

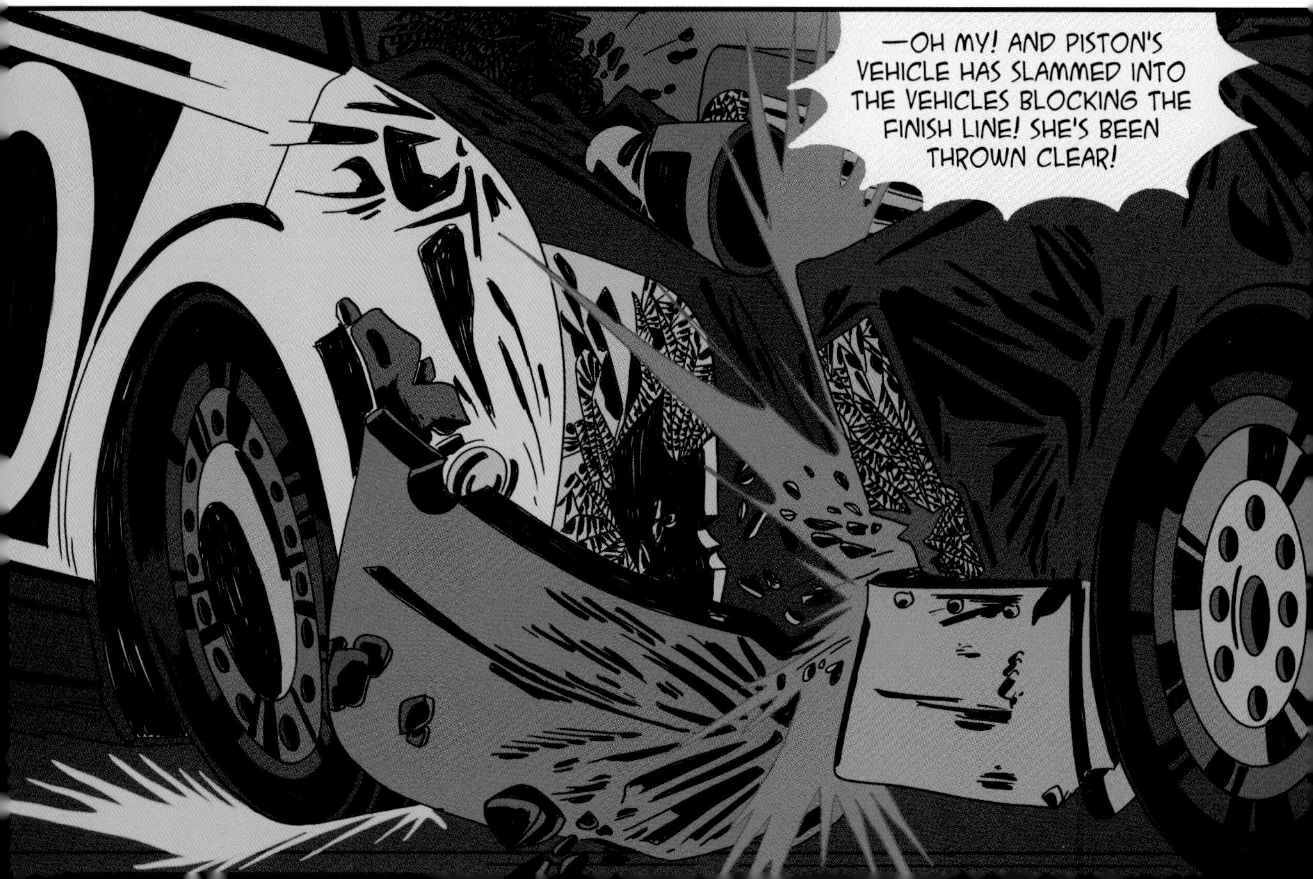
—OH MY! AND PISTON'S VEHICLE HAS SLAMMED INTO THE VEHICLES BLOCKING THE FINISH LINE! SHE'S BEEN THROWN CLEAR!

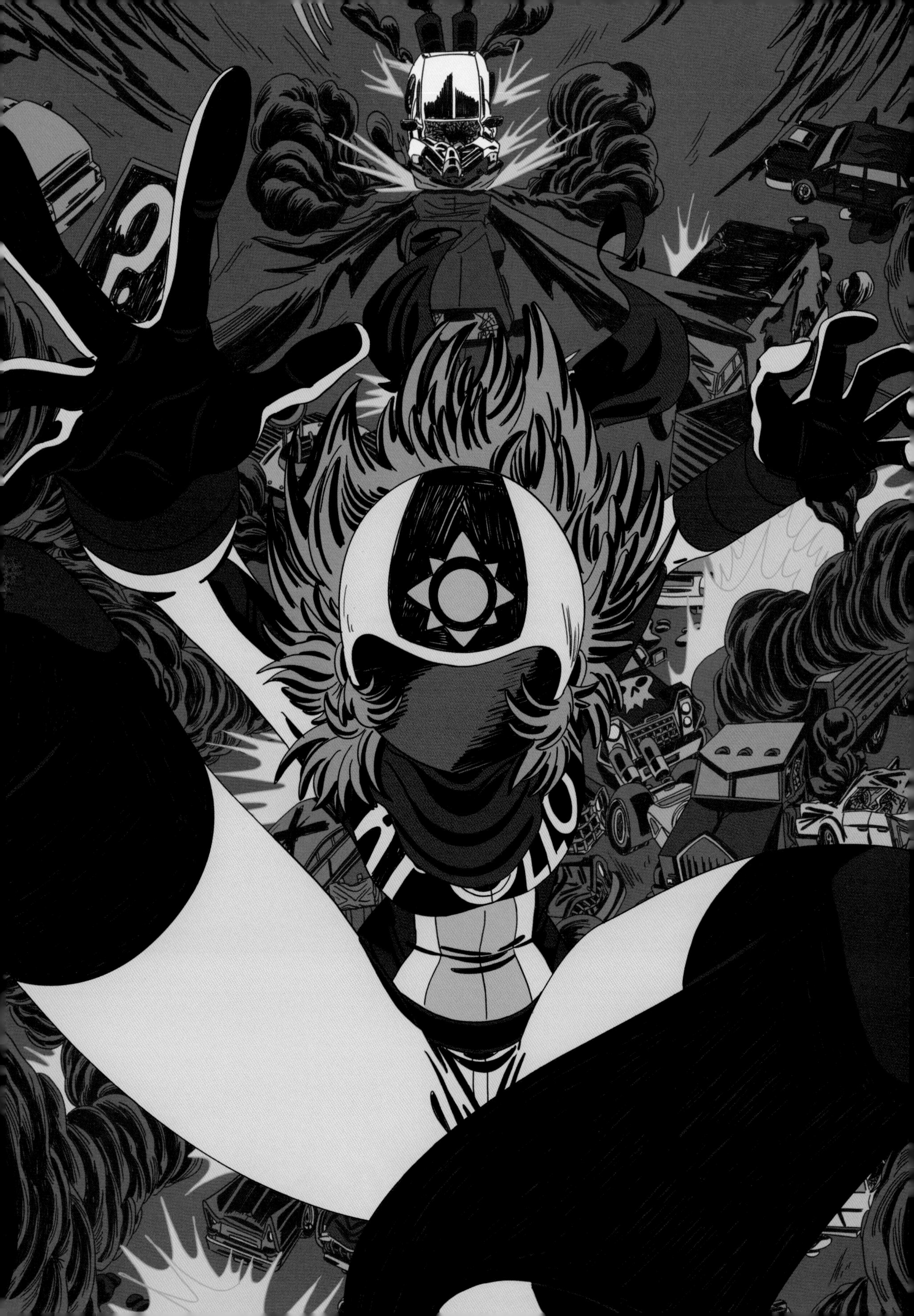

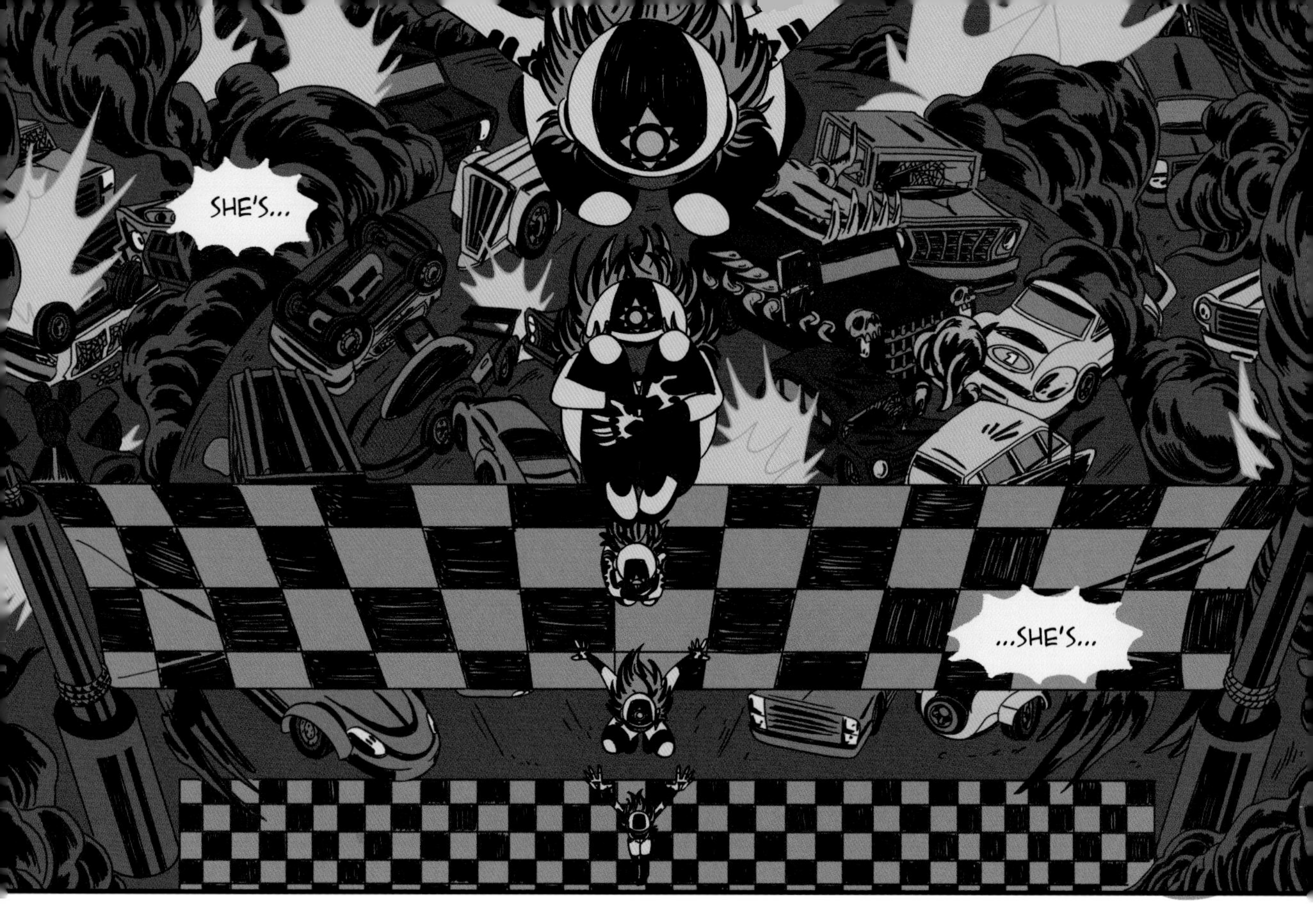
SHE'S...
...SHE'S...
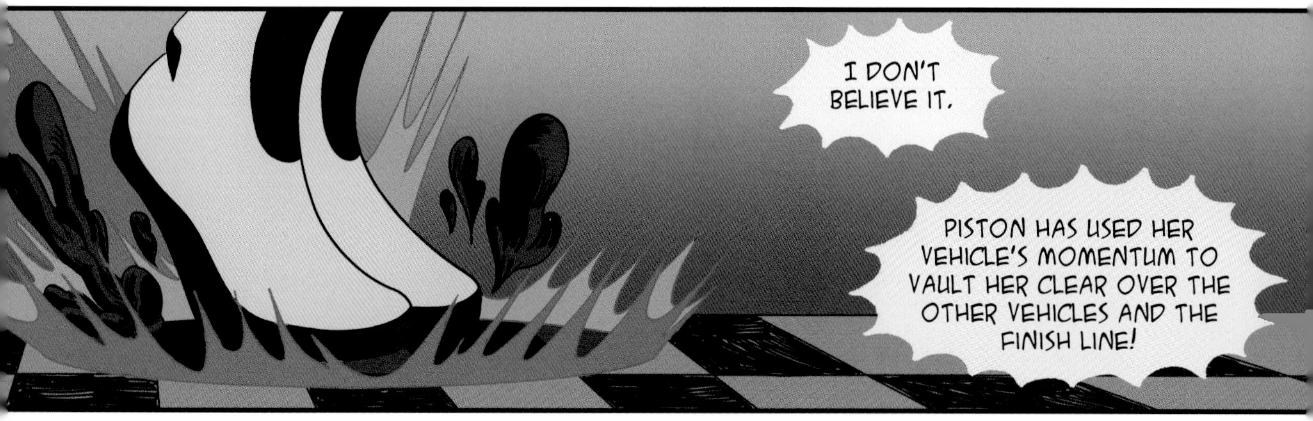
I DON'T BELIEVE IT.
PISTON HAS USED HER VEHICLE'S MOMENTUM TO VAULT HER CLEAR OVER THE OTHER VEHICLES AND THE FINISH LINE!
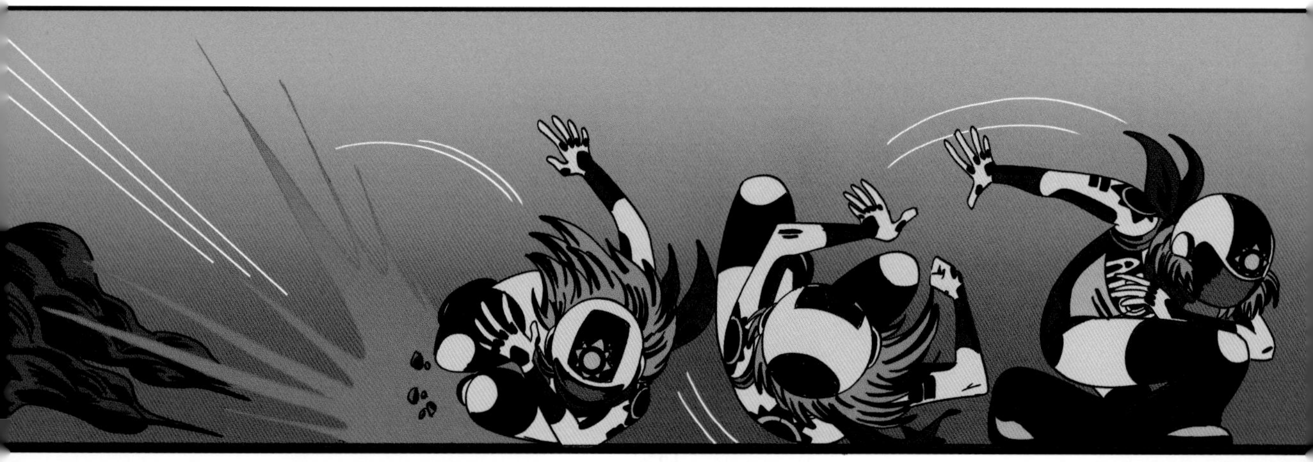

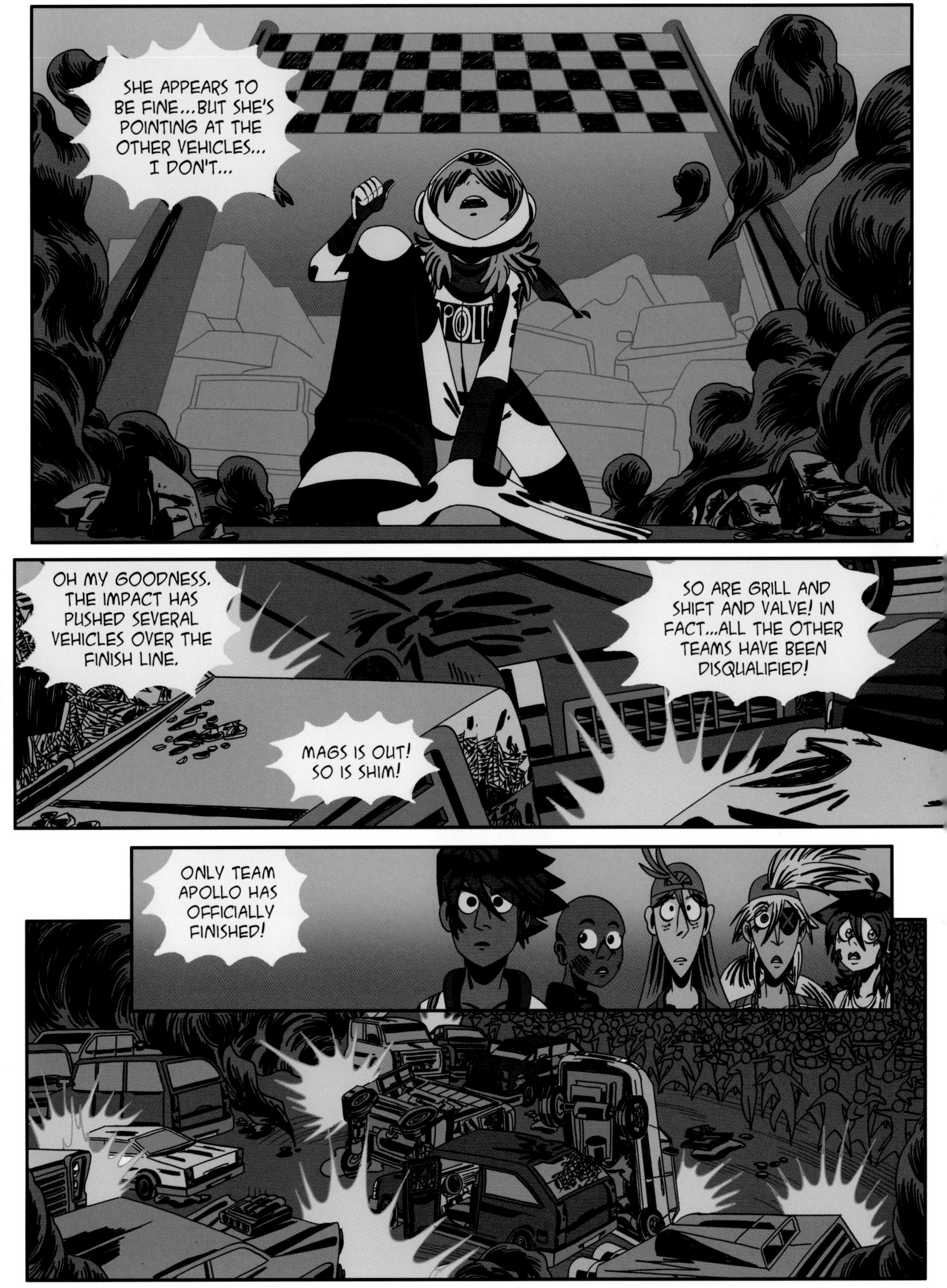
SHE APPEARS TO BE FINE...BUT SHE'S POINTING AT THE OTHER VEHICLES... I DON'T...
OH MY GOODNESS. THE IMPACT HAS PUSHED SEVERAL VEHICLES OVER THE FINISH LINE.
MAGS IS OUT! SO IS SHIM!
SO ARE GRILL AND SHIFT AND VALVE! IN FACT...ALL THE OTHER TEAMS HAVE BEEN DISQUALIFIED!
ONLY TEAM APOLLO HAS OFFICIALLY FINISHED!

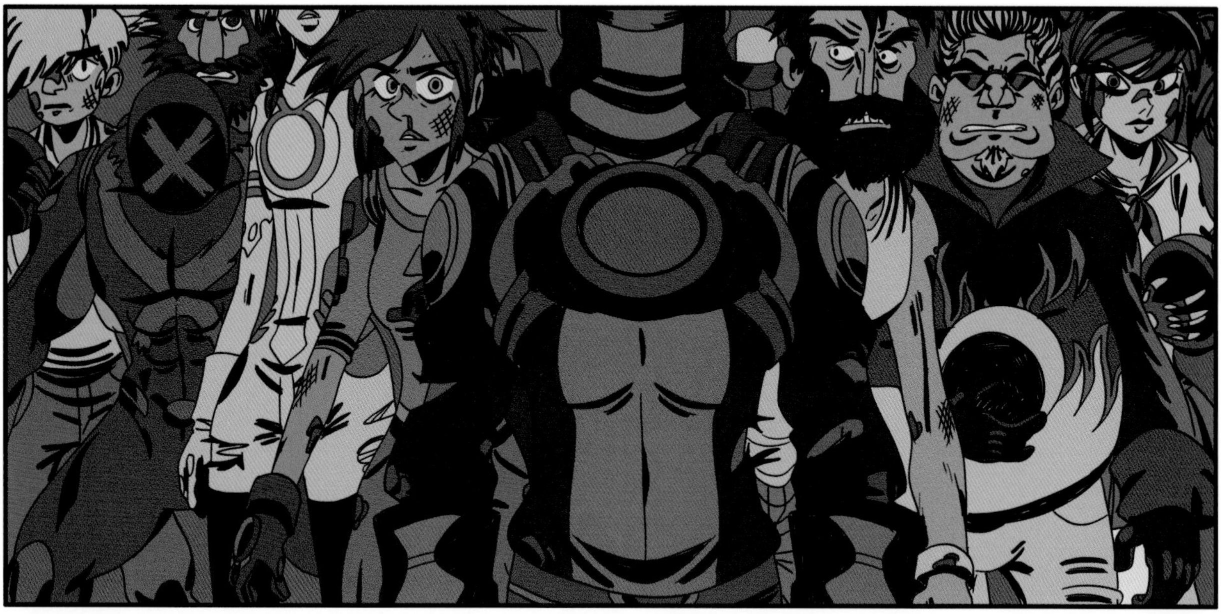

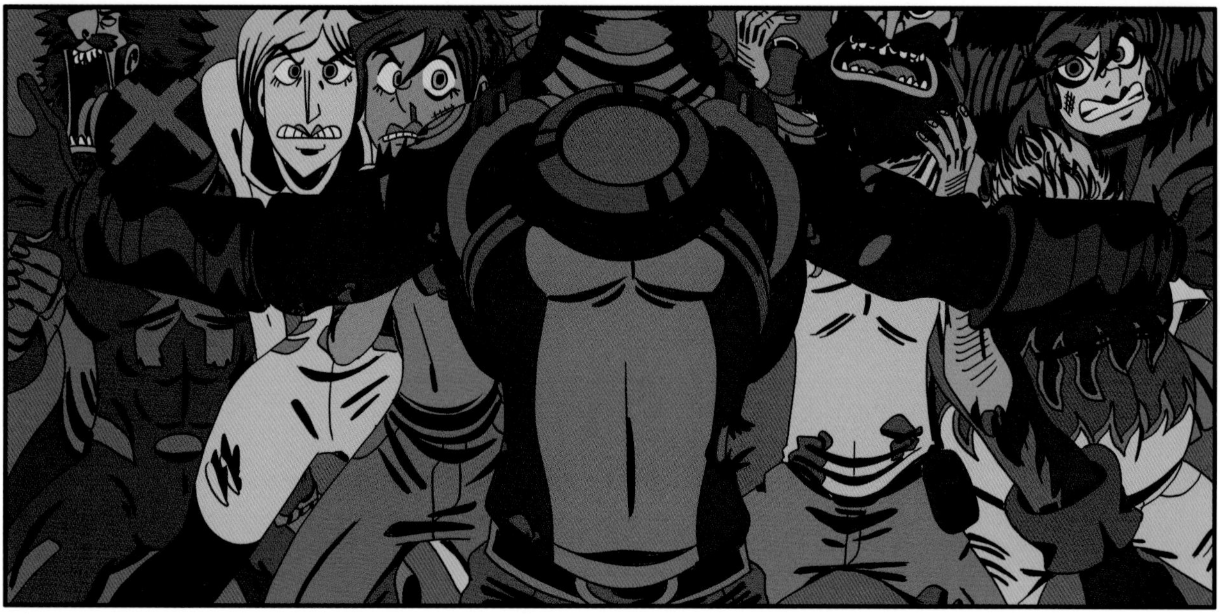

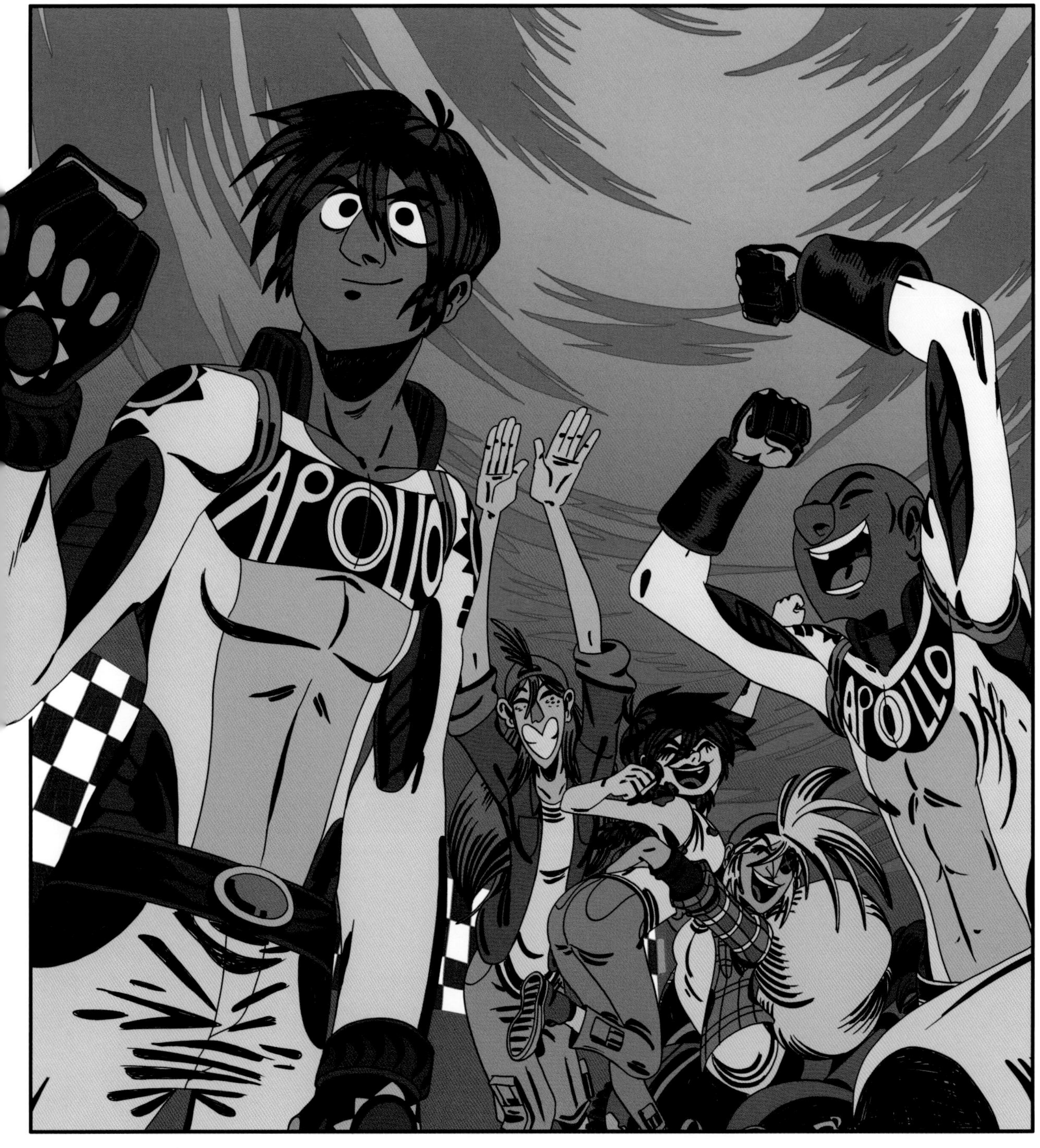

APOLLO
APOLLO

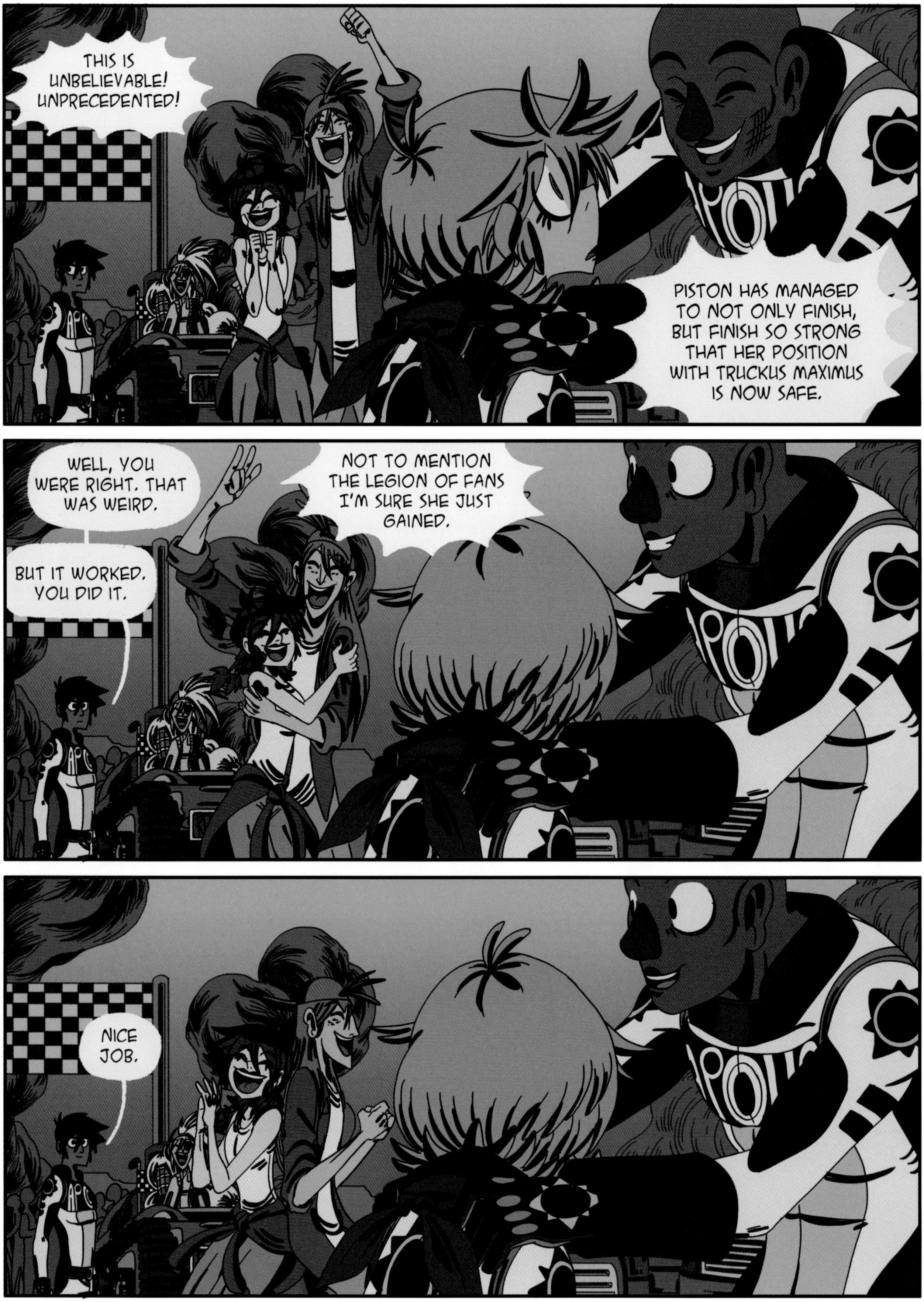
THIS IS UNBELIEVABLE! UNPRECEDENTED!
PISTON HAS MANAGED TO NOT ONLY FINISH, BUT FINISH SO STRONG THAT HER POSITION WITH TRUCKUS MAXIMUS IS NOW SAFE.
WELL, YOU WERE RIGHT. THAT WAS WEIRD.
NOT TO MENTION THE LEGION OF FANS I'M SURE SHE JUST GAINED.
BUT IT WORKED. YOU DID IT.
NICE JOB.

SO, I SEE THE NEW GIRL IS WORKIN' OUT REAL GOOD.

YOU WERE RIGHT. YOU JUST NEEDED THAT ONE DRIVER.

I'LL TELL YA, I SURE DO LIKE THE ATTENTION I GET WHEN TEAM APOLLO DOES WELL. AND I SURE DON'T LIKE IT WHEN APOLLO DON'T DO WELL, 'CUZ IT MAKES ME LOOK BAD. SO I'M HAPPY THESE DAYS, RIGHT?

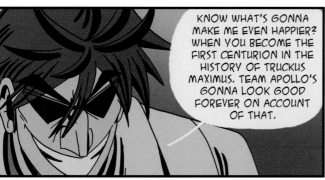

KNOW WHAT'S GONNA MAKE ME EVEN HAPPIER? WHEN YOU BECOME THE FIRST CENTURION IN THE HISTORY OF TRUCKUS MAXIMUS. TEAM APOLLO'S GONNA LOOK GOOD FOREVER ON ACCOUNT OF THAT.

YESSIR, YOU GO RIDIN' OFF INTO THE SUNSET, HAPPY AS A CLAM, NOT A CARE IN THE WORLD...AND TEAM APOLLO FALLS APART WITHOUT YOU.

THESE MISFITS AND RAGAMUFFINS YOU PUT TOGETHER WORK GREAT, PROVIDED YOU'RE THERE.

WITHOUT YOU, THEY'RE JUST A LOTTA MISMATCHED PARTS. IT WON'T TAKE LONG 'TIL THEY'RE AT ONE ANOTHER'S THROATS.

AND WHEN THAT HAPPENS? I'LL BREAK UP THE TEAM. TRADE THE ONES I CAN OFF TO OTHER TEAMS.

AND THE REST? WELL, I RECKON IT'S THE SALT MINES FOR THEM.

BUT NOT FOR LONG, I'M GUESSIN'. I DON'T EXPECT MANY OF THEM'LL LAST LONG THERE.

AND THEN? THEN I REMAKE TEAM APOLLO THE WAY I WANT. IN MY IMAGE.

YOU SLEEP WELL NOW. DREAM OF YOUR FREEDOM. AND ALL THAT'LL COME WITH IT.

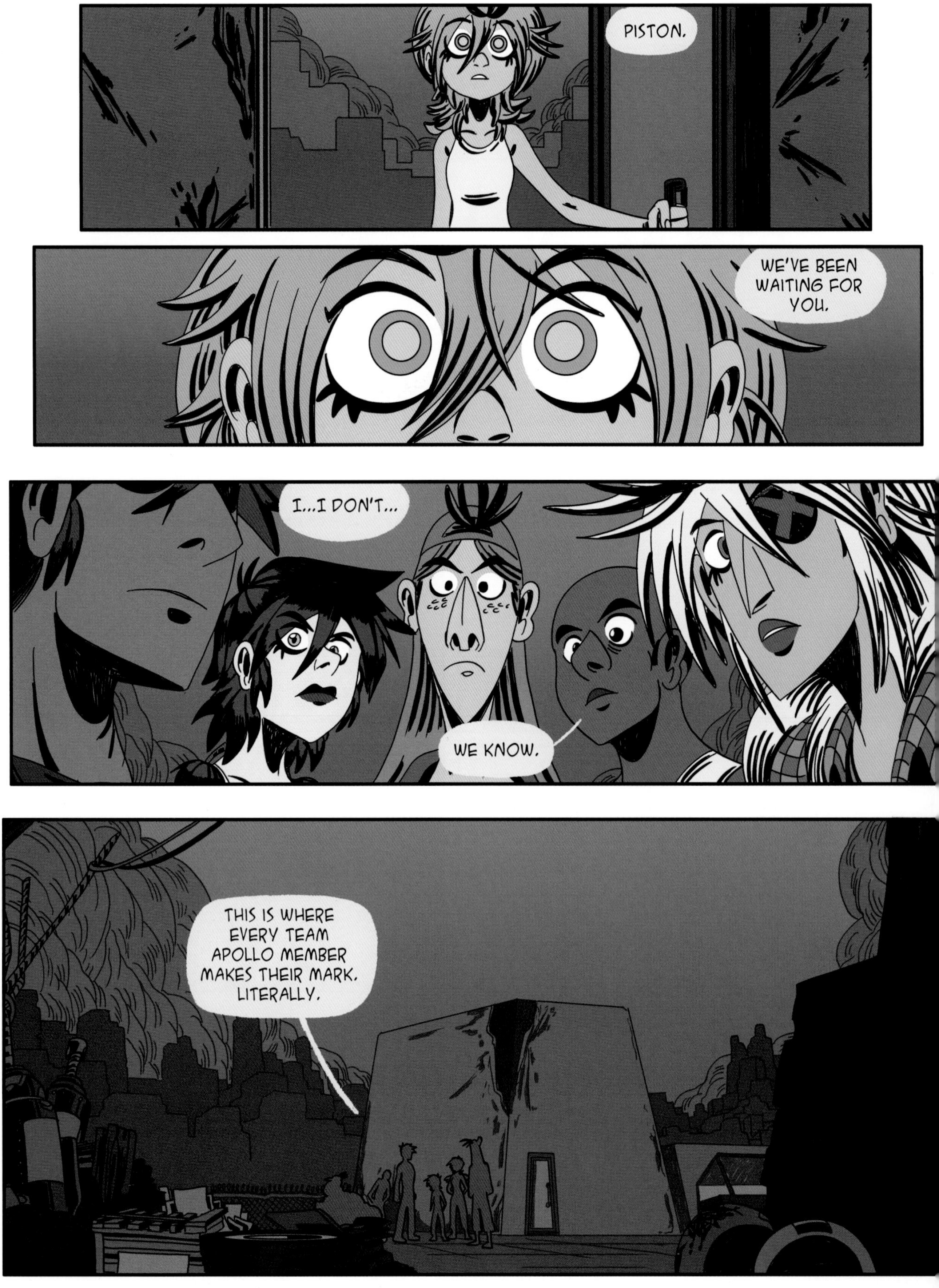
PISTON.
WE'VE BEEN WAITING FOR YOU.
I...I DON'T...
WE KNOW.
THIS IS WHERE EVERY TEAM APOLLO MEMBER MAKES THEIR MARK. LITERALLY.

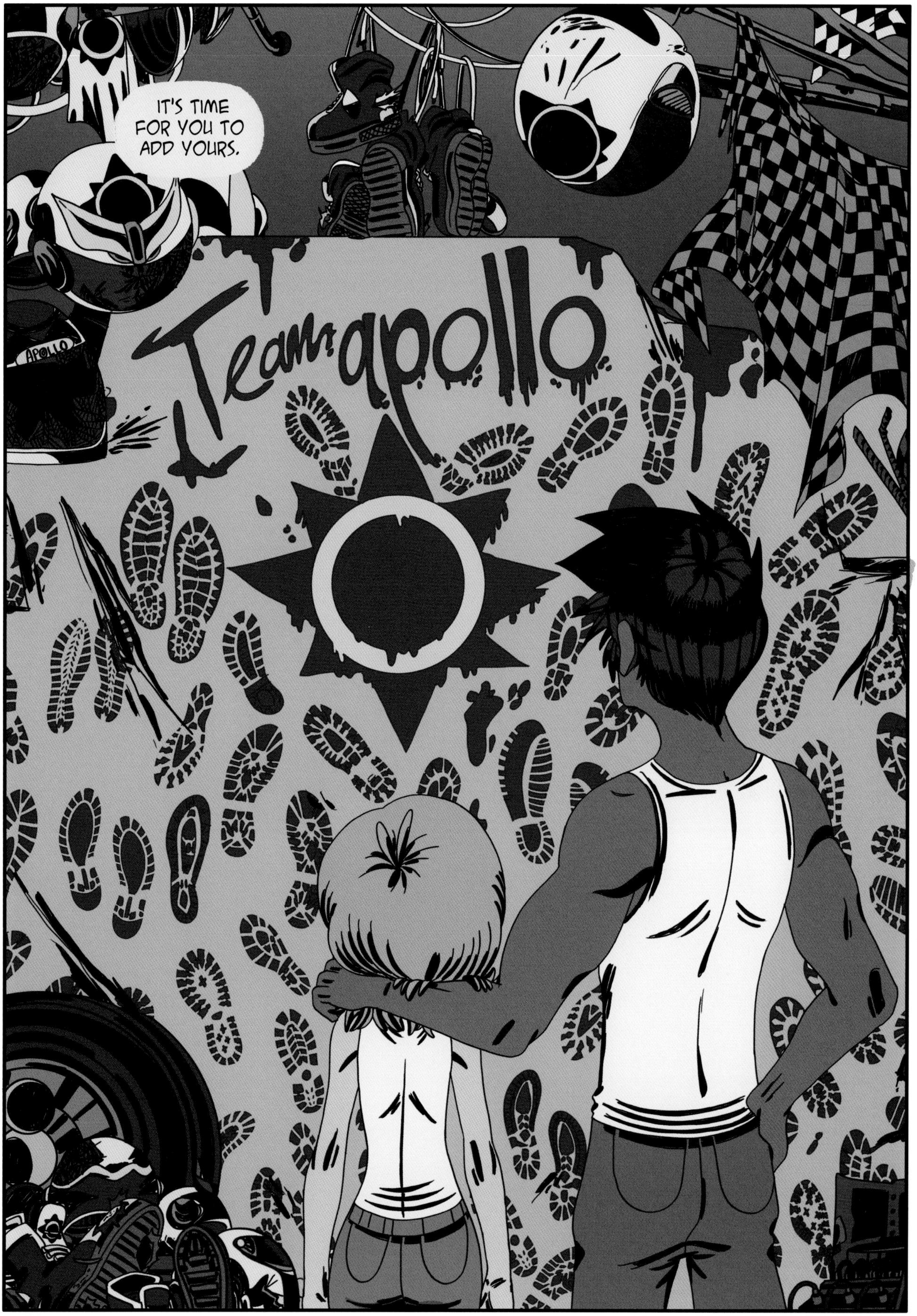
IT'S TIME FOR YOU TO ADD YOURS.
APOLLO
Team apollo

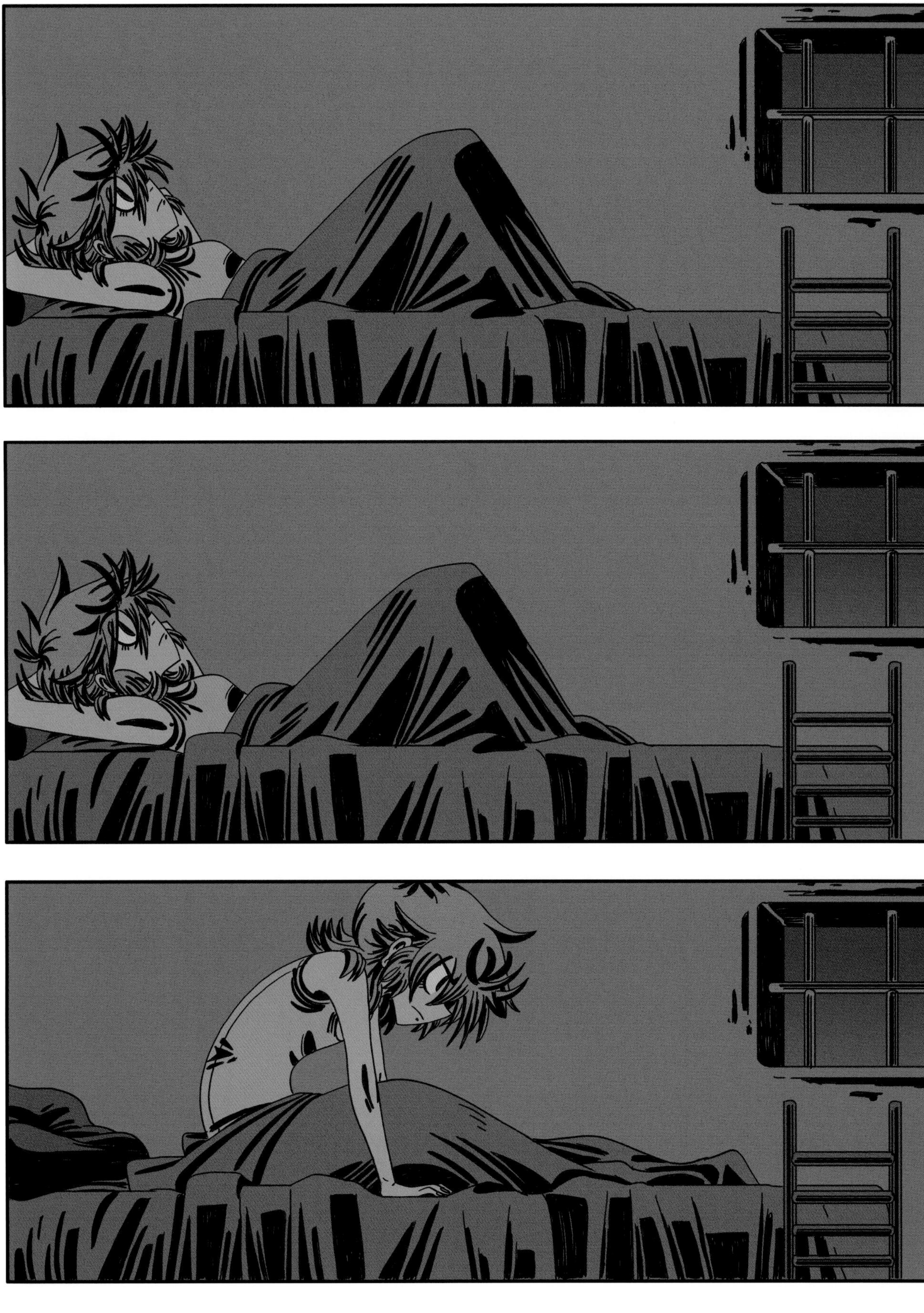

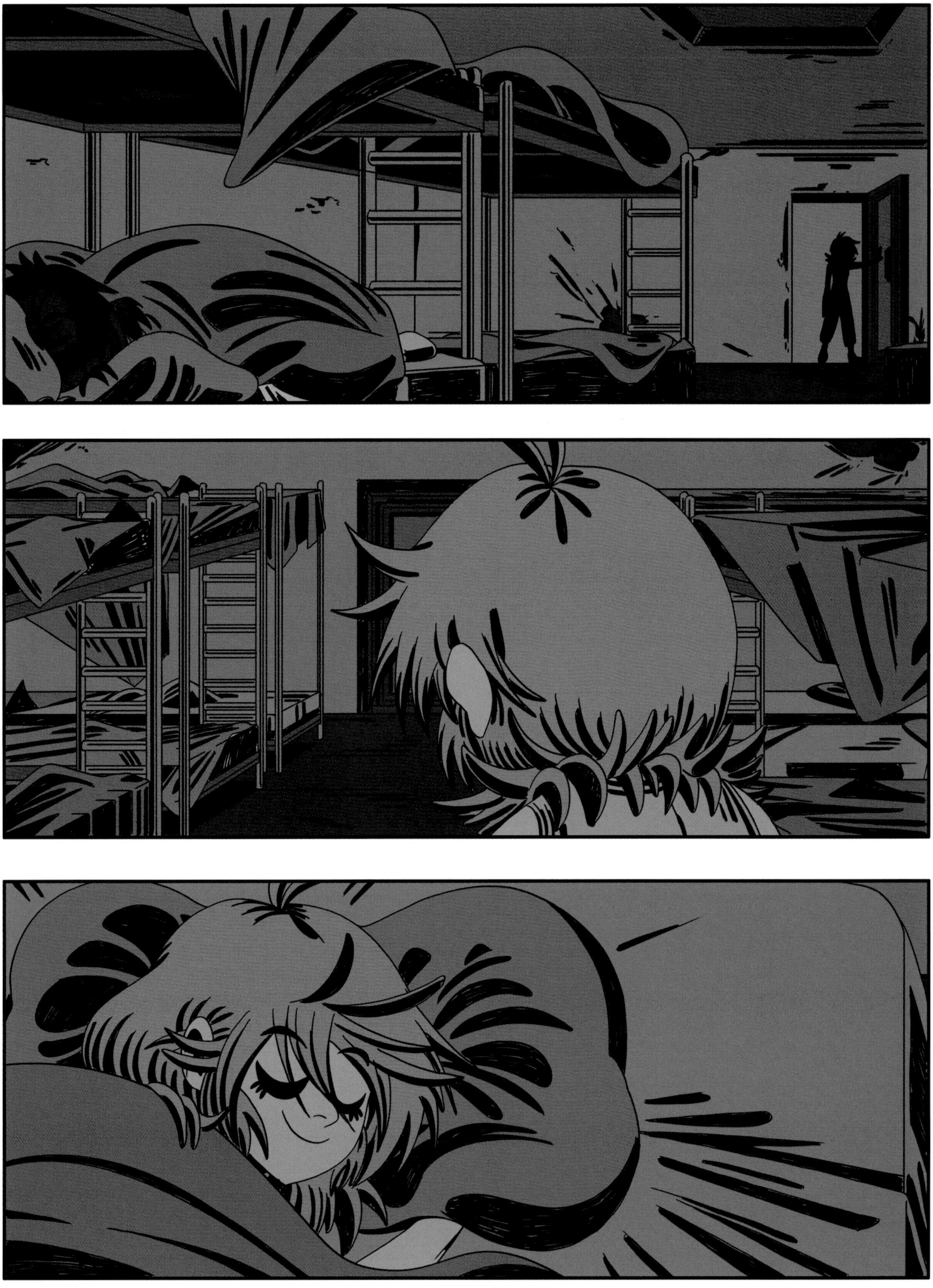

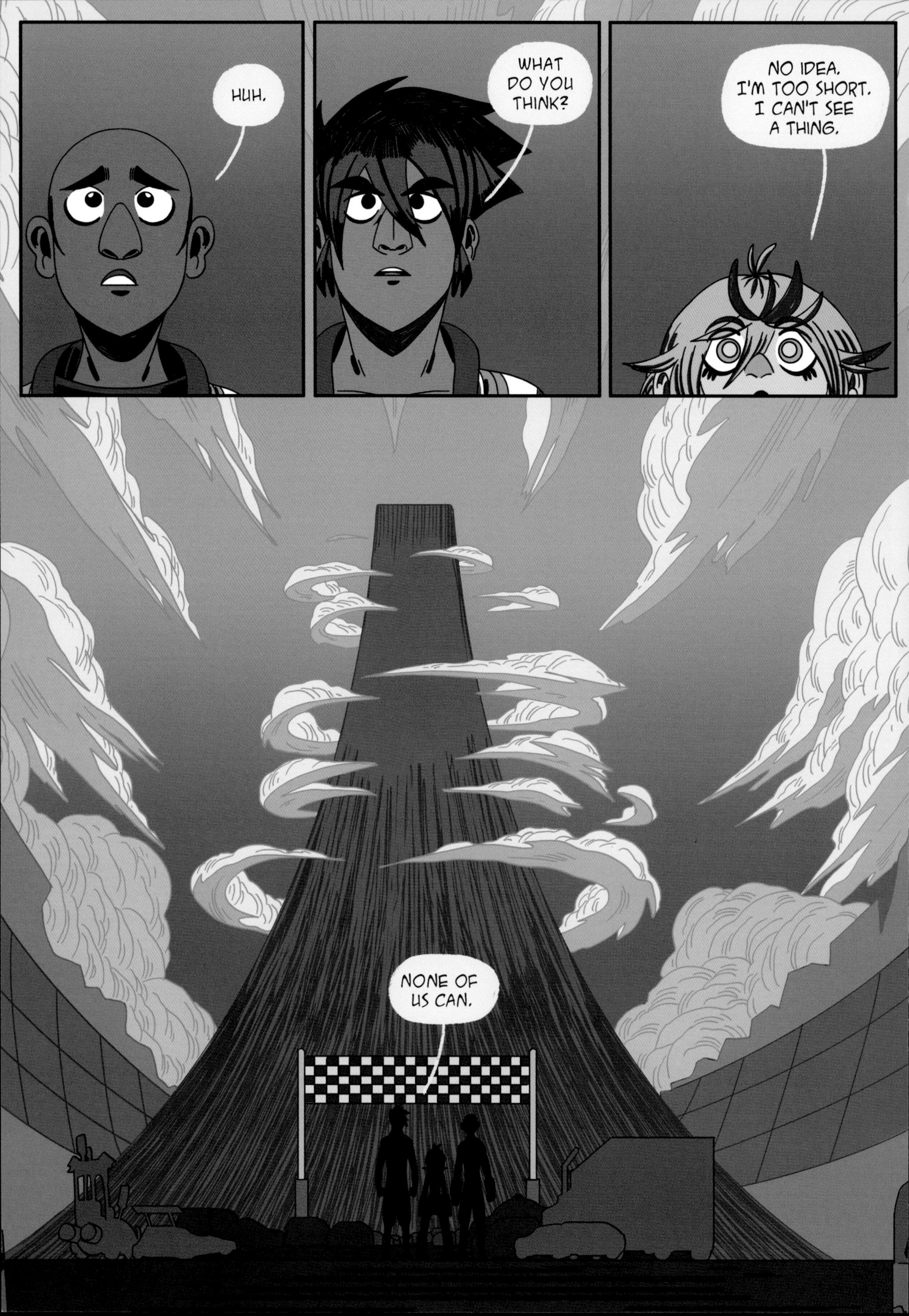
HUH.
WHAT DO YOU THINK?
NO IDEA. I'M TOO SHORT. I CAN'T SEE A THING.
NONE OF US CAN.

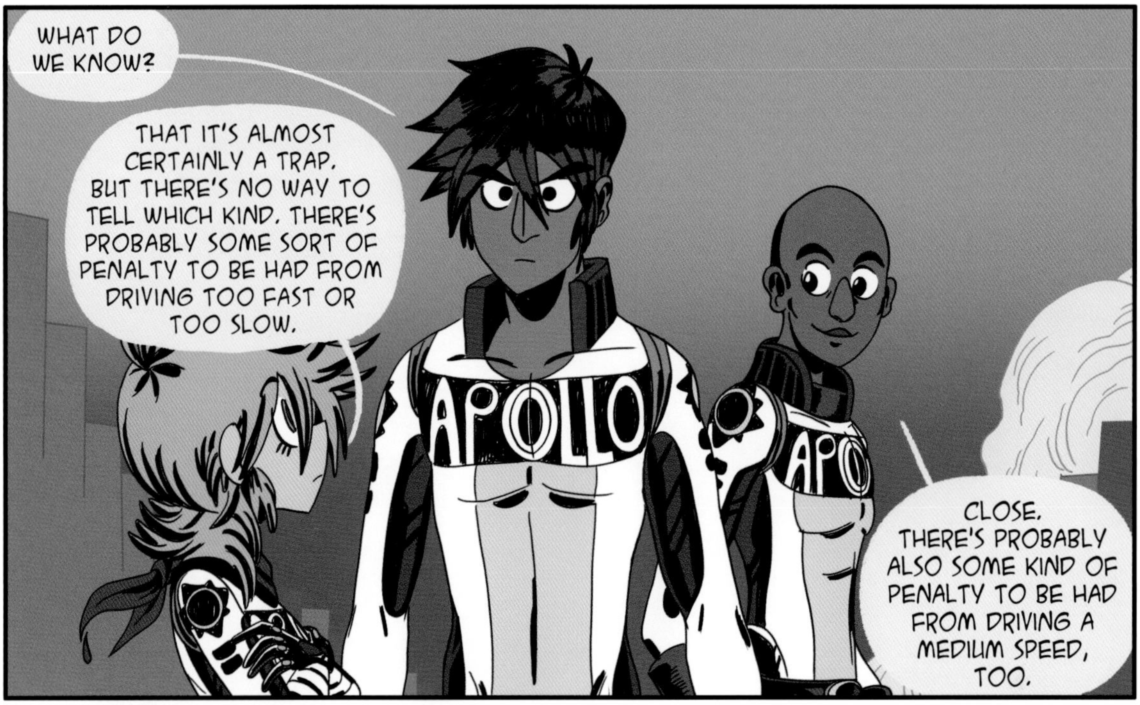
WHAT DO WE KNOW?
THAT IT'S ALMOST CERTAINLY A TRAP, BUT THERE'S NO WAY TO TELL WHICH KIND. THERE'S PROBABLY SOME SORT OF PENALTY TO BE HAD FROM DRIVING TOO FAST OR TOO SLOW.
APOLLO
CLOSE. THERE'S PROBABLY ALSO SOME KIND OF PENALTY TO BE HAD FROM DRIVING A MEDIUM SPEED, TOO.

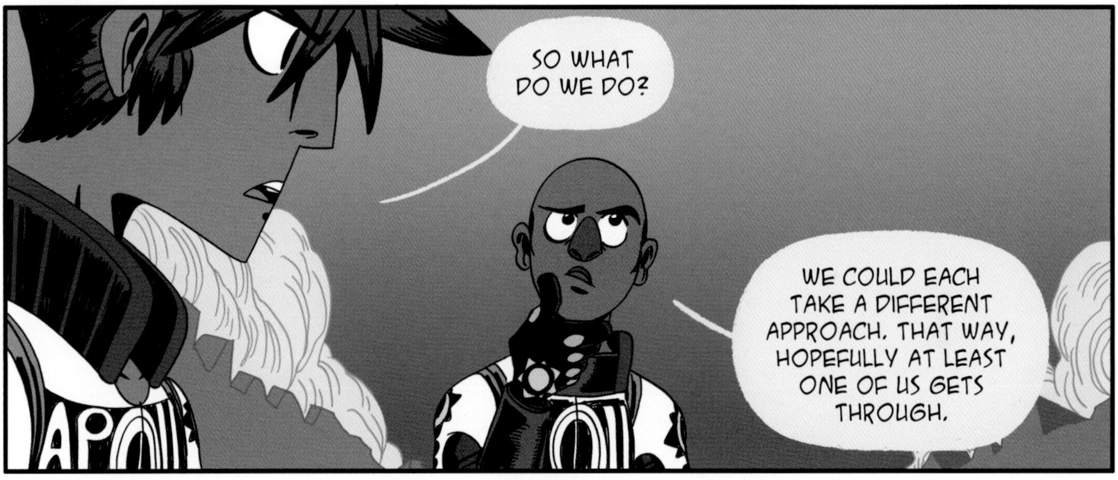
SO WHAT DO WE DO?
WE COULD EACH TAKE A DIFFERENT APPROACH. THAT WAY, HOPEFULLY AT LEAST ONE OF US GETS THROUGH.

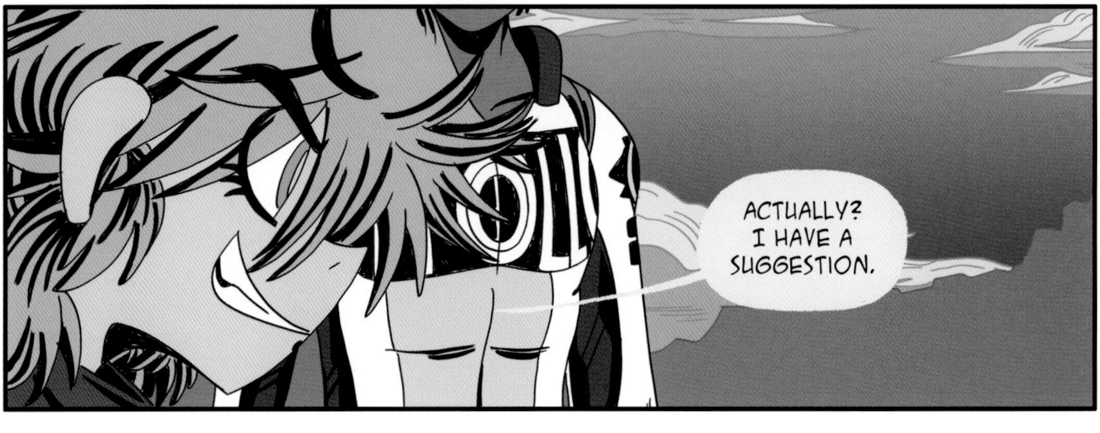
ACTUALLY? I HAVE A SUGGESTION.

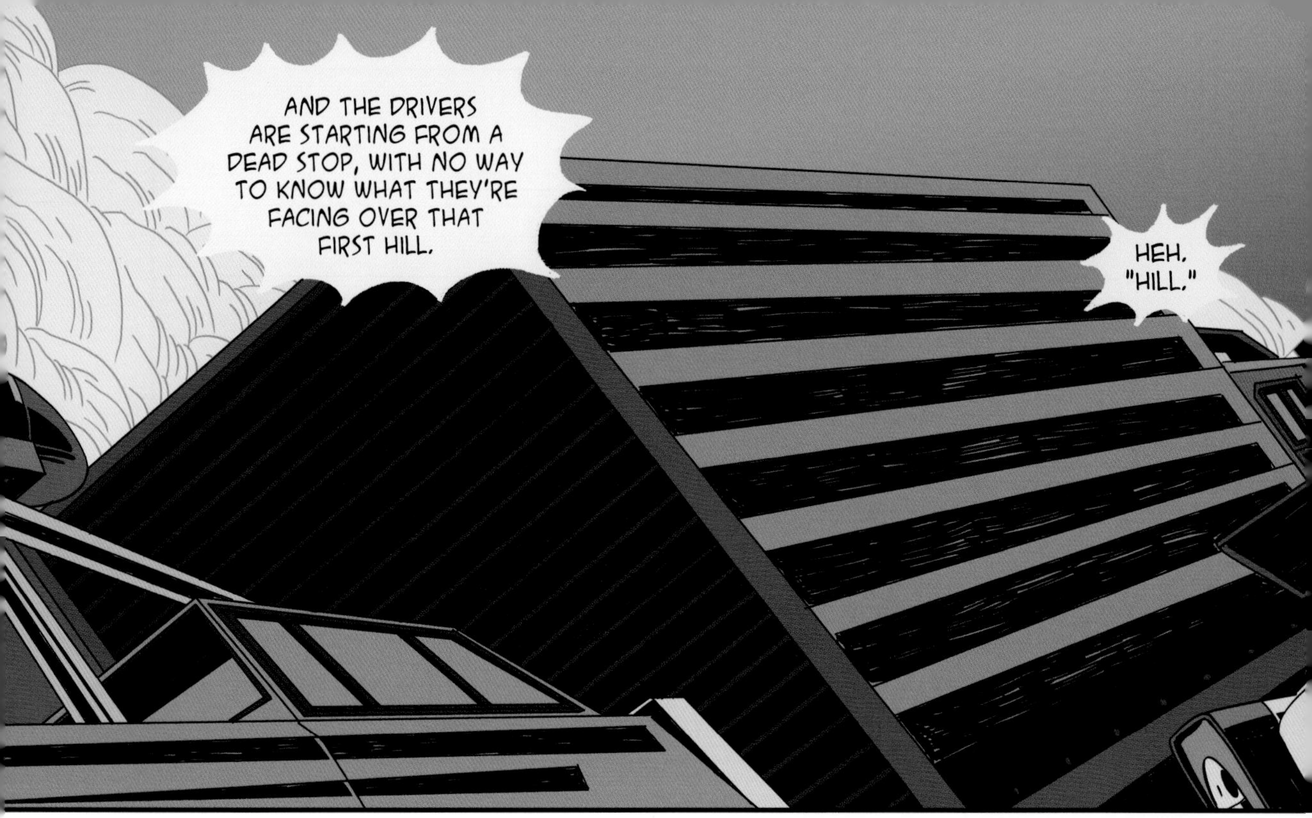
AND THE DRIVERS ARE STARTING FROM A DEAD STOP, WITH NO WAY TO KNOW WHAT THEY'RE FACING OVER THAT FIRST HILL.
HEH. "HILL."

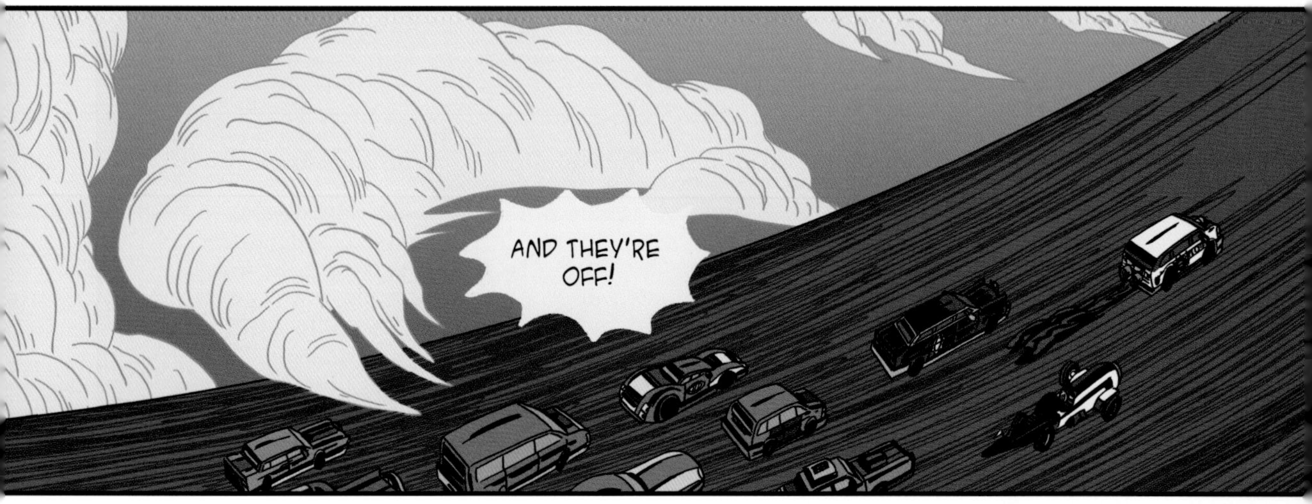
AND THEY'RE OFF!

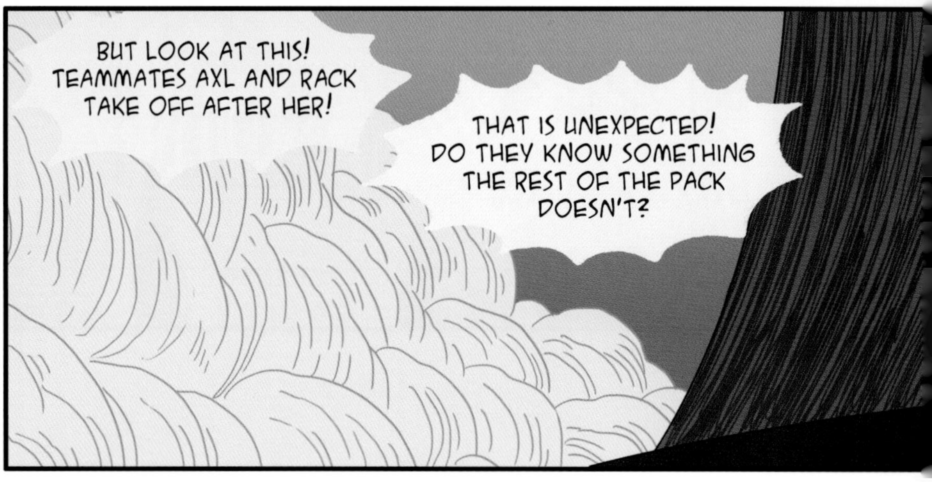
BUT LOOK AT THIS! TEAMMATES AXL AND RACK TAKE OFF AFTER HER!
THAT IS UNEXPECTED! DO THEY KNOW SOMETHING THE REST OF THE PACK DOESN'T?

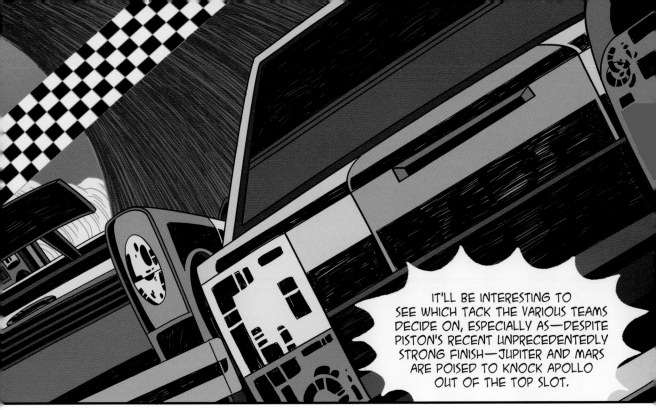

IT'LL BE INTERESTING TO SEE WHICH TACK THE VARIOUS TEAMS DECIDE ON, ESPECIALLY AS—DESPITE PISTON'S RECENT UNPRECEDENTEDLY STRONG FINISH—JUPITER AND MARS ARE POISED TO KNOCK APOLLO OUT OF THE TOP SLOT.

TO THE SURPRISE OF FEW, PISTON JUMPS INTO THE LEAD, GOING FULL THROTTLE.

THE OTHER DRIVERS APPEAR TO THINK SO, AS THE REST OF THE FIELD IS NOW RUNNING FULL OUT AS WELL, TRYING TO CATCH UP.

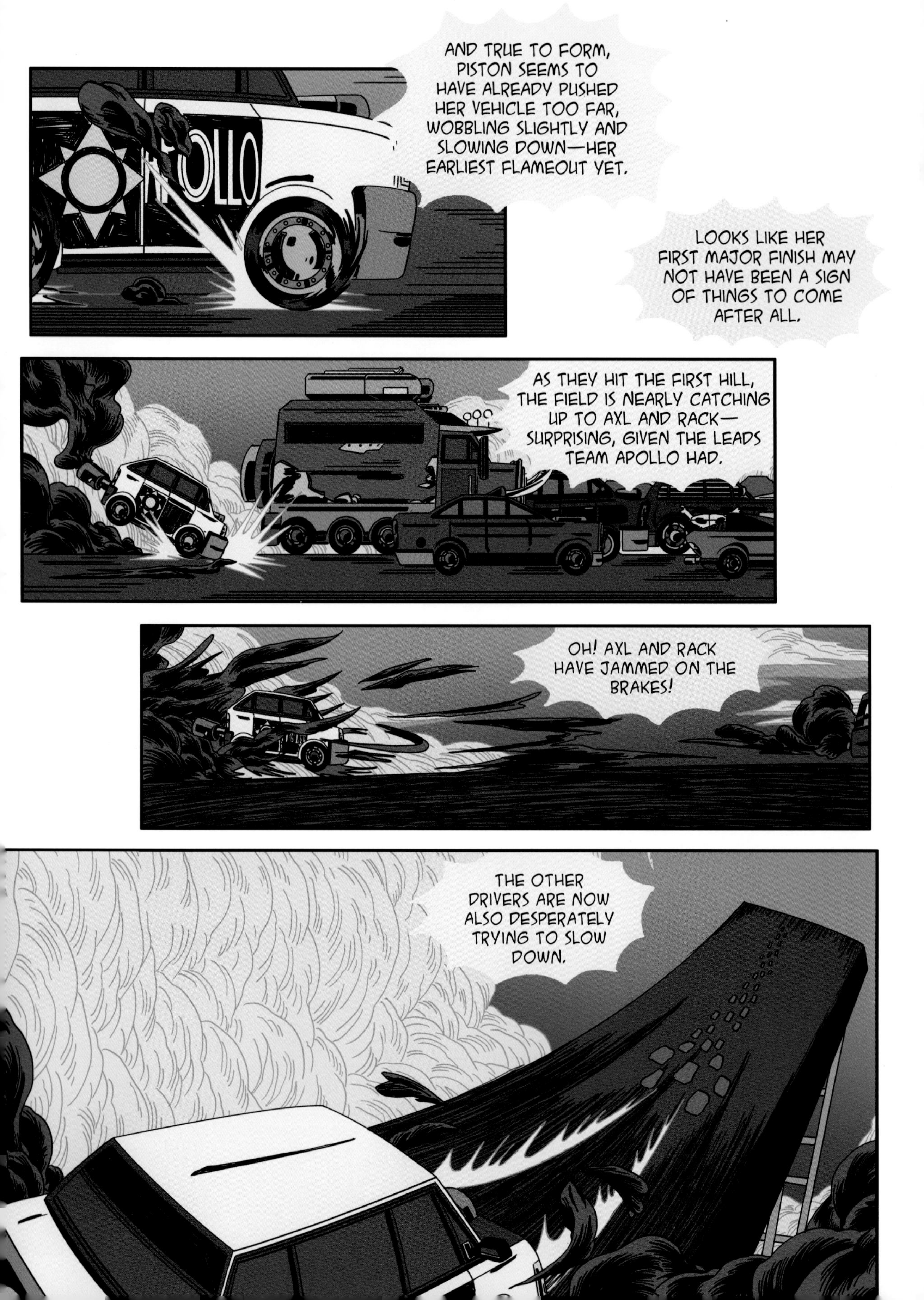
AND TRUE TO FORM, PISTON SEEMS TO HAVE ALREADY PUSHED HER VEHICLE TOO FAR, WOBBLING SLIGHTLY AND SLOWING DOWN—HER EARLIEST FLAMEOUT YET.
APOLLO
LOOKS LIKE HER FIRST MAJOR FINISH MAY NOT HAVE BEEN A SIGN OF THINGS TO COME AFTER ALL.
AS THEY HIT THE FIRST HILL, THE FIELD IS NEARLY CATCHING UP TO AXL AND RACK—SURPRISING, GIVEN THE LEADS TEAM APOLLO HAD.
OH! AXL AND RACK HAVE JAMMED ON THE BRAKES!
THE OTHER DRIVERS ARE NOW ALSO DESPERATELY TRYING TO SLOW DOWN.

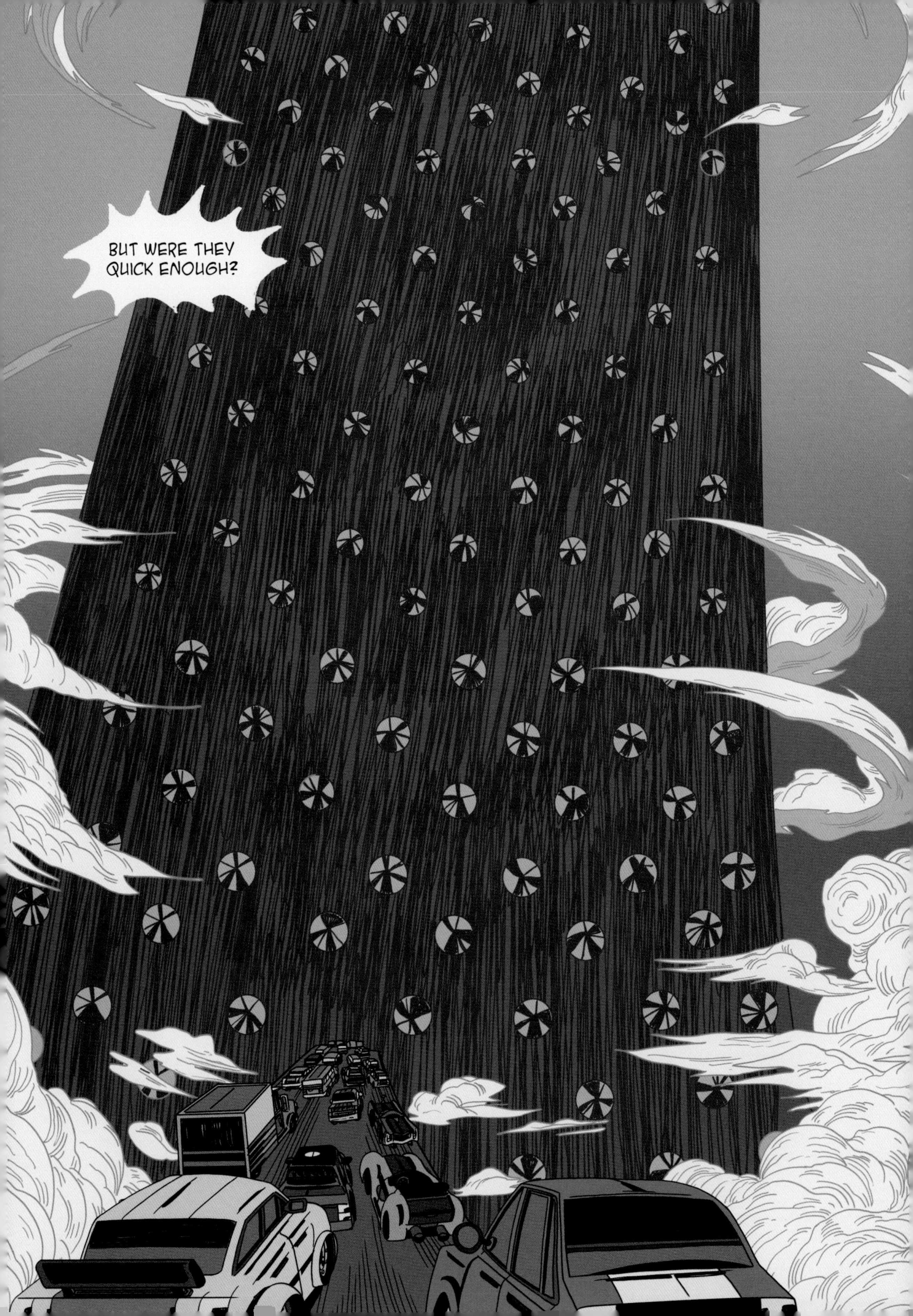
BUT WERE THEY QUICK ENOUGH?

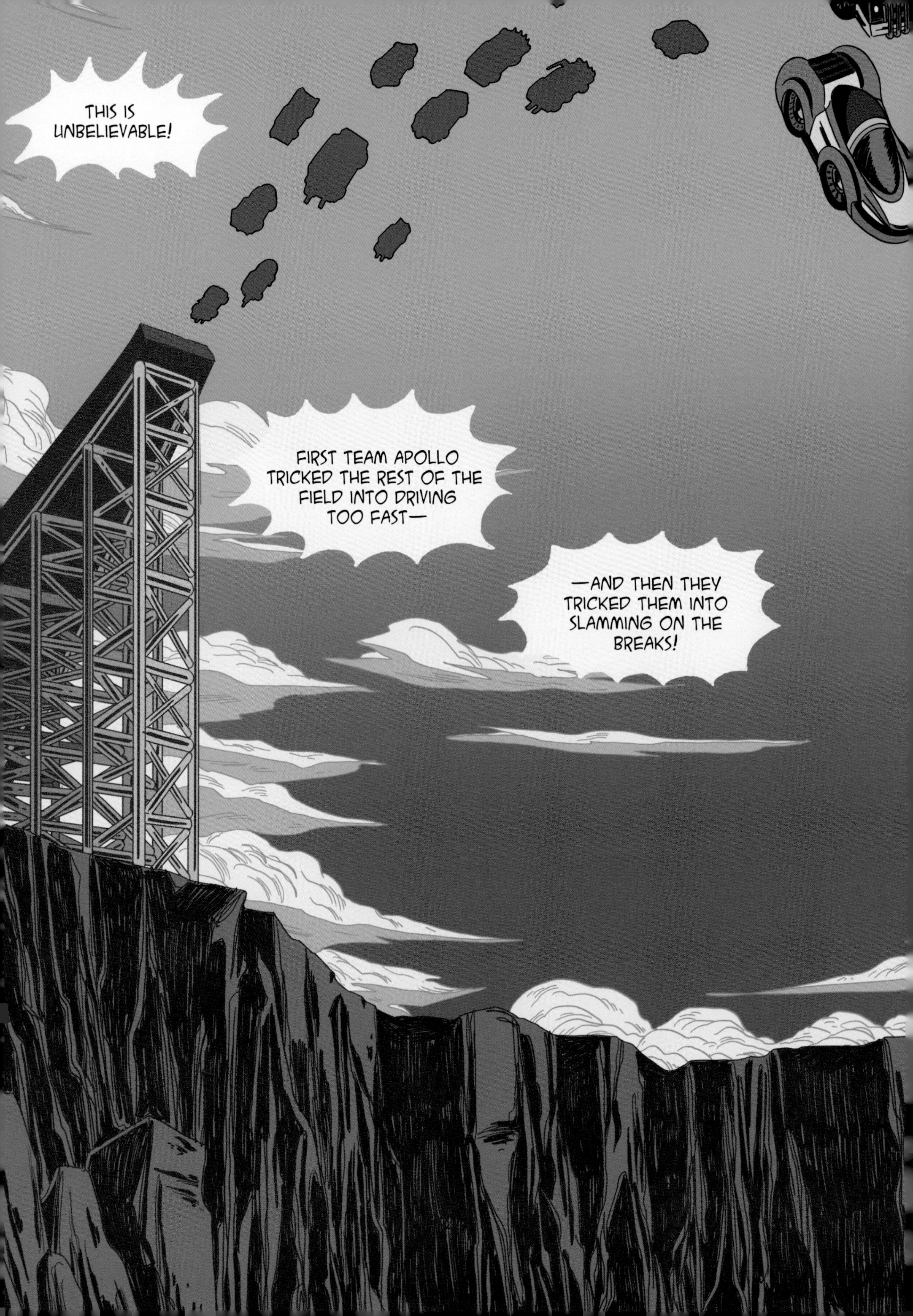

THIS IS UNBELIEVABLE!
FIRST TEAM APOLLO TRICKED THE REST OF THE FIELD INTO DRIVING TOO FAST—
—AND THEN THEY TRICKED THEM INTO SLAMMING ON THE BREAKS!

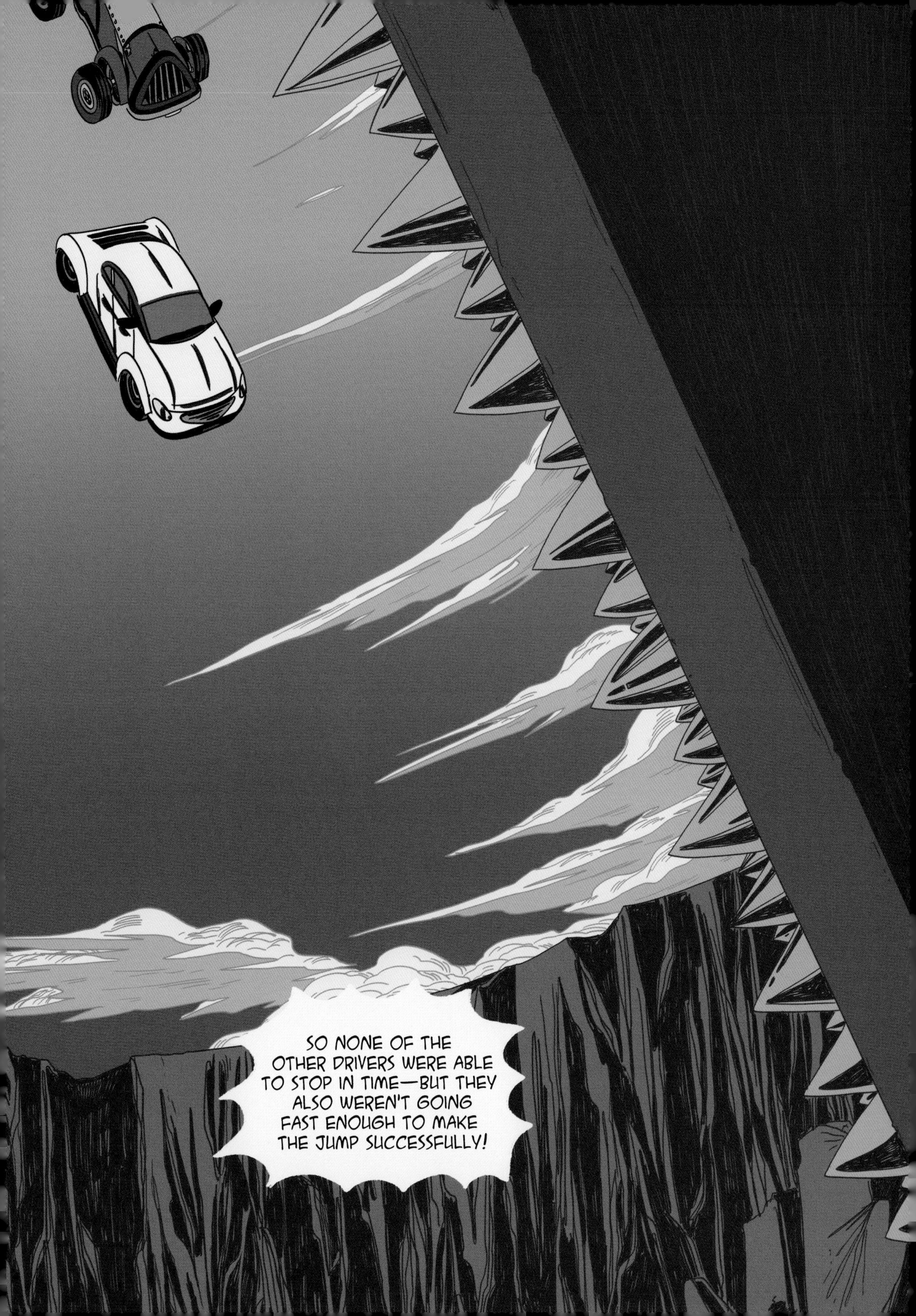
SO NONE OF THE OTHER DRIVERS WERE ABLE TO STOP IN TIME—BUT THEY ALSO WEREN'T GOING FAST ENOUGH TO MAKE THE JUMP SUCCESSFULLY!

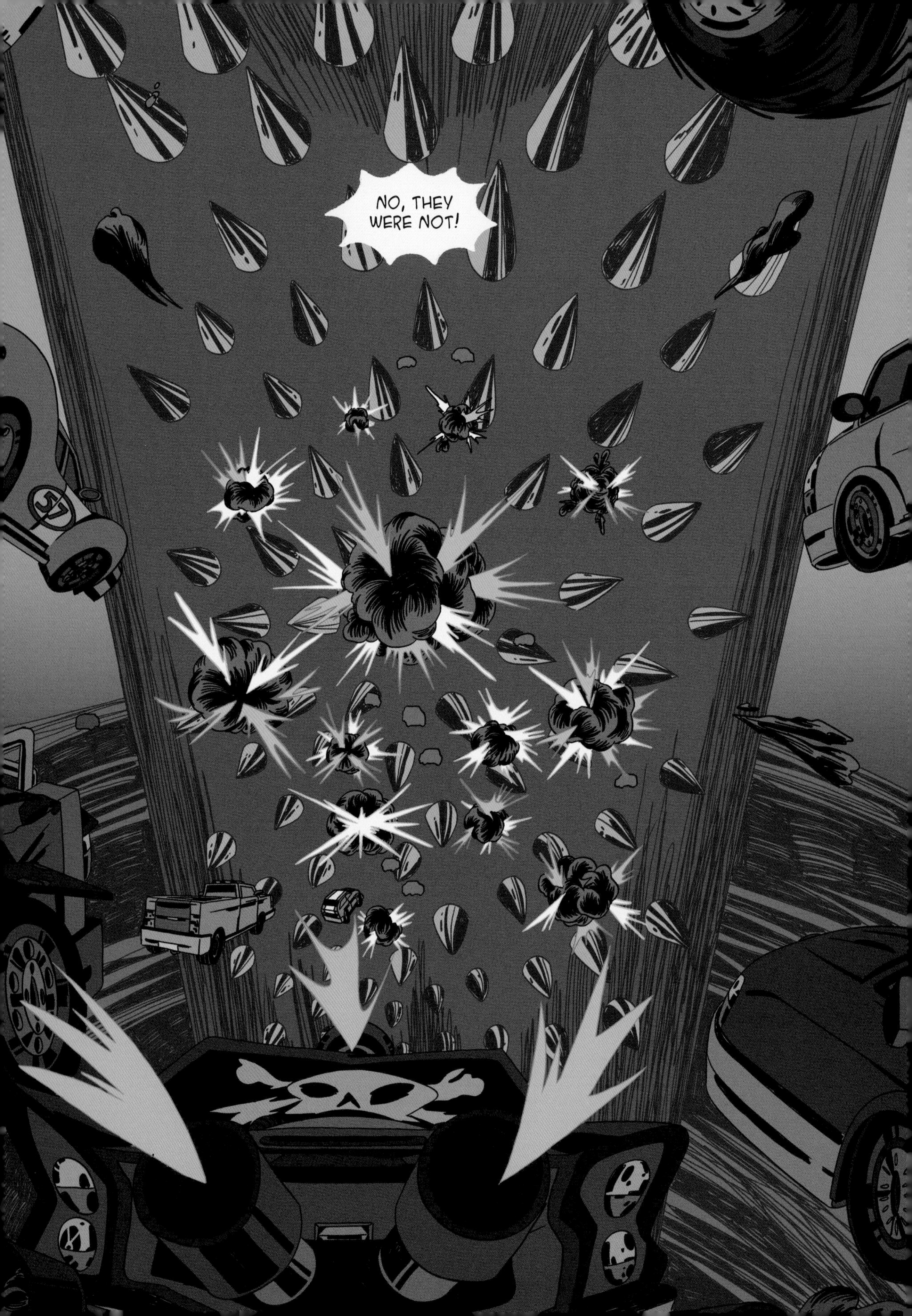
NO, THEY WERE NOT!

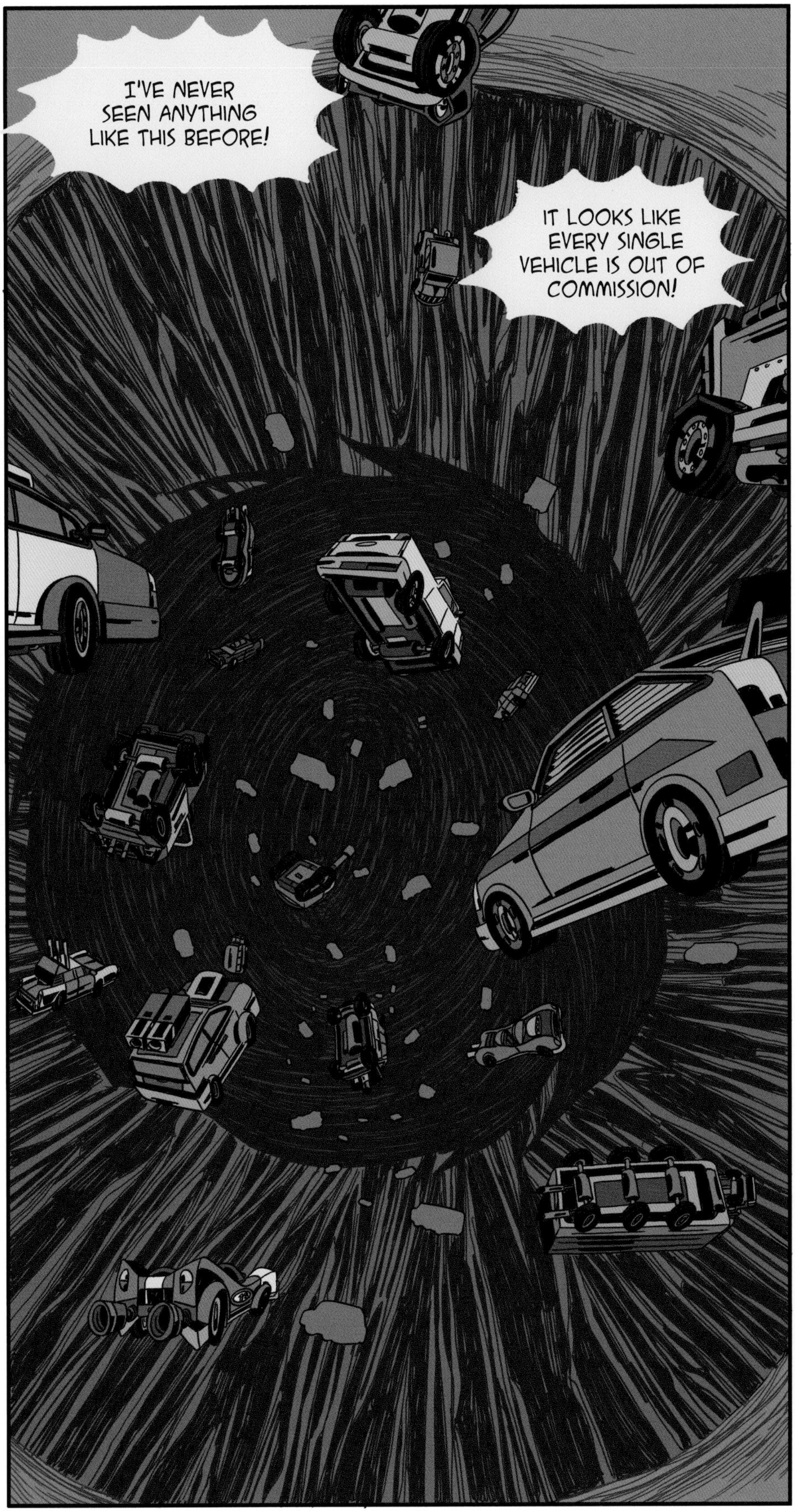
I'VE NEVER SEEN ANYTHING LIKE THIS BEFORE!
IT LOOKS LIKE EVERY SINGLE VEHICLE IS OUT OF COMMISSION!

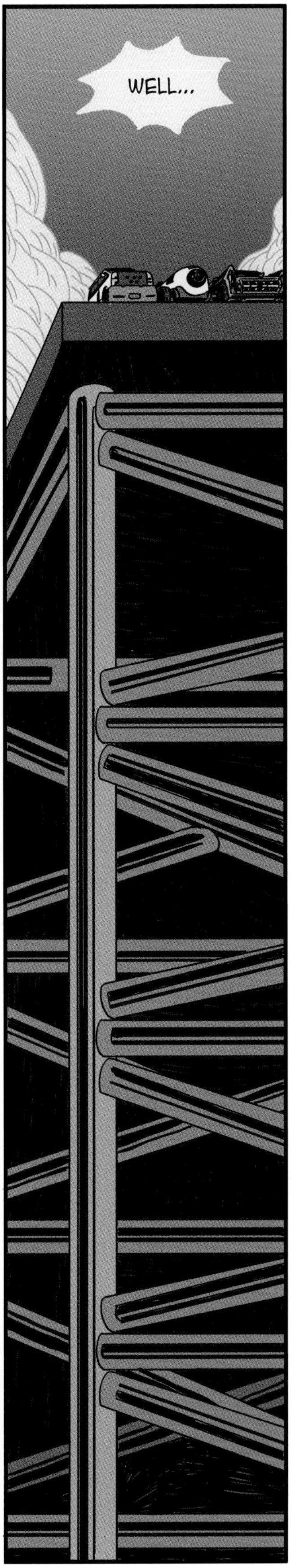
WELL...

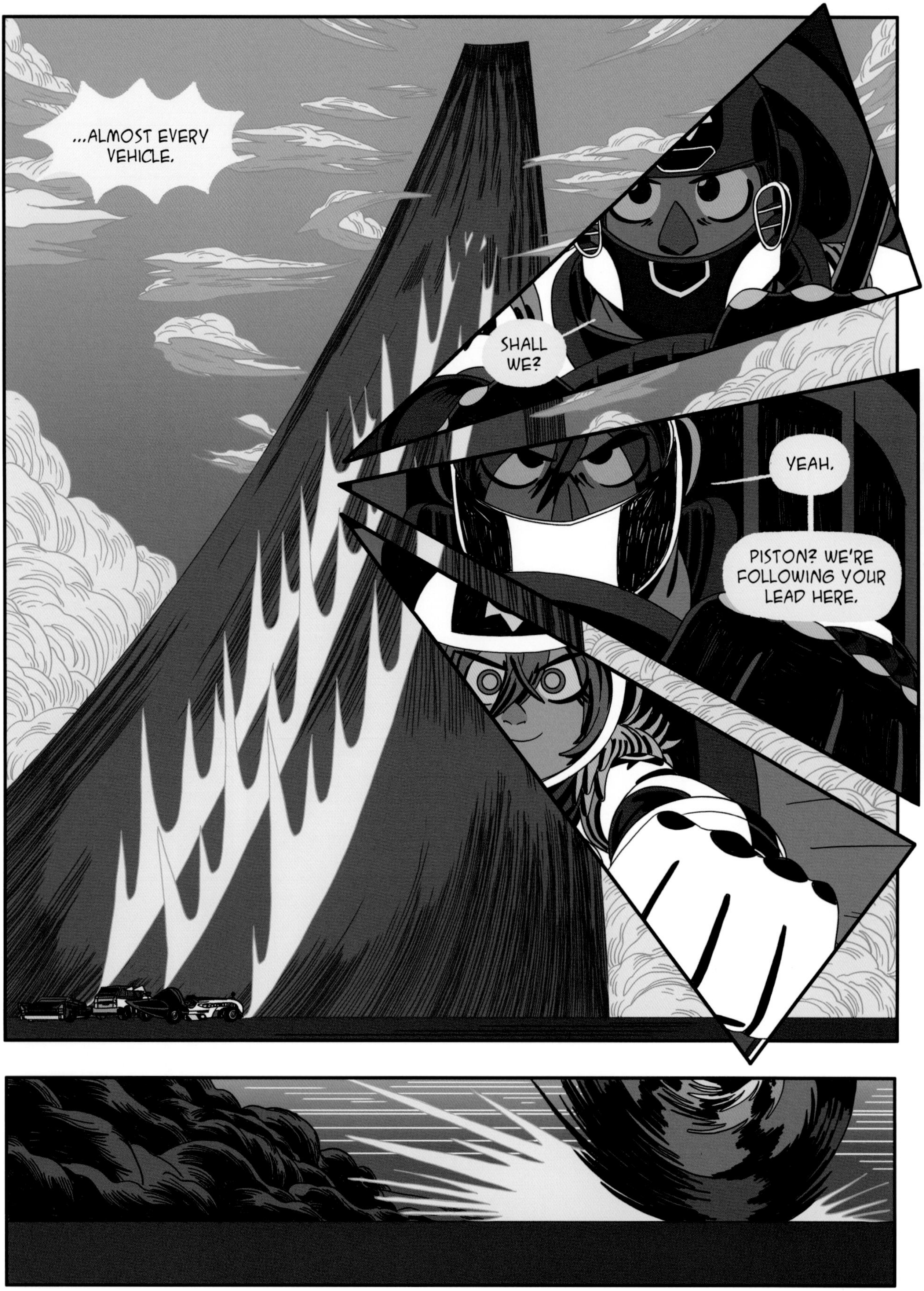
...ALMOST EVERY VEHICLE.
SHALL WE?
YEAH.
PISTON? WE'RE FOLLOWING YOUR LEAD HERE.

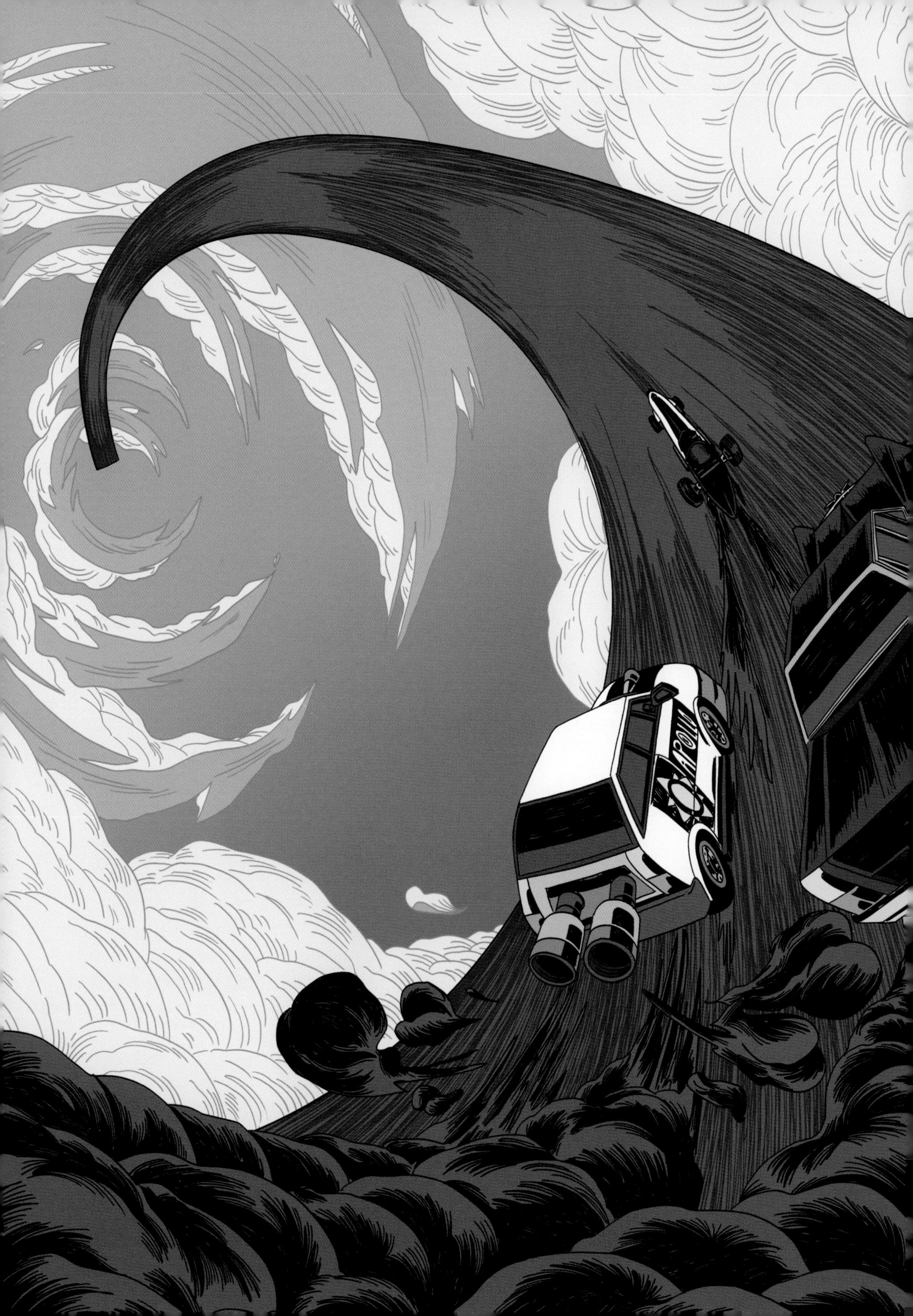
APOLLO

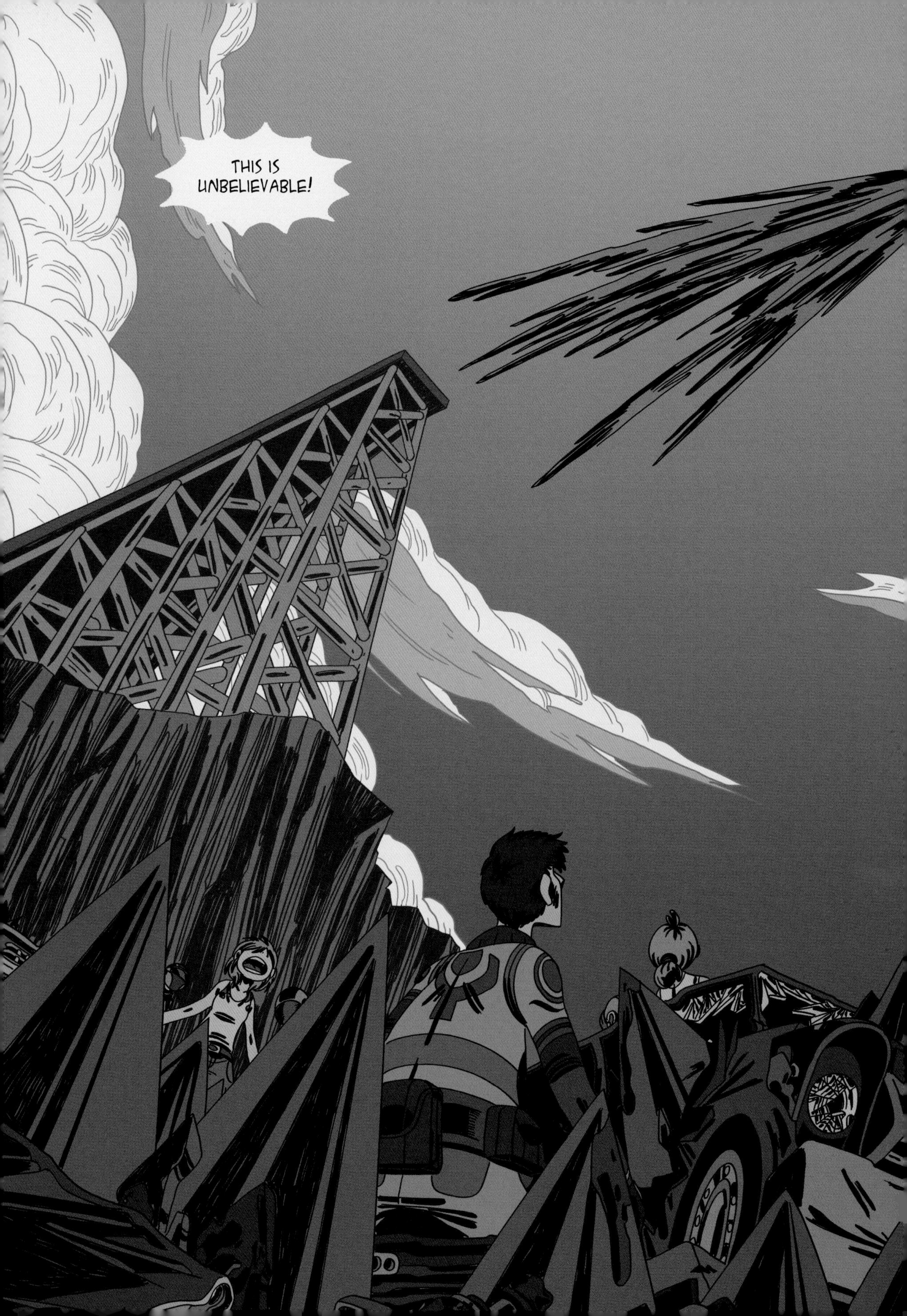
THIS IS UNBELIEVABLE!

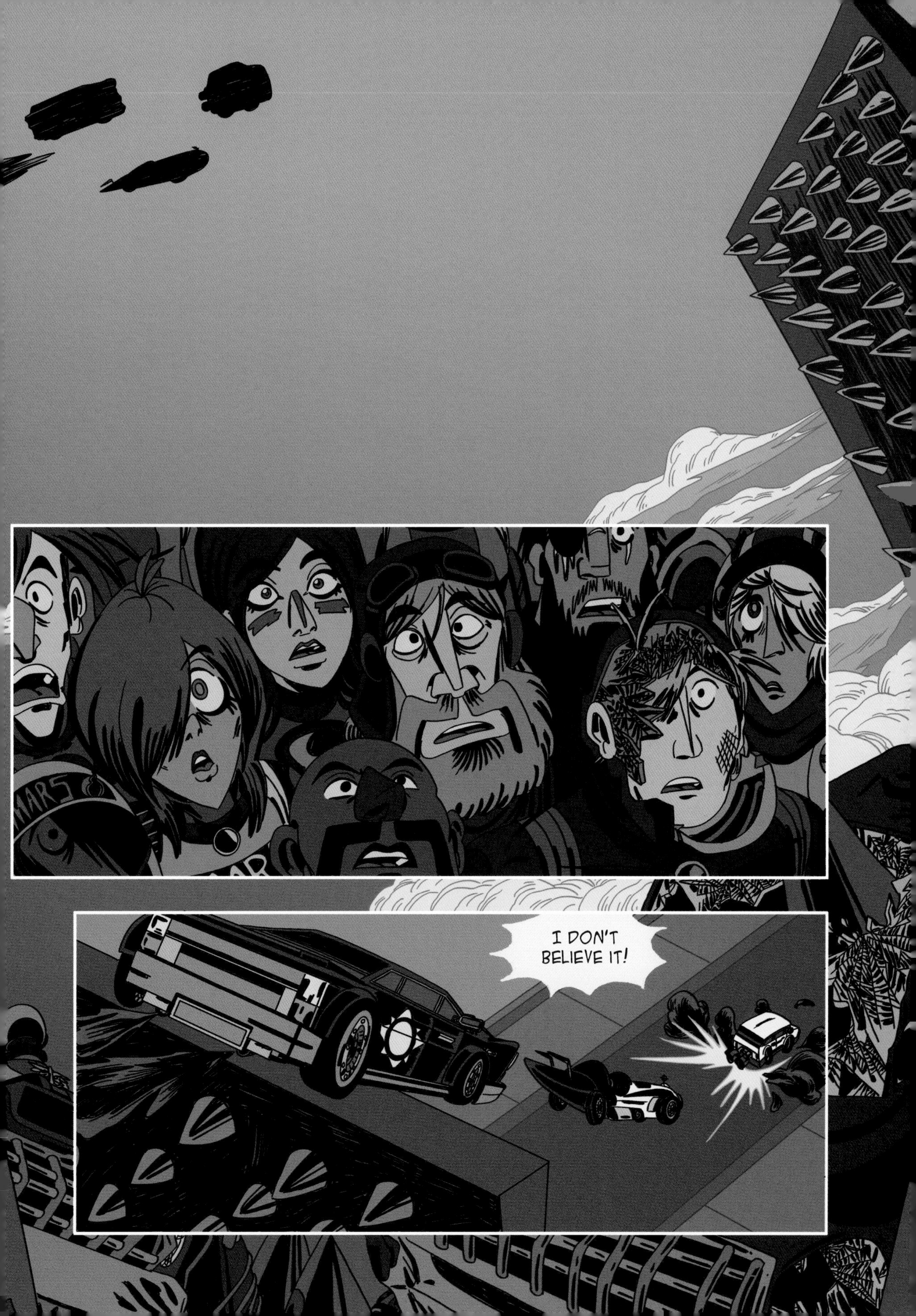
MARS
I DON'T
BELIEVE IT!

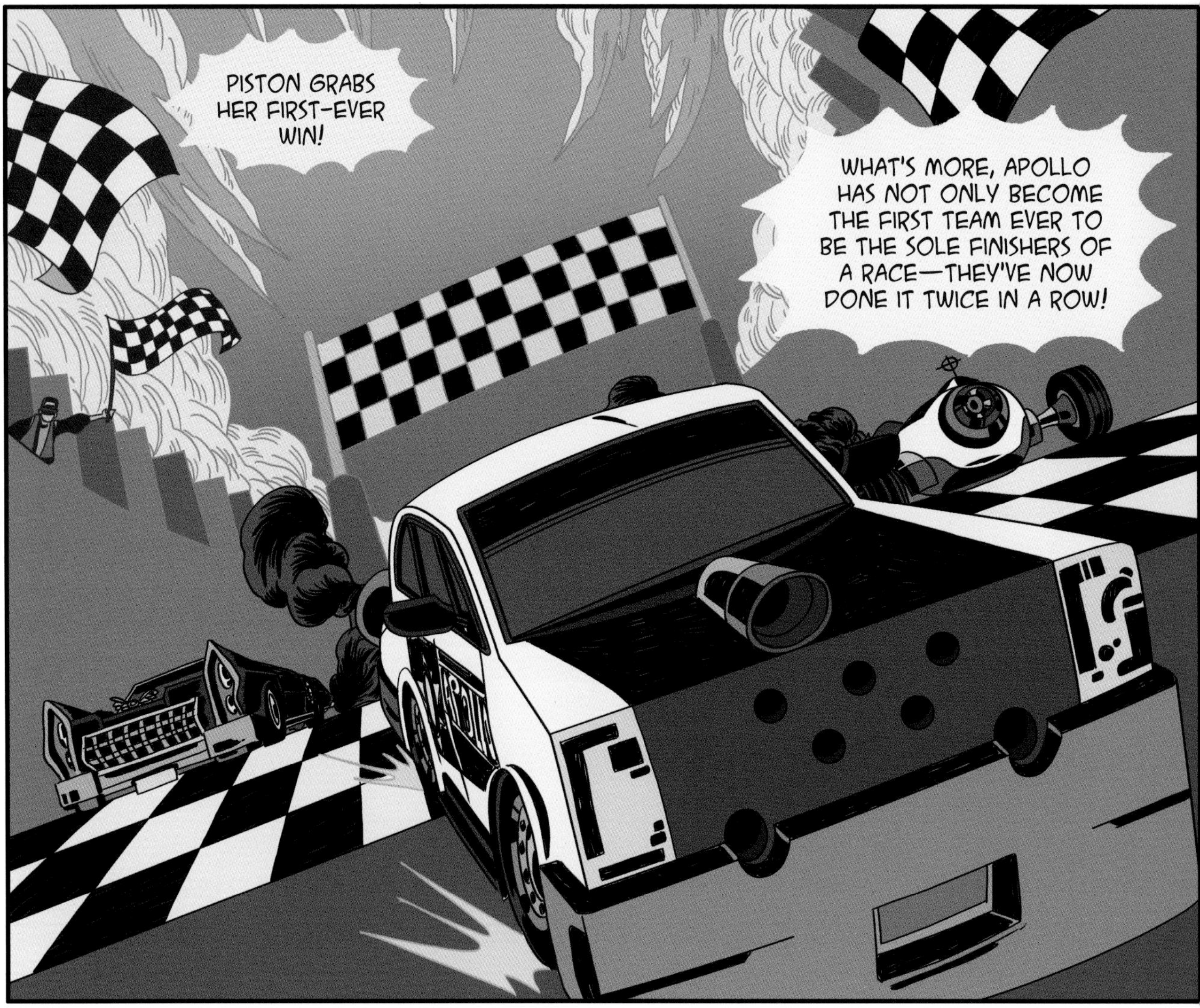
PISTON GRABS HER FIRST-EVER WIN!
WHAT'S MORE, APOLLO HAS NOT ONLY BECOME THE FIRST TEAM EVER TO BE THE SOLE FINISHERS OF A RACE—THEY'VE NOW DONE IT TWICE IN A ROW!
APOLLO

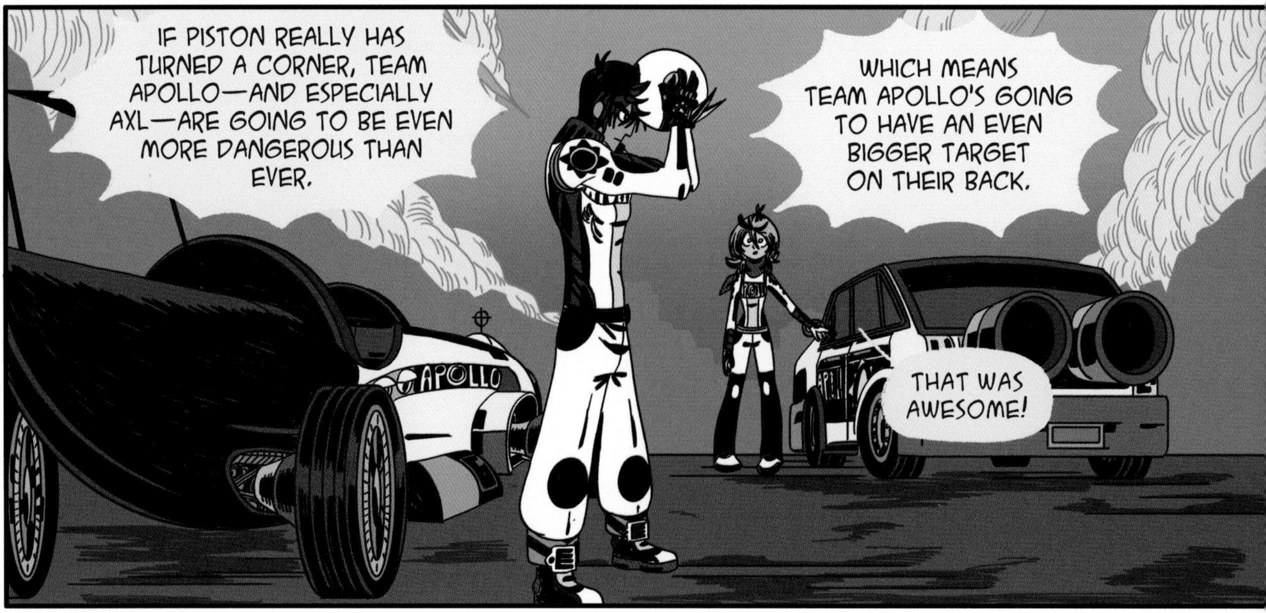
IF PISTON REALLY HAS TURNED A CORNER, TEAM APOLLO—AND ESPECIALLY AXL—ARE GOING TO BE EVEN MORE DANGEROUS THAN EVER.
WHICH MEANS TEAM APOLLO'S GOING TO HAVE AN EVEN BIGGER TARGET ON THEIR BACK.
THAT WAS AWESOME!
APOLLO

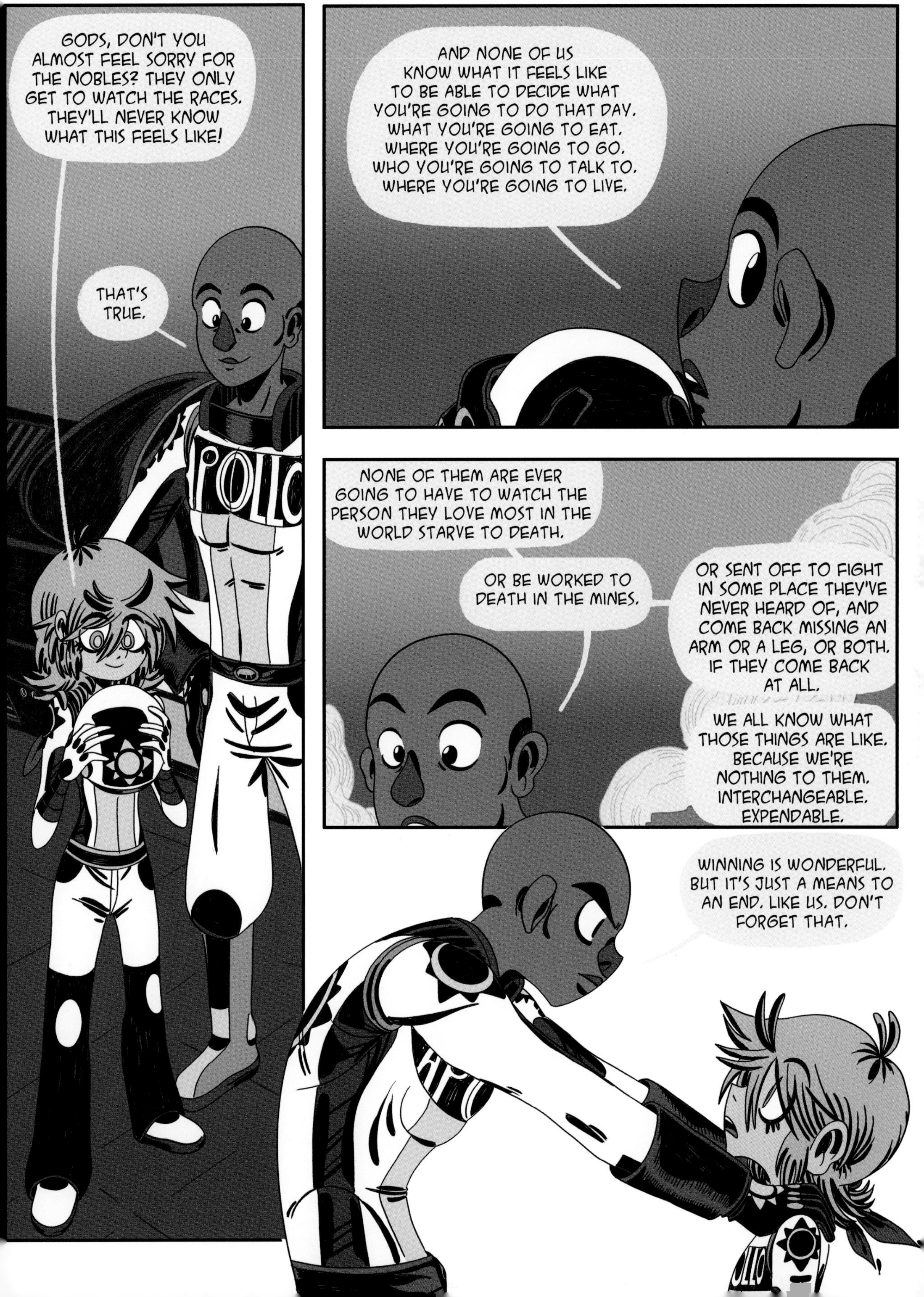
GODS, DON'T YOU ALMOST FEEL SORRY FOR THE NOBLES? THEY ONLY GET TO WATCH THE RACES. THEY'LL NEVER KNOW WHAT THIS FEELS LIKE!
THAT'S TRUE.
AND NONE OF US KNOW WHAT IT FEELS LIKE TO BE ABLE TO DECIDE WHAT YOU'RE GOING TO DO THAT DAY. WHAT YOU'RE GOING TO EAT. WHERE YOU'RE GOING TO GO. WHO YOU'RE GOING TO TALK TO. WHERE YOU'RE GOING TO LIVE.
NONE OF THEM ARE EVER GOING TO HAVE TO WATCH THE PERSON THEY LOVE MOST IN THE WORLD STARVE TO DEATH.
OR BE WORKED TO DEATH IN THE MINES.
OR SENT OFF TO FIGHT IN SOME PLACE THEY'VE NEVER HEARD OF, AND COME BACK MISSING AN ARM OR A LEG, OR BOTH. IF THEY COME BACK AT ALL.
WE ALL KNOW WHAT THOSE THINGS ARE LIKE. BECAUSE WE'RE NOTHING TO THEM. INTERCHANGEABLE. EXPENDABLE.
WINNING IS WONDERFUL. BUT IT'S JUST A MEANS TO AN END. LIKE US. DON'T FORGET THAT.

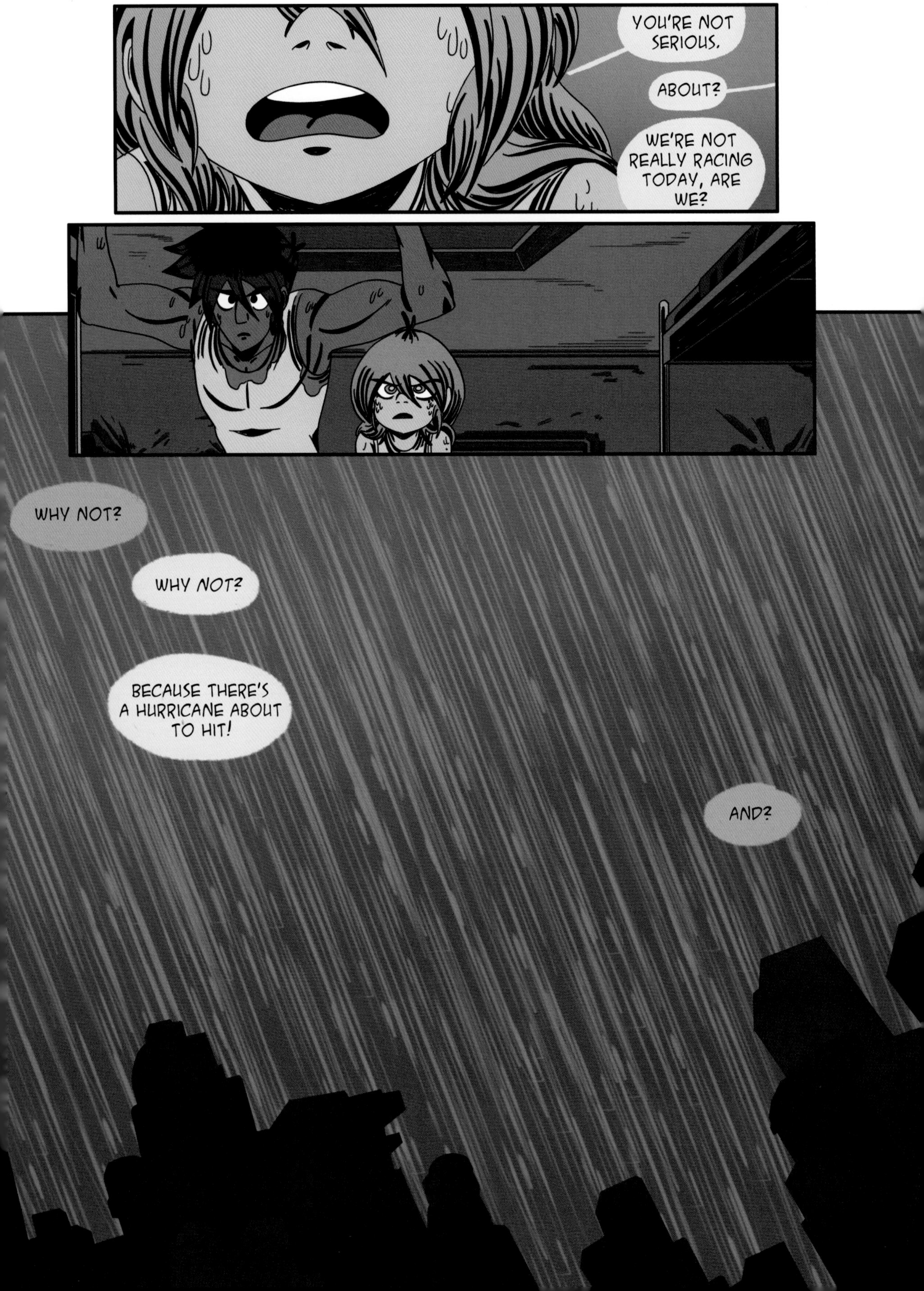
YOU'RE NOT SERIOUS.
ABOUT?
WE'RE NOT REALLY RACING TODAY, ARE WE?
WHY NOT?
WHY NOT?
BECAUSE THERE'S A HURRICANE ABOUT TO HIT!
AND?

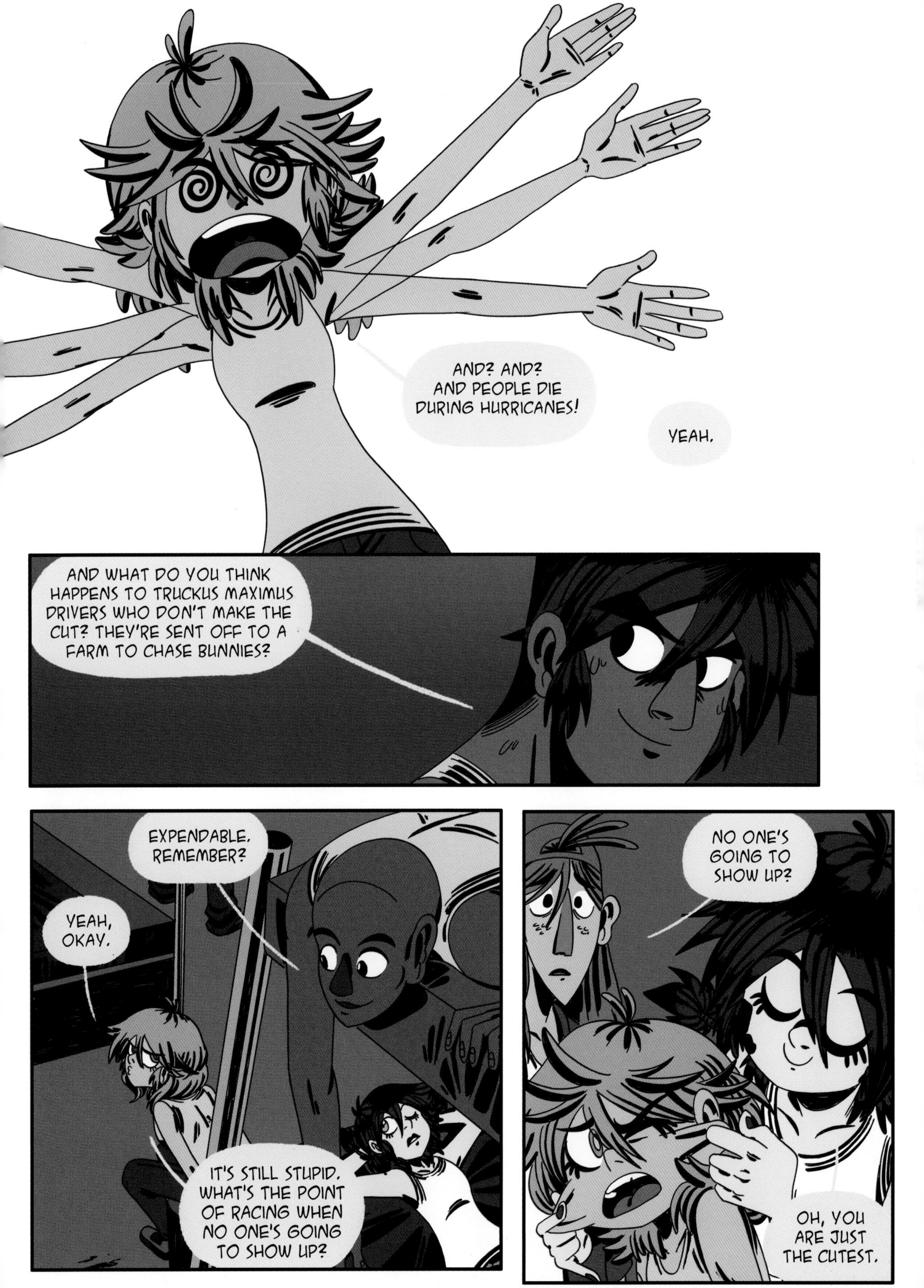
AND? AND? AND PEOPLE DIE DURING HURRICANES!
YEAH.
AND WHAT DO YOU THINK HAPPENS TO TRUCKUS MAXIMUS DRIVERS WHO DON'T MAKE THE CUT? THEY'RE SENT OFF TO A FARM TO CHASE BUNNIES?
EXPENDABLE. REMEMBER?
YEAH, OKAY.
IT'S STILL STUPID. WHAT'S THE POINT OF RACING WHEN NO ONE'S GOING TO SHOW UP?
NO ONE'S GOING TO SHOW UP?
OH, YOU ARE JUST THE CUTEST.

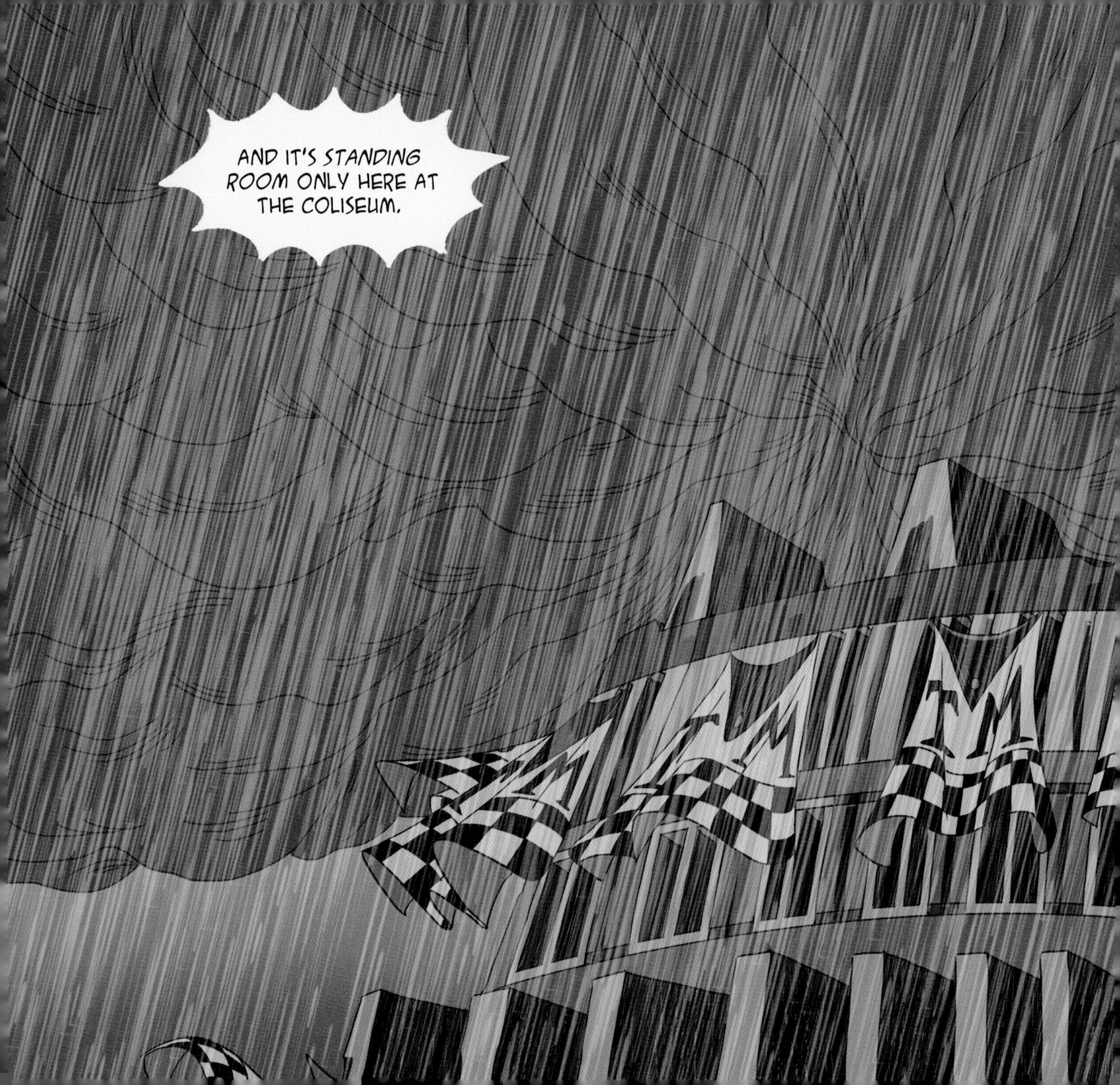
AND IT'S STANDING ROOM ONLY HERE AT THE COLISEUM.

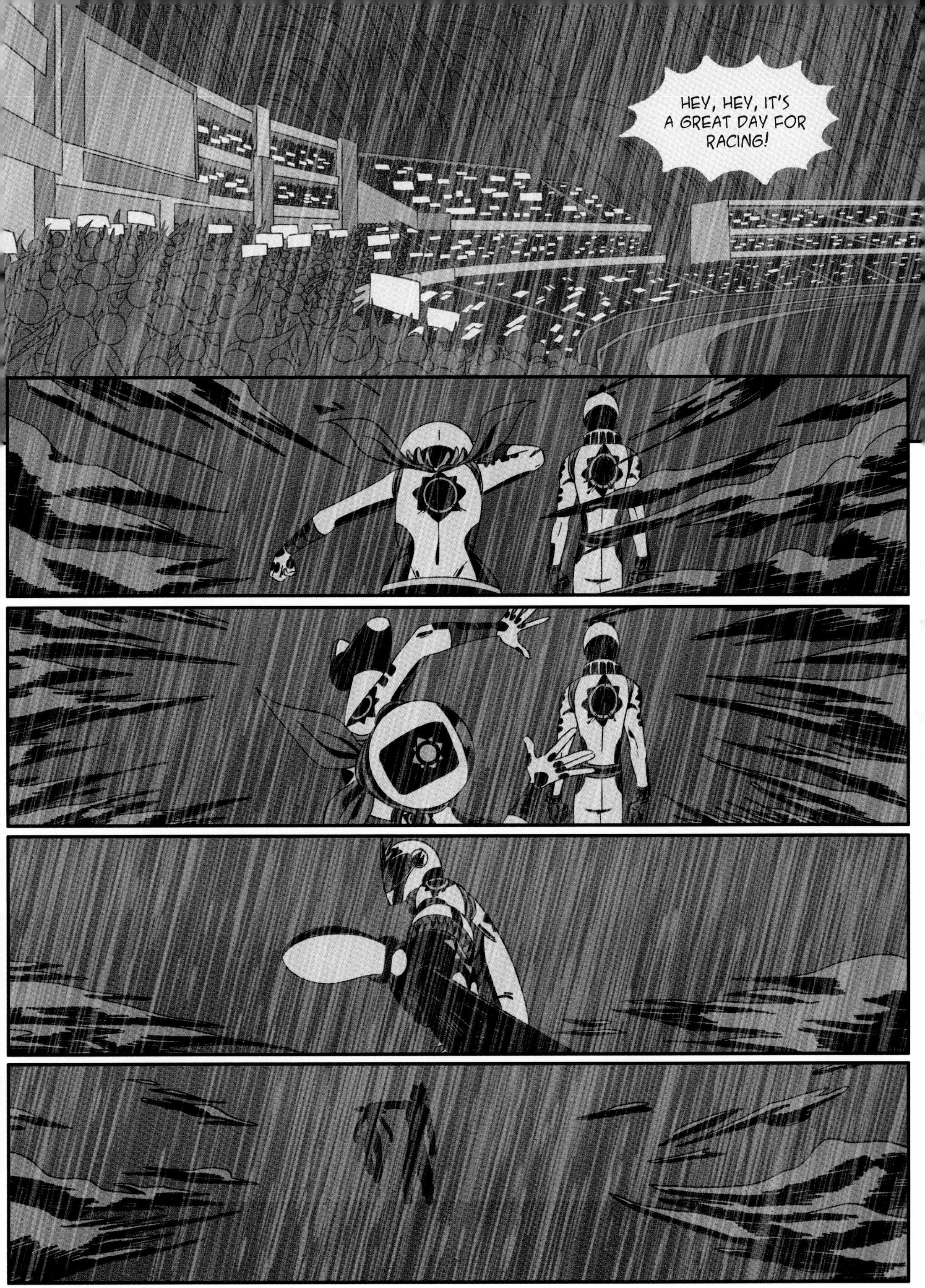
HEY, HEY, IT'S A GREAT DAY FOR RACING!

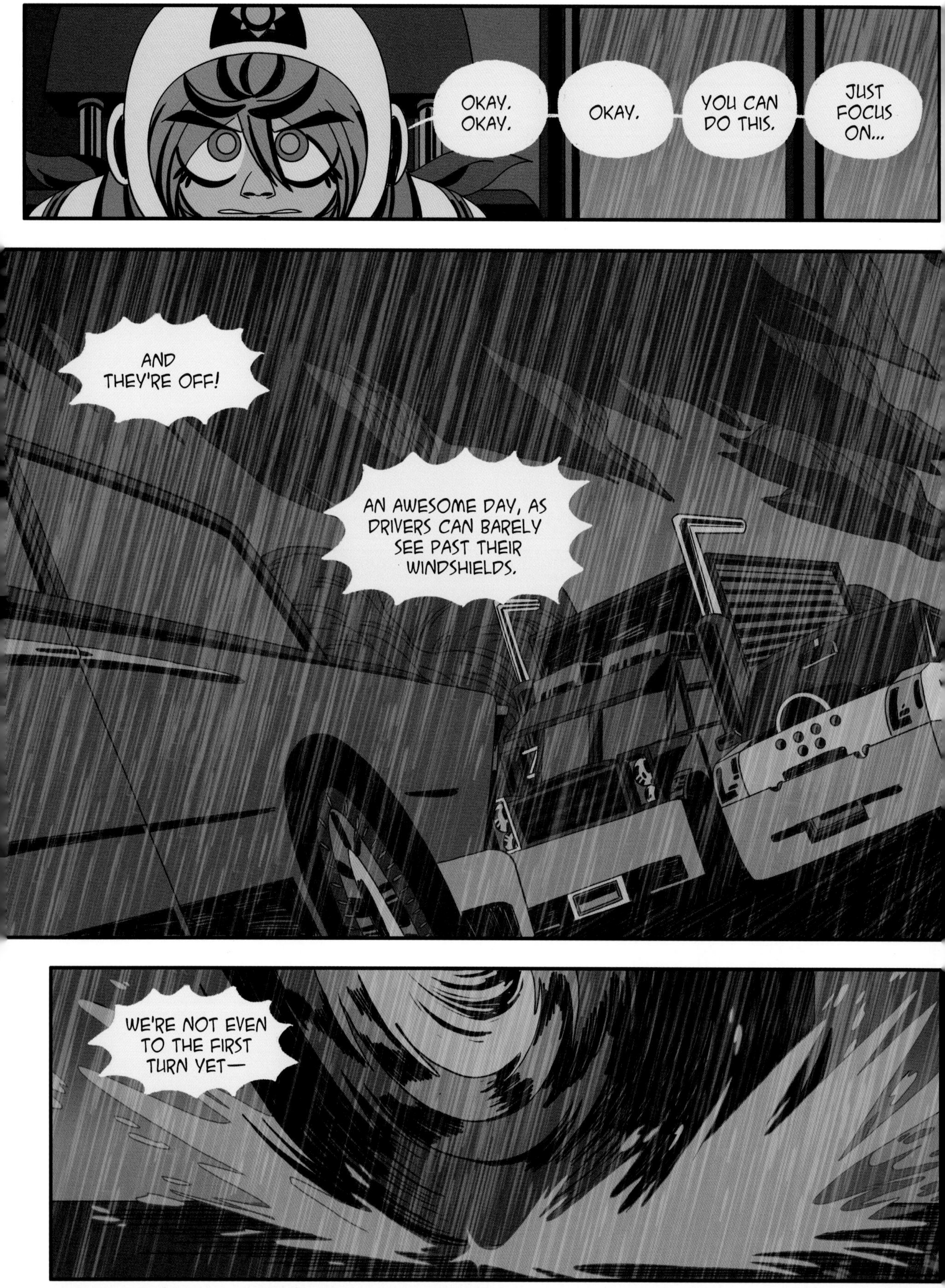
OKAY. OKAY.
OKAY.
YOU CAN DO THIS.
JUST FOCUS ON...
AND THEY'RE OFF!
AN AWESOME DAY, AS DRIVERS CAN BARELY SEE PAST THEIR WINDSHIELDS.
WE'RE NOT EVEN TO THE FIRST TURN YET—

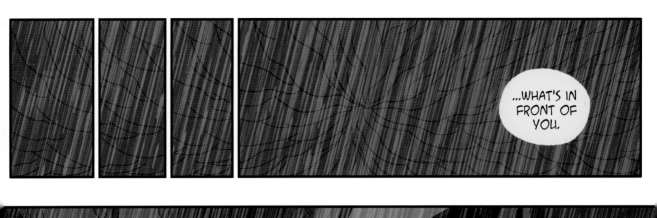

...WHAT'S IN FRONT OF YOU.

—AND PISTON'S ALREADY SPINNING OUT.

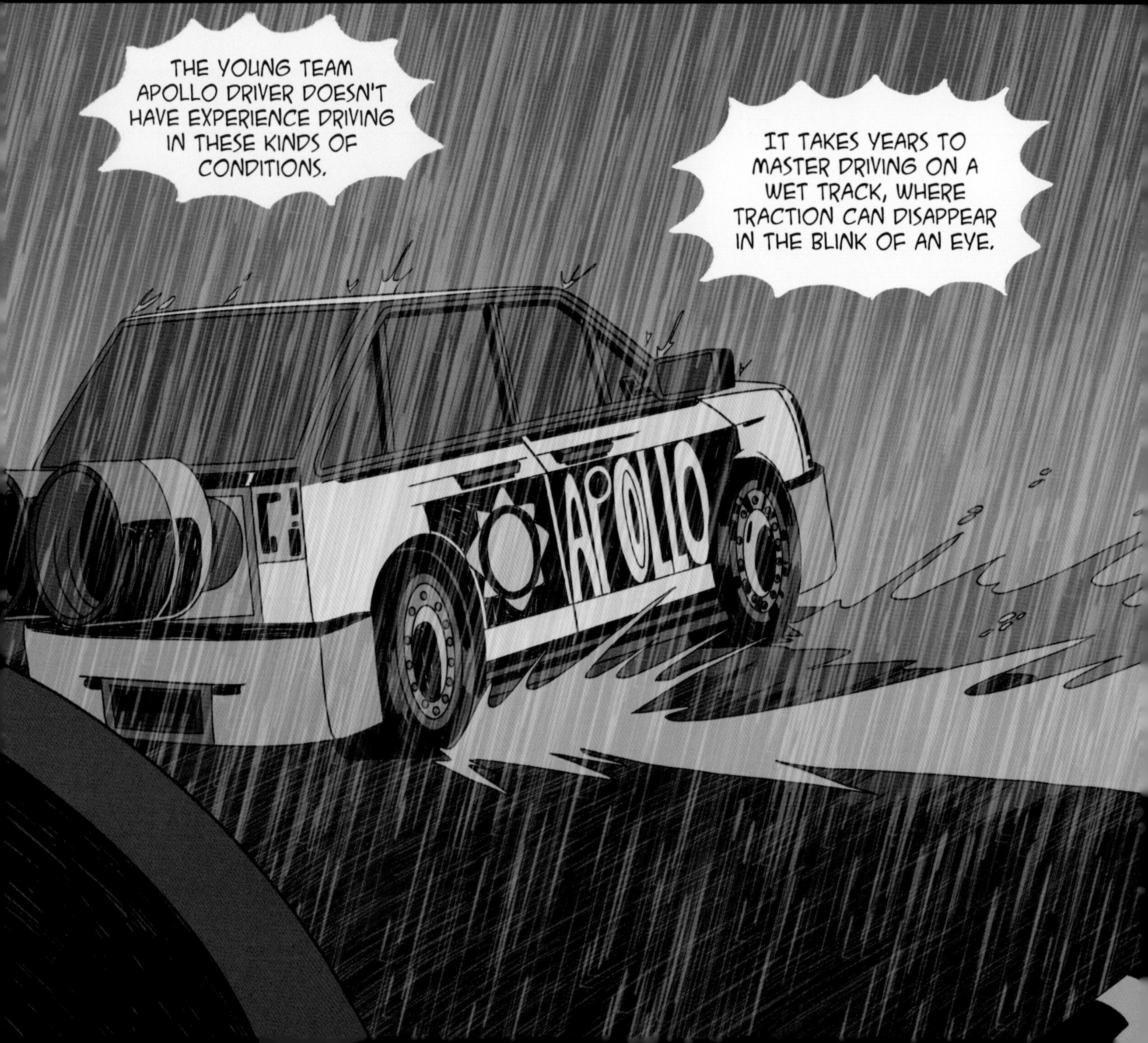
THE YOUNG TEAM APOLLO DRIVER DOESN'T HAVE EXPERIENCE DRIVING IN THESE KINDS OF CONDITIONS.
IT TAKES YEARS TO MASTER DRIVING ON A WET TRACK, WHERE TRACTION CAN DISAPPEAR IN THE BLINK OF AN EYE.
APOLLO

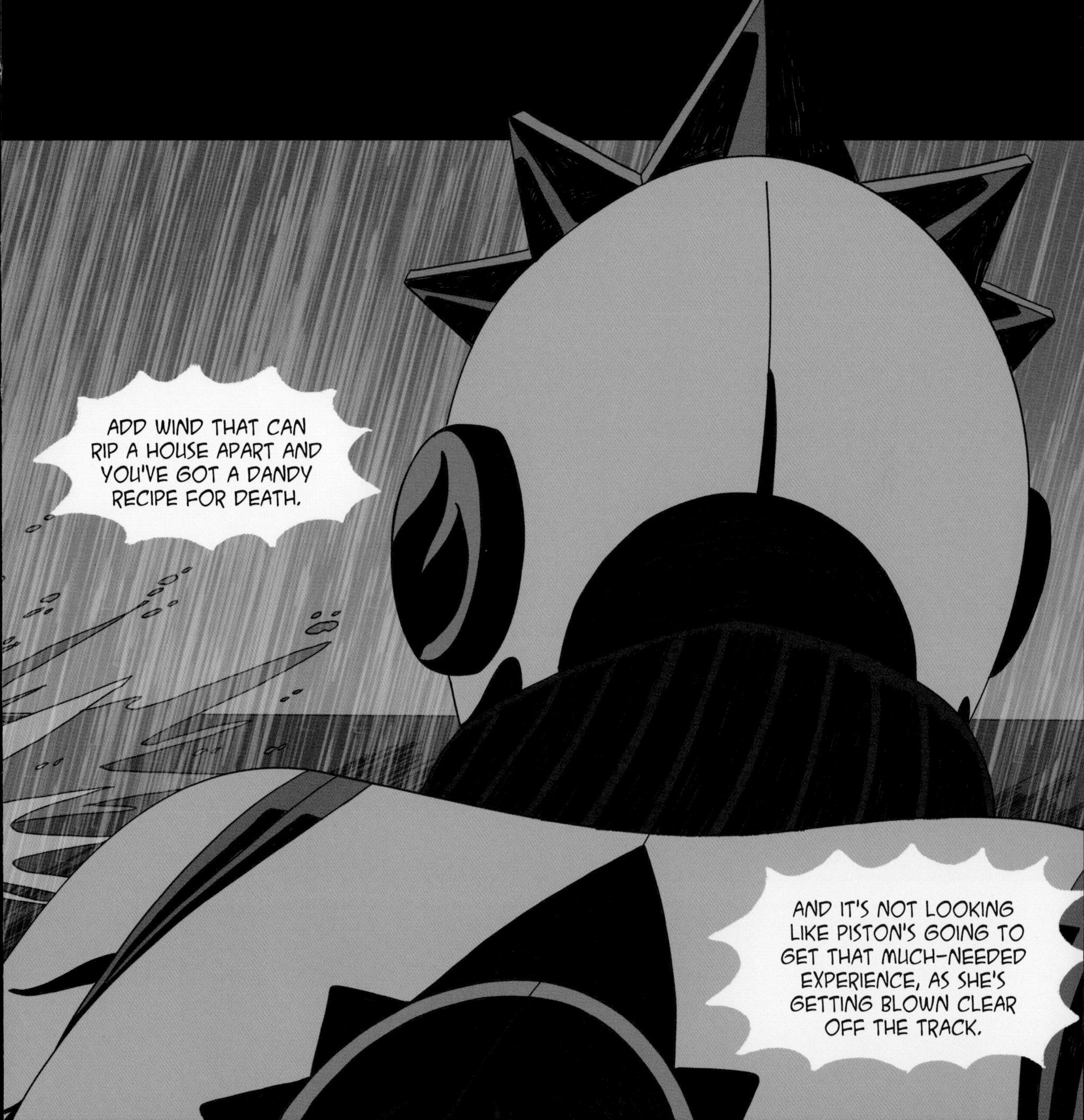
ADD WIND THAT CAN RIP A HOUSE APART AND YOU'VE GOT A DANDY RECIPE FOR DEATH.
AND IT'S NOT LOOKING LIKE PISTON'S GOING TO GET THAT MUCH-NEEDED EXPERIENCE, AS SHE'S GETTING BLOWN CLEAR OFF THE TRACK.

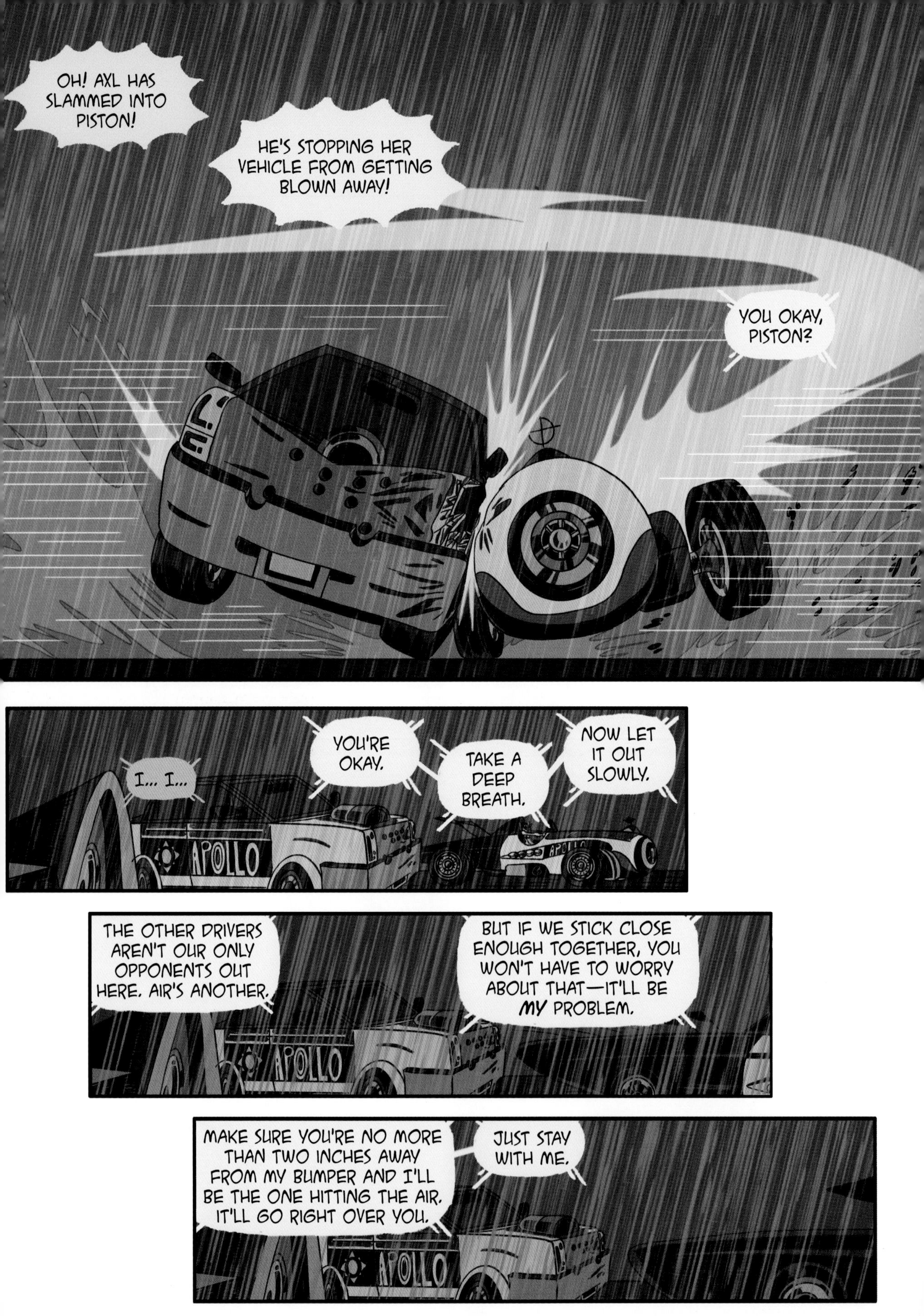
OH! AXL HAS SLAMMED INTO PISTON!
HE'S STOPPING HER VEHICLE FROM GETTING BLOWN AWAY!
YOU OKAY, PISTON?
I... I...
YOU'RE OKAY.
TAKE A DEEP BREATH.
NOW LET IT OUT SLOWLY.
APOLLO
THE OTHER DRIVERS AREN'T OUR ONLY OPPONENTS OUT HERE. AIR'S ANOTHER.
BUT IF WE STICK CLOSE ENOUGH TOGETHER, YOU WON'T HAVE TO WORRY ABOUT THAT—IT'LL BE *MY* PROBLEM.
APOLLO
MAKE SURE YOU'RE NO MORE THAN TWO INCHES AWAY FROM MY BUMPER AND I'LL BE THE ONE HITTING THE AIR. IT'LL GO RIGHT OVER YOU.
JUST STAY WITH ME.
APOLLO

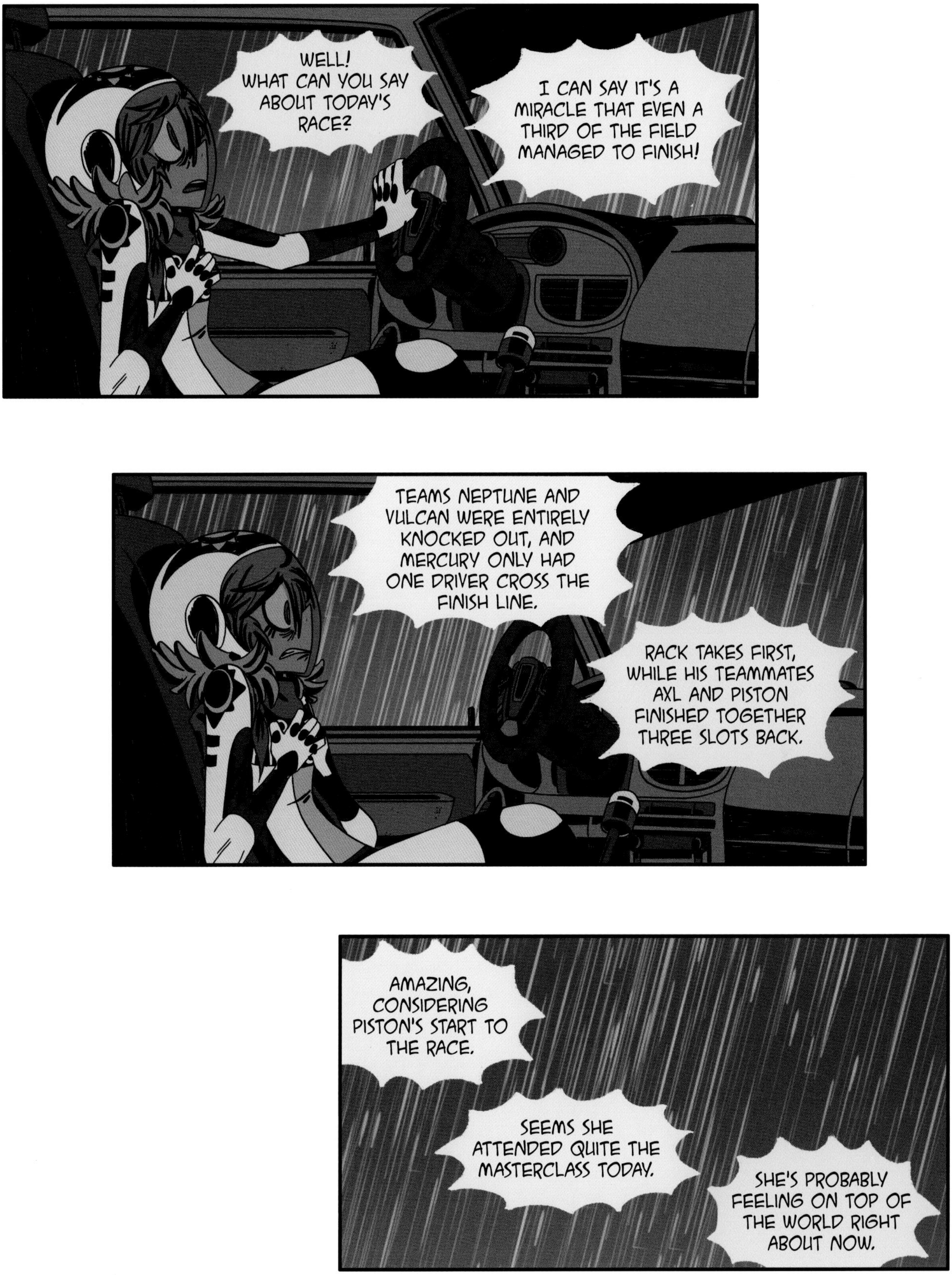
WELL! WHAT CAN YOU SAY ABOUT TODAY'S RACE?
I CAN SAY IT'S A MIRACLE THAT EVEN A THIRD OF THE FIELD MANAGED TO FINISH!
TEAMS NEPTUNE AND VULCAN WERE ENTIRELY KNOCKED OUT, AND MERCURY ONLY HAD ONE DRIVER CROSS THE FINISH LINE.
RACK TAKES FIRST, WHILE HIS TEAMMATES AXL AND PISTON FINISHED TOGETHER THREE SLOTS BACK.
AMAZING, CONSIDERING PISTON'S START TO THE RACE.
SEEMS SHE ATTENDED QUITE THE MASTERCLASS TODAY.
SHE'S PROBABLY FEELING ON TOP OF THE WORLD RIGHT ABOUT NOW.

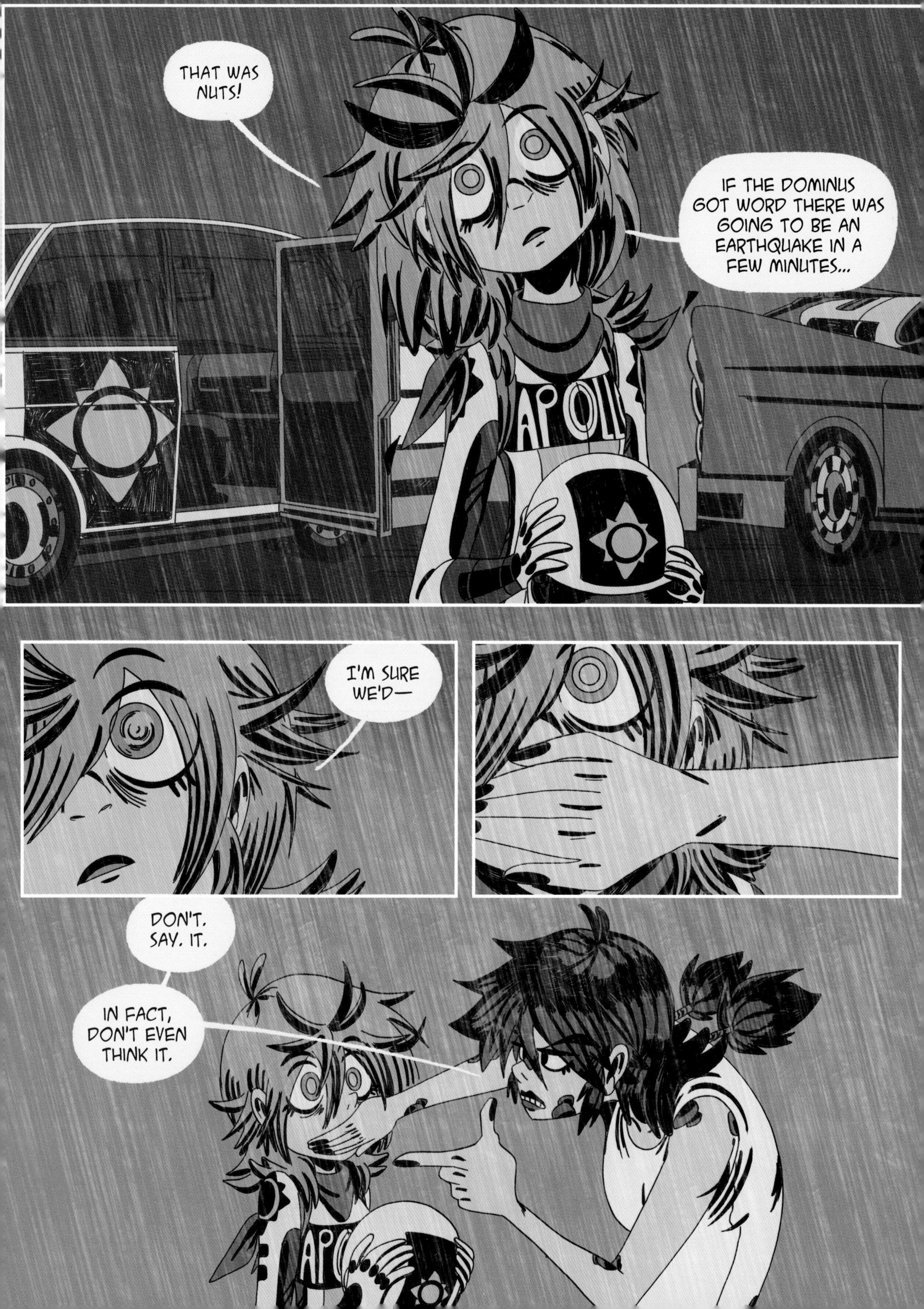
THAT WAS NUTS!
IF THE DOMINUS GOT WORD THERE WAS GOING TO BE AN EARTHQUAKE IN A FEW MINUTES...
I'M SURE WE'D—
DON'T. SAY. IT.
IN FACT, DON'T EVEN THINK IT.

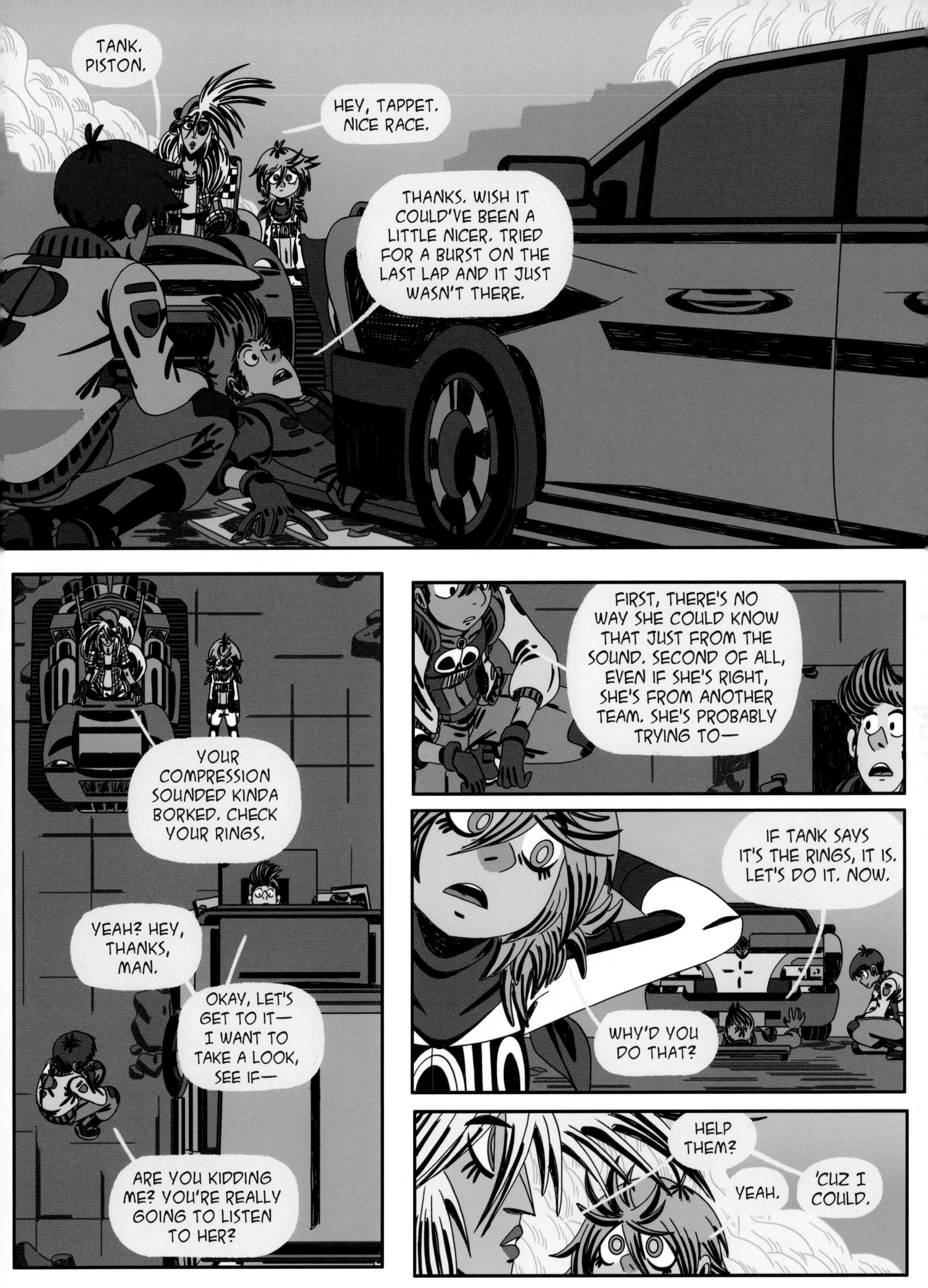
TANK. PISTON.
HEY, TAPPET. NICE RACE.
THANKS. WISH IT COULD'VE BEEN A LITTLE NICER. TRIED FOR A BURST ON THE LAST LAP AND IT JUST WASN'T THERE.
YOUR COMPRESSION SOUNDED KINDA BORKED. CHECK YOUR RINGS.
YEAH? HEY, THANKS, MAN.
OKAY, LET'S GET TO IT— I WANT TO TAKE A LOOK, SEE IF—
ARE YOU KIDDING ME? YOU'RE REALLY GOING TO LISTEN TO HER?
FIRST, THERE'S NO WAY SHE COULD KNOW THAT JUST FROM THE SOUND. SECOND OF ALL, EVEN IF SHE'S RIGHT, SHE'S FROM ANOTHER TEAM. SHE'S PROBABLY TRYING TO—
IF TANK SAYS IT'S THE RINGS, IT IS. LET'S DO IT. NOW.
WHY'D YOU DO THAT?
HELP THEM?
YEAH.
'CUZ I COULD.

BUT...YOU MIGHT HAVE JUST HELPED THEM BEAT ONE OF US. THEY'RE OUR COMPETITION.

IN ONE SENSE, YEAH. BUT NOT IN THE BIGGER PICTURE, AND YOU ALWAYS GOTTA KEEP THE BIGGER PICTURE IN MIND, RIGHT?

DON'T GET SO FOCUSED ON YOUR NEXT MOVE YOU FORGET WHERE ON THE TRACK YOU ARE, REMEMBER?

BESIDES...THOSE GUYS ARE PRETTY DECENT, RIGHT?

WHAT, AS PEOPLE? YEAH, I GUESS. YEAH.

THEY BETTER DRIVERS THAN YOU?

ACCORDING TO THE STANDINGS, THEY ARE.

ARE THEY BETTER THAN YOU?

NO.

BETTER THAN RACK?

NO.

BETTER THAN AXL?

HELL NO.

SO WHY NOT?

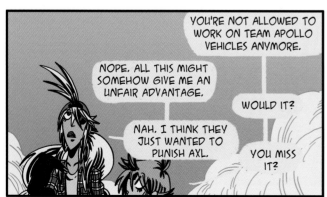

YOU'RE NOT ALLOWED TO WORK ON TEAM APOLLO VEHICLES ANYMORE.

NOPE. ALL THIS MIGHT SOMEHOW GIVE ME AN UNFAIR ADVANTAGE.

WOULD IT?

NAH. I THINK THEY JUST WANTED TO PUNISH AXL.

YOU MISS IT?

OH MY GODS, YES.

SO WAS THAT FUN?

MAYBE A LITTLE.

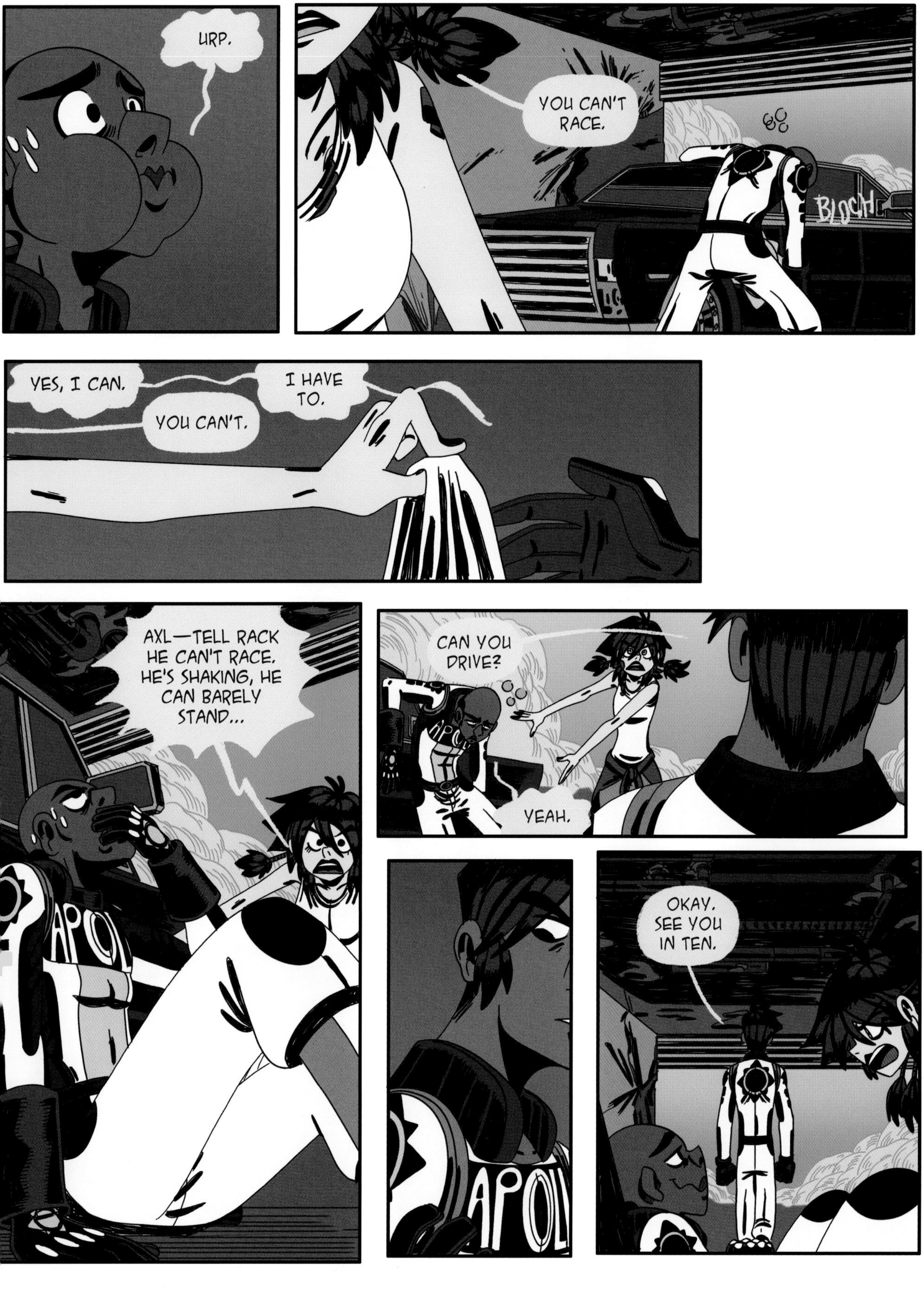
URP.
YOU CAN'T RACE.
BLOCH
YES, I CAN.
YOU CAN'T.
I HAVE TO.
AXL—TELL RACK HE CAN'T RACE. HE'S SHAKING, HE CAN BARELY STAND...
CAN YOU DRIVE?
YEAH.
OKAY. SEE YOU IN TEN.

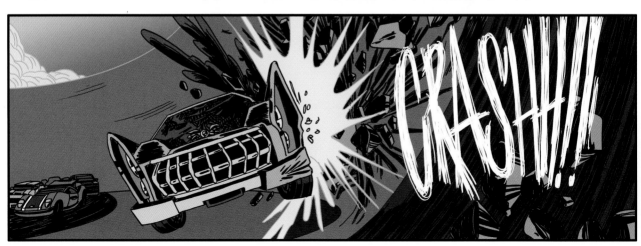

CRASHH!!

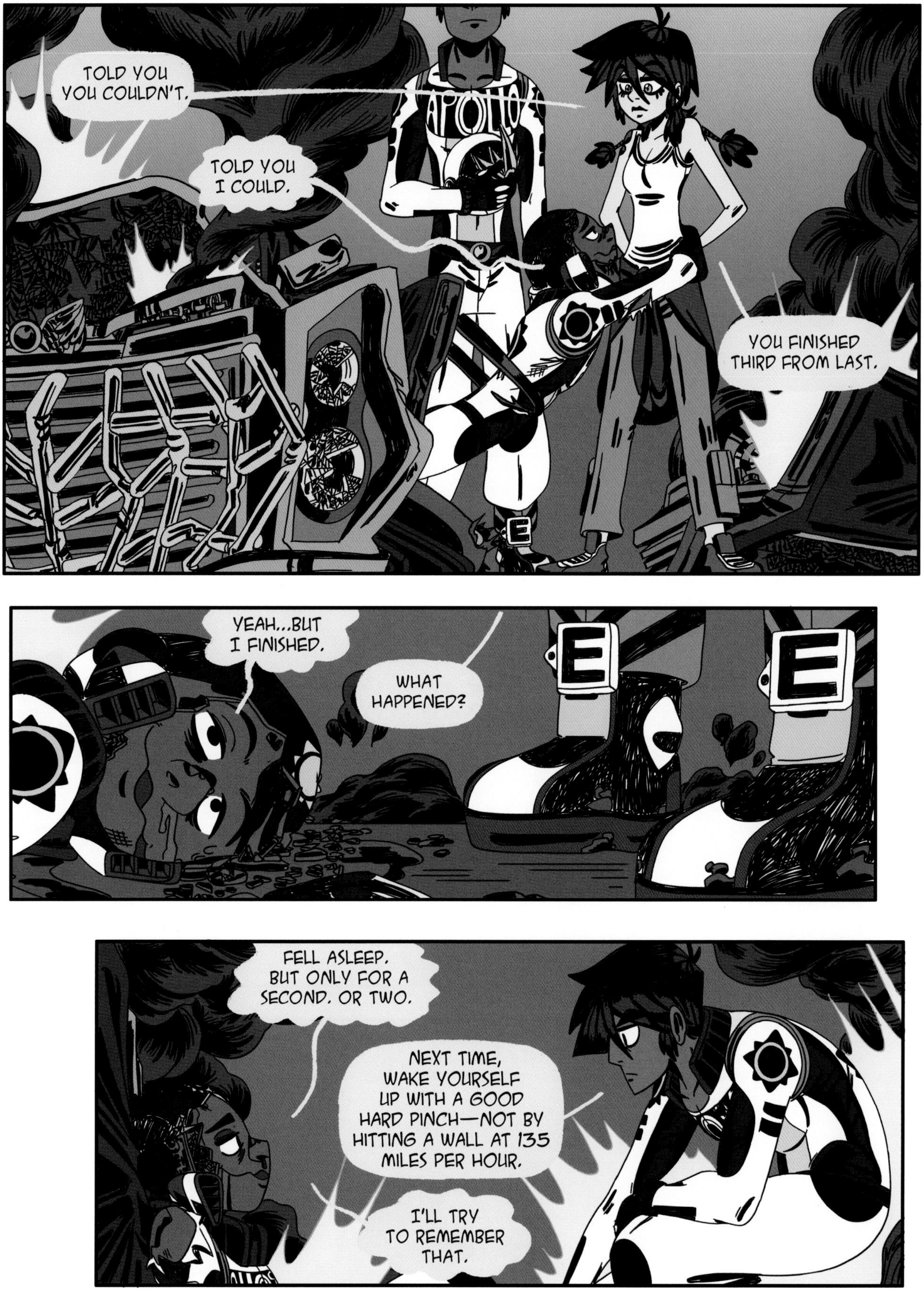
TOLD YOU
YOU COULDN'T.
TOLD YOU
I COULD.
YOU FINISHED
THIRD FROM LAST.
YEAH...BUT
I FINISHED.
WHAT
HAPPENED?
FELL ASLEEP.
BUT ONLY FOR A
SECOND. OR TWO.
NEXT TIME,
WAKE YOURSELF
UP WITH A GOOD
HARD PINCH—NOT BY
HITTING A WALL AT 135
MILES PER HOUR.
I'LL TRY
TO REMEMBER
THAT.

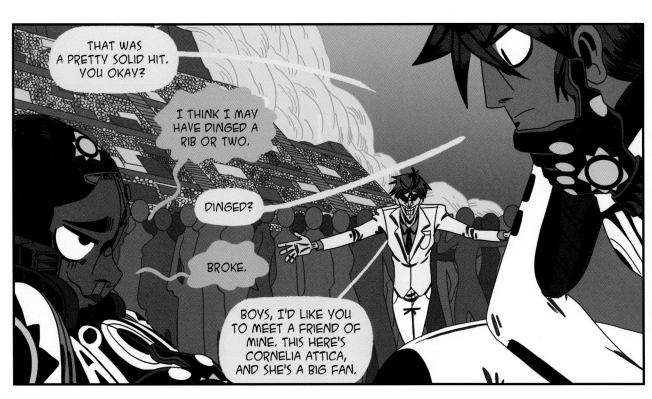

THAT WAS A PRETTY SOLID HIT. YOU OKAY?

I THINK I MAY HAVE DINGED A RIB OR TWO.

DINGED?

BROKE.

BOYS, I'D LIKE YOU TO MEET A FRIEND OF MINE. THIS HERE'S CORNELIA ATTICA, AND SHE'S A BIG FAN.

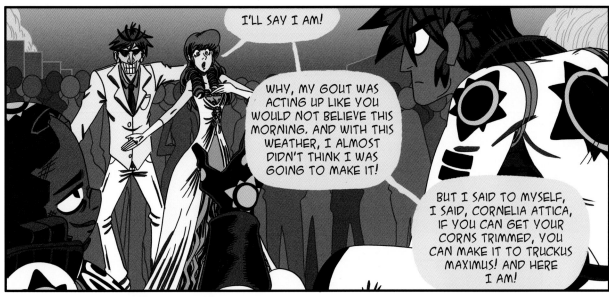

I'LL SAY I AM!

WHY, MY GOUT WAS ACTING UP LIKE YOU WOULD NOT BELIEVE THIS MORNING. AND WITH THIS WEATHER, I ALMOST DIDN'T THINK I WAS GOING TO MAKE IT!

BUT I SAID TO MYSELF, I SAID, CORNELIA ATTICA, IF YOU CAN GET YOUR CORNS TRIMMED, YOU CAN MAKE IT TO TRUCKUS MAXIMUS! AND HERE I AM!

WELL, NOW, IF THAT'S NOT DEVOTION!

WE SURE ARE RELIEVED YOU WERE ABLE TO MAKE IT.

I HOPE YOU FEEL BETTER SOON.

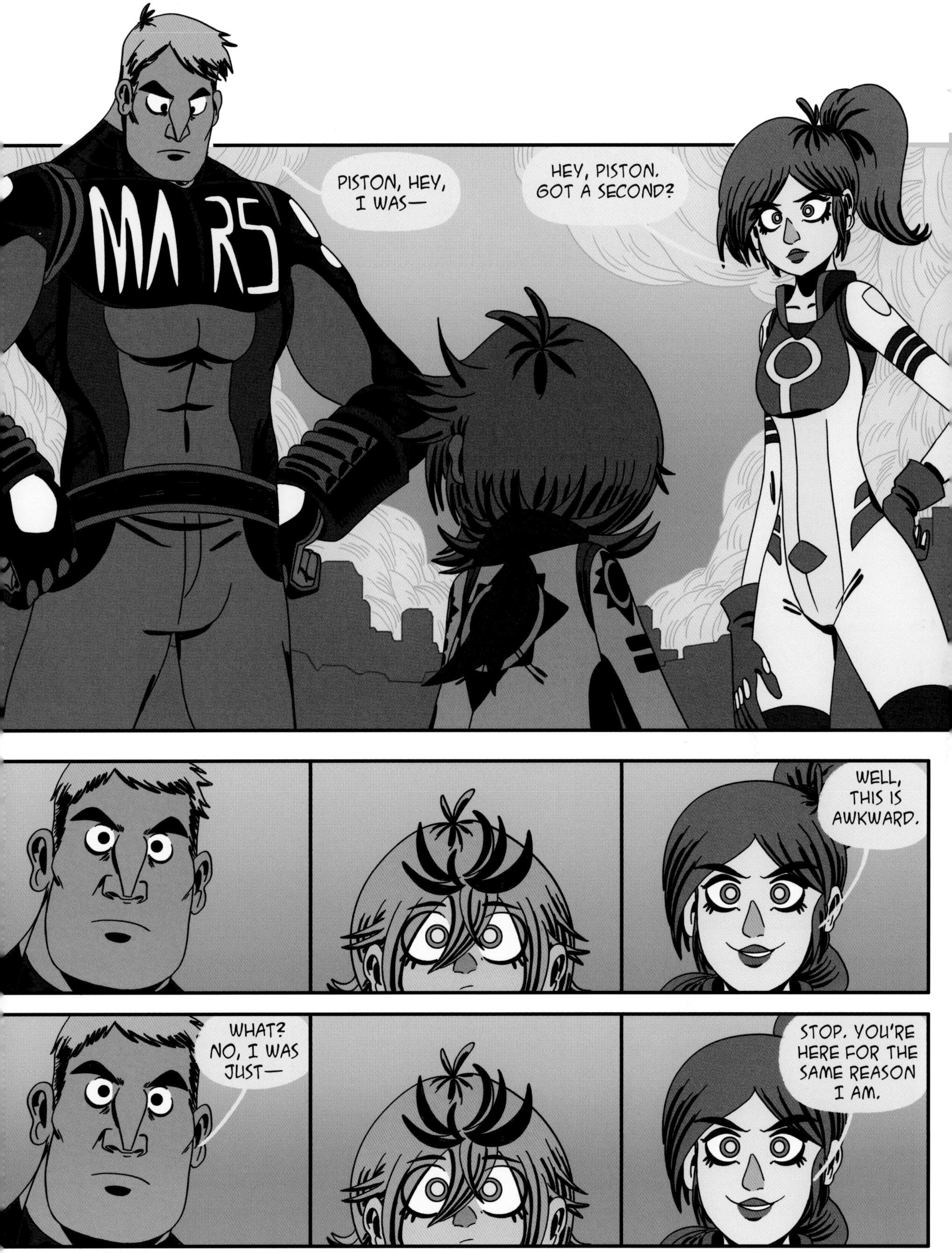
MARS
PISTON, HEY, I WAS—
HEY, PISTON. GOT A SECOND?
WELL, THIS IS AWKWARD.
WHAT? NO, I WAS JUST—
STOP. YOU'RE HERE FOR THE SAME REASON I AM.

WHICH IS...?

WELL, APPARENTLY MAGS IS TRYING TO POACH YOU FROM TEAM APOLLO FOR TEAM JUPITER. WHEREAS I WAS JUST GOING TO INVITE YOU TO COME BACK HOME TO TEAM MARS.

WHAT? BUT YOU—

I KNOW. BUT THAT WAS THEN. AND WATCHING YOU THESE PAST FEW WEEKS, I COULDN'T HELP REMEMBERING HOW WELL WE ALL WORKED, AS A TEAM, WHEN YOU WERE WITH US. ALMOST LIKE A FAMILY. AND I—

OH, FOR PITY'S SAKE. HOW DUMB DO YOU THINK SHE IS?

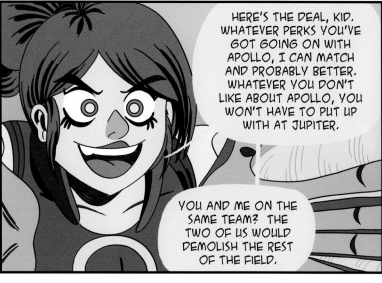

HERE'S THE DEAL, KID. WHATEVER PERKS YOU'VE GOT GOING ON WITH APOLLO, I CAN MATCH AND PROBABLY BETTER. WHATEVER YOU DON'T LIKE ABOUT APOLLO, YOU WON'T HAVE TO PUT UP WITH AT JUPITER.

YOU AND ME ON THE SAME TEAM? THE TWO OF US WOULD DEMOLISH THE REST OF THE FIELD.

WHAT ABOUT TACH AND TORQUE? WHO WOULD GO?

DOES IT MATTER? WHICHEVER DRIVER YOU WANT GONE IS HISTORY.

YOU AND AXL USED TO BE A THING, RIGHT?

THAT'S RIGHT.

WHY'D YOU BREAK UP?

NONE OF YOUR BUSINESS.

WELL, I CAN SEE WHY YOU WERE A COUPLE.

AND I CAN SEE WHY YOU'RE NOT ANYMORE.

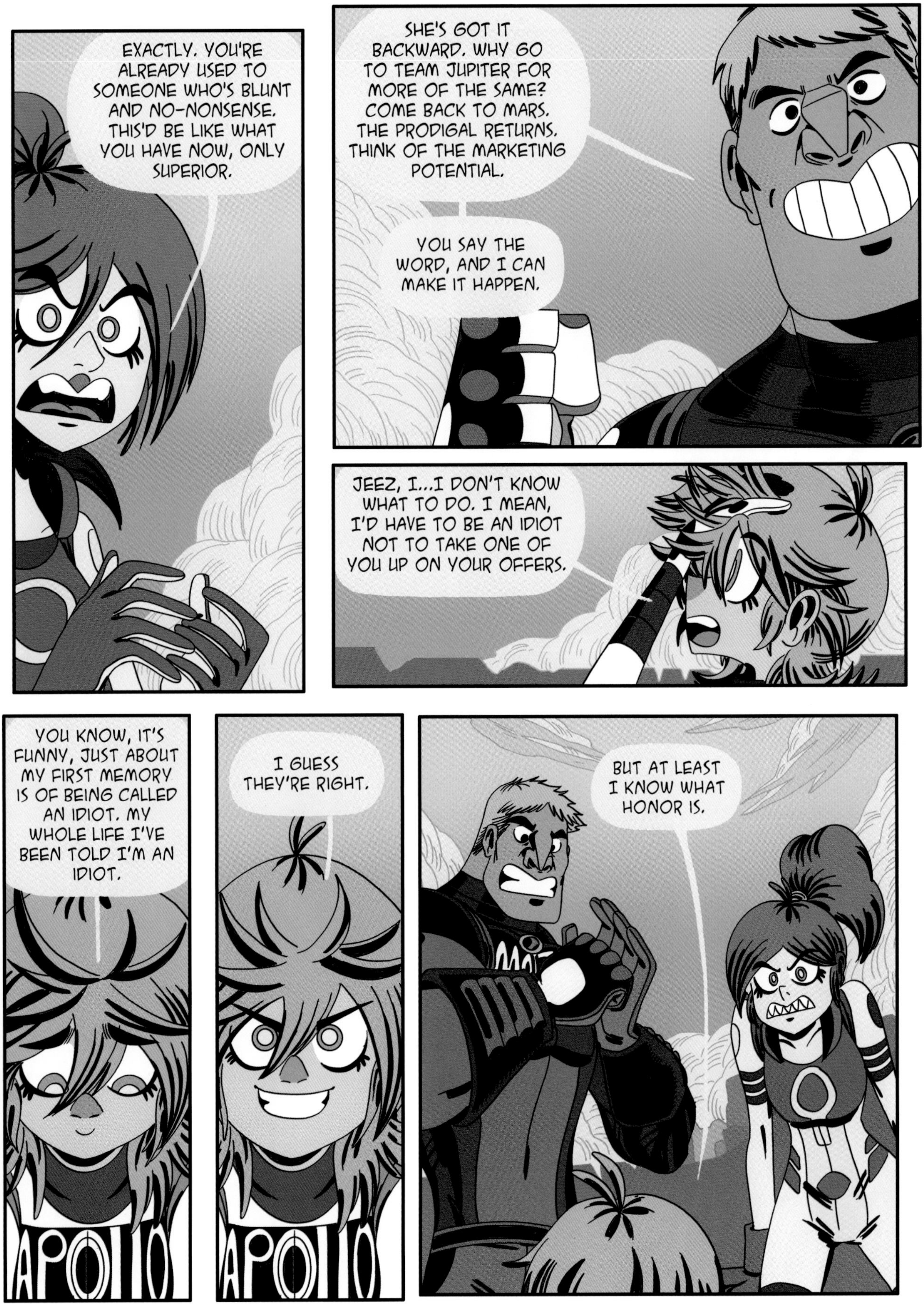
EXACTLY. YOU'RE ALREADY USED TO SOMEONE WHO'S BLUNT AND NO-NONSENSE. THIS'D BE LIKE WHAT YOU HAVE NOW, ONLY SUPERIOR.
SHE'S GOT IT BACKWARD. WHY GO TO TEAM JUPITER FOR MORE OF THE SAME? COME BACK TO MARS. THE PRODIGAL RETURNS. THINK OF THE MARKETING POTENTIAL.
YOU SAY THE WORD, AND I CAN MAKE IT HAPPEN.
JEEZ, I...I DON'T KNOW WHAT TO DO. I MEAN, I'D HAVE TO BE AN IDIOT NOT TO TAKE ONE OF YOU UP ON YOUR OFFERS.
YOU KNOW, IT'S FUNNY, JUST ABOUT MY FIRST MEMORY IS OF BEING CALLED AN IDIOT. MY WHOLE LIFE I'VE BEEN TOLD I'M AN IDIOT.
APOLLO
I GUESS THEY'RE RIGHT.
APOLLO
BUT AT LEAST I KNOW WHAT HONOR IS.

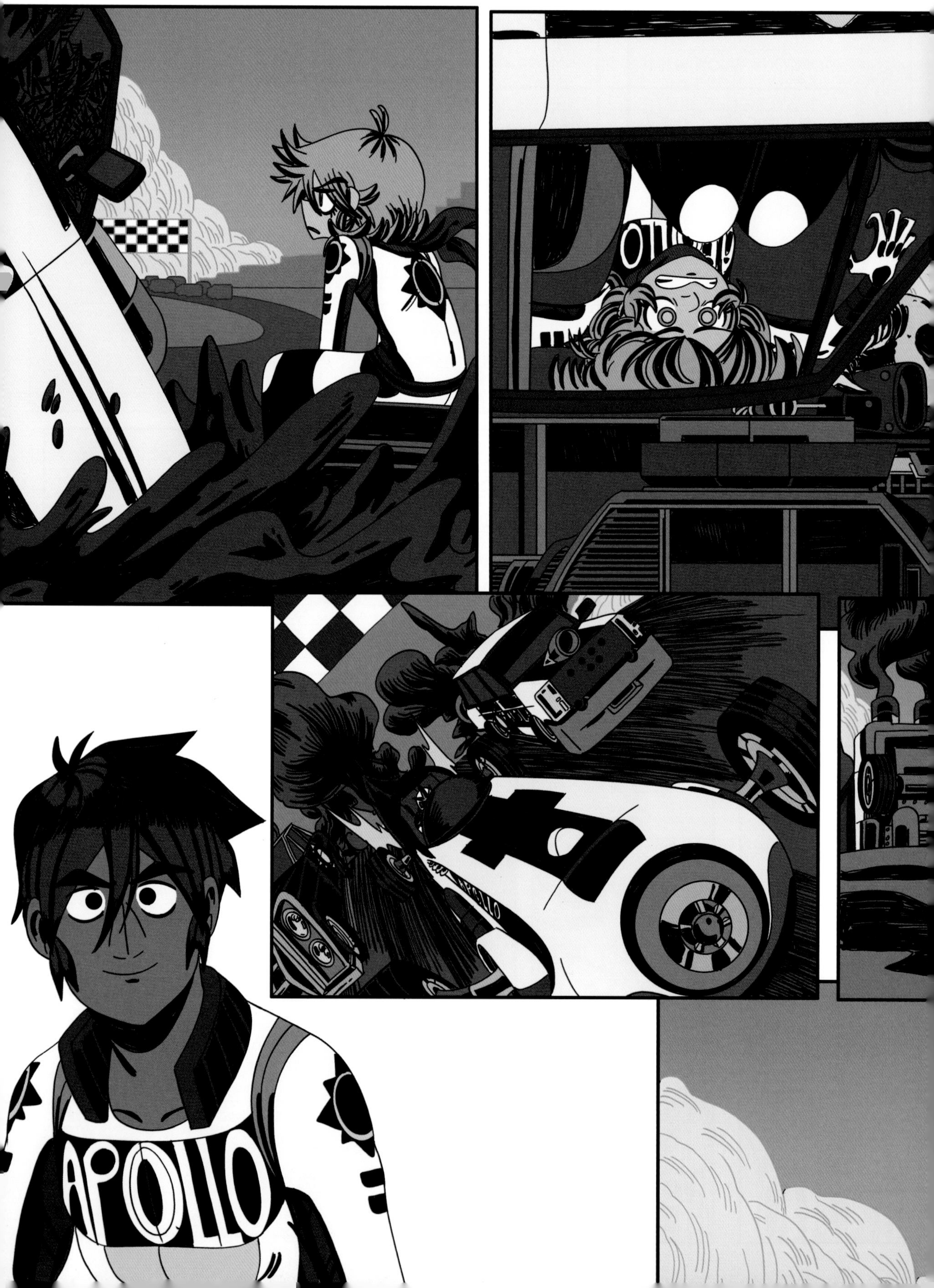
APOLLO

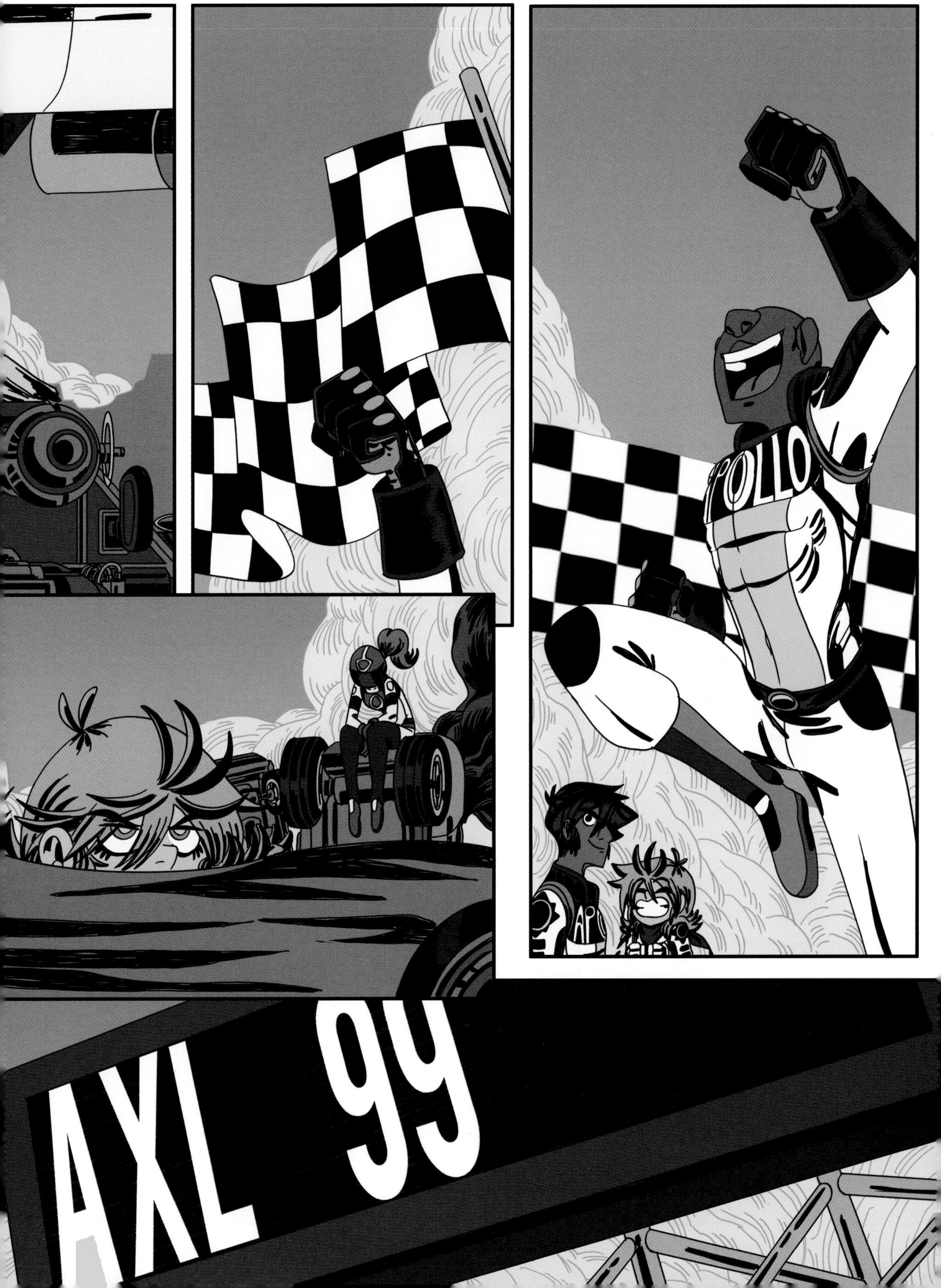
APOLLO
AXL 99

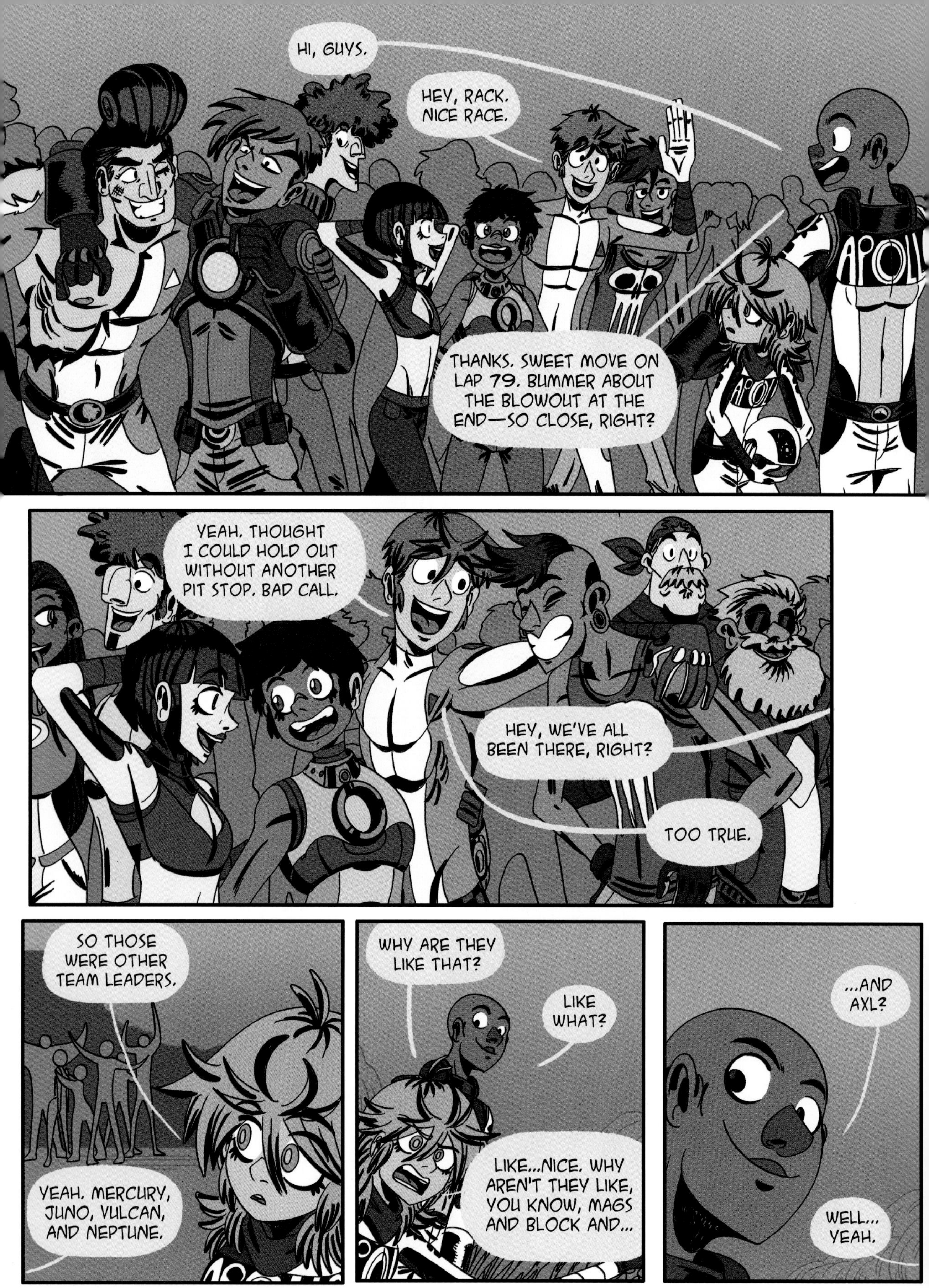
HI, GUYS.
HEY, RACK. NICE RACE.
THANKS. SWEET MOVE ON LAP 79. BUMMER ABOUT THE BLOWOUT AT THE END—SO CLOSE, RIGHT?
YEAH. THOUGHT I COULD HOLD OUT WITHOUT ANOTHER PIT STOP. BAD CALL.
HEY, WE'VE ALL BEEN THERE, RIGHT?
TOO TRUE.
SO THOSE WERE OTHER TEAM LEADERS.
YEAH. MERCURY, JUNO, VULCAN, AND NEPTUNE.
WHY ARE THEY LIKE THAT?
LIKE WHAT?
LIKE...NICE. WHY AREN'T THEY LIKE, YOU KNOW, MAGS AND BLOCK AND...
...AND AXL?
WELL... YEAH.

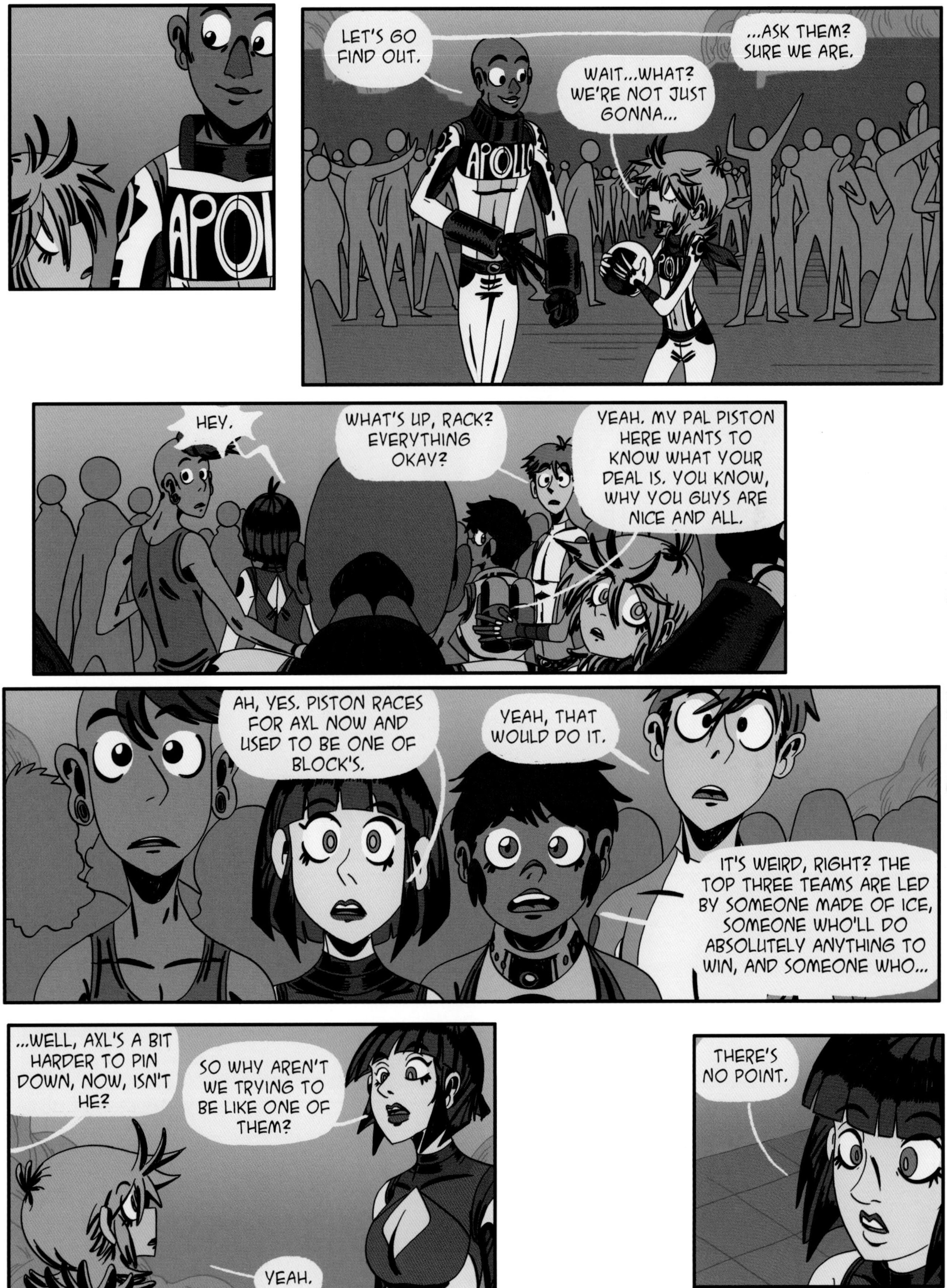
LET'S GO FIND OUT.
WAIT...WHAT? WE'RE NOT JUST GONNA...
...ASK THEM? SURE WE ARE.
HEY.
WHAT'S UP, RACK? EVERYTHING OKAY?
YEAH. MY PAL PISTON HERE WANTS TO KNOW WHAT YOUR DEAL IS. YOU KNOW, WHY YOU GUYS ARE NICE AND ALL.
AH, YES. PISTON RACES FOR AXL NOW AND USED TO BE ONE OF BLOCK'S.
YEAH, THAT WOULD DO IT.
IT'S WEIRD, RIGHT? THE TOP THREE TEAMS ARE LED BY SOMEONE MADE OF ICE, SOMEONE WHO'LL DO ABSOLUTELY ANYTHING TO WIN, AND SOMEONE WHO...
...WELL, AXL'S A BIT HARDER TO PIN DOWN, NOW, ISN'T HE?
SO WHY AREN'T WE TRYING TO BE LIKE ONE OF THEM?
YEAH.
THERE'S NO POINT.

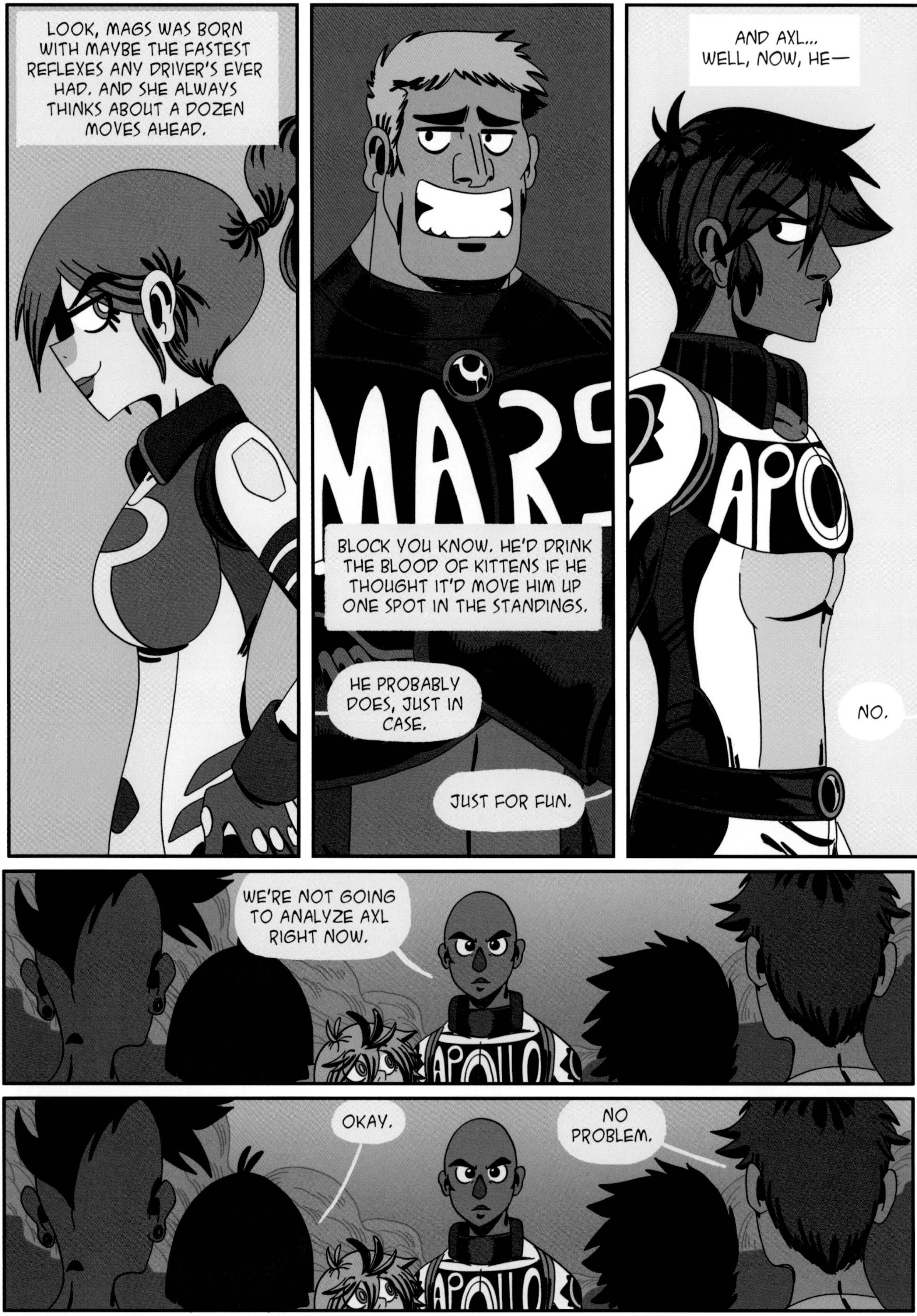
LOOK, MAGS WAS BORN WITH MAYBE THE FASTEST REFLEXES ANY DRIVER'S EVER HAD. AND SHE ALWAYS THINKS ABOUT A DOZEN MOVES AHEAD.
MARS
BLOCK YOU KNOW. HE'D DRINK THE BLOOD OF KITTENS IF HE THOUGHT IT'D MOVE HIM UP ONE SPOT IN THE STANDINGS.
HE PROBABLY DOES, JUST IN CASE.
JUST FOR FUN.
AND AXL... WELL, NOW, HE—
APO
NO.
WE'RE NOT GOING TO ANALYZE AXL RIGHT NOW.
APOLLO
OKAY.
NO PROBLEM.
APOLLO

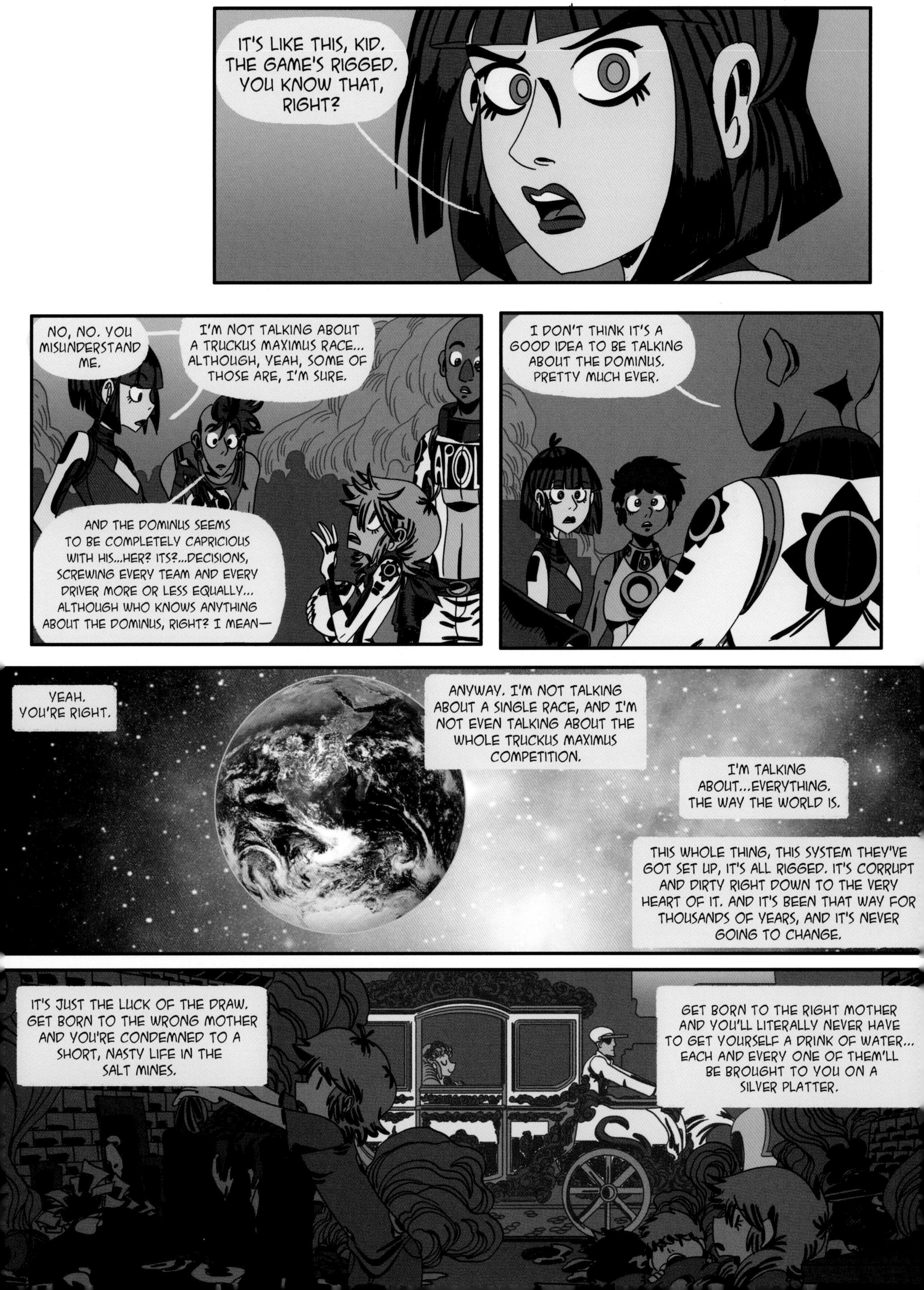
IT'S LIKE THIS, KID. THE GAME'S RIGGED. YOU KNOW THAT, RIGHT?
NO, NO. YOU MISUNDERSTAND ME.
I'M NOT TALKING ABOUT A TRUCKUS MAXIMUS RACE... ALTHOUGH, YEAH, SOME OF THOSE ARE, I'M SURE.
AND THE DOMINUS SEEMS TO BE COMPLETELY CAPRICIOUS WITH HIS...HER? ITS?...DECISIONS, SCREWING EVERY TEAM AND EVERY DRIVER MORE OR LESS EQUALLY... ALTHOUGH WHO KNOWS ANYTHING ABOUT THE DOMINUS, RIGHT? I MEAN—
I DON'T THINK IT'S A GOOD IDEA TO BE TALKING ABOUT THE DOMINUS. PRETTY MUCH EVER.
YEAH. YOU'RE RIGHT.
ANYWAY. I'M NOT TALKING ABOUT A SINGLE RACE, AND I'M NOT EVEN TALKING ABOUT THE WHOLE TRUCKUS MAXIMUS COMPETITION.
I'M TALKING ABOUT...EVERYTHING. THE WAY THE WORLD IS.
THIS WHOLE THING, THIS SYSTEM THEY'VE GOT SET UP, IT'S ALL RIGGED. IT'S CORRUPT AND DIRTY RIGHT DOWN TO THE VERY HEART OF IT. AND IT'S BEEN THAT WAY FOR THOUSANDS OF YEARS, AND IT'S NEVER GOING TO CHANGE.
IT'S JUST THE LUCK OF THE DRAW. GET BORN TO THE WRONG MOTHER AND YOU'RE CONDEMNED TO A SHORT, NASTY LIFE IN THE SALT MINES.
GET BORN TO THE RIGHT MOTHER AND YOU'LL LITERALLY NEVER HAVE TO GET YOURSELF A DRINK OF WATER... EACH AND EVERY ONE OF THEM'LL BE BROUGHT TO YOU ON A SILVER PLATTER.

THAT'S WHERE TRUCKUS MAXIMUS COMES IN.

WE'RE THE THING THAT KEEPS THE WORKING CLASS FROM PAYING ATTENTION TO HOW THEY'RE GETTING SCREWED, AND HOW THEIR GRANDPARENTS GOT SCREWED, AND HOW THEIR GRANDCHILDREN ARE GOING TO GET SCREWED.

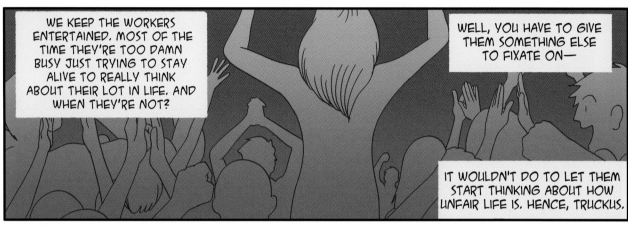

WE KEEP THE WORKERS ENTERTAINED. MOST OF THE TIME THEY'RE TOO DAMN BUSY JUST TRYING TO STAY ALIVE TO REALLY THINK ABOUT THEIR LOT IN LIFE. AND WHEN THEY'RE NOT?

WELL, YOU HAVE TO GIVE THEM SOMETHING ELSE TO FIXATE ON—

IT WOULDN'T DO TO LET THEM START THINKING ABOUT HOW UNFAIR LIFE IS. HENCE, TRUCKUS.

SO, US? WE'RE GOOD DRIVERS. WE'RE REALLY GOOD, BETTER THAN ALL BUT A TINY HANDFUL OF THOSE EVER BORN.

ESPECIALLY ME.

BUT WE'RE NEVER GOING TO BE BLOCK OR MAGS OR AXL.

WE DON'T HAVE IT IN US—WE WEREN'T BORN WITH THE THINGS THEY'VE GOT, THE REFLEXES, THE VISION, THE DRIVE, THE HUNGER. THE DIFFERENCES ARE TINY AND THEY MAKE ALL THE DIFFERENCE.

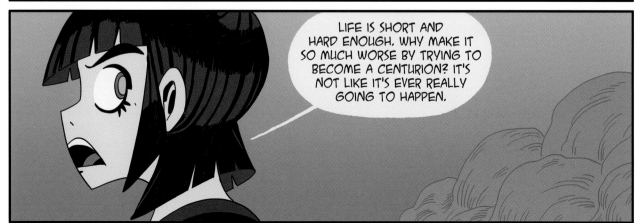

LIFE IS SHORT AND HARD ENOUGH. WHY MAKE IT SO MUCH WORSE BY TRYING TO BECOME A CENTURION? IT'S NOT LIKE IT'S EVER REALLY GOING TO HAPPEN.

WHAT? BUT... I THOUGHT AXL—

NOPE. NEVER. THAT'S NOTHING BUT A DREAM, DANGLED JUST OUT OF REACH, TO KEEP ALL OF US OCCUPIED, JUST LIKE WE KEEP THE PROLES DISTRACTED.

NO. I THINK AXL MIGHT DO IT.

NO. NO WAY. THE DOMINUS...HELL, THE EMPEROR— WON'T EVER LET THAT HAPPEN.

I THINK THEY MIGHT.

LOOK, WHAT WOULD BE BETTER ENTERTAINMENT... AND WHAT WOULD KEEP THE REST OF US HUNGRIER—THAN IF ONE OF US DID MAKE IT SOMEDAY?

I THINK IT'S IN THEIR BEST INTEREST TO LET ONE OF US WIN. AND, I MEAN, AXL'S ALREADY AT 99 WINS... HE ONLY NEEDS ONE MORE. HAS HE EVER EVEN GONE THREE OR FOUR RACES WITHOUT A WIN BEFORE?

DOESN'T MATTER. STILL NOT GONNA HAPPEN.

SO, THERE YOU GO, KID. THAT'S WHY WE'RE THE WAY WE ARE. WE TRY TO WIN, EVERY TIME...MAKE NO MISTAKE ABOUT THAT. WE TRY AND WE TRY HARD—HARD AS WE CAN.

BUT AT SOME POINT YOU REALIZE THERE'S JUST NO POINT IN MAKING THAT THE ENTIRE FOCUS OF OUR LIVES. WE'RE NOT GOING TO WIN IT ALL. WE'D LOVE TO. BUT WE WON'T.

SO IF EACH OF US GETS EVEN A FEW MORE YEARS HERE, WE'LL CONSIDER OURSELVES LUCKY.

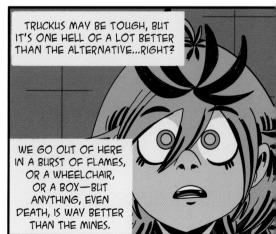

TRUCKUS MAY BE TOUGH, BUT IT'S ONE HELL OF A LOT BETTER THAN THE ALTERNATIVE...RIGHT?

WE GO OUT OF HERE IN A BURST OF FLAMES, OR A WHEELCHAIR, OR A BOX—BUT ANYTHING, EVEN DEATH, IS WAY BETTER THAN THE MINES.

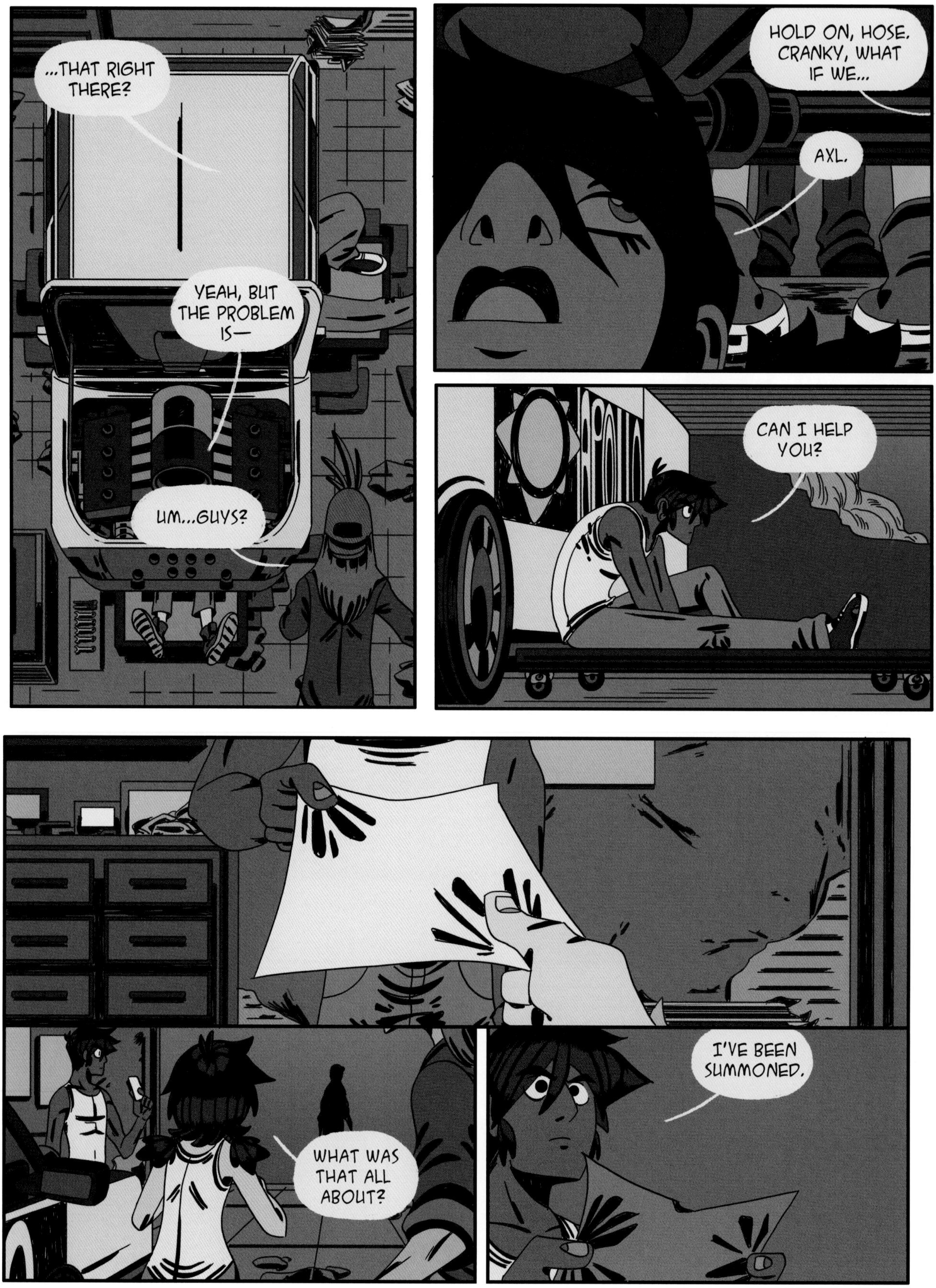
...THAT RIGHT THERE?
YEAH, BUT THE PROBLEM IS—
UM...GUYS?
HOLD ON, HOSE. CRANKY, WHAT IF WE...
AXL.
CAN I HELP YOU?
APOLLO
WHAT WAS THAT ALL ABOUT?
I'VE BEEN SUMMONED.

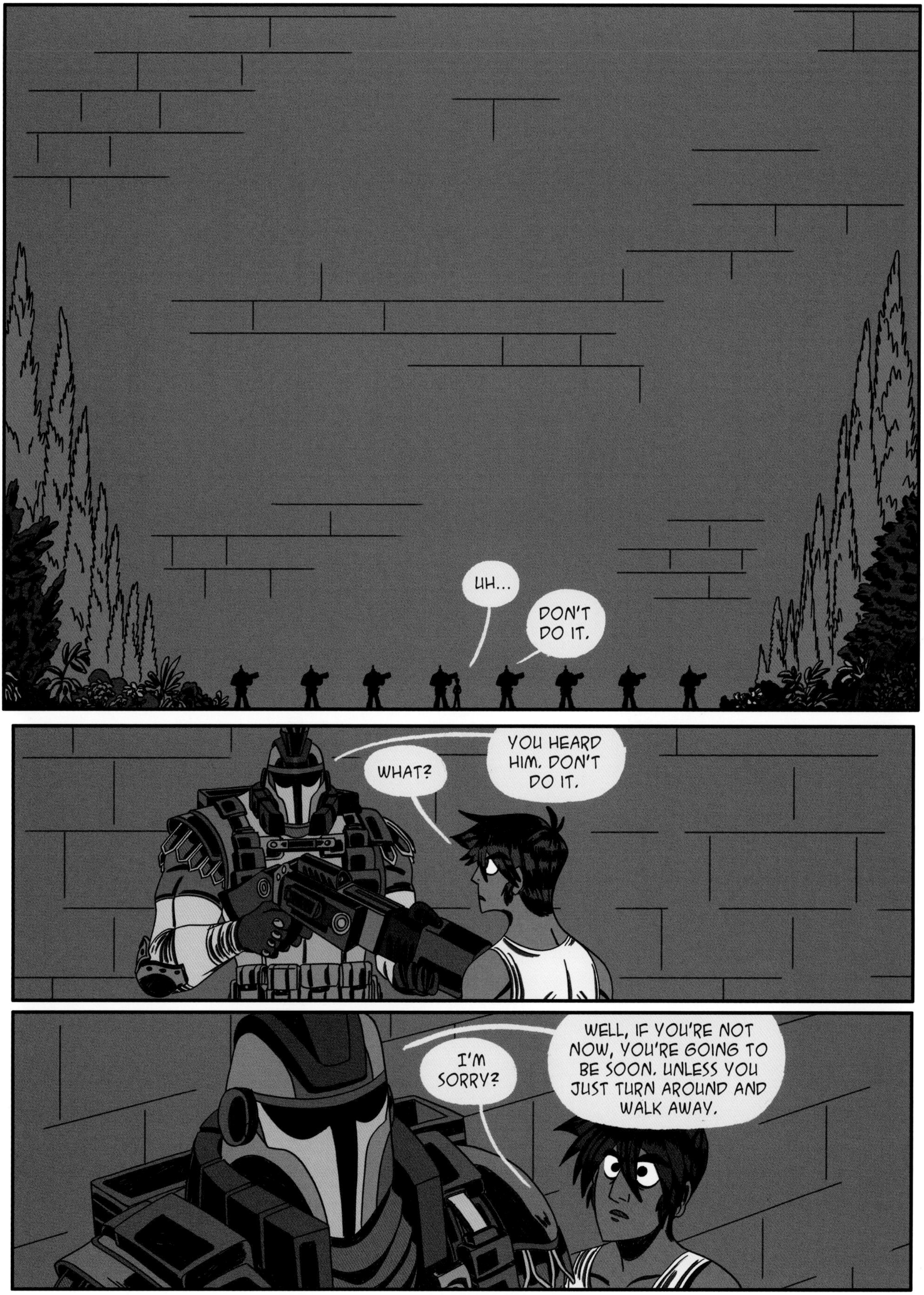
UH...
DON'T DO IT.
WHAT?
YOU HEARD HIM. DON'T DO IT.
I'M SORRY?
WELL, IF YOU'RE NOT NOW, YOU'RE GOING TO BE SOON. UNLESS YOU JUST TURN AROUND AND WALK AWAY.

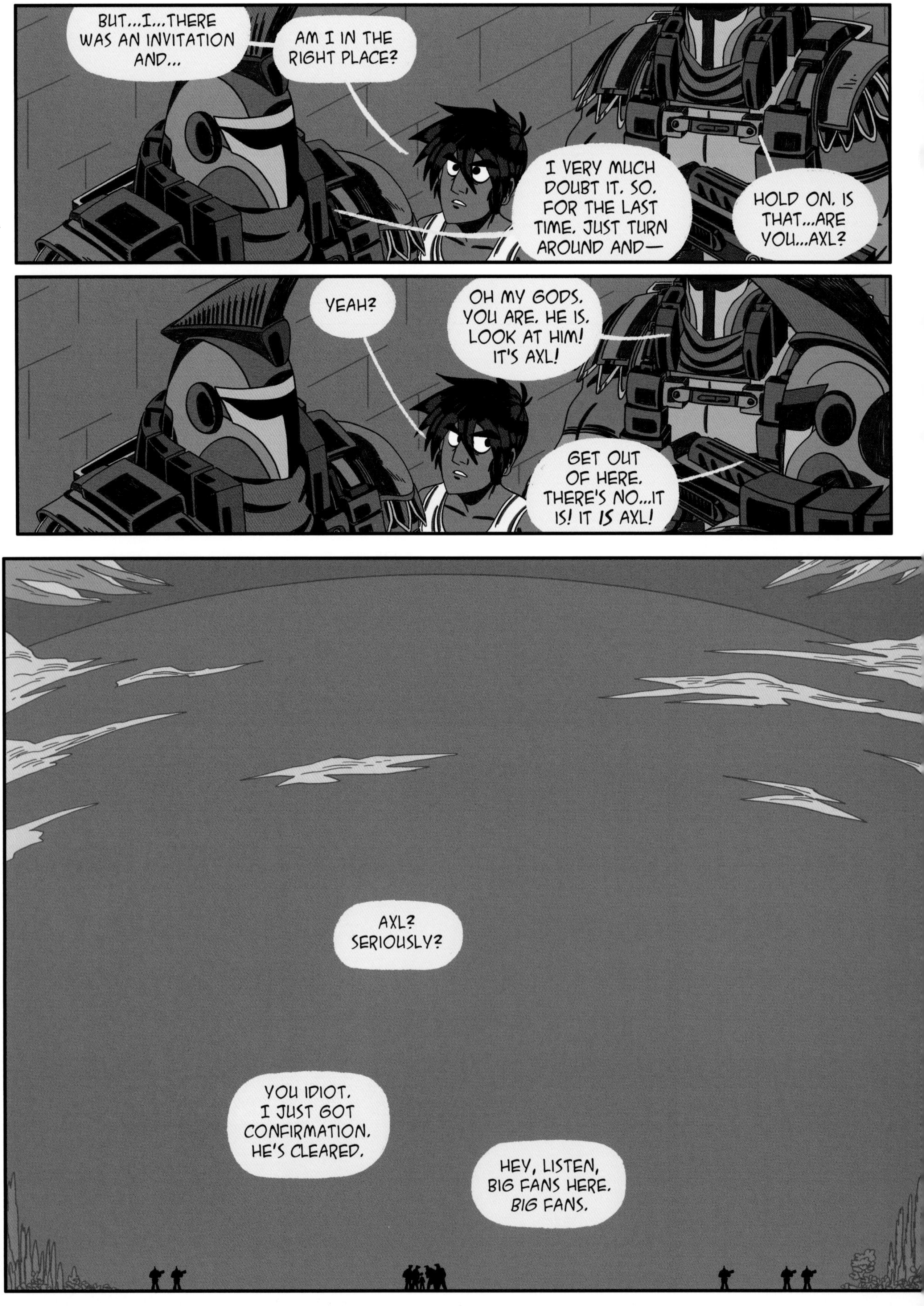
BUT...I...THERE WAS AN INVITATION AND...
AM I IN THE RIGHT PLACE?
I VERY MUCH DOUBT IT. SO, FOR THE LAST TIME, JUST TURN AROUND AND—
HOLD ON, IS THAT...ARE YOU...AXL?
YEAH?
OH MY GODS, YOU ARE. HE IS. LOOK AT HIM! IT'S AXL!
GET OUT OF HERE. THERE'S NO...IT IS! IT **IS** AXL!
AXL? SERIOUSLY?
YOU IDIOT. I JUST GOT CONFIRMATION. HE'S CLEARED.
HEY, LISTEN, BIG FANS HERE. BIG FANS.

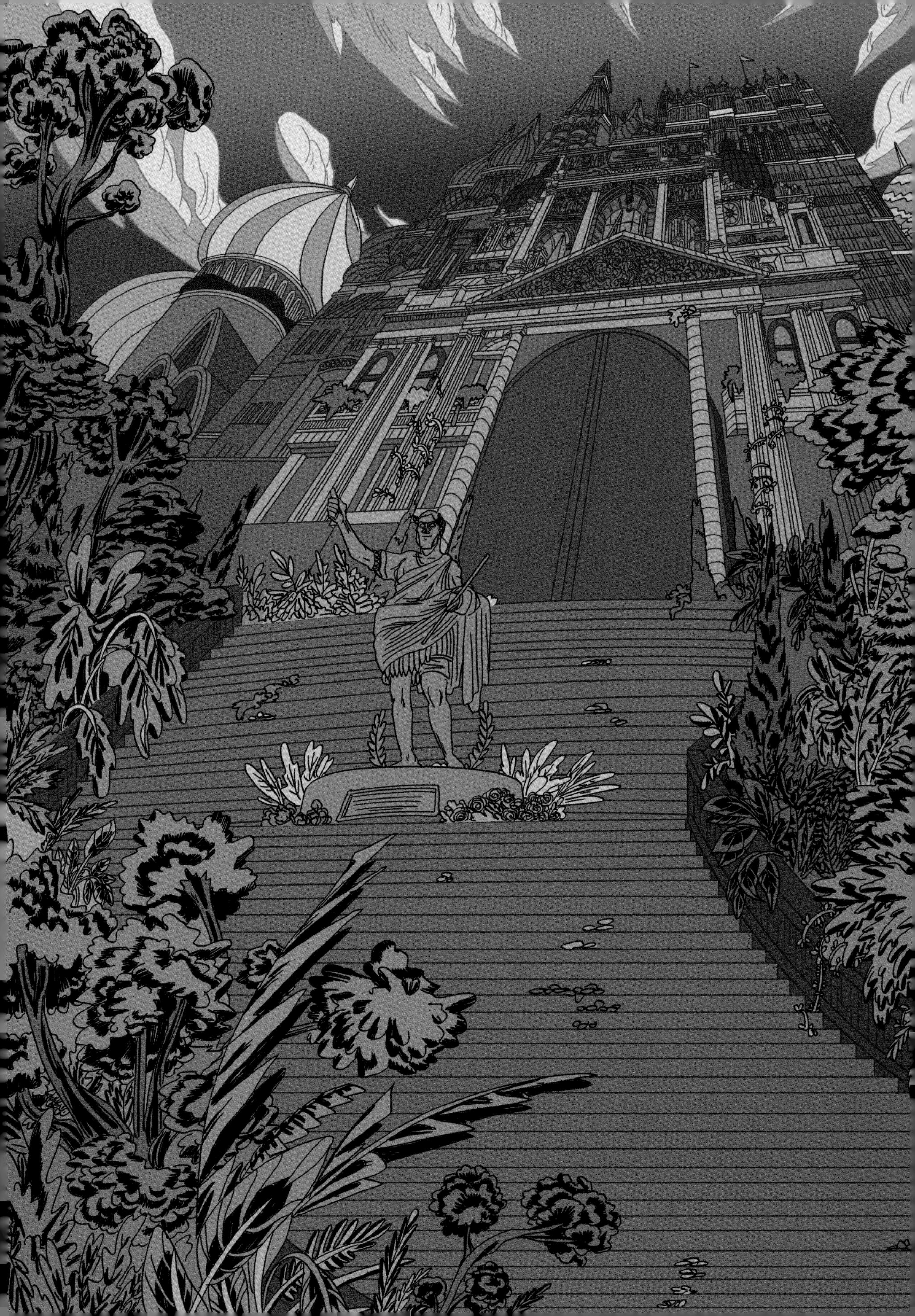

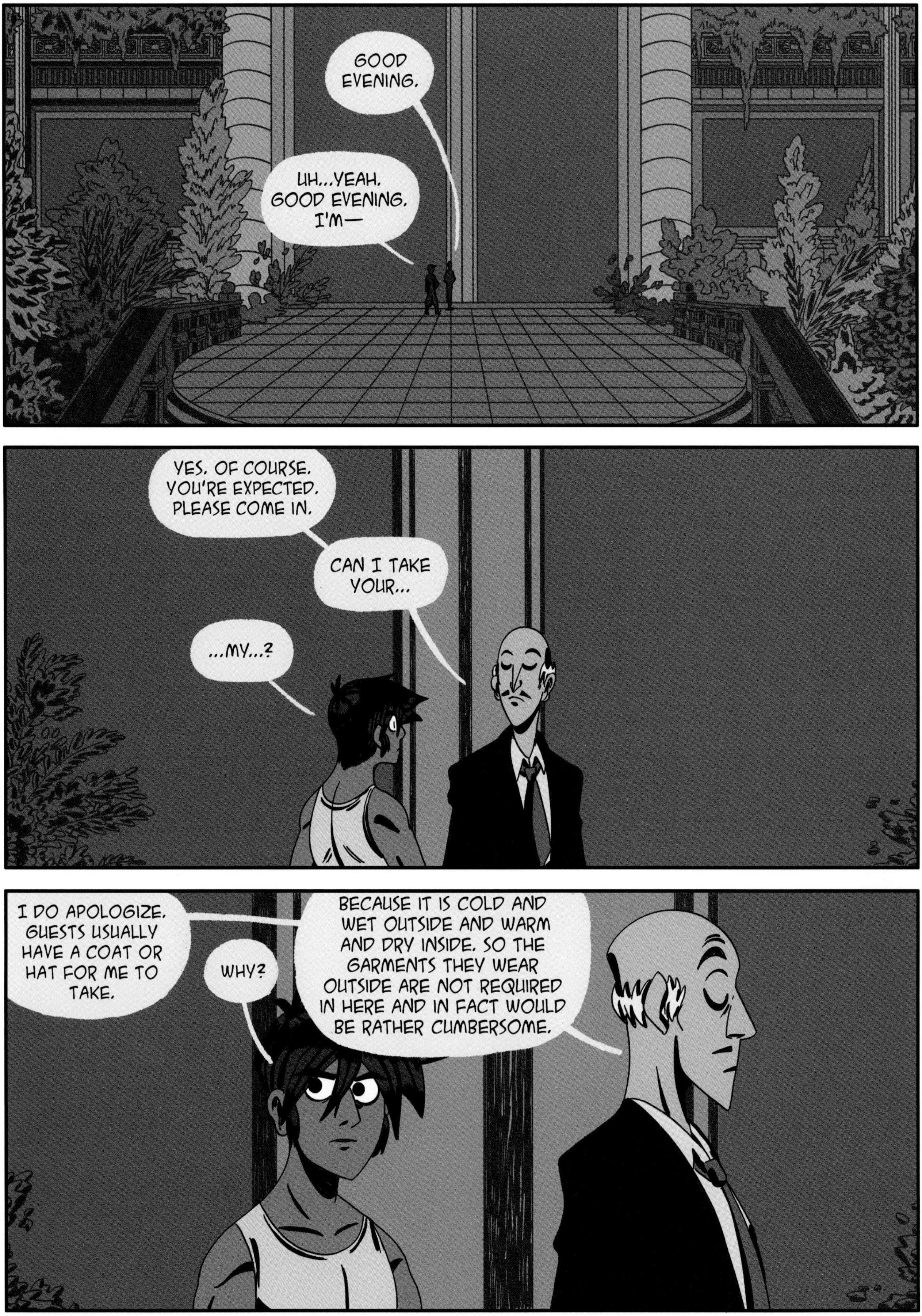
GOOD EVENING.
UH...YEAH. GOOD EVENING. I'M—
YES. OF COURSE. YOU'RE EXPECTED. PLEASE COME IN.
CAN I TAKE YOUR...
...MY...?
I DO APOLOGIZE. GUESTS USUALLY HAVE A COAT OR HAT FOR ME TO TAKE.
WHY?
BECAUSE IT IS COLD AND WET OUTSIDE AND WARM AND DRY INSIDE. SO THE GARMENTS THEY WEAR OUTSIDE ARE NOT REQUIRED IN HERE AND IN FACT WOULD BE RATHER CUMBERSOME.

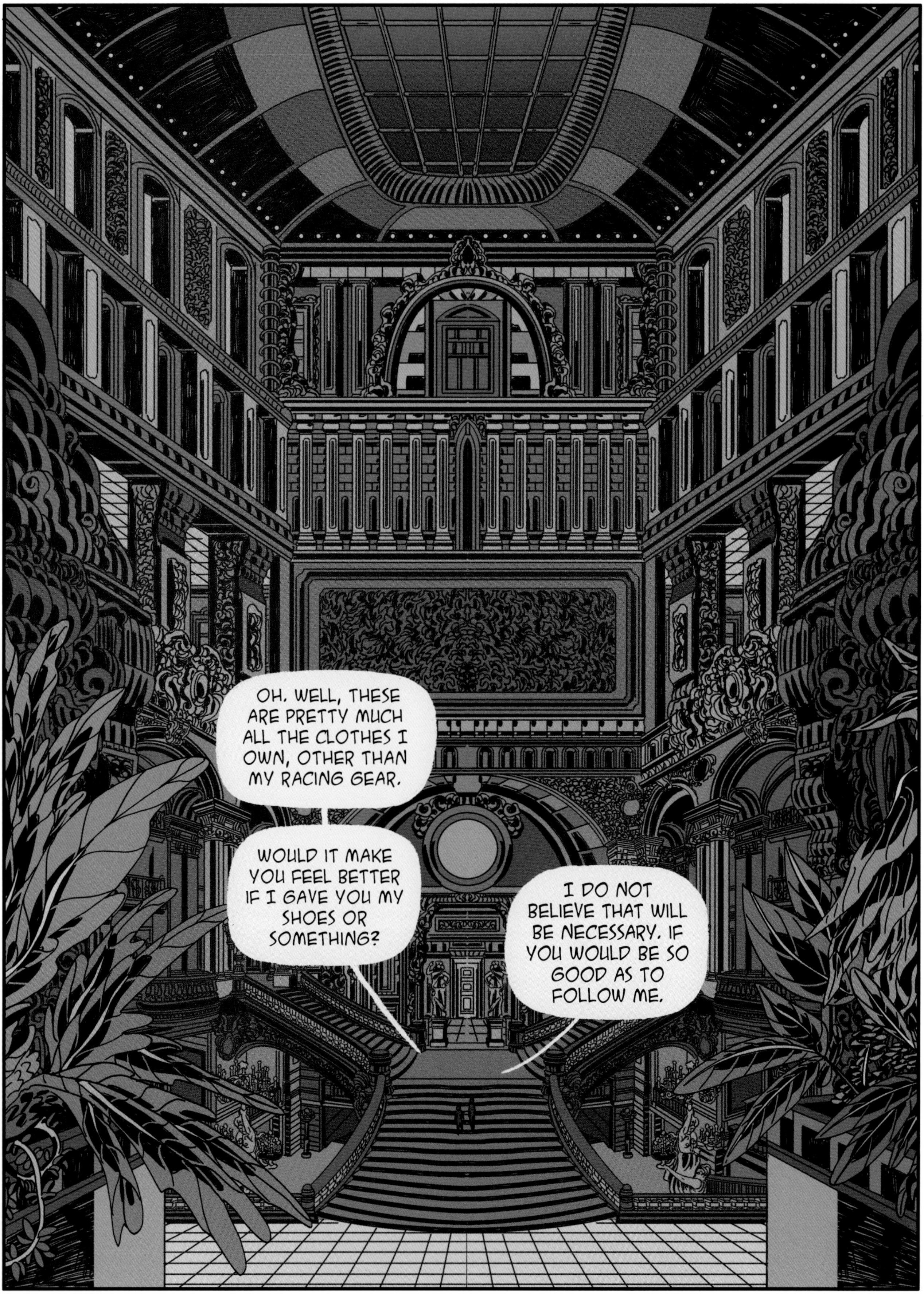
OH. WELL, THESE ARE PRETTY MUCH ALL THE CLOTHES I OWN, OTHER THAN MY RACING GEAR.
WOULD IT MAKE YOU FEEL BETTER IF I GAVE YOU MY SHOES OR SOMETHING?
I DO NOT BELIEVE THAT WILL BE NECESSARY. IF YOU WOULD BE SO GOOD AS TO FOLLOW ME.

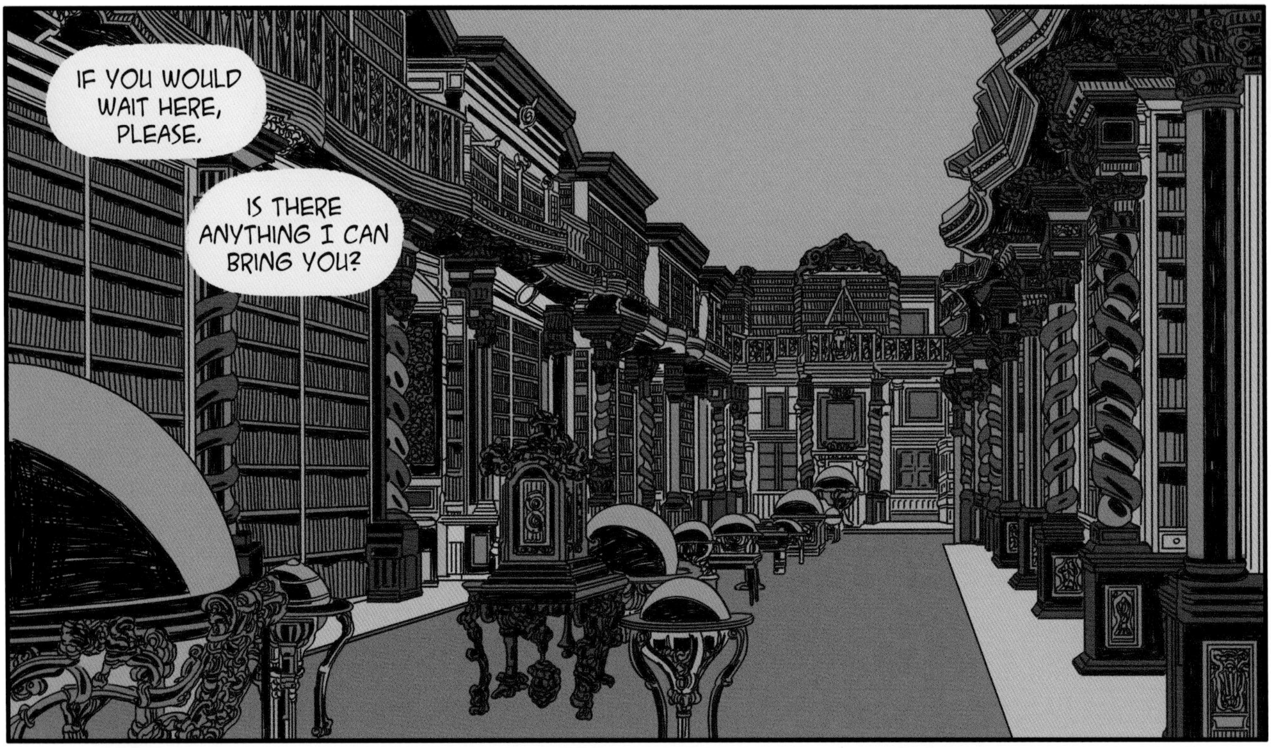
IF YOU WOULD WAIT HERE, PLEASE.
IS THERE ANYTHING I CAN BRING YOU?

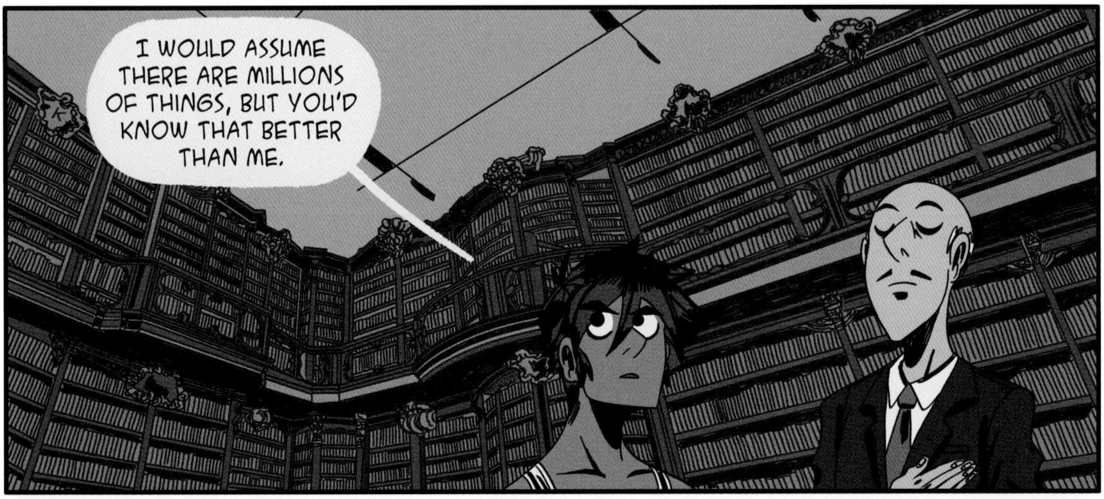
I WOULD ASSUME THERE ARE MILLIONS OF THINGS, BUT YOU'D KNOW THAT BETTER THAN ME.

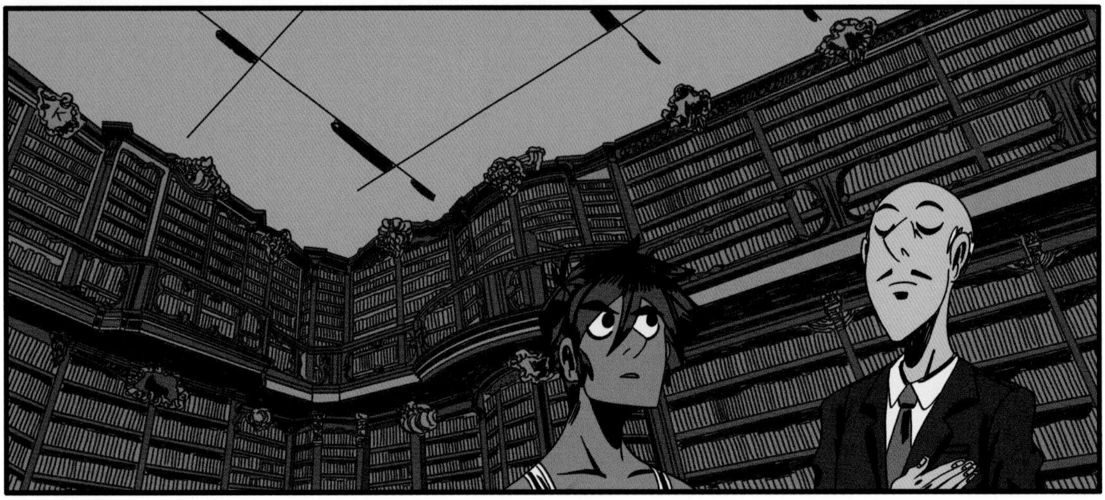

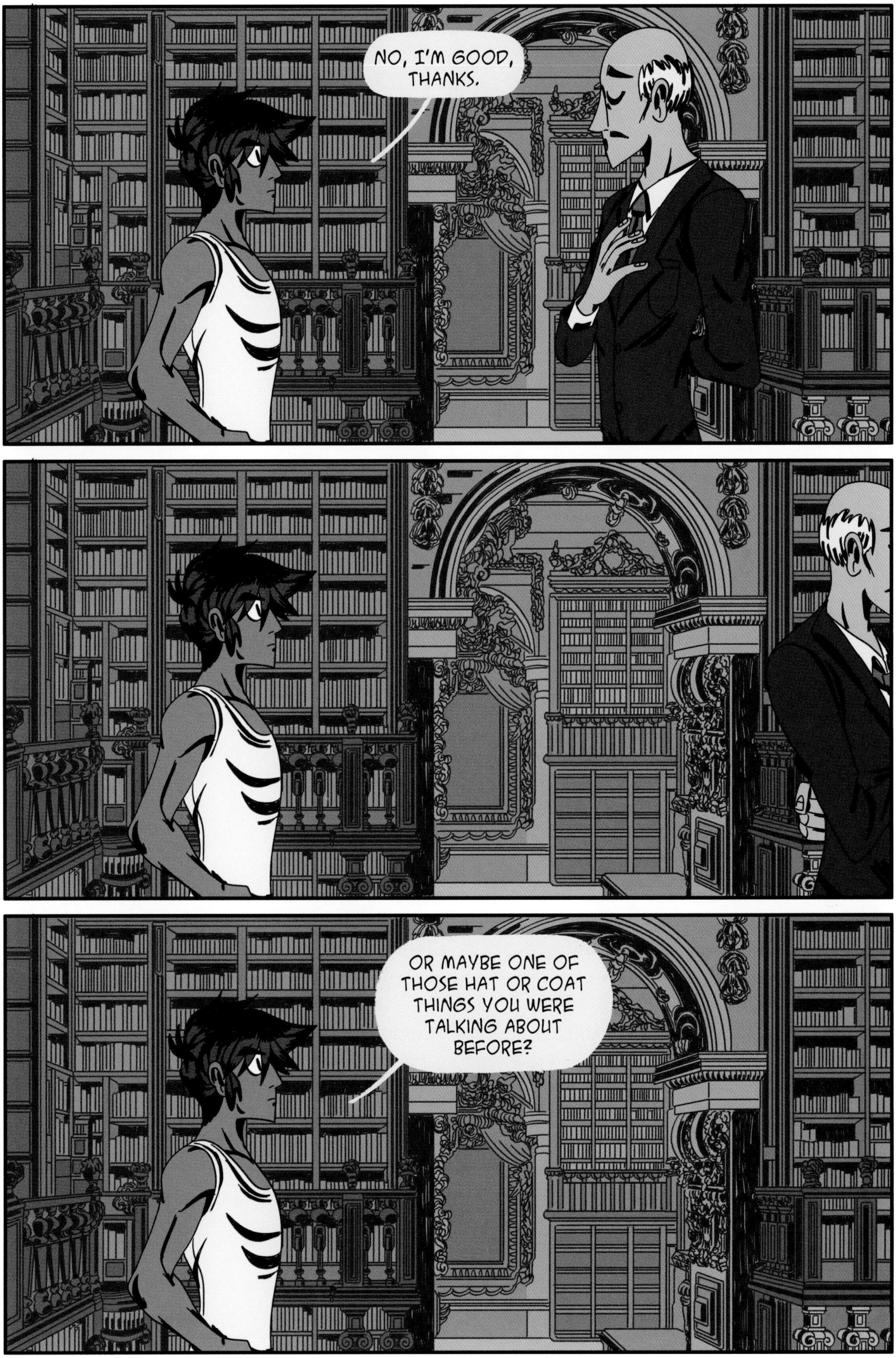
NO, I'M GOOD, THANKS.
OR MAYBE ONE OF THOSE HAT OR COAT THINGS YOU WERE TALKING ABOUT BEFORE?

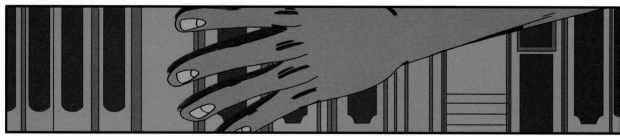

MAGNIFICENT THINGS, AREN'T THEY?

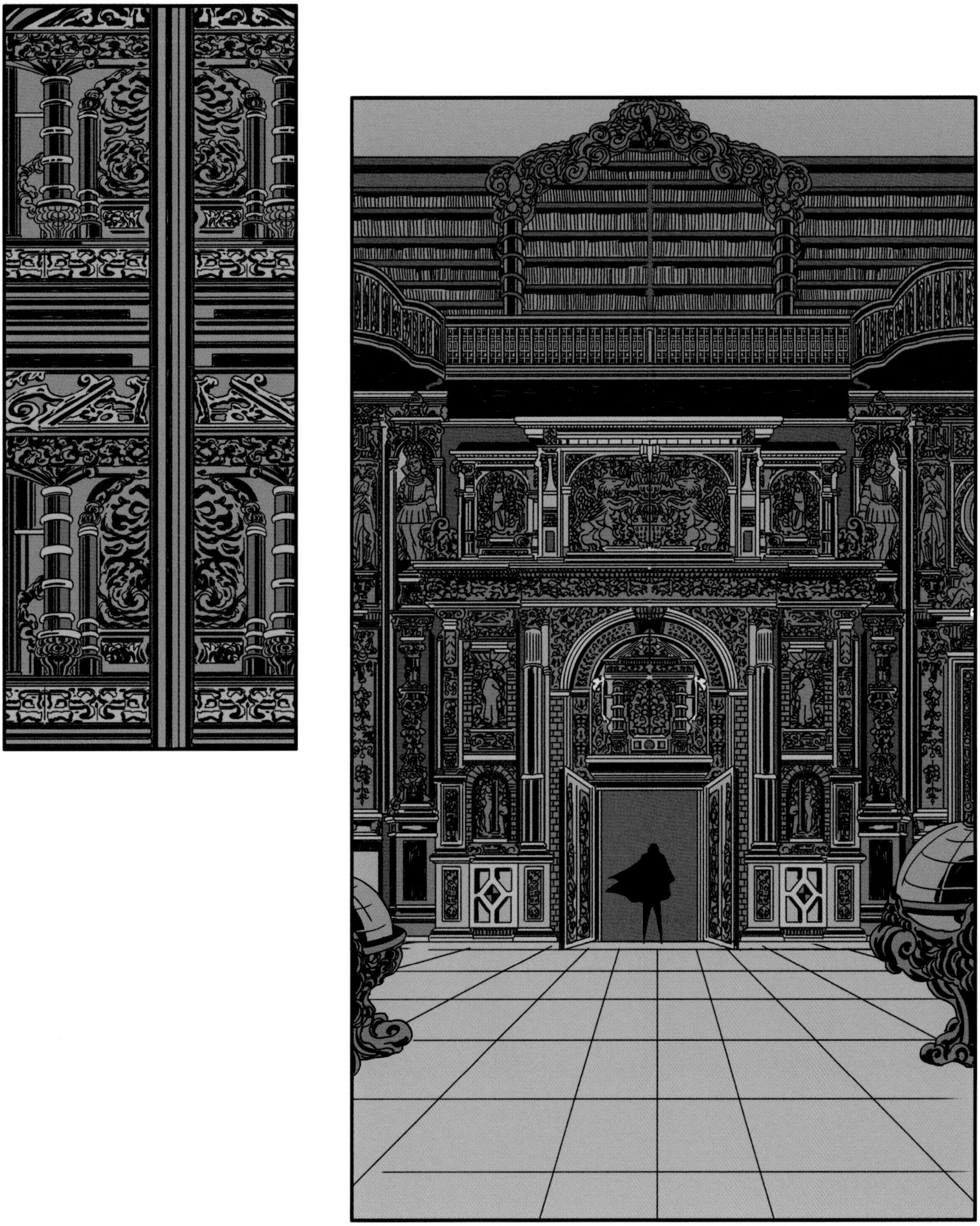

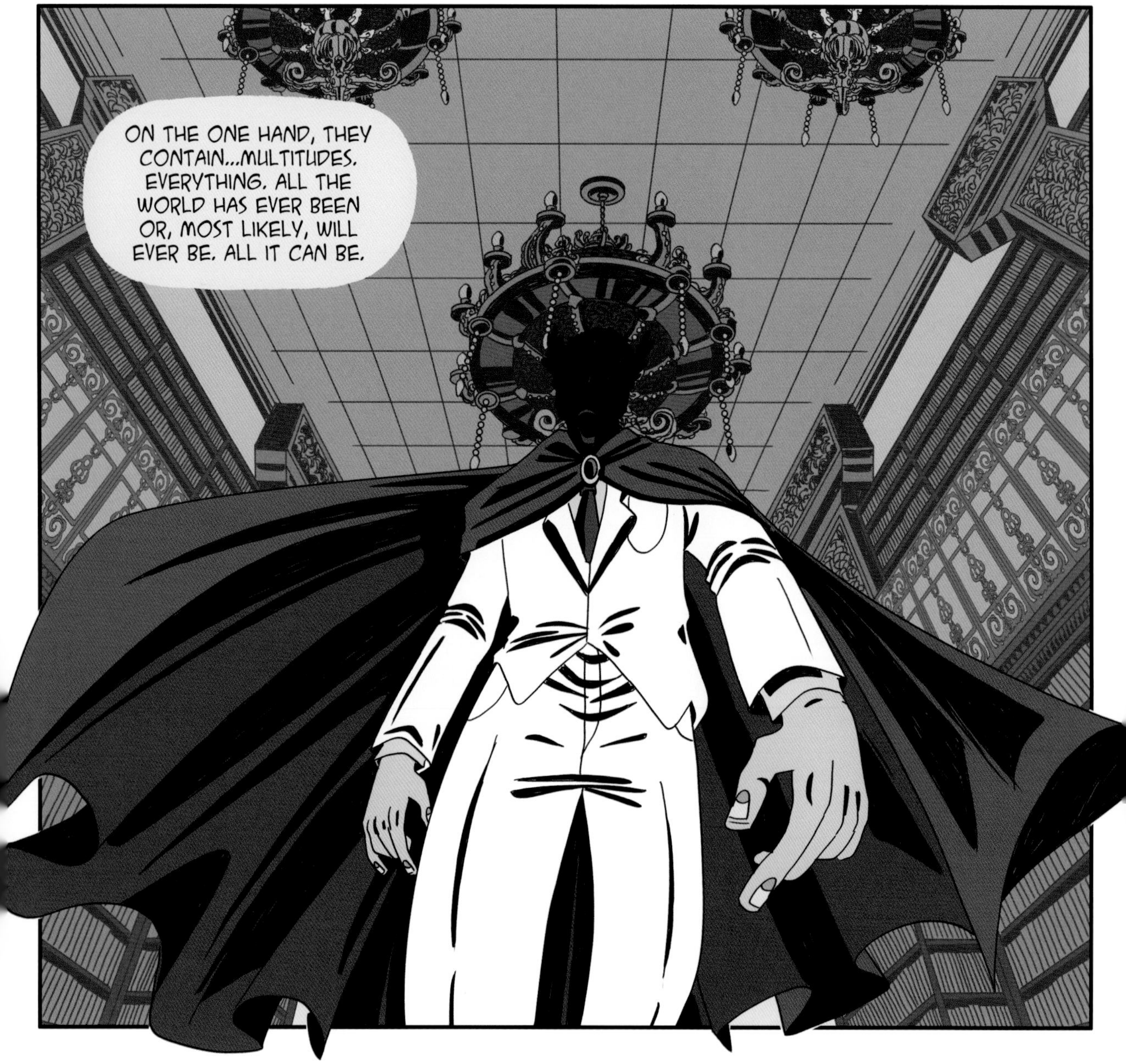
ON THE ONE HAND, THEY CONTAIN...MULTITUDES. EVERYTHING. ALL THE WORLD HAS EVER BEEN OR, MOST LIKELY, WILL EVER BE. ALL IT CAN BE.

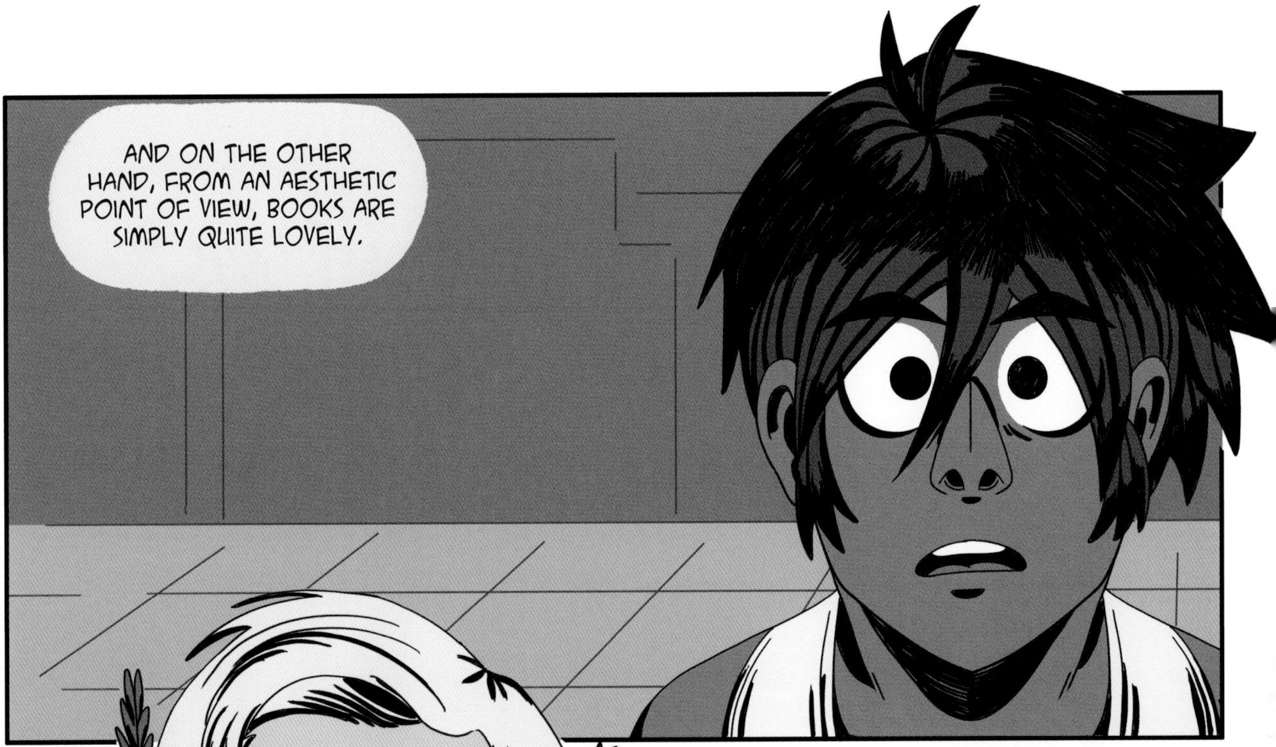
AND ON THE OTHER HAND, FROM AN AESTHETIC POINT OF VIEW, BOOKS ARE SIMPLY QUITE LOVELY.

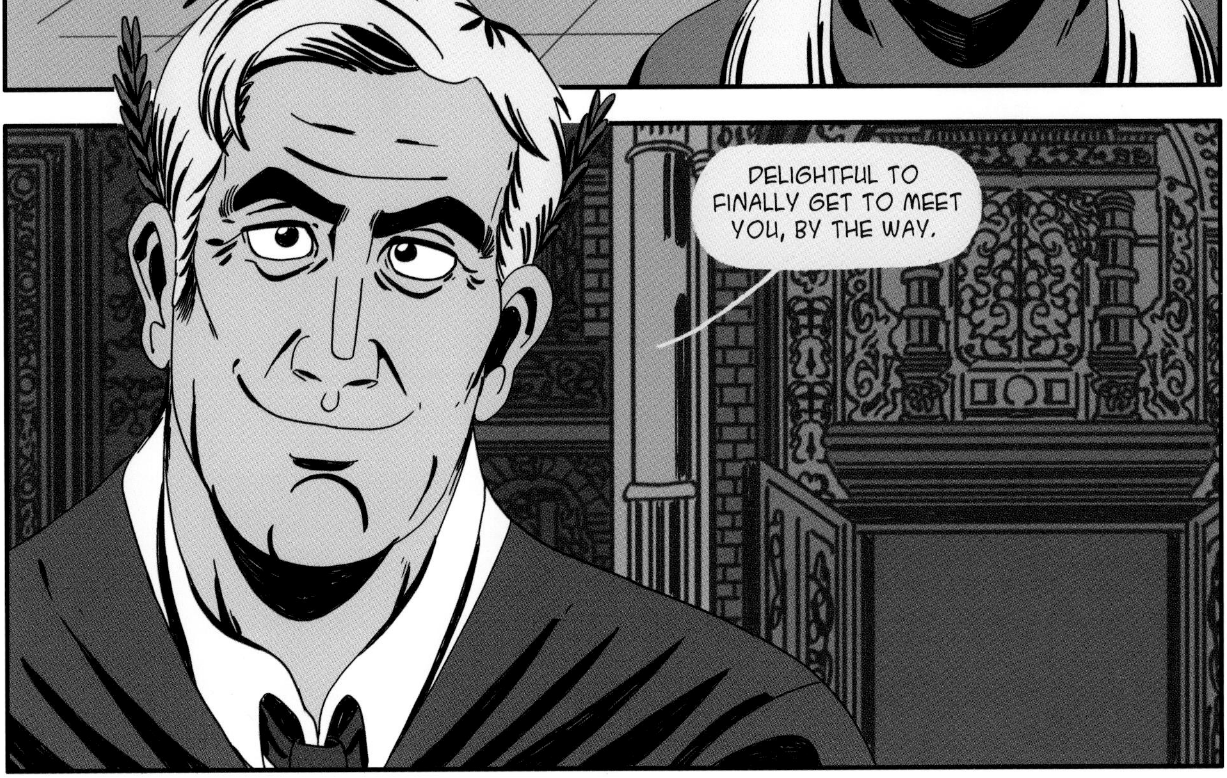
DELIGHTFUL TO FINALLY GET TO MEET YOU, BY THE WAY.

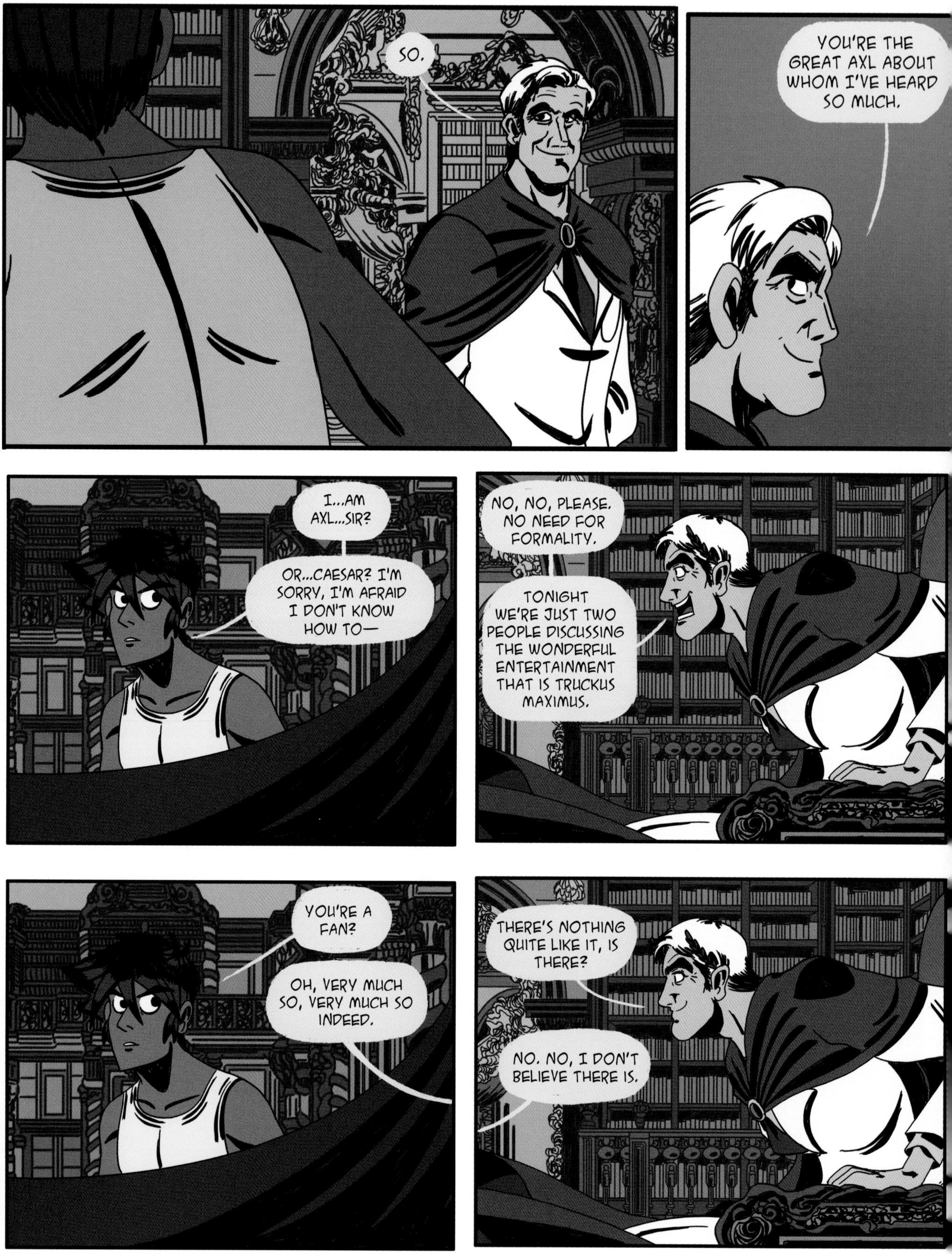
SO.
YOU'RE THE GREAT AXL ABOUT WHOM I'VE HEARD SO MUCH.
I...AM AXL...SIR?
OR...CAESAR? I'M SORRY, I'M AFRAID I DON'T KNOW HOW TO—
NO, NO, PLEASE. NO NEED FOR FORMALITY.
TONIGHT WE'RE JUST TWO PEOPLE DISCUSSING THE WONDERFUL ENTERTAINMENT THAT IS TRUCKUS MAXIMUS.
YOU'RE A FAN?
OH, VERY MUCH SO, VERY MUCH SO INDEED.
THERE'S NOTHING QUITE LIKE IT, IS THERE?
NO. NO, I DON'T BELIEVE THERE IS.

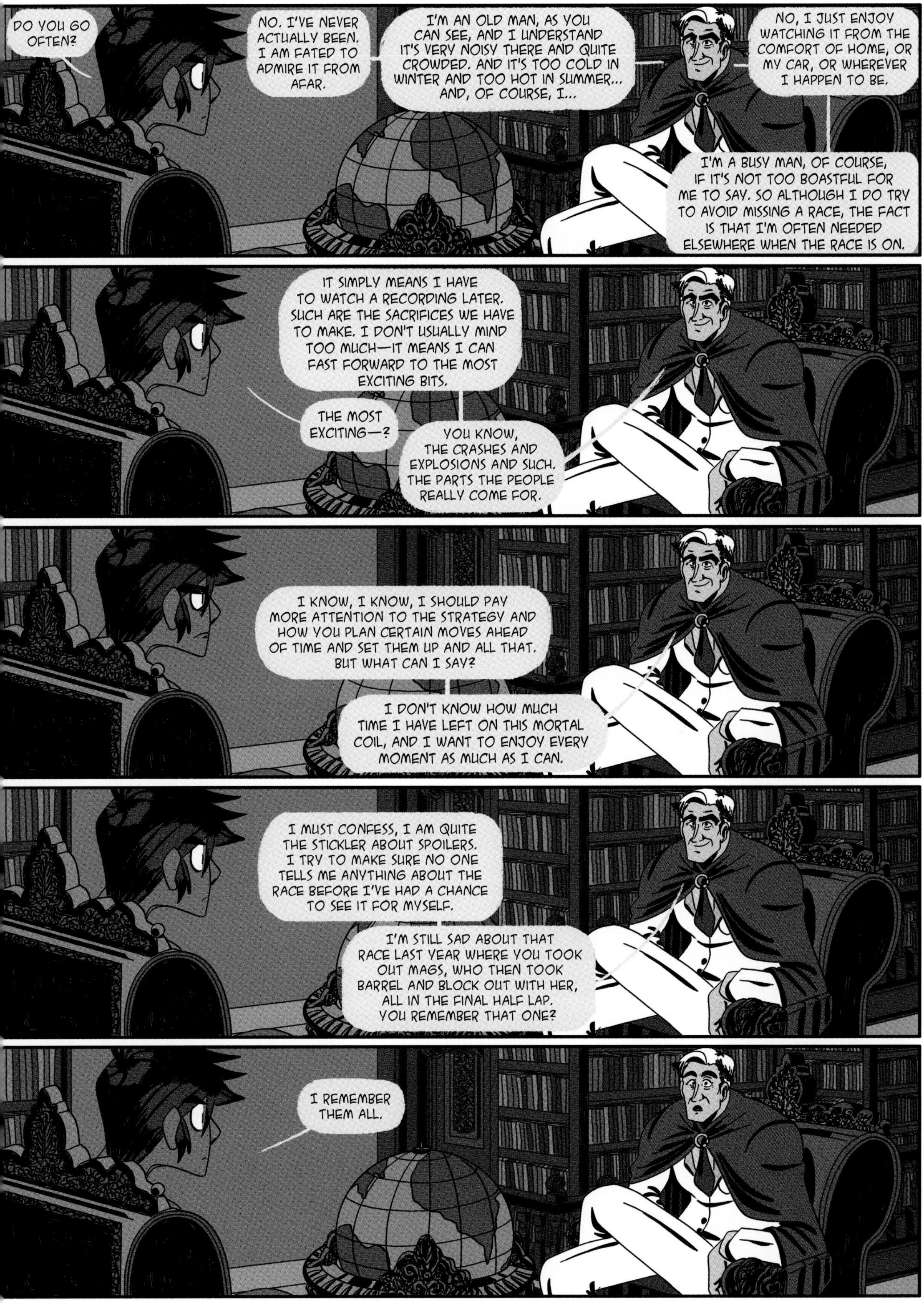
DO YOU GO OFTEN?
NO. I'VE NEVER ACTUALLY BEEN. I AM FATED TO ADMIRE IT FROM AFAR.
I'M AN OLD MAN, AS YOU CAN SEE, AND I UNDERSTAND IT'S VERY NOISY THERE AND QUITE CROWDED. AND IT'S TOO COLD IN WINTER AND TOO HOT IN SUMMER... AND, OF COURSE, I...
NO, I JUST ENJOY WATCHING IT FROM THE COMFORT OF HOME, OR MY CAR, OR WHEREVER I HAPPEN TO BE.
I'M A BUSY MAN, OF COURSE, IF IT'S NOT TOO BOASTFUL FOR ME TO SAY. SO ALTHOUGH I DO TRY TO AVOID MISSING A RACE, THE FACT IS THAT I'M OFTEN NEEDED ELSEWHERE WHEN THE RACE IS ON.
IT SIMPLY MEANS I HAVE TO WATCH A RECORDING LATER. SUCH ARE THE SACRIFICES WE HAVE TO MAKE. I DON'T USUALLY MIND TOO MUCH—IT MEANS I CAN FAST FORWARD TO THE MOST EXCITING BITS.
THE MOST EXCITING—?
YOU KNOW, THE CRASHES AND EXPLOSIONS AND SUCH. THE PARTS THE PEOPLE REALLY COME FOR.
I KNOW, I KNOW, I SHOULD PAY MORE ATTENTION TO THE STRATEGY AND HOW YOU PLAN CERTAIN MOVES AHEAD OF TIME AND SET THEM UP AND ALL THAT. BUT WHAT CAN I SAY?
I DON'T KNOW HOW MUCH TIME I HAVE LEFT ON THIS MORTAL COIL, AND I WANT TO ENJOY EVERY MOMENT AS MUCH AS I CAN.
I MUST CONFESS, I AM QUITE THE STICKLER ABOUT SPOILERS. I TRY TO MAKE SURE NO ONE TELLS ME ANYTHING ABOUT THE RACE BEFORE I'VE HAD A CHANCE TO SEE IT FOR MYSELF.
I'M STILL SAD ABOUT THAT RACE LAST YEAR WHERE YOU TOOK OUT MAGS, WHO THEN TOOK BARREL AND BLOCK OUT WITH HER, ALL IN THE FINAL HALF LAP. YOU REMEMBER THAT ONE?
I REMEMBER THEM ALL.

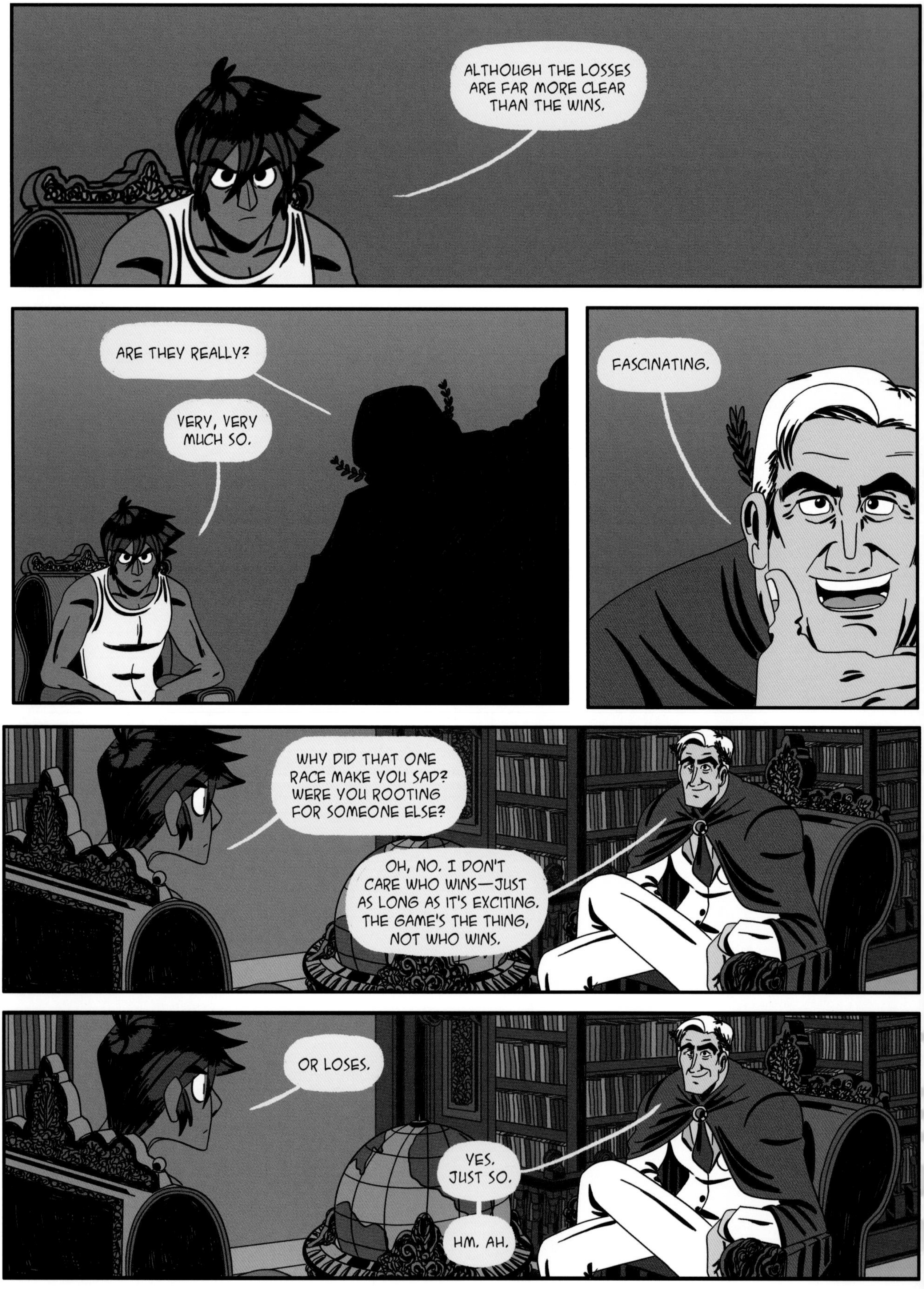
ALTHOUGH THE LOSSES ARE FAR MORE CLEAR THAN THE WINS.
ARE THEY REALLY?
VERY, VERY MUCH SO.
FASCINATING.
WHY DID THAT ONE RACE MAKE YOU SAD? WERE YOU ROOTING FOR SOMEONE ELSE?
OH, NO. I DON'T CARE WHO WINS—JUST AS LONG AS IT'S EXCITING. THE GAME'S THE THING, NOT WHO WINS.
OR LOSES.
YES. JUST SO.
HM. AH.

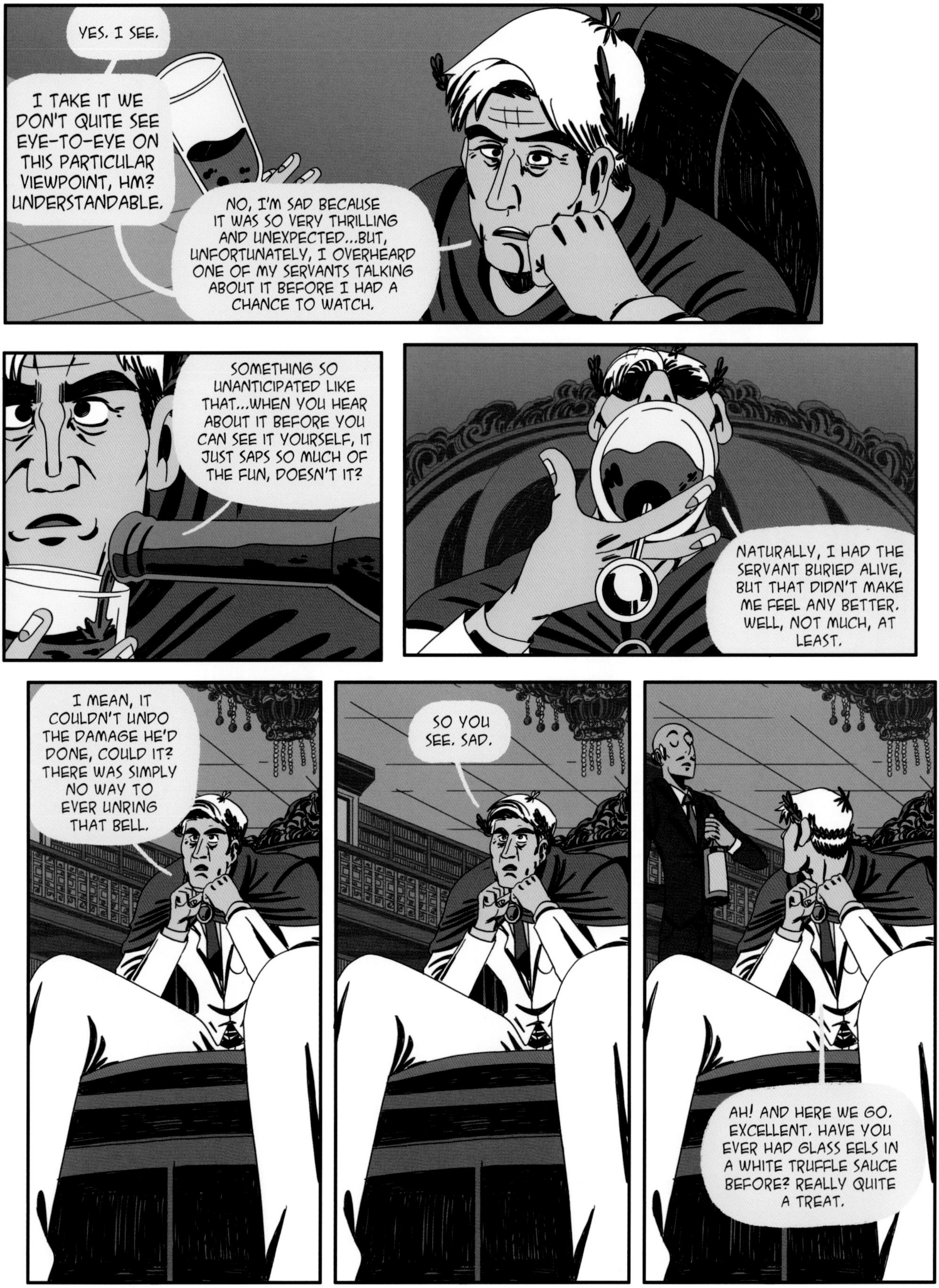
YES. I SEE.
I TAKE IT WE DON'T QUITE SEE EYE-TO-EYE ON THIS PARTICULAR VIEWPOINT, HM? UNDERSTANDABLE.
NO, I'M SAD BECAUSE IT WAS SO VERY THRILLING AND UNEXPECTED...BUT, UNFORTUNATELY, I OVERHEARD ONE OF MY SERVANTS TALKING ABOUT IT BEFORE I HAD A CHANCE TO WATCH.
SOMETHING SO UNANTICIPATED LIKE THAT...WHEN YOU HEAR ABOUT IT BEFORE YOU CAN SEE IT YOURSELF, IT JUST SAPS SO MUCH OF THE FUN, DOESN'T IT?
NATURALLY, I HAD THE SERVANT BURIED ALIVE, BUT THAT DIDN'T MAKE ME FEEL ANY BETTER. WELL, NOT MUCH, AT LEAST.
I MEAN, IT COULDN'T UNDO THE DAMAGE HE'D DONE, COULD IT? THERE WAS SIMPLY NO WAY TO EVER UNRING THAT BELL.
SO YOU SEE. SAD.
AH! AND HERE WE GO. EXCELLENT. HAVE YOU EVER HAD GLASS EELS IN A WHITE TRUFFLE SAUCE BEFORE? REALLY QUITE A TREAT.

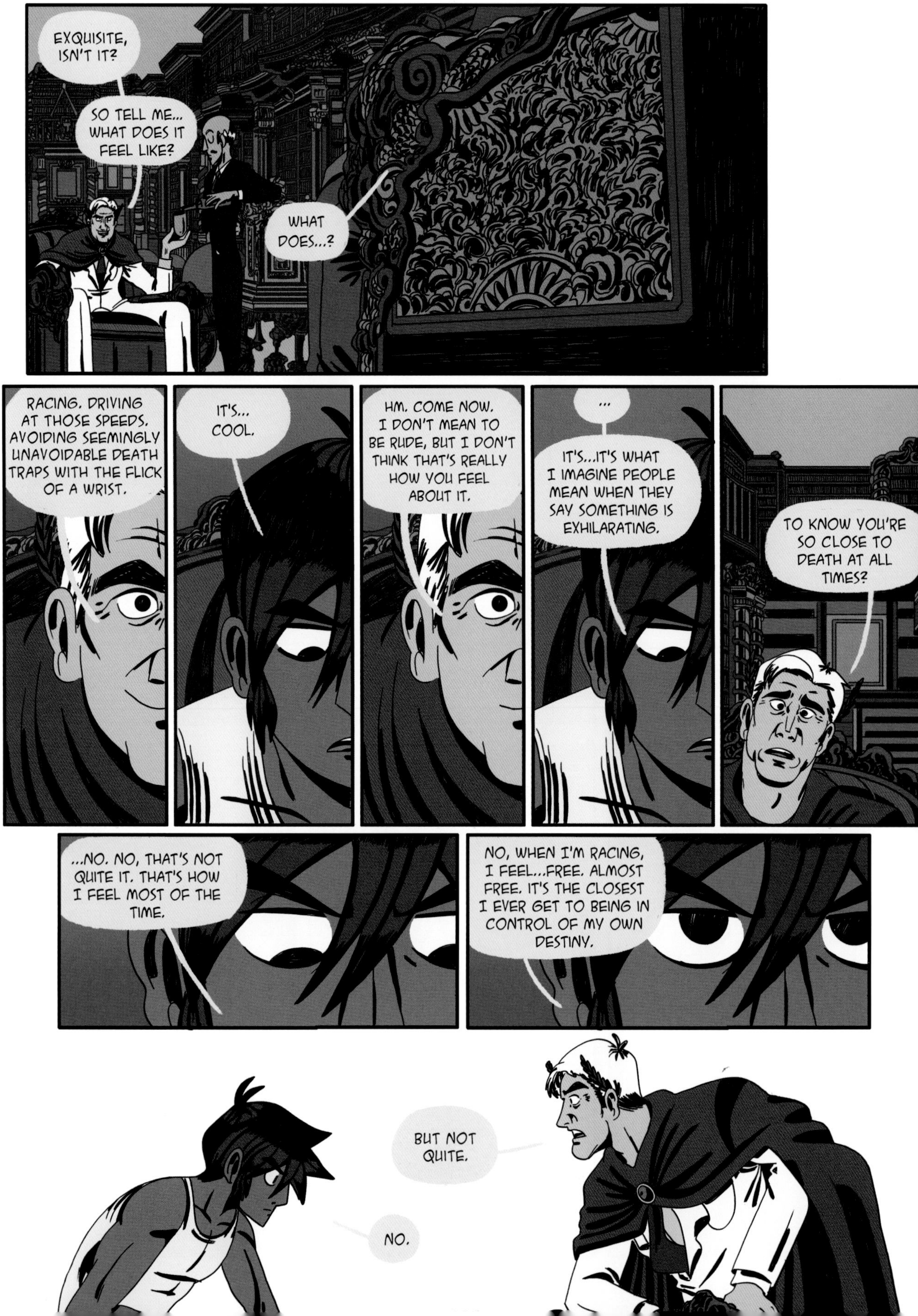
EXQUISITE, ISN'T IT?
SO TELL ME... WHAT DOES IT FEEL LIKE?
WHAT DOES...?
RACING. DRIVING AT THOSE SPEEDS. AVOIDING SEEMINGLY UNAVOIDABLE DEATH TRAPS WITH THE FLICK OF A WRIST.
IT'S... COOL.
HM. COME NOW. I DON'T MEAN TO BE RUDE, BUT I DON'T THINK THAT'S REALLY HOW YOU FEEL ABOUT IT.
...
IT'S...IT'S WHAT I IMAGINE PEOPLE MEAN WHEN THEY SAY SOMETHING IS EXHILARATING.
TO KNOW YOU'RE SO CLOSE TO DEATH AT ALL TIMES?
...NO. NO, THAT'S NOT QUITE IT. THAT'S HOW I FEEL MOST OF THE TIME.
NO, WHEN I'M RACING, I FEEL...FREE. ALMOST FREE. IT'S THE CLOSEST I EVER GET TO BEING IN CONTROL OF MY OWN DESTINY.
BUT NOT QUITE.
NO.

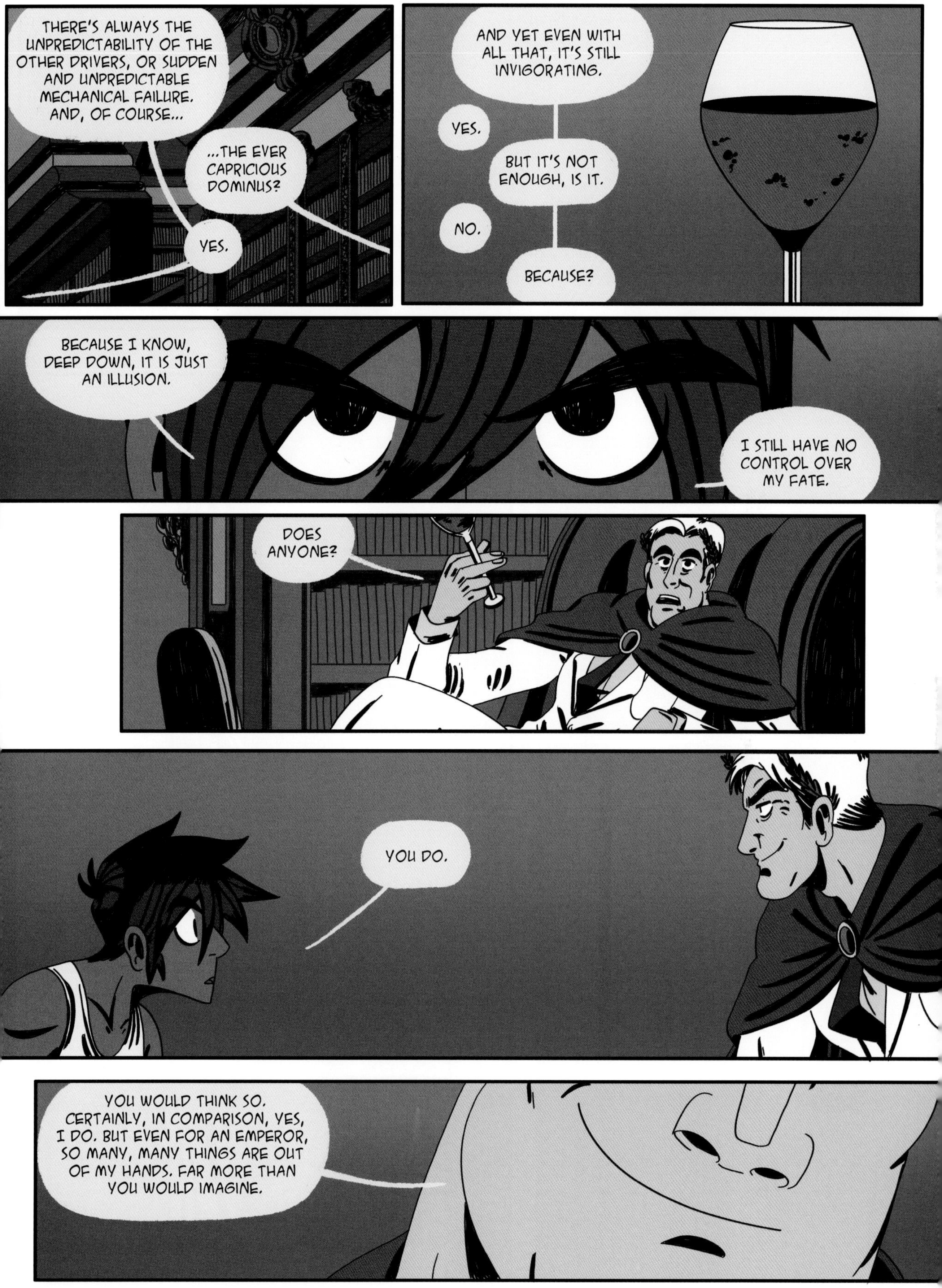

THERE'S ALWAYS THE UNPREDICTABILITY OF THE OTHER DRIVERS, OR SUDDEN AND UNPREDICTABLE MECHANICAL FAILURE. AND, OF COURSE...
...THE EVER CAPRICIOUS DOMINUS?
YES.
AND YET EVEN WITH ALL THAT, IT'S STILL INVIGORATING.
YES.
BUT IT'S NOT ENOUGH, IS IT.
NO.
BECAUSE?
BECAUSE I KNOW, DEEP DOWN, IT IS JUST AN ILLUSION.
I STILL HAVE NO CONTROL OVER MY FATE.
DOES ANYONE?
YOU DO.
YOU WOULD THINK SO. CERTAINLY, IN COMPARISON, YES, I DO. BUT EVEN FOR AN EMPEROR, SO MANY, MANY THINGS ARE OUT OF MY HANDS. FAR MORE THAN YOU WOULD IMAGINE.

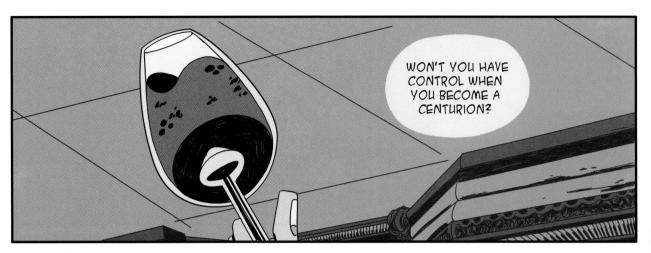

WON'T YOU HAVE CONTROL WHEN YOU BECOME A CENTURION?

I DON'T THINK THAT'S GOING TO HAPPEN.

REALLY? IT WOULD SEEM AS THOUGH YOU HAVE A LOCK ON IT. WHY DON'T YOU BELIEVE IT'S GOING TO HAPPEN?

BECAUSE I THINK I'M MORE VALUABLE RIGHT WHERE I AM.

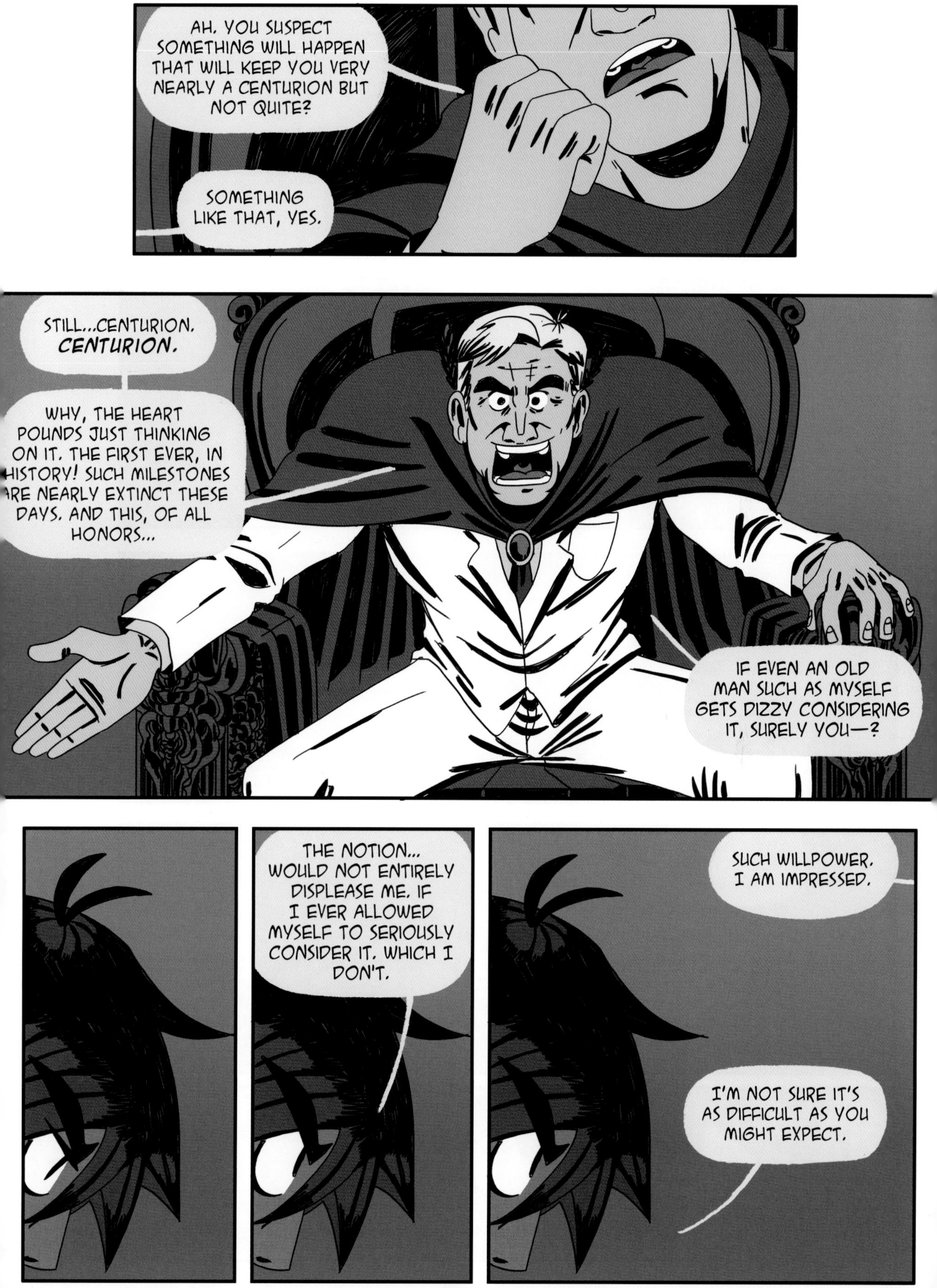
AH. YOU SUSPECT SOMETHING WILL HAPPEN THAT WILL KEEP YOU VERY NEARLY A CENTURION BUT NOT QUITE?
SOMETHING LIKE THAT, YES.
STILL...CENTURION. ***CENTURION.***
WHY, THE HEART POUNDS JUST THINKING ON IT. THE FIRST EVER, IN HISTORY! SUCH MILESTONES ARE NEARLY EXTINCT THESE DAYS. AND THIS, OF ALL HONORS...
IF EVEN AN OLD MAN SUCH AS MYSELF GETS DIZZY CONSIDERING IT, SURELY YOU—?
THE NOTION... WOULD NOT ENTIRELY DISPLEASE ME. IF I EVER ALLOWED MYSELF TO SERIOUSLY CONSIDER IT. WHICH I DON'T.
SUCH WILLPOWER. I AM IMPRESSED.
I'M NOT SURE IT'S AS DIFFICULT AS YOU MIGHT EXPECT.

I'M SORRY SOMEONE SO YOUNG IS ALREADY SO JADED.

DO YOU THINK I SHOULDN'T BE?

OH, NO, I'M SURE IT'S THE BEST APPROACH.

AFTER ALL, AS THEY SAY, THE DOMINUS IS THE ONLY THING THAT'S NEARLY AS CAPRICIOUS AS LIFE ITSELF, NO? THAT EVEN THE GODS ARE MORE PREDICTABLE?

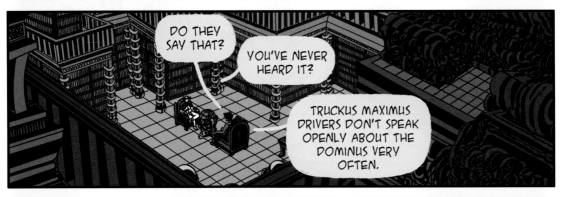

DO THEY SAY THAT?

YOU'VE NEVER HEARD IT?

TRUCKUS MAXIMUS DRIVERS DON'T SPEAK OPENLY ABOUT THE DOMINUS VERY OFTEN.

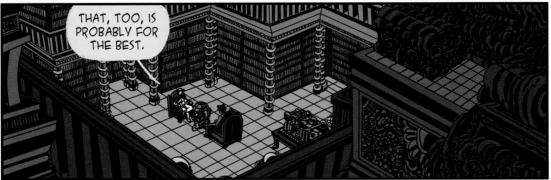

THAT, TOO, IS PROBABLY FOR THE BEST.

ARE YOU THE DOMINUS?

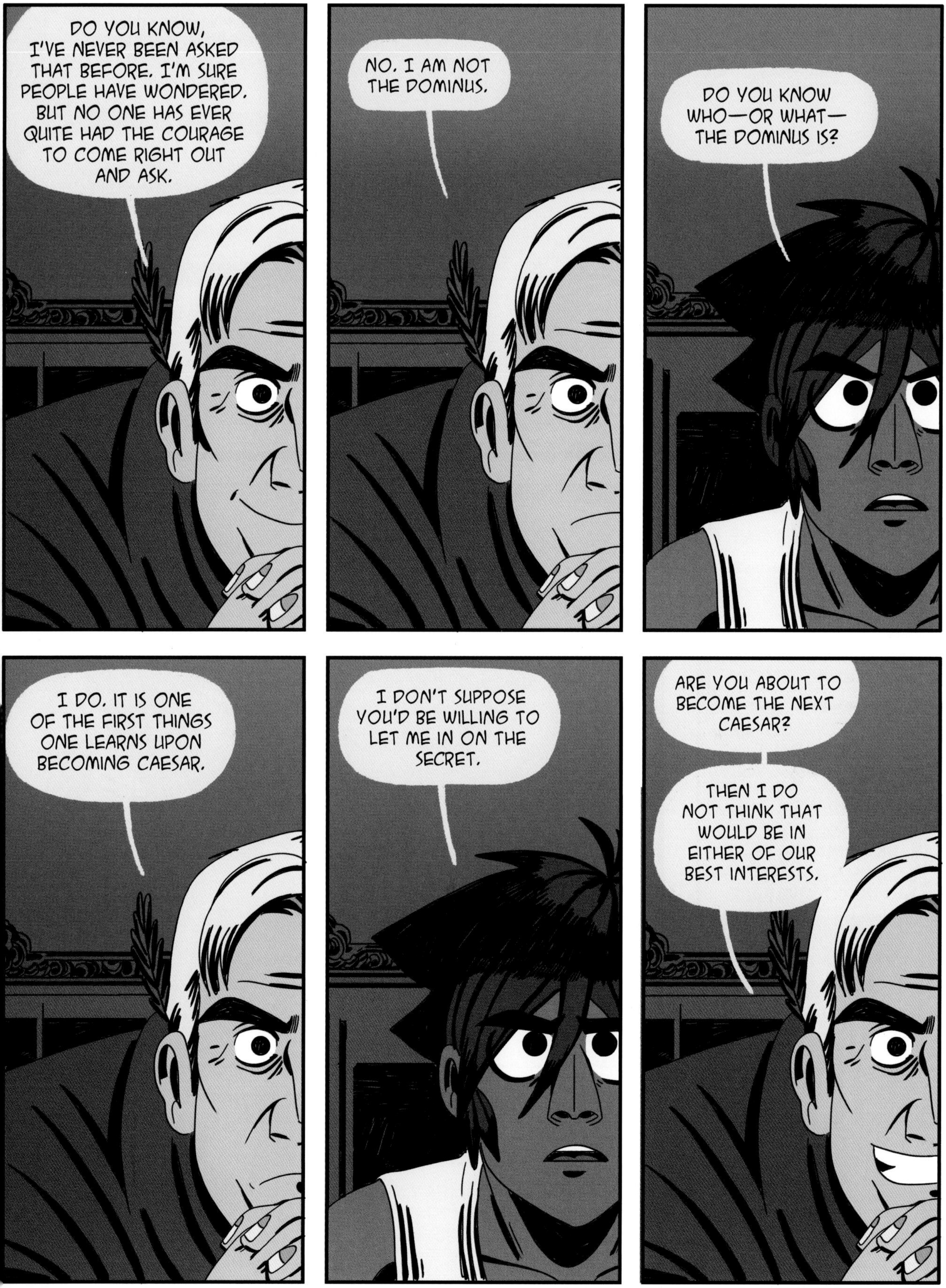
DO YOU KNOW, I'VE NEVER BEEN ASKED THAT BEFORE. I'M SURE PEOPLE HAVE WONDERED. BUT NO ONE HAS EVER QUITE HAD THE COURAGE TO COME RIGHT OUT AND ASK.
NO. I AM NOT THE DOMINUS.
DO YOU KNOW WHO—OR WHAT—THE DOMINUS IS?
I DO. IT IS ONE OF THE FIRST THINGS ONE LEARNS UPON BECOMING CAESAR.
I DON'T SUPPOSE YOU'D BE WILLING TO LET ME IN ON THE SECRET.
ARE YOU ABOUT TO BECOME THE NEXT CAESAR?
THEN I DO NOT THINK THAT WOULD BE IN EITHER OF OUR BEST INTERESTS.

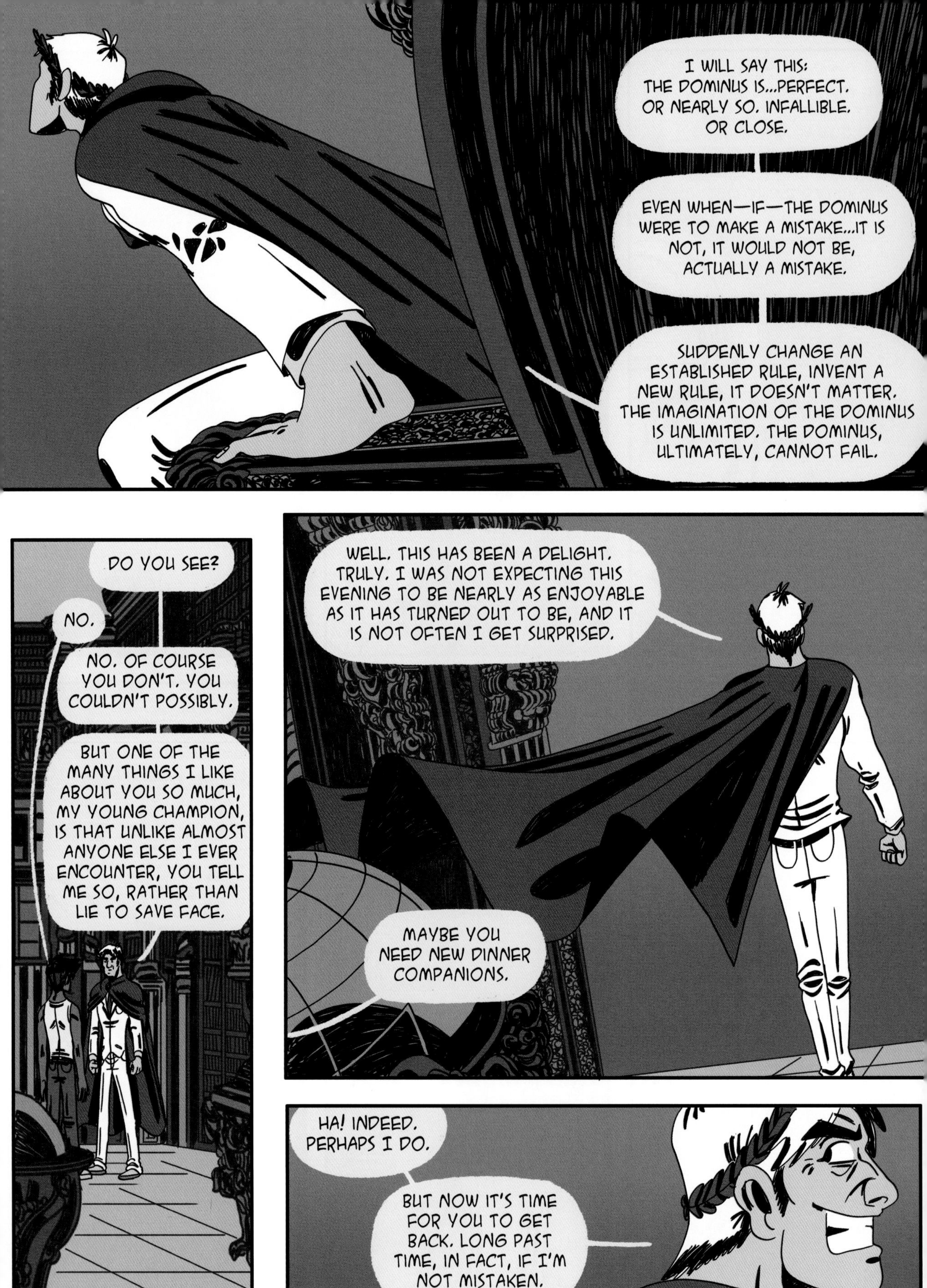

I WILL SAY THIS: THE DOMINUS IS...PERFECT. OR NEARLY SO. INFALLIBLE. OR CLOSE.
EVEN WHEN—IF—THE DOMINUS WERE TO MAKE A MISTAKE...IT IS NOT, IT WOULD NOT BE, ACTUALLY A MISTAKE.
SUDDENLY CHANGE AN ESTABLISHED RULE, INVENT A NEW RULE, IT DOESN'T MATTER. THE IMAGINATION OF THE DOMINUS IS UNLIMITED. THE DOMINUS, ULTIMATELY, CANNOT FAIL.
DO YOU SEE?
NO.
NO. OF COURSE YOU DON'T. YOU COULDN'T POSSIBLY.
BUT ONE OF THE MANY THINGS I LIKE ABOUT YOU SO MUCH, MY YOUNG CHAMPION, IS THAT UNLIKE ALMOST ANYONE ELSE I EVER ENCOUNTER, YOU TELL ME SO, RATHER THAN LIE TO SAVE FACE.
WELL. THIS HAS BEEN A DELIGHT. TRULY. I WAS NOT EXPECTING THIS EVENING TO BE NEARLY AS ENJOYABLE AS IT HAS TURNED OUT TO BE, AND IT IS NOT OFTEN I GET SURPRISED.
MAYBE YOU NEED NEW DINNER COMPANIONS.
HA! INDEED. PERHAPS I DO.
BUT NOW IT'S TIME FOR YOU TO GET BACK. LONG PAST TIME, IN FACT, IF I'M NOT MISTAKEN.

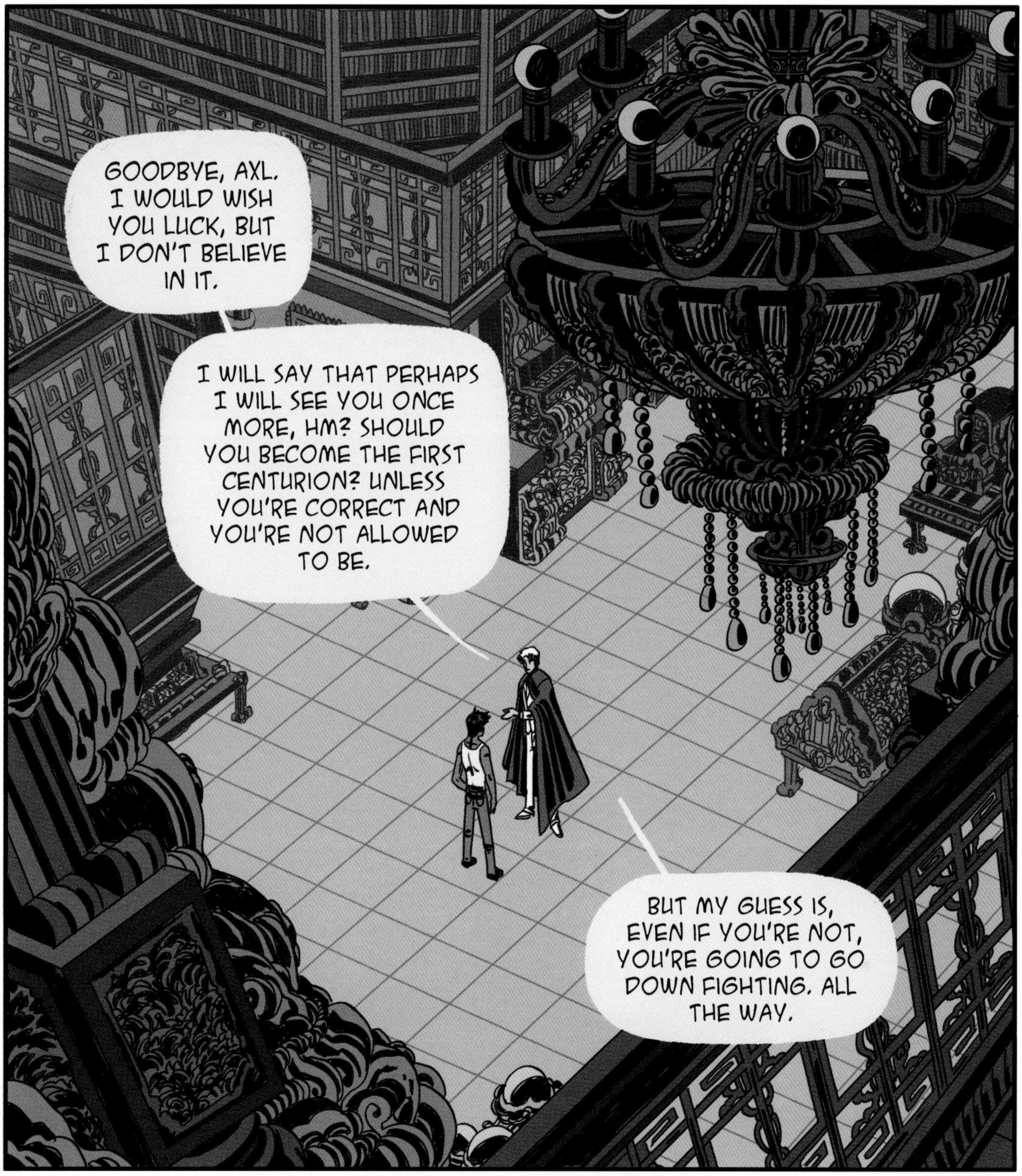
GOODBYE, AXL. I WOULD WISH YOU LUCK, BUT I DON'T BELIEVE IN IT.
I WILL SAY THAT PERHAPS I WILL SEE YOU ONCE MORE, HM? SHOULD YOU BECOME THE FIRST CENTURION? UNLESS YOU'RE CORRECT AND YOU'RE NOT ALLOWED TO BE.
BUT MY GUESS IS, EVEN IF YOU'RE NOT, YOU'RE GOING TO GO DOWN FIGHTING. ALL THE WAY.

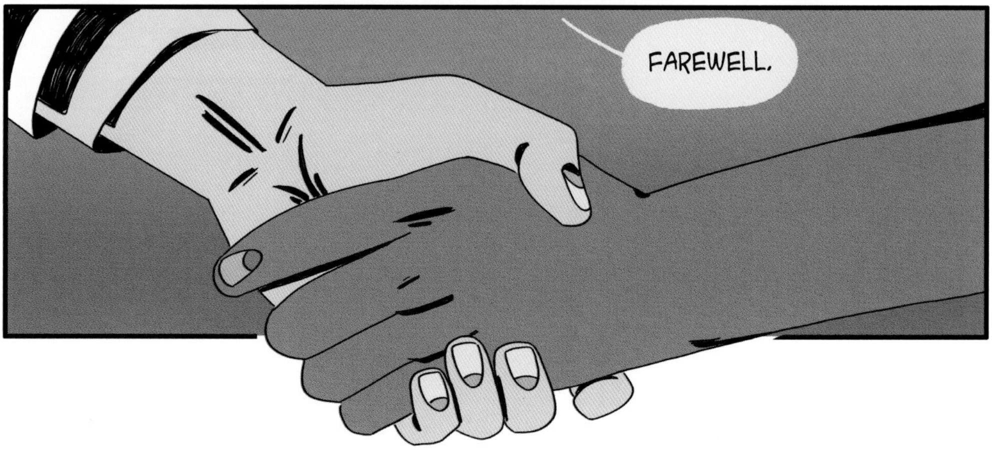
FAREWELL.

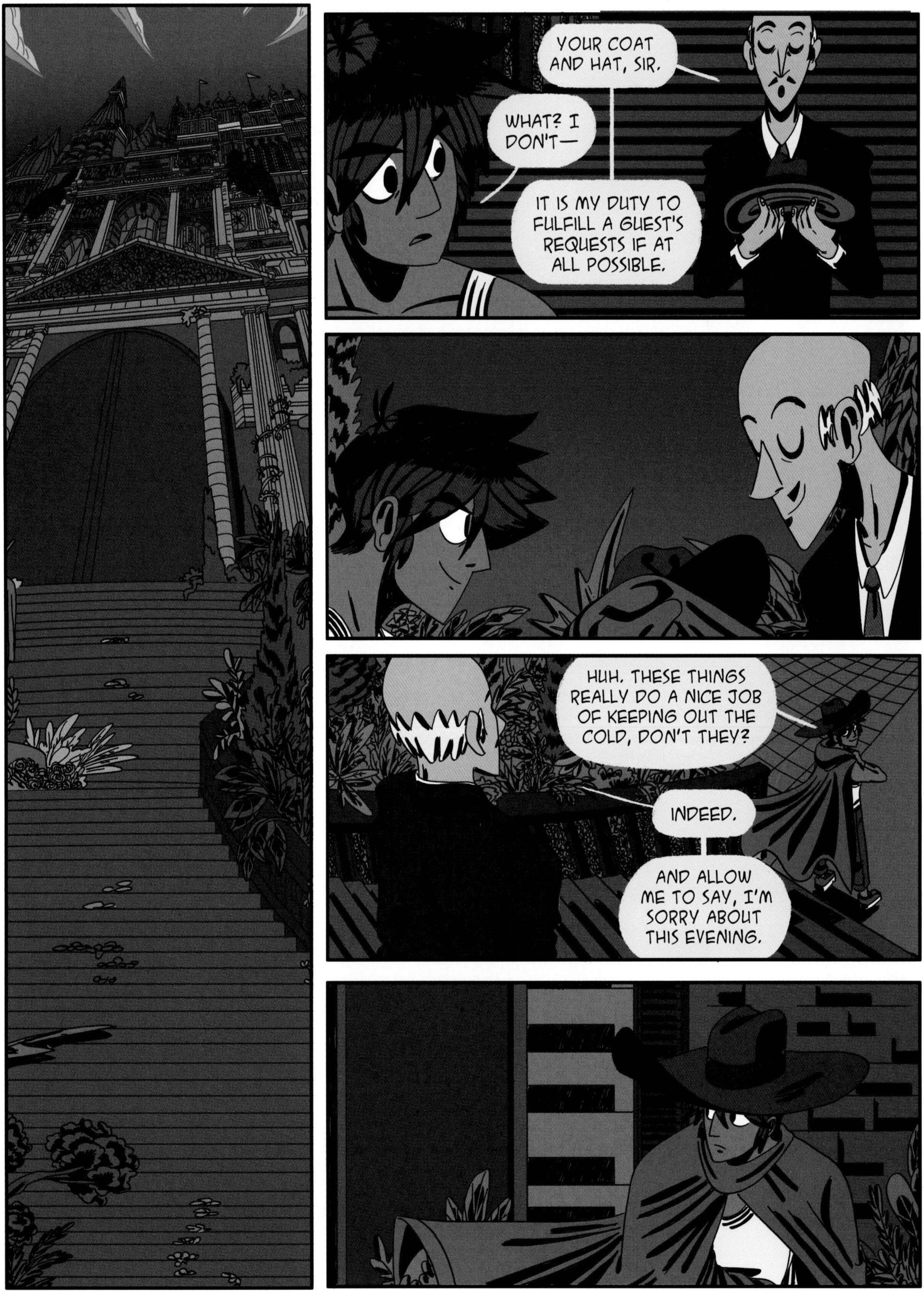
YOUR COAT AND HAT, SIR.
WHAT? I DON'T—
IT IS MY DUTY TO FULFILL A GUEST'S REQUESTS IF AT ALL POSSIBLE.
HUH. THESE THINGS REALLY DO A NICE JOB OF KEEPING OUT THE COLD, DON'T THEY?
INDEED.
AND ALLOW ME TO SAY, I'M SORRY ABOUT THIS EVENING.

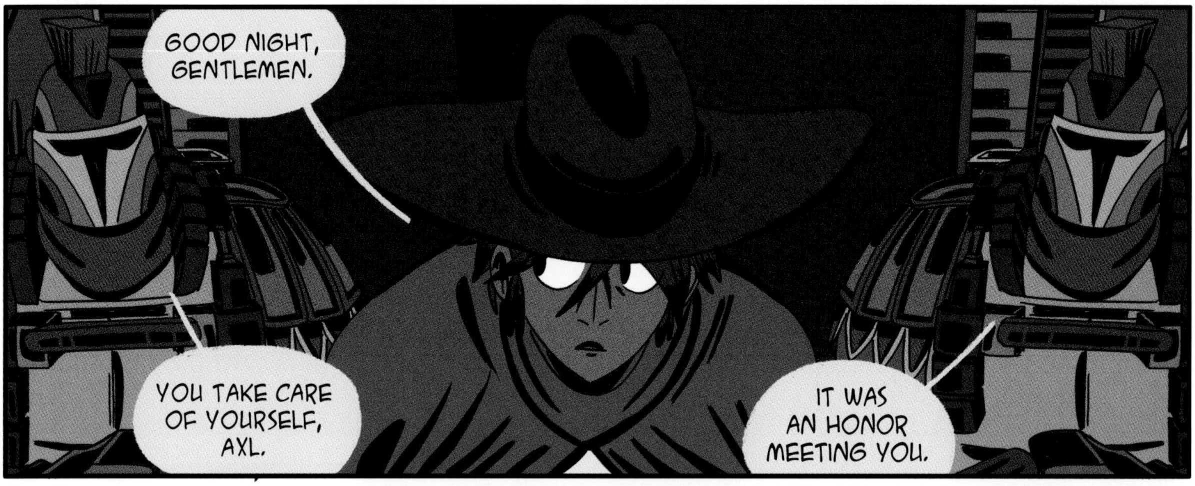
GOOD NIGHT, GENTLEMEN.
YOU TAKE CARE OF YOURSELF, AXL.
IT WAS AN HONOR MEETING YOU.

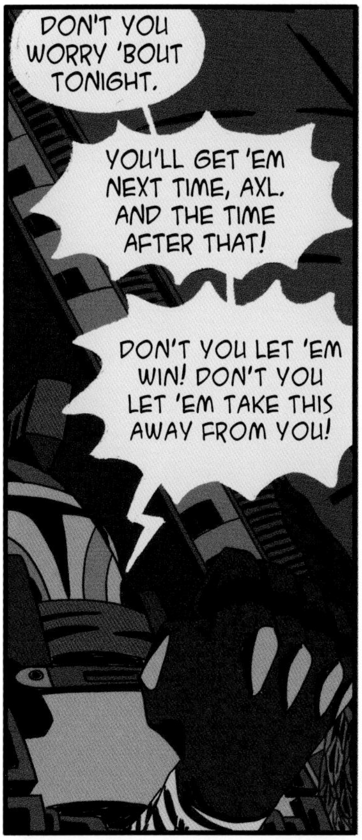
DON'T YOU WORRY 'BOUT TONIGHT.
YOU'LL GET 'EM NEXT TIME, AXL. AND THE TIME AFTER THAT!
DON'T YOU LET 'EM WIN! DON'T YOU LET 'EM TAKE THIS AWAY FROM YOU!

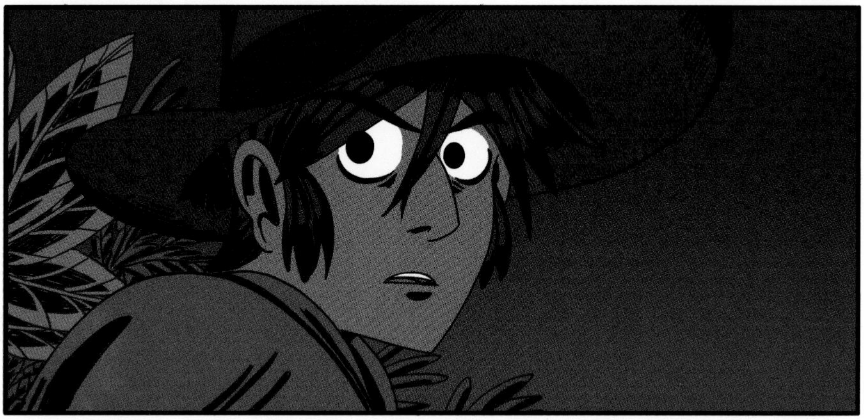

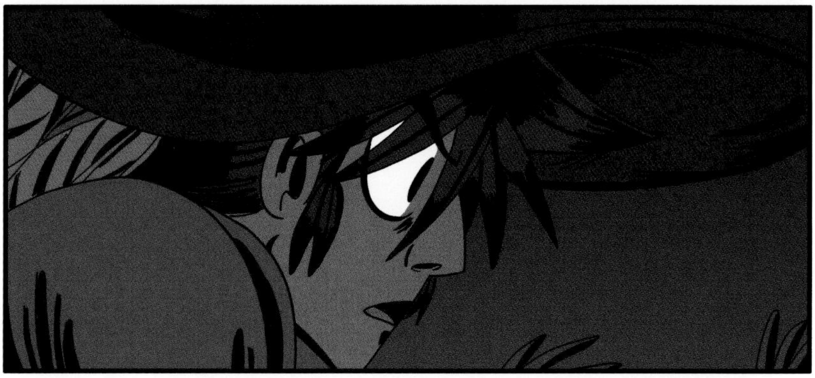

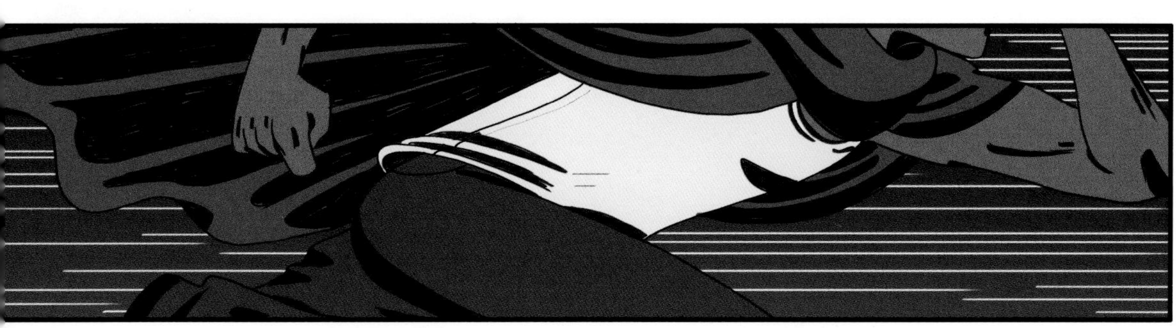

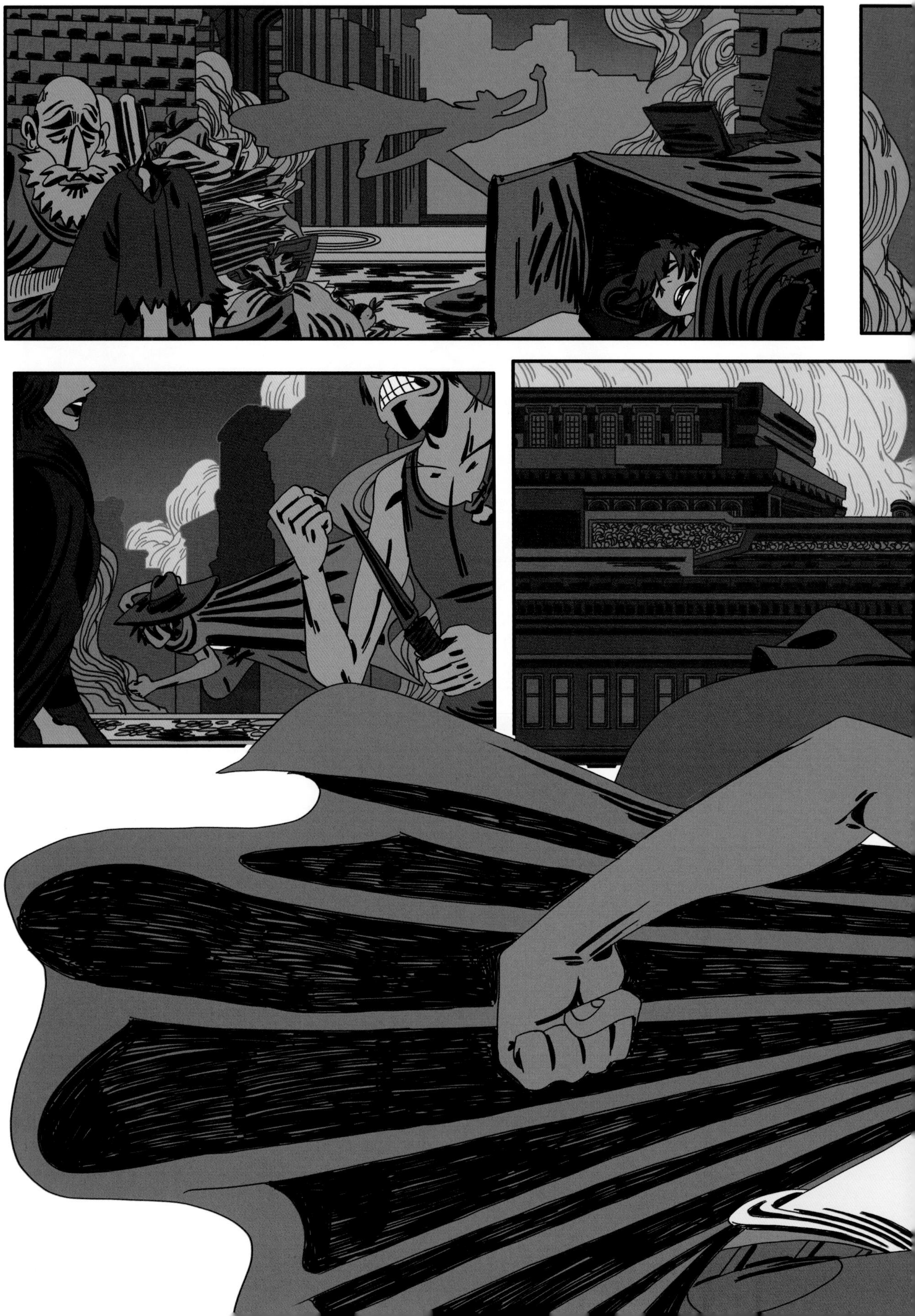

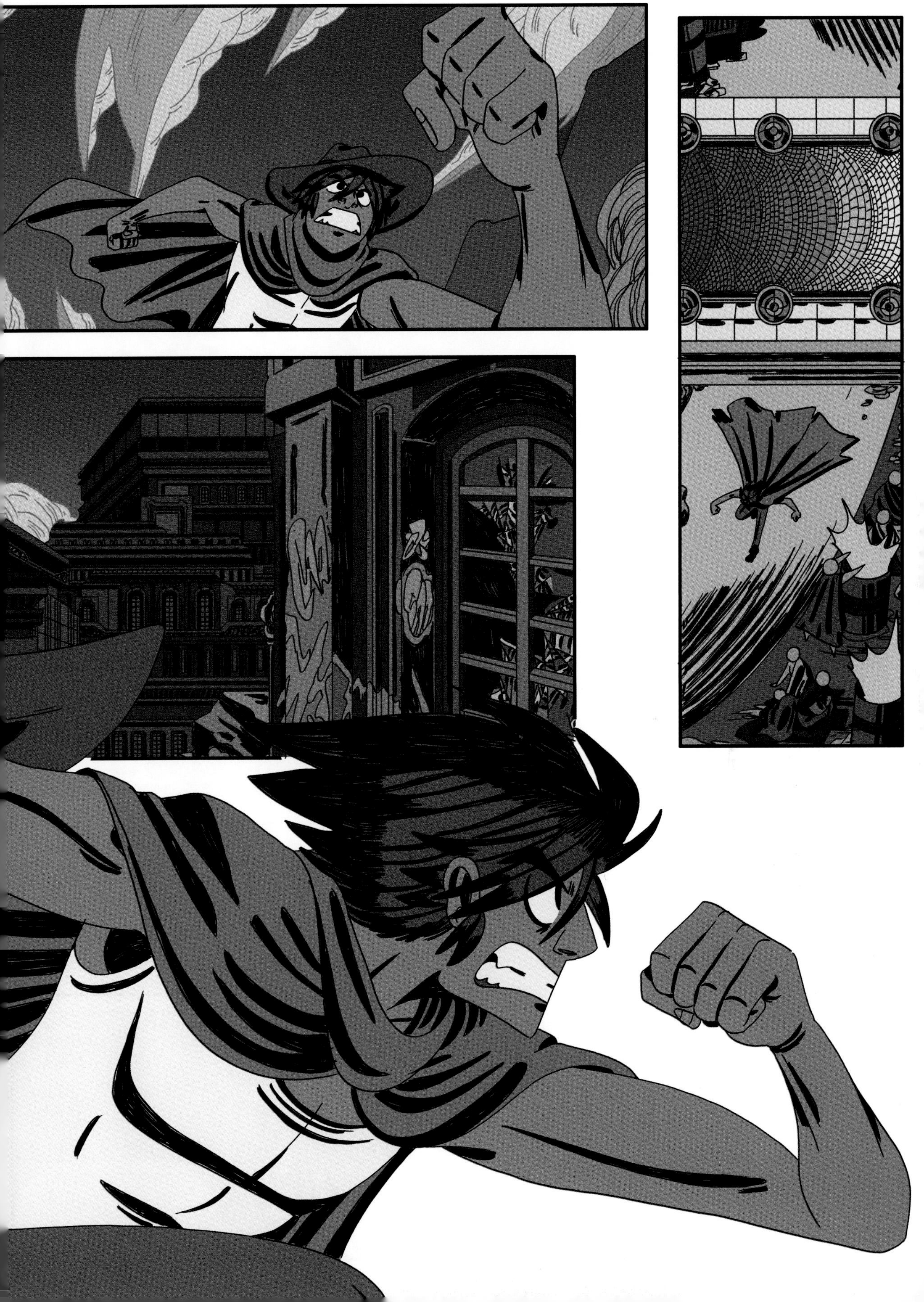

WHAT HAPPENED?

THERE WAS A RACE.

RIGHT AFTER YOU LEFT.

JUST OUT OF THE BLUE.

SAID IT WAS STARTING IN FIFTEEN MINUTES, AND THAT IT WAS "MANDATORY." THAT ALL DRIVERS HAD TO RACE, REGARDLESS OF HEALTH OR VEHICLE CONDITION OR WHATEVER.

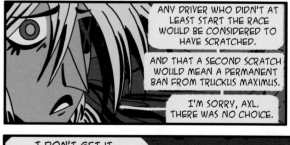

ANY DRIVER WHO DIDN'T AT LEAST START THE RACE WOULD BE CONSIDERED TO HAVE SCRATCHED.

AND THAT A SECOND SCRATCH WOULD MEAN A PERMANENT BAN FROM TRUCKUS MAXIMUS.

I'M SORRY, AXL. THERE WAS NO CHOICE.

I DON'T GET IT. WHY ARE THEY DOING THIS? DO THEY WANT YOU TO WIN OR DON'T THEY?

I DON'T KNOW. I THINK THEY'RE DOING IT BECAUSE THEY CAN. TO KEEP RATINGS UP. AND TO KEEP ME GUESSING.

SO...I KNOW THIS SOUNDS WEIRD...AND WE DON'T REALLY TALK ABOUT...YOU KNOW...*IT*...BUT...

ARE WE GOING TO...I DUNNO...DO SOMETHING? FOR AXL? IF HE...YOU KNOW...

BECOMES A CENTURION?

YEAH.

YOU'RE RIGHT. WE DON'T REALLY TALK ABOUT THAT.

BUT WE SHOULD DO SOMETHING.

YOU DON'T THINK THERE'S GOING TO BE SOME SORT OF HUGE OFFICIAL CEREMONY OR SOMETHING?

I'M SURE THERE IS.

BUT YOU HAVEN'T HEARD WHAT IT IS?

I KNOW THIS COMES AS A SHOCK, BUT I'M NOT KEPT INFORMED OF SUCH DECISIONS.

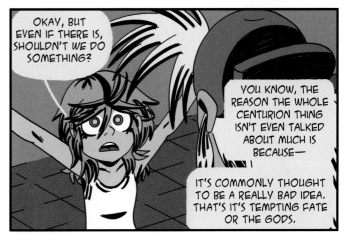

OKAY, BUT EVEN IF THERE IS, SHOULDN'T WE DO SOMETHING?

YOU KNOW, THE REASON THE WHOLE CENTURION THING ISN'T EVEN TALKED ABOUT MUCH IS BECAUSE—

IT'S COMMONLY THOUGHT TO BE A REALLY BAD IDEA. THAT'S IT'S TEMPTING FATE OR THE GODS.

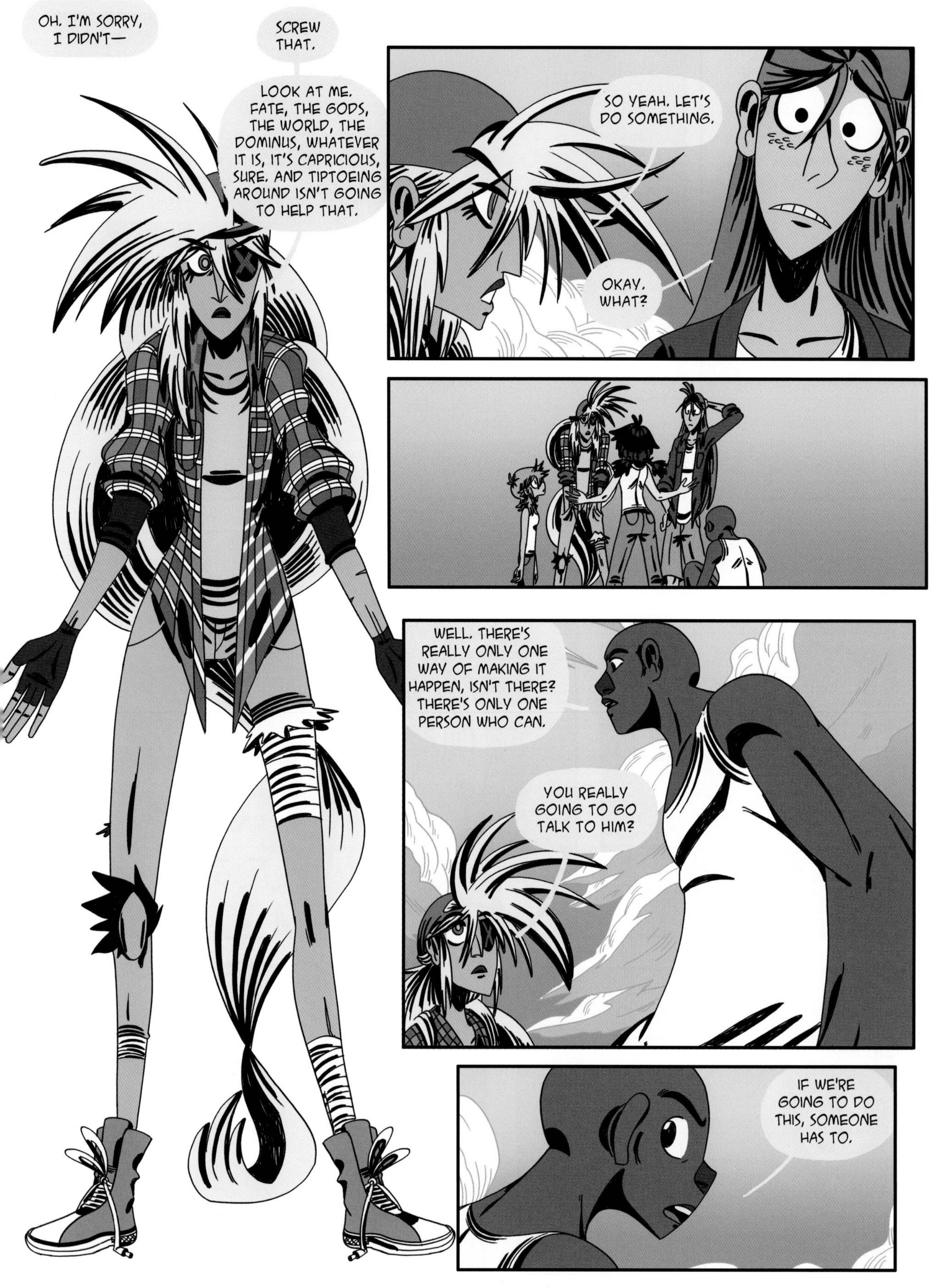
OH. I'M SORRY, I DIDN'T—
SCREW THAT.
LOOK AT ME. FATE, THE GODS, THE WORLD, THE DOMINUS, WHATEVER IT IS, IT'S CAPRICIOUS, SURE. AND TIPTOEING AROUND ISN'T GOING TO HELP THAT.
SO YEAH. LET'S DO SOMETHING.
OKAY. WHAT?
WELL. THERE'S REALLY ONLY ONE WAY OF MAKING IT HAPPEN, ISN'T THERE? THERE'S ONLY ONE PERSON WHO CAN.
YOU REALLY GOING TO GO TALK TO HIM?
IF WE'RE GOING TO DO THIS, SOMEONE HAS TO.

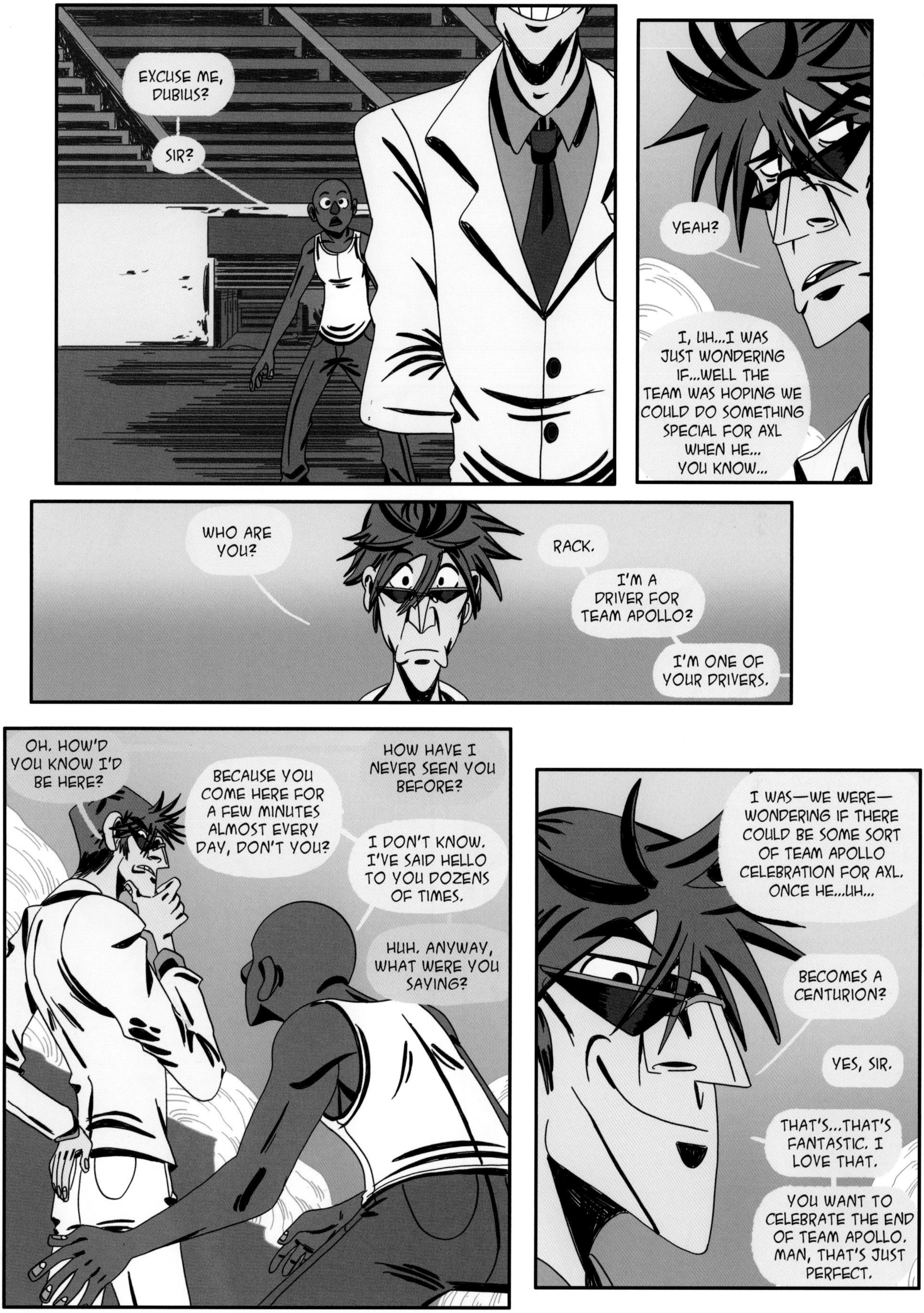
EXCUSE ME, DUBIUS?
SIR?
YEAH?
I, UH...I WAS JUST WONDERING IF...WELL THE TEAM WAS HOPING WE COULD DO SOMETHING SPECIAL FOR AXL WHEN HE... YOU KNOW...
WHO ARE YOU?
RACK.
I'M A DRIVER FOR TEAM APOLLO?
I'M ONE OF YOUR DRIVERS.
OH. HOW'D YOU KNOW I'D BE HERE?
BECAUSE YOU COME HERE FOR A FEW MINUTES ALMOST EVERY DAY, DON'T YOU?
HOW HAVE I NEVER SEEN YOU BEFORE?
I DON'T KNOW. I'VE SAID HELLO TO YOU DOZENS OF TIMES.
HUH. ANYWAY, WHAT WERE YOU SAYING?
I WAS—WE WERE—WONDERING IF THERE COULD BE SOME SORT OF TEAM APOLLO CELEBRATION FOR AXL. ONCE HE...UH...
BECOMES A CENTURION?
YES, SIR.
THAT'S...THAT'S FANTASTIC. I LOVE THAT.
YOU WANT TO CELEBRATE THE END OF TEAM APOLLO. MAN, THAT'S JUST PERFECT.

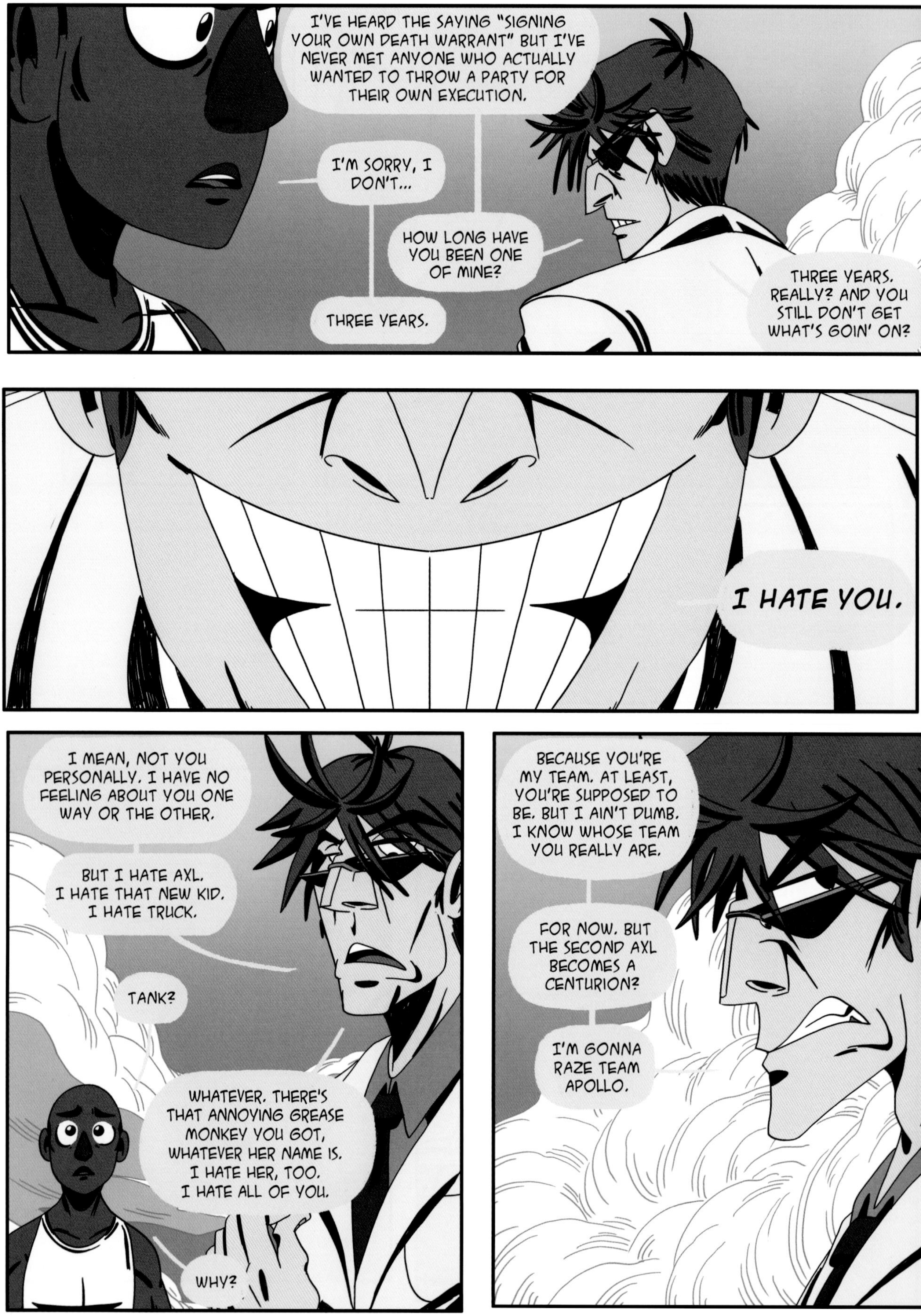
I'VE HEARD THE SAYING "SIGNING YOUR OWN DEATH WARRANT" BUT I'VE NEVER MET ANYONE WHO ACTUALLY WANTED TO THROW A PARTY FOR THEIR OWN EXECUTION.
I'M SORRY, I DON'T...
HOW LONG HAVE YOU BEEN ONE OF MINE?
THREE YEARS.
THREE YEARS. REALLY? AND YOU STILL DON'T GET WHAT'S GOIN' ON?
I HATE YOU.
I MEAN, NOT YOU PERSONALLY. I HAVE NO FEELING ABOUT YOU ONE WAY OR THE OTHER.
BUT I HATE AXL. I HATE THAT NEW KID. I HATE TRUCK.
TANK?
WHATEVER. THERE'S THAT ANNOYING GREASE MONKEY YOU GOT, WHATEVER HER NAME IS. I HATE HER, TOO. I HATE ALL OF YOU.
WHY?
BECAUSE YOU'RE MY TEAM. AT LEAST, YOU'RE SUPPOSED TO BE. BUT I AIN'T DUMB. I KNOW WHOSE TEAM YOU REALLY ARE.
FOR NOW. BUT THE SECOND AXL BECOMES A CENTURION?
I'M GONNA RAZE TEAM APOLLO.

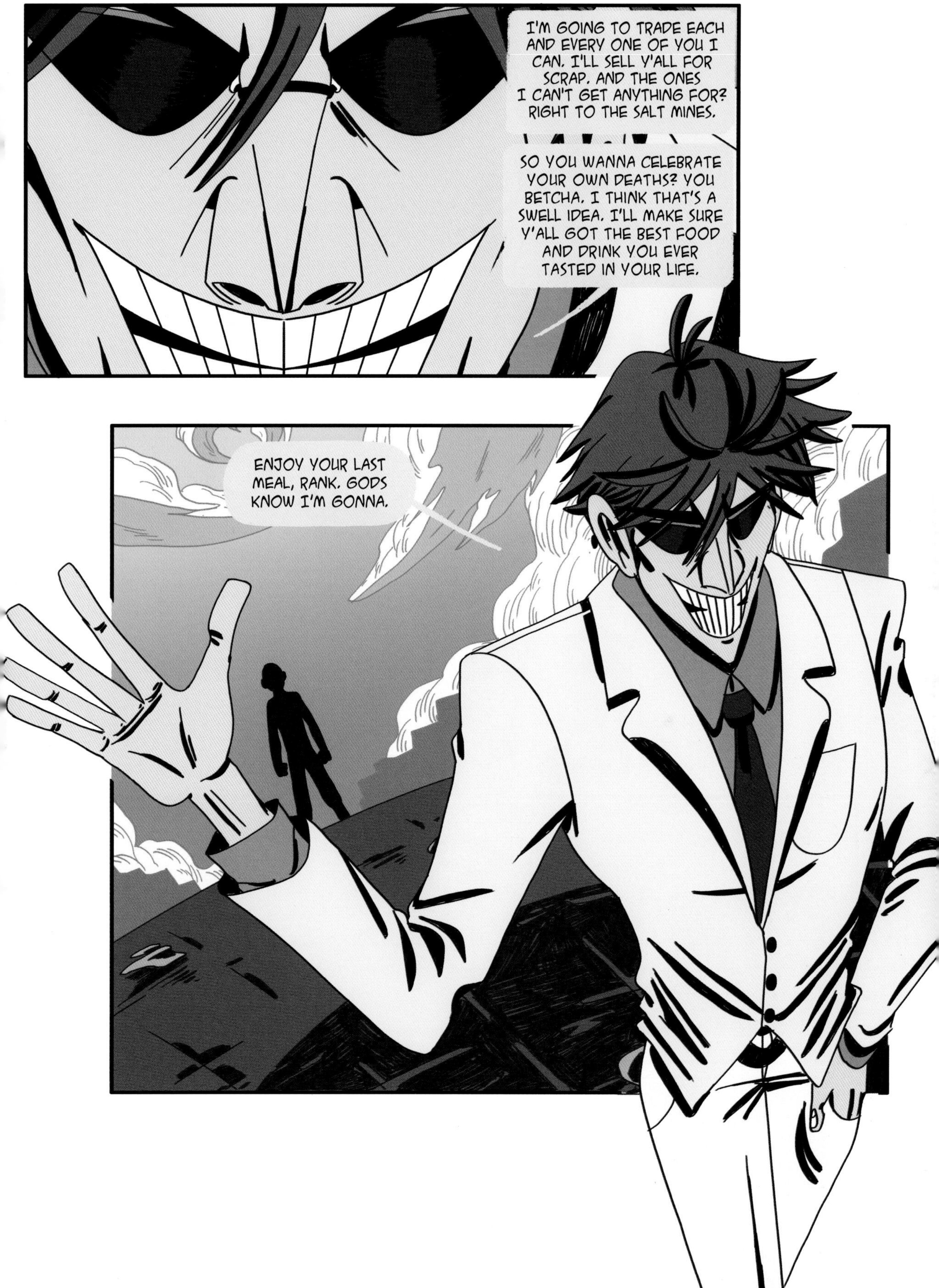
I'M GOING TO TRADE EACH AND EVERY ONE OF YOU I CAN. I'LL SELL Y'ALL FOR SCRAP. AND THE ONES I CAN'T GET ANYTHING FOR? RIGHT TO THE SALT MINES.
SO YOU WANNA CELEBRATE YOUR OWN DEATHS? YOU BETCHA. I THINK THAT'S A SWELL IDEA. I'LL MAKE SURE Y'ALL GOT THE BEST FOOD AND DRINK YOU EVER TASTED IN YOUR LIFE.
ENJOY YOUR LAST MEAL, RANK. GODS KNOW I'M GONNA.

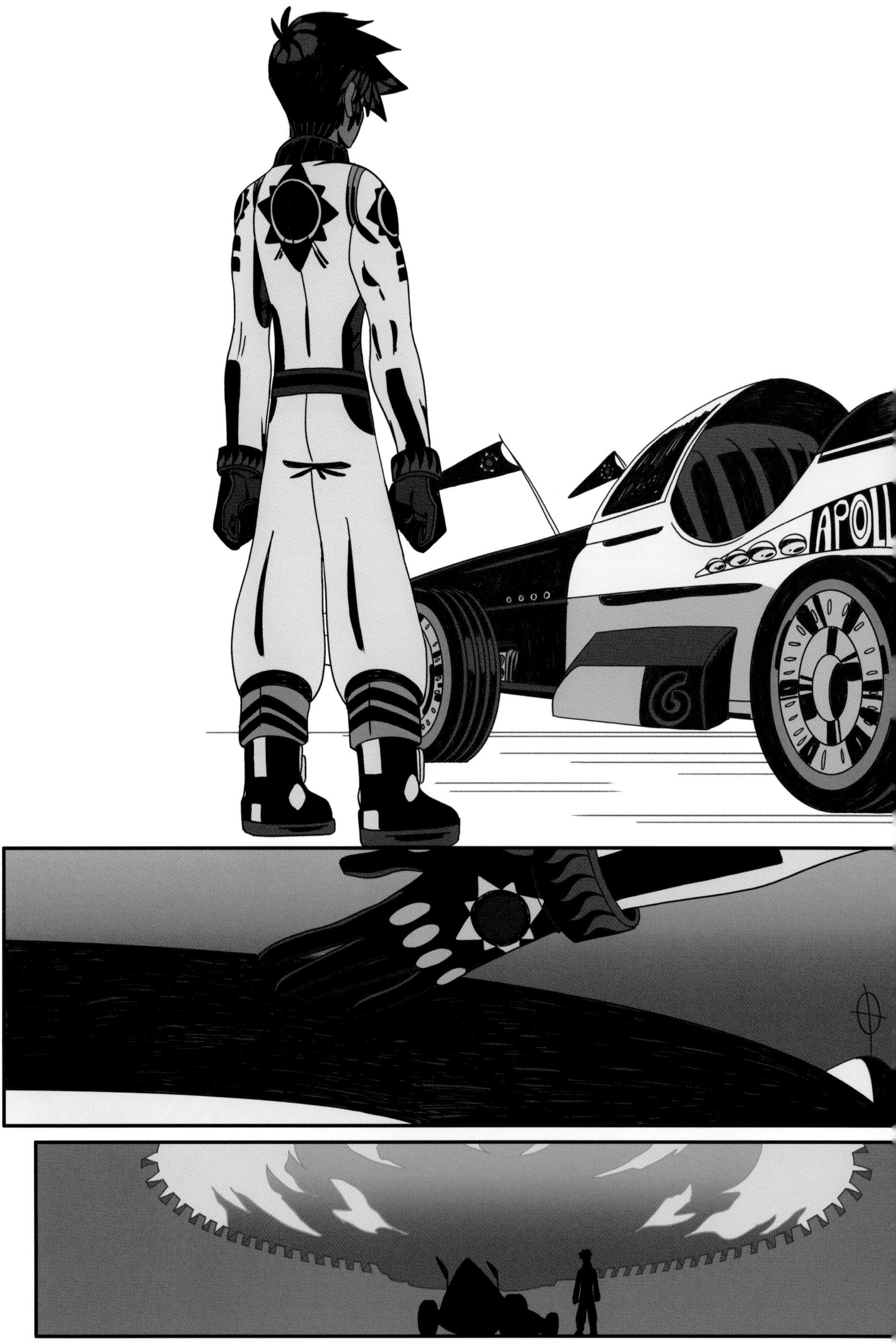

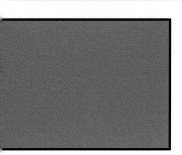

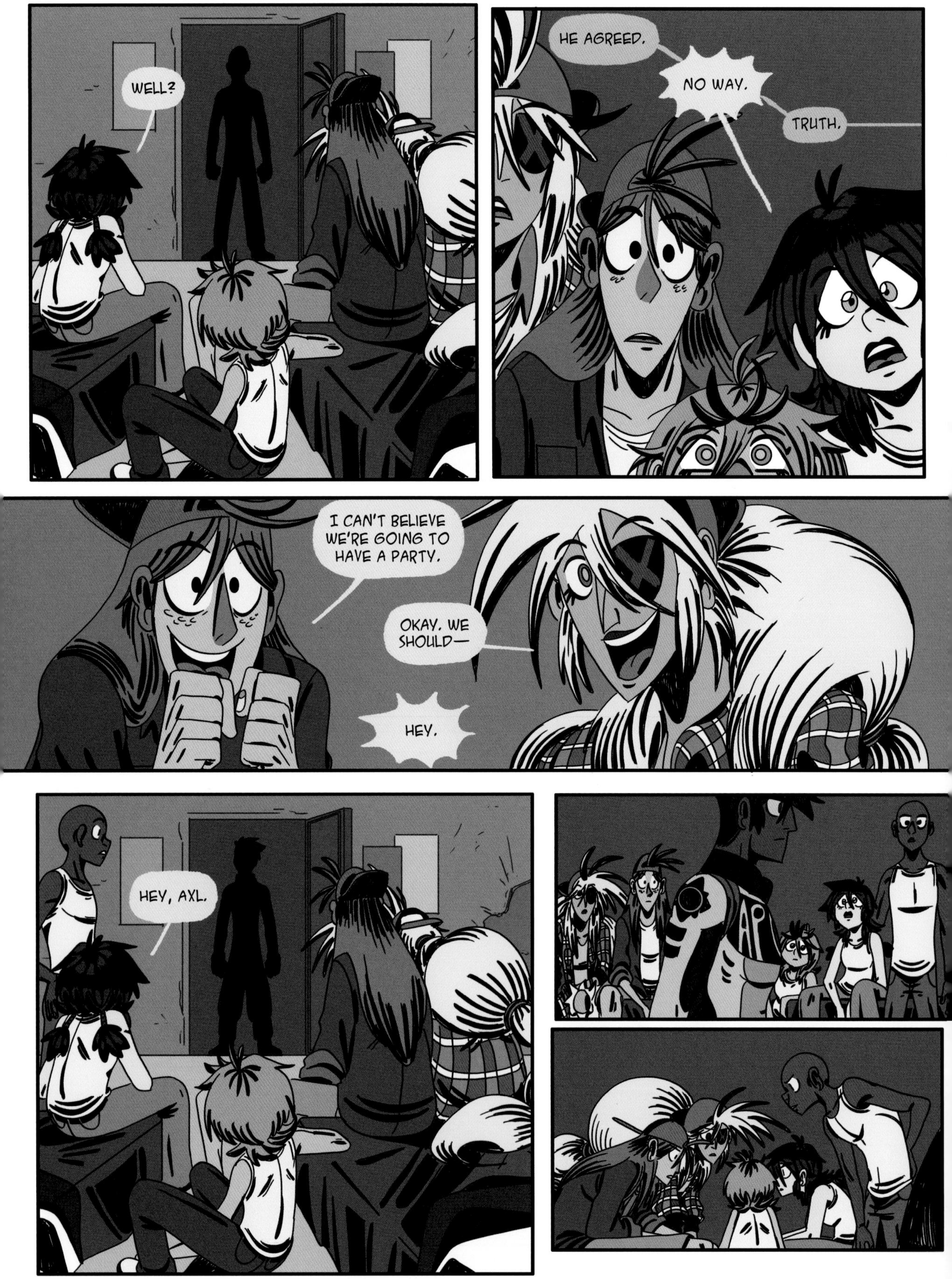
WELL?
HE AGREED.
NO WAY.
TRUTH.
I CAN'T BELIEVE WE'RE GOING TO HAVE A PARTY.
OKAY. WE SHOULD—
HEY.
HEY, AXL.

HEY, RACK?

YEAH?

I DON'T MEAN TO SOUND...BUT...WE'RE SUPPOSED TO, YOU KNOW, THINK AHEAD, SO...

WHAT'S GOING TO HAPPEN TO US IF AXL WINS? TO TEAM APOLLO?

WHEN AXL WINS, YOU MEAN?

YEAH.

I DON'T KNOW.

BUT DON'T WORRY TOO MUCH ABOUT IT. WE'LL BE FINE.

YOU REALLY BELIEVE THAT?

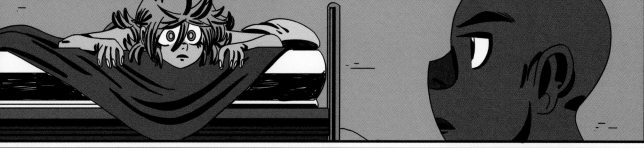

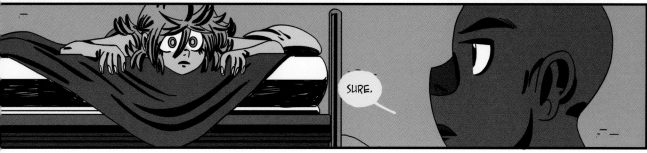

SURE.

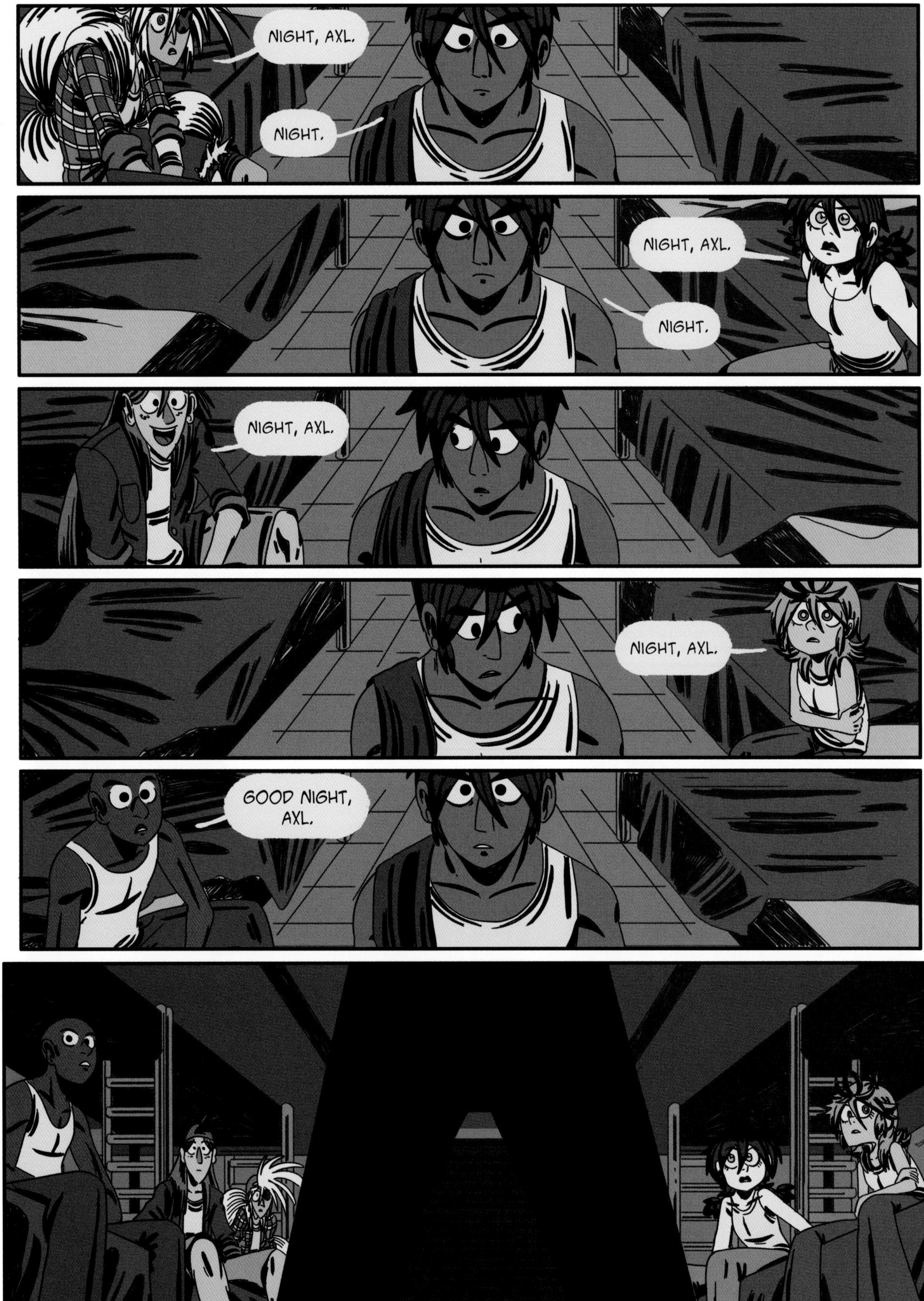
NIGHT, AXL.
NIGHT.
NIGHT, AXL.
NIGHT.
NIGHT, AXL.
NIGHT, AXL.
GOOD NIGHT, AXL.

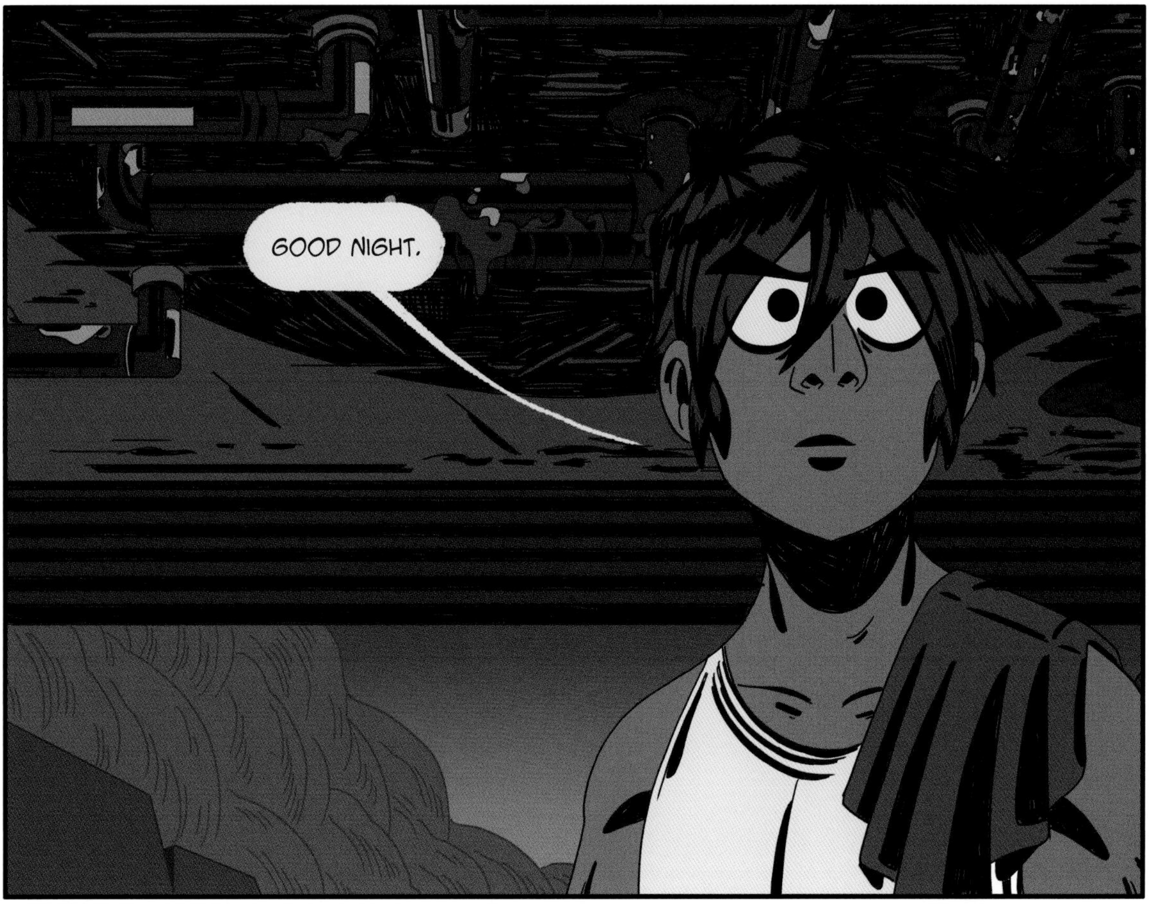
GOOD NIGHT.

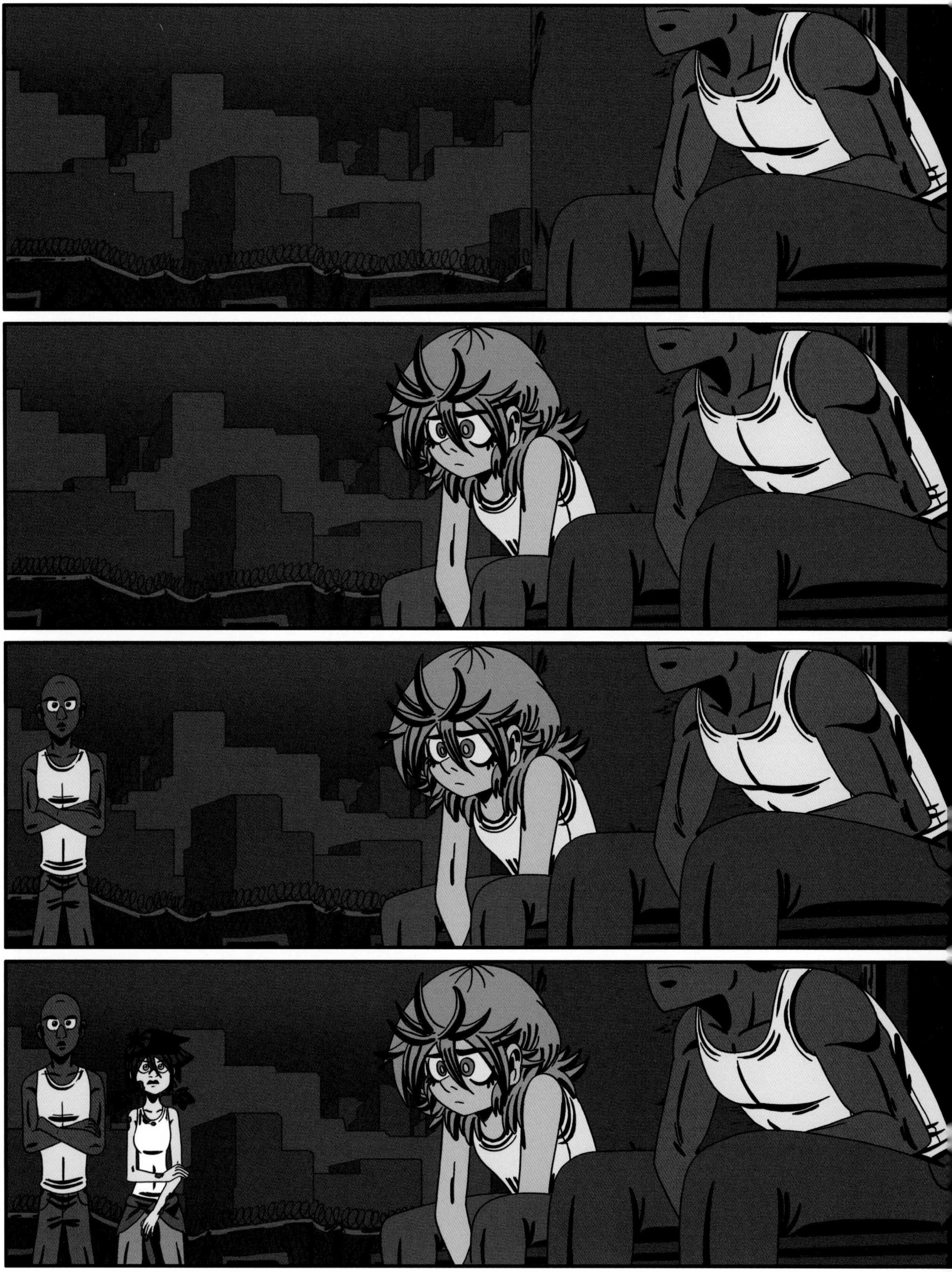

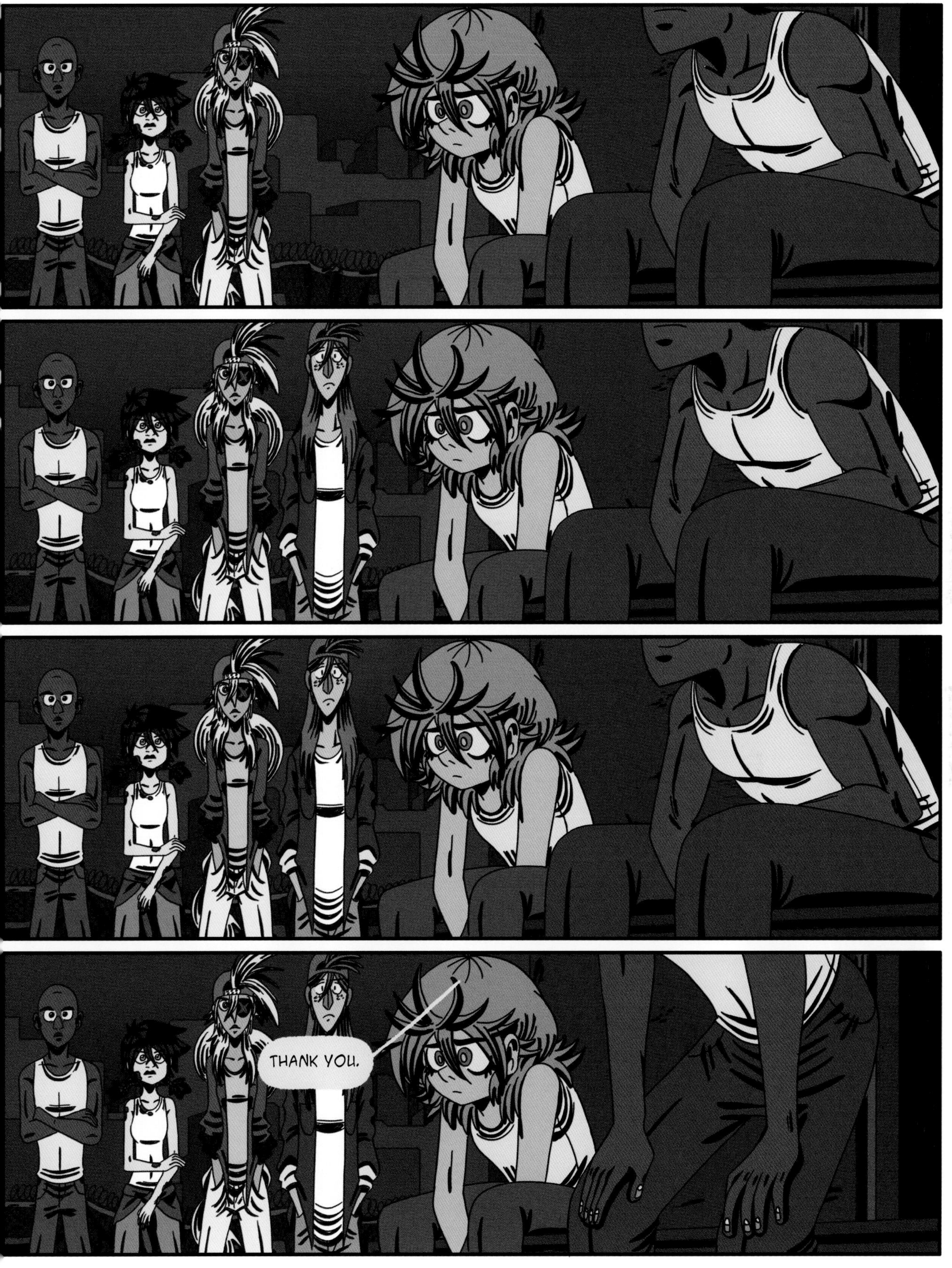
THANK YOU.

WHAT DO YOU THINK?
I THINK IT LOOKS...STANDARD. LIKE THEY DON'T WANT ANYTHING TO DISTRACT FROM WHAT TODAY'S REALLY ABOUT.
'COURSE, THAT COULD BE WHAT THEY WANT US TO THINK.
AND...I THINK...
I THINK YOU SHOULD...STOP WORRYING ABOUT US. YOU'VE DONE ALL YOU CAN. NOW IT'S UP TO US. WE'LL BE OKAY.
OF COURSE YOU WILL.
RIGHT. EXACTLY.
OH, AND AXL?

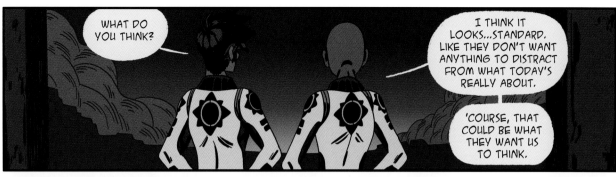

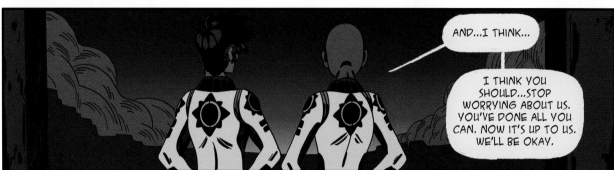

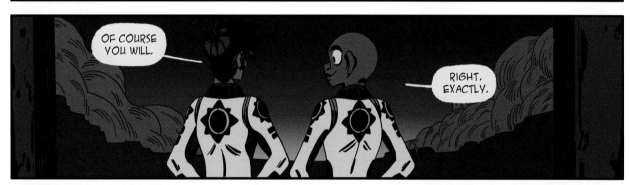

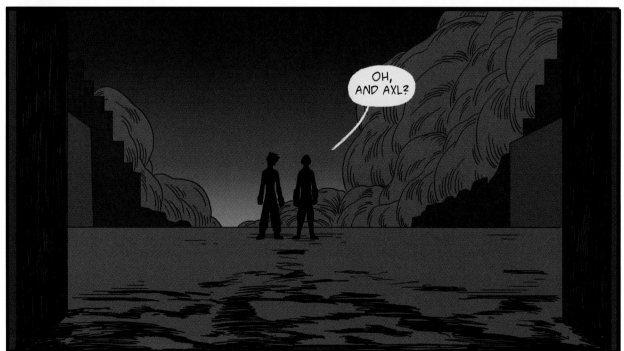

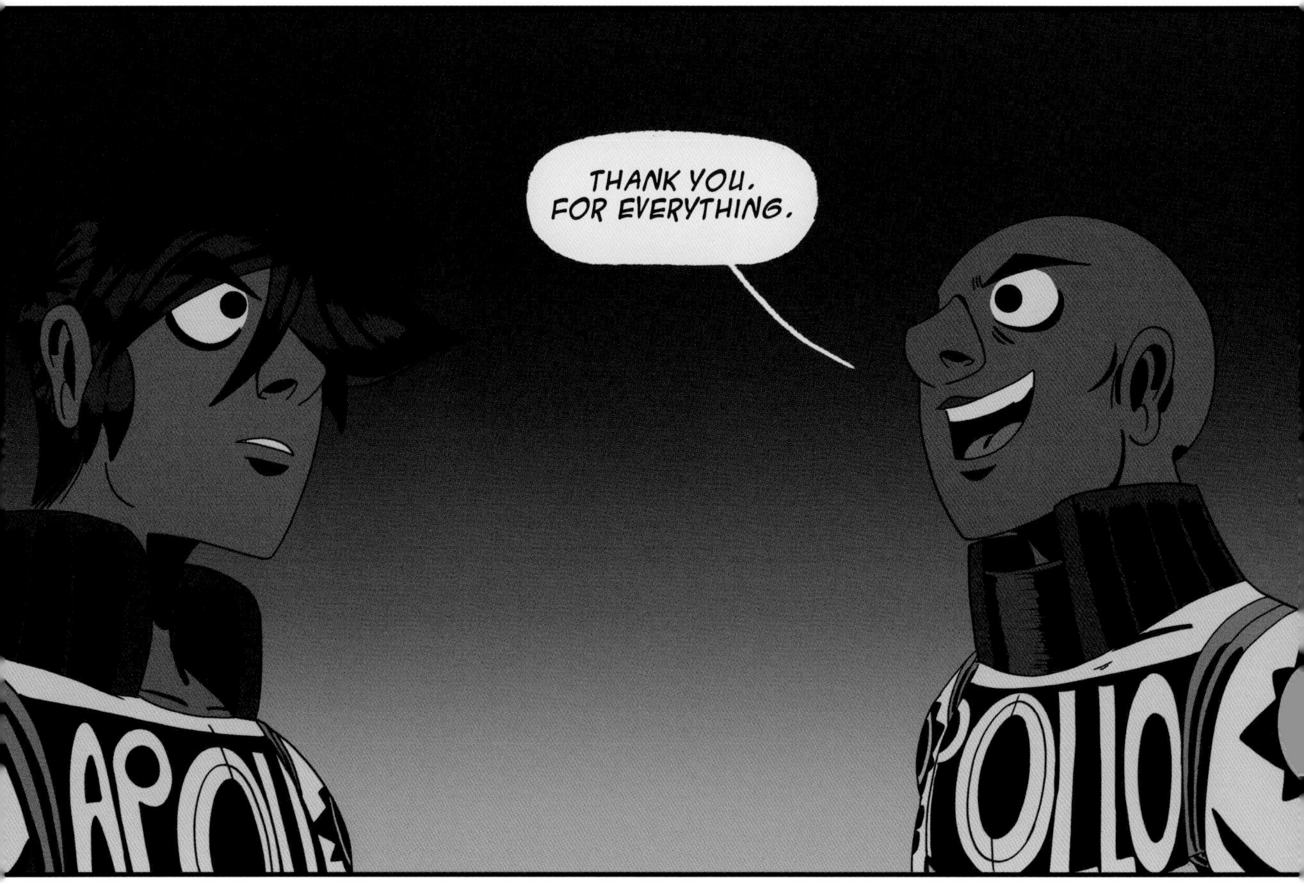
THANK YOU.
FOR EVERYTHING.
APOLL
POLLO

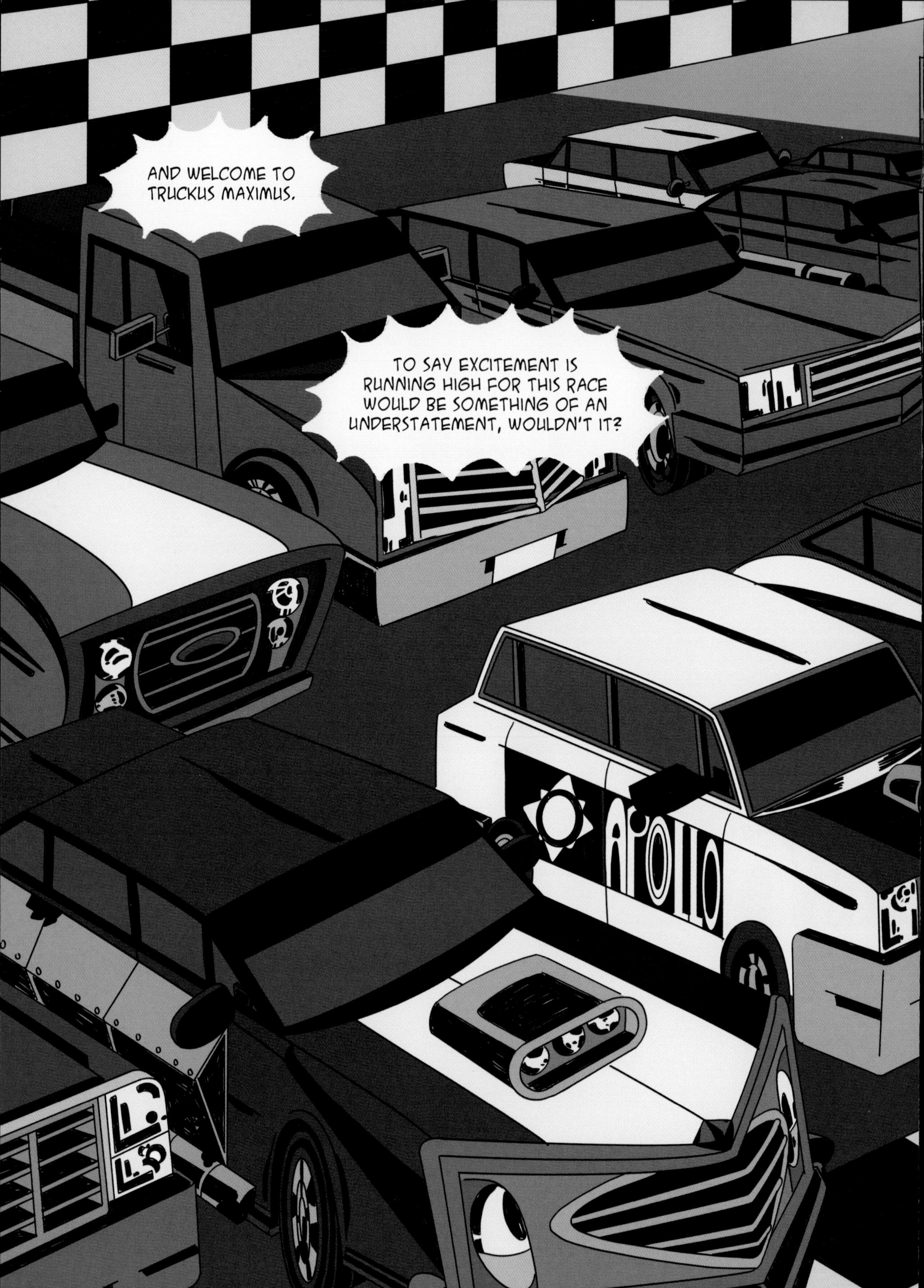
AND WELCOME TO TRUCKUS MAXIMUS.
TO SAY EXCITEMENT IS RUNNING HIGH FOR THIS RACE WOULD BE SOMETHING OF AN UNDERSTATEMENT, WOULDN'T IT?
APOLLO

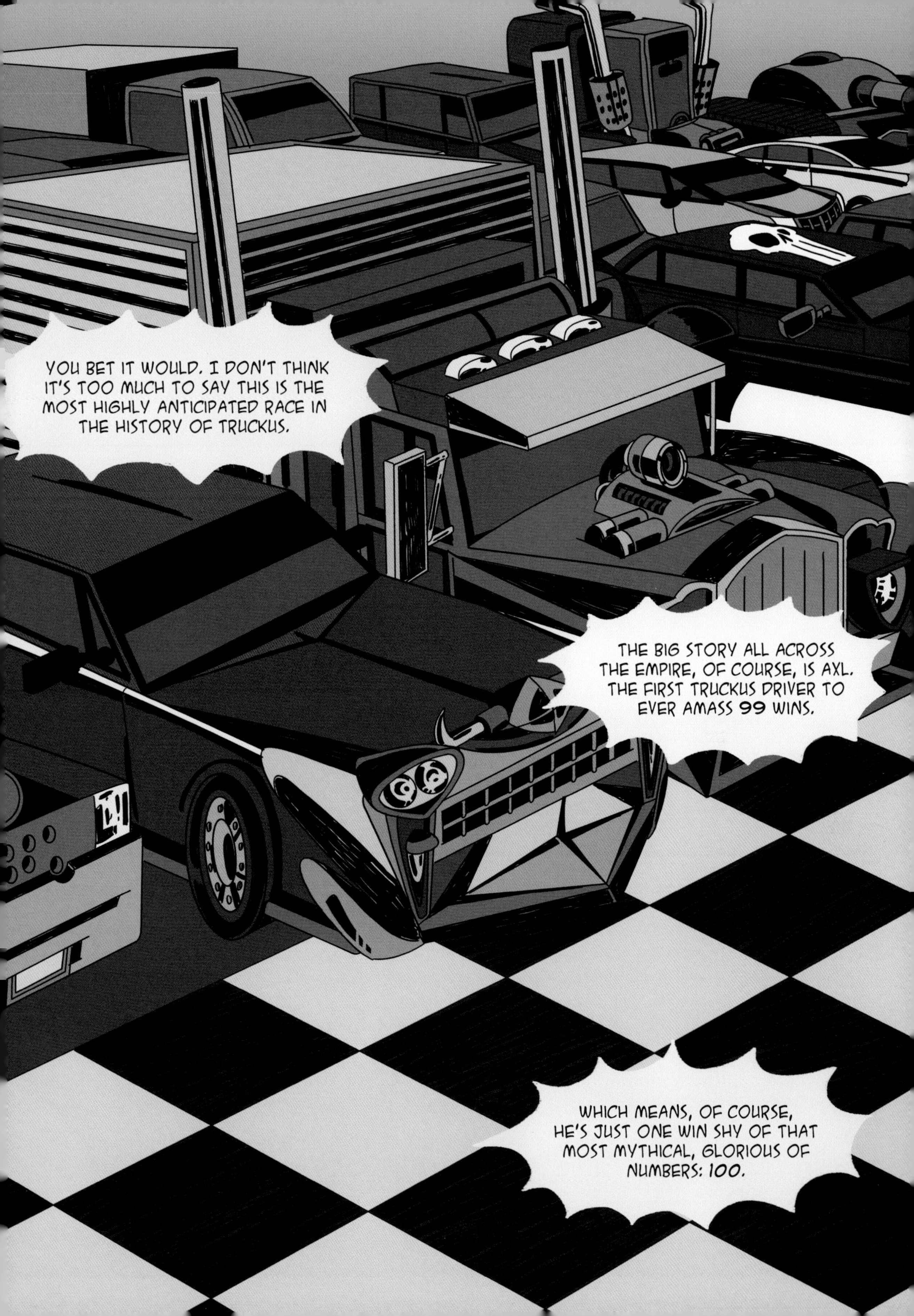
YOU BET IT WOULD. I DON'T THINK IT'S TOO MUCH TO SAY THIS IS THE MOST HIGHLY ANTICIPATED RACE IN THE HISTORY OF TRUCKUS.
THE BIG STORY ALL ACROSS THE EMPIRE, OF COURSE, IS AXL. THE FIRST TRUCKUS DRIVER TO EVER AMASS 99 WINS.
WHICH MEANS, OF COURSE, HE'S JUST ONE WIN SHY OF THAT MOST MYTHICAL, GLORIOUS OF NUMBERS: *100.*

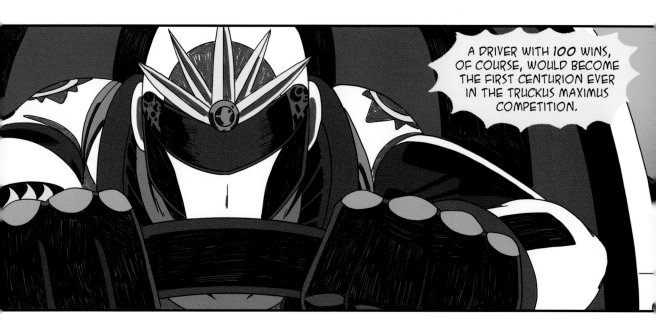

A DRIVER WITH *100* WINS, OF COURSE, WOULD BECOME THE FIRST CENTURION EVER IN THE TRUCKUS MAXIMUS COMPETITION.

NOW, AXL'S STARTING ALL THE WAY AT THE BACK OF THE PACK, DUE TO HIS MYSTERIOUS SCRATCH IN THE PREVIOUS RACE—THE FIRST TIME IN HIS ENTIRE CAREER THAT HE MISSED A START.

THAT'S RIGHT. AND THE DOMINUS ANNOUNCED THAT A DRIVER WHO SCRATCHES A SECOND RACE IS AUTOMATICALLY OUT OF TRUCKUS FOR GOOD. SO YOU KNOW AXL'LL BE DRIVING TODAY.

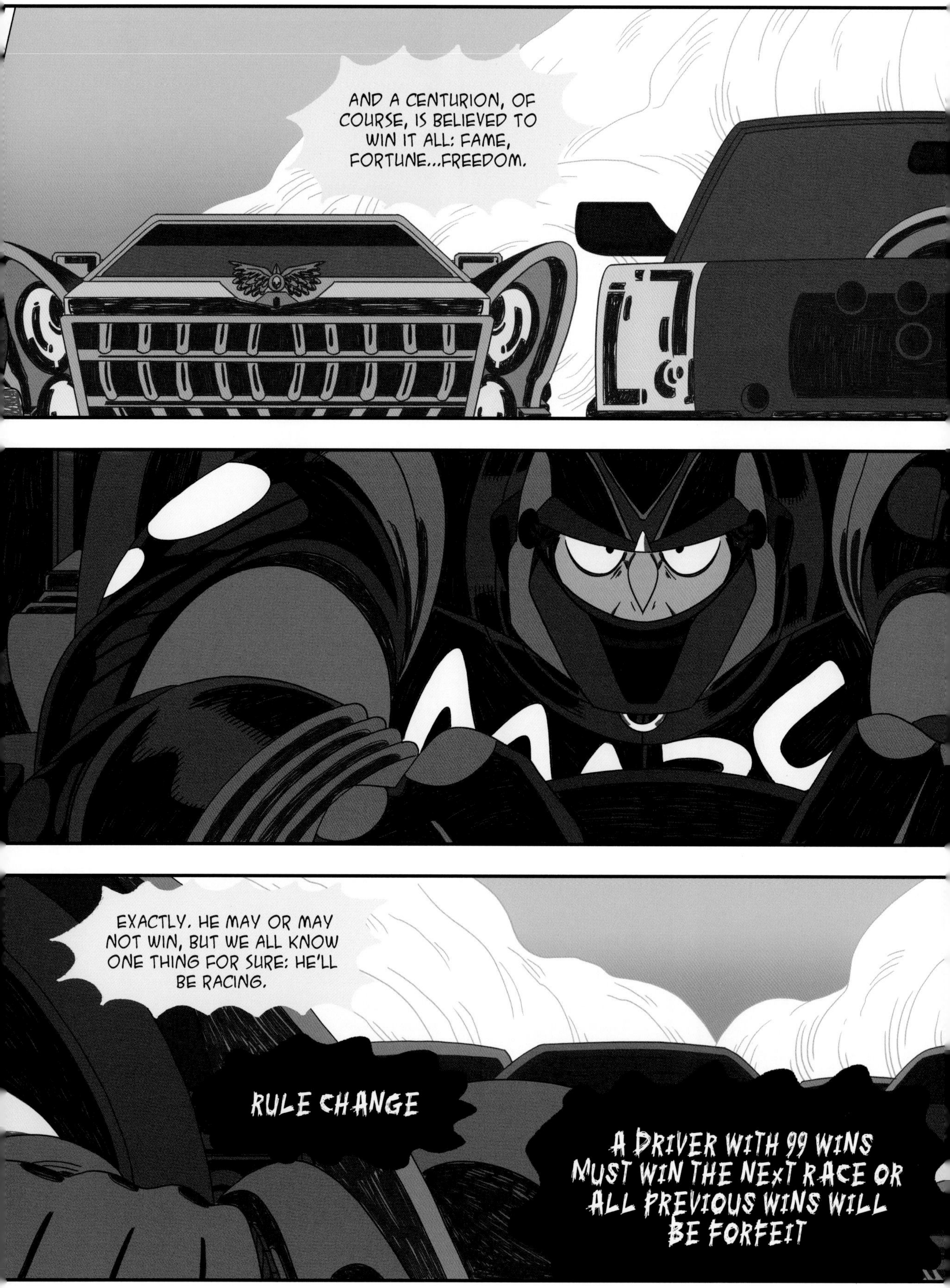
AND A CENTURION, OF COURSE, IS BELIEVED TO WIN IT ALL: FAME, FORTUNE...FREEDOM.
EXACTLY. HE MAY OR MAY NOT WIN, BUT WE ALL KNOW ONE THING FOR SURE: HE'LL BE RACING.
RULE CHANGE
A DRIVER WITH 99 WINS MUST WIN THE NEXT RACE OR ALL PREVIOUS WINS WILL BE FORFEIT

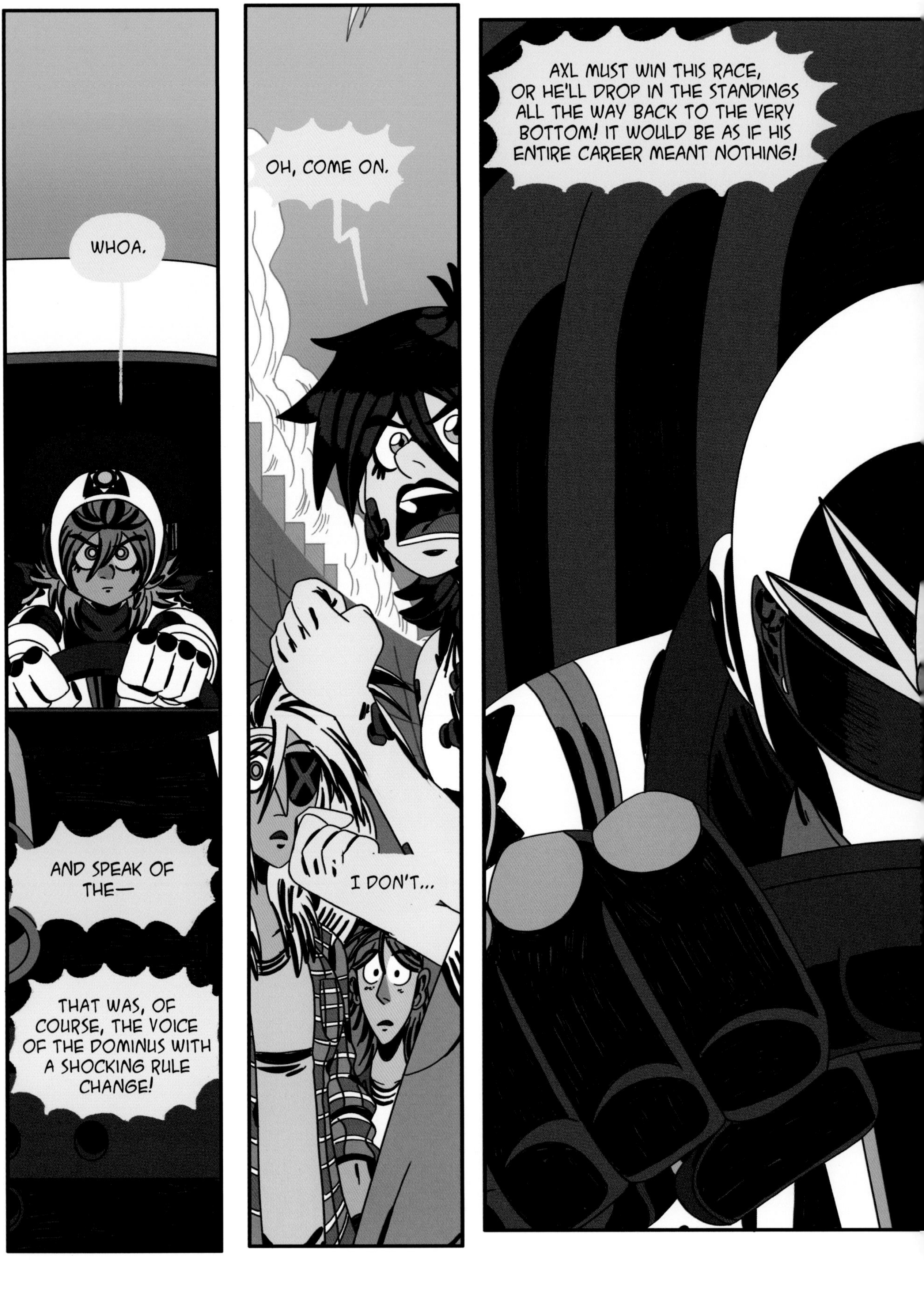
WHOA.
AND SPEAK OF THE—
THAT WAS, OF COURSE, THE VOICE OF THE DOMINUS WITH A SHOCKING RULE CHANGE!
OH, COME ON.
I DON'T...
AXL MUST WIN THIS RACE, OR HE'LL DROP IN THE STANDINGS ALL THE WAY BACK TO THE VERY BOTTOM! IT WOULD BE AS IF HIS ENTIRE CAREER MEANT NOTHING!

DESPITE BEING ONE OF THE OLDEST DRIVERS—AND BY FAR THE MOST SUCCESSFUL—HE'LL BE ESSENTIALLY A WINLESS ROOKIE AGAIN.

AND LET'S BE HONEST, THIS TIME THERE'S NO CHANCE EVEN THE GREAT AXL WILL BE ABLE TO GET ANYWHERE CLOSE TO TRIPLE DIGITS.

SO. NO PRESSURE, RIGHT?

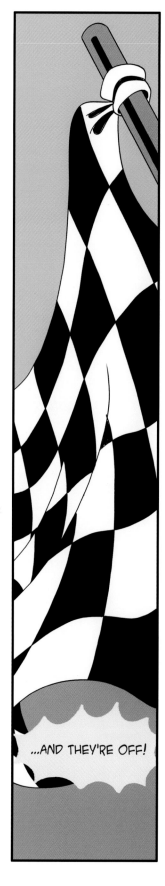

...AND THEY'RE OFF!

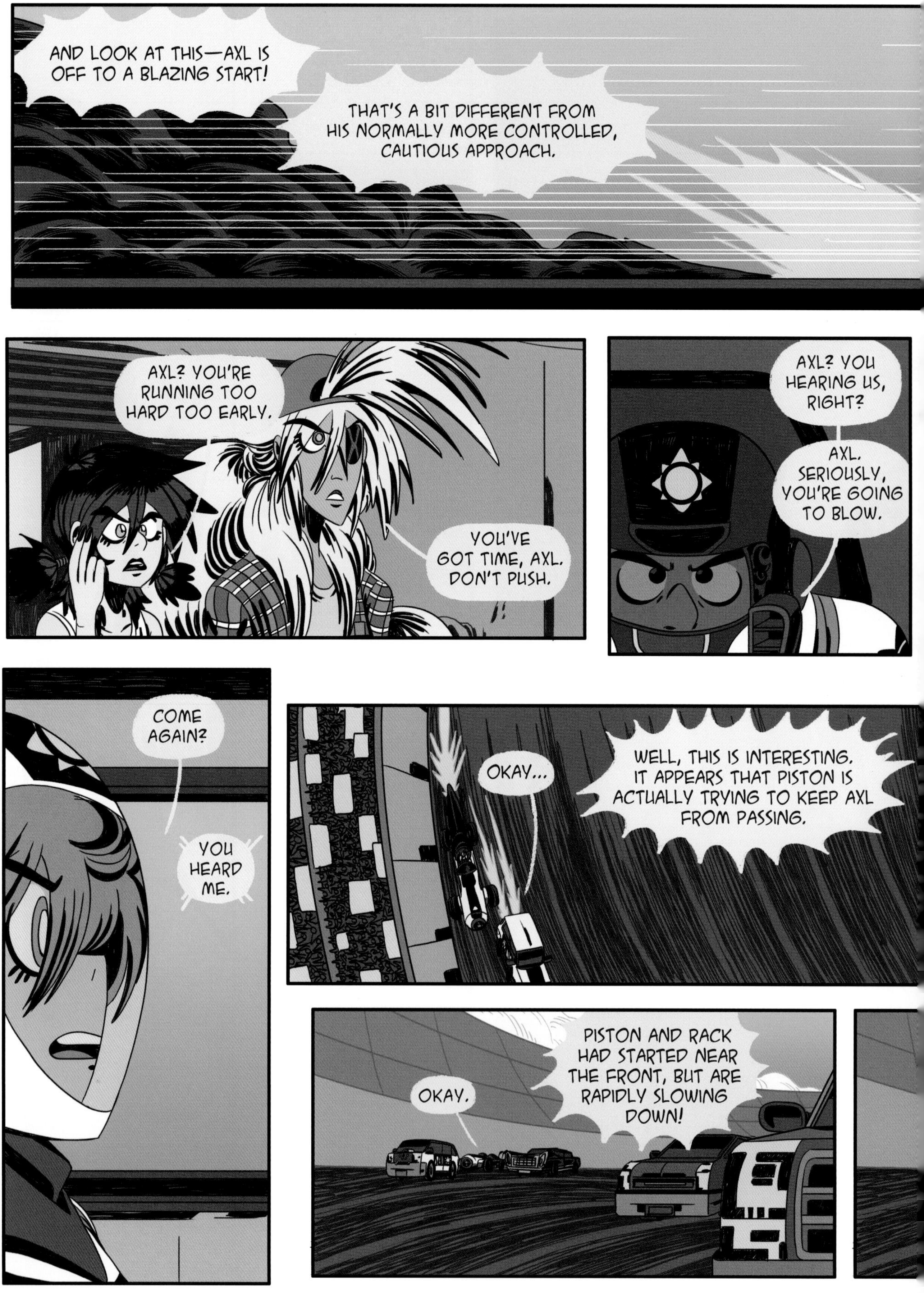
AND LOOK AT THIS—AXL IS OFF TO A BLAZING START!
THAT'S A BIT DIFFERENT FROM HIS NORMALLY MORE CONTROLLED, CAUTIOUS APPROACH.
AXL? YOU'RE RUNNING TOO HARD TOO EARLY.
YOU'VE GOT TIME, AXL. DON'T PUSH.
AXL? YOU HEARING US, RIGHT?
AXL. SERIOUSLY, YOU'RE GOING TO BLOW.
COME AGAIN?
YOU HEARD ME.
OKAY...
WELL, THIS IS INTERESTING. IT APPEARS THAT PISTON IS ACTUALLY TRYING TO KEEP AXL FROM PASSING.
OKAY.
PISTON AND RACK HAD STARTED NEAR THE FRONT, BUT ARE RAPIDLY SLOWING DOWN!

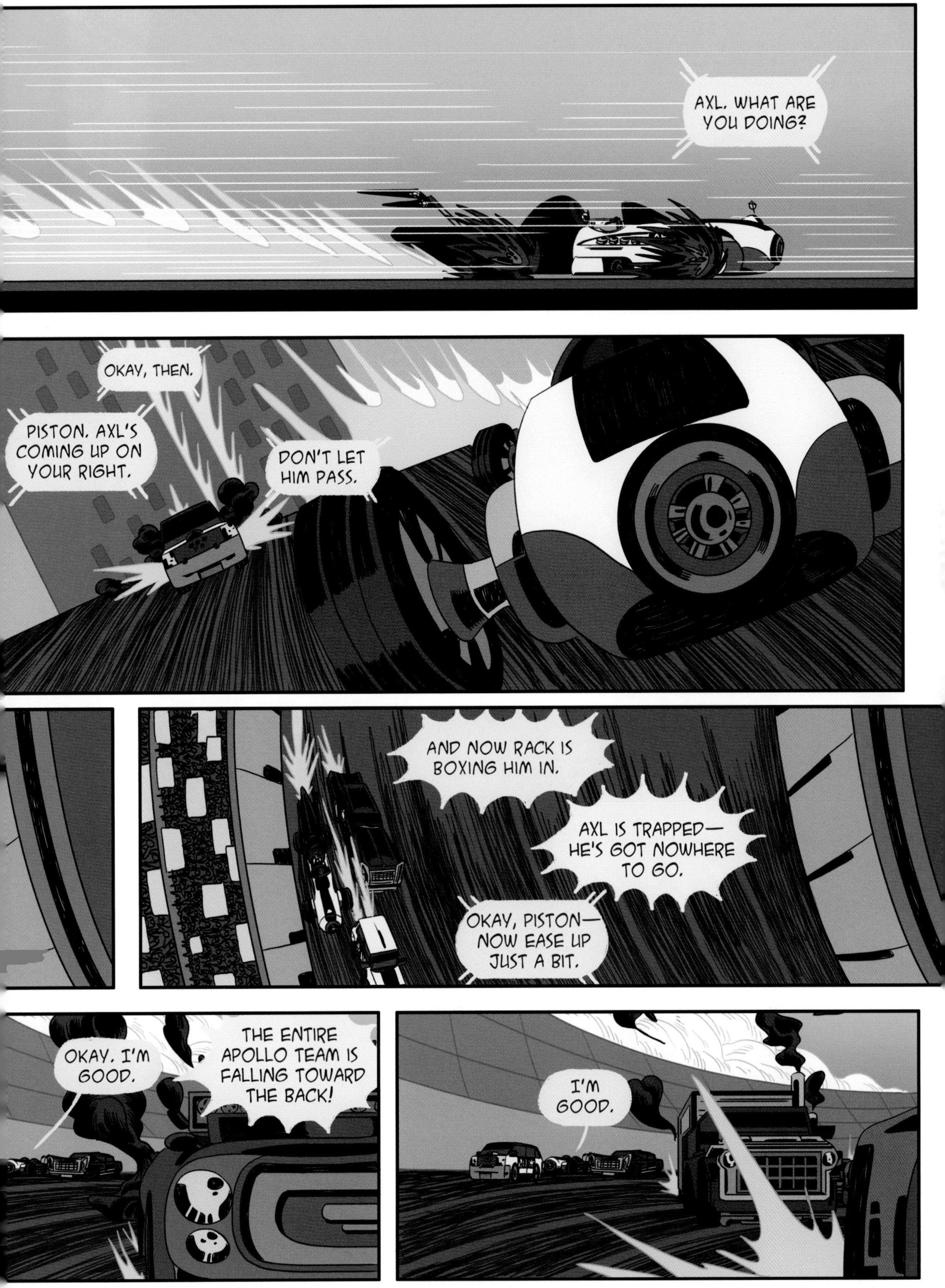
AXL, WHAT ARE YOU DOING?
OKAY, THEN.
PISTON, AXL'S COMING UP ON YOUR RIGHT.
DON'T LET HIM PASS.
AND NOW RACK IS BOXING HIM IN.
AXL IS TRAPPED— HE'S GOT NOWHERE TO GO.
OKAY, PISTON— NOW EASE UP JUST A BIT.
OKAY. I'M GOOD.
THE ENTIRE APOLLO TEAM IS FALLING TOWARD THE BACK!
I'M GOOD.

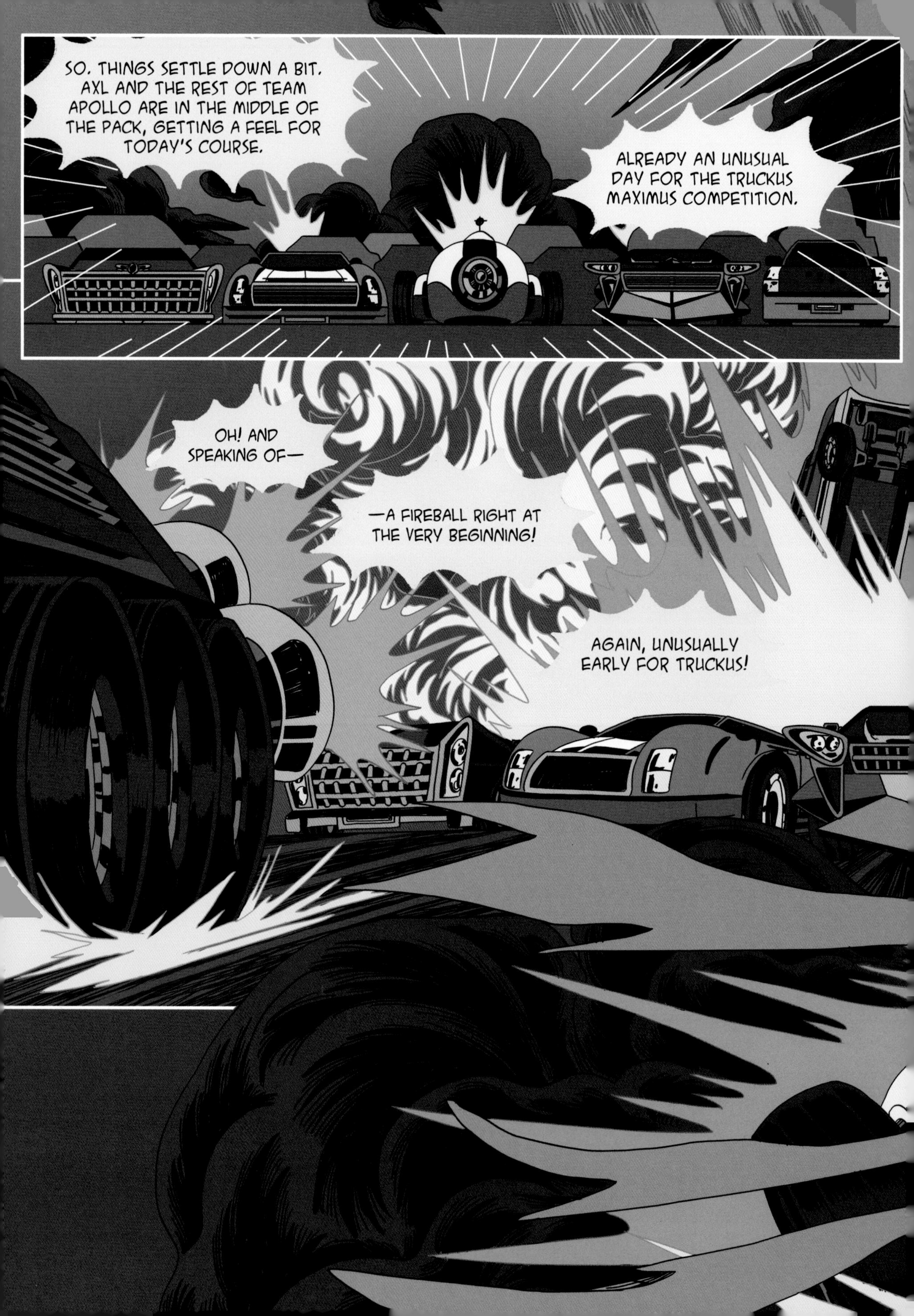
SO. THINGS SETTLE DOWN A BIT. AXL AND THE REST OF TEAM APOLLO ARE IN THE MIDDLE OF THE PACK, GETTING A FEEL FOR TODAY'S COURSE.
ALREADY AN UNUSUAL DAY FOR THE TRUCKUS MAXIMUS COMPETITION.
OH! AND SPEAKING OF—
—A FIREBALL RIGHT AT THE VERY BEGINNING!
AGAIN, UNUSUALLY EARLY FOR TRUCKUS!

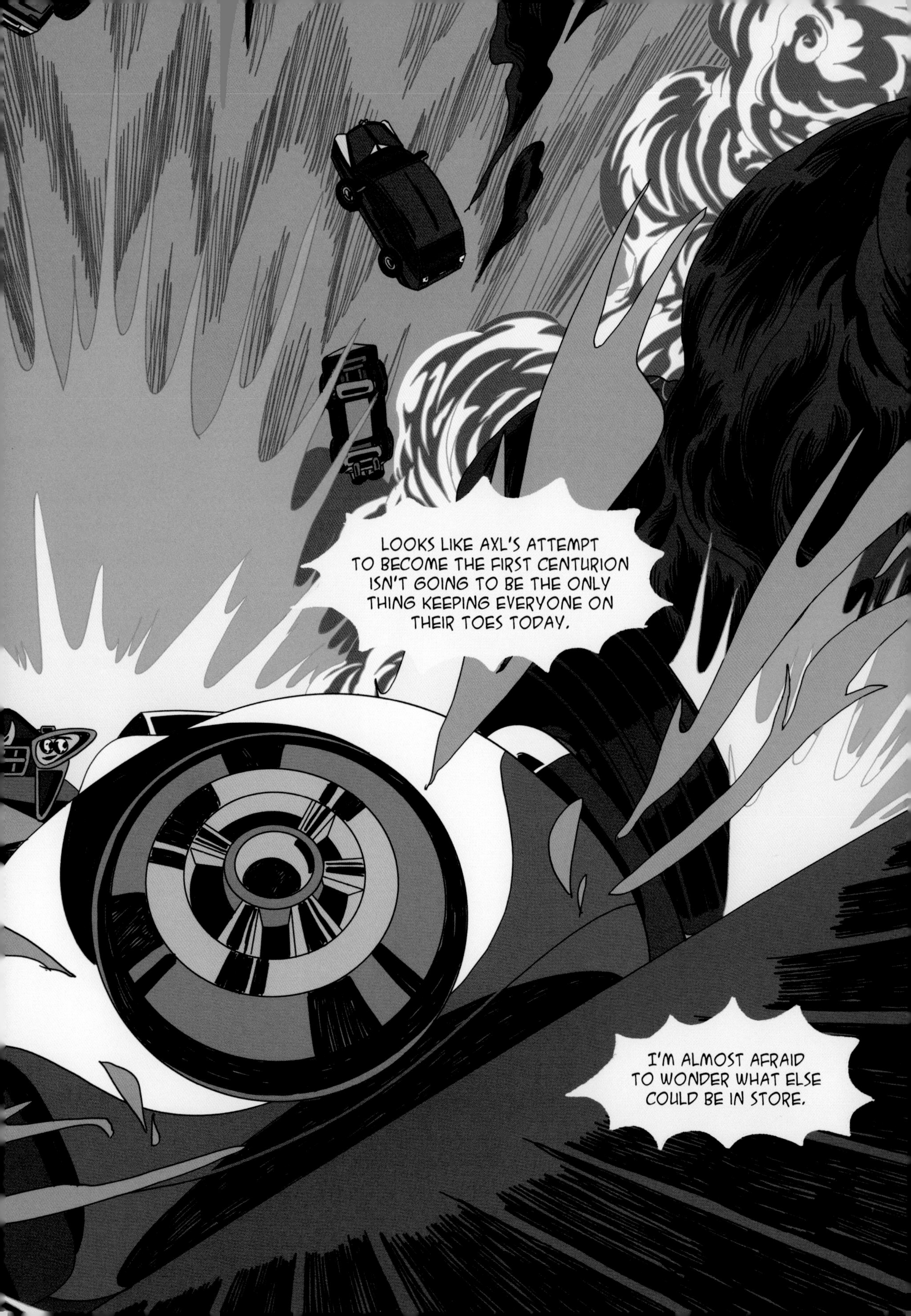
LOOKS LIKE AXL'S ATTEMPT TO BECOME THE FIRST CENTURION ISN'T GOING TO BE THE ONLY THING KEEPING EVERYONE ON THEIR TOES TODAY.
I'M ALMOST AFRAID TO WONDER WHAT ELSE COULD BE IN STORE.

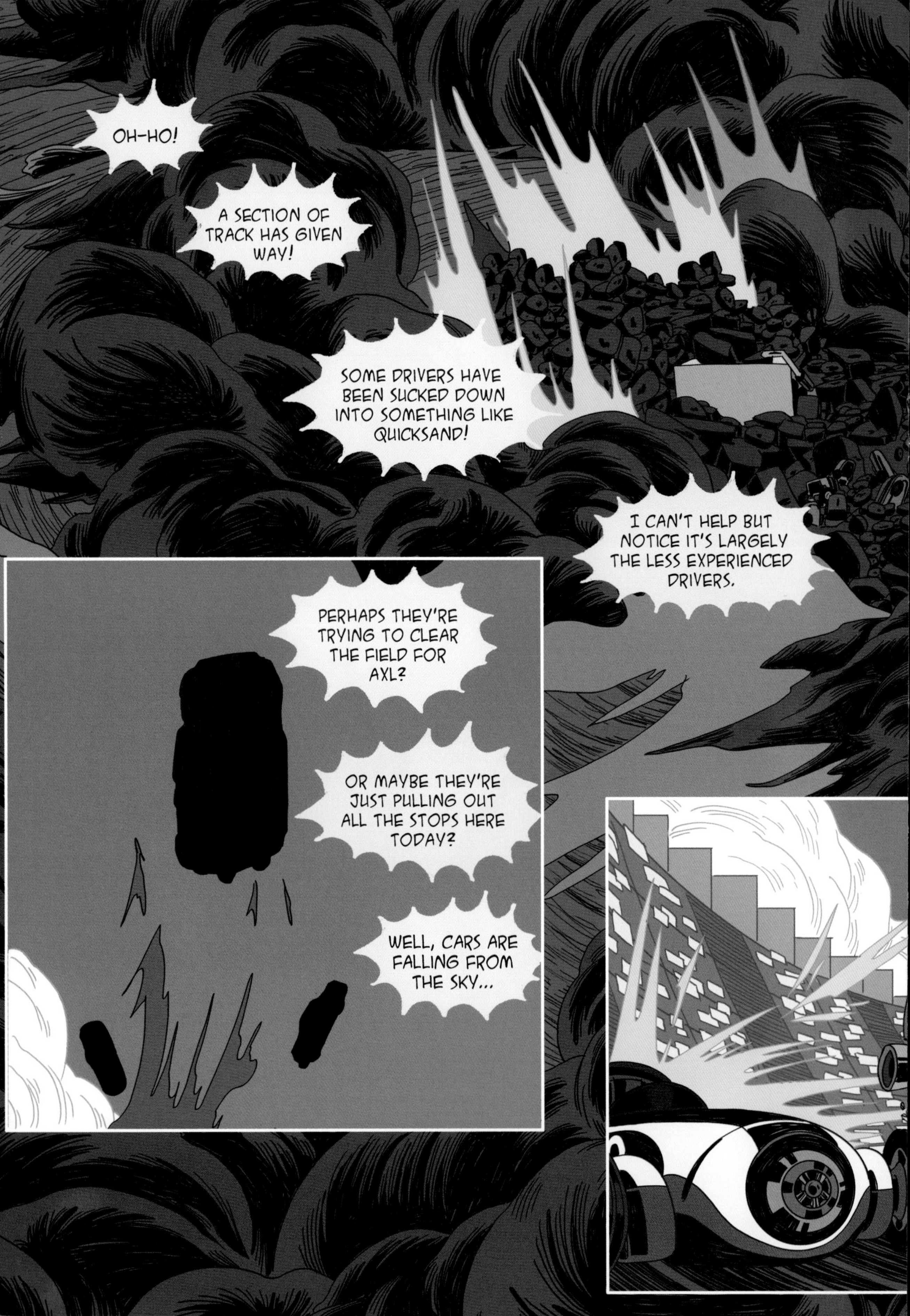
OH-HO!
A SECTION OF TRACK HAS GIVEN WAY!
SOME DRIVERS HAVE BEEN SUCKED DOWN INTO SOMETHING LIKE QUICKSAND!
I CAN'T HELP BUT NOTICE IT'S LARGELY THE LESS EXPERIENCED DRIVERS.
PERHAPS THEY'RE TRYING TO CLEAR THE FIELD FOR AXL?
OR MAYBE THEY'RE JUST PULLING OUT ALL THE STOPS HERE TODAY?
WELL, CARS ARE FALLING FROM THE SKY...

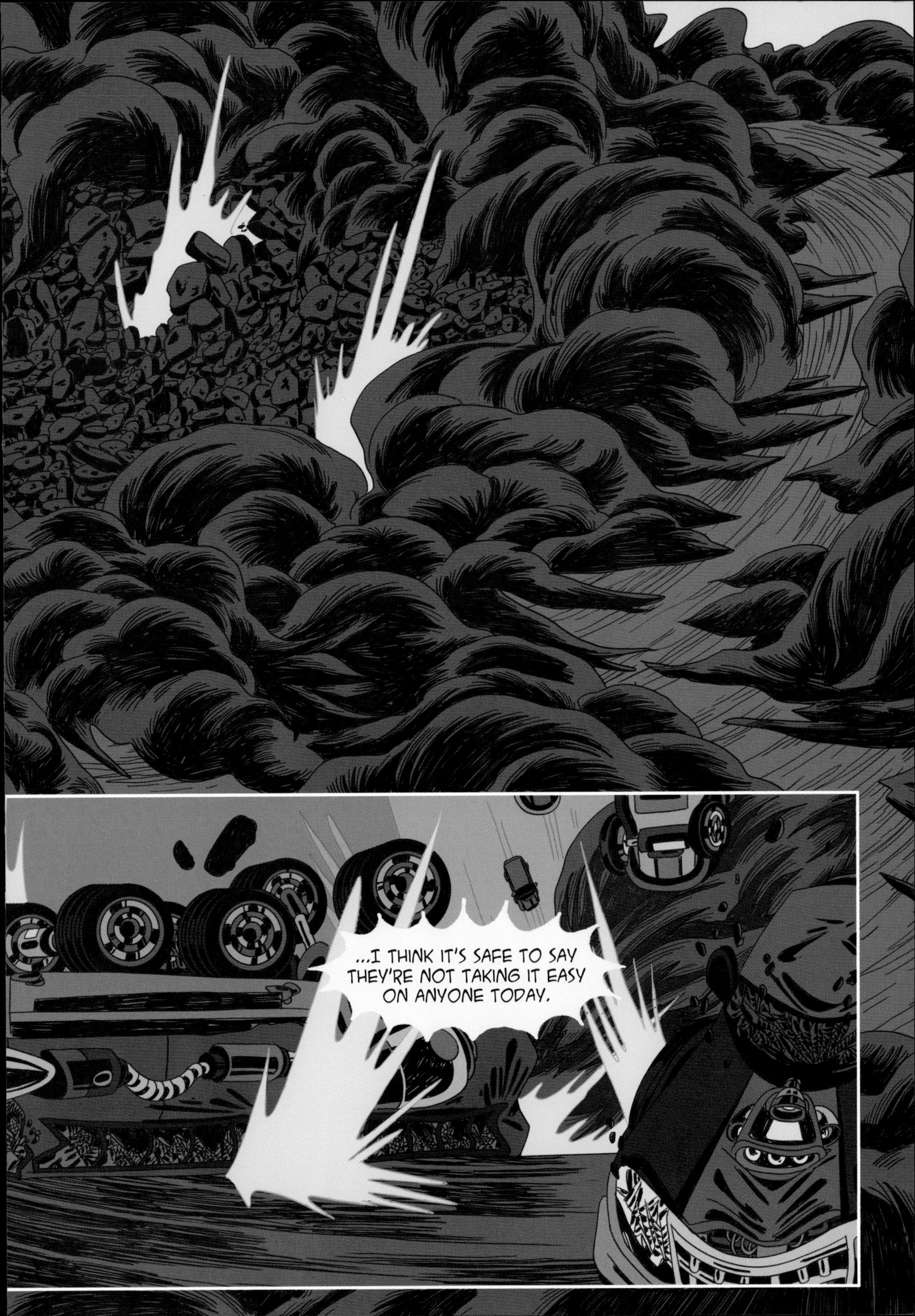
...I THINK IT'S SAFE TO SAY THEY'RE NOT TAKING IT EASY ON ANYONE TODAY.

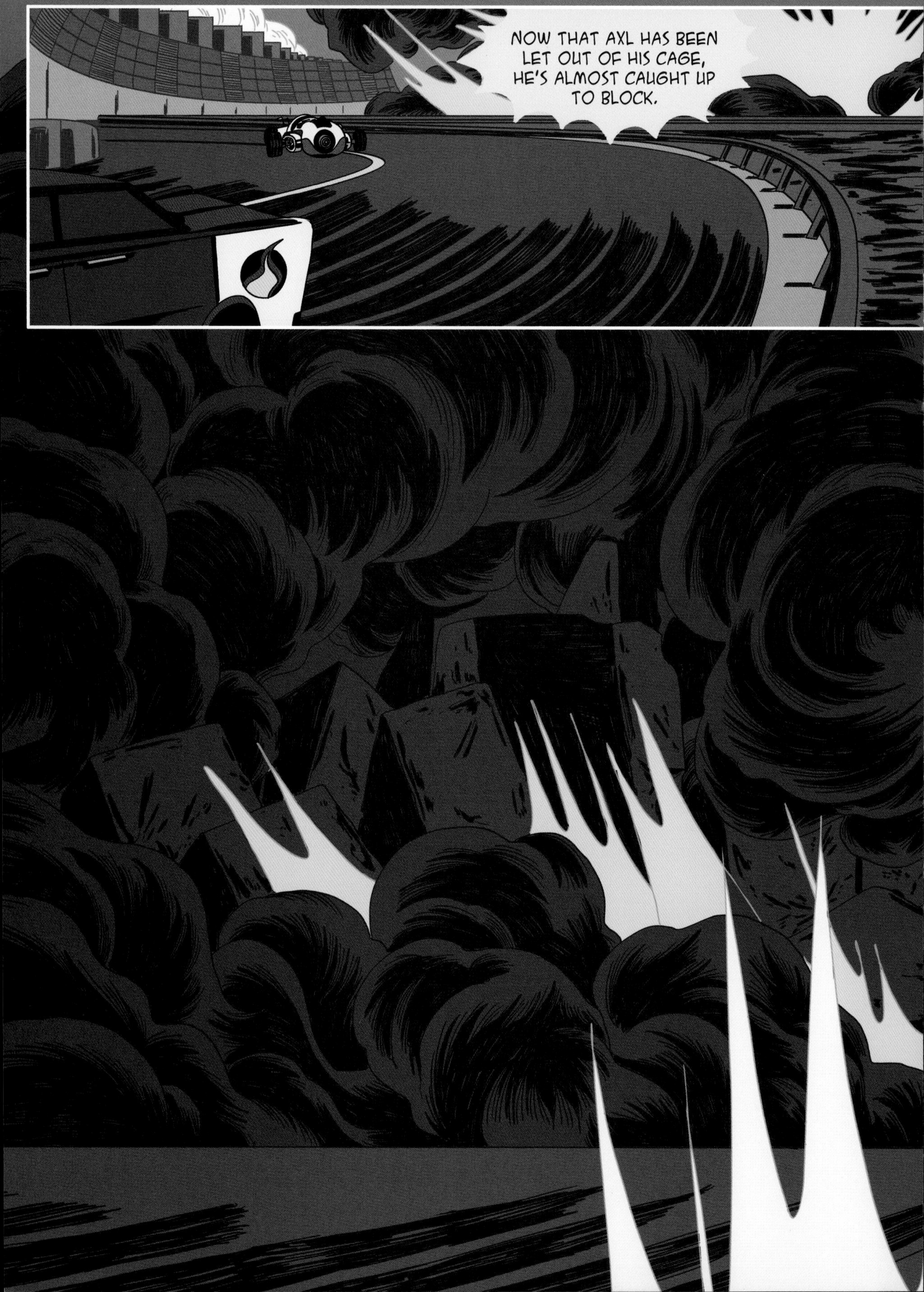
NOW THAT AXL HAS BEEN LET OUT OF HIS CAGE, HE'S ALMOST CAUGHT UP TO BLOCK.

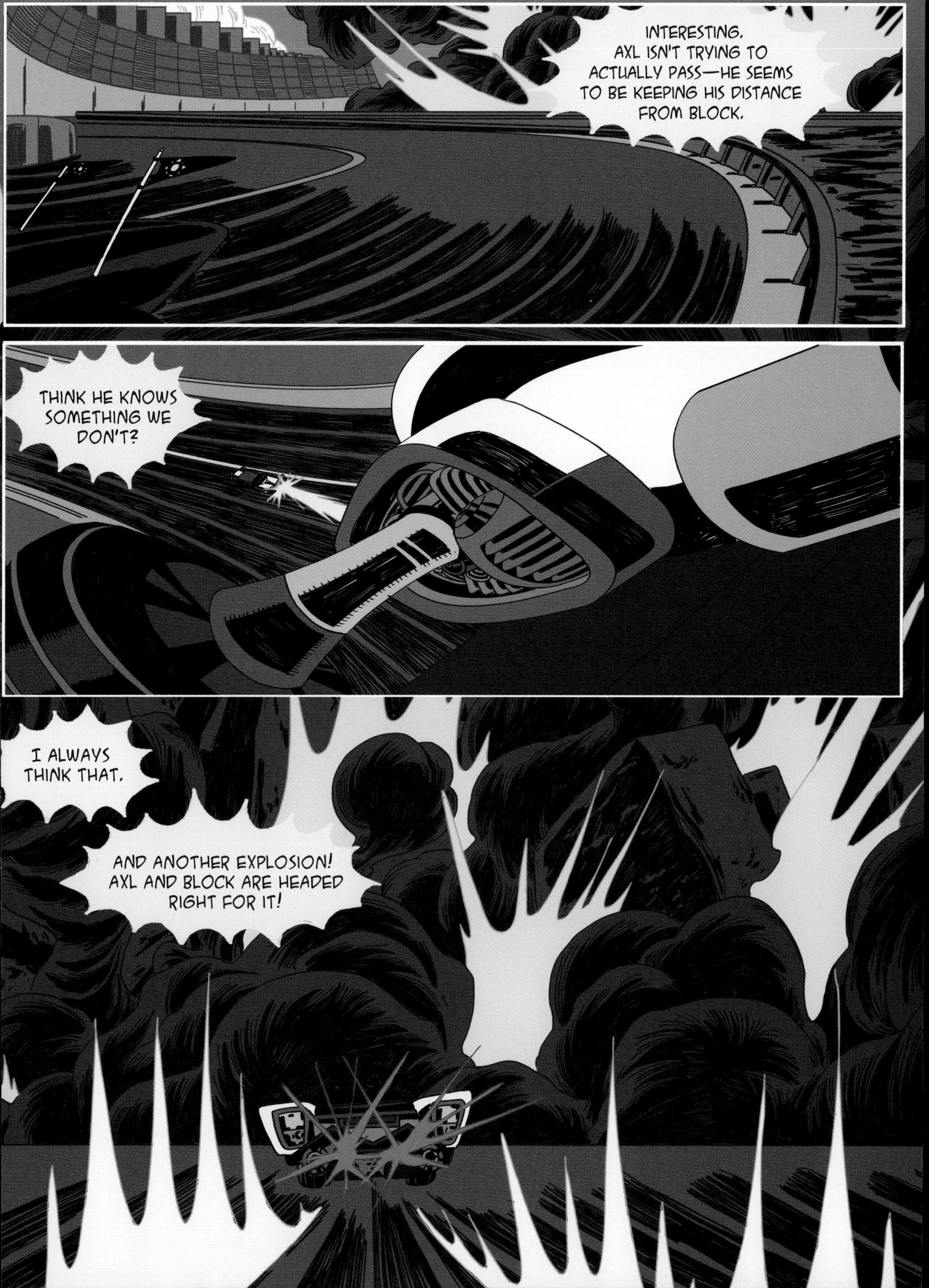
INTERESTING. AXL ISN'T TRYING TO ACTUALLY PASS—HE SEEMS TO BE KEEPING HIS DISTANCE FROM BLOCK.
THINK HE KNOWS SOMETHING WE DON'T?
I ALWAYS THINK THAT.
AND ANOTHER EXPLOSION! AXL AND BLOCK ARE HEADED RIGHT FOR IT!

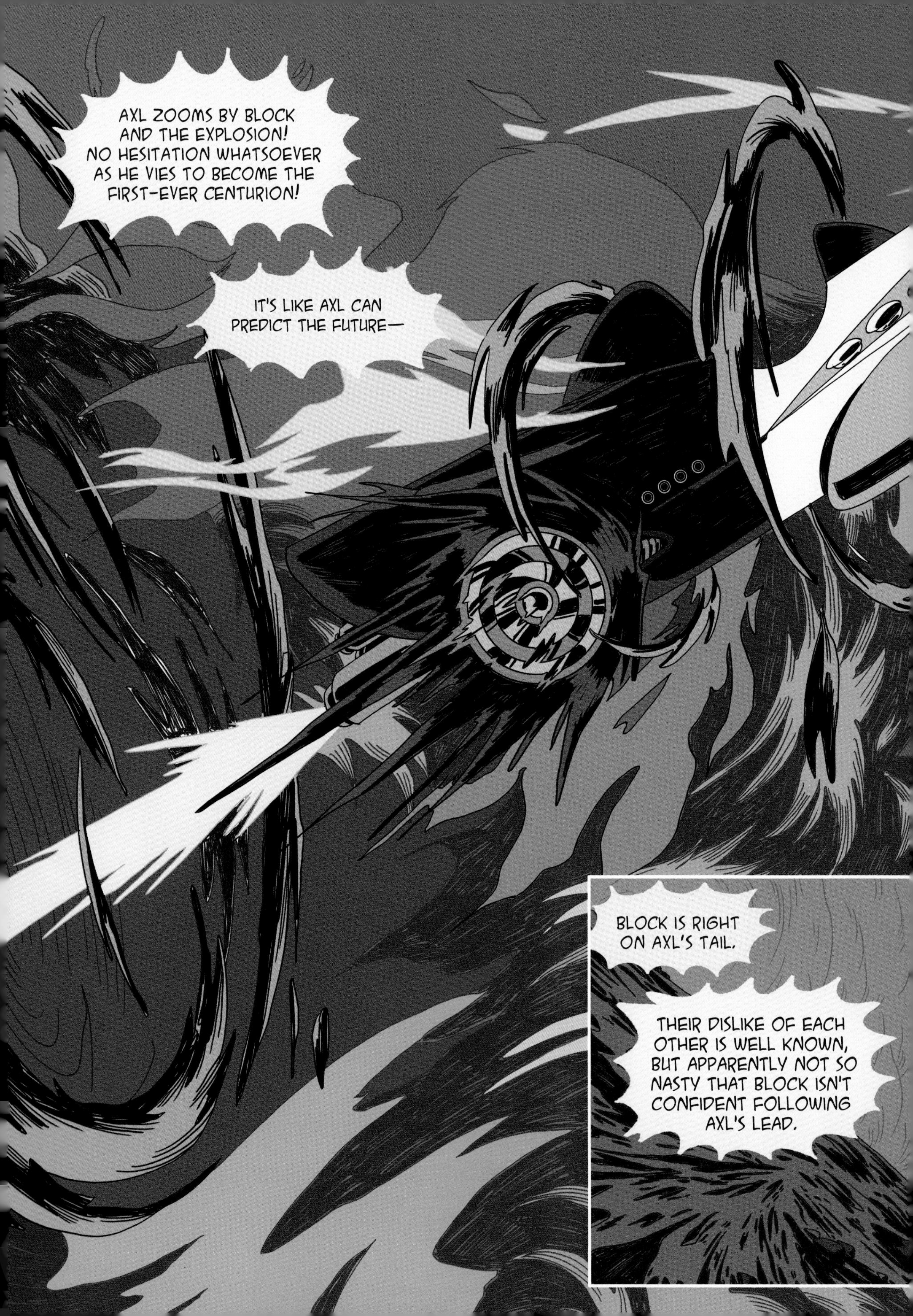
AXL ZOOMS BY BLOCK AND THE EXPLOSION! NO HESITATION WHATSOEVER AS HE VIES TO BECOME THE FIRST-EVER CENTURION!
IT'S LIKE AXL CAN PREDICT THE FUTURE—
BLOCK IS RIGHT ON AXL'S TAIL.
THEIR DISLIKE OF EACH OTHER IS WELL KNOWN, BUT APPARENTLY NOT SO NASTY THAT BLOCK ISN'T CONFIDENT FOLLOWING AXL'S LEAD.

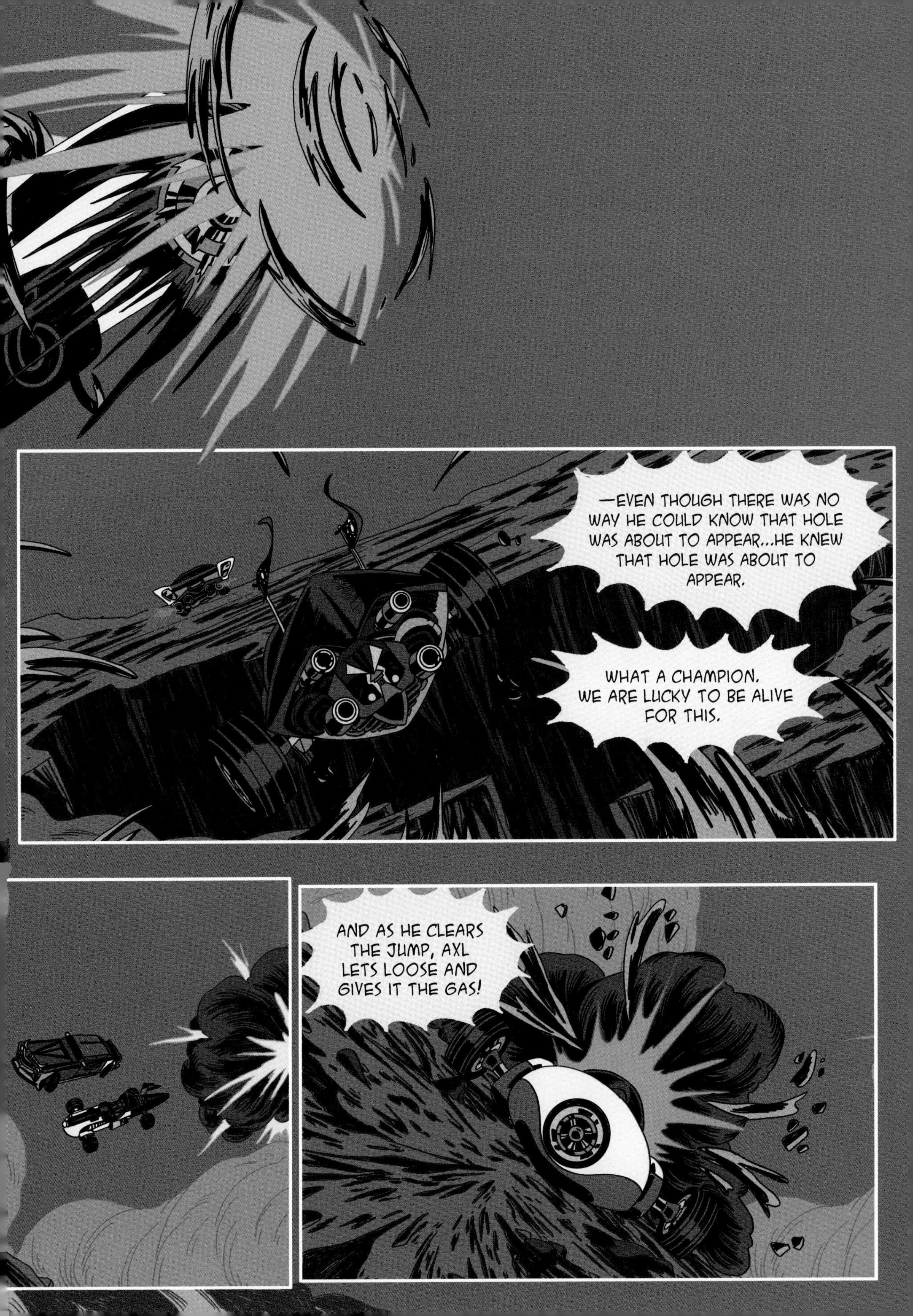
—EVEN THOUGH THERE WAS NO WAY HE COULD KNOW THAT HOLE WAS ABOUT TO APPEAR...HE KNEW THAT HOLE WAS ABOUT TO APPEAR.
WHAT A CHAMPION. WE ARE LUCKY TO BE ALIVE FOR THIS.
AND AS HE CLEARS THE JUMP, AXL LETS LOOSE AND GIVES IT THE GAS!

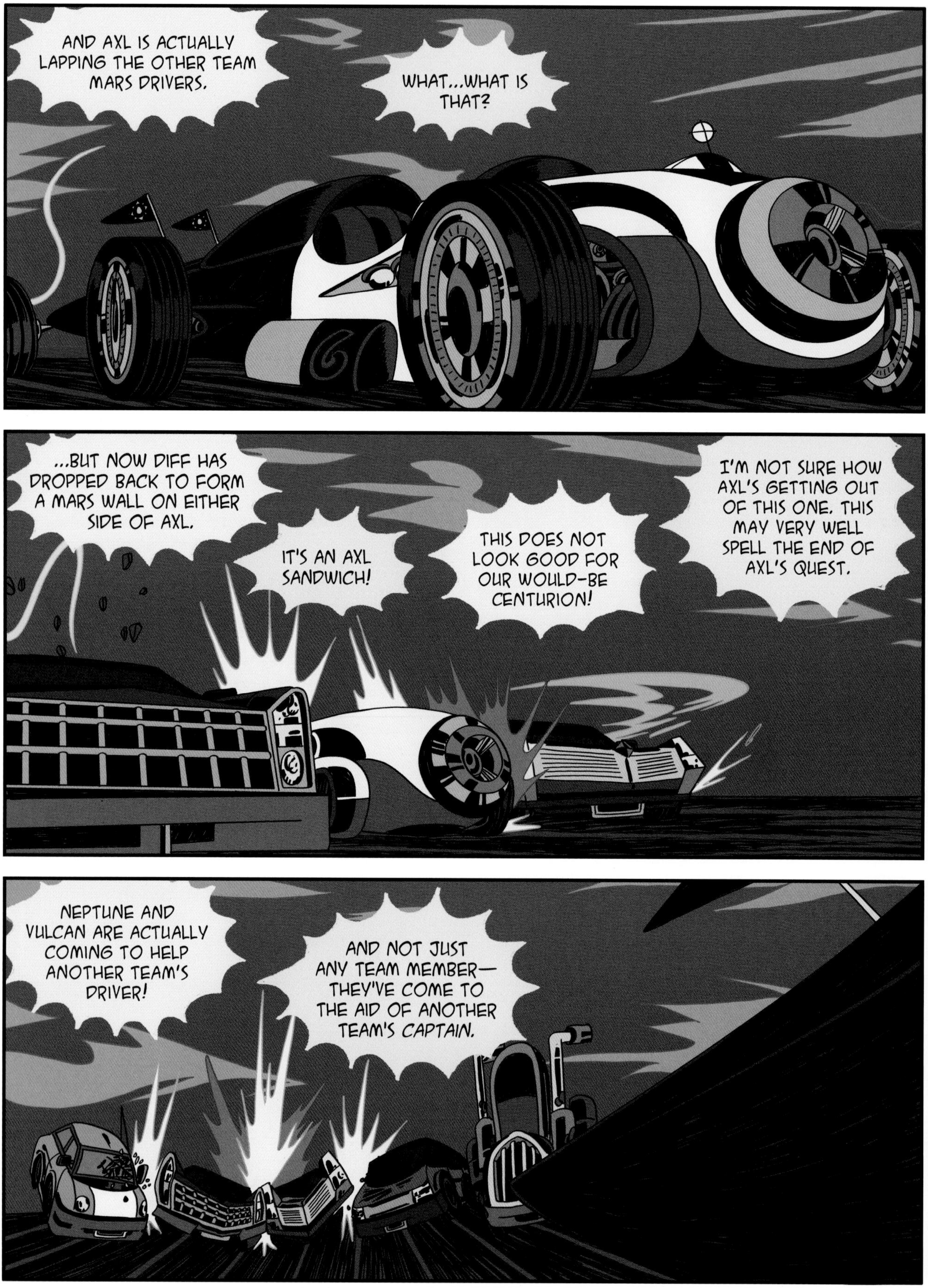
AND AXL IS ACTUALLY LAPPING THE OTHER TEAM MARS DRIVERS.
WHAT...WHAT IS THAT?
...BUT NOW DIFF HAS DROPPED BACK TO FORM A MARS WALL ON EITHER SIDE OF AXL.
IT'S AN AXL SANDWICH!
THIS DOES NOT LOOK GOOD FOR OUR WOULD-BE CENTURION!
I'M NOT SURE HOW AXL'S GETTING OUT OF THIS ONE. THIS MAY VERY WELL SPELL THE END OF AXL'S QUEST.
NEPTUNE AND VULCAN ARE ACTUALLY COMING TO HELP ANOTHER TEAM'S DRIVER!
AND NOT JUST ANY TEAM MEMBER— THEY'VE COME TO THE AID OF ANOTHER TEAM'S CAPTAIN.

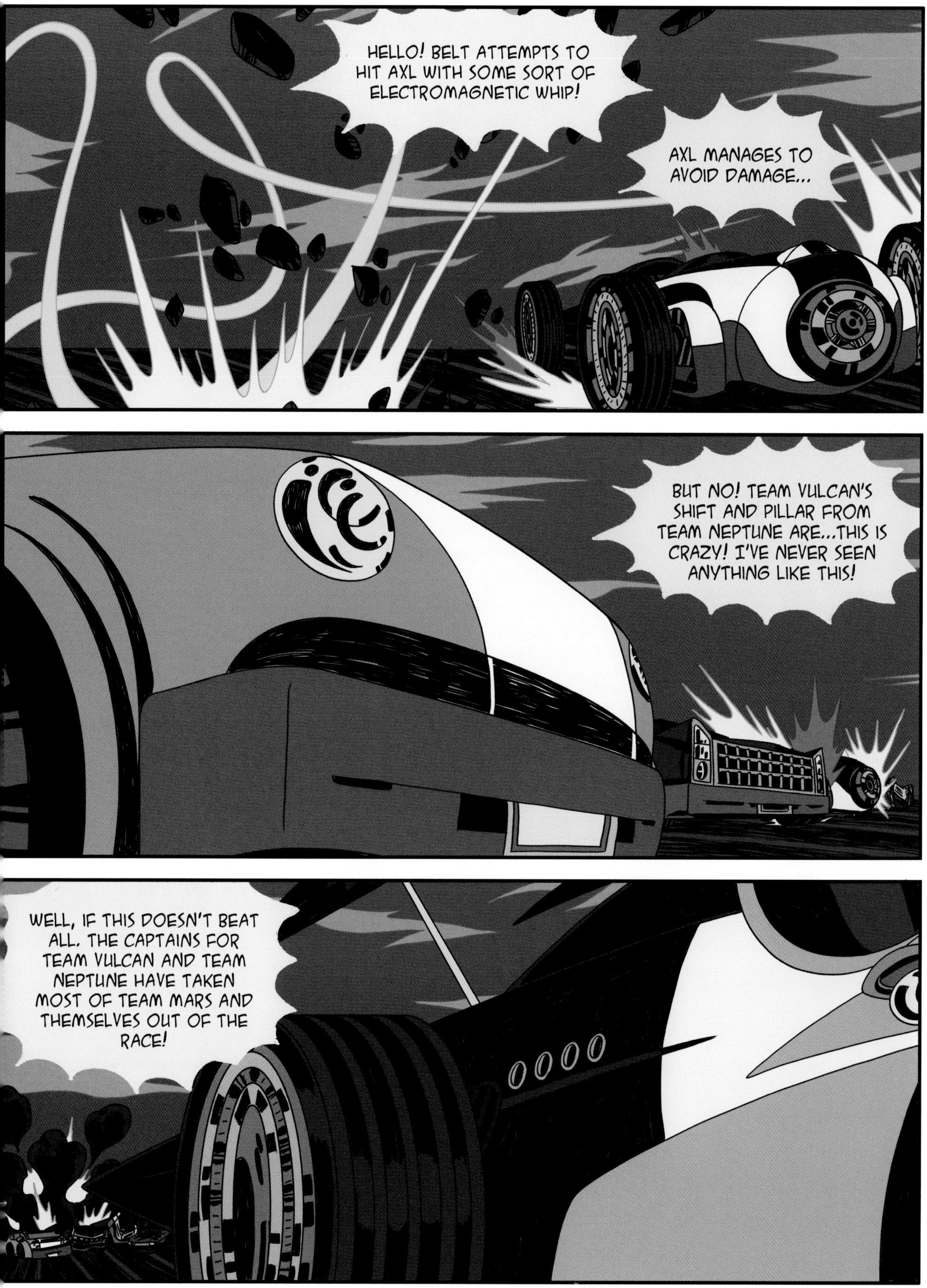
HELLO! BELT ATTEMPTS TO HIT AXL WITH SOME SORT OF ELECTROMAGNETIC WHIP!
AXL MANAGES TO AVOID DAMAGE...
BUT NO! TEAM VULCAN'S SHIFT AND PILLAR FROM TEAM NEPTUNE ARE...THIS IS CRAZY! I'VE NEVER SEEN ANYTHING LIKE THIS!
WELL, IF THIS DOESN'T BEAT ALL. THE CAPTAINS FOR TEAM VULCAN AND TEAM NEPTUNE HAVE TAKEN MOST OF TEAM MARS AND THEMSELVES OUT OF THE RACE!

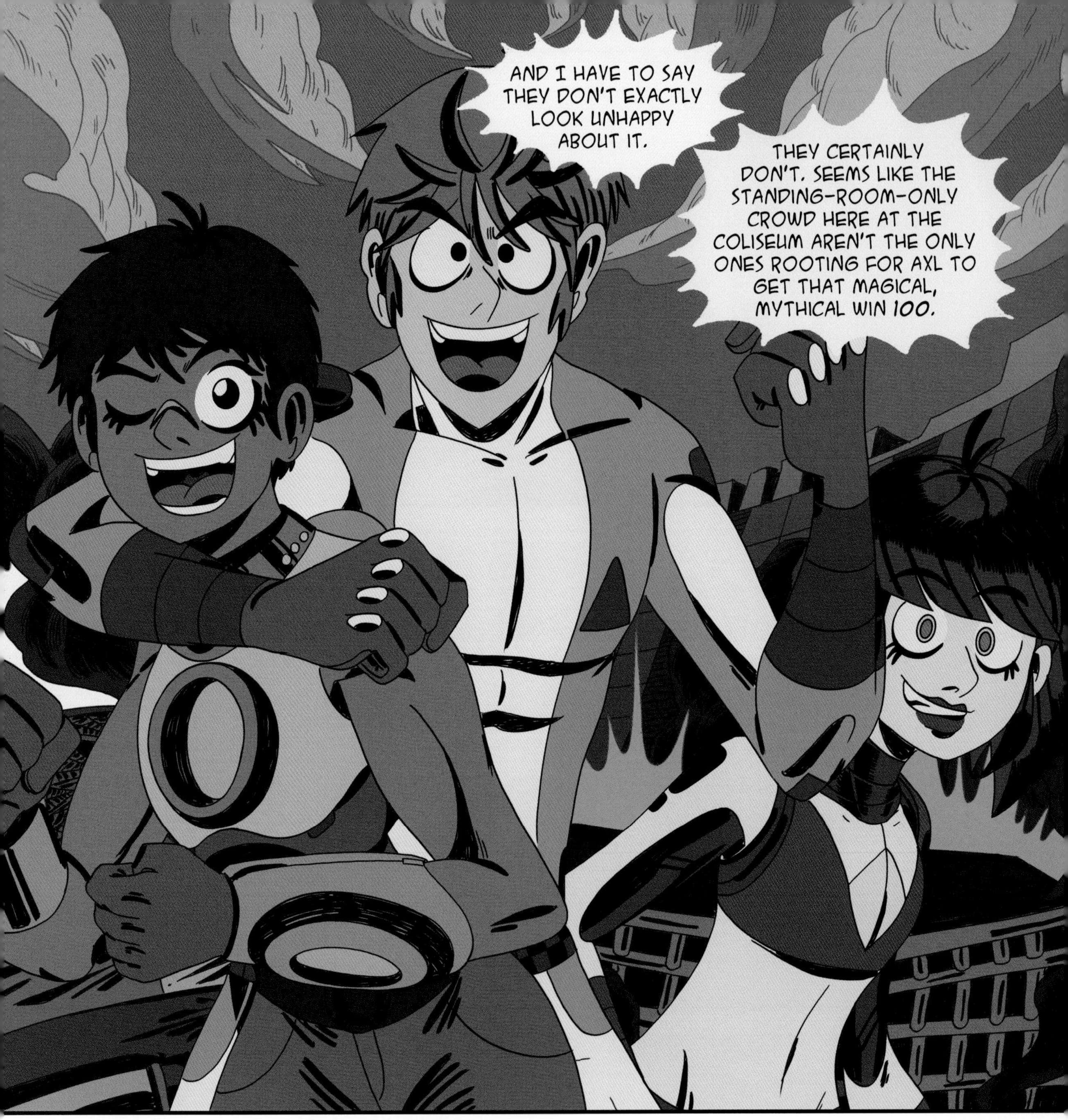
AND I HAVE TO SAY THEY DON'T EXACTLY LOOK UNHAPPY ABOUT IT.
THEY CERTAINLY DON'T. SEEMS LIKE THE STANDING-ROOM-ONLY CROWD HERE AT THE COLISEUM AREN'T THE ONLY ONES ROOTING FOR AXL TO GET THAT MAGICAL, MYTHICAL WIN *100*.

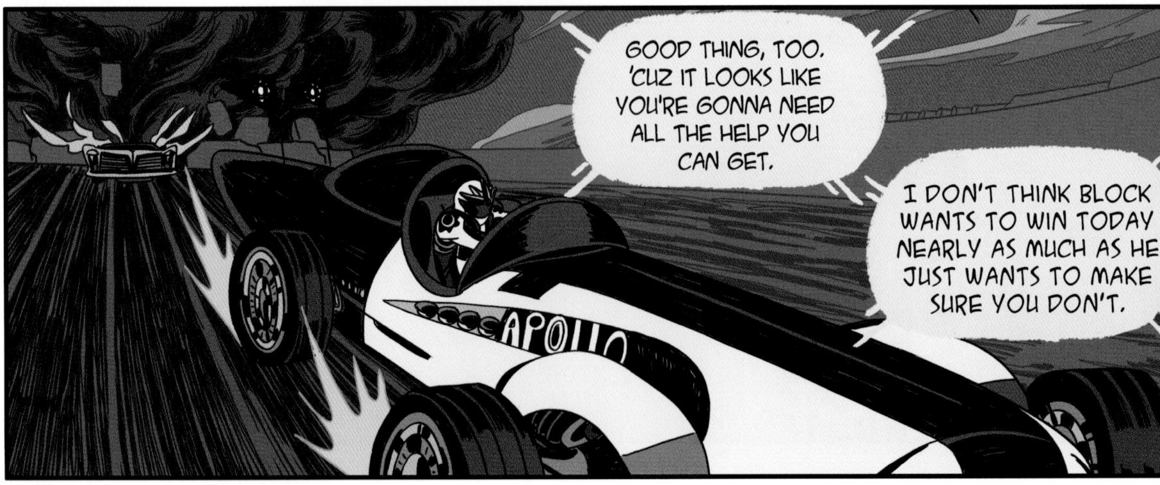
GOOD THING, TOO. 'CUZ IT LOOKS LIKE YOU'RE GONNA NEED ALL THE HELP YOU CAN GET.
I DON'T THINK BLOCK WANTS TO WIN TODAY NEARLY AS MUCH AS HE JUST WANTS TO MAKE SURE YOU DON'T.
APOLLO

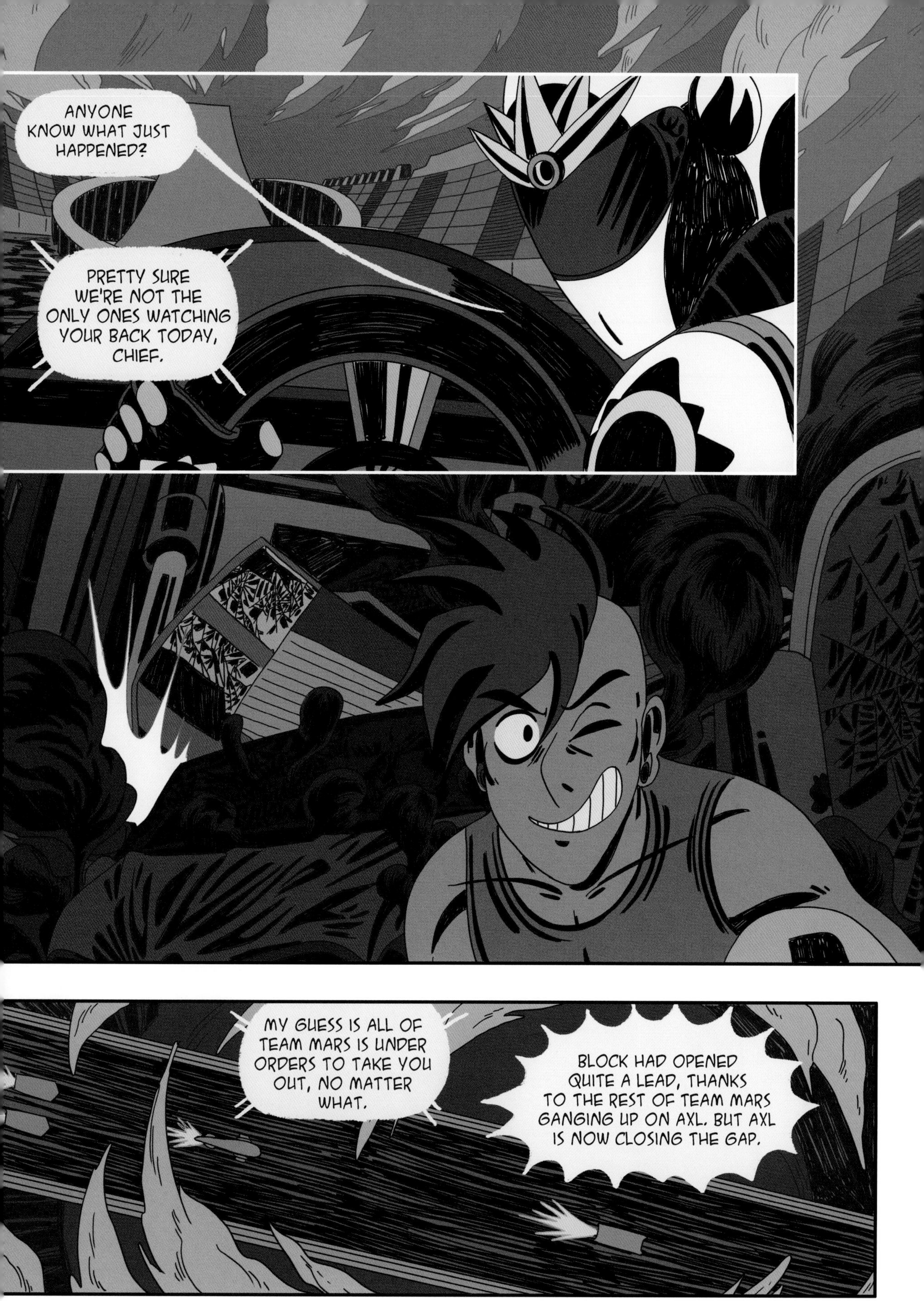
ANYONE KNOW WHAT JUST HAPPENED?
PRETTY SURE WE'RE NOT THE ONLY ONES WATCHING YOUR BACK TODAY, CHIEF.
MY GUESS IS ALL OF TEAM MARS IS UNDER ORDERS TO TAKE YOU OUT, NO MATTER WHAT.
BLOCK HAD OPENED QUITE A LEAD, THANKS TO THE REST OF TEAM MARS GANGING UP ON AXL. BUT AXL IS NOW CLOSING THE GAP.

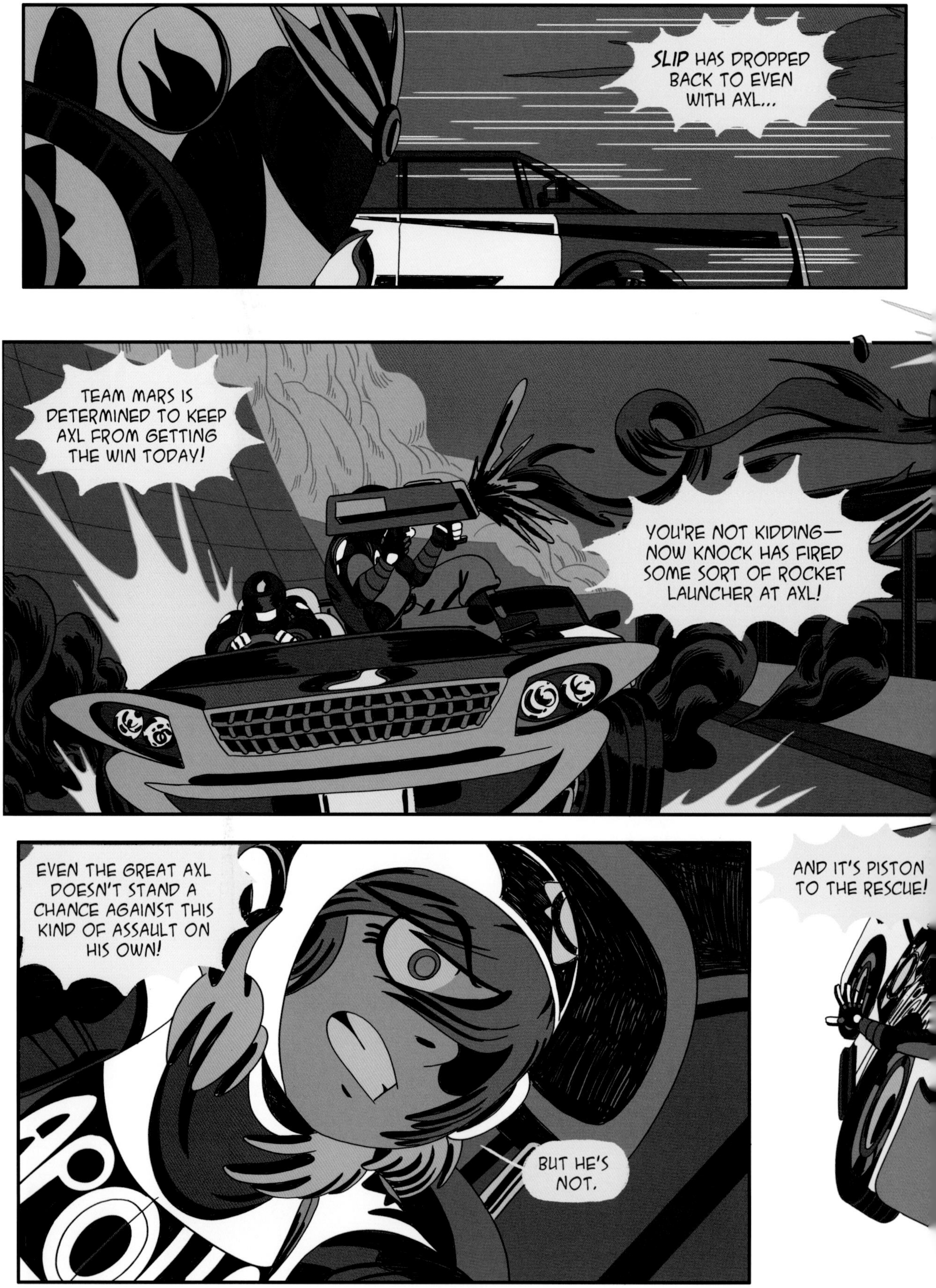

SLIP HAS DROPPED BACK TO EVEN WITH AXL...
TEAM MARS IS DETERMINED TO KEEP AXL FROM GETTING THE WIN TODAY!
YOU'RE NOT KIDDING— NOW KNOCK HAS FIRED SOME SORT OF ROCKET LAUNCHER AT AXL!
EVEN THE GREAT AXL DOESN'T STAND A CHANCE AGAINST THIS KIND OF ASSAULT ON HIS OWN!
BUT HE'S NOT.
AND IT'S PISTON TO THE RESCUE!

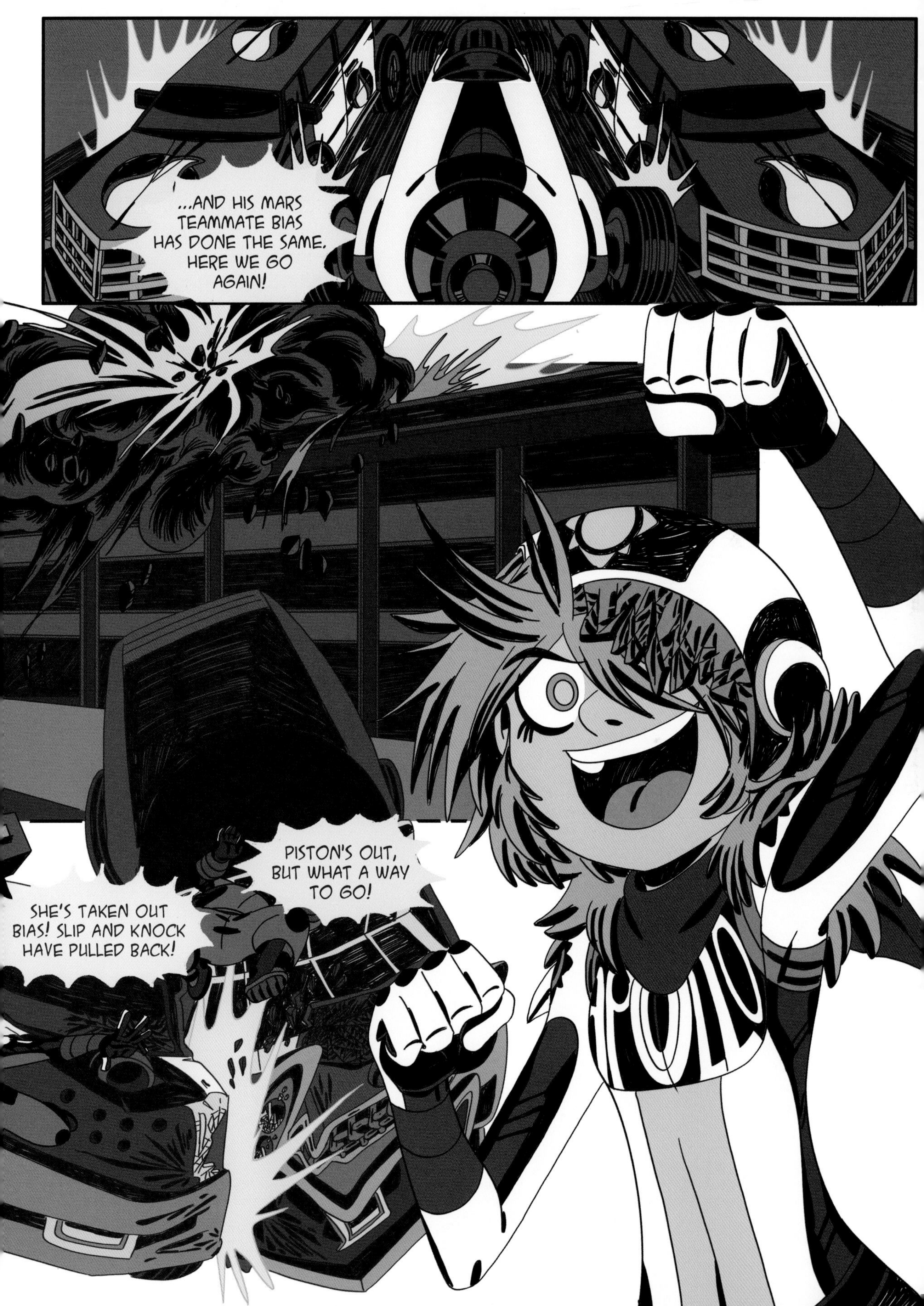
...AND HIS MARS TEAMMATE BIAS HAS DONE THE SAME. HERE WE GO AGAIN!
SHE'S TAKEN OUT BIAS! SLIP AND KNOCK HAVE PULLED BACK!
PISTON'S OUT, BUT WHAT A WAY TO GO!
APOLLO

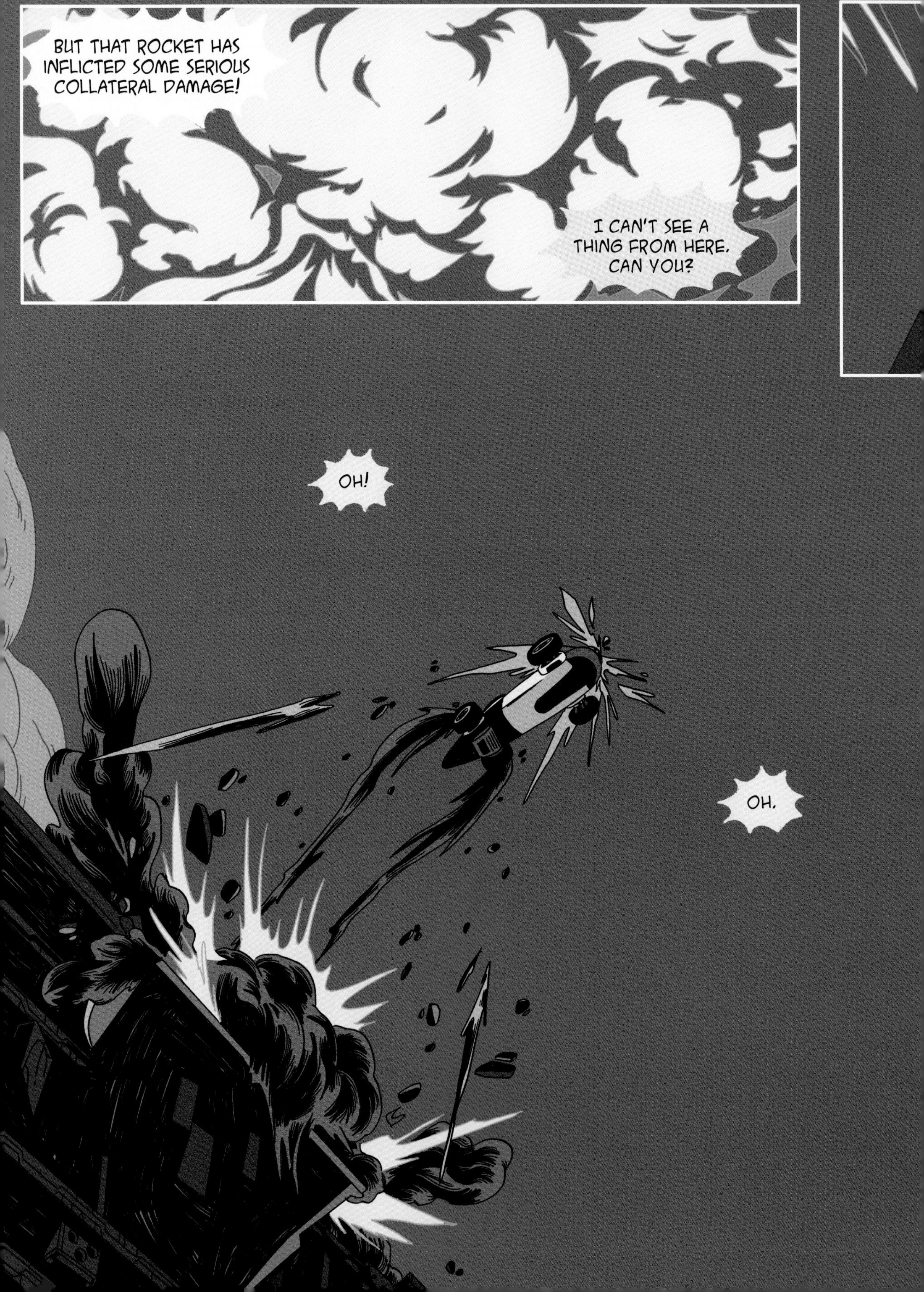
BUT THAT ROCKET HAS INFLICTED SOME SERIOUS COLLATERAL DAMAGE!
I CAN'T SEE A THING FROM HERE, CAN YOU?
OH!
OH.

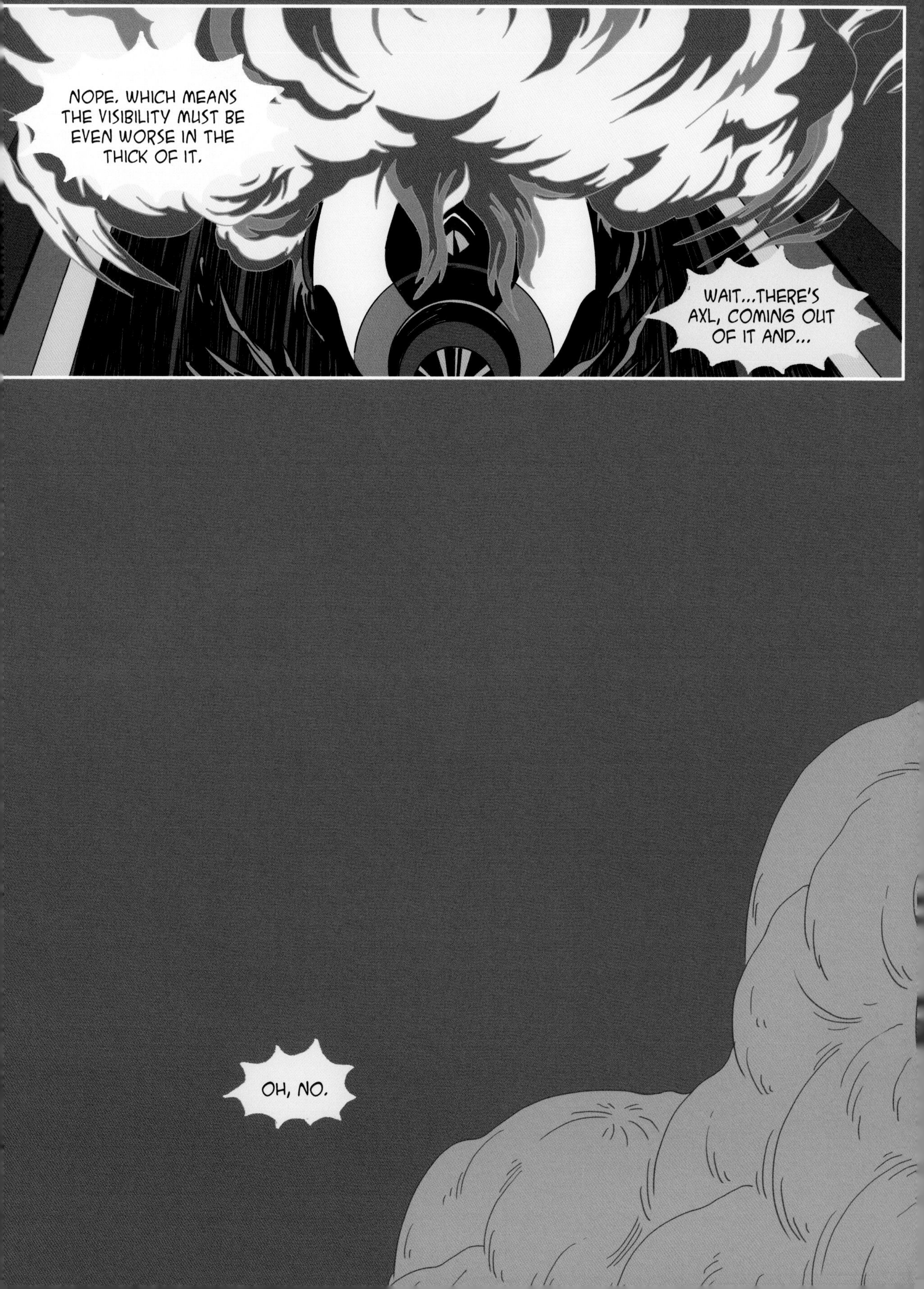
NOPE. WHICH MEANS THE VISIBILITY MUST BE EVEN WORSE IN THE THICK OF IT.
WAIT...THERE'S AXL, COMING OUT OF IT AND...
OH, NO.

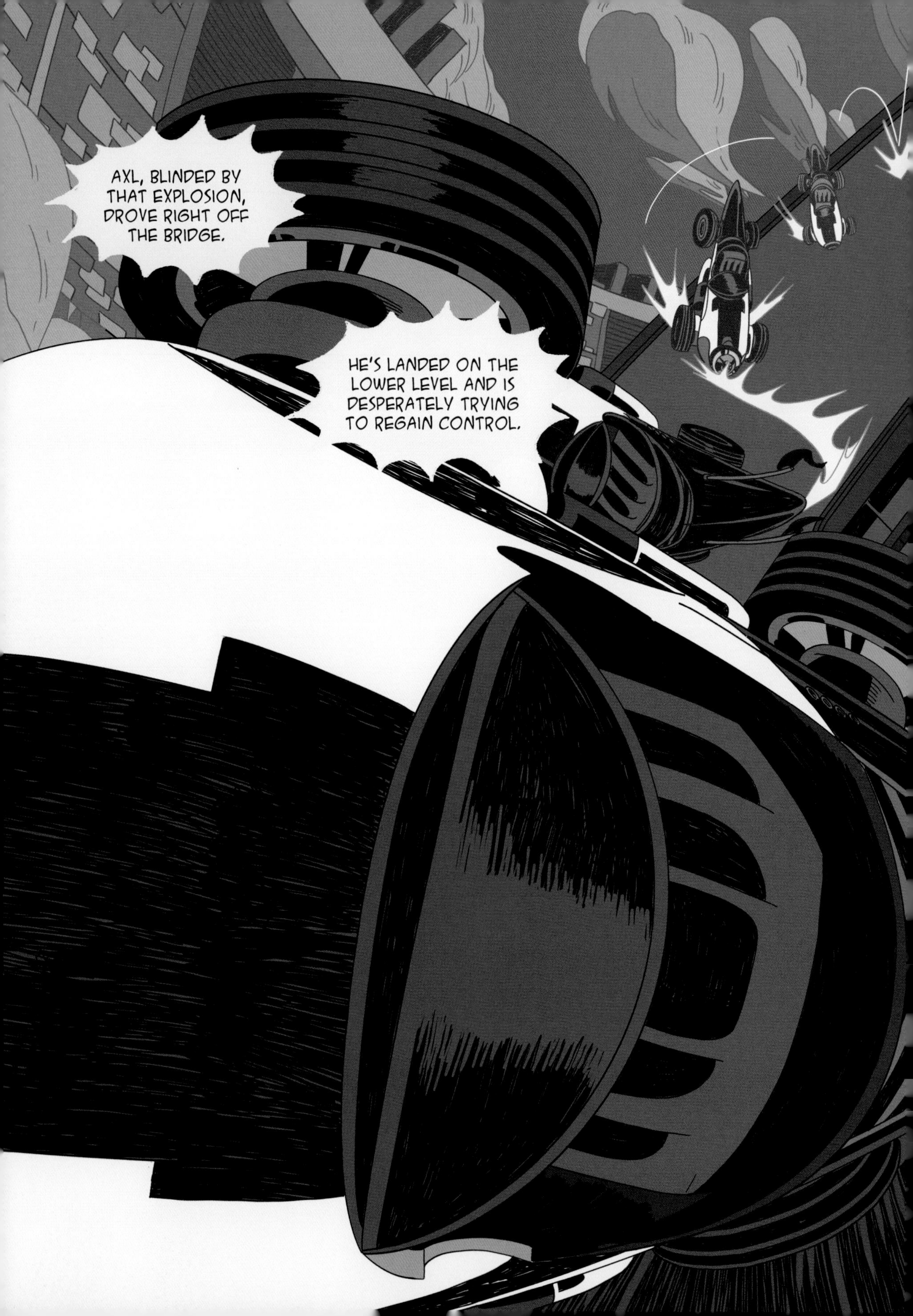
AXL, BLINDED BY THAT EXPLOSION, DROVE RIGHT OFF THE BRIDGE.
HE'S LANDED ON THE LOWER LEVEL AND IS DESPERATELY TRYING TO REGAIN CONTROL.

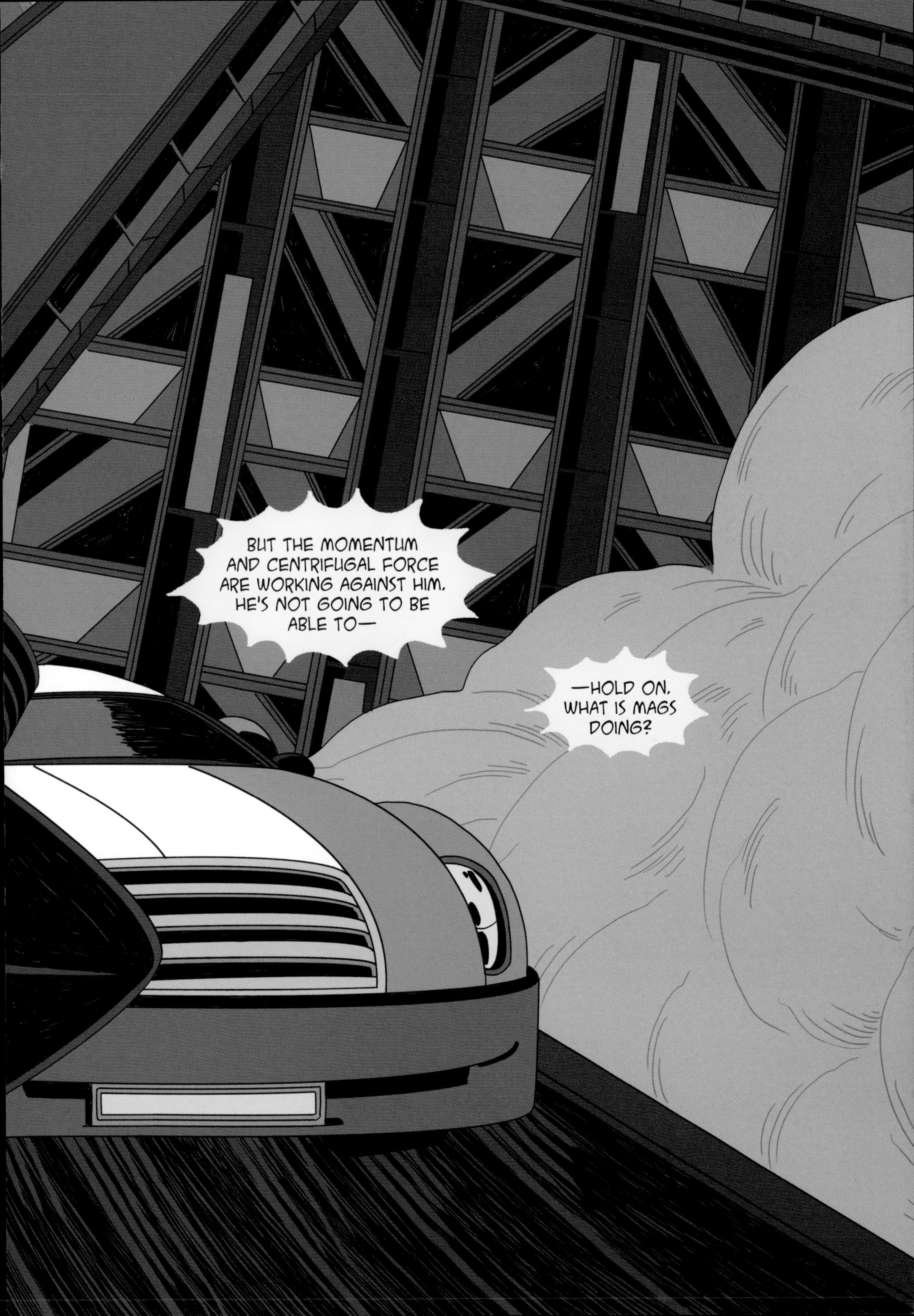
BUT THE MOMENTUM AND CENTRIFUGAL FORCE ARE WORKING AGAINST HIM. HE'S NOT GOING TO BE ABLE TO—
—HOLD ON. WHAT IS MAGS DOING?

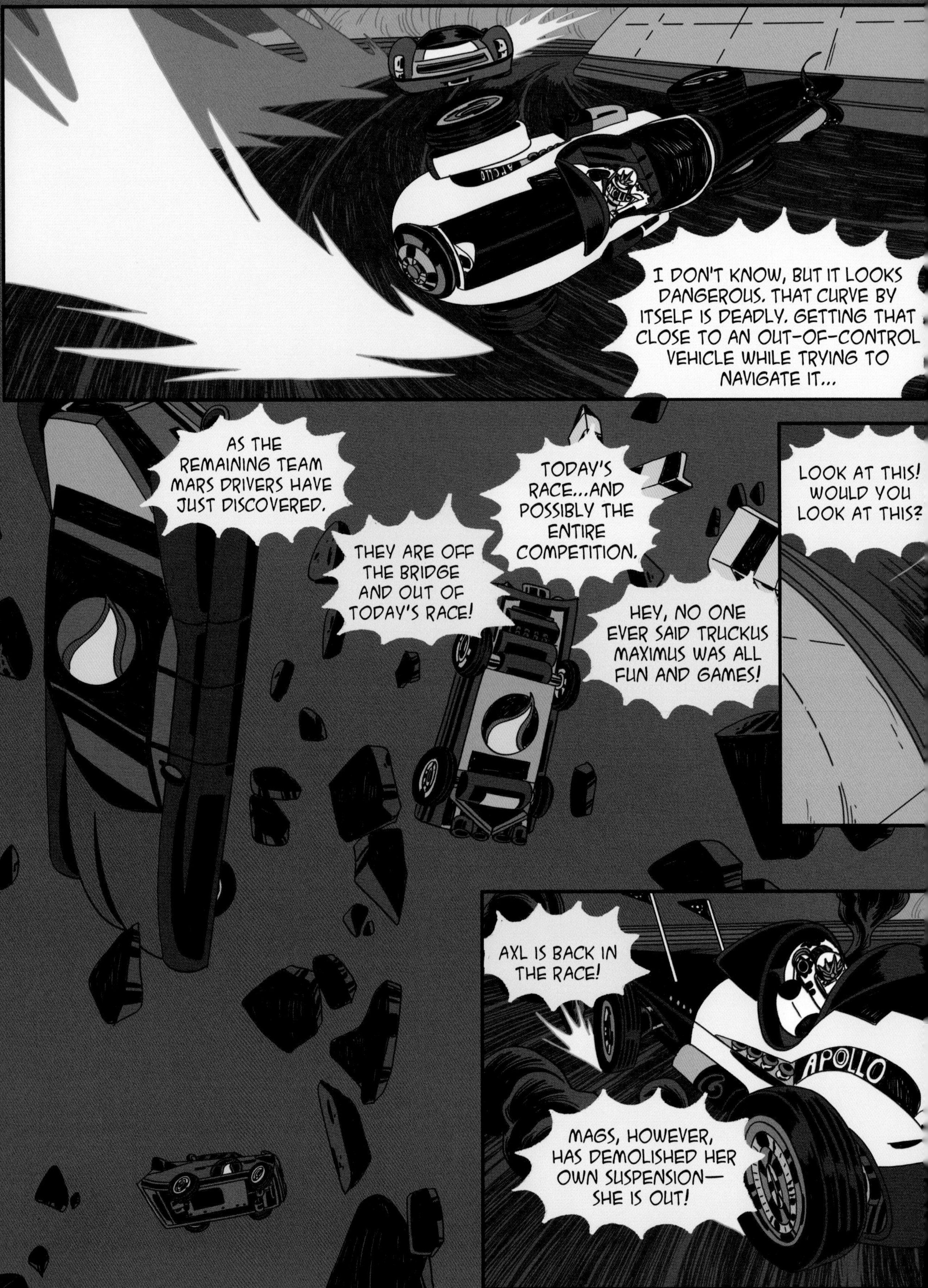
I DON'T KNOW, BUT IT LOOKS DANGEROUS. THAT CURVE BY ITSELF IS DEADLY. GETTING THAT CLOSE TO AN OUT-OF-CONTROL VEHICLE WHILE TRYING TO NAVIGATE IT...
AS THE REMAINING TEAM MARS DRIVERS HAVE JUST DISCOVERED.
TODAY'S RACE...AND POSSIBLY THE ENTIRE COMPETITION.
THEY ARE OFF THE BRIDGE AND OUT OF TODAY'S RACE!
HEY, NO ONE EVER SAID TRUCKUS MAXIMUS WAS ALL FUN AND GAMES!
LOOK AT THIS! WOULD YOU LOOK AT THIS?
AXL IS BACK IN THE RACE!
APOLLO
MAGS, HOWEVER, HAS DEMOLISHED HER OWN SUSPENSION— SHE IS OUT!

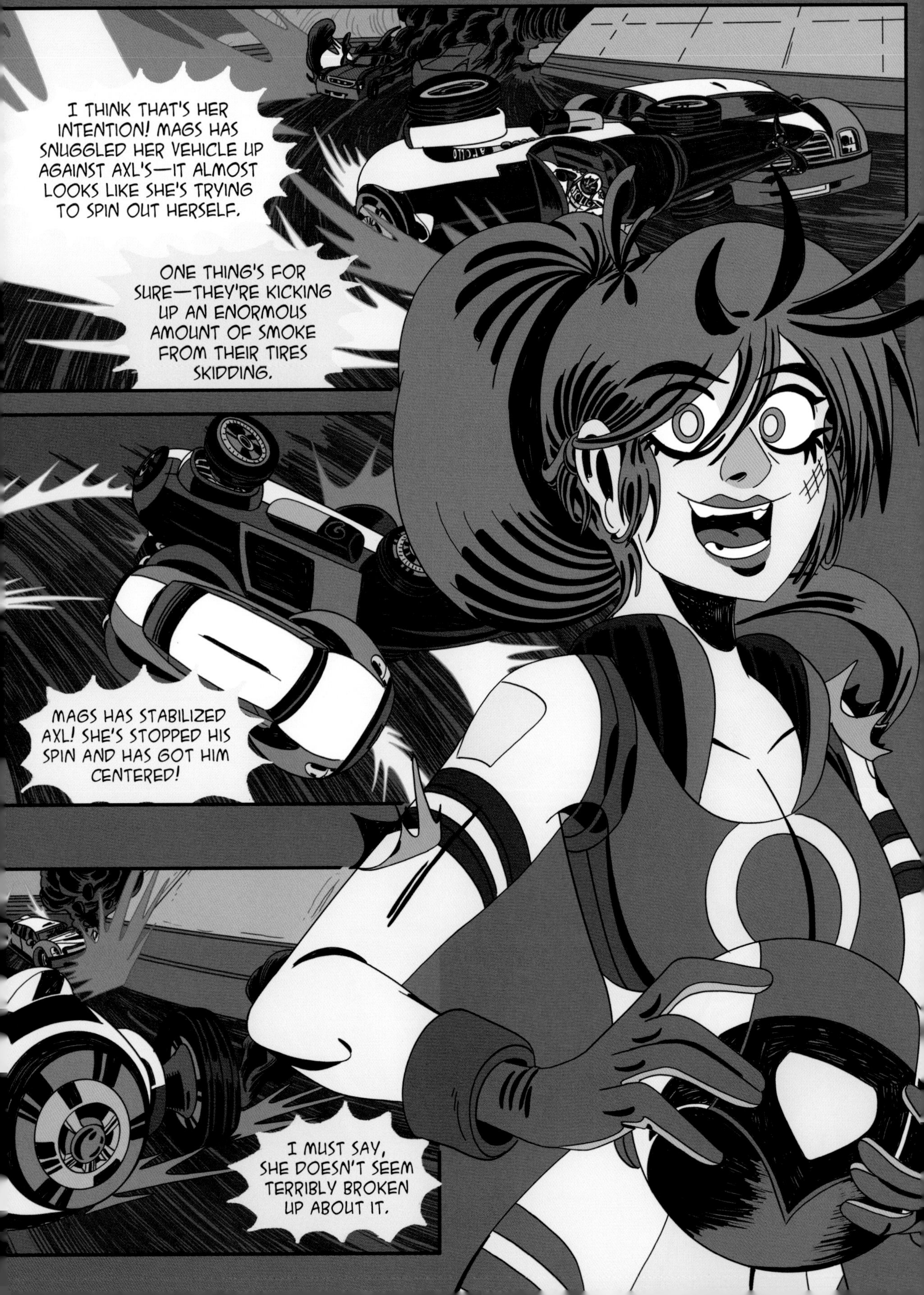
I THINK THAT'S HER INTENTION! MAGS HAS SNUGGLED HER VEHICLE UP AGAINST AXL'S—IT ALMOST LOOKS LIKE SHE'S TRYING TO SPIN OUT HERSELF.
ONE THING'S FOR SURE—THEY'RE KICKING UP AN ENORMOUS AMOUNT OF SMOKE FROM THEIR TIRES SKIDDING.
MAGS HAS STABILIZED AXL! SHE'S STOPPED HIS SPIN AND HAS GOT HIM CENTERED!
I MUST SAY, SHE DOESN'T SEEM TERRIBLY BROKEN UP ABOUT IT.

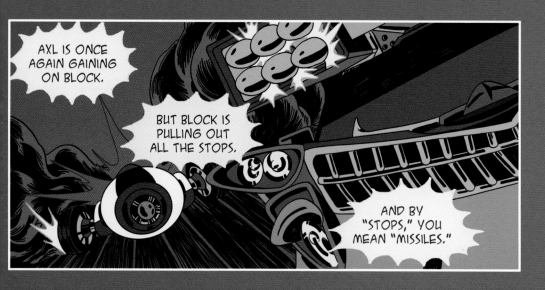

AXL IS ONCE AGAIN GAINING ON BLOCK.

BUT BLOCK IS PULLING OUT ALL THE STOPS.

AND BY "STOPS," YOU MEAN "MISSILES."

...AND HE LOOKS POSITIVELY OVERJOYED ABOUT IT!

NO MATTER WHAT HAPPENS, THIS RACE HAS ALREADY BEEN ONE FOR THE BOOKS!

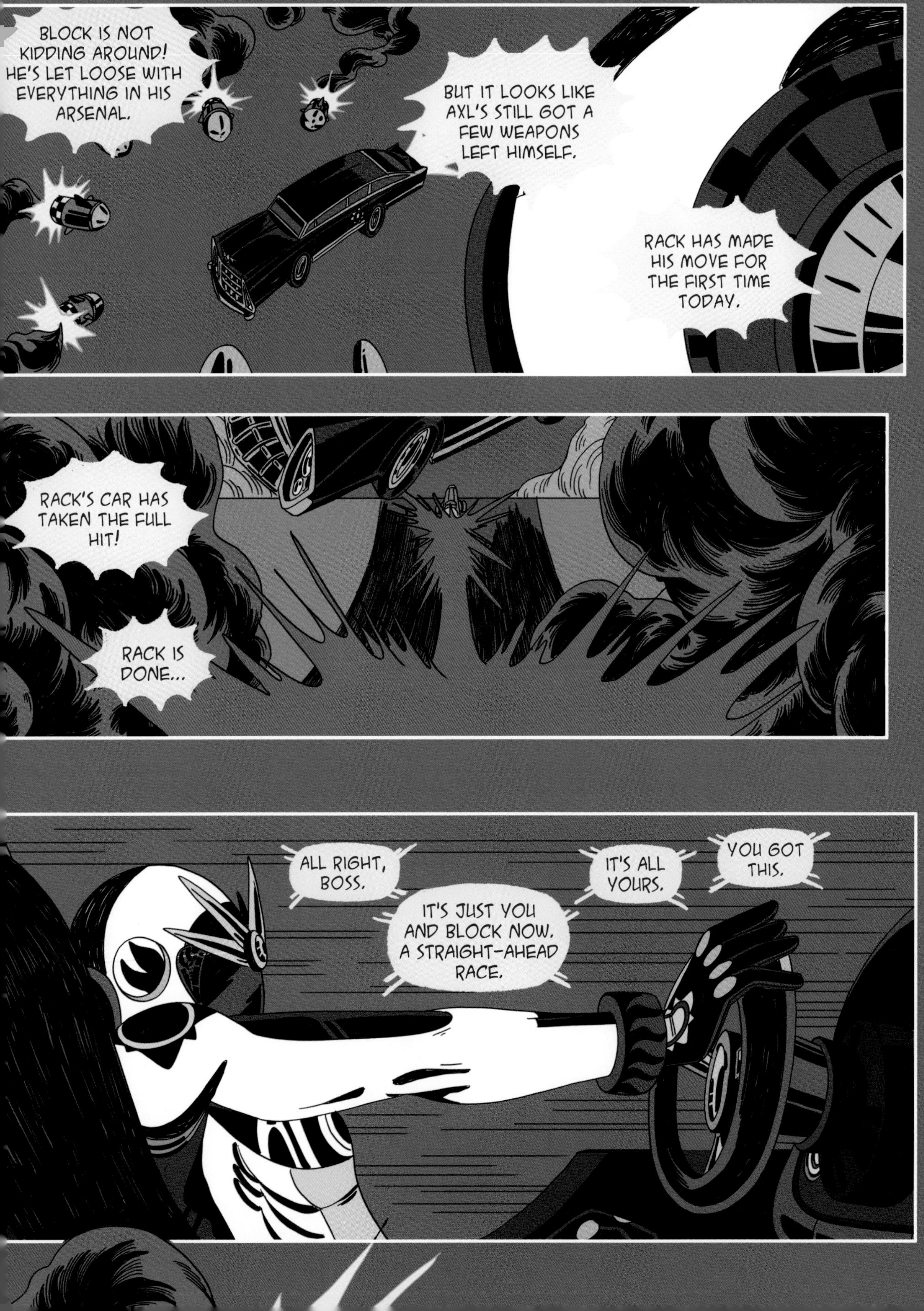
BLOCK IS NOT KIDDING AROUND! HE'S LET LOOSE WITH EVERYTHING IN HIS ARSENAL.
BUT IT LOOKS LIKE AXL'S STILL GOT A FEW WEAPONS LEFT HIMSELF.
RACK HAS MADE HIS MOVE FOR THE FIRST TIME TODAY.
RACK'S CAR HAS TAKEN THE FULL HIT!
RACK IS DONE...
ALL RIGHT, BOSS.
IT'S JUST YOU AND BLOCK NOW. A STRAIGHT-AHEAD RACE.
IT'S ALL YOURS.
YOU GOT THIS.

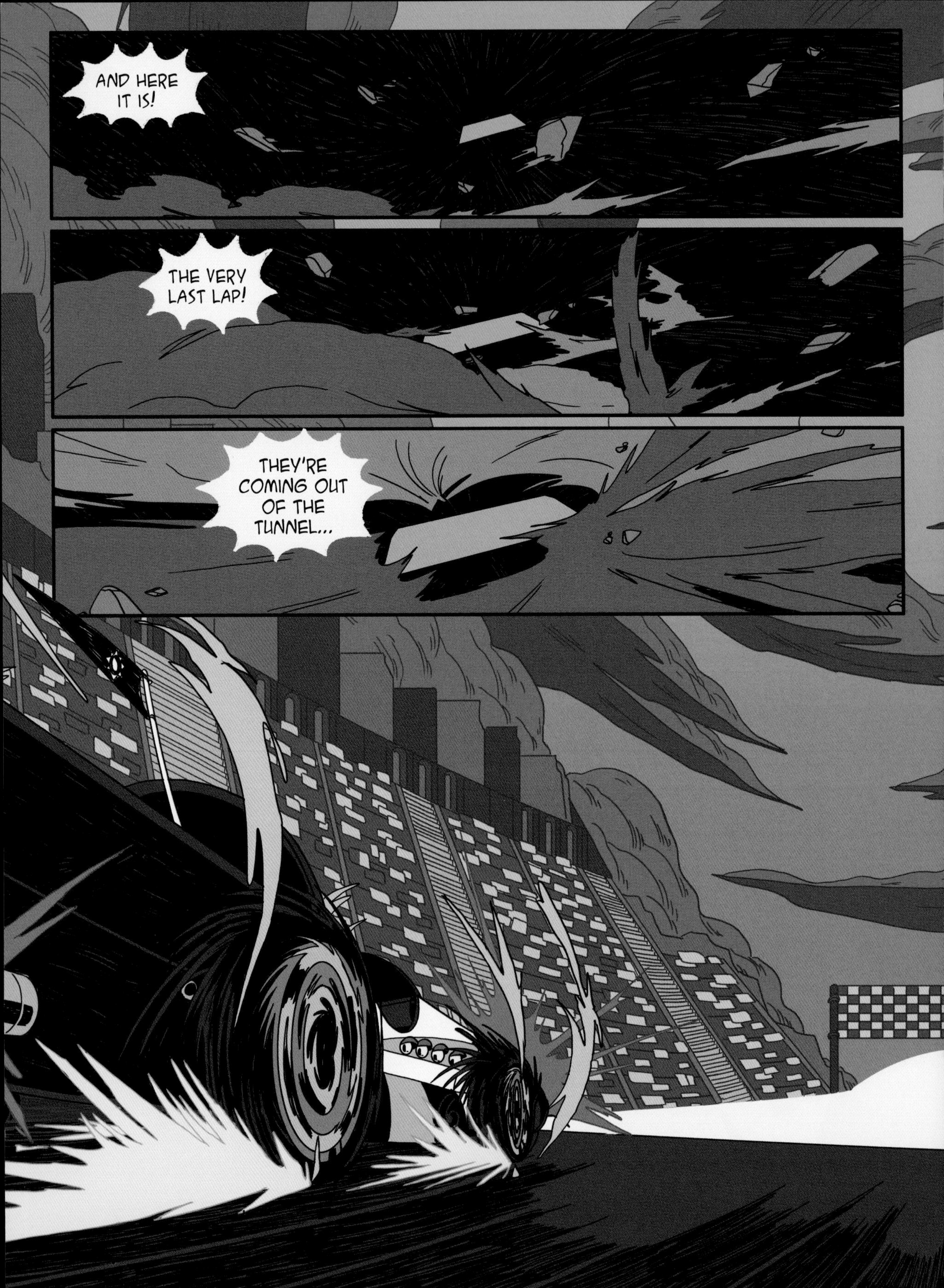
AND HERE IT IS!
THE VERY LAST LAP!
THEY'RE COMING OUT OF THE TUNNEL...

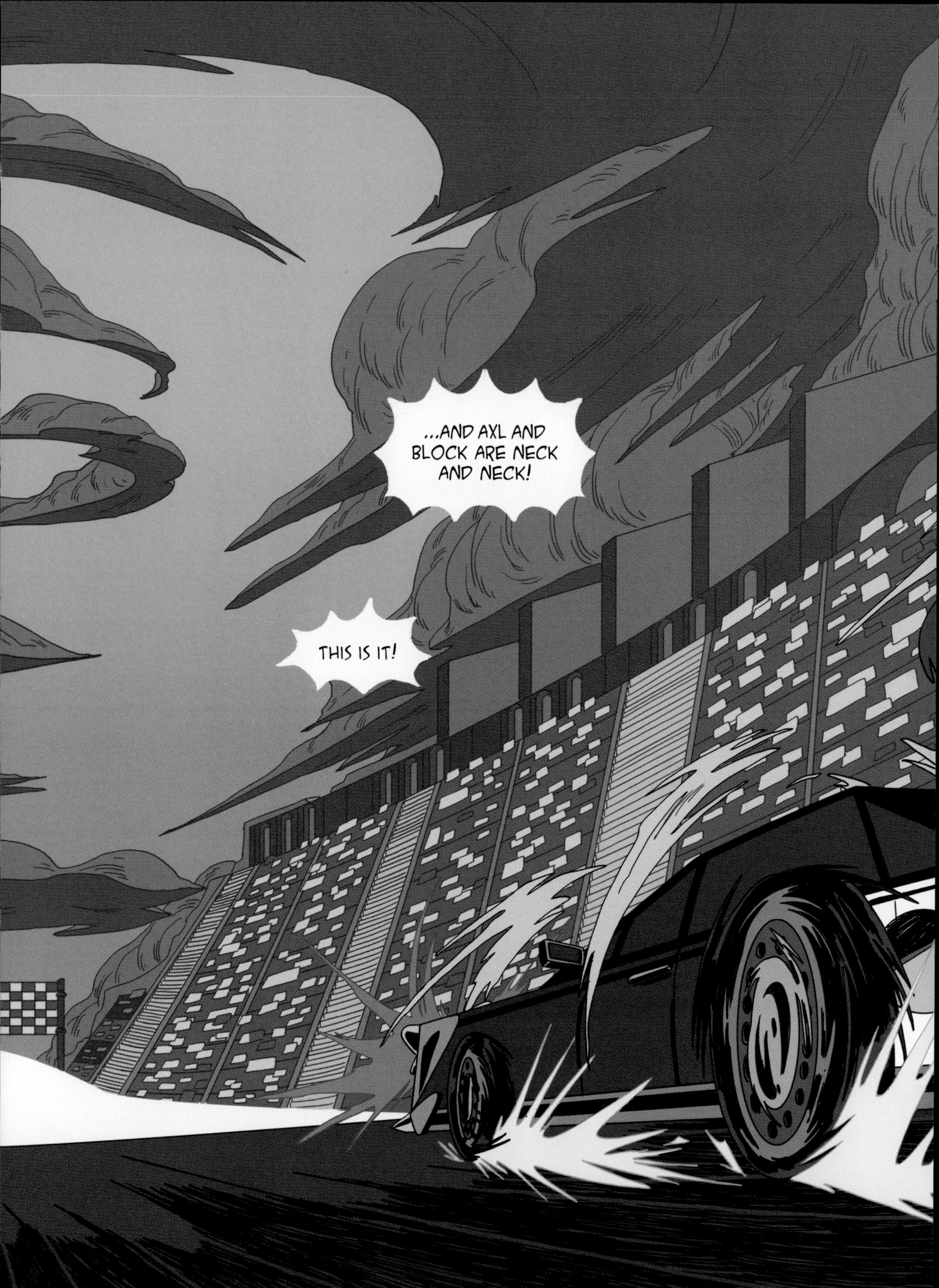
...AND AXL AND BLOCK ARE NECK AND NECK!
THIS IS IT!

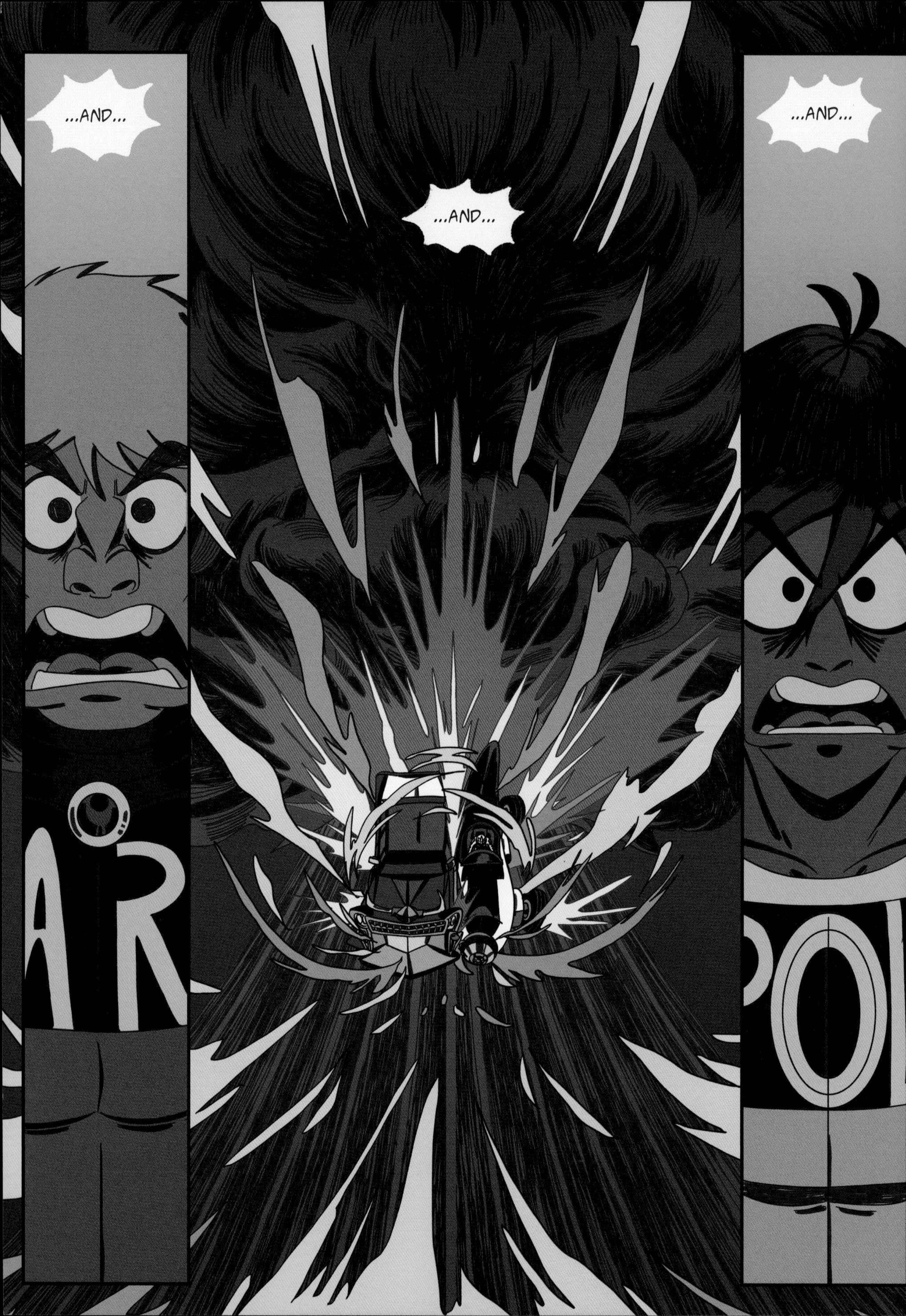
...AND...
...AND...
...AND...

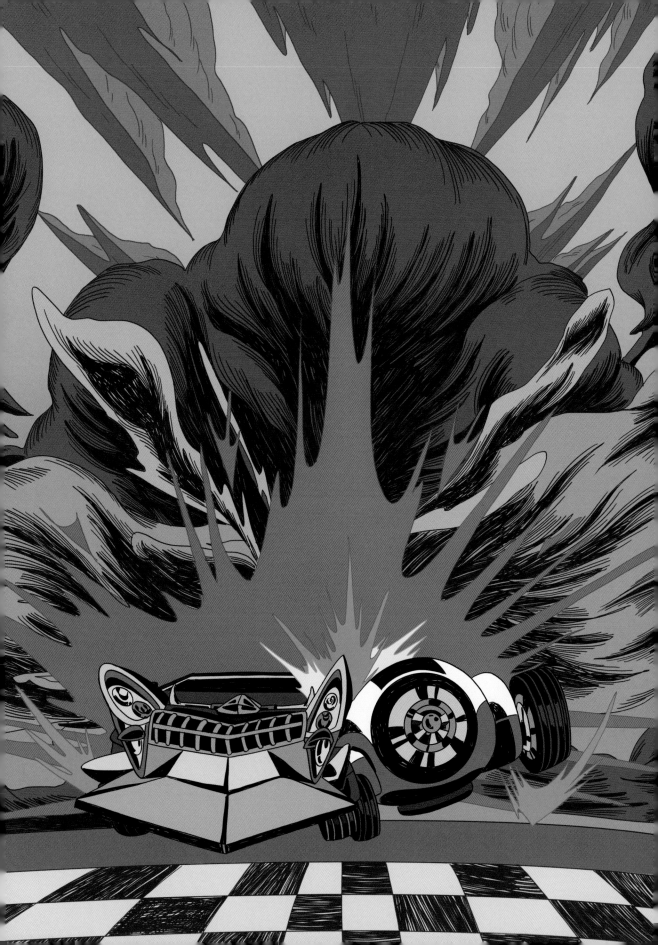

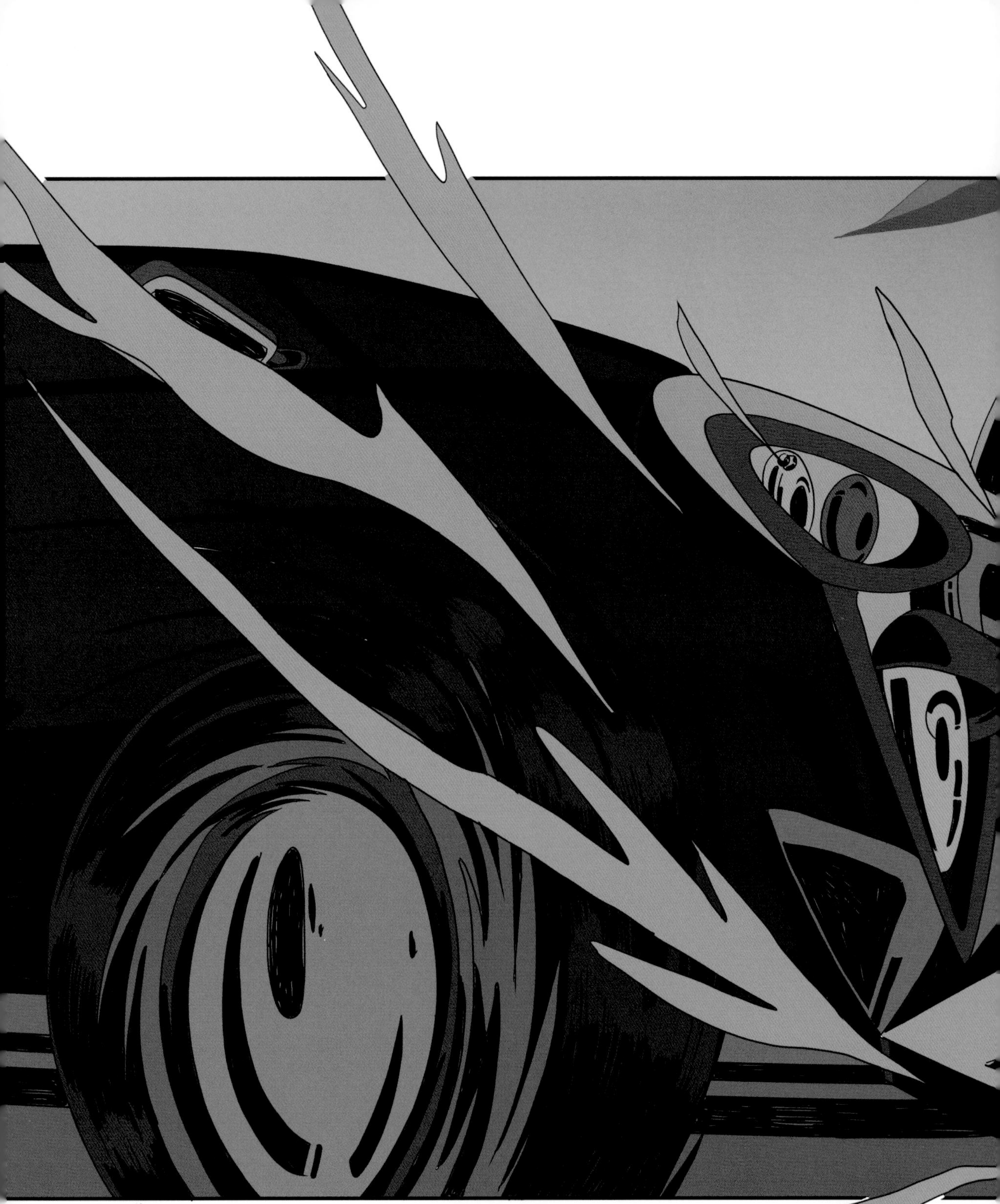

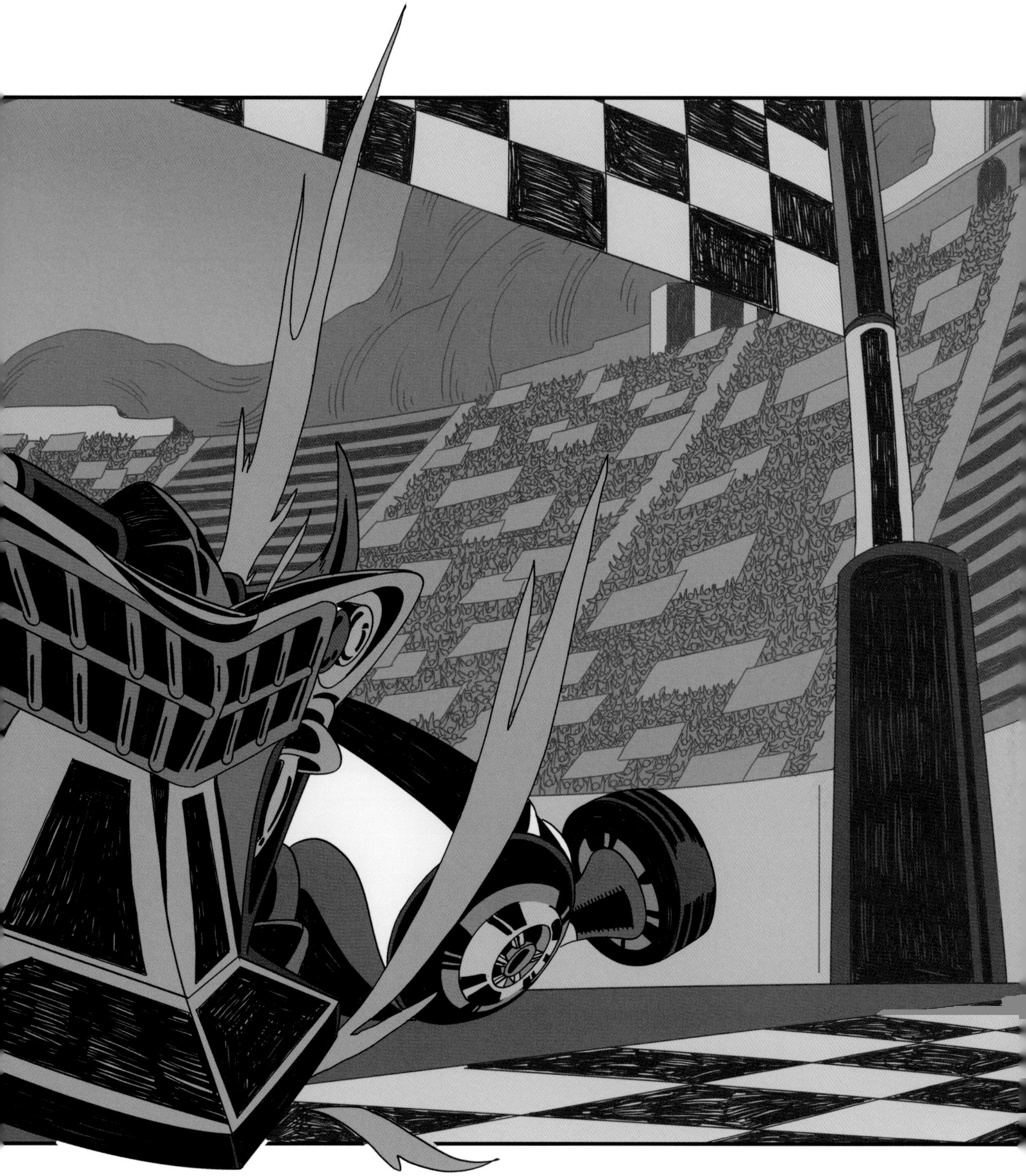

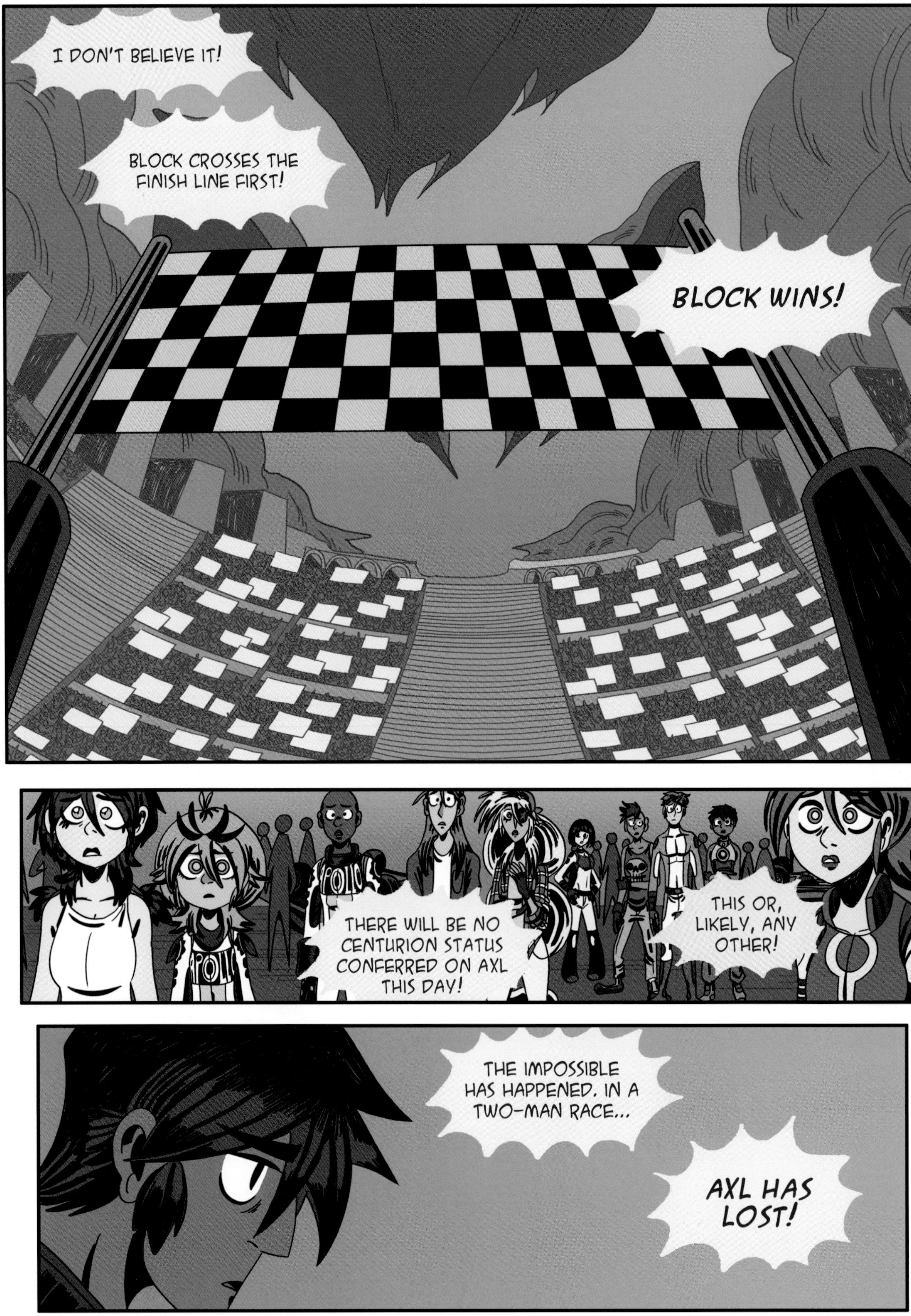
I DON'T BELIEVE IT!
BLOCK CROSSES THE FINISH LINE FIRST!
BLOCK WINS!
THERE WILL BE NO CENTURION STATUS CONFERRED ON AXL THIS DAY!
THIS OR, LIKELY, ANY OTHER!
THE IMPOSSIBLE HAS HAPPENED. IN A TWO-MAN RACE...
AXL HAS LOST!

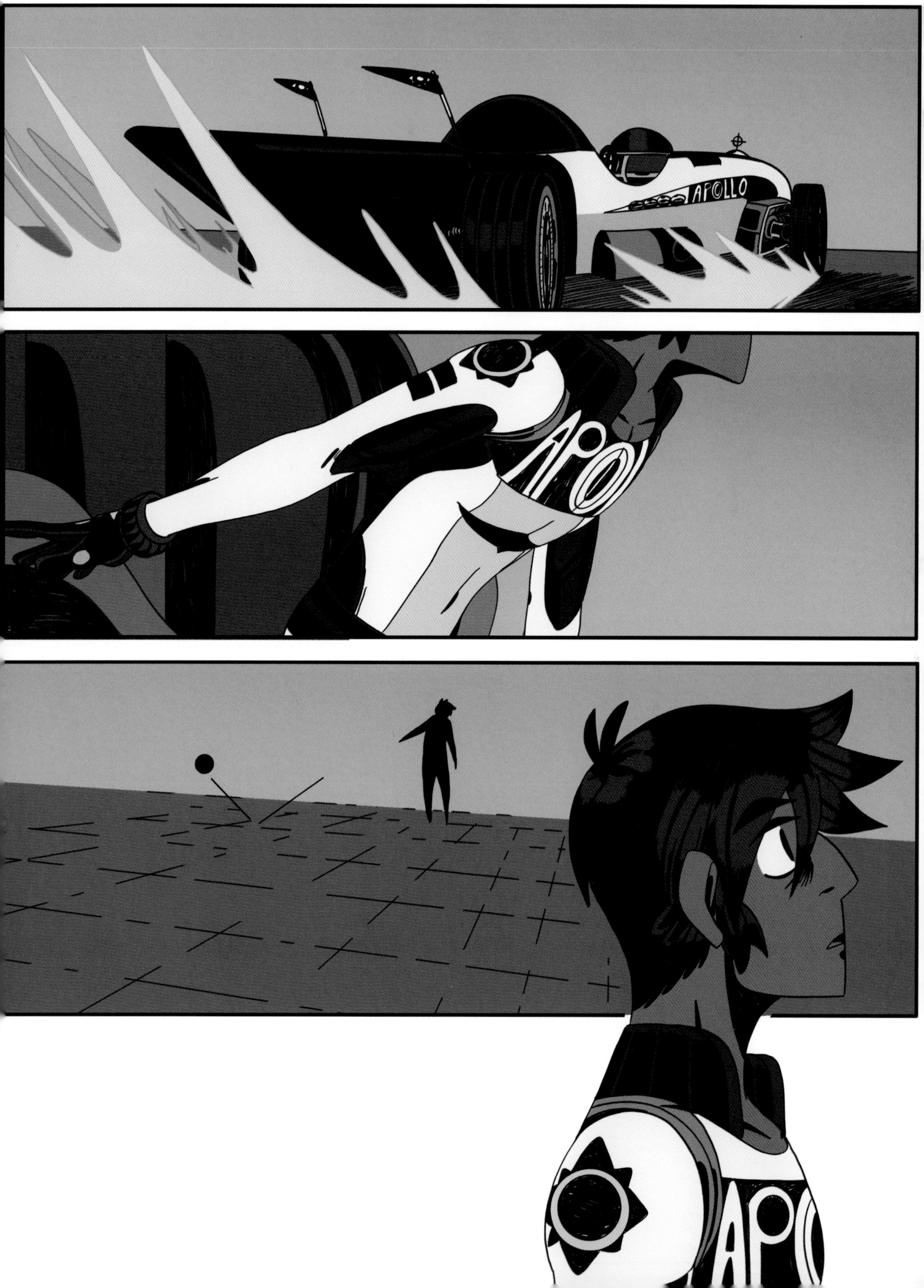
APOLLO

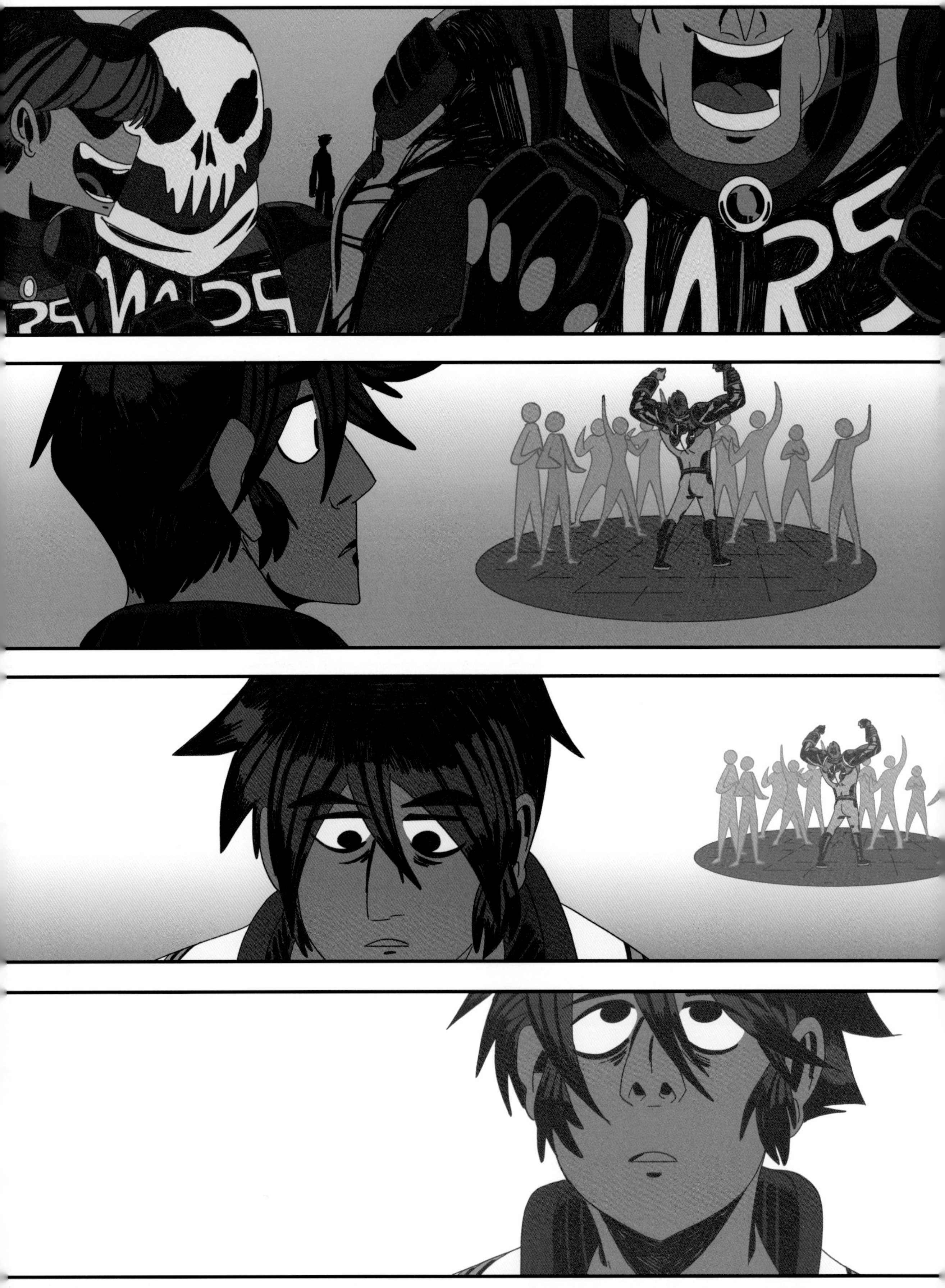

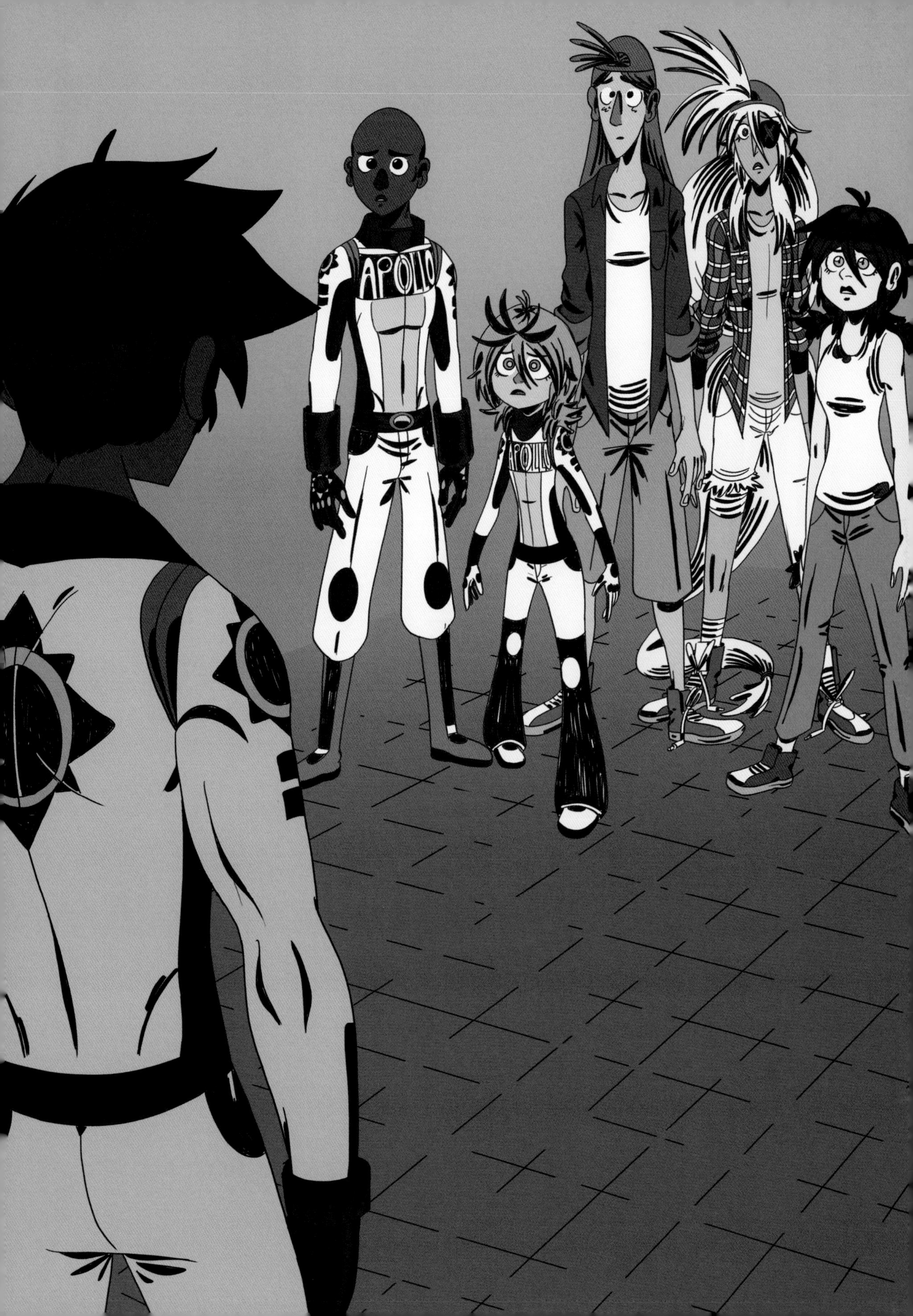
APOLLO
APOLLO

I'M SORRY.

HOLD ON. AXL...ARE YOU...

YOU DON'T THINK WE'RE DISAPPOINTED, DO YOU?

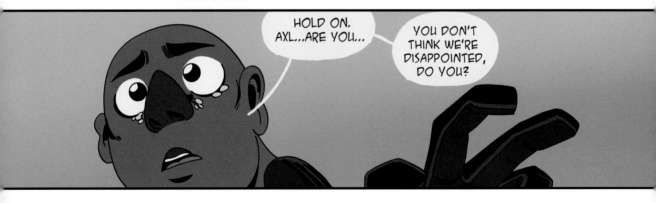

I DISHONORED MYSELF.

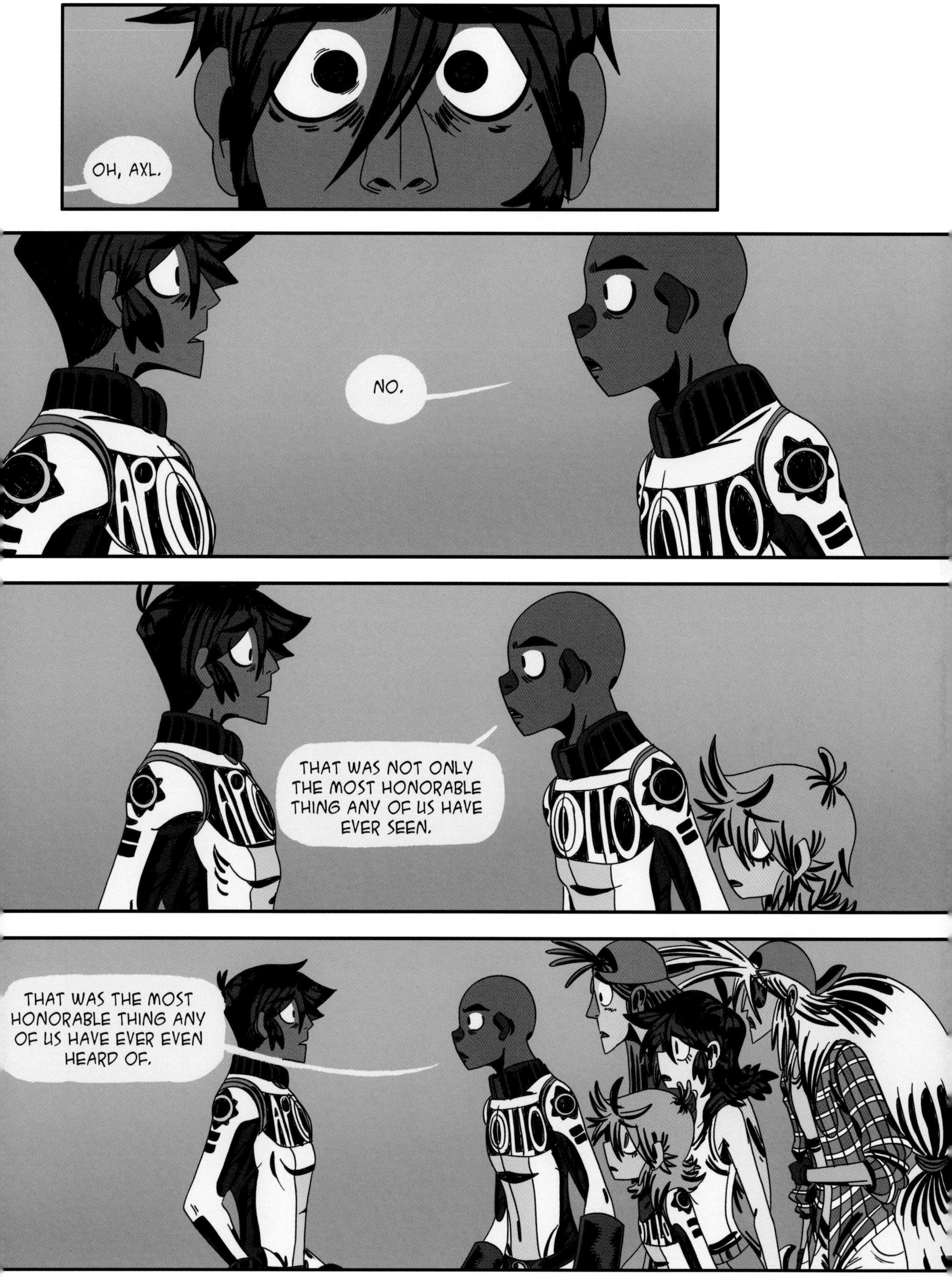
OH, AXL.
NO.
THAT WAS NOT ONLY THE MOST HONORABLE THING ANY OF US HAVE EVER SEEN.
THAT WAS THE MOST HONORABLE THING ANY OF US HAVE EVER EVEN HEARD OF.

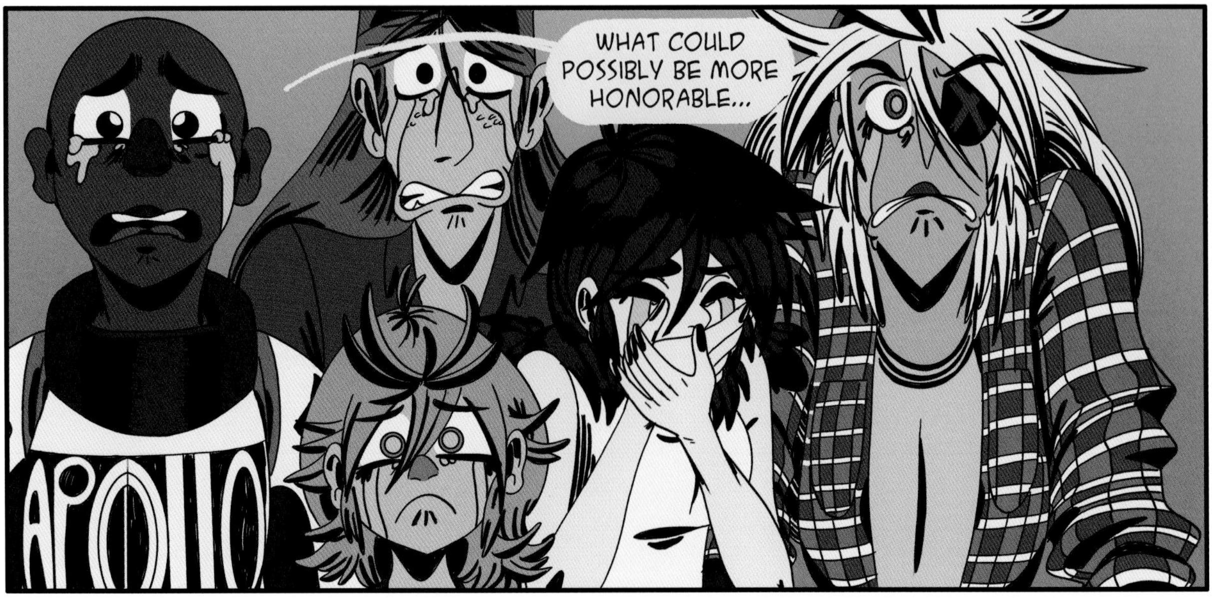
WHAT COULD POSSIBLY BE MORE HONORABLE...

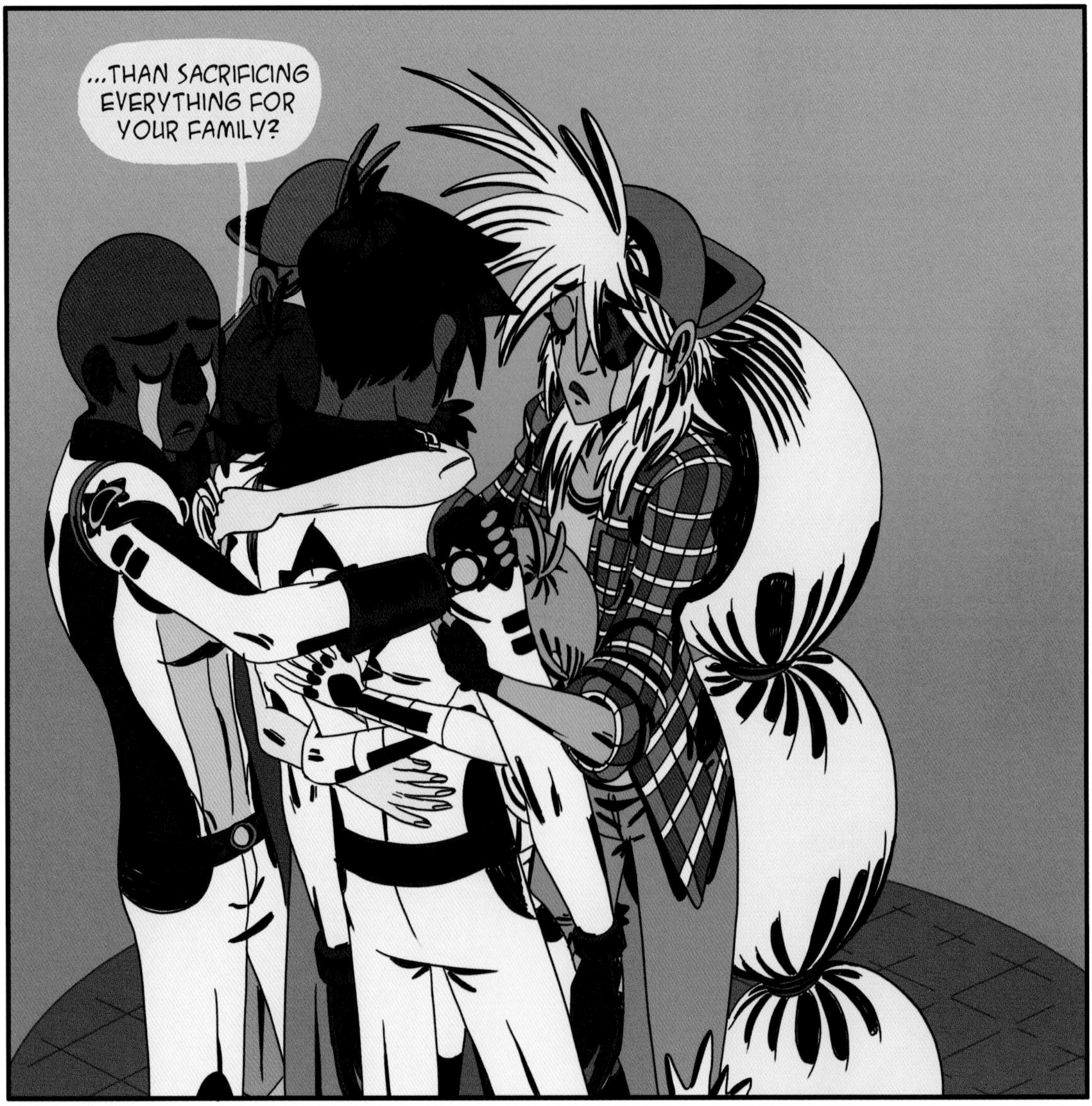
...THAN SACRIFICING EVERYTHING FOR YOUR FAMILY?

YOU DID IT. YOU ACTUALLY DID IT.

I GOTTA ADMIT, I DIDN'T THINK YOU WOULD—HELL, IT NEVER EVEN OCCURRED TO ME YOU MIGHT. NOT YOU.

NOT MISTER "HONOR IS ALL" AXL.

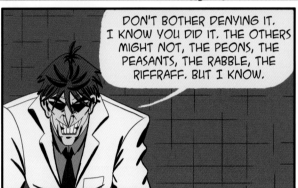

DON'T BOTHER DENYING IT. I KNOW YOU DID IT. THE OTHERS MIGHT NOT, THE PEONS, THE PEASANTS, THE RABBLE, THE RIFFRAFF. BUT I KNOW.

I KNOW YOU THREW IT. YOU THREW THE RACE. YOU LOST ON PURPOSE.

I NEVER WOULD'VE BELIEVED IT. IF SOMEONE'D WANTED TO BET ME, I'D HAVE LOST A LOT OF MONEY. SURE, NO ONE'D EVER DO SOMETHING LIKE THAT—BUT ESPECIALLY YOU, OF ALL PEOPLE.

SOMETHING SO UNDERHANDED, SO TREACHEROUS, SO DECEITFUL. SO LACKING IN HONOR.

WELL, LIVE AND LEARN. LIVE AND LEARN.

YOU KNOW WHAT, THOUGH? I MIGHT JUST BREAK UP THE TEAM ANYWAY. HOW'D YOU LIKE THAT?

YOU BROKE YOUR WORD TO ME—AND I DON'T WANNA HEAR THAT WE DIDN'T HAVE AN AGREEMENT, IT WAS AN UPSPOKEN ONE AND YOU KNOW IT—SO I'M UNDER NO OBLIGATION TO KEEP MINE TO YOU.

SO CONGRATULATIONS, BOY. YOU DIDN'T WIN YOUR FREEDOM TODAY, AND YOU DIDN'T KEEP YOUR TEAMMATES OUT OF THE SALT MINES AFTER ALL. ALL YOU DID WAS LOSE YOUR SOUL.

WELL, NOW, I'M NOT SURE I'D GO QUITE THAT FAR.

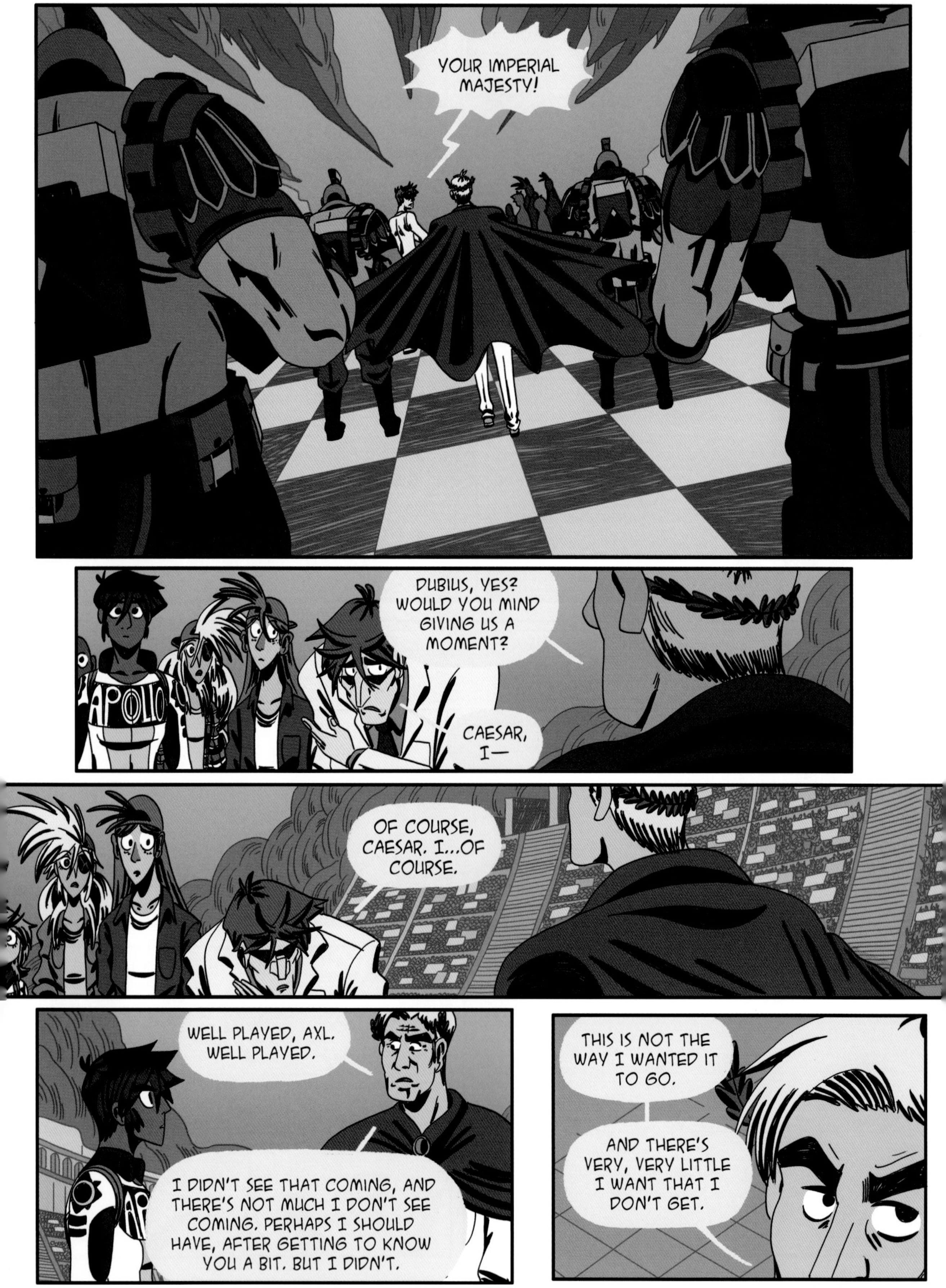
YOUR IMPERIAL MAJESTY!
DUBIUS, YES? WOULD YOU MIND GIVING US A MOMENT?
CAESAR, I—
OF COURSE, CAESAR. I...OF COURSE.
WELL PLAYED, AXL. WELL PLAYED.
I DIDN'T SEE THAT COMING, AND THERE'S NOT MUCH I DON'T SEE COMING. PERHAPS I SHOULD HAVE, AFTER GETTING TO KNOW YOU A BIT. BUT I DIDN'T.
THIS IS NOT THE WAY I WANTED IT TO GO.
AND THERE'S VERY, VERY LITTLE I WANT THAT I DON'T GET.

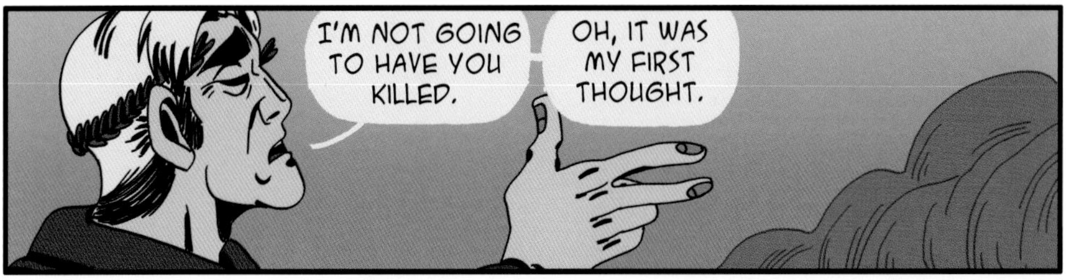
I'M NOT GOING TO HAVE YOU KILLED.
OH, IT WAS MY FIRST THOUGHT.

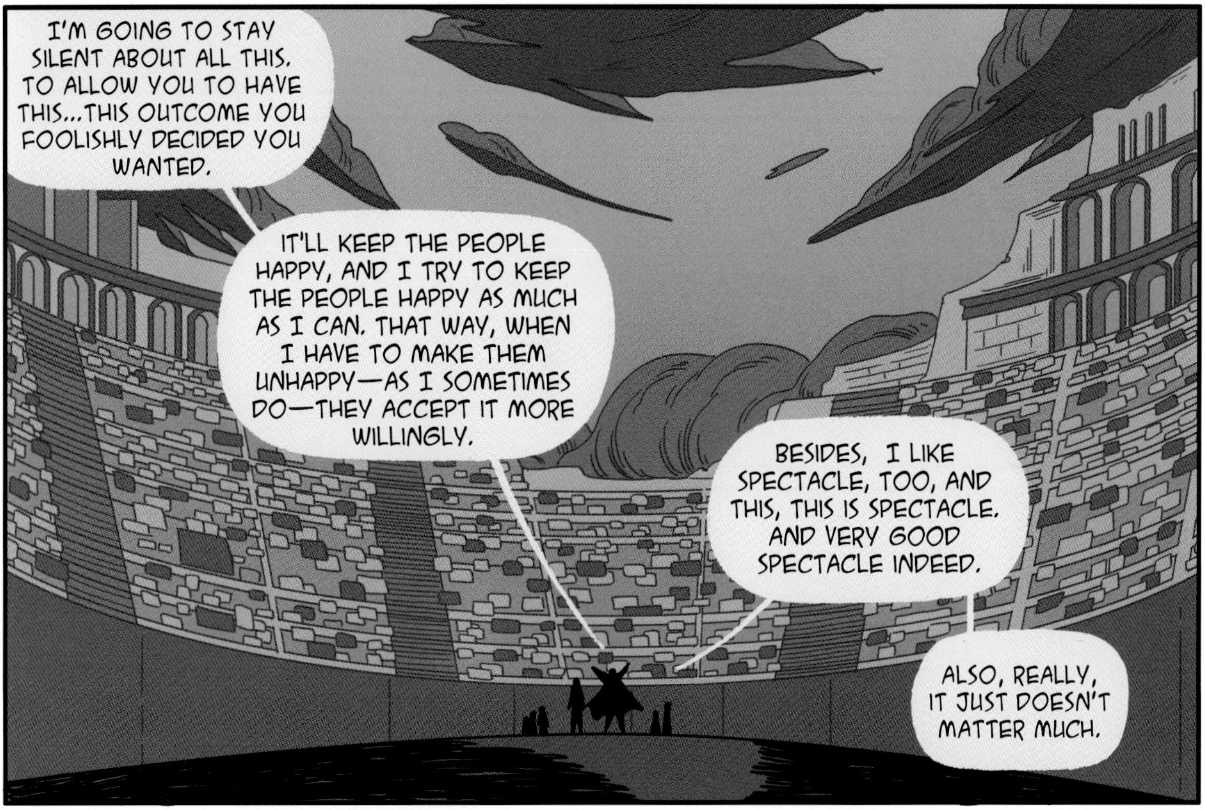
I'M GOING TO STAY SILENT ABOUT ALL THIS. TO ALLOW YOU TO HAVE THIS...THIS OUTCOME YOU FOOLISHLY DECIDED YOU WANTED.
IT'LL KEEP THE PEOPLE HAPPY, AND I TRY TO KEEP THE PEOPLE HAPPY AS MUCH AS I CAN. THAT WAY, WHEN I HAVE TO MAKE THEM UNHAPPY—AS I SOMETIMES DO—THEY ACCEPT IT MORE WILLINGLY.
BESIDES, I LIKE SPECTACLE, TOO, AND THIS, THIS IS SPECTACLE. AND VERY GOOD SPECTACLE INDEED.
ALSO, REALLY, IT JUST DOESN'T MATTER MUCH.

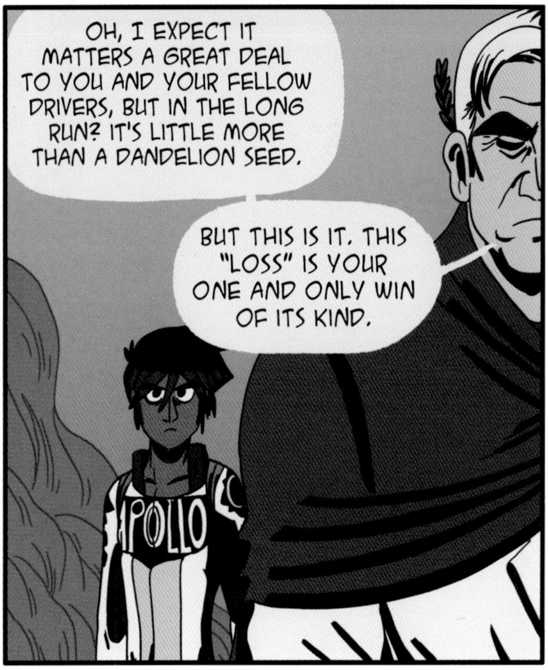
OH, I EXPECT IT MATTERS A GREAT DEAL TO YOU AND YOUR FELLOW DRIVERS, BUT IN THE LONG RUN? IT'S LITTLE MORE THAN A DANDELION SEED.
BUT THIS IS IT. THIS "LOSS" IS YOUR ONE AND ONLY WIN OF ITS KIND.
APOLLO

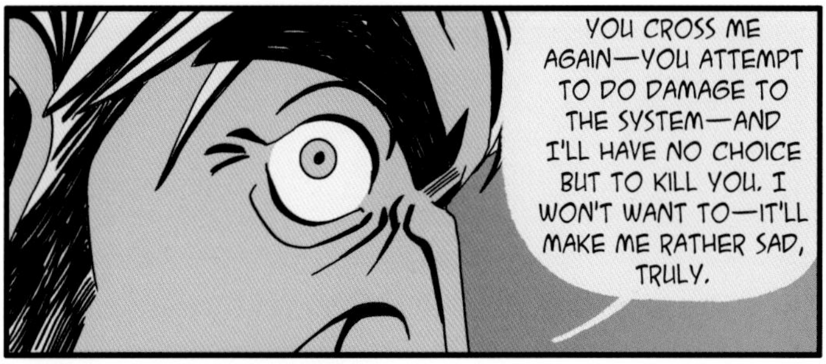
YOU CROSS ME AGAIN—YOU ATTEMPT TO DO DAMAGE TO THE SYSTEM—AND I'LL HAVE NO CHOICE BUT TO KILL YOU. I WON'T WANT TO—IT'LL MAKE ME RATHER SAD, TRULY.

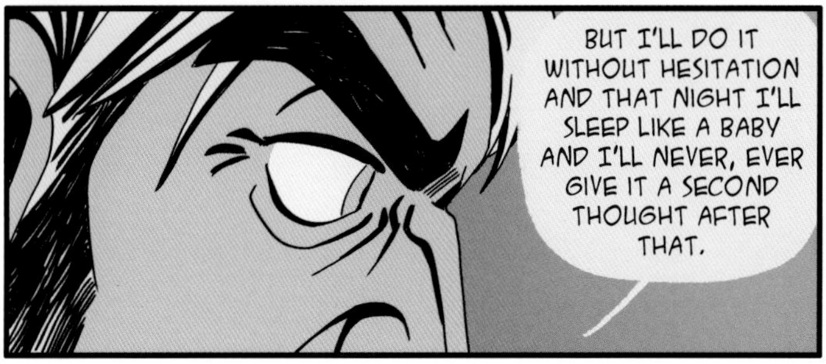
BUT I'LL DO IT WITHOUT HESITATION AND THAT NIGHT I'LL SLEEP LIKE A BABY AND I'LL NEVER, EVER GIVE IT A SECOND THOUGHT AFTER THAT.

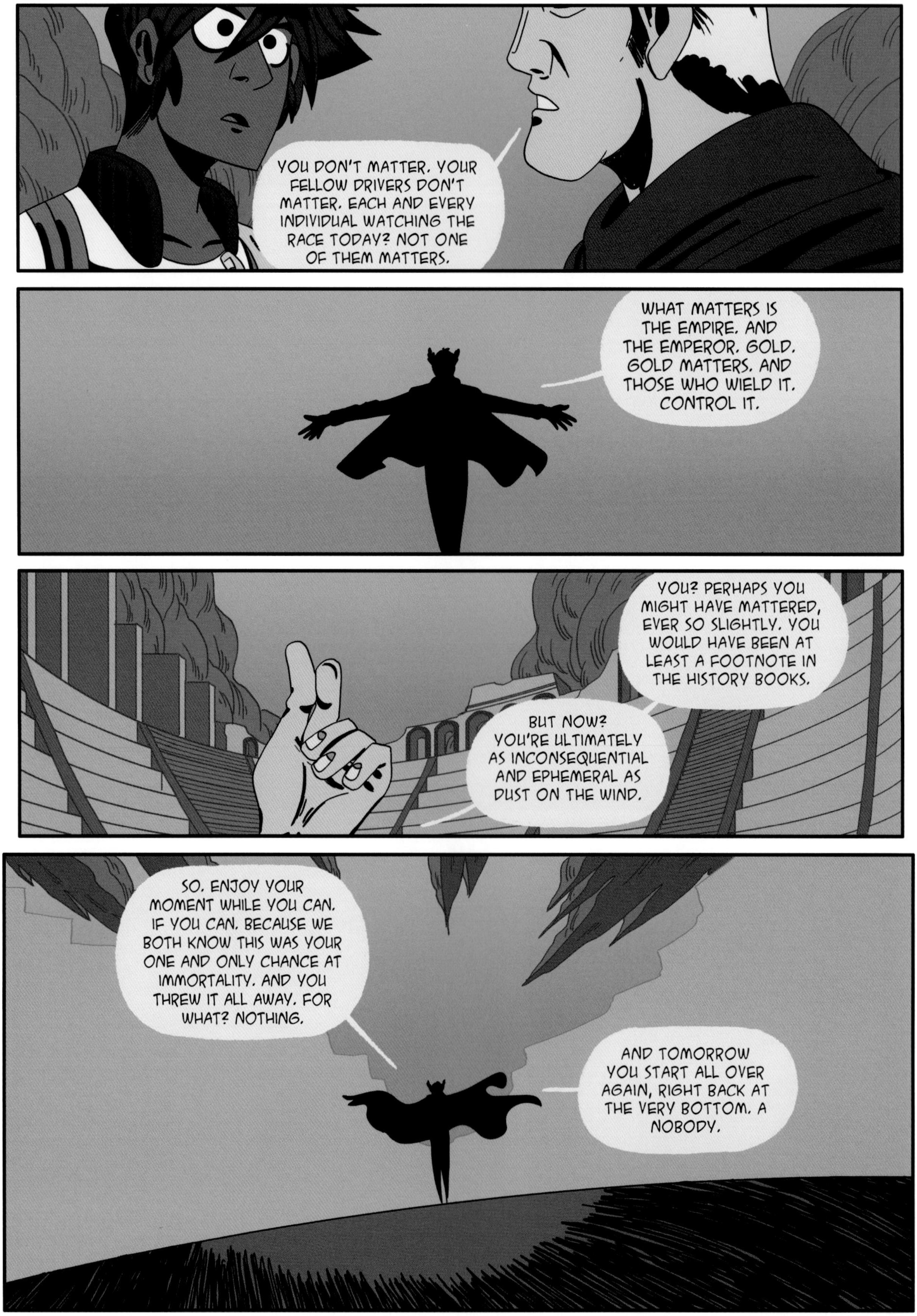
YOU DON'T MATTER. YOUR FELLOW DRIVERS DON'T MATTER. EACH AND EVERY INDIVIDUAL WATCHING THE RACE TODAY? NOT ONE OF THEM MATTERS.
WHAT MATTERS IS THE EMPIRE. AND THE EMPEROR. GOLD. GOLD MATTERS. AND THOSE WHO WIELD IT. CONTROL IT.
YOU? PERHAPS YOU MIGHT HAVE MATTERED, EVER SO SLIGHTLY. YOU WOULD HAVE BEEN AT LEAST A FOOTNOTE IN THE HISTORY BOOKS.
BUT NOW? YOU'RE ULTIMATELY AS INCONSEQUENTIAL AND EPHEMERAL AS DUST ON THE WIND.
SO. ENJOY YOUR MOMENT WHILE YOU CAN. IF YOU CAN. BECAUSE WE BOTH KNOW THIS WAS YOUR ONE AND ONLY CHANCE AT IMMORTALITY. AND YOU THREW IT ALL AWAY. FOR WHAT? NOTHING.
AND TOMORROW YOU START ALL OVER AGAIN, RIGHT BACK AT THE VERY BOTTOM. A NOBODY.

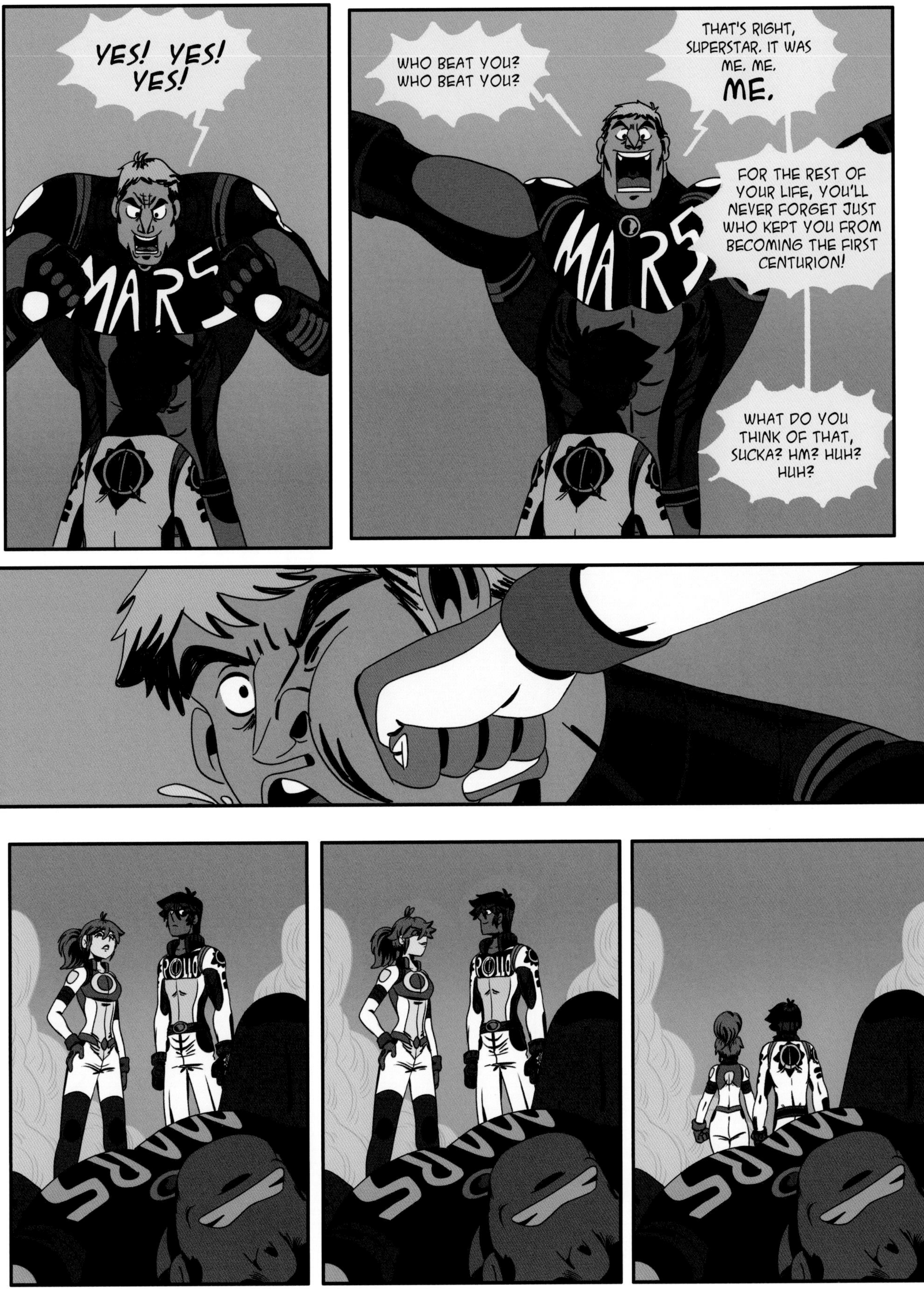
YES! YES! YES!
WHO BEAT YOU? WHO BEAT YOU?
THAT'S RIGHT, SUPERSTAR. IT WAS ME. ME. ME.
FOR THE REST OF YOUR LIFE, YOU'LL NEVER FORGET JUST WHO KEPT YOU FROM BECOMING THE FIRST CENTURION!
WHAT DO YOU THINK OF THAT, SUCKA? HM? HUH? HUH?

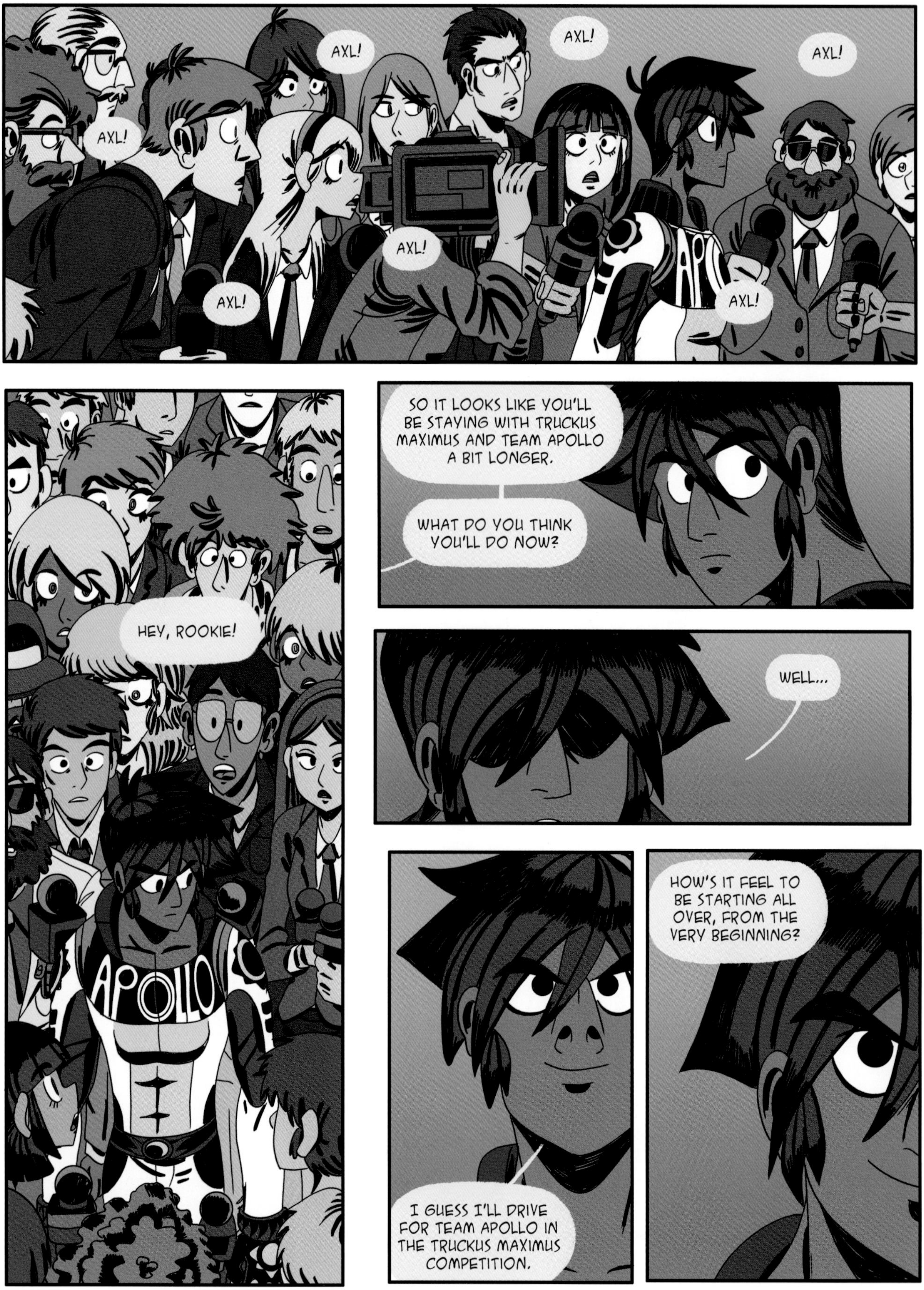
AXL!
AXL!
AXL!
AXL!
AXL!
AXL!
AXL!
HEY, ROOKIE!
SO IT LOOKS LIKE YOU'LL BE STAYING WITH TRUCKUS MAXIMUS AND TEAM APOLLO A BIT LONGER.
WHAT DO YOU THINK YOU'LL DO NOW?
WELL...
I GUESS I'LL DRIVE FOR TEAM APOLLO IN THE TRUCKUS MAXIMUS COMPETITION.
HOW'S IT FEEL TO BE STARTING ALL OVER, FROM THE VERY BEGINNING?

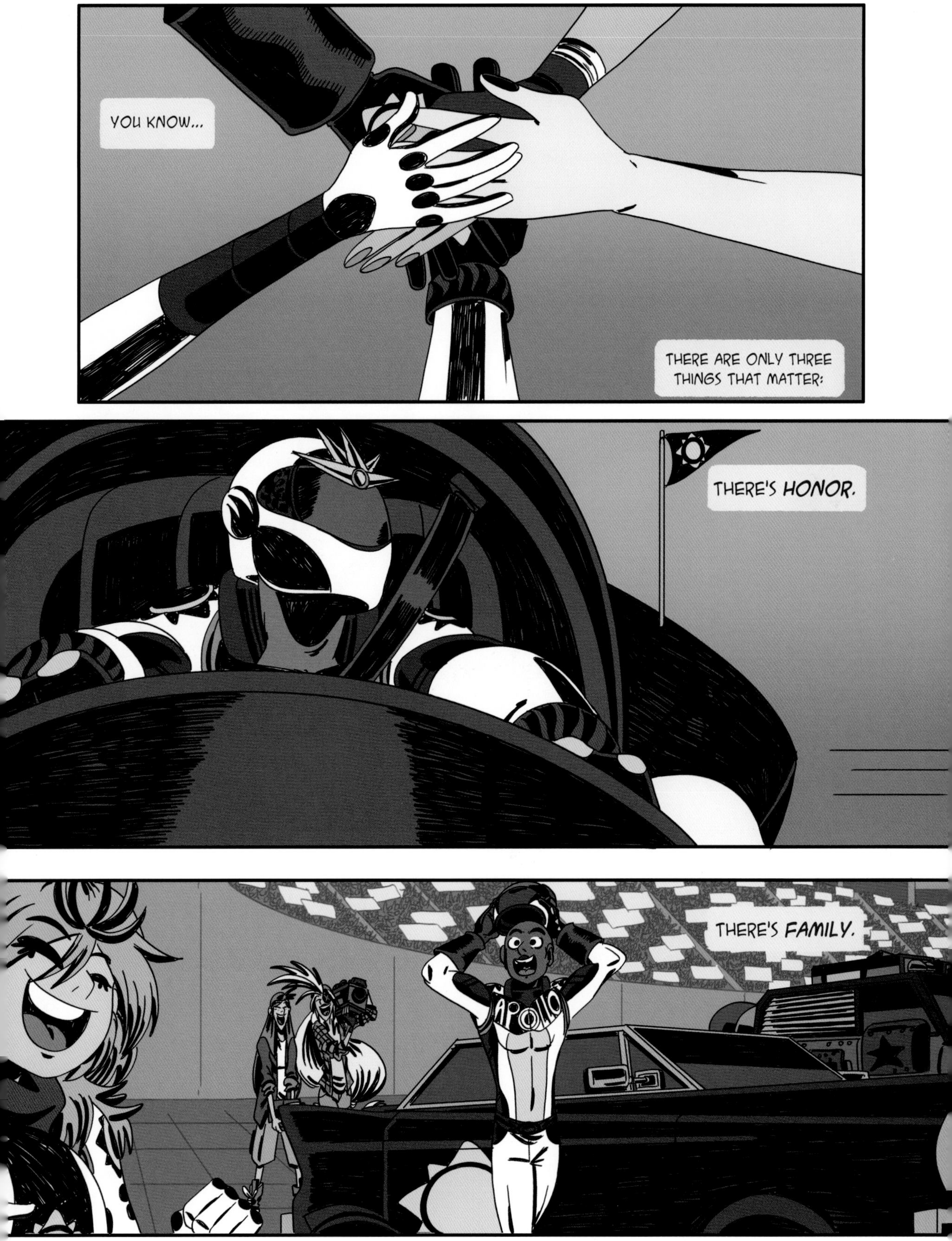
YOU KNOW...
THERE ARE ONLY THREE THINGS THAT MATTER:
THERE'S HONOR.
THERE'S FAMILY.
APOLLO

AND THERE'S THE GAME.

END.

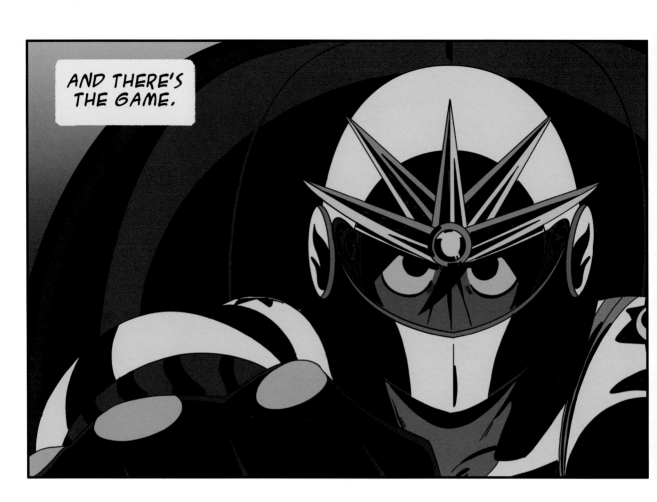

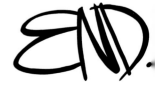

First Second

Text Copyright © by Scott Peterson
Art Copyright © by José García

Published by First Second
First Second is an imprint of Roaring Brook Press,
a division of Holtzbrinck Publishing Holdings Limited Partnership
120 Broadway, New York, NY 10271

Don't miss your next favorite book from First Second! For the latest updates go to
firstsecondnewsletter.com and sign up for our enewsletter.

Library of Congress Control Number: 2018953669
Paperback ISBN: 978-1-59643-814-9
Hardcover ISBN: 978-1-250-19696-5

Our books may be purchased in bulk for promotional, educational, or business use. Please
contact your local bookseller or the Macmillan Corporate and Premium Sales Department at
(800) 221-7945 ext. 5442 or by email at MacmillanSpecialMarkets@macmillan.com.

First edition, 2019
Edited by Calista Brill and Steve Behling
Book design by Molly Johanson
Printed in China

Sketched, inked, colored, and lettered in Photoshop.

Paperback: 10 9 8 7 6 5 4 3 2 1
Hardcover: 10 9 8 7 6 5 4 3 2 1